A Shout for the Dead

THE ASCENDANTS OF ESTOREA
BOOK 2

A Shout for the Dead

THE ASCENDANTS OF ESTOREA
BOOK 2

James Barclay

GOLLANCZ

LONDON

The right of James Barclay to be identified as the author of this work has
been asserted by him in accordance with the
Copyright, Designs and Patents Act 1988.

First published in Great Britain in 2006 by
Gollancz

An imprint of the Orion Publishing Group
Orion House, 5 Upper St Martin's Lane, London WC2H 9EA

A CIP catalogue record for this book is available
from the British Library.

ISBN-13 978 0 57507 621 1 (cased)
ISBN-10 0 57507 621 6 (cased)
ISBN-13 978 0 57507 622 8 (trade paperback)
ISBN-10 0 57507 622 4 (trade paperback)

1 3 5 7 9 10 8 6 4 2

Typeset by Input Data Services Ltd, Frome

Printed in Great Britain by
Mackays of Chatham, Chatham, Kent

www.orionbooks.co.uk

Dedication

This book is dedicated to the memory of David Gemmell. A great friend and a peerless mentor. The world is the poorer without you.

Acknowledgements

One day in January 2006, I went to visit David Gemmell and as a result, this book is the one I hoped it would be. David had a way of visualising and solving problems when we talked that I will never be able to replace. Sadly, it is a debt I will never be able to repay.

I also want to thank Simon Spanton for (still) putting up with the job of editing my work; my wife, Clare, who tries damned hard to make sure I sit in front of the PC and actually put finger to keyboard for enough hours every day; William Montanaro for producing a terrific and growing web resource for the Ascendants (address below); and Ariel, Lizzy Hill and Paul Maloney for their fantastic help with the website, forum, maps, and all that online stuff. I am more grateful than you know.

www.theascendants.co.uk
www.jamesbarclay.com

Cast List

OFFICERS OF THE ASCENDANCY ACADEMY

Hesther Naravny MOTHER OF THE ASCENDANCY, LAND WARDEN

Andreas Koll ASCENDANCY ECHELON, LAND WARDEN

Meera Naravny ASCENDANCY ECHELON, FIREWALKER

Harkov GENERAL OF THE ASCENDANCY GUARD

Arducius ASCENDANT OF THE 9TH STRAND

Mirron ASCENDANT OF THE 9TH STRAND

Ossacer ASCENDANT OF THE 9TH STRAND

Cygalius ASCENDANT OF THE 10TH STRAND

Yola ASCENDANT OF THE 10TH STRAND

Petrevius ASCENDANT OF THE 10TH STRAND

Mina ASCENDANT OF THE 10TH STRAND

Bryn ASCENDANT OF THE 10TH STRAND

Kessian ASCENDANT, SON OF MIRRON

OFFICERS OF THE ESTOREAN CONQUORD

Herine Del Aglios ADVOCATE OF THE ESTOREAN CONQUORD

Paul Jhered EXCHEQUER OF THE GATHERERS

Felice Koroyan CHANCELLOR, ORDER OF THE OMNISCIENT

Roberto Del Aglios AMBASSADOR TO SIRRANE

Arvan Vasselis MARSHAL DEFENDER OF CARADUK

Katrin Mardov MARSHAL DEFENDER OF GESTERN

Megan Hanev MARSHAL DEFENDER OF ATRESKA

Orin D'Allinnius CHIEF SCIENTIST TO THE ADVOCATE

Marcus Gesteris SENATOR

Tuline Del Aglios SECRETARY TO THE CONSUL GENERAL

Yuri Lianov HARBOUR MASTER OF WYSTRIAL, GESTERN

Fleet Corvanov CONQUORD MESSENGER, WYSTRIAL, GESTERN

SOLDIERS AND SAILORS OF THE CONQUORD

Karl Iliev PRIME SEA LORD OF THE OCETANAS

Kashilli LEAD MARINE, OCENII SQUAD VII

Elise Kastenas MARSHAL GENERAL OF THE ARMIES

Pavel Nunan GENERAL, 2ND LEGION

Dina Kell GENERAL, 2ND LEGION

Adranis Del Aglios MASTER OF HORSE, 2ND LEGION

Davarov GENERAL OF THE ATRESKAN LEGIONS

Cartoganev MASTER OF HORSE, ATRESKAN LEGIONS

CITIZENS AND OTHERS

Dahnishev MASTER SURGEON, 2ND LEGION

Julius Barias ORDER SPEAKER, 2ND LEGION

Harban-Qvist KARKU GUIDE

Khuran KING OF TSARD

Rhyn-Khur PRINCE OF TSARD

Gorian Westfallen ASCENDANT OF THE 9TH STRAND

Kreysun PROSENTOR, TSARDON FORCES

Thomal Yuran KING OF ATRESKA

Chapter One

859th Cycle of God, 15th day of Dusasfall

It was the second time he had seen Icenga die.

The first time had been a fall. And through his magnifier Harban had seen the broken body and the stain of blood on the snow far below.

It was an unusual way for one of the Karku to die. Yet the body had gone by the time Harban had finished his descent and he had felt pure joy. No animal had taken Icenga. There were no drag marks but there was a single set of footprints leading into the maze of rocks. Hope flared within him.

Immediately, he had known it could not be. Icenga could not possibly have survived such a fall. Fear had settled on him. Glancing up at the surrounding mountains, he had seen the glint of sun on glass as a magnifier turned his way. Rock dust and grit fell from the same place.

And then he had heard the rasp of shoe on ice and had seen Icenga walking towards him. He was sure-footed, as he had always been. But every few paces he had staggered as if pain was shearing through his head and he had lost all coordination, able only to grip his skull hard with his hands.

Harban had stood mute, unable to offer assistance or to flee. Icenga had not fallen. The broken shaft of an arrow jutted from his ribs over his heart. Icenga had collapsed into his arms and the pair of them had sagged to the frozen ground. Harban had stroked the dead man's hair while he breathed his last once again. The confusion in Icenga's eyes had turned Harban's fear to pity. He had whispered words of comfort but none could possibly be adequate. He wasn't even sure if Icenga could hear him.

And then at the very end, Icenga's expression had cleared and words had issued from his mouth, bound to the sour taint of sick breath.

'You know what this means,' he had said, his voice a dry rasp. 'We all know.'

Dimly, Harban heard the beat of hoofs on stone and ice. The fear deepened then, bringing a shortening of his breath. Harban sat with Icenga in his arms until his body was numbed by the cold and all his prayers were spoken.

Only then did his mind begin to function. Harban looked around him. The carved marble memorial to the Conquord dead in the slaughter a decade past stood cracked and creeper-covered. It had once been a grand obelisk with the bust of Jorganesh, the fallen general, proud at its head. But through the creepers could be seen scrawled Tsardon insults and threats should the Conquord ever return this way. It was smeared with long-dried goat's blood and the nose of the general had been shorn away.

Dusas chill ran deep and abiding. A gale charged with ice howled along Lubjek's Defile, rustling the ivy on the memorial. Nothing else remained to mark the single worst defeat of Conquord forces during her war with Tsard. No bones remained, no onager stones sat among the leaves. Not even an arrowhead poked through. All long cleared by Atreska's impoverished southern peoples.

Harban had seen the immediate aftermath. The images still haunted his dreams and filled his prayers to the Heart of the Mountain. This was not a place any Karku, let alone Harban, would choose to come any more. Though the scorched trees had grown afresh and flowers would carpet the ground when genastro warmed the earth, it would forever be tainted.

Harban was on Kark's northern border with Atreska, there with Icenga because of the rumours that had now proved true. Icenga had not been the only one to perish this way. Others had been used. Testing a power that the Karku had feared down the long centuries of history but had never really believed would be made flesh. That it was being tested here and Harban could take back undeniable evidence was the realisation of the darkest of Karku fears.

Harban stood, Icenga's body limp in his arms, finally granted the peace he deserved. He began to walk back up the slope towards the passageway under the mountains. The deep rumble of a distant avalanche reverberated over him. He stopped and stared up at the white peaks above, many lost in dense grey cloud. Another portent giving credence to Icenga's words from beyond death?

'Perhaps we are already too late,' he said and moved on again.

There was a great deal to be done. Icenga had to be interred in the rock catacombs under the village of Yllin-Qvist where he had lived his whole life; a place from where he could never be reawakened again. And Harban had to speak with the guardians of Inthen-Gor, the Heart of the Mountain. They had to know what he had seen and determine whether the prophecy was coming to pass. And if it was, it would be Harban who would make the journey to seek the few who could save them.

Deep in the mountain, the prophecies and writings of the ancients were already under close scrutiny. In the most sacred place in Kark, where the Eternal Water lapped the shores of the island on which the Heart Shrine stood, where the priests and guardians kept unflinching vigil, there had been a theft. Truth had been stolen. Disaster would surely follow. He lived. And He would come for them.

King Thomal Yuran of Atreska accepted the parchment but did not open it, knowing it would represent his last act as monarch of his country. In front of him, a man and a woman stood a respectful distance away. They were flanked by guards, polished armour reflecting the firelight of the cold throne room, faces emotionless. There would be more in every corridor of the castle and thousands of others, all bearing the Del Aglios crest, securing every inch of his country. It had gone with scarcely a whimper.

'This is what I think it is?' he asked.

His throne felt uncomfortable beneath him. The throne room, long divested of its Conquord accoutrements, was stale and bare. Outside, a dusas gale scoured the aged stone and mourned around the turrets and arches. This was not how he imagined it would end. By the lord of sky and stars, looking at the woman in front of him his dreams had ever been different and full of light and love.

Not like this. This miserable end. They wouldn't understand he had never had any real choice. Any decision he had made during those fateful days would have led to disaster for ordinary Atreskans. His people. The ones who had chanted his name and now demanded his deposition.

'I'm fulfilling my destiny as a servant of the Conquord,' she said quietly.

There was strength in her. He had seen the same ten years before.

'It is not the destiny I envisaged for you, Megan,' said Yuran.

'That was before you turned from the Conquord,' said Megan.

'And you turned from me.'

Yuran couldn't keep the edge from his voice. The years in Estorr had been very good to Megan Hanev. Her authoritative bearing had heightened her beauty. She was elegant, dressed in a toga and stola of finest Tundarran weave, and she wore a gold circlet with a woven leaf motif in her hair. Her long black hair was brushed to hang perfectly down between her shoulder blades and those deep brown eyes still retained such youthful energy.

She glanced to her right, to receive a nod from her companion before stepping forwards. Yuran felt his bravado begin to crumble. Megan reached a hand out to him and brushed his face.

'Have you seen the world outside this castle? The Tsardon have raped it. There's nothing left. You must have known they would take everything when it suited them.' She sighed. 'What happened, Thomal? Why did you do it?'

'I couldn't stand by and watch our people be slaughtered.'

'Instead, they died in their thousands at your borders with Neratharn and Gestern,' growled the man standing next to Megan. 'All because you were gutless in the face of your enemy.'

'You were not there, Exchequer Jhered. They would have crushed Haroq City without breaking sweat.'

Jhered's face was almost sympathetic. He still looked strong and vital, though grey dominated his hair, which was cut viciously short as a consequence. He had to be almost sixty years old by now. Lines marked his face but you wouldn't mistake age for weakness. Not in this man.

'You never really understood, did you?' said Jhered. 'We were then, and are now, one Conquord. Some must always die in order to save others. But you didn't ever see the world beyond Atreska's borders.'

'Don't patronise me, Jhered.'

'You and your people should have died for the Conquord when the Tsardon stood at your gates. Instead you fell meekly into line and listened to their lies about liberation. If what I saw when I rode through your once beautiful country is liberation then I would rather be a slave.

'Every hour you held them up would have brought the rest of the

Conquord time to marshal a more effective defence. And when we had won, we would have had the strength to take Atreska back then and there.'

'But we would have been torn to pieces,' said Yuran, aware of the whine in his voice. 'We were outnumbered ten to one.'

Jhered nodded. 'And your sacrifice would have saved five times the numbers that might have died within these walls. Atreska would have been a hero nation, blessed by the Advocate and feted by the whole of the Conquord. And you would have been its greatest son.

'Instead, you chose cowardice and betrayal. Did you really think we would not dare come back? Did you really believe the Tsardon would defend you when our legions massed again on your borders? Atreska belongs to the Conquord.'

'I chose the lives of my people,' whispered Yuran.

'And we hear their gratitude sounding from every window,' said Jhered. 'And we see it daubed on every wall.'

Yuran let his head drop. His mind raced. Curse the man. Always, his words sounded so simple, so plausible. Yet he had not been there. He had not tasted the terror of the people Yuran had sworn to protect. He felt Megan's hand raising his chin. Her face was very close, her eyes deep with regret.

'I dreamed for so long of our life together,' she said quietly.

'As did I.'

'Even after I knew Atreska had turned, I didn't want to believe it was you. But you never came back to me to prove it was not your doing. You gave me no choice but to pledge my allegiance to the Conquord above Atreska.'

Yuran smiled and reached out a hand, yearning to feel her skin one more time. But she leaned back from his touch and the first tear spilled on to her cheek.

'You remain my greatest triumph and proudest moment,' said Yuran. 'Don't make the mistakes I made.'

'Undoubtedly, she will listen more closely to her teachers,' said Jhered. He paused. 'Megan.'

Yuran frowned at the Exchequer's tone and looked questioningly at Megan. She stood up and stepped back.

'You must read the order,' she said, voice strained as if the words were hard to say. 'I'm sorry.'

Yuran shook his head. 'Don't be. You know in some ways, this even represents relief. I fear I am no longer secure in my own castle.'

He focused on the parchment and broke the Conquord seal. He unrolled it, reading the declaration of Conquord rule over Atreska and naming his country's new ruler and Marshal Defender. Further down, his own name was listed as deposed ruler to be dealt with under the law as prescribed by the Advocate. A half-smile crept across his lips. It was almost word for word the document he had handed to the then King of Atreska almost twenty years before.

'It is true then, that some things never change in the Conquord,' he said. He unrolled the parchment further and his next words withered on his lips.

'Not all things,' said Jhered.

Yuran shook his head and stared again at the lines he had just read. Chill cascaded through him and a pit opened in his stomach, leaving him feeling physically sick. His vision swam for a moment before he clutched hard to his fading hope.

'This is wrong,' he said. 'It has to be. This is not the Conquord way, please. I know how it works. We all know. The deposed ruler has choice. Exile, swearing of loyalty, not just ...'

'But you are not the deposed ruler of a once independent state,' said Jhered. 'You are a traitor of the Conquord and a self-imposed king of a Conquord territory. Those rules do not apply to you.'

Yuran's heart beat so loud he barely heard Jhered's words. He was aware he was shaking but could do nothing to stop it. He looked down at the parchment once more then across to Megan who was staring back at him, her lips quivering.

'And you signed it?' he said showing her the proof beneath the execution order.

'I am fulfilling my destiny,' she said again. 'Guards, please escort King Yuran to the cells.'

Men moved in on him from left and right. He wanted to be dignified but the moment one of them touched his arm, his courage failed him completely. Fear swamped him and he searched for something, anything that might save him. And there was something. Something he had thought to use to buy his freedom. Now it might buy his life.

'You cannot do this to me. You need me alive. You don't understand why the Tsardon left.'

The guards were hustling him to the door. He could no longer see Megan and Jhered but knew they would be staring at his back.

'Only I can help you. They are coming back to finish the job and you won't be strong enough to defeat them. No power is. Even your precious Ascendants won't be able to stop what He will unleash. Please—'

Jhered barked a single word and the guards stopped and turned Yuran around. The Exchequer marched up to him and grabbed him by the jaw, strong fingers gripping him hard. Jhered made to speak but Yuran saw his chance.

'Guarantee commutation of my sentence or I'll tell you nothing. Let me live and I'll help you to do the same.'

Jhered considered for a heartbeat then nodded minutely.

'What do you mean, "he"?' he asked.

The room seethed with the dead.

Khuran took a pace backwards. None who saw this could fail to recoil. And this was the nucleus of his army. The forces that would march across the tatters of the Conquord and see its remaining defence run in terror. So it was said.

It was also said that these would herald the troops that would fly his banner and sing his name utterly without question. Unconditional loyalty. Belief submerged beneath blind subservience. It was a force given new voice. Small yet but he could see the potential. One would have to be simple to understand otherwise.

But the fact was that they were not *his*. Not truly. And the man who controlled them, who freed them to new directed life, was a power beyond his thinking. Yuran had brought him as a gift but had left Tsard relieved of a burden.

'Isn't it beautiful?' said Gorian.

'What? A dance of the dead?' asked Khuran.

Gorian stood by him, unafraid.

'Surely beauty can be seen in an irrepressible army. One without fear, which can feast off the earth beneath its feet and fight day and night. It is a perfection no Conquord legion will ever attain. Without thought to self. Without family. The perfect fighting force. And if there are enough of them, unstoppable.'

'But without love or honour too. Without drive and belief. Without a reason to die in service of their king. Without loyalty, an army is nothing.'

Gorian chuckled. 'You're confused by ancient values, my King.

There is nothing sweeter than the second chance. And there is nothing more terrible than the fear of losing that chance. We hold that power over each and every one of these dead people. There is nothing they would not do for us. Is that not loyalty?'

Khuran shuddered. The day outside was warm but deep in the heart of his castle the cold endured. He gazed at the dead, trying not to feel repulsed. The pervasive sense of wrongness threatened to overwhelm him. And his distaste was heightened by Gorian's obvious delight at what he had created.

The dead were confused. A dozen of them standing, walking and seeing in the pre-burial chamber. Thinking and understanding. But in a thrall that kept them silent. Bemused. These were young children dead of the pox the day before and a man whose heart had failed him. Another who had been hanged for stealing livestock, his head fallen forwards onto his chest, and a woman who had died in the act of childbirth.

Their last thoughts had been desperate, agonised and frightened. And now they had been reawakened. Khuran wondered if they thought of this as an afterlife. Because that is exactly what it was. But not the one laid down in the words of any god he had ever read about. There was no glory in this death and certainly no peace. Animated by Gorian and sustained by the rumbling power of the ground beneath their feet and by each other. A circuit, Gorian called it. Khuran didn't really understand. It hardly mattered. The proof was standing before him, dull-eyed people wearing the clothes in which they had died.

Still Khuran fought the idea that this was some trick though he had seen them all lying lifeless. He had felt for a pulse or for the warmth of blood below the skin. They had all been dead and now they all drew breath.

And in the next moment, they dropped silently to the ground and were still once more. Khuran looked at Gorian. A frown passed across the Ascendant's face.

'What happened?' asked Khuran, relieved of a dread he had tried not to show.

'It is a new ability,' said Gorian. 'Tried but sparingly and never on so many at one time. But it works. And I know how to make it better. But to make it overwhelming, I will need help.'

'Help? Where from?'

Gorian smiled. 'Just prepare your country for war, despatch your armies to where we agreed and leave it to me. I'll be back almost before you realise I'm gone.'

Khuran looked at Gorian. Just in his mid-twenties but so authoritative and confident in his power. His eyes shone from a face much coveted by the women of his court. The face of one of the Conquord's dramatic heroes, framed in glorious curled fair hair. He was tall, powerful and dressed in one of the togas Khuran found ridiculous but which he insisted were woven for him. Gorian liked his games and this was a particularly trivial one. And most people did not dare contradict Gorian Westfallen's wishes. But Khuran was not most people.

'Oh no, Gorian. You will not leave my sight. I will lead my people and you will follow me.'

'As you wish, my King.'

Chapter Two

859th cycle of God, 20th day of Dusasfall

The energy map was sick. Grey flecks coursed through veins and infested vital organs. Ossacer could feel the strength of the infection like heat washing over his face. The boy he was tending was gripped by his fever and barely conscious. His body was soaked in sweat though the wind blew cold around the small house in which he lay. Ossacer moved his hands down to the boy's stomach and winced at the picture that his mind's eye read in the fine detail of the energy trails. The liver and kidneys were strained to the point of shutdown. The boy didn't have long to live.

He and Arducius had come to the Morasian port of Okiro on the back of strong rumours of Ascendancy potential there and in outlying villages. But they had arrived in the midst of an epidemic that was sweeping the poor quarter of the port adjacent to the harbour. Something in the water, so Arducius said. And while he tried to divine the source with a fledgling passive Land Warden they'd met the day before, Ossacer was assessing the impact on the local population. The strong could fight it. The old, the young and the weakened were being taken back to the embrace of God in their hundreds.

'Can you save him?'

Ossacer turned to the doorway. The boy's mother stood there. She was a young woman, beauty submerged by her distress. Her voice trembled and the map of her lifelines was riddled with her anxiety. It was almost palpable. Mixed with her fear for her son was her fear of Ossacer himself. Desperation had overcome her suspicion and she had been prepared to let him try. It was the history of the Ascendancy repeated yet again.

She shifted under his gaze. A reaction he was long used to. Eyes that saw nothing but sensed everything, that penetrated to the heart straight through skin and bone.

'If you will let me, I can.'

The colours of her life energy pulsed bright with hope and relief.

'Anything,' she said. 'Please.'

She reached out to touch Ossacer but stopped herself before making contact. He knew what she saw. So normal in most respects. Neat short hair, friendly face a little careworn before its time, and an easy smile. But the shifting colour of his blind eyes and the fact of who he was could not be denied. Ossacer nodded.

'It's all right,' he said. 'I understand. Trust me. Don't be scared by anything you see. I will not hurt him.'

He turned back to the boy and placed a hand on his brow, the heat and damp a shock.

'Stay with me,' he whispered. 'Don't let go.'

Ossacer focused on the sick and dying body before him. The frenzy of energy outside in the harbour and through the port softened and faded from his mind. He sought sources closer to him. He was fresh but knew he couldn't risk too much of himself. There was so much work to do elsewhere in the slums when this one child was saved. Outside the window grew an old olive tree, roots deep, branches twisted and gnarled. Inside, candles and lanterns were lit and a fire was going in the tiny kitchen next door. It would be enough.

Ossacer lifted one hand, palm up, above his head and crabbed his fingers as if holding a bowl. He opened his mind to the energies of tree and fire and let their maps coalesce before him. The tree, strong, slow-pulsing brown and deep green, shot with the pale shades of youth where new growth awaited the warmth of genastro. The fire a chaotic, vibrant mass of red and yellow, dark at its tips where energy escaped the circuit and bled into the air around.

He remembered how alien and difficult it had been when he was younger, when he and the others had first emerged and seen the true colours of life, the glory of this earth under God. Then, to link with another energy source had seemed all but impossible; to direct it a ludicrous notion and an effort that was instantly exhausting.

Now it was different, natural, though no less tiring in the long run. Ossacer pushed out with his own energy map to link with the sources he wanted. He teased breaks in their circuits to allow the energy to flow into him. He felt the quick jolt of fire and the lumbering power of the olive tree. Within his body, he contained and amplified what he took and reformed it to a map of his own design.

He projected this map on to the boy and drove its energies through his veins and organs. It was the map of health, a pure construct that overwhelmed the infection. The grey flashed to brightness and then was gone. Ossacer kept up the tide of health until no trace remained of the disease. Only then did he relax and release himself from the energies and let in the sounds of the day once again.

Ossacer sat back on his haunches and breathed out heavily. He shook his head at the exertion and wiped a hand across his brow. In the bed, the boy was calm. His fever was gone and he slept. Ossacer smiled and turned back to the mother. She was in the doorway still, her hands clutching hard at the frame. In the room, the lantern and candles were extinguished and in the kitchen, the fire smoked, its last embers dim. There was new growth on the olive tree despite the cold of dusasfall.

'Let him sleep,' said Ossacer. 'And boil all your water until we make the supply safe.'

She nodded mutely, unwilling to come near him even though she must be desperate to go to her son. Ossacer stood up.

'I understand your fear. I see it every day. But you must forget what you have been told. This is what the Ascendancy can bring to you, to the whole Conquord. We are not against God, we act with God and do his work. We seek only to help. I was born to heal.'

'Thank you,' she managed, her voice choked with a confusion of emotion. 'I just—'

'It's all right,' said Ossacer. 'All I ask is that you think about what you have seen here today. What will you tell your son, your friends? That your son has been cured by an evil that must be stamped out, or that by God's will, he has been granted another chance at life, a chance he so richly deserves? Think. We do not ask for thanks, only acceptance.'

He bowed his head and walked past her towards the front door. Harkov, general of the Ascendancy Guard, intercepted him. He was an instantly comforting figure. His strong lifelines surrounded a commanding frame. Harkov was a former palace guardsman respected by Paul Jhered and hence the perfect choice to lead the Ascendancy Guard. His natural energy map oozed authority and control.

'Trouble at the fountain,' he said.

'Bad?' asked Ossacer, putting a hand on Harkov's arm and relaxing his mind. The world faded to black before him. Harkov led him out into the chill day.

'Bad enough. It's Koroyan.'

Ossacer sighed and sagged, feeling suddenly tired. 'Will that woman dog my footsteps forever?'

'Unless she meets with a nasty accident,' said Harkov.

'You don't mean that,' said Ossacer.

'Not all the time.'

'Where's Arducius?'

'Three guesses,' said Harkov.

'Then we'd better be quick,' said Ossacer.

The two men were joined by another six Ascendancy guardsmen, each armed with gladius and shield and with bows slung across their backs. Their livery, red, with the Ascendancy crest of sun over tree in a pair of cupped hands, was becoming a common and accepted sight throughout the Conquord. Made up of ex-levium and palace guard for the most part, the Ascendancy Guard were quickly gaining respect. They were also making powerful enemies.

It was a short walk to the fountains through slums that stank of death. The streets were tight and full of fear. Refuse was strewn across muddy cobbles. The stench of sewage was strong. Ossacer felt a little anxious. This far from the heart of the Conquord, not all the advances it boasted had penetrated to the poorest. It would ever be so.

The tension travelled in waves through the latent energies surrounding them. And in a few paces, he could hear it too. The wind carried the harsh sound of angry voices.

'The fountain's crowded,' said Ossacer. 'I can see the interference in the energies above it. Heat and emotion carried on the wind.'

'Don't leave my side,' said Harkov. 'This might get ugly.'

'If Koroyan is there, it already is,' said Ossacer.

They hurried down a right-hand turn. The fountain was at the end of the alley. Ossacer could see the confused mass of people in the lifelines. Beyond them, the lively blues of the fountain waters. Harkov signalled two of his men to move ahead while he slowed almost to a halt. Ossacer searched the blaze of human energy, searching for Arducius's map. So hard to divine.

'Where is he?'

'He'll be all right,' said Harkov.

Ossacer's heart was pounding. He fought himself to calmness. Energy signatures ceased their flaring and resolved to detail once again. But he still couldn't see Arducius. There was shouting, a brief scuffle and into the silence that followed walked Ossacer with Harkov. The general filled in the detail.

'Koroyan is with Vennegoor and twenty or so Order guards. Arducius is facing them behind a line of our people. No swords are out but it's getting twitchy. Trouble is that citizens are crowding in quickly. If this goes the wrong way, we'll have nowhere to go.'

'We'll be fine,' said Ossacer. 'Just get me next to Ardu.'

Harkov's men put their shoulders to the gathering crowd and forced a path through to the fountain. The multiple images in Ossacer's mind thinned. He could see Arducius now. His aura was calm, his body map even. But within his frame, the brittleness of his bones was a dominant shifting pale grey. A sickness not even Ossacer could cure.

Around him, the guards showed more signs of stress while across from them, just a few yards away, the Order flooded his senses with their anger. Conversation broke out around them and Arducius looked round as he approached.

'Can't leave you alone for a moment without trouble breaking out,' said Ossacer.

'Nothing I can't handle,' said Arducius. 'Glad you're here though.'

The two of them moved in front of the line of guards. Before them, Chancellor Koroyan stood haughty and disdainful.

'Ah,' she said. 'The blind one too. Fresh from peddling your perverse healing, no doubt?'

Quiet spread again among the crowd, now several hundred strong, in the tight square which housed the fountain. Ossacer could feel them wavering. The Chancellor remained a dominant figure and despite the work he and Arducius had done here, their security was by no means guaranteed. Everyone listening and watching was an Order devotee.

'You are of course welcome to accompany me and talk to some of those I have helped,' said Ossacer, raising his voice loud. 'Ask them how they feel about my work.'

'It is interesting, and I think all of us would be fascinated to know,' said Arducius. 'What exactly is it you are doing here?'

Ossacer sucked in a breath.

'Risky, Ardu, very risky,' he whispered.

'Best get it out of the way now.'

Indeed, Koroyan did seem a little taken aback at the invitation but she recovered quickly and strutted into the gap.

'Is she still wearing the old robes of state?' asked Ossacer.

'Still. Lot of grey in her hair since last time though.'

'Good people of Okiro, of Morasia and the Conquord,' said Koroyan, indulging them with a smile. 'Faithful servants of the Omniscient. I am glad that you have had the opportunity to see at first hand what these so-called Ascendants can do. They can heal your sick, but what do they use to do it? And what else can they do that they would not be so pleased to demonstrate?

'I have seen what they can do and it chills my blood that they are allowed to walk among you. They can raise waters that could drown you all in your beds. They can summon gales that would flatten your homes. They play with the elements as if they own them. They do not. This earth is the province of God the Omniscient. None of us has the right to call on the powers of God and use them as our own. Can you possibly feel secure with them moving amongst you?

'The Omniscient cares for you. And this tragic disease that has afflicted you means that you are utmost in my prayers and in my thoughts. Curious, is it not, that the Ascendants choose to come here at the very outbreak of disease. Almost as if they knew it was going to happen.' Koroyan shrugged. 'Who knows, perhaps they are so powerful that they could sense the coming of the disease. Or perhaps they are the cause of it. After all, what is more powerful than live demonstration. They would not command your attention if there was nothing to improve, no?

'I denounce them. They are criminals under the Conquord's mistaken protection. They are heretics under the Omniscient. These people must be stopped. All here who worship Him know this and know the penalty. They should burn.'

There was a movement in the crowd. Anger stirred and voices were raised. The majority in support of the Chancellor but not all. None risked a move to action with guards flanking both parties.

'This is becoming a trial,' said Harkov quietly. 'I suggest you choose your next words very carefully.'

Arducius jumped on to the lip of the fountain, raising himself head and shoulders above the crowd which quietened quickly. Ossacer could see the confidence radiating from him, a warm green ripple in his aura.

'We've been here five days now. Five days in which we have sat with you, eaten with you, prayed with you and, yes, used the abilities we have to heal the sick. I recognise many of you as I look around. Some of you once heading for a premature return to the earth, are now walking, with your strength returning.

'The Chancellor is right. The Omniscient does care for you. And we do the Omniscient's work, saving those who can be saved. Helping those who can be helped and who ask us for it.

'The Chancellor is right. We can raise wind, we can raise water and fire. But only in the Omniscient's name. Only to protect our people. You. That is the worth of us. We are here to serve you. Have we harmed a single one of you?'

Arducius turned his attention square on the Chancellor. 'It is an enduring tragedy that we want nothing more than to be welcomed into the bosom of the Order. We would happily swear loyalty to the Chancellor. She denies us that opportunity and so we are forced to work without her blessing.

'I stand before you now and tell you that you have nothing to fear from the Ascendants. If you choose not to believe us, then see us burn. But it will not stop the destiny of the Conquord. The Ascendancy is here forever. It has the support of the Advocate. And as the generations pass, more and more of your children will demonstrate similar abilities.

'Some will accompany us back to Estorr today. Others will follow. See the good in us for that is all that there is. The Chancellor is mistaken. We are not heretics. It is only she who talks of death. We prefer a discourse on life. I can think of no greater pleasure than to worship the Omniscient and I urge you all to maintain your faith and bring others to you. All we ask for is that you understand that we work within the faith of the Omniscient, never ever against Him.'

The crowd had fallen completely silent while Arducius spoke. He jumped down from the fountain and walked across the space to face the Chancellor.

'It's tired, Felice, this declamation of yours. In a decade, we have saved hundreds, liberated thousands and harmed no one. We will take those who wish to go with us back to Estorr and you will not stop us, nor will your lap dog draw his sword.'

Beside the Chancellor, Horst Vennegoor, Prime Sword of the Armour of God tensed and growled.

'Save it, Vennegoor,' said Arducius. 'When you first crossed us in

Westfallen a decade ago, you were past your best. Now you're just old.'

Felice Koroyan hushed Vennegoor's retort and took a pace forward to stand toe-to-toe with Arducius.

'You have always been, and will always be, an abomination,' she said quietly. 'And one day, you or one of your bastard brothers and sisters will transgress. The ear of the Advocate will turn back to me and you will have no friends. All I have to do is wait.'

Arducius smiled and Ossacer saw the anger settle on him. 'We will never give you the satisfaction, Felice. I know why you fight us. It is because you fear one day your crimes against us will come back and bite you. It is only by the grace of the Advocate and the laws of tolerance in our Conquord that you are still alive, let alone still the Chancellor. But while the Advocate might forgive and forget, we Ascendants never will. One day, you will be gone and the Ascendancy and the Order will be as one, as the Omniscient surely intends.'

The Chancellor's face was grey and angry.

'Your words speak your guilt,' she said. 'And one day I will watch you burn.'

'Don't hold your breath,' said Arducius. He turned back to Ossacer and Harkov. 'Come on. Plenty of work to do yet.'

Chapter Three

859th cycle of God, 1st day of Genasrise

'All right, you can come in now.'

Her son's voice swelled Mirron's heart as it had done from his first newborn cry. She turned from the window overlooking the splendour of Estorr and walked from her bedroom to the main reception room. Through the partially open doors, she could hear the shuffling of feet and a low murmur. The beautiful scents of fresh-cut flowers and greenery wafted out and water trickled in the decorative fountain.

Her son was at her side.

'Look left first. Don't look right,' said the boy, putting a hand up to her face to shield the rest of the room from her eyes.

'All right,' she said.

The fountain was there in the left-hand corner of the room. In the pool, a carved wooden boat with a cloth sail on its mast scudded around in gentle circles. She gasped and put a hand to her mouth. The sail was filled with a breeze that chased the boat, propelling it in its course.

'Oh, darling, you can do it!' she said, kneeling and pulled him into a crushing hug.

The boat slowed and stopped, his concentration on it broken.

'Oh, Mother!'

'Kessian, I am so proud of you. I knew you could do it.'

'Happy birthday, Mother.'

She kissed his cheek and let him go. 'How did you do it?'

'Well, he needed a little help but it was there all along, just like you said.'

Mirron swung round on her haunches, having to steady herself against the marble side of the fountain pool. She'd forgotten there were others in the room. Actually, it was quite crowded with friends.

But the voice belonged to a man she hadn't seen in a year. She flew to her feet and into his embrace.

'Ardu! When did you get back? Why didn't you tell me?'

'Because your son got to me first and wanted to organise this surprise,' said Arducius. His eyes swam from green to a gentle warm blue.

'And then we thought we might as well have a joint birthday party.'

Another voice. Mirron almost burst into tears. She pushed Arducius away. Standing to his left was Ossacer. All three of them came together. Applause broke out.

'Happy birthday all of us,' said Mirron.

Her words were chorused around the room. Goblets were raised in salute.

'Twenty-four now,' said Ossacer. 'Getting on . . .'

'Sometimes I feel twenty years older,' said Mirron.

'Well you look ten years younger,' said Arducius.

'Liar.' She shook her head and stepped back so she could see them both, looking tired but wonderful in white togas slashed with deep Ascendancy red, Ossacer with his hair cut short and Arducius who sported long, slightly wavy dark locks these days. 'Neither of you is supposed to be here until solastro. It's been lonely without you.'

'Never miss a birthday,' said Ossacer.

Mirron smiled at him. He was studying her closely, his sightless eyes flickering up and down her body, irises a chaotic rush of colour. It was disconcerting if you weren't used to it. But Mirron, Ossacer and Arducius had been together almost every day for the first twenty years of their lives. Ossacer was examining her energy map and lifelines in the way only he could, trying to discern the emotions underpinning her words.

Mirron didn't need to look inside Ossacer to understand his mood. He was unhappy and he was anxious. It was written on his face and in the way he held himself. That little stoop and the rounding of the shoulders as if he had been given something too heavy to carry.

'Come on, Ossie, think I buy that even for one moment?'

Ossacer shrugged. 'Well, you know, we were just passing through . . .'

'No one passes through here from Morasia to Westfallen,' said Mirron. 'But I couldn't be happier you're here, today of all days. See what my son can do?'

'I saw the trails,' said Ossacer. 'Very impressive in a ten-year-old. Glad he's coming into his potential so soon. Still, I shouldn't be surprised by the talents of the offspring of Mirron and ... well, you know.'

Mirron nodded and looked round at Kessian. He was playing with his boat, sending it in a figure-of-eight with the breeze he created. Hesther Naravny, Mother of the Ascendancy, was looking over his shoulder, encouraging him. Others were watching too, along with a couple of the teenage Ascendants. The room was breaking up into small groups to talk and drink, or try snacks from the serving platters set around. Much of the Ascendancy project hierarchy was here, testament to the reverence in which Mirron was held. In which all three of the original Ascendants were held.

Kessian could feel her eyes on him and he turned round, favouring her with a huge smile. Mirron smiled back but behind her expression, she felt the pain that would never truly die. Those gorgeous blue eyes and that mass of curly blond hair. So much like Gorian.

'At least that's where the similarity ends,' whispered Ossacer into her ear.

Mirron let go a breath she hadn't realised she was holding.

'I'll never work out how you do that.'

'It's quite simple, dear Mirron. Be blind most of your life. It gives you such an uncluttered perspective on the nuances of energy.'

Even when he tried to joke, Ossacer managed to sound serious and analytical.

Mirron turned to face him. 'What is it, Ossie?'

'What do you mean?' Ossacer looked at the floor.

'Like I don't know something's amiss? You and Ardu show up here unannounced from your duties in the west. I know it's our birthday but I can't imagine the Advocate agreeing that you break off your tour for a party, can you?'

'Just enjoy it,' said Arducius. 'It's a beautiful genastro day in Estorr, the Advocate is paying for the wine and we've brought back some fantastic potential for you and Hesther to meet. And taken from beneath that lovely snarl the Chancellor has when she gets beaten.'

'She was there?'

'Like always,' said Arducius.

'And is there nothing we can do about it?' asked Mirron.

Arducius shook his head. 'The Advocate won't change the law. And anyway, it isn't the Order who is at fault, it's just her and her cronies. We have to persuade people of our faith through demonstration and understanding. We need acceptance, not religious conflict.'

Mirron chewed her lip, worry nagging at her mind. 'One day you won't be able to talk your way out of it. What then? We know the Chancellor would use force, given the merest opportunity. I can't bear the thought of you two getting burned in some far-flung corner because you've spoken out of turn.'

Arducius spread his hands. 'What else can we do? This is the only way to get the message across. And look at the hundreds we've taken from self-imposed repression. People who thought they were freaks and who lived in fear of the Order can now walk in daylight with confidence.'

'That's still a naïve vision, Ardu,' said Mirron. 'Maybe they can here on the Hill, but there are parts of Estorr where we still can't go without protection, and this is the capital city for God's sake. It doesn't matter what the Advocate says and what she decrees. At best, most people are wary of us. And out in the wilds most of them still hate us. The Order still represents the Advocate and we are still a splinter faith, no matter what we believe.'

'It changes nothing,' said Arducius. 'We have to spread our message. Like the Order did in centuries gone by. It has its risks but if we don't do it now, our future generations will be no further forward. What would you have us do?'

Mirron shook her head. 'Oh, I don't know. Just be careful. Don't provoke the Chancellor. And don't deny that's what you do. I've seen you at it.'

Arducius laughed and kissed her cheek. 'Come on, let's mingle. Relax for a change. You worry too much.'

'With good reason.' She accepted the goblet Arducius took from a tray for her and drank. 'And don't think I won't find out the real reason you've shown up here today.'

'I know that you will,' said Arducius and for a moment, his sparkle dimmed. 'Please, it has to be later.'

Mirron nodded and turned to her son and Hesther, trying hard not to think about it.

Roberto Del Aglios, eldest son of the Advocate, and the first Conquord Ambassador to the closed nation of Sirrane, felt energised and far younger than his forty-eight years today. Season upon season, year upon year of difficult, delicate and frustrating negotiations and at last, in his hand he held a Sirranean government signature.

It was short of full alliance but it was an agreement to closer ties, to an exchange of technologies and to a broad range of commodity quotas that would benefit territories across the Conquord. And more important than all of these, it was an agreement to share information on Tsard to the south, Omari to the west and the vast desert and plain kingdom of Garanth to the north of Sirrane. The once-blind now had eyes everywhere.

Roberto waited until they stepped outside the Sirrankjor, the seat of the government in this extraordinary country, before letting himself go and embracing Gesteris. The two men slapped each other's backs.

'This,' said Roberto, breaking away. 'Is going to make the Conquord great once more. Just think what this does for Gosland, for Dornos ...'

'It strengthens your mother's hand in every corner of the Conquord.'

Roberto looked at his companion. Senator Marcus Gesteris, hero of the Conquord. The man who held the Tsardon at bay on the Neratharnese border until Roberto himself came to relieve him in the defining battle of the 848th cycle in the war with Tsard. A great soldier and a clever diplomat. There were few that did not recognise and respect the one-eyed general with the signature scar down the right-hand side of his face. It still flared red in cold weather and the eye socket remained a constant irritation.

'I cannot thank you enough. So long away from your family.'

'It is an honour and a pleasure to serve,' said Gesteris. 'But there is more to do. Our intelligence from Tsard suggests they are arming again. It might be in response to our retaking of Atreska and the build-up of legions in the border states but I don't think so. We need Sirrane's help militarily. They have such strength should they choose to use it.'

'Interesting, isn't it?' said Roberto. 'And in Conquord history, they have never chosen to invade anywhere. No desire for expansion.'

Gesteris chuckled. 'Hard to credit when you're a Conquord citizen, eh? But think about it. How many people have we seen. How much of the country have they let us see? It could be empty. Maybe the talk of strength here is just that.'

'I very much doubt that. What is it really, do you think?'

'Well, no doubt part of it is in their psyche. They aren't a united people and that will undermine any thought of invasion. This is a country ruled by consent, not declaration. But more than that, and laugh if you want, I think they're a race of agoraphobics. Very unhappy out of the shade of trees. Take the city. No parks, no big open spaces.'

'You know, you might be right,' said Roberto. 'If it wasn't for the spires.'

'No. They're safe because they are protected. The spires are enclosed and they are blessed, so I understand.'

Roberto looked around him at the stunning and extraordinary capital city of Mytarinos, which translated roughly as 'meeting place'. It was a city of low domes and towering spires; tree-lined streets and walled woods; covered markets and secluded glades. The predominant colours were those of the forest, greens, browns and reds.

The trees, so the Sirranean saying went, were the roof of the world. And to pierce the roof was to toy with the power of the sky. Not that it meant they were scared of the heavens. The highest spires soared hundreds of feet above the tallest tree and were monuments to engineering excellence. They were places for solitude and reflection, to bask in the glories of the world above the roof, to offer respect and worship to the myriad gods the Sirraneans followed and, with typical Sirranean practicality, to monitor the weather.

Roberto hadn't considered it before. The Sirraneans were an eclectic mix, happy to live in sprawling low houses that seldom reached above two storeys but equally comfortable in their swaying spires or the upper boughs of their trees. He had never seen climbing like it. Nor camouflage. Nor the breathtaking acrobatics they undertook to get from tree to tree. Fearless. You could easily see why they had never suffered serious threat from invasion. No conventional army could hope to counter them, short of felling or burning every tree. And getting close enough to wield the axe would be a task in itself.

And yet Gesteris had nailed it. On their journey through the vast forests, studded with stunning mountain ranges, broad lakes and impenetrable valleys and gorges, the Sirraneans had been uncomfortable the few times they had been forced to cross open spaces.

'I'm right, I promise,' said Gesteris. 'Look.'

Their translator, Tarenaq, had just emerged from the building along with Huatl a senior member of her delegation. As they emerged into sunlight, they made a brief gesture, passing their hands across their eyes and over their heads.

'The Omniscient save me, I had assumed they were waving away flies.'

Gesteris chuckled. 'Sometimes they probably are. I swear some of these bites will leave permanent scars.'

'Marcus, your minute observation has embarrassed me again.'

'Don't be down on yourself. It's a rare enough gesture.'

'Superstition?'

'Religion, I think,' said Gesteris. 'Tarenaq was vague in the extreme when asked.'

'You do surprise me,' said Roberto with a raising of the eyebrows.

Tarenaq and Huatl were hurrying towards them. Typical of the Sirranean build, they were tall, slender people, sinuous, with large strong hands. The Sirraneans had been an arboreal race. Bony ridges ran down the sides of their necks and continued, he had been informed, the length of their torsos and along the undersides of their arms. A membrane had once grown from the ridges, providing limited glide, balance and enormous control in the leap between branches. Some still had an elongated coccyx. A vestigial reminder of a past long forgotten, as was the faint green tint within their deep brown skin. It was a history they held dear and which still governed much of their mythology, religion and ceremony.

'You've forgotten an important clause?' ventured Roberto as the two Sirraneans neared, trotting down a short flight of stone steps. Both were clothed in tight-fitting leggings and shirts. Lightweight cloaks were about their shoulders, floating in the breeze.

Tarenaq did not smile though she was used to Roberto's sense of humour by now. Her large, brown eyes locked on him and her brow creased.

'We have informations,' she said.

Her voice was strong and guttural, like that of so many of her kind, designed to carry through the sound-sapping foliage. Roberto couldn't help but smile.

'Lucky we signed when we did, then.'

'Yes.' Still no smile.

Roberto sobered. There was deep disappointment in Tarenaq's eyes. And sadness.

'What is it?'

Tarenaq turned to Huatl and motioned him to speak. It was slow and Tarenaq had to stop often, struggling for the right Estorean words but she did her best.

'The armies of Khuran cover the ground again. Their westerly progress is swift, an angry beast rumbling on mountain and plain. They have not scale but they have cruel purpose. Blood is in their eyes, it is all that they see. Something moves behind them and they dare not turn aside though fear bids them scatter. They will fall upon our friends. You are unready.'

Roberto found himself staring at Gesteris. All their joy was turned to ash. Both had spent long enough with Tarenaq to interpret nearly all she said first time around. And this message was simple enough.

'Where are they?' asked Roberto. 'How far have they got?'

'They stand south and east of us now. By the Gor of Halor. They travel our southern borders. Goscapita, surely their journey end.'

'The Halorian mountains? How can they be that close and you didn't tell us?'

Tarenaq passed on the question and Roberto saw Huatl frown as if it was obvious.

'Only our friends hear what we see. Yesterday, it was not written that you were. Today, you are.'

Roberto bit back a retort. Instead he nodded and turned sharply to Gesteris.

'My mother must hear of this immediately. Take your team and take the samples. Neristus and D'Allinnius will need them rather sooner than we thought. Send birds, send fast riders on the message service ahead of you. We must mobilise and we have no time.'

Gesteris thumped his right arm into his chest. 'My arm and heart are yours, Roberto. What about you?'

'I'm going to take a look for myself. Get numbers and weapons. Then I'm going to Gosland to command the defence. Make sure they know I'm coming.' Roberto slapped his palm on the stone rail at his side. 'Damn Khuran. Damn his ashes to the devils on the wind. How can he have rebuilt so quickly?'

He didn't really believe it. It could just be posturing. The Sirraneans might have got the intent wrong. But seldom were they so direct and detailed in their opening words on any subject. And that was something that worried Roberto more than he was prepared to say. Tsardon invasion. The Conquord simply wasn't ready.

Chapter Four

859th cycle of God, 1st day of Genasrise

Mirron walked with Arducius and Ossacer across the grand courtyard, with its fountains, lawns and marble-tiled paths. They passed the basilica and moved into the palace itself, under the flags of the members of the Conquord, some of whose allegiance remained in considerable doubt.

They were shown to a small, luxuriously appointed reception chamber. The day was growing cold and the hypocaust warmed the floor beneath their feet. But amongst all the splendour, the busts, the tapestries and the furniture Mirron would never quite get used to, was yet another surprise on this day of surprises.

'Paul!' she shouted and ran into his embrace.

The huge man enveloped her almost completely and she lost herself in his strength; the father she had never known and the man to whom she owed her life more times than she could easily count. Paul Jhered, Exchequer of the Conquord treasury.

'Happy birthday,' he said.

'So why weren't you at the party?'

'Affairs of state, that sort of thing.' He released her and stepped back, indicating a recliner. 'Talking of which, sit down, Mirron. All of you.'

'What's going on?' Mirron looked at her brothers. 'Well?'

'We just know the Exchequer wanted to talk to us all. That's why we were called back from Morasia,' said Ossacer.

'Former Exchequer,' said Jhered. 'Remember I retired on setting foot back on Estorean soil. Just plain old head of palace security now, and looking forward to my dotage.'

'Except ...' said Mirron, taking a seat and accepting a goblet of water from a servant.

Jhered sat opposite the Ascendants. He was looking good on his fifty-seven years, if a little tired from the journey back from Atreska. He had lost none of his authority. The crow's feet around his eyes gave him a fatherly look when he smiled as he was doing now.

'We had a disturbing conversation with the erstwhile King of Atreska,' said Jhered. 'Look, there's no easy way to say this. If Yuran is to be believed, Gorian is alive.'

Mirron's vision tunnelled and her senses closed in around her. She dropped her water. She felt heat across her face. She couldn't sense the energy maps of her brothers and Jhered any more and the isolation was dark. She was dimly aware she was breathing too quickly but did not have the coherence to stop it.

She closed her eyes and swayed as his name washed through her. Images flashed before her. His beauty, his fury. All from a time long ago that would always remain yesterday. A decade past that she could only ever push aside, never forget.

There were arms about her, trying to calm her. She couldn't settle her mind. She didn't know if she was going to laugh in relief or cry in desperation. For all they had grown to hate his memory, they had never wished him dead. But the knowledge of his survival brought such problems with it. It was a boulder dropped into the slowly calming pool of all their lives.

'What do we do?' It was her voice speaking, but distant as if through a closed door. 'What do we do?'

She felt the same heat in her gut she had first experienced when she was just a little girl, seeing his beauty for the first time. She cursed herself for it and for the confusion it sparked within her.

'Hey, it's all right.' Arducius's voice laid calm across the torrent of her mind. 'Take it easy. Come on. Have a drink.'

Mirron opened her eyes. They were fogged with her tears and she wiped at them angrily.

'Sorry,' she said, taking the goblet of watered wine from Arducius. 'Thank you, Ardu.'

'No, it is I who should be apologising to you,' said Jhered.

Mirron took a sip and looked at her brothers. Ossacer's face had fallen and he was biting back tears. Arducius just looked achingly sad.

'I think we all knew that he would resurface one day,' said Ossacer quietly. 'We haven't talked about it for years but I don't think any of us ever really believed he had died out there.'

Jhered's forehead creased. 'If you thought that, then we should have been searching for him all this time.'

'And where would we have looked?' asked Arducius. 'The Conquord is massive, Tsard an unmapped vastness. We would never have found him. He was always clever.'

'But we left him unmolested,' said Jhered. 'Roberto Del Aglios wanted him dead when we had the chance. We decided to let him go free. Will we live to regret that decision, I wonder?'

'He was just fourteen,' shouted Mirron, finding release for her anger. 'We were all just fourteen. And despite what he did, we couldn't stop caring for him, not for years after. Even you, Paul, because you supported us at the time. We can't afford to dwell on the past. What do we do now? And how is it he has reappeared?'

The Ascendants' attention switched back to Jhered.

'What did Yuran say?' asked Arducius.

Jhered leaned forward and took a deep breath. Mirron could see him recalling unsettling memories.

'You know he was actually relieved when he was deposed?' Jhered shook his head. 'When he began to speak I thought it was because he was scared at the prospect of his execution. I mean, he was, but that wasn't the whole of it, not deep down. Gorian terrified him. Used him to gain access to King Khuran and then deserted him when the Conquord was building to retake Atreska.

'Yuran says he has quickly grown to prominence in Tsard and is the key adviser and power behind the throne already. That's if you choose to believe it.'

'But that wouldn't scare Yuran on its own though, would it?' said Ossacer. 'He's done something, hasn't he? What?'

'This sounds absolutely ridiculous I know but Yuran says he is experimenting with animating the dead. And that he has succeeded. Yuran believes he has taken the ability to Khuran and wants him to begin a new war with the Conquord, using this new weapon.'

Mirron heard the words and felt the distasteful sensation of perverse sense. A memory as clear as yesterday filled her.

'You remember, don't you?' said Ossacer. He was exhibiting the same fear in his lifelines.

Mirron nodded. 'He spoke about it in Lubjek's Defile. What did he see, I wonder?'

'Hold on,' said Jhered. 'What did he speak about?'

'Back when we saw all the dead in Lubjek's Defile during the war with Tsard,' said Arducius. 'We all stood about feeling sick and Gorian was fascinated. He said something about the dead having their own energy. I said it would be the rats under the piles of bones. He didn't buy that. Mirron's right. He saw something, he must have done.'

'You believe Yuran's story? It still may be the words of a desperate man, who'd say anything to save himself.'

'But you said yourself it wasn't to do with his execution. You saw him. What do you think?' asked Ossacer.

'I think it the most outrageous thing I have ever heard. And I wanted to believe that he was doing it simply to prolong his sorry life. But Megan was there too. We both questioned him. And we both came to the same conclusion. He believes utterly in what he says he saw. Now, whether he has drawn flawed conclusions, I don't know, but I do know that we can't ignore him just yet. Not until you have had the chance to speak with him yourselves. Not until you three and the Echelon have had a chance to establish whether this concept of reanimating the dead is possible or simply a, I don't know, an illusion or a trick of the light or something.'

Mirron stared at Jhered. Through their long friendship she had come to know him as a realist without peer as well as being someone with a nature far more generous and kind than his outward persona would ever show. But for the first time, she saw uncertainty there.

'This is beyond any of us,' said Mirron. 'If it's true, it's something we have never researched, never even considered.'

'Where's Yuran now?' asked Arducius.

'In the cells below the palace,' said Jhered. 'Look, I'm finding this hard to rationalise.'

'No surprise there,' said Ossacer.

'No indeed. But if there is a threat, we need to assess it. I'm going to see the Advocate now to brief her on what we know so far. She's going to want quick action on this so we have to assess the truth of it and also the potential of this ability, if it is true. We can't afford to place our border forces on alert unless we are sure Khuran is coming for the Conquord again. You know the delicacy of relations across our territories.'

'And we also know the delicacy of our own position,' said Arducius.

Jhered nodded. 'I was going to mention it. As and when this gets out, the Ascendancy will gain more enemies and have a lot of questions to answer. You will take the blame whether you like it or not. Be careful. All of you.'

Jhered rose and smiled unconvincingly.

'Go and speak to Yuran. Get your own account of this. Get the Echelon working on it. The trouble is, I don't really know what it means. Is it a theory that has no application or something else? Yuran was sure there was real weapon potential in it. I have to know if he's right. I have to know if we need to be gearing up for a war we do not want and may not be able to repel. I have to know what the legions might face.'

There was a prolonged silence following Jhered's departure. The void inside Mirron felt like grief. It wasn't hard to look forward and see the collapse of all that they had been building.

'So, he's alive, then,' said Ossacer.

'We have to be strong,' said Arducius. 'Don't let him obsess us or change us.'

'How can we possibly do that?' said Mirron. 'He's already got to the Exchequer.'

'I mean, the work of the Academy must go on. We have to believe in the ethos of the Ascendancy and never deviate from the education of our new Ascendants and of the wider public. But we have a blight on us now and we have to counter it.'

'That's all lovely talk Ardu, and I look forward to hearing you repeat it to the Advocate and the Echelon. But what are we actually going to *do*?' said Mirron.

'It's quite simple,' said Ossacer. 'I don't see the point of investigating whether Gorian can do what is rumoured. All we have to do is track him down to wherever he is hiding and when we do, kill him.'

'This is nothing more than opportunism. And you will regret it.'

Herine Del Aglios, Advocate of the Estorean Conquord, stood up from her recliner and walked to the open balcony. Estorr sparkled in the cool sunlight. The air was fresh, scented with dawn rain and drenched in the taste of the new season. But Herine's heart remained set in dusas ice.

'We regret the necessity, not the decision itself.'

Herine turned back and stared hard at Ambassador Tharin of Dornos. He had grown very old in the years since the Tsardon had all but torn the Conquord apart. His huge eyebrows were completely white now and his face had sagged alarmingly, giving him the look of an ageing bloodhound. Liver spots covered his hands and he was unsteady on his feet. His toga, slashed with Dornosean lilac, covered a body that was withering quickly.

Yet he was still proud and authoritative in his dealings. Herine had watched his position regarding Dornos and the Conquord harden. She had seen it from a number of her territories. Tharin, though, had played his hand with the assured timing of a master. Bahkir, under marshal law for four years now and with an Estorean consul sitting in the palace at Sungmai, should have watched him.

'That statement makes no sense, Tharin.' Herine sighed. 'You have waited until we are committed to the pacification of Atreska to take your disastrous course of action. Presumably, you feel we will ever be too weak to enforce our will on Dornos in the future. You will find that you are mistaken. Though perhaps you will be safe in the embrace of God by that time.'

Herine stopped herself from scoffing at the expression of hurt on the man's face.

'Herine, please. We are friends.'

'Were. Be happy I am not having you tried for treason. Diplomats have many rights not granted to the common citizen. Sometimes I regret the passing of certain of my more inclusive laws.'

'I've been trying to tell you for years how badly we have been struggling. Yet still Jhered or his lackeys come every season with their criminal demands for levies, both men and money. We cannot, we will not, sustain it.' Tharin coughed. His whole body shuddered with the effort. A little blood flecked his lips.

Tharin wiped his mouth with a cloth. Herine signalled a servant to pour him some water. She looked away from the ambassador again, seeking to compose herself. She caught her reflection in a mirror glass hanging above an ornate, leaf-carved fire mantle.

Her make-up had covered most of the lines on her face but she was always careful to ensure she looked authoritative, ignoring the trend to try and appear as young as possible. That did not befit the Advocate at the age of eighty-two. She was proud of the grey in her hair. Signs of a life spent in the service of her citizens. Nonetheless, Herine still felt vibrant and refused to contemplate old age. She adjusted the circlet of gilded leaves in her hair and ran her finger along her nose, wishing as ever that it had been more sculpted. She smiled to herself before turning back to Tharin; that she should still suffer vanity at her age.

'You know there is a man not two hundred yards from here who could cure you, whatever it is you have. And there will be more like him. Able to save citizens who once had no hope.'

'They represent your greatest weakness, Herine,' said Tharin. 'I would rather die than have one of your Ascendants touch me.'

'You will undoubtedly get your wish,' snapped Herine.

'Don't you see they are the root cause of the Conquord's struggles since the war?'

'I know the job of education is not complete.' Herine retook her seat and stared across the table at Tharin, wondering where she had gone wrong with this man.

'Is that what they tell you? Your advisers and the Ascendants? The sweetened story that nothing is wrong that a little teaching won't cure?'

'You think I don't know the poison that the Order is spreading?'

'And there you sum up the problem you face,' said Tharin.

Herine paused and frowned. 'Speak.'

Tharin took a deep breath and composed himself, dabbing at his mouth and his forehead. Sweat was on his brow.

'You are the appointed representative of the Omniscient on this earth. And yet your disdain for your own Chancellor is common knowledge. In pursuit of your Ascendants, you have turned your back on your own religion.'

'Oh!' Herine threw up her hands in exasperation. 'A decade and still you don't understand? The Ascendants are part of the Omniscient, they do his work. They are not a replacement. You know what we have uncovered. You know this strand of our religion existed before it was outlawed by those who feared its capacity to undermine their power. That fear still drives Felice Koroyan. So be it. I no longer recognise the religion the Chancellor claims to follow. It is not mine. I only regret the Senate's refusal to let me remove her.'

'I understand exactly what you think you are doing, Herine. But the ordinary citizen has not seen what you have and you cannot be surprised that they remain scared of this new power they see you supporting. The citizen is confused. He no longer knows if the generations of Omniscient beliefs he has taken to his heart are true. He feels undermined by you, his Advocate, and he fears the violent influence of the Chancellor.

'He cannot trust what he always took to be the truth. You should talk to Felice. She'll tell you. For every citizen who keeps faith with her doctrine or who chooses to turn to the Ascendancy strand, ten revert to the ancient faiths that dominated before the Conquord came. You're breaking the Conquord more effectively than any action Dornos takes ever could.'

'You're attempting to render me responsible for Dornosean treachery? Ridiculous. Refusal to pay levies has nothing to do with religion.'

'No, no,' said Tharin. 'Your refusal to read the accounts has done that. Your confusing signals over the Omniscient are merely cement over the cracks. My people are poor and they are hungry. And they will not pay any more to keep you in wine, Estorr in fresh paint and your legions staffed to wage war. That time has passed. Peace and stability must rule. We want the friendship of the Conquord. We want trade and alliance. We can no longer suffer dominion. It is ruining us.'

Herine laughed. She couldn't help herself.

'You think the Conquord is no longer in danger? God-embrace-me, do you never look beyond your borders? The Omari have not ceased their aggression and Conquord legions stand on your borders keeping them back. The Tsardon have not gone away. Like us, they await a return to full strength. My own son is in Sirrane, trying to forge an alliance that might just save us next time they threaten invasion. You think you will be safe because my flag doesn't fly over the palace of Cabrius? You and your Marshal Defender are deluded if you believe that. Remove yourself from the Conquord and make yourself weak.'

'Not so, Herine. We are only under threat because we are part of the Conquord. The Omari are no threat to those who do not threaten them. We have alliances going back generations which were only broken when your flag began to fly in our lands. There is no other way for Dornos. You cannot force your will upon us any longer. When I return to Cabrius, the Estorean consul and all non-Dornosean legions will be expelled. Our agreement with Omari is already in place.'

Herine rose. 'Then go,' she said. 'And do not look to us for aid when your folly is revealed to you and your people are dying in front of you. You think you're clever, timing this when we are diverted to Atreska and Bahkir. It is indeed a clever piece of work. But flawed. Because as all Atreska now knows, and as you will discover, we always come back for what is ours. And the second time, we are not so flexible with our rule.

'Go home and look to your borders north, south and east. Enemies will come and you will beg me for forgiveness before the end. You will get none. I do not know you, Ambassador Tharin.'

'We must still work together as independent nations,' said Tharin.

'We will do no such thing. Dornos belongs to the Conquord. And any who think our relative weakness permanent is making a grave mistake. It is now that I look to my friends and know those who believe in my vision. This chamber is bereft of them.'

Chapter Five

859th cycle of God, 4th day of Genasrise

Herine walked towards the Ascendancy Academy with Jhered at her side. She'd ignored the problems too long. She had hoped the citizens would see the good running through the veins of the Ascendants. But the suspicion had lingered. And the mistrust was stoked by the Chancellor, her large army of faithful Readers and Speakers and, of course, the Armour of God.

Felice Koroyan had proved an implacable opponent. Herine had believed that nothing but time would expose her fears for the falsehoods they were. Nothing but numbers of Ascendants growing to maturity and being seeded from all across the Conquord. The process had begun but it would be a long one. And in the intervening period, more of her doubting territories would question their allegiance. Something had to change.

Herine was scared she was losing the battle for the hearts of her citizens.

They walked into the Academy, its hypocaust-fed warmth comforting now the genastro sun had lost its potency. The former halls of the Chancellor of the Omniscient had been quickly converted into a centre of excellence for all that Felice despised. Herine still remembered the moment. Sweet at the time but she had miscalculated the persistency of Koroyan's hate and the groundswell of support that the Chancellor had maintained this past decade.

It wasn't just Dornos or Bahkir. There was discontent everywhere. Even in Estorr, capital of the Conquord. And she needed strength and solidarity right now or her rule might begin to slip.

Jhered directed her along a marbled corridor, recessed and set with busts of Chancellors and heroes of the Omniscient past. It also held a bust of Ardol Kessian at its western end, welcoming all to the

Academy. The most famous recent Father of the Ascendancy, killed by a Chancellor whose faith he followed so unstintingly. A man Herine had never met but whom Jhered had respected enormously.

'Was it folly, do you think, bringing the Ascendancy in here?' asked Herine.

'It was the only place,' said Jhered. 'Not just because they needed the security of the palace complex. You had to make a statement of their place in the eyes of the Omniscient. And you did. It is an enduring shame that so few seem to have listened to you and believed you.'

'Not even my eldest son,' said Herine. 'And it is he who will succeed me.'

Jhered chuckled. He towered above Herine and she had to hurry to keep up with his easy long stride. Here was one man at least who would never question her authority, even if he sometimes disagreed with her methods.

'I wouldn't worry about Roberto. He'll always be a soldier at heart and he worries about their power as a battlefield weapon in the wrong hands. He doesn't know them like we do. He's been away so long. He hasn't seen them grow as we have.'

'So he's going to be very unhappy to hear Gorian is still alive,' said Herine.

Jhered inclined his head. 'It will feed his concern. But he's not stupid. It makes the Academy even more important.'

'Well that depends on your point of view. An investigation of purity or a school of evil.'

'Don't lose heart, Herine. You're the head of this religion. The people will come round.'

'But how long will it take? Another decade, twenty years. Forty? We can't afford these divisions. God-surround-me, they should have closed by now but I actually think they are beginning to widen. Why is that, do you think?'

'Ah well,' said Jhered. 'I think I have an answer to that.'

'And?'

'The Order has a House of Masks in every hamlet in the Conquord. Readers and Speakers numbering thousands teach the scriptures every day. And they are backed by almost nine hundred years of history. More if you want to trace the roots back before the Conquord. And the Ascendancy, for all your support, is effectively a guerrilla movement. They ride into towns with your seal, seek out people who would once have hidden and spirit them away. Those that are left behind have nothing but the Order to explain what had just happened. Think about it, Herine. There are only three Ascendants in adulthood.'

'Four.'

'We don't count the other one. They are not enough to lift their deeds beyond rumour. People are yet to believe. Perhaps they never will.'

They passed the library where all the accumulated knowledge of the Ascendancy was stored. A room that creaked with secret history. Herine felt nervous even stepping through the door. On the right, there was a reception room where those displaying signs of active or passive talent were inducted into the Ascendancy. And further on, administration and record-keeping rooms where a knowledge base was building. Over the generations, it would guide and chart the germination of the Ascendancy until, with everyone exhibiting talent sometime in the far future, it would itself become a historical curiosity.

That, Herine had to assume, was progress. Yet there were times when she awoke, anxious at what she was nurturing. It was a feeling that wouldn't quite die.

'So was I wrong to believe in them myself?'

'No,' said Jhered, and Herine could feel the force of his response. 'You made a decision that history will mark as both brave and inspired. But the result is unsettled times.'

Herine nodded and her mood eased. She smiled. 'Great. You know I had thought I might be revered while I was still alive. Posthumous deification is of no use to me.'

Jhered laughed out loud, the sound bouncing from the walls.

'Think yourself lucky. My legacy is one of being the thorn in the side of every citizen. What is of no use to you would be wonderful for me.'

'I know your worth.'

Jhered bowed. 'And in truth, that is enough.'

They stopped outside a small classroom. Mirron was teaching five emerged Ascendants under the watchful eye of Hesther Naravny, the Mother of the Ascendancy. The students were all seventeen years old. They were the tenth strand and developing beautifully. Elsewhere, small groups of citizens, young and old, from across the Conquord were being schooled in an ancient knowledge that until recently had been submerged beneath a tide of prejudice. Most would lose their talents. Some would be asked to become mothers and fathers of future strands. Some would refuse. The wheel turned so slowly.

Jhered opened the door and Herine walked in, waving everyone back into their seats. There was a hush in the classroom.

'I am sorry to disturb, Mirron. Do you mind if we sit in and listen?'

Mirron smiled. 'No, of course not, my Advocate. It is an honour.' She turned back to her class. 'Real pressure on those answers now, eh?'

The laughter was nervous.

'Right. Back to the lesson. Not long to go now. Cygalius, you were in the midst of telling us the theory behind moulding the energy map of quick energy, like fire, from a slow energy. You correctly suggested a tree would be an ideal example. Continue.'

'Um—' The flame-haired youth glanced around at Herine and blushed across his pale features. 'Well, I – um – like I was saying, they – um—'

'Oh, I am sorry,' said Herine, suppressing a laugh. 'I've put you off. Please don't worry. You can say anything you like and I won't know whether you are right or wrong.'

More nervous giggles in the classroom. Cygalius managed a smile, took a deep breath and began to speak. Herine sat back in her chair and listened. Next to her, Jhered settled uncomfortably into a chair far too small for him, grumbling very quietly. For his part, Cygalius grew in confidence under the encouraging nods of Mirron and by the end, he had plainly forgotten who it was sat behind him.

'Very good,' said Mirron. 'Very good.'

Jhered leaned into Herine. 'Just like old times. An Ascendant speaks and I have no idea what they're talking about.'

'Quiet at the back there,' said Mirron.

'Sorry, teacher,' said Jhered. 'It won't happen again.'

The classroom dissolved into laughter. Mirron clapped her hands.

'All right, you lot. As you can see, I have a meeting to attend so you can go. Now I want you all to study Arducius's texts on amplifying rain clouds and prepare yourselves for a practical with the man himself in two days. Today has been excellent. And before you ask, getting you outside to work for others is coming. Very soon. Now go.'

Herine stood with Jhered while the students left the room, giving them a salute which Jhered returned. Their excited babble rose in volume outside in the corridor.

'Do you mean what you said about working outside?' asked Herine.

'We've been assessing them for a season,' said Hesther, taking the lead. 'Their development has been exceptional for a year. Psychologically, they are ready. It's fine control they lack.'

'Good, good,' said Herine. 'We'll take that on in the meeting. Where are the others?'

'In the Chancellery,' said Mirron. 'After you, my Advocate.'

The Chancellery had lost none of its splendour. Tapestries and paintings hung on veined marble walls, depicting the glories of the Omniscient. Statues and busts stood in huge galleries around grand gardens where the sound of fountains lent an idyllic quality to the air. Tundarran weave and Morasian leather upholstered every piece of furniture. Scripture quotes topped every lintel. Sirranean timber formed every table, desk and bed frame. Felice Koroyan certainly had an eye for the finer things in life. None of the scriptures she chose for the Chancellery referred to abstinence. Leastways, not amongst Order ministers.

They were shown into a dining room overlooking an open but netted rockery in which a dozen species of small bird fluttered and water tumbled over beautifully carved stone. Carp lazed in a deep pond.

Food and wine were on the central table. Ossacer and Arducius were already seated and talking. Mirron sat with them as she always would. Herine placed herself in an upright chair while Jhered chose to stand and look out over the rockery. Hesther took her leave. The teaching day had not finished for all.

'You still haven't changed anything in here,' said Herine, taking in statues, furnishings and wall coverings.

'We are tenants,' said Ossacer. 'One day, a Chancellor will live here again and we will sit and eat together as one under the Omniscient.'

'Not any time soon,' said Herine.

'We can but pray,' said Arducius.

'I fear that may not be enough,' said Herine. 'But our theological future is a debate for another day, I'm afraid.'

She paused and studied the Ascendants. All were struggling with the news they'd heard and she had some sympathy with that.

'I don't know quite where to start,' she said, then smiled briefly. 'At home seems the best place.'

'What do you want to know?' asked Arducius.

Herine waved a hand back towards the palace. 'I've just had the Dornosean ambassador telling me that Dornos is leaving the Conquord. He blames the levy of course but deep inside, I think he blames you and your effects on the ordinary citizen, who is confused by the direction our faith is taking. Tell me, is he right? I've heard what my Exchequer has to say. What do you think? Is the Ascendancy tearing the Conquord apart? Am I losing my own people because I chose to support you?'

Arducius blew out his cheeks and scratched at an ear while he sought a response. Mirron was looking a little angry. Ossacer remained stone-faced.

'That was not quite the question I was expecting,' said Arducius.

'Clearly,' said Herine. 'But surely one for which an answer is at your fingertips.'

'The records—'

'Damn the records, Mirron,' snapped Herine. 'They say everything about who you have saved and who has been brought to the Academy and who has been persuaded by your arguments. They say nothing about who has turned their backs on the Omniscient entirely and are now lost to me, you and the Chancellor. I cannot afford any further fracturing of the religious authority on the Hill. Certainly not in the light of our new information. So tell me. What is it really like out there? How long will my servants have to keep scouring the graffiti from my walls—' she pointed in the direction of the Victory Gates '— and from the statues of our great generals out there beyond our little sanctuary?'

'Generations,' said Ossacer quietly.

Herine nodded. 'Well, that's honest at least. Why?'

'We're trying to adapt hundreds of years of teaching. We're trying to bring a truth to people who are mostly unwilling to hear it. And every time we open our mouths, the Chancellor is there to call us liars and heretics. If you want us to educate more effectively and more quickly, you have to remove or gag her.'

At the doorway to the rockery, Jhered drew in a sharp intake of breath and looked round, catching Herine's eye. He shook his head minutely. Herine relaxed just a little.

'As I have said to more people than you have seen dawns, there is nothing I *have* to do. Being the Advocate has its few privileges.'

'I didn't mean to—'

Herine held up a hand. 'I'm talking now, Arducius.'

She stopped speaking and looked down at the table. She took a plate and helped herself to some cut fruit and cured meat. She poured herself a goblet of wine having waved away the servant. She leant back.

'A long time ago, well before the Advocacy had even heard of your existence, Felice Koroyan used to implore me to give her more power. Ban religions, hire more legions, remove difficult individuals. But it is not the Del Aglios way. Felice disagrees with my stance on the Ascendancy and has exiled herself from the Hill to preach her brand of the Order. That is not in itself a crime. That she still calls herself Chancellor is a borderline offence but it is merely the name all know her by. Can I put someone in chains for using the name with which they are familiar? Well, actually, I can in this case but there's another problem.'

Herine sipped her wine and caught Jhered's growing smile. She leaned forward.

'Let me ask you, what do you think would happen if I were to remove Felice from her role as Chancellor? A role that, conservatively, ninety-five per cent of the citizens of my Conquord revere her for?'

Arducius spread his hands. 'Well, surely it would send out the message that the Order must embrace the Ascendancy because you, as His representative on earth want it to be so.'

'Then thank the Omniscient you will never be Advocate. "Must" and "want" are no good to me. You're young, Arducius, but this naïvety is alarming in one in whom I have trusted so much. The moment I depose the Chancellor, I make enemies out of most of my people. They won't see a message. They will see the seeds of tyranny. They will see repression. And how can I be seen to repress the Order? Me. Felice knows it, I know it. So I will tell you what I always told her. You must win the theological argument. I believe in you. Make others do the same.'

'It isn't quite that simple,' said Ossacer. 'But it will get easier. The next strand is almost ready to stand by you. The numbers of passive-ability citizens is growing. The balance is shifting. You have to trust that we will bring the people round however long it takes.'

'So Paul tells me,' said Herine. 'But I don't have the luxury of time. Neither do you. I will not be around for generations, Ossacer, and when I'm gone, Roberto will be Advocate. But even in the intervening period, if I feel I am losing the support of the citizenry, my hand may be forced.'

'But you can't go back,' said Mirron. 'You can't afford to show such weakness.'

'Oh my dear, it would never appear as weakness, believe me,' said Herine.

'You think our approach has been wrong?' asked Arducius.

'Not entirely,' said Herine. 'I support the need to bring Ascendancy potential here to the Hill from wherever it is found. But I think you've recently been neglecting problems which are very close to home. I look out on my capital city and it is still uneasy about you. Ten years on. I know you've only been active for five but even so ... we've all seen the protests and we've read what has been daubed on the walls.

'You shouldn't need a bodyguard to visit Taverna Alcarin, should you?'

Arducius scratched at his head. 'You could argue that this is the hardest place to convince.'

'You could argue but I don't much care,' said Herine. 'Felice Koroyan never comes here because she believes her position to be so strong. And she isn't far wrong is she? The Speakers of the Winds, the Oceans and the Earth have a stranglehold over large parts of the citizenry and you have not been out to oppose them seriously in what, three years?'

Mirron frowned. 'Surely we all felt that with there only being three of us, our priority was communication to the furthest reaches of the Conquord, the message that talents were not evil and should not be hidden. We sat here and decided Estorr could wait.'

'And that has proved to be a mistake, one that I expected you to raise with me.' Herine ate a quarter of an orange. 'But I'm not here to apportion blame. We have new emerged talent ready to take the message outside and they will do so at the earliest opportunity. This will leave you three free to respond to the news Yuran gave up with the torch all but touching his pyre.

'The principal reason Felice cannot win the battle for the hearts of my citizens is that nothing the Ascendancy has done, no action you Ascendants have made, has been anything other than overwhelmingly positive. Is what is coming out of Tsard about to change all that?'

A firm rap on the door to the Chancellery heralded General Harkov's entrance.

'I apologise for interrupting your meeting, my Advocate, but this won't wait.'

'Did you model your behaviour entirely on Paul Jhered's penchant for dramatic interruption?' asked Herine, tight-lipped. 'It is more important than the future of the Ascendancy and perhaps, my Advocacy?'

Harkov paused and darted a glance at Jhered.

'I think it is pertinent to the conversation,' he said carefully.

'Then I am all ears,' she said.

Harkov made a beckoning gesture with his hand and a man walked in behind him. He was wearing lightweight clothes for such a chill day, grey woollen weave and with mountains embroidered on the chest. But then, he was a Karku. Genastro evenings were probably uncomfortably hot for him. He had thick curled hair and a beard and walked barefoot, his long limbs and short body giving him an unbalanced appearance that Herine found very unattractive.

He was clearly tired after a long journey but Harkov had at least seen to it that he was clean from the trail. Finally, Herine noticed his eyes. He was studying them all, brow creased, with a look bordering on sympathy. But there was something else in there too. Herine had seen it often. He was afraid.

'Who—?' she began but was interrupted by the sound of Jhered's steel-shod road boots on the marble and stone floor.

'Harban?' he said. 'Is it you?'

'Exchequer Jhered,' said the man in an accent so thick it was close to impenetrable. 'Please. You must help us. The Ascendants must come.'

Chapter Six

859th cycle of God, 4th day of Genasrise

Harban didn't really want to sit down but the Advocate wasn't going to talk to him until he did. Jhered had spoken quiet words to him and he had acquiesced eventually.

Arducius watched while Harban calmed and accepted a goblet of wine with hands that were shaking so much he needed both to guide the cup to his lips. His breathing was ragged, as though he was in pain, but the fear they had all seen in his eyes had gone for the moment, replaced by a sadness that pulsed all the way through his energy map. It was so powerful that Arducius had to fight back the tears. Ossacer and Mirron were not able to.

'What's all this about?' asked Jhered of Harkov.

'He wouldn't say too much. Just that he had to speak to the Ascendants and it was about Gorian and the dead.'

'They are coming. The mountain will shiver,' said Harban. 'It will fall.'

Ossacer laid a hand on his arm. Immediately, the Karku relaxed and some colour came to his cheeks. His trembling subsided.

'By the Heart of the Mountain, if only every Ascendant was as you are,' said Harban.

'Only one of us has . . .' said Arducius.

'One is enough.'

Across the table, the Advocate cleared her throat.

'Yes. All very dramatic. Now let's have detail and reality. I have other appointments today.'

Harban was silent for a time, gathering his thoughts. Arducius could see the Advocate weighing him up. That Jhered knew and respected Harban had given him significant credibility.

'Many of my people have what you call passive Ascendant abilities.

It has always been so. It is inscribed on the stones of Inthen-Gor.'

'Which is?' asked the Advocate.

'Our most sacred shrine. The Heart of Kark in the mountain.'

'I'm terribly pleased you're so accepting of the Ascendancy but is this history lesson leading to anything significant?'

Harban shot her a sharp glance. 'Had you followed our way, you would not face what you do now. The shunned turn from the light.'

'And what do we face now, Harban?' asked Jhered, interrupting the Advocate's retort.

'A prophecy was written when Inthen-Gor was founded. Its roots are ancient and until the appearance of your four Ascendants, its message went unheeded by most, the inscription a curiosity, a tale of doom that could never come to pass. Now it seems it will.'

'Look ... Harban,' said the Advocate. 'I respect your ways and your beliefs but in this world, my world, ancient prophecies are ridiculed for lots of good reasons. Mostly because they are utter rubbish that you can bend to current events if you really try hard enough. But also because they never suggest a solution. All they do is describe what we already know and can see. Or indeed some inescapable doom which never, ever comes to pass. Don't waste my time.'

Arducius sensed Harban's mood change. His energy map flooded a bright blue, pulsing with white.

'Then you will die in your ignorance.' He stood, flung his goblet to the floor and jabbed a finger at her. 'You insult the Karku. Your clever words will be as acid in your throat when you are overrun. I have no need of your Conquord, only the Ascendants. It is my time wasted talking to you.'

'How dare—'

'Herine!' Jhered was back at Harban's shoulder, pushing him firmly back into his seat. 'Please. And you, Harban. Sit. This gets us nowhere. No one is wasting anyone's time. Harban, you will take care with your words when you speak to my Advocate. Herine, he has travelled well over a thousand miles at his own behest. The least we can do is listen to him.'

The stand-off was brief but the air between them was alive with their anger. Energy from their bodies coiled and spat so bright Arducius had to block it from his eyes. Poor Ossacer had no choice but to stare. It was all he had.

Harban nodded. Herine's eyes narrowed but she sat, smoothing her toga over her legs.

'Perhaps I should relate the prophecy,' said Harban quietly.

'Perhaps you should apologise,' said Herine.

'For what?'

'I am the Advocate.'

'And I want to keep you in that position.'

Jhered coughed and glared.

'All right,' said Herine, waving a hand. 'Get on with it. The suspense is almost overwhelming.'

Harban shook his head. Arducius's heart was hurrying along in his chest, the atmosphere deeply uncomfortable and in his mind a clash of unruly energies played out all around the table.

'"The lost will be plucked from rest by malign hands. Their footfalls will shiver the mountain. Purpose without reason. Triumph without glory. Should the mountain fall, so shall he ascend. And from the new peak shall he and his spawn preside over the tipping of the world."'

Harban spoke with reverence and passion. It was one of those moments old Father Kessian would have called 'portentous'. The discomfort in the Chancellery dissipated. And despite the fact that the prophecy matched much of the Advocate's opinion, she had a frown on her face and was leaning forward.

'Almost poetic,' she said. 'A literal translation, I presume?'

Harban nodded. 'As close as we can match to native Estorean.'

'And what makes you believe this prophecy is coming to pass?'

Arducius saw Ossacer wince at the strength of Harban's emotional reaction. The Karku dropped his head and wrung his hands in his lap. When he looked back up, his eyes were full of tears.

'Because I have seen it,' he said, his voice cracking at the memory. 'My mentor, my guide, my oldest friend.'

'Icenga,' breathed Mirron.

'Dead. I saw him fall. Shot from the mountain like an animal. And then I saw him walking though life had left him.' Harban shuddered and choked off.

The Advocate was nonplussed. 'Presumably he simply survived the fall?'

'Do you think I don't know death when I see it?' Harban's spittle flew out over the table. 'He fell more than two thousand feet on to rock. His body was broken, his blood scattered across the ice. I climbed down to him but he was gone. A single set of footprints were in the snow. And then he was coming towards me. An arrow was in his heart ... how can I describe the walk of a dead man? How can I do that?'

His tears fell and Ossacer's touch calmed him again.

'It must have been terrible,' said the Advocate. 'But let me get this straight. There was no way you could be mistaken? It was your friend, not another? We are discussing you seeing a dead man moving, walking, presumably seeing and hearing. Indistinguishable in any way from the living.'

Harban nodded. 'Excepting that I knew him to be dead. And that in his eyes was all the fear of knowing what he had become.'

'Become?' asked Arducius.

'Even in death, the spirit of a Karku has will. Walking beyond death, Icenga no longer had free will. No man should ever be allowed to master a Karku. Not in life, not in death.'

'I don't—' began Ossacer.

'He was not just made to walk and then cast free,' said Jhered. 'Something – someone – was controlling him.'

'What happened to Icenga after you saw him?' asked the Advocate. 'Where did he go?'

'He died again. This time in my arms. And only when he was released could he tell me what he feared.'

'He could speak too?' said Jhered.

'And he breathed like a living man. But he was not.'

'This is almost all just as Yuran reported,' said Jhered.

Harban started. 'We've had other sightings and rumours in the borders of Kark but no news of anything elsewhere. This Yuran, what is his knowledge?'

'Gorian was with him for almost ten years,' said Jhered. 'If this is Gorian's doing.'

'Who else could it be? The rest of you are here. Where is Yuran? Where did Gorian go?' Harban's eyes were wild and scared again and this time Ossacer was unable to force calming energy on him.

'Yuran is in the cells, Gorian deserted him in Tsard when he met the king,' said Jhered. 'But you need to take a deep breath or two, Harban.'

'I cannot rest. I must know what Yuran has seen. We must know the extent of Gorian's powers.'

'I absolutely agree,' said the Advocate. 'Because at the moment, I don't see that we have a lot to worry us besides losing the theological argument. Difficult in itself but hardly threatening to the Conquord or Kark.'

Harban gaped. 'Gorian can control the dead.'

'By the sounds of it, if we believe it, one dead person at a time. I appreciate the fear it is bound to inspire but one man does not a legion make.'

'One is only the beginning,' said Harban.

The Advocate raised her eyebrows. 'All right. So let's speculate. And let's begin by realising that the only reason we are talking about something as ridiculous as the walking dead is that the things I have seen since I first heard the word "ascendant" make me willing to contemplate almost anything.'

Arducius couldn't help but smile. There were times when being in the presence of the Advocate was a truly terrifying experience. Other times were merely uncomfortable, like today. But always, the capacity for sense wrapped around a little genuine humour, no matter the occasion. It made her a little hard to read at times and Arducius reckoned that was just the way she liked it.

'So, you three,' said the Advocate. 'How does he do it and how many can he control today, tomorrow, next year?'

They looked at each other. Arducius cast his eyes up to the heavens and pointed at himself. Mirron shrugged.

'It's always you who speaks for us,' she said.

'I guess so,' said Arducius. 'In short, we have few answers right now. How he does it, we haven't a clue. All our work is based on the use of life energies. We can't bring life, only amplify it. When something is dead, it's dead.'

'Apparently not,' said Jhered.

Arducius shrugged. 'I can only tell you what we know. Assuming everything we're hearing is true, Gorian has a ten-year head start on us. He was always fascinated by controlling animals, not just healing them. But the most I ever saw him impose his will on were those three gorthock.'

The Advocate leaned back. 'I am hearing nothing that gives me any cause for concern. Certainly nothing that's going to bring down mountains and tip the world, whatever that actually means.'

'You can't dismiss this,' said Harban. 'If we act now, we can stop him before it is too late.'

'For what?' The Advocate was smiling. 'Beyond playing straight into Felice Koroyan's hands, I don't think we have a problem here, do we? I mean, barring a desire to see the little bastard caught and burned.'

'You have no idea what he will be capable of doing,' said Harban. 'He must be stopped and destroyed.'

'There we agree,' said Ossacer.

'Ossie!' said Mirron.

'He will wreck everything we are trying to do,' said Ossacer. 'I said it in the palace and I'll say it again now. We find him, we kill him.'

Mirron sat back, looking at him askance. 'You don't mean that, Ossie. You can't.'

'You cannot cage him,' said Ossacer quietly. 'There is no other choice.'

Jhered had moved to stand behind Mirron and his hand was on her shoulder.

'You all agree with him, don't you?' she said.

When she was younger, she would have cried. Now her overwhelming emotion was one of disappointment. Arducius could see it in her energy map.

'Can you see an alternative?' he asked.

'Yes,' she said. 'We catch him and put him on trial. That's the Conquord way. If he's guilty, he dies. If not, he goes free.'

'We already know he is guilty,' said Ossacer.

'Do we really?' said Mirron. 'How clever of you to be able to decide guilt based on hearsay and a single witness.'

'He murdered Appros Menas and he raped you,' snapped Ossacer. 'What more do we need?'

'That was ten years ago.' Mirron's voice rose a notch.

'Time makes no difference,' said Ossacer. 'It was only our misplaced loyalty to him that left him alive. We can't repeat the mistake.'

'And what do I tell my son when he asks about his father? That we found Gorian and killed him and that one of the crimes we condemned him for resulted in Kessian's own birth?'

'Mirron, we all love your son,' said Arducius. 'But it has been a long time since we thought of Gorian as his father. And as Kessian is subject to Ascendancy rules, you will never tell him who his father was. It has always been the way.'

'And I've never understood it,' said Mirron. 'What possible harm can it do?'

'Oh come on, Mirron. Early Ascendancy history is littered with the deaths of young talents at the hands of their fathers. That is why the decision was taken to keep fathers from knowing the identities of their children.'

'Mirron,' said Herine. 'Too many men fear what they create. And think, if those same men had talents that have gone only to see their children achieve what they cannot.'

'It doesn't matter if it's fair or not,' said Arducius. 'All we need to know is that there were no more deaths after the rule was made. Fathers have to deal with it, children have to understand it. We all did. And Ossie and I do not know who our children are, do we? It hurts but we understand. It is why we do not teach the strand potential where our children might be. We don't know if they have talent and are in the classroom, or are without talent and back in Westfallen. Kessian can be treated no differently.'

'All right, all right,' said Mirron, both hands in the air. 'It doesn't change the fact that what we are planning to do is wrong.'

'Give us a solution that doesn't involve bringing his menace into my city and I'll think about it,' said Herine. 'Until then, I move with the majority. Paul, sorry but I don't think I can let you retire just yet. I need the ears and eyes of every member of the levium in the hunt. And there is no one I trust more to get this job done.'

But Jhered wasn't really paying her any attention.

'Are you all right, Harban?' he asked.

Arducius looked along the seats to the Karku. Harban was staring at Mirron. His eyes were wide and the tremble was back but this time over much more than his hands.

'Gorian has a son? Your son?' he managed.

Mirron nodded.

'Then he must also be destroyed,' said Harban.

A moment's silence.

'You lay one finger on him and I will melt your skull,' said Mirron.

Arducius winced, Ossacer gasped at the weight of her fury through the energy lines.

'He cannot be allowed to join with Gorian. He cannot be allowed to develop to maturity,' said Harban, the desperation of hideous knowledge bringing sweat to his brow. 'The prophecy—'

The Chancellery dissolved into shouts and threats. The Ascendants were on their feet. Harban was protesting his truth. Herine remained in her seat.

'Quiet!'

Jhered's voice bounced from the walls and shuddered through everyone in the room.

'I feel like I've stepped back ten years,' he continued. 'And you are doing it in the presence of my Advocate. You will have more control, do I make myself clear?'

Silence. Nodding.

'Mirron, no one is going to kill your son. He is in the safest place in the Conquord. Untouchable. Harban, I am speechless. What sort of statement was that? We all understand you're scared but that sort of outburst is unacceptable.'

Arducius could see that Harban was unrepentant. He stood up and immediately Jhered motioned to two guards.

'See him to his rooms. See he doesn't leave them without you.'

'Yes, Lord Jhered.'

'I will not kill him,' said Harban. 'That is for you. But you do not understand what you face, and every day you delay he gets stronger. And think on this too. We have been misreading the prophecy for hundreds of years. In Kark our best scholars have always assumed that the "spawn" of the Ascendant is a reference to the dead he controls. But it isn't, is it?'

Chapter Seven

859th cycle of God, 5th day of Genasrise

Mirron stood at the door to Kessian's room at the end of that day. Her beautiful son was sleeping peacefully. She had left the Chancellery in Harban's footsteps and there were guards on her rooms and patrolling the gardens beneath her balconies. Jhered had seen to that but even so, she was scared.

'No one will harm you while I live,' she whispered. 'I will never leave your side.'

Both Arducius and Ossacer had offered to stay with her through the night but she had locked the doors on everyone, determined to face her fear alone and try not to let any change affect her son. She was lucky he wasn't attuned enough to read her true emotions through her energy map but through the afternoon, she had seen him watching her closely. More than once, it was his hand laid on her to provide comfort. He didn't say anything, or ask any questions but it wouldn't last.

'What will I tell you, because it cannot be the whole truth?'

Mirron walked across to the shutters in Kessian's room and checked them again. They were strong and thick against the dusas chill that swept up the hill every year and they covered beautiful stained glass windows that must have cost a small fortune. She leaned over and kissed Kessian's forehead.

'Good night, darling,' she said.

She walked out of his room and closed the single door. Across a hall the doors to her reception and bedrooms both stood open. She didn't approach either of them. In the hall was a recliner stacked with cushions and set with blankets. It faced Kessian's door and was about as far as she could bear to be from him this night. The recliner looked comfortable but it hardly mattered. Mirron couldn't imagine sleep.

She sat down, picked up some papers she was marking. At least just this once, the tedium of the task wouldn't send her to sleep.

Mirron awoke to find lantern lights still burning away at the night. She had no idea what time it was but felt calmer and a little refreshed. The marking papers were scattered across the white marble floor, one or two having travelled almost to Kessian's door over the smooth surface. She felt a breeze on her face coming from her bedroom and shook her head.

'Idiot,' she said.

She pushed herself upright and kneaded the back of her neck where she'd slept at an angle. The palace was quiet. Mirron padded on bare feet to Kessian's door, feeling the chill of the marble on her soles. She cracked his door quietly and looked in on him, pale light from the hallway splashing across his head. Lost to sleep, he lay with his arms flung out and his head cocked to one side.

She smiled and closed the door once more, deciding she really ought to take a leaf out of his book. Guards on the doors and in the gardens, latched shutters. The Omniscient-protect-her, the Ocenii squadron would have a job getting in here, let alone one scared man of Kark.

'Right.'

Mirron walked into her bedroom and felt the cold inside through her stola. She pulled the window closed and latched the shutters. The bed looked very tempting. Lavender bags scented the pillows and the sheets were fresh and crisp. But now she was here it felt just that little bit too far away.

The bedroom door closed. A shape moved from the shadows behind it. Mirron's heart lurched and she stepped back towards the window. It was surely a trick of her eyes.

'Who's there?' she said.

It was no trick. She focused her mind and saw the flares of an energy map in front of her.

'Not another pace or I will burn you where you stand.'

'Harsh words, dear Mirron. And empty. Where will you draw your energy from in a cold, dark room, I wonder? And to what purpose. No Ascendant is prey to flame.'

Mirron flushed so hot her vision blurred. The strength left her body and she sat down hard on the stone floor, grabbing at the bed frame to keep herself from falling prone. He walked forward slowly, a hand outstretched. In the dark, his energy map shone with barely suppressed power and to her struggling mind he appeared wreathed in fire. But it was him. The signature was burned within her forever. She recoiled from the hand. She opened her mouth but no words came out.

'Don't shy from me. I am not your enemy,' said Gorian.

Her vision was clearing. His features began to resolve from the gloom to add substance to the energy map. Memories came tumbling through her mind. Beauty and power. The smile that melted her. The touch under Genastro Falls. And the fury in those eyes.

'You can't be here,' she said. 'It's impossible. Go away.'

He was still walking towards her. She dragged herself to her feet and felt her way back to the shutters. Nowhere else to go. Her heart was slamming so hard in her chest she thought she was going to be sick. She could feel sweat over her whole body and a quiver in her legs that she could not control. She fought to slow her breathing.

'Why are you frightened?' Gorian was frowning. 'I could never hurt you. Not you, Mirron. The only woman I ever loved. The mother of my child.'

Mirron gasped. She wanted to shout. To scream for help. But there was nothing in her but a terror that cast a sheet of white across her energy map, obliterating all else.

'How could you—'

'Oh, Mirron, do you think King Khuran is blind inside Estorr? I know what is going on here. The work that you do and that my brothers are doing across the Conquord. Finally, the Ascendancy is achieving its rightful place. I am proud of you all. But mostly you. Bringing up our son on your own. And what a talent he will surely be. Indeed, already is.'

'You can never see him, never know him,' she said, dredging deep for courage.

'Don't be naïve. Why do you think I am here?' asked Gorian, a smile on his face.

'The prophecy was right,' she whispered. 'You're here for my son.'

'And for you.'

'I'll die before I—' Mirron shook her head. 'What did you say?'

'You must have known I would come back for you, Mirron. I love you. I always have. And you have always loved me.'

Something grew within Mirron that was stronger than fear. She surged forwards and pushed him away so hard he staggered and had to grab at the bed frame to stop himself falling.

'I hoped you were dead,' she hissed. 'You raped me and ran, you bastard. Too scared to face what you'd done. Ten years I learned to live with what you did to me. I have a life. The Academy and my son. From the moment you ran, it didn't include you. And it never will. I grew up, Gorian. Why didn't you?'

Gorian's face hardened and his energy map solidified to a malevolent deep red.

'I know you, Mirron. I know that's not true.'

'I was *fourteen*,' she snapped, clinging on to her self control. 'You know nothing of me. How dare you come here and expect me to pander to your puerile fantasies. You don't scare me, Gorian. For all your cleverness you have no courage. Courage is spreading the word of the Ascendancy over the scars of hate. It is bringing truth to those who could not see it and feared what they couldn't comprehend.'

She gazed at him, finding herself almost pitying him. 'Whatever powers you think you have developed, they will serve only to destroy us all.'

'Ah but what powers they are,' said Gorian, voice low and resonant, his anger gone. 'And how much I can show you. Expand your horizons. I know the real truth.'

'Get out of here, you're making me sick. Just one scream and you'll be ashes tomorrow.'

'You won't do that,' said Gorian, taking a step towards her.

She met his gaze. 'Try me.'

But he only laughed and when he reached out towards her and his energy flooded out over her, she found she had no voice with which to carry out her threat.

The morning sun edging around her shutters woke her. She was in bed, the covers neat around her. The relief of a fading bad dream warmed her and her anxiety on waking already seemed preposterous.

She turned her head. Something was lying on the pillow beside her. She frowned. One of her shutters slapped gently in its frame.

'I loc—'

She flew from her bed, Kessian's name on her lips. She cast aside her bedroom door, past the papers strewn on the marble and the people standing in her hallway. Kessian's door was open. His bed was empty and cold.

Mirron spun round. Arducius stood there. So did Ossacer. And men from the Ascendancy guard. And Jhered. Why were they all here? And why did they wear such pain on their faces?

'Where is he? Where's Kessian?'

She knew she was screaming. None of them spoke. They could only stare at her.

'Help me,' she said, a roaring in her head. 'You have to help me.'

Mirron gasped and ran back into her bedroom. She snatched the ring that lay on her pillow. They all had them, the original Ascendants. Bryn Marr, the Westfallen blacksmith, had made them. They had been too big then, of course and he had not lived to see the teenage Ascendants put them on. She still had hers and was certain that Ossie and Ardu had kept theirs safe too.

She opened her fist and looked at the beautifully engraved Ascendancy symbol surrounding a single letter. Gorian had kept his too. She sat on the bed and let the tears come. They were all standing in the doorway.

'He's taken him. Gorian has taken my son.'

Mirron had Kessian's sailing boat cradled in her arms. She was sitting on his bed, the scent of his room drifting through her, vestiges of comfort quickly diluting, fleeting motes of energy. Gone too soon. Just like Kessian.

It was surreal. The news had spread too quickly to be contained and the palace complex was in uproar. Three ancient corpses had been found. Once young palace guards who'd had the misfortune to encounter Gorian last night. The inquest had begun. The Advocate was demanding answers, the Academy was frightened and messages had gone out to Westfallen to be on their guard. Harban had expressed his regret but it was nothing to do with Mirron's loss. He'd already left to return to Kark, speaking about impending conflict.

Mirron found herself calm and with only the vague sense that she had misplaced something important. She felt she ought to be more desperate and panicked but after the first moments of terror and with the arms of Hesther Naravny about her, she had almost recovered her self control. She knew it was transitory. Like being in the eye of the storm.

'At least we know he will not harm the boy,' said Jhered.

'That is of no comfort,' said Mirron.

'But we must remember it nonetheless,' said Jhered. 'Cling on to it for sanity if not for comfort. This is no kidnap for ransom, no snatching of a child from a loving parent for reasons of rage or revenge. He needs Kessian. And Kessian will slow him down.'

'But we know nothing. No one who saw him enter is alive and no one saw him leave at all. How can that be?' Mirron forced her hands to unclench. She put the boat down before she broke it. 'This is the palace of the Advocate.'

Ossacer shrugged. 'For ten years, we've been teachers and messengers. Gorian's been developing new abilities. Never mind this animation of the dead or whatever it turns out to be, he can obviously do other things we haven't a clue about. Imagine it and don't be surprised if he can do it.'

'Even he will have his limits, Ossie,' said Arducius.

'All I'm saying is, rule nothing out,' said Ossacer.

'We'll find him,' said Jhered. 'But first of all, we need information on how he got in and out, where he's gone. And from you, we must know what he might want Kessian for, assuming it isn't just the desire of a father to be with his son.'

Mirron snorted. 'My son has no father.'

'You know what I mean,' said Jhered. 'It's then we can form a plan and go and get him.'

'We can't take too long,' said Mirron. 'I won't risk Gorian changing him, turning him against me.'

'Don't worry, I'll have him back in your arms before you know it,' said Jhered.

'Even sooner than you think,' said Mirron. 'Because I'm coming with you.'

'And we'll be by her side,' said Arducius.

'I don't think so,' said Jhered.

'Think what you like,' said Mirron. 'But nothing and no one is stopping me going out to get my son.'

'And to kill the one who took him,' said Ossacer.

Mirron bit her lip and wished it wasn't so.

'That too,' she whispered.

Yuri Lianov, Harbour Master of the Gesternan port of Wystrial, put his magnifier to his eyes and looked again at the ship making steady progress under oar towards its allocated deep-water berth. He was uneasy and couldn't put his finger on why.

Since the arrival of a Tsardon invasion fleet ten years before, this bleak port on Gestern's eastern seaboard had been cautious under his charge. Every incoming vessel was watched from the harbour-mouth fortifications and met by harbour officials riding fast boats. Lianov didn't care what flag they flew, he would not be caught out again by one ship or a hundred.

His people had flagged all-clear. Just another independent Tsardon trader from a port in the Bay of Harryn and flying the kingdom's flag proudly from her single mast. It caught in the throat to let them in but Gestern needed the trade and Marshal Defender Mardov had been particularly explicit in her orders. And the ship appeared entirely normal. The skipper was on deck by the tiller, his deckhands were at the rails and the stroke drum beat a standard pace.

Lianov looked beyond the ship and away towards the dockside. It was busy with morning trade. Loading and unloading was taking place at six of the port's ten berths. Shouts floated across calm waters and the smell of the sea, fresh fish and seaweed mingled pleasantly. Lianov handed the magnifier to the fort captain.

'Watch that ship. If it deviates from its given course by one degree, sound the alarm. Something's wrong here, I can smell it.'

'Yes, Master Lianov.'

'I know what you're thinking captain. Too many of these feelings, isn't it?' The captain looked at him, unable to deny his words. 'This time. This time.'

Lianov hurried down the slope from the wide floor of the fort that housed his onagers and ballistae. He ran through the dark and cold of the fort and back out into the sun along the causeway that curved towards the dock. He barely took his eye from the Tsardon ship. Three banks of oars dipped and rose; clumsy like a rookie crew in training. Its wake ran away from the bow, the distance between him and the ship shortening as it neared its anchorage.

Lianov increased his pace. The paintwork on the ship was poor. Peeling and without the aggressive images of Tsardon sea gods that adorned most hulls he had seen. It was clear to him then what it was that had bothered him from afar through the magnifier. It wasn't that the images weren't there. They'd been painted out. It was a sign he understood only too well. Whatever this ship was here to do, the gods did not want to see.

The alarm bell rang out its flat tone from the fort behind him. Lianov broke into a run.

'Archers to the dockside!' he shouted. 'Dock guard to ready. Prime catapults.'

No one heard him at first but the alarm sent the defences into standard order anyway. He saw men and women looking out into the harbour, searching for the source of the threat. Onager arms were winched back. Ballista windlasses rattled and creaked as they cranked. On the surface of the water, gulls put to flight. More bells joined the clamour.

'Tsardon Trireme. Bearing south south-west. Berth seven.'

Lianov pumped his arms harder. The vessel's drum beat faster. She was going to ram the dock, surely. What could they hope to achieve? One ship. He reached the berth. Sailors, dockers and traders had scattered or been cleared from the concrete wall. Bows bristled. Swordsmen stood by. On the artillery towers, flags signalled their crews' readiness.

The bells ceased and the silence fled across the harbour and through the dock. The beating of the drum, the cries of the gulls and the sound of wavelets slapping stone became unnaturally loud. Lianov stood in front of his guards.

'Steady.'

The trireme came on, oars driving her through the water. She had to be making nine knots. Lianov frowned and shook his head. He sensed unease and confusion behind him.

'Tsardon trireme!' he bellowed though he doubted the skipper could hear him. 'Turn your vessel or we will fire on you. You may not land here. This is your only warning.'

The ship came on. It was under a hundred yards distant now. Deck hands were moving forward but without urgency and without any attempt to hide themselves or brace themselves from the inevitable impact. Lianov moved to the right. He could not order artillery fire. There were too many innocents in the bay. But he had no such problem with his archers.

'Ready to fire. On my order, let's wipe that deck clean. And if anyone makes it on to my dock, shoot them too. We'll question anyone who's still breathing later.'

Lianov raised his hand. The ship loomed large now. He could hear the individual creaks of oars and the hull pushing through the water. It was unnerving. The bow was strengthened but would split apart on the deep, heavy walls of the dock. Her ramming spike would miss entirely and the whole would ride up before falling back into the water unless by some mischance, it stuck fast.

'Fire at will,' he said, dropping his hand.

Arrows crossed the shortening gap, coming in across bow, starboard and port rails. Thirty shafts in the first volley and with more archers gathering all the time. Lianov saw most of them miss but two or three found targets. Sailors were knocked from their feet or stumbled to their knees. At the stern, the skipper did not flinch.

A second volley flew. More accurate this time. Six men struck down. Lianov's grunt of satisfaction died in his throat. He hadn't seen it immediately but there was no doubting it now. Every single one of those hit by an arrow, whether in head, body or limbs got straight back to his feet and continued on as if nothing had happened. He could see blood on shirts and bare chests but not one of them reached down to check their wounds or even so much as look at them. Like they didn't know or care that they had been pierced.

'God-surround-us all,' he breathed.

Two volleys later, the ship struck the dock. Lianov felt the vibrations through the thick concrete. He saw chips fly away from the impact zone and watched timbers buckle and crash inwards. The ship drove hard up the side of the berth. His guards backed off a pace. Swords were drawn, more arrows were nocked and ready. Fear washed across the dockside. He could almost taste it and looking down at his hand, he saw his fingers trembling.

But no one came to the rails to lead the assault on to the dockside. Through the smashed timbers, Lianov thought he could see movement but it might have been a trick of the light. He could hear a scrabbling sound from within. None of it made sense, certainly not the fact that the drum was still beating time and as many oars as could were still moving, apparently trying to keep the ship against the dock.

Something moved on the bow deck. A flash of black. Lianov looked again but it was gone. Smoke billowed into the air. There was a fire below. Some of the guards started cheering but a heartbeat later there was black everywhere, and the cheer faded to nothing. Driven by smoke and flame they came. Thousands of them, scrambling over each other in their desperation to escape. Over the bow rail and boiling from the smashed hull. Rats. Tens, dozens, tumbled into the sea. But for every one that fell, ten more made it to dry land.

This wasn't any accident. This was cargo.

'Kill them!' shouted Lianov, drawing his gladius. 'Kill them all.'

Hopelessly, guards dropped bows and pulled swords and daggers. Two men were carrying a pitch fire down towards the ship. Rats scurried towards them.

'Pour it over the dock,' ordered Lianov. 'I want every one of these little bastards gone.'

But it was already too late. Lianov stamped and slashed as the rodent tide coursed around him and his men. The rats were already scattering towards nearby buildings and the streets that led into the town. He heard screams and cries and saw people running.

Lianov gave up and tried to ignore the hideous feeling of rats running over his boots. He stared back at the ship from which flames and smoke were spiking and clouding. The last few stragglers were coming out now. One of his guards had taken the brave decision to leap on to the broken bow timbers. Below, the oars had stopped moving but the ship was jammed fast. Archers came up in support, other swordsmen with them.

'Get me one of the crew,' said Lianov. 'I don't care who it is just so long as he talks.'

The guard shook his head and jumped back onto the harbour wall.

'It's an inferno in there,' he said.

'Well why aren't they trying to get off?'

The guard shrugged. 'Because they're already all dead, sir.'

Lianov made a move towards the ship but that wasn't his priority despite what he'd just heard. There was only one reason a ship would deliver such a cargo. Instead he turned back to the town and watched his guards chasing a last few rats. Most had already escaped into the town to spread whatever it was they were carrying.

He had to get hold of the Praetor and the Order Speaker to quarantine the whole port. And then he had to send a message to Katrin Mardov. It was just like he'd always suspected. The Tsardon were coming back to finish what they had started ten years ago.

Chapter Eight

859th cycle of God, 6th day of Genasrise

He pitied them even while he respected their diligence and determination. An extraordinary effort backed by undimmed belief. But all misplaced. They had sought the supplication of the masses when all they really needed was time to experiment, to learn and to grow.

He had a little time to think on his way back to his ship out in the sound beyond Estorr's harbour. The boy clutched to his powerful body was so stricken with fear he did not so much as twitch a muscle or utter a word. This was beyond his comprehension. Indeed it was beyond everyone's. Yet it should not be. It was merely the extension of a theory all four Ascendants had known since they were teenagers.

Moulding the elements. They could thin cloud and earth, so they could thicken both too. And the air. With a tiny gale at his back and the molecules pulled into dense form below, he skated across thickened air two hundred feet above the ground. It was exhausting and he'd broken bones developing the ability but to anyone looking from below it would look simply astonishing.

Gorian could fly.

'It'll be over soon, little one,' he said. 'And one day, I will teach you and we will rule the sky as well as the earth together.'

The boy clutched harder but there was only self-preservation in the gesture. Gorian was beyond the harbour now. He lost some height and speed, feeling the lessening drain on his mind and body like a cool healing balm. His ship was already sailing north and east as instructed, benefiting from the prevailing winds blowing up the Tirronean Sea.

Every day was vital now. The Karku already had their suspicions and now his actions in Estorr had inevitably alerted the attentions of the only people who could realistically stop him. But none of them yet had any notion of the scale of his plans. It was an advantage he meant to keep for as long as he could.

He dropped lightly on to the deck just aft of the mast and set the boy down, keeping him close despite the smell of urine that wafted up now they had ceased travel. He understood Kessian's reaction as he did that of the crew. All around them on the ship he could sense unease and fear. It suited him for the most part. They thought him evil, touched by the same gods that they warded against sending them to the bottom of the ocean. They wore charms around their necks and made their symbols and gestures in the air whenever he passed or even so much as looked at them.

Captain Nahran was coming down from the tiller deck. He was a sour-faced man with a shaven head. His powerful frame was scarred from a lifetime at sea and his eyes were hard and cold.

'You have the cargo, I see,' he said.

Gorian prised the terrified boy from him.

'His name is Kessian,' said Gorian, his Tsardon faultless. 'It is a name that speaks greatness and you will treat him as such.'

'As you wish.'

'As you should treat me and address me.'

Nahran raised an eyebrow. 'I have one lord and he is not aboard my ship, Gorian Westfallen. We will make land in Gestern in less than four days if this weather holds. Your boy shares your quarters. See he doesn't get under the feet of my crew.'

Gorian squeezed Kessian's shoulder.

'Go to the rail. See if you can sense dolphins. I'll bet you can if you try. Go on.'

The boy nodded minutely and wandered across the gently rolling deck. His eyes were everywhere, his confusion complete. Gorian turned back to Nahran.

'Remember one thing, Captain. To me, you are transport. A service given to me by your king. And I can always find new transport.'

Nahran chuckled. 'Then do so. Leave whenever you wish.' He gestured at the open sea. 'You are but one man. I have two hundred men and you do not scare me. Fly to the coast if you're able. Otherwise save your threats for those who care to hear them.'

Nahran turned on his heel and stalked back towards the tiller. Gorian watched him go.

'Ocean men. When will you really understand who commands the sea?'

Kessian's knuckles were white on the starboard gunwale. The day was young and the spray ice cold. Dolphins were a remote possibility here.

'What do you see?'

'Nothing.' Kessian shrugged but didn't look around.

'And sense?'

Kessian turned then and Gorian dropped to his haunches, happy to be out of the breeze in the lee of the gunwale timbers.

'Well?'

'Everything.' Kessian stared at him, face and eyes full of uncertainty and dislocation. The stare was long and intense. Gorian began to feel uncomfortable before it was broken. 'You're Gorian.'

'You've heard of me.'

Kessian shrugged. 'They talk about you sometimes. They hate you.'

'They are scared of me,' said Gorian, finding the thought disappointing.

'No. They thought you were dead. They wished you were.'

'Well now they know different.'

Abruptly, Kessian's eyes filled with tears. 'I don't want to be here. I want to go home now.'

Gorian reached out a hand. Kessian flinched backwards and clung more tightly to the rail.

'You're with me,' said Gorian. 'You *are* home.'

'No! I want to go home. I want to go back to my mother.'

'But she wanted you to come with me, didn't she tell you?'

'Liar. She hates you.' Kessian's shout had heads turning on deck. 'You're bad. You're what we must not be.'

Gorian felt like he'd been slapped. 'Who told you that?'

'Everyone knows it,' said Kessian, distracted for the moment. 'Mother Naravny teaches us and everyone says the same thing.'

'What do they say?' Gorian wasn't sure he wanted to hear the answer.

'They say you hurt people with your abilities and you shouldn't have. They say you ran from justice and that you are the one who will spoil it for all the rest of us.' Kessian frowned.

'Don't they say how I helped save the Conquord? Don't they tell how I helped us escape Westfallen when the Order would have killed us all?'

Kessian shook his head. 'They say we must control ourselves or become like you. Now take me home. Please.'

Gorian sat with his back to the side of the ship and shook his head. That they would do this to him after all he had meant to them. Still meant to them.

'I want to go home!'

Kessian's voice was rising to a shout. Gorian glared at him.

'Calm down, Kessian. You know you aren't going home. You're with me now. Father and son on an adventure.'

Kessian froze and his face reddened with an anger Gorian well recognised. 'You aren't my father,' he screamed, voice carrying clear through the ship and across the water. 'You aren't anything. I don't want to be on this ship. I don't know what I'm *doing* here! Take me home. Take me home.'

Gorian's look made the boy flinch backwards. In his mind's eye he had seen Kessian running into his embrace, desperate to be with the one who had given him life. Instead he got this ... this screeching abuse. He grabbed Kessian's left arm above the elbow and hauled him to his feet.

'You need to learn your destiny,' he said. 'Come with me.'

'I don't want to—'

Gorian let it happen. He pulsed cold down his arm and let it flow into Kessian's arm through the break he made in the boy's energy map. Kessian yelped and tried to pull away. He was strong in Gorian's image but he did not yet have Gorian's build.

'You have pushed me far enough.'

He pulled the boy towards the fore hatch and thrust him down the steep stair. Kessian half-fell and sprawled at the bottom, looking up and trying to back away. Gorian jumped down after him, grabbed him to his feet again and marched him to the quarters they were going to share. Behind a rough curtain, two narrow cots were crammed into the tiny space. Gorian's few belongings were strewn across his bed. He threw Kessian onto the other cot.

'Does it hurt?' he asked, indicating the boy's upper arm where it was being clutched.

There were tears in his eyes when he nodded. The fury had gone, replaced by new fear.

'I didn't mean to hurt you,' said Gorian quietly, feeling a stab of guilt. 'I had to make you quiet.' He sat on the bed next to him. 'You have to understand that I cannot be undermined in front of the crew like that. I will not stand for it. You must respect me as they must, do you see?'

'I don't know what I'm doing here,' whined Kessian. 'I just want to go home.'

Gorian sucked his lip and breathed in slowly, desperate to calm himself. The thoughts chased themselves around his head. Over-whelming the rest was a sense of deep disappointment. The boy was not what he expected at all. Weak. More like Ossacer than himself. He pushed his forefingers into the corners of his eyes and cleared his throat.

'Look, Kessian, I know this must be hard for you to accept but your life has changed.' An idea struck him. 'Did Mirron, your mother, ever tell you how her life changed very suddenly one day?'

'Father Kessian Day,' said Kessian quietly. 'We remember him and the day every year.'

Gorian smiled and with it came the sense of loss that he experienced every time he dwelt too long on memories of Westfallen and all those he had loved and who had abandoned him.

'It's right he is remembered,' said Gorian. 'It's a tragedy you could never know him. But at least, the others won't sully his memory, will they?'

'They loved him.'

'As did I.'

'Why did you bring me here?'

'To fulfil your promise. To achieve that which the Academy and all who run it would deny you with their teaching.'

Kessian stared at him, face blank and confused. There were tears in his eyes and he was kneading the thin blankets rhythmically.

'I don't know what to say to you,' said Gorian. 'Your mother had to leave Westfallen to find the strength within herself. So did I and Ossacer and Arducius. We were all unhappy about it at the time but we can all see what it did for us now. That's what is happening to you.'

'But I didn't ask for it to happen,' said Kessian.

'Do you think I did?' Gorian shot to his feet. 'Do you think I chose to see Father Kessian murdered before my eyes and be chased from my own home? Do you? Stupid child. At least you are in a safe place. We were cast adrift without friends or sanctuary. No one asks for things like this to happen. They just do. And the mark of who you are is how you rise to meet the problems you face. Your mother did, I did. You must.'

Kessian stared up at him. His chin was wobbling as he fought to contain his tears.

'But I can't do anything. You had to stop a war. You've just taken me from my home. Isn't that my only problem?'

Gorian sat back down. 'No. Your problem is facing up to who you are. And welcoming your destiny. And that is to sit with me while I rule this world of ours.'

Kessian's eyes widened in surprise but at the same time, a smile tugged at the corners of his mouth.

'The Advocate is the ruler. She won't let you do that.'

'No?' Gorian shrugged. 'I can see you don't believe me but one day soon, you'll stop laughing. You see, I know more about you than you think. You're a very special boy. The only male child born of the original Ascendants.'

'I'm still too young,' said Kessian. 'I can't do much.'

'Really?' Gorian's voice dropped low and he felt pride through his veins when he spoke. 'I have felt you ever since you were born though I was thousands of miles away. It is how I knew the time was right to come for you, to free you.'

'I don't—'

'Shh.' Gorian held a finger to his lips. 'I'm speaking. Listen to me. You can do so much more than any other Ascendant of your age, can't you?'

'No,' said Kessian sharply. 'Everyone knows that I won't fully emerge until I'm thirteen or fourteen.'

'Everyone but you and I,' said Gorian. 'Your mother doesn't look so she doesn't see. But I have. I felt it happen across the endless miles but it was so brief a thing that even those closest to you missed it. You emerged, didn't you? Over the course of a few hours not days like everyone expected. And early. Years early. I have touched your life energies and I know. Don't deny it, Kessian. You have the power at your fingertips now, today.'

Kessian's head dropped and he scratched the top of his head. Gorian put a hand under his chin and tilted his face back up.

'What's wrong?'

'Everything!' shouted Kessian. 'It shouldn't have happened. It means I'm not like the others. Not normal. It means something is wrong with me.'

Gorian drew in a sharp breath. 'You're *ashamed*?'

Kessian nodded. 'I have to hide it until I'm ready.'

'No, no,' whispered Gorian, happy to accept the gift he had been given. He stroked Kessian's beautiful blond hair and for the first time the boy didn't recoil from the gentle touch. 'Don't be ashamed, be proud. Can't you see why I was right to liberate you from the Academy? From your mother just for now? You felt you had to hide what you were because you think they won't understand. And you're right, they won't. They'd want to study you, hold you back until they thought you were safe to be taught again.

'With me, that won't happen. You are far ahead of any other Ascendant. Far ahead of where I was at your age. But I'm not scared by that, I'm excited by it. Because it means your potential for shaping your abilities in the right way is that much bigger.'

Kessian's face had cleared a little and Gorian felt that for the first time, he actually had his son's attention.

'I will teach you to understand what you are feeling and how to tap the well of your power. I'll teach you the things you would never have been taught at the Academy. The things they think are dangerous but are the birthright of every Ascendant. You want to learn, don't you?'

Kessian nodded.

'Well, I will help you and in return, you will help me. I won't ask you to do anything you don't want to do. You won't harm anyone, I promise. And neither will I harm anyone who believes in me. In us. And one other thing I promise is that you will see your mother again. I can't say when but you will. One day, we will all stand together. A proper family.

'So, what do you say? Do you want to try?'

The confusion was back on Kessian's face. Gorian could understand it readily enough. He smiled and ruffled the boy's hair before standing up.

'All right, look, this is all too much to take in, isn't it. I'm sorry to have to do it to you, all right?'

Kessian nodded and the tiniest smile appeared.

'You're scared, you don't know me and you don't know where you are or where you're going. Hey, are you hungry?'

'A bit.'

'All right then, here's what I'm going to do. I'm going to leave you to think about all that we have spoken about. And then I'll bring you some food and see what you think. And Kessian. Let me promise you one thing more. I will never let anyone harm you. While you are with me, you are safe and secure. You're my son, whatever you think about that right now and that makes you precious beyond measure.'

Gorian pulled the curtain across the opening and walked back to the stair and up to the deck. Whether he had turned Kessian at all, he was unsure. But one thing was certain. He had been right about the enormous capacity for his power. And it could be tapped and used. It would make Gorian ten times the man. More.

The first keystone was in place. He looked west towards Gestern and imagined the snow-capped heights of Kark.

'And you're next,' he said into the wind. 'Then it can truly begin.'

Chapter Nine

859th cycle of God, 8th day of Genasrise

Katrin Mardov, Marshal Defender of Gestern, asked an aide to bring back the messenger from Wystrial. She rested her head in her hands as she sat at her desk in Skiona's basilica. It had been impossible to ignore the signs for some time now but this was a direct strike. This was an act of war.

The Tsardon had been camped in some numbers to the north of Kark throughout dusas. Estorr had dismissed the move as posturing but Mardov had reinforced the northern border with Atreska and offered troops to Kark nonetheless. A thousand legionaries were in the mountain country even now, scouting and advising. She didn't like the tenor of the reports she was getting.

And now this. She'd always said Tsard would be back to finish the job they'd so nearly completed ten years ago. That they were better prepared in every respect. Only Paul Jhered really listened to her. Everyone else in the Conquord hierarchy was too busy assuming Tsard would be in a position identical to their own: no funds, no armies of any real significance, licking deep wounds and considering reinvasion a monumental folly in the short term. They didn't know the Tsardon mind like she did.

The messenger returned and stood in front of Mardov's desk in the small office. She was tired but had been granted time for a wash and a change of clothes. Mid-height, young and plain, she stood to attention until waved to be at ease.

'What's your name?' asked Mardov.

'Fleet Corvanov, Marshal.'

'Really? A bit young to be a Fleet already, aren't you?'

Corvanov blushed. 'I ride well,' she admitted.

'That much is clear by your timely arrival.' Mardov paused. 'So tell me. Any exaggeration in this message?'

'No, Marshal.'

'And how do we know it is Bitter's Plague?'

'I suppose we don't know for certain. But it's what sea rats from Tsard typically carry, so the doctors say.'

'Assume the worst, eh?'

Corvanov dropped her gaze. 'Yes, Marshal.'

In fairness, a deliberate attack by a plague ship was the only likely explanation and hence the only likely plague was Bitter's. Mardov sighed. It would reduce Wystrial to a ghost port. So-called because of the bile that eventually clogged the throat, Bitter's Plague was a virulent blood disease that carried in the air and attacked through the lungs. It could be passed by touch too.

It killed ninety per cent of the affected within five days, poisoning the bloodstream, starving the vital organs of nourishment so that they simply shut down. It was a painful and frightening way to die. The only reason Mardov knew Corvanov was not a carrier was that she was still alive. The grace, if it could be termed such, was that the airborne spores died quickly and could not travel far without a new host.

'How effective is the quarantine?' asked Mardov.

'It was in place as I left but some may have escaped the net,' said Corvanov. 'I think we're all relieved Wystrial is remote.'

'Indeed. Damn but this is low even for the Tsardon. No reports of naval build-up offshore?'

'None,' said Corvanov.

'Something else that confused me. A note Harbour Master Lianov made on the message. Here ... "They seemed impervious to our arrows, though they appeared to wear no armour. Yet when we boarded the ship after the rats had fled into the town, all on board were dead." Presumably they took their own lives?'

'That isn't my understanding, Marshal,' replied the Fleet. 'If the reports are accurate, they all appeared to have been dead for some days. There was decomposition evident in them all.'

'I beg your pardon?'

'I'm sorry, Marshal, but it was the last I heard before Lianov had me leave to lessen my chances of contracting the plague.'

'It makes no sense. Whoever made the report must be mistaken, surely some ship-borne problem or they were all dying of the plague themselves. Makes you wonder what sort of man will willingly sail to his death, doesn't it?' Mardov shook her head. 'And Lianov?'

'I don't know. He wouldn't come close to the messenger post. He shouted the message to us from the gates and had me read it back to him. That's why there is no seal.'

'I guessed as much. Well, decisions are simple. Tsard will invade through Wystrial and the western coast, I have no doubt. Corvanov, I will give you a choice. You can either take my messages to Estorr and speak to Exchequer Jhered and the Advocate or you can travel ahead of whatever force I can muster to defend Wystrial. Which is it to be?'

Corvanov shrugged. 'Wystrial is my home. I would be nowhere else.'

'Good answer. Go and get some rest and you'll receive your orders at dawn tomorrow. But before you do, go to the messenger office and send me the best two Fleets there. Someone has to go and tell the Advocate I was right and someone else has to warn the Karku, assuming they don't already know.'

Corvanov slapped her right fist into her chest. 'Marshal.'

'Dismissed. And thank you.' Mardov watch Corvanov go. She called over her senior aide. 'I'll need signals sent across the country to prepare for war. I'll need a fast ship and the coastal flags to alert Kester Isle. I need the military and naval councils convened and I have to have some Gatherers sent to Wystrial to enforce the quarantine, together with the Order to sanction the burning of bodies as necessary. Some must fall to protect the mass. And I need it all to happen right now. We can't afford to lose a single day.'

'Anything else?' the aide had a small smile on his face as he finished scribbling the instructions.

'Yes. I want a miracle because I have no idea how we are going to repel a full scale invasion if such it is.'

The smile disappeared. 'I'll report back before dusk.'

Mardov pushed her hands back through her thick grey hair. Something about all this wasn't right. It was piecemeal, a sort of poking at the seams too see if anything tore. But not organised, as if King Khuran was breaking in a new warmaster. Unless she was missing something. One thing she did know was that it smelled bad. Gestern was going to be the front line in a new war and in the quiet of her chambers that night, she would let herself weep at the pain her citizens were going to face.

Roberto Del Aglios was confused. The Sirraneans had taken leave of their collective senses. The force they had described needed to be somewhere in the region of forty thousand strong to believe it could fight its way south to Estorr via Goscapita. Roberto had come to the edge of the forest country to see the Conquord's doom approaching.

And there they were a mile to the south, marching towards the Gosland border. Roberto put down his magnifier and turned to his retinue of six immaculately turned-out green-cloaked palace cavalry, having left the bulk of his people under cover with their Sirranean guides.

'This is either a joke in poor taste or I am looking at the vanguard of a far larger army that we have no intelligence of at present. Captain?'

The young palace guard captain shifted uncomfortably on his feet.

'We are assured this is the full complement,' he said.

'Really,' said Roberto. 'The Sirraneans' definition of an invasion force is clearly somewhat at odds with my own. Invasion farce would be more accurate. This is a hunting party, isn't it?'

'Perhaps a little more than that, my Lord Del Aglios,' said the captain.

Roberto glared at him. 'Just bring the guide to me. And don't ask him the definition of irony while you're there or you'll never learn.'

He took up his magnifier again and had another look. Six thousand men, no more. No horses, a handful of catapults pulled by oxen, a scattering of supply wagons behind them. This was by Tsardon standards of war a force designed for skirmishing, causing trouble and provoking a response, no more. They were still many days from the Gosland border and Roberto was certain they would not cross it. While the Goslander borders were not heavily manned due to their straitened circumstances, they would, given any sort of warning, be capable of holding off this small army.

'So what are they doing?' he asked himself.

'My Lord?' ventured a soldier.

'Nothing, nothing,' said Roberto.

It had to be some sort of show of force or future intent. Either that or they were engineers coming to build fortifications and staging. But there was no other army within a season that the Sirraneans knew about. Ridiculous. Behind him, his captain cleared his throat. Roberto turned.

'Ah, my embellisher in chief,' he said. 'I am surprised you aren't walling in the whole of Sirrane, such is the magnitude of the threat before us.'

The Sirranean frowned and gestured for explanation. Roberto had to remind himself he was a diplomat, not a legion general any more.

'Simply put, Hadadz, the army I can see through my magnifier does not present a threat to the Conquord.'

Hadadz's frown deepened further. The deep coloured skin on his face darkened further with irritation.

'You make a mistake that will soon be too long forged to reverse with any hope of success,' he said. 'You must look further than your eyes see.'

Roberto passed a hand over his face and dragged it hard across the growth of stubble on his chin.

'You're going to have to do better than that,' said Roberto. 'Marcus Gesteris is rushing to Estorr to warn of imminent invasion. I am supposed to be warning Gosland that they are about to be attacked. When they see this lot come over the last hills before the border, they will laugh me out of the country. Do you understand?'

Hadadz nodded after a pause and a smile crossed his face, lighting up his eyes.

'Your mind's clarity will be viewed as obscured,' he said.

'Something like that,' said Roberto.

The smile faded. 'There is more driving this enemy than numbers. More than songs speaking victory and dominion.'

Roberto stared at him. 'Hadadz, they do not have Ascendants and they do not have secret weapons. There are six thousand at best and they will not get across Gorneon's Bridge before they are routed. If you know something different, please, share it with me. Our alliance is new. It would be a shame if it was to be wounded so soon.'

'At their backs is fear of a power their comprehension fails in discerning. Tarenaq said it. And you make a second mistake, Lord Del Aglios. They do have an Ascendant.'

'How do—?' Roberto stopped. 'I'm sorry, you're telling me they have developed Ascendants in ten years? Impossible.'

'No,' said Hadadz. 'Yours that ran has found his home.'

Roberto felt the strength desert him. 'Gorian.' He shook his head.

'Little bastard, I should have cut his throat when I had the chance.' He looked at Hadadz. 'But even so, even if you're right, he's just one man. An arrow will take him. We will find him in the field and kill him. Is he with them now?'

'No. He is distant yet he dominates them.'

'All right, all right. Look, while I think on this, show me what it is you think I should be seeing.'

Hadadz shrugged. 'It is in every face. It bleeds from their souls. They march hard to distance themselves from their masters yet his hand can reach them anywhere. And they do not relish whatever task has been set for their accomplishment.'

While not as poetic as the diplomat, Tarenaq, Hadadz was certainly as verbose. Roberto put his magnifier to his eye again and studied a few faces. He saw nothing immediately out of the ordinary. Unease, anxiety perhaps but . . .

'No, no,' he said. 'That doesn't make sense.'

'My Lord?' it was the guard captain.

'They're over a hundred miles from the Gosland border,' said Roberto. 'And they're scared. I mean I'd expect it when they closed with their enemy but now? Half of them have the look of people being marched to their own executions. Their eyes are everywhere and they are silent, aren't they?'

Roberto looked again. At the head of the march, the commander had stopped, the column following his order. In his eyes there was no fear, only anticipation. He was a tall man, massively built. And what Roberto had taken for a skull cap was nothing of the sort. His face and shaven head were covered completely with tattoos; circular and stud patterns, geometric shapes too.

'Haven't seen his like before,' he said.

'No,' said Hadadz. 'He is from Khuran, from the temples of the damned, where the King's enemies are destroyed.'

'He's an ugly bastard, I'll give him that. So what's he doing at the head of an army marching to Gosland?'

'He brings his trade to the hinterland,' said Hadadz.

'And is it him that the rest of them are scared of?'

'It is what he represents.'

'And what's that, exactly?'

'The shroud that falls upon us all. The net from which none may ultimately escape. Death.'

Roberto laughed. 'I'm sorry, Hadadz but this is like some poor melodrama. I have the utmost respect for the ways and beliefs of the Sirranean peoples but when steel clashes with steel, it is courage, skill and numbers that win the day. They may have none, my legions do. It will be us who bring death if the Tsardon march into battle like that.'

Hadadz didn't appear to be offended. He studied Roberto for a moment while he fought for the right words.

'In the far south, the Karku barricade the mountains though no overwhelming force stands at their gates. And Sirrane shudders though we cannot fathom why. I understand the paths to our truths elude you but they would not elude your Ascendants. They would see. They would feel.'

'I cannot light the invasion beacons on the basis of a feeling,' said Roberto.

But within, Hadadz's persistence was getting to him.

'Then accept there is danger and prepare. Do not cover the sky in flame but never slip your vigilance. We have watched the Tsardon across the centuries. Their respect of time is undimmed, a commodity they do not fritter away. Something is happening and this army holds the key to the floodgates.'

'What?' snapped Roberto. 'It's all just talk and speculation, most of it barely makes sense.'

'Our knowledge is incomplete. This is a warning.'

'And we thank you for bringing it to our attention. I do not mean to be dismissive but you have to see the problem from my perspective.'

'I understand.' Hadadz bowed. 'You should continue to the Goslander border.'

Roberto nodded. 'The honour of your company is bettered only by the promise of more to come.'

Hadadz smiled again. 'My arm and heart are yours.'

'Well, at least we've learned one thing about each other's ways.'

'That road has no conclusion.'

'End, Hadadz. We'd say, "has no end".'

'As you wish.'

Roberto turned back to the Tsardon army. His first sight of them had left him confused and he felt no different now. What he had was a sense of unease that would not go away. Out there was a force any sane man would all but ignore as a serious attempt at invasion. But

Hadadz was right, the Tsardon were not in the habit of wasting time and men on anything. And Roberto had learned enough that if the Sirraneans thought it worrying, then he should do the same.

Convincing the Marshal Defender of Gosland though, that would be something else entirely.

Chapter Ten

859th cycle of God, 10th day of Genasrise

Commonsense had prevailed in the end. That and a few sharp words from Jhered and the Advocate once the boiling emotions had begun to subside. Mirron and fifty Ascendancy guard under Harkov's command would travel with Jhered and two hundred levium to Kark via Gestern to assess any threat and try to gain intelligence on Gorian's whereabouts. Ossacer and Arducius would remain on the Hill to school the new Ascendants who, if Harban was right, would be required in the field rather sooner than anticipated.

'Bit of a role reversal, isn't it?' Arducius tried to sound bright but the joke fell flat.

'Not really,' said Mirron.

She still couldn't quite get to grips with what she was doing or what had happened to her. That Kessian was gone remained almost unreal but for the emptiness in her rooms and the roar of loss that overwhelmed her on an instant. His little sailing boat was drifting in the fountain. She had promised herself that only he would pick it up and move it now she had placed it there.

'You sure you'll be all right?' asked Ossacer.

'I think I'll be safer with Paul than you are around here. Don't think I haven't heard about your plans to go into the city and upset the Order.'

'Well, the Advocate was right; we haven't been to the heart of the Conquord to win them over. Looks like we're getting our chance now,' said Arducius.

'Be careful. The Chancellor won't be far away if she isn't here already. It's not good out there. Harkov says the protests are growing again now news is out that Gorian is still alive.'

There was a knock on the door. A spearman opened it and the

Advocate swept in with Jhered in her wake. She approached down the hall and came to stand by the fountain. Her eyes lingered on the model boat for a moment.

'I'm not happy you're going on this fool's chase,' she said. 'I understand your desire to rescue your son but I think the Exchequer is capable of doing it on his own.'

'I can't stay here, Herine,' said Mirron. 'I can't pace the floor waiting for news. It will kill me.'

'Do not place yourself at risk. This isn't going to be a time for diplomacy, do you understand?'

'Yes, she does,' said Jhered at the Advocate's shoulder. He was looking harassed. 'Now please, say what you came to say.'

The Advocate looked round at him sharply and hissed a few words Mirron didn't quite catch. She had composed herself by the time she looked back at the Ascendants. Jhered was tight-lipped and angry.

'The Order have their demon,' she said. 'It seems much of my staff couldn't wait to spread the story to all that would hear. The mood in the city is ugly concerning you, and Felice will bask in it when she inevitably arrives. So while you two do what you can to shore up my belief in you with our dear citizens, I want you to bear this in mind. Mirron, I want no ifs and no buts. There is no redemption. The future of the Ascendancy hangs on one thing, so far as I am concerned and so I am giving you this order. Gorian is to be caught and he is to be killed, that much has not changed. But when he is, I want his body brought back here because I am going to parade it around the city as a demonstration of my authority. Then I will burn it.'

Mirron made to speak but the Advocate held up a hand.

'No ifs, no buts. I do not care about personal feelings and who used to love who or who is whose father. He is an enemy of the Conquord and he will be hung out for every citizen to see. The people want proof and I will give it to them or you lot can all pack your bags. Do I make myself clear? Good, now get going. My Exchequer assures me the tide is about to turn.'

The Advocate turned on her heel and swept out.

'Short and sweet,' muttered Arducius.

'It is often the way,' said Jhered. 'Come on, Mirron, the carriage is at the gates.'

'Why are you so shocked, anyway?' asked Ossacer. 'It is no more than he deserves.'

'He is still one of us,' she said. 'Even though he must die, we shouldn't disrespect where he came from and what he used to mean to us.'

'Wrong,' said Ossacer. 'He was never really one of us and I for one would love to have the eyes to see him swinging in his gibbet.'

Mirron started. 'You don't mean that.'

'Don't I?'

'You're a bastard sometimes, Ossacer,' she said.

'No, Mirron, I'm a realist. I think you should be too.'

'Much though I hate to break up these loving goodbyes.' Jhered glared at Ossacer. 'The carriage *is* waiting, Mirron Westfallen. We have to go.'

Mirron nodded, confused by her anger. 'Fine. Let's get it done.'

'Good luck, Mirron,' said Ossacer.

'Right,' said Mirron.

'Look after yourself,' said Arducius.

'You too, Ardu. We'll send word.'

'Mirron!' called Jhered from the door to her rooms.

'Who are you, my father?'

'No, but I am the man who'll throw you into the harbour if we miss the tide. Come on.'

She raised her eyebrows and closed the door on her brothers, her fountain and Kessian's sailing boat. Tears threatened.

'Stay afloat,' she whispered.

There were no obvious signs of panic on the river and road journey back to Wystrial, for the most part at any rate. The news of the outbreak had spread halfway to Skiona but those a long way from the port were simply happy to be where they were and reports were that the quarantine had been very effective.

But in the last thirty miles or so, Fleet Corvanov began to feel uneasy. She saw plainly abandoned farmsteads, empty of livestock and human life. The traffic, hardly heavy at the best of trading times, was non-existent, and the last messenger station had passed on rumours and stories that made no sense whatever.

They had warned her not to go near the port, that the station just beyond the gates was abandoned and its staff gone but she could not ignore her Marshal's orders. She had asked others to come with her but they had refused and the fear in their voices and faces was confusing and worrying.

Plague was a strange demon, she considered on the last mile to the messenger station. The gates to the port itself were a couple of hundred yards beyond it. The spectres of unstoppable disease were powerful and difficult to oppose. Rumour and myth grew and spread faster than any virus. But medical facts were, in Corvanov's opinion, the more persuasive weapon. And they told her that anyone moving about in the port today would be free of the disease. Either a survivor or one whom it had passed by. But not sick and not a carrier.

She smiled and shook her head when the crest of a rise granted her sight of Wystrial. The gates stood open. Flags flew across the port. Sails moved distantly, in and out of the harbour. It was quiet but that was no surprise. The breeze was offshore and little sound would reach her ears here. She was heartened to find the ring of soldiers enforcing the quarantine had gone. They'd be inside, helping where they could.

Corvanov pushed her horse on past the abandoned station and down the gentle slope towards the port. It was mid afternoon and the warmth of a bright early genas day was waning. Trepidation moved through her. The reality of what she might find inside began to gnaw. If the plague had swept through the whole population, she could expect to find decay, desperation and grief beyond measure. At least she brought hope with her. People were coming. Help was at hand.

She slowed to a gentle trot on approaching the gates. There were no guards. No one to acknowledge. She breathed deep and carried on. Just a couple of strides inside the port, her horse skittered, snorted and stopped. He was shivering all over, his nostrils were flared and his eyes were wide. He backed up.

'Shh, it's all right. Come on, young fella, I won't let anyone harm you.'

She kicked at his flanks and clucked but he didn't budge. A nervous whinny escaped him. He backed further up and lost control of both bladder and bowels. Corvanov stroked his neck and looked around her.

'All right, all right. Take it easy, there's a good boy.'

Wystrial was tightly packed this close to the gates. Roads led left, right and straight away from her. Buildings crowded close. Doors were hanging open, shutters too. The streets were dusty and strewn with the rubbish of days. And it was silent. There was no one at all as far as she could see in any direction. And inside the walls, with the breeze captured, she could smell the foul reek of decay. She shuddered and dismounted, throwing the reins back over her horse's head.

'All right, boy, see you back at the stables.'

He knew where to go and, released of control, cantered back out of the gates and towards the messenger station. Corvanov became acutely aware of her solitude. She was armed with gladius and buckler like any Conquord messenger but the very fact she gained comfort from them here in her home port was frightening itself.

She walked down the Portsway and into the forum. It clearly hadn't been open for days. Was everyone dead? There had been the sails in the harbour so surely not, and anyway, the town didn't *feel* deserted.

Corvanov stood in the centre of the forum and turned a full circle. She felt like screaming for someone, anyone, to walk in so she knew she wasn't alone. There had to be survivors here. If the plague had wiped out everyone, there would be rotting bodies everywhere. Corvanov shivered. Nothing. Not a dog or a cat. Nor a single bird flying overhead or perched on a rooftop.

She drew her gladius. It didn't make her feel any better. The stench of death was not so prevalent here but it lingered in the air. A shout filtered to her across the dense quiet. Relief cascaded through her. She realised she was sweating. The noise had come from the dock and she sheathed her blade and hurried out of the forum.

Down the hill from the forum she went, passing street upon empty street, devoid of any life or sound. Rounding a gentle right-hand bend, the harbour came into view ahead of her. Ships crowded the wharfs. Flags were flying and sails were raised out in the deep water just off shore. And there were people thronging the dockside. Every inch was crammed, or so it seemed.

Corvanov broke into a run for a few paces before the peculiarity of the situation stopped her. There were *so* many people at the dock. Bitter's should have destroyed at the very least three quarters of Wystrial's eight thousand population. There had to be at least six thousand people down there.

They weren't moving either, for the most part. Just standing as if awaiting instruction or for something to appear. Statuesque. But not everyone. By each of the seven ships tied up along the wharf, men stood bellowing orders. Without the break of the buildings, the sound was loud over the silence dominating the rest of the dock. Corvanov blinked. It really was true. No one else was making a sound. She craved the barking of a dog. Anything that would make this scene in any way normal.

Abruptly, the tenor of the shouting changed. Three people moved through the still mass and trotted up the slope towards her. Not a single other head so much as flickered in her direction. Corvanov didn't know what to do. Part of her still grabbed at the tendrils of possibility that there was some rational explanation for all this. That those heading her way were coming to warn her away from the plague.

But it wasn't that. What she was looking at ... God-embrace-her, what *was* she looking at? Bizarre and frightening. She fought the urge to turn and run from the people of Wystrial. But her desire to find out what was going on overcame the crawling of her skin and the screaming of her mind. This wasn't an occupation and she could see no enemy. She had no reason to flee.

So why was that urge almost overwhelming?

Corvanov clung to her courage and stood her ground, watching the three men approach. They were in no particular rush. Their trotting had become a steady walk up the incline away from the harbour and none had a weapon drawn. She recognised the man in the middle and relaxed a little. He was twenty yards away when she hailed him.

'The plague must have been kind to leave this many survivors, Master Lianov,' she said.

There was no response. Not even an acknowledgement that she had spoken. How could he not have heard her?

'What's everyone doing down there? Supply boats is it? I'm bringing a message from Marshal Mardov. She's sending help and reinforcements. They're ...'

Corvanov trailed off. Lianov and the other two were looking at her but they weren't hearing her. They just walked on towards her. Worry gripped her again and she took a step backwards. Now Lianov's head turned fractionally and the three of them hurried the final paces.

They weren't right, none of them. Their skin didn't have the weathered tan of the harbour-dweller. It was a sick tinge, like plague still clung to them though she knew it could not. And one of the men had an ugly cut across one arm, now she looked. A cut that had not been dressed or seen to. It was filthy and crawling.

'Oh dear God,' she breathed.

Maggots. And at the last, a base instinct bade her turn and run. A hand grabbed at her back but didn't snag her cloak. She heard renewed shouts from behind her. She was a Fleet, faster than any of them on foot or horse back. God-surround-her, she wished she'd paid attention to her stallion now. He'd sensed the wrong, whatever it was.

A pain seared through her lower back, a heavy impact sending her stumbling. The knife was long, its blade sharp. She tried to get back to her feet but her strength was draining away, like her blood on to the dusty cobbles.

'Master Lianov,' she said, holding up a hand. 'It's me. Fleet Corvanov. Please. I'm not an enemy.'

The three men stood over her where she lay, lying on one side, a hand grasping uselessly at the knife in her back. She gasped at the pain that washed over her, shook her head to clear her eyes and stared at Lianov, searching for recognition. Perhaps there was a flicker but nothing more. He was as blank as a corpse and his eyes were empty of feeling.

'What's happened to you?' she said, the tears coming, the hopelessness suffocating. 'Why would you do this? Please, don't do this.'

Harbour Master Lianov drew the gladius from his belt and plunged it through her ribs and into her heart. They had turned and walked away from Corvanov before her sight faded.

Chapter Eleven

859th cycle of God, 16th day of Genasrise

The three Gatherer ships had made good progress west across the Tirronean Sea towards the eastern Gesternan port of Kirriev Harbour, a six-day journey at a steady five knots. From there it would be a further two days or so upriver to Ceskas, the border town that held indistinct but uncomfortable memories for all the Ascendants.

Jhered walked across the deck of the *Hark's Arrow*. It was as if he had stepped back in time ten years. Mirron stood alone, staring out at the Gesternan coastline that closed in on both sides as they sailed up Kirriev Inlet. It was a staggeringly beautiful landscape. Mists partially obscured soaring cliffs covered with lush green vegetation that hung down over ledges and adorned sweeping narrow terraces. Flowers were just starting to burst through where the rock protected the soil from wind erosion and the first genastro birds were beginning to nest. Their calls were echoing and somehow haunting, like a warning. Apt.

He stood behind her, silent for a while. She was wearing a thick cloak against the breeze off the sea. The hood was up and it was hard to see where exactly she was looking. Straight ahead, probably, as with every day.

'How are you feeling?' he asked.

She turned to him, face framed by her hood making her look so beautiful. He felt it deep in his heart and the vulnerability and loss in her eyes tore a hole in him.

'I don't know what to feel,' she said. It was more than he had prised from her in the last four days. 'Every moment we draw closer but I feel more distant.'

Jhered frowned. 'I don't follow you.'

'I'm sure we're going the right way but there's so much we don't know. He could take my son anywhere and I would never see him again. He could take him into terrible danger and I wouldn't be there to protect him. How do we know he's even still alive?'

This last was a whisper and Mirron turned her face back to the sea.

'Needle and haystack, I know,' said Jhered. 'And he's alive, I stake my life on it. Anyway it's not as bad as you fear. Gorian is not going to stay quiet. If anything Harban said happens, we will have found Gorian and if we do, we find Kessian too. Kark is readying for a war they believe is coming and that, if nothing else, is a reason to travel there. They have eyes across southern Tsard and into Atreska. If anyone has information, it will be them.'

Mirron shook her head. Long hair fell from where it had been tucked inside her hood and she scraped it back.

'You make things sound so simple and they aren't. He stole my son for a reason and he isn't going to let him get away without a fight. And Gorian knows how to fight, doesn't he? And if the Karku do have information, do you think they'll share it with us? Harban wants Kessian dead. They have no interest in us rescuing him.'

'Yet Harban came to Estorr specifically to ask for the Ascendants' help.'

'And look what we're sending. A mother who can barely keep a cogent thought in her head. Some help I'll prove to be.'

'For one thing, that's rubbish and for another, that isn't what I meant. They need our help, they'll have to give us information in return. Simple trade.'

Mirron sighed and turned to face Jhered once more.

'Why are you doing this, Paul? God-embrace-me, why didn't you retire and relax five years ago. You don't need to do this any more. More than anyone I know, you've earned the right to some peace and quiet.'

'Think I'm too old?' His reply was a little more gruff than he'd intended.

Mirron put a hand on his arm and even managed a smile. 'Oh, Paul, I'm not trying to insult you. Although you are a little grey. Seriously, though, I feel safer because you're with me. But Harkov could easily have led. You know the Advocate wouldn't have forced you to go. Why did you put yourself back in the front line again?'

'It ought to be obvious.'

Mirron blushed. 'That's not enough, though, is it?'

'Yes it is,' said Jhered. 'Look, I made a promise to protect you and

Ossacer and Arducius when the war was won. And I don't break my promises. There'll come a time when you don't need my protection and I'll gladly retire to my villa at Lake Phristos that same day. Anyway, I like travelling with you. It's a rare thing to indulge in these days so I'd like to make the most of it.'

'Ah, promises,' said Mirron.

'Yes. Badges measuring a man's respect and honour. You know there's one I have yet to fulfil? Made it to a man called Han Jesson from a village called Gull's Ford in Atreska before the war started. Tsardon raiders had taken his wife and son and I promised I'd return them. Think I've forgotten that promise? You know he disappeared from his home years ago. Probably went to look for them himself. Doesn't make any difference. If we end up in Tsard, I will look for them. Even if it's to return their bones, I will look.'

'Isn't that just personal pride?'

'Probably,' said Jhered. He tapped his chest above his heart. 'But in here, I feel a pang whenever I think about it. I haven't given it my best and that sits badly.'

'But if this man is already dead ...'

'It doesn't matter. Like you said, pride. But what if they are still alive out there and wanting rescue? I don't make promises lightly.'

Mirron understood. He could see it in her eyes.

'Why did you ask, Mirron? Really?'

'Because I worry about you,' she said. 'It's the law of averages. How many more times can you put yourself in harm's way before you fall?'

Jhered laughed. 'I'm the Exchequer of the Gatherers, Mirron, not your father.'

'But I wish you were.'

Jhered stared at his shoes while the wind rattled the mast lines and snapped the sail canvas.

'So do I,' he said and put a hand to her cheek. 'I couldn't ask for better.'

The new Marshal Defender of Atreska, Megan Hanev, had endured the worst fifty days of her life and from the look on General Davarov's face, the situation was not about to improve. An endless procession of misery, that's what her tour of Atreska had been. Unadulterated desperation and poverty. She had seen the ruin of lives, the ruin of her country.

She barely recognised it. Only Haroq City had remained largely intact. Outside of the capital, farmland was weed-grown when it should be prepared for seed or showing the first of the spring crops; the roads were similarly overgrown, imperial highways cracked and ill-maintained, local roads gone to ruin, no more than mud and wagon ruts; and in the towns and cities, basilicas were rubble, forums defaced and broken up for their stone. Houses of Masks were burned and defiled.

Everything the Conquord had built in Atreska had been systematically destroyed or plundered. It would take another decade to put it to rights. Megan seriously wondered if there was the will to do so. Refugees travelled north, south and west to try and find better lives in other Conquord territories now the borders were open again. Many had even chosen Tsard to the east. She didn't blame them.

But they blamed her. Or rather the Conquord for abandoning them while the Tsardon occupation force, for such it had been despite Yuran's protestations, raped the country. What depressed Megan the most was the manner in which those who remained had returned to a bare subsistence way of life. It was out of necessity of course but it had made them insular and aggressive, prepared to fight their own to keep what they understood to be theirs.

And now, like the turning of a great wheel, the Conquord was back, attempting to impose order and reinstitute the systems that had begun to make Atreska work before the war. She could see the resentment in the eyes of her citizens and didn't really know how to placate them.

Megan had sat at more meetings than she had had hours' sleep and listened to pleas for assistance and succour. Yet when she suggested that the Conquord forces and administrators moving through the country would provide just that, she was often shouted down. They couldn't explain what they really wanted. Megan knew, just as she knew they could never have it. Ten years of misrule really should have demonstrated how independence, or what they thought of as independence, was not the way forward.

And now here she was at a principal border crossing into Tsard and about to hear something else she didn't want to. The Advocate had been bleak in her assessment of Megan's task. And accurate, as it turned out. She had a penchant for exaggeration, did Herine Del Aglios, but when it came to affairs of state, she was always, always right on the mark.

'General Davarov,' she said, walking the short distance from her carriage to the barrel-chested Atreskan hero.

He was one of the key figures in the victory at Neratharn that had finally broken the Tsardon advance. A man who would live on in history when his cycle was complete and he returned to the earth. A man of whom statues and busts were already made and standing in the corridors of Conquord power. She felt in awe of him and he knew it. He stood proud before the border fortress gate under the flag of the Conquord, the rearing white horse over crossed spears. His armour shone in the sunlight and his dark blue, green-trimmed cloak blew gently in the wind.

'My Marshal,' he said, slapping his right arm into his chest. 'I trust your journey was at least reasonable under the circumstances.'

'None of the last fifty days has been reasonable, General,' said Megan. 'But it's good to see a friendly face in welcome. I've been rather used to scowls and frowns of late.'

Davarov chuckled briefly, a sound that bounced from the stone of the fort.

'Friendly faces often bring the worst of news. I am sorry to report this is the case today. Come with me, if you will.'

Megan nodded and Davarov marched inside. The fort was small, one of many in varying poor states of repair spread along the exposed Atreskan border north and south of a mountain range which provided a natural barrier. It was a basic circular construction with its inners divided between barracks, administration and rough armoury facilities. Cellars had been dug for storage. Weeds sprouted from cracks in the walls inside and out. The general took her up a spiral stair to the roof. It was concrete and supported by heavy timbers. Solid enough but cracked and poorly maintained.

There were battlements up here, archer positions and small artillery pieces. But these forts were all largely watch emplacements, not designed to hold off a major invasion as much as to provide staging for attacks into Tsard. To that end, the building was reduced to a folly.

'We've got almost eight hundred miles of border,' said Davarov in answer to her question. 'When the Conquord first came, one fort was built every ten miles or so along the stretches most at risk of invasion. I've travelled the border personally and this piece of dressed-up rubble is among the best we have left. Most of the others, and there were over seventy of them, have been taken apart, stone by stone. We're rebuilding but we won't be quick enough.'

'Quick enough for what?'

'Ah,' said Davarov. 'That's what I want to show you.'

Davarov led the way across the roof to the eastern wall. In the bright sunlight of a clear genas day, the view was glorious. Tsard was a country of staggering contrasts. Megan could see distant mountains, rolling plains and forest. Nearer at hand, the old highway ran off towards a line of crags behind which smoke blotted the purity of the sky. Quite a lot of smoke. Her heart fell. This sort of thing she had seen before.

'What is that?' she asked, expecting exactly the answer she received.

'That is a Tsardon army. It isn't huge. Twelve thousand, cavalry and infantry. Light on artillery which is a little odd but I presume they want to be able to move fairly quickly. They're about six miles from the border. Arrived here three days ago. I knew you were heading this way so I thought you might like to see for yourself.'

'You sound like you're describing a travelling fair,' said Megan. Her heart was thumping.

'No sense in being over-dramatic,' said Davarov.

'*Over-dramatic?* There's an invasion force on our doorstep. How much more dramatic can we get?'

Davarov looked about him. His guards were all staring out at Tsard, ignoring their Marshal's outburst. He smiled a little indulgently. How old must he be? Mid-forties, certainly. And world-wise.

'If there's one thing Roberto Del Aglios taught me it is that the only time to get really excited is when the sword actually enters your flesh. Until then, the only option is restraint in one form or another. If I panic, every citizen under my command does the same. So do their families, the local tradesmen, bloody hell even the dogs and cats. You get my meaning.'

Megan nodded, finding his calm suddenly very reassuring. 'Do you still hear from Roberto?'

'Probably not as much news as you do, being a Marshal Defender these days.' Davarov's eyes twinkled. 'Still chasing the chalice of a Sirranean alliance last time I heard. I hope he succeeds. We could do with allies like them just about now.'

Megan looked back to the smoking fires of the Tsardon camp. 'But you don't think there's imminent danger of a sword entering your flesh, though?'

Another chuckle. 'From the last recruit I bawled out for having a smudge on his helmet, yes, every day. From the Tsardon, well, no, but then again if they decided to march, I'd only have two hours to reflect on the poor quality of my judgement.'

'But that's why you're here, though, isn't it? And that's why you brought all this lot with you?'

Megan indicated back over her shoulder. Behind her, Davarov's legions were encamped. Around nine thousand in all and representing much of the force that should be policing Atreska in the service of the Gatherers. Davarov had the good grace to look embarrassed.

'I wanted to get messages to you but your itinerary wasn't being communicated to me too well. I've riders all over Atreska trying to track you down.'

'So, General, what is your judgement?'

'They're waiting.'

'What for?'

'That I do not know. If they'd marched straight in they'd be close to Haroq by now so it's a bizarre decision. But their camp has permanency about it.'

'You're sure they mean to invade?' Megan hadn't wanted to ask. The question sounded stupid in her ears.

'We're the only enemy within four hundred miles so I'd have to say, yes. But this could be just a show of strength and a demonstration of future intent.'

'But you don't think so.'

'No. Even with my legions here, we are outnumbered and I don't have anyone else to call on. What I don't understand is that there are not enough out there to make inroads all the way to Neratharn. I know there's trouble down south on the Karku border so this could be a two-pronged attack. The fact is, if they know they can push us back, they can walk in whenever they feel like it. Whenever they get the word or whatever it is they're waiting for.'

'More troops?'

'I know it seems the obvious thing but our scouts don't see anything coming.'

'So what are you going to do?' Megan was a little confused. 'These soldiers are expensive to keep sitting here if they aren't going to invade.

We need them inland. There's plenty of trouble at our backs, let alone ahead of us.'

Davarov's expression cooled, the twinkle in his eyes gone. 'They are legion soldiers and cavalry and they are here to fight and defend. That is what they will do. I cannot walk away from here leaving the gate wide open, my Marshal. Are you suggesting I should?'

'No, no,' said Megan. 'But how long will you have to wait here?'

'Well I can go and ask the Tsardon if and when they intend to invade, if you like.' Davarov spread his hands wide. 'I have no choice but to wait and track them and repel them if necessary. I hope it doesn't come to that. In the meantime, I need you to try and find me reinforcements, a steady supply line and approve my messages back to Estorr. In the end, I expect they are just testing our resolve and reaction to an attack. That means we have to appear strong and determined. If not, we can expect them back in greater numbers.'

Megan paused and looked at Davarov. She didn't know the general all that well but she saw in him something she had not seen before.

'You're confused about something. What is it?' she asked.

'You noticed. Looking back at what I've told you today, I'm not surprised. It's inconsistent, I know. The point is that this is behaviour unlike any invading army I have ever seen or read about. This isn't a sport, it's about winning with minimal casualties. It's like they want us to gather our forces to make it a fair fight and that is plainly ridiculous. That is why I'm confused. Half of me wonders what would happen if I *did* turn round and march away ten miles. Would they still attack? Or would they just sit there? It doesn't make sense. Why, as-God-warms-the-earth, when they marched all this way did they pitch camp and wait?'

'Whatever you decide to do, I will support your decision,' said Megan.

'Whatever I decide to do, no Tsardon is setting foot in my country. That I promise.'

Chapter Twelve

859th cycle of God, 18th day of Genasrise

Mirron felt ill. It wasn't sea sickness. It had been coming on for days. Growing in intensity, an indefinable sense of ill-being was surrounding her. She kept it to herself at first, attempting to dismiss it as anxiety over her son. Quite understandable and only natural. But it wasn't that. As soon as the river journey to Ceskas began, she knew.

Everywhere, the glory of God shone through. Early genastro was so wonderful. Growth and new life filled the senses and warmed the core of her body and mind. The earth awoke and heralded the beginning of a new cycle blessed by God. It was a time when Mirron had no desire to temper the clamour that rushed through her every moment of every day. But this cycle, the taste was sour.

Mirron thought back over Harban's assertions and Gorian's words and the conclusions scared her. She wanted to be able to talk to Ossie and Ardu. They'd have placed it all in perspective. Beneath the fresh strong life of genastro, there was rot and decay. Death. And with every dip of the oars, it was growing stronger. She shivered.

'Cold?'

She turned from the bow rail. 'No, Paul, I'm fine. Lovely genastro afternoon like this? How could I be cold?'

'You tell me. I know the view's beautiful – and at least this time, I haven't had to drag you on deck to get you to see it – but your study has gone well beyond intricate. What's wrong?'

The mountains sweeping up before them, black, grey and dazzling white weren't beautiful. Their aura was foreboding just like everything else the land had to offer. Warning her away, telling her not to look because she would fear what she found.

'It's hard to say. The energy map of everywhere is unsettled. Jumbled almost like an illness was upon it, but not grey like disease.'

'Then how is it?'

Jhered had tried to understand what the Ascendants felt and saw as no one else. He'd admitted his desire to sample their world just once. This wouldn't be the time.

'Like something core to the way of things has grown beyond its natural proportion and unbalanced everything.'

'Something like dead people walking about the place, you mean?'

Mirron felt herself blush. 'Sorry, I—'

'It doesn't matter but you all do it, you know.'

'Do what?'

'Talk like it's a mystery play and you're working up to the last dramatic line. Just say it, that's my advice.'

'Oh. I see.' Mirron laughed and felt the tension seep out of her.

Jhered put an arm round her shoulders and she snuggled in a little. It felt good. Safe.

'I thought you'd think me mad,' she said.

'Why? Harban said things back in Estorr that sounded insane but your missing son isn't the only reason we're out here, is it? We have to know if he's right or not. And you think he might be. That's not mad, it's frightening.'

'We should be careful in Ceskas,' said Mirron, after a pause. 'More careful, that is.'

Jhered nodded. 'Noted.'

'I don't know what we'll find.'

By the time they arrived, however, she knew the answer to that question too. She walked the deserted streets of Ceskas hugging herself over her cloak. It was a cold day but that barely registered. Wind blew over slushy cobbles, blowing debris against closed doors and shutters. Rats scurried to cover as the Gatherers searched every room, shed and warehouse. They found blood, evidence of struggle and obvious signs that the town had been plundered but there was no one to ask what had happened.

The House of Masks was destroyed, and so was every shrine to Atreskan, Gesternan and Karku gods. That the Tsardon had been here was not in question. Mirron knew that was worrying Jhered deeply. She wasn't great on geography but even she knew this was way too close to secure Conquord lands. Actually, he'd called it an act of war and coming on the back of stories they'd heard in Kirriev about attacks at eastern ports, it sent a shudder through her.

Mirron stood at the central fountain in Ceskas, waiting for the inevitable. The fountain was smashed. And somewhere else the feed pipes had been damaged or were frozen because there was no water. It stank of urine and excrement this close to so she moved away a few paces. She watched Jhered's Gatherers and her Ascendancy guard emerge from building after building, shaking their heads, shrugging their shoulders and moving on.

She didn't have to wait too long before Jhered and Harkov walked over to her. Her guards moved discreetly aside to let them speak to her. Both men looked bemused, Harkov a little scared. Not emotions she associated with either of them.

'I could have told you before you did all that searching.'

'You did tell us,' said Harkov. 'But we had to search anyway.'

'But it's worse than you think,' said Jhered. 'There's no livestock here. No dogs or cats either. About the former, I am not surprised. But a cat? The Tsardon won't have taken them. No point. So where are they? Only rats and mice. It's like God reached down his hand and scooped them all up. I've never seen anything like it.'

'But the Tsardon might have cleaned this place out for a statement mightn't they?'

'It's not their way,' said Jhered.

'No. They take prisoners but always leave people behind to tell the tale. It's been an effective tactic in the past.' Harkov looked round and shook his head again.

'What do you think, Mirron?' Jhered rubbed a gloved hand over his chin.

'Me?'

'Why not? You sensed something wrong. Are they all dead and walking elsewhere? That's what my people are guessing and who can blame them, eh? It's as sensible an explanation as anything else right now.'

Mirron almost laughed but caught herself.

'You should listen to those words again, Paul.'

'I know. Ridiculous isn't it? How easily the unbelievable can become real. But that's what you're left with, isn't it, when everything else has been dismissed.' Jhered sucked his top lip. 'I don't like this at all. It feels wrong. And if it feels wrong to me, God-surround-us, it must feel dreadful to you.'

Mirron raised her eyebrows. 'Not here, it doesn't. This is almost like standing in a fallow field. It's had life and will have again. But right now, apart from what's always here, it's dormant. It's up there where the problem is.'

She gestured away to the mountains of Kark. Somewhere in there or maybe beyond, was her son. And Gorian, perpetrating something unspeakable.

'Don't you corrupt him, you bastard.'

'Sorry?'

Mirron sighed. 'Sorry, I didn't realise I said it out loud.'

'What?' asked Jhered.

'Nothing.' The tears threatened, quite suddenly. She felt tight across her chest and the pit in her stomach yawned. 'We should go. I want my son back.'

The enemy would attack uphill over the ice and snow. For four days, they had been gathering. The Karku had watched them from the mouth of the Canas Valley, the only mass entry point into Kark along the border with Tsard. They were not afraid. They knew this would happen. The writings stolen from Inthen-Gor made it inevitable. He had come back and they knew where He wanted to go and who He needed to take.

Harban stood and gazed down on the assembly. The main body of the enemy was marching from the camp spread to the west. Fires still burned bright under dark morning skies. More snow was coming. There were some thousands of foot soldiers forming up.

The others came from the east. The ones who needed no fire or cover. Who stood or sat silent and who marched with no will but with purpose. He knew who they were and who it was that drove them.

Where were the Ascendants?

Harban ruffled his gorthock's head and ears, dragging his fingers through her dense, tough white fur. The beast growled. She was tense, staring at the invaders and unsure of the scents carried on the breeze.

'Come, Drift. Time to be with our people.'

Harban tugged on the gorthock's thick leather collar and she turned. Graceful, powerful, with the speed of a lion and the bulk of a bear. Jaws that could pierce metal. The Karku's most potent weapon.

They began to walk up the valley. Karku with spear, arrow and sling lined both edges. Most appeared grim-faced. So long since a war. Already the mountain was angry. Those taken to the roots this day would not be at peace.

The valley was six hundred feet deep at its mouth, the ground broken and difficult all the way up a sharp slope to the head a mile to the south. The mass of the Karku was clustered there. Their breath mingled in a great cloud around them. Their gorthock, two hundred and more, howled, growled and strained, impatient to attack. The had not smelled the wind like Drift had.

Harban studied his people. Blades, axes and hammers were held in hands still dark with dusas hair. Bare feet were planted firmly in the snow. Mountain men and women. Long-limbed and short-bodied. Enough to repel an army four times their number such was the advantage of height and terrain. The valley was a killing ground and still more Karku arrived.

Facing them were perhaps twice their number but it was no ordinary army. Courage and a willingness to commit hideous acts were the factors that would win this fight.

Harban stood by his army's commander, nodding that all was in place at the valley mouth. The man nodded back, his face betraying his nervousness. He wasn't a true commander. He was no Prosentor of Tsard or General of the Conquord. No Del Aglios. None of them were. How long since any serious threat worth the name? A hundred and seventy years. Border skirmishes and mineral disputes, yes. Little fights quickly resolved. But this. This was an assault on the fabric that bound the Karku. No preparation was adequate.

The gorthock scented enemies, an alien irritant in the nose that dragged their voices to full cry. The howling spread across the army. It was deafening, boosting the blood and calling the mountains to keep them strong. It was all they had. The determination to live on as they always had. And indignation that any should try to take from them.

But along the valley floor came order, discipline and something none had seen the like of before. Harban prayed to stone and sky that he lived to see another dawn.

Mirron retched. Her legs felt leaden and she dropped to her knees. Her hands touched the ground to steady herself but she snatched them away, unable to bear the sick crawling directed through her fingers.

'Exchequer!' called Harkov, kneeling down beside her on the icy slope that led high and deep into Kark. 'Mirron?'

She gasped for air, feeling the sickness surge through her, leaving a bitter aftertaste in her mouth, a thundering in her head and a roiling pain in her stomach. She fought down the nausea. Every muscle shook and she couldn't focus her mind to calm herself. She dared another touch on the ground. Nothing. Just the cold and dormant life beneath her and as far in any direction that she could sense. And away to the north-west, a sense of bleakness covering the earth. That was where it had come from and the knowledge of what it meant brought tears to her eyes.

The column had stopped and Mirron could hear Jhered barking Gatherers and Ascendancy guards out of the way. She pushed herself upright and managed a weak nod at Harkov.

'I'm all right,' she said.

Harkov raised an eyebrow. 'Really?'

She shook her head. The ache was fading from her, letting her think.

'He's started,' she said. 'I think we might already be too late.'

'Mirron?' It was Jhered. 'What's wrong?'

She leaned against him for a moment while her vision swam.

'God-surround-me, that was horrible.'

'What was it?'

'Like tasting rotten meat. Meat that crawled with maggots. It went through my whole body. Dammit but I can still taste it.' She spat a little phlegm on to the snow, watching it sink a little way before it cooled. 'It's him. He's making the dead walk, I know it.'

'Where?'

'Way to the north and west. Days from here. I can't imagine what it will feel like closer to. I've got to work out how to push it away or it'll swamp me.'

Jhered rubbed at the stubble on his chin. It was grey and flecked with white. He was always so smart back on the Hill. Out here though, he became the rough soldier he'd been since his youth.

'How many days?'

'I don't know. Depends if we can find a Karku to take us through the mountains. Still, I'd guess at three days, maybe four.'

'Too many,' said Jhered. 'Far too many. Whatever's happening will be over for good or ill. We can do no more than walk inland until we find the Karku. Persuade them to take us to Yllin-Qvist and Harban. Are you all right to go on?'

Mirron nodded. 'There's not much choice is there?'

'You said it,' said Jhered.

'I wish we had mules like last time.'

Jhered chuckled. 'Had Ceskas been at the height of trade, two hundred mules might have been hard to come by. And they'd have bankrupted the treasury. Thieves. Listen, I want you to be careful. Don't hide those feelings from me. They could help us. Give us warning. But more important, look after yourself. We're going to need you, Mirron. Everyone on this path knows the pain you carry every day your son is missing. We'll walk until we drop but you have to tell me or Harkov when you need to stop. Don't be a martyr, it won't do any of us any good. We're here for you, all of us. All right?'

Mirron blinked back fresh tears. 'Yes,' she said quietly.

'Good,' he said. He turned to the column and Mirron saw him studying the steep, slender path ahead, the dizzying drop to their left. He sighed and gathered himself. 'Let's move! Keep your eyes open. We need contact and we need it quickly. March.'

The hail of missiles was unrelenting. The scale of the violence meted out on the advancing invaders was sickening and shocking. Arrows, spears, sling shots, loose rocks tipped over the sides to start small avalanches of stone and earth. Men and women were cast from their feet under the weight of the assault.

Through his magnifier, Harban saw skulls staved in. He saw limbs torn from bodies and chests impaled. He saw blood and flesh scattered across the valley, defiling the pure ground. And he saw almost every single body pull itself back to its feet and move on.

He could not deny the fear that crawled through him just as it did every Karku, every gorthock around him. He didn't know who they had been before they were taken and driven to this fate. Gesternan, Atreskan, Tsardon, dead but walking. They moved despite arrows piercing chest, throat and skull. Arms hung by a thread, dripping blood to the earth. Some had legs clearly broken, torn or mangled. Still they dragged themselves forwards, impelled by something he simply could not comprehend.

Behind them waited the regular Tsardon army. They stood in ranks, watching in near silence while the Karku, with no alternative, wasted their weapons on the dead. Harban could see the faces of those in the Tsardon front line. There was no triumph in their expressions. The misgivings were plain but so was the relief they were not facing the barrage. They would look to either side, talking to their comrades, seeking explanation and reassurance they would not get. Not a one of them was smiling.

Somewhere, He would be. Out of sight, separate, working his thralls.

Harban refocused on the dead moving implacably up the slope. Soldiers all of them, a thousand and more carrying weapons if they had the limbs left to do so. Armour ragged if they wore any, damaged by exposure and lack of care. Only three hundred yards distant now. Their faces betrayed nothing but the scars of their deaths and the wounds of today. Some were covered in sores. He could see bone and tooth through rents in pallid flesh. But in their eyes, those that still had them, there was no understanding, nor fear, nor determination. Not even the confusion he had seen in Icenga. Just blind subservience to their new master.

The barrage was decreasing in intensity. Those standing and looking down saw their efforts come to nought. The enemy didn't even pull arrows free unless they directly hindered movement. Spears had been torn out and the innards that came with them were casually discarded.

With every onward step, the realisation that they would be confronting this implacable enemy face-to-face was creeping through the Karku standing and waiting. Harban looked left, right and behind. It was in every eye and quickened breath. It was plastered across the expression of the commander, Jystill-Rek.

'What can we do?' he asked, catching Harban's eye. 'What can we do?'

Harban looked back at the approaching dead. Staggering, striding, advancing.

'No man can fight if he lies flat on the earth, whether he is driven dead, or still alive under mountain and sky,' said Harban, his next words tainting his heart. 'We must divide their bodies.'

'And fire,' said Jystill. 'We need fire.'

Harban bowed his head briefly. 'Yes. Fire.' May they all be judged honestly when their time came. 'But act now. You can feel we are losing our men.'

Anxiety was spreading like a virus through the Karku and the gorthock alike.

'Listen to me!' Jystill raised his voice to a shout after a brief survey of the situation ahead. 'We must face what comes against us. We are Karku and we must defend our home. But I understand your fear. I share it. But now is our opportunity. These abominations are well ahead of their masters. They are isolated and we outnumber them. We will bring fire and we will bring blade to bear. Don't try to kill them, render them unable to move and then burn them. Pray to sky and stone and remember who waits behind us, relying on us.

'Handlers, prepare to release your gorthock. Runners to the peaks. Tell them to attack the Tsardon, should they move. Light fires, light torch and branch. Karku, for your people, fight.'

Jystill's words passed quickly through the Karku on this curious, quiet battlefield. Harban heard the shouts of objection filter back even as others readied gorthock or broke away to bring wood from their camp for fires and torches.

'We cannot stop them! Even with heads smashed, still they move.'

'They are innocents forced to fight beyond death.'

'We may not judge and so burn them.'

Harban unclipped the lead from Drift. She looked up at him, expression almost pleading under her heavy bony brow. The noise around them was growing, Karku encouraging one another, arguing with the objectors. Jystill opened his mouth to add his voice. Harban stopped him.

'You have said all you must. They will follow us or they will not.'

'We cannot march divided.'

'We may have no choice.' Harban knelt by Drift, placed his hands around her jaws and staring deep into her eyes. 'Go from me and tear the flesh of our foe. Fear not death or wound. You are gorthock.'

He felt the rumble in her body as his words pierced her fear and stoked her lust for blood. He straightened and stepped back a pace. Drift turned to face the dead, sat back on her haunches and let rip the cry of the gor. It was an ululating sound, picked up in the throats of all gorthock. It reverberated against the sides of the valley, half scream, half howl. It struck deep in the bones of men and even Karku shuddered.

Yet as Drift led the gorthock charging down the slope, the dead had not flinched from their path. And behind them, beyond the valley mouth, the Tsardon had not yet reacted either. Harban's fundamental sense of the sheer wrong in the situation threatened to overwhelm him. Part of him had to believe these dead were simply husks with nothing left of their original selves. But he had seen Icenga. Icenga had spoken to him before he had died the second time. The person was left inside the body, trapped and with no way out. They wanted help and all they would get would be flames.

'Karku, for sky and stone!'

Jystill raised his short blade high and led his army after the gorthock. Harban matched him stride for stride, pushing thoughts of the horror they would perpetrate from his mind. The time for guilt was later. Now, Kark had to survive. The mountain had to stand against the tide.

Harban was no fighter. He was a hunter and a farmer. He had a sword as they all did for ceremonies, and for the passing of boy to man deep inside Inthen-Gor. He drew his as they all did and ran on, hoping the gorthock would check the advance. Yet already ahead of him, the animals had begun to slow.

'Drift!' he called. 'Don't fear. Enemy. Prey.'

Whether she heard him or not, he didn't know. But the charge became a lope and the lope became a cautious walk, and so quickly the gorthock stopped. Scant yards from the dead and all they could do was snarl and growl. The dead did not pause and in front of them, the gorthock backed off, pace by pace. Like so many cubs scared of a mountain ass. Toothless and unsure. The moment they backed up to the faltering line of Karku, they turned and scattered back behind cover.

'Stand! Stand!' Jystill shouted, though his own voice was wavering.

In front of them the dead came on. Their march was untidy but they were in ranks and their weapons and shields were held ready. Harban took a deep breath. The Karku had halted, many had turned and fled after their gorthock. Those that stood were ready to follow them.

'Stand!' Jystill again, forcing steadiness into his tone.

The Karku stood. The dead advanced. Harban heard the crackle as torches were brought up to the back of the line.

'Only if we have to,' said Jystill.

Harban was shaking his head. 'These are not our enemies. Remember Icenga. Remember what I saw.'

The dead came on.

'Stop,' ordered Jystill. 'You cannot go further. Please. You are Atreskan and Gesternan. You are friends. You can hear me. I know you can. Turn aside. Turn against the one who sent you.'

There was not a flicker from any one of them. Harban shivered and gripped his sword a little more tightly. They were ten yards away. Utterly silent but for the dragging of feet over the ice and snow and the dull clank of armour and sword.

'God of the sky protect me,' whispered Harban.

He could see their faces. The clouding of breath in some but by no means all. The magnifier had not told the whole truth. Jaws hung slack. Tumours, pustules and sores covered flesh. Many had tears in their flesh and clothing where killing blows had been struck. Maggots crawled in uncovered wounds. Bone gleamed white from beneath flaps of flesh. Rot and decay surrounded them. The smell was extraordinary, hideous. One man, and it had been a man, wearing the livery of the Atreskan border guard, had lost most of his head. The left side of his skull was smashed. Brain was smeared over the shards, rested in the base of the skull and had dripped on to his shoulder.

Harban was shaking. Gasps and prayers surrounded him. He heard running feet.

'Jystill,' he managed. 'Before we lose the rest.'

Beside him, Jystill swallowed. 'I can't,' he said. 'I can't.'

The dead marched slow and steady. Five yards. The Karku backed off just as their gorthock had done. Helpless, Harban went with them.

'Give the order, Jystill. Please.'

Jystill opened his mouth, his voice loud and dominating. 'Run! Save yourselves. To the paths of Inthen-Gor. Run!'

Harban gaped, unable to speak in defiance. As if bindings had been cut, the army of Karku burst backwards, fleeing back up the slope. Jystill was roaring them on, hurrying through the lines away from the dead. Harban had no choice. He and the very few others who had been prepared to fight were already at risk of being overwhelmed. So he turned and retreated too.

Not a run. He discovered pride within himself. Only twenty walked with him, secure in the knowledge that the Tsardon were too far back and the dead were not about to change the pace of their march.

But with every pace, he felt the strength of the Karku fade. Beneath his feet, the mountain would weaken and the roots that held the Karku people and their lands together would wither. Jystill spoke of defending Inthen-Gor and perhaps they would. Perhaps the outcome would be precisely the same.

Harban couldn't find it in his heart to blame anyone but as the roar of the commencing Tsardon advance reached his ears, he couldn't find in his heart any hope for survival either. His people had turned their backs on the tumbling of the world.

Chapter Thirteen

859th cycle of God, 20th day of Genasrise

'Come walk with me.'

Gorian held out his hand. Kessian kept his firmly inside his cloak. He was cold. Very cold indeed. He didn't know what was going on but he felt scared and ill. He hadn't wanted to eat and now he was starving too. Today had been horrible. It had dawned wet and freezing. Something had happened that he hadn't been able to see because Gorian wanted him to help with something else. And that had been horrible too. Gorian had placed hands on him and sucked energy from him, or so it felt like. It had made him tired but he was all right now.

But now it was just as horrible because he was being made to walk from the camp where all the soldiers were and up past the place where they'd all been sent to fight. Them and the ones who went before them whom he could feel but didn't understand. The ones Gorian told what to do whilst using him. It was all very confusing. He wished he was still at home but he'd learned that crying got him nowhere. So he just got angry instead.

'Why?'

'Because I am going to show you what it is you have helped come about.'

'I didn't do anything.'

Gorian beckoned. 'Yes, you did. Or you made it so I could. Come and see.'

'I don't want to. It's cold.'

Kessian regretted saying that but this time, Gorian only smiled. 'If you come with me now, I'll show you an easy way to keep yourself warm, how about that?'

Kessian frowned. 'I can't do any of these things you say I can. I'm too young.'

Gorian squatted down in front of him. 'I keep telling you, I know you have emerged. You are a fully-fledged Ascendant, potentially the best of us all. Your mother might not have seen it, or she might have been keeping it from you. But it's true. All you have to do is believe.'

Kessian sighed. This wasn't any good. Gorian gripped his arms quite hard.

'Ow.'

'You can drop that expression for a start and listen to me. There's a man came into the camp last night. He's a little further ahead now with his soldiers, working out which direction we should go next. I can help him because I've been here before. I need to tell you that because I am going to introduce you to him. He is King Khuran. He is king of all the Tsardon and I have told him how important you are. So you will not embarrass me and you will be polite to him, do you understand?'

'Why do you want me to—'

'Do you understand!' Gorian shook him.

'Ow, yes. Yes. Let go.'

Gorian did so and stood back up, the smile on his face again. 'We shouldn't fight, you and I. We are father and son, no matter what you think right now.'

'We wouldn't fight if you took me back home.'

Gorian's eyes flashed. Kessian backed off a pace.

'Last time,' he said quietly but in a tone of voice that made Kessian shiver. 'I mean it.' He reached down and grabbed Kessian's hand. 'Let's go. Keep quiet until you're spoken to.'

Kessian felt sick all over again. But he'd lost his appetite now. Gorian was gripping his wrist too tight. He wanted to pull away but dared not. Instead, he looked about him and tried to see what the fuss was about. The snow was all turned to slush where the soldiers had marched on it, churned with mud. It was very slippery. Kessian shook his arm to try and free his hand.

'It's all right, I'm not going to run or anything.'

Gorian looked down briefly and let him go. 'No, I don't suppose you are.'

They passed between two dazzling white cliffs and were heading up a slope towards more and more mountains and snow. The wind was cold in the valley and Kessian rubbed his mittened hands together.

'How far are we going?'

'Can you see those people at the top of the rise?'

'Yes.'

'There. That's where everyone is that I need you to see.'

'Why?'

'Because I said so, and because it will teach you some important things.'

More learning. It was always learning. Even at the Academy they had time to play. Here, there was no time at all.

'And don't think that about me, boy,' said Gorian.

'I wasn't thinking anything,' said Kessian, unable to keep the whine from his voice.

Unexpectedly, Gorian laughed.

'You know I was just like you at your age.'

'Were you?' Kessian didn't think it very likely.

'Of course. Like father, like son. Always picking at the corners, always kicking against authority, testing my boundaries. And so you should. It'll make you strong in mind.'

Kessian smiled.

'Just try and learn when to stop,' said Gorian, patting his shoulder. 'That's the difficult part.

Kessian wondered if he should try and be a bit like Gorian. At the Academy, understanding and tolerance were everything. Out here, being in charge was the best thing. And everyone listened to Gorian. They might even be scared of him. Gorian didn't seem to mind which it was.

'What did I help you do?'

'Watch out.'

Gorian's sharp tone stopped him in his tracks. At his feet lay a whole human arm. The fingers were curled around an axe and there was a ring on one finger. Kessian choked on a scream and stepped back, looking away. But suddenly, all he could see were arrows, spears, stones, blood and bones. Bits of people. And even one or two almost whole bodies, crushed and mangled. He gagged and put his hand to his mouth and nose though there was no smell. Just this horrible mess.

'What is it?' he asked weakly.

'This is a battlefield,' said Gorian. 'But a very special one.'

Kessian wanted to back away. To turn and run. Dark was smeared over the slush. He'd thought it mud only it wasn't.

'Why?' It was the last thing he wanted to ask.

'Because if a man loses his arm on a normal battlefield, he falls beside it to die. Not our men, not our army. They carry on, do you see?'

Kessian shook his head. 'I don't—'

'Come over here.'

Gorian was moving to stand by a body with a spear in its lower back. A rock had all but crushed its head. Kessian tried to be strong but he gagged again. His heart was pounding and he thought he was going to be sick. It felt so bad here. Like sickness. Ossacer would know what it was.

Gorian knelt by the broken body and placed a hand on its neck. Kessian felt a rush of energy through the earth and the man's legs jerked and his fists clenched and unclenched.

'You're healing him!' breathed Kessian, his nausea forgotten.

'Oh no,' said Gorian. 'You cannot heal a man who is dead already. But you can make him live again. And move. Come and touch him. Tell me what you feel.'

Kessian backed off shaking his head but with his eyes locked on the reanimated man. The body twitched and writhed. It made no sound. He felt a pain low in his stomach. The man clawed at the back of his head, trying to move the rock that lay on his shattered skull. Gorian rolled it away, wiping gore off on his cloak. Kessian dropped to his knees and was sick. He couldn't help it. There was nothing left of his head. The whole back of it was splintered and the brain inside was smeared over rock, bone and slush. His face was pressed into the ground. He was trying to turn it up but he couldn't do it.

'It's all right, Kessian. Don't be ashamed. This one doesn't look too pretty, does he?'

'We mustn't meddle with the cycle of life,' said Kessian. 'He should be returned to the embrace of God.' He retched and spat. His mouth tasted horrible.

'Direct from the Omniscient's scriptures no doubt,' said Gorian. 'But the scriptures are old. We are the new power and the Order is scared of us because of what we understand. We all worship the Omniscient, Kessian, but we must be allowed to do his work in the best ways we can.'

'But—'

'Do you think this man wants to return to the earth? I gave him another chance. Is that not a miracle?'

Kessian was confused. This man was broken beyond repair. He reached out with his mind and recoiled from what he felt.

'He is in agony,' he said.

Gorian looked across at him, a slight frown on his face.

'Does that matter? He was not breathing and now he is. Now, admittedly this subject isn't useful to me. His back is broken so he cannot support his torso and there is little muscle left in his neck to turn his head. It doesn't matter. The point is that I can do it and you can do it too, if I show you. And to answer an earlier question, your natural use of energies is amazing. I can use the well of power you draw in to help me make these people live again.'

Kessian heard him. He even understood all the words. But it made no sense.

'Why?'

'Come here.' Gorian's gesture was insistent and Kessian pushed himself back to his feet and dragged himself over to the body that was still jerking soundlessly. 'I know you can do this so just listen. Ossacer will have taught you. Place your hand where mine is and open your mind to the energy map of this subject. Remember, he was dead until I touched him. I want you to tell me how you think I managed to make him live and move again.'

'I don't want to touch him,' said Kessian. 'Please don't make me.'

The wind was whistling north along the valley, gaining strength. He was cold and he was scared. He shivered, wanting the nightmare to end only he knew it wouldn't. Tears broke around his eyes and ran down his face. At his feet, the body twitched violently and was still.

'All right,' said Gorian, sounding irritable. 'He isn't in pain any more if that makes you feel better.'

Kessian felt some semblance of normality return to the earth and the world around him. The clamouring and complaint he sensed in the fibres of energy subsided.

'The earth is angry you did that,' said Kessian.

Gorian's eyes locked on to his, the power in that gaze almost overwhelming. But there was light in his eyes, and joy.

'You could feel that?'

'I couldn't shut it out. Why do you think I was sick?'

'Don't get sharp with me, Kessian. This is important.'

'Why?'

'Because it means you can feel something it took me years to feel.

It makes you even better, even more useful, than I thought you were.'

'Oh.'

Gorian frowned. 'You should feel glad about that. This is a wild land. Power is everything.'

Kessian said nothing for a moment. He felt uncomfortable, like he'd seen something he shouldn't and was about to be found out.

'I still don't know what we're doing here.'

'I've told you,' said Gorian. 'Taking the Ascendants from the shadows. Putting us where we belong.'

'All of us?'

Gorian ruffled Kessian's hair inside his cloak hood. 'All who believe as I do. Come on.'

Kessian stared down at the body one last time.

'Why do you want to make the dead live again?'

'Because we need our own army. We have no country of our own like the Conquord or the Kingdom of Tsard and we must not rely on others. These people, the dead that I can give life to once again, will be ours to command. They will fight for us and be loyal only to us.' There was an odd light in Gorian's eyes, a grim delight. 'They will want nothing, they will need nothing but our blessing to continue walking. What do you think about that? Your own fighting force?'

Kessian had wooden soldiers at home. One of the carpenters on the Hill made him a whole maniple and a miniature catapult. Gorian's tone made the dead sound like toys.

'They should be granted rest in God's embrace,' said Kessian.

'These are soldiers!' Gorian's shout bounced off the valley sides and Kessian winced. 'There is not one among them who wanted to die or whose time had been called by God. Every one of them wanted to live on. I give them that chance. Don't you understand? I am helping them and in return, they fight for me. It's so simple, Kessian, why don't you get it?'

'But in that place you took me to . . .'

'Wystrial,' said Gorian.

'They were not soldiers. Just ordinary people.'

Gorian sighed. 'There was a plague there. Terribly unfortunate. And you're right, it killed ordinary people. Some of those we managed to make live again and they helped us load ships, didn't they? And now they are returned again to God's embrace. But there were soldiers too. The garrison and lots of legionaries. None of these people chose to

die. These were good honest people and a horrible death found them.
I gave them life again and here they are. Is that not a good thing?'

'I suppose,' said Kessian.

'And if you were in their shoes, and your life was snatched from
you even though you were faithful to the Omniscient, would you not
choose to live and breathe and walk again if you could?'

Kessian considered for a moment and felt his mood brighten. 'I
would.'

Gorian nodded and smiled. 'As would I. However briefly. And
whatever I was asked to do. And if an Ascendant has saved them, is
it not right that they leave their prior allegiance and work for that
Ascendant?'

'I suppose so,' said Kessian.

'That's all there is to it. Now come on, come and meet the king and
think on the good we are doing for the unfortunate dead.'

He was right, of course. No one chose to be dead. Old people, like
very sick people, sometimes said they'd had enough and welcomed a
return to the earth but that was about as far as it went. It was a
strange thing to consider. You could get second chances at many things
but never at life once you were dead. Until now.

'What does it feel like to be woken up after you've been dead?'
asked Kessian once they were well on their way.

Ahead, he could see the slope rising up to the top of the valley. A
lot of people were up there. They were standing in two groups. One
was still and he realised who they were. The other was bigger and
hard at work setting up a new camp. There were already a lot of fires
alight. He could already imagine the warmth just as he could see it
through the excited energy trails in the air. His mother had taught him
loads about fire. He loved it.

'I don't know,' said Gorian. 'It's a very good question. We'll research
it together, how's that?'

'Why don't we just ask one of them?' asked Kessian.

'Because they may not speak their opinion,' said Gorian.

'Why not?'

'Because they do not need to speak to do the work they must do.
How do you think someone feels if their last memory is of death and
they open their eyes on God's blessed earth once again?'

Kessian thought for a moment. 'I think they might be frightened.
They might think it was their next cycle on the earth beginning but

then they might think they were lucky that they had another chance at the old one.'

Gorian chuckled. 'I think so too. And because of that, there is no need to speak, is there? I speak for them instead.'

Kessian shook his head although it didn't make much sense. Gorian was sure and there were things he understood better than anyone. The two of them fell silent and Kessian found his eyes drawn more and more towards the reawakened dead standing or sitting silent up on the rise to his left. There was quite a distance between them and the regular Tsardon army.

Gorian angled them well up to the right and Kessian surprised himself by feeling a little disappointed. He wanted to know what they felt right now. But he knew the king wouldn't wait. It was a bit like having to see the Advocate. She made all the rules.

The two of them walked through the Tsardon army. Kessian drew closer to Gorian. The men were huge, covered in thick furs or dark metal and leather armour. Their voices sounded harsh and came from mouths full of broken and rotten teeth, surrounded by stubble and beard and mired in dirt and grime.

They looked down at Kessian and over at Gorian with obvious distaste and although some of them showed some fear, most wouldn't move aside for them. Some even got in the way. Gorian didn't react, just kept a firm hand on Kessian's shoulder and steered him through the camp. He was heading for a grand-looking set of pavilions with flying pennants, set a little way from the bulk of the army.

The king was standing warming his hands over a fire and talking to a couple of other men. Kessian could tell he was the king right away. The energy map surrounding him pulsed strong and calm like the Advocate's always did. Although he wore clothes similar to many of his soldiers, they were of fine tailoring. A chain of gold hung from his left shoulder to his right hip and a shining dark cloak was clasped about his shoulders. His face was clean and shaven, his mid-brown skin looked scrubbed and oiled in the firelight and his hands were adorned with thick gold rings. He had a single tattoo across his forehead depicting galloping horses.

'He's from a steppe cavalry high family,' said Gorian when Kessian asked about it. 'And royalty in Tsard always displays its lineage like that.'

'What happens if he stops being king?'

'I don't think the thought has ever crossed his mind,' said Gorian.

He marched them straight up to the fire. None of the guards near the king challenged them or gave them any more than a glance. The king noticed them, dismissed one of the men and nodded at the other to make him see who was coming. The man turned round and Kessian's breath caught in his throat. He was so ugly. His face looked like it had been hit with a rock. His small eyes stared out of a face absolutely covered with tattoos. Kessian couldn't make any of them out. They were just meaningless squiggles and dots and lines. But it wasn't just the face that made Kessian scared, it was his aura. It was cold. Cold like death though he was not a reawakened one. Whoever he was, he bowed to Gorian.

'My Lord Gorian,' he said in a thick accent. His voice was like stone dragged over stone.

Gorian nodded to him but bowed to the king. 'King Khuran, if I may?'

The king shrugged and gestured.

'Condition?' demanded Gorian of the tattooed man.

'Significant damage. Wear was considerable. Projectile impacts from that height are difficult. I am suggesting forty per cent will not go further without repair. A waste of thread and subsequently a waste of your energy, my Lord.'

'Muscle depletion?'

'Mostly. Some limbs. Fractures of legs and lower back are common. They will walk but they will decline quickly and the drain on you will be out of proportion with their worth.'

'Suggestion?'

'I will sort them. You can inspect at your leisure and administer the touch to those you agree are of no further use.'

Gorian nodded. 'You seem a little saddened, Lord Hasheth. I do hope you aren't developing any emotional attachments.'

'They are my boys and girls,' said Hasheth, a smile cracking his face and revealing painted teeth, the centre ones sharpened to points. 'Every general cares for his charges.'

'Thank you, Hasheth, I will inspect later. Dismissed.'

Hasheth bowed once more and marched away through the Tsardon ranks. Kessian watched him go and saw how every soldier stepped aside even if they weren't looking in his direction. He was desperate to ask about Hasheth but the king was waiting and everyone knew you didn't keep kings waiting.

'And despite all that you consider this a success, do you?' Khuran's face was stone.

'You did not lose a single man to the enemy, my King,' said Gorian. 'None has so much as a scratch.'

'And the dead did not land a single blow,' said Khuran. 'No new dead, no dead army, wouldn't you say?'

Gorian looked confused for a moment. 'One can always create dead. The battlefield is the most convenient place but it is by no means the only resource available to us.'

Khuran's eyes narrowed and his face flushed. 'You know what we agreed, Gorian. You know the weaknesses in your "other resources". You know why we must have fresh fighting dead, not fat town garrison soldiers.'

Gorian glanced quickly at Kessian who had felt a chill across his body that wasn't due to the weather. He wasn't sure why but what Khuran said left him deeply uneasy all over again.

'My King. We are all of us new to this warfare. We will perfect our tactics.'

'I do not have the weight of arms to win the fight we have started,' said Khuran sharply. 'The mathematics are very simple indeed. If you do not deliver, or if I think for one moment you cannot deliver me what I must have, I will withdraw. I will not leave my country open again. Do you understand me?'

'You worry unnecessarily,' said Gorian smoothly. 'We are halfway to Inthen-Gor. When we take what we came for, the entire front north to south is at our mercy. We cannot lose this, Khuran. Trust me.'

Khuran let his gaze linger on Gorian before he turned to Kessian. Kessian gulped, feeling as if the weight of those powerful, confident eyes would be enough to drive him to his knees.

'Your Majesty,' said Kessian.

'And you are?'

'I am Kessian,' he replied, bowing his head. 'Your Majesty.'

'Oh dear,' said Khuran.

Kessian felt as if he had been slapped. Next to him, Gorian tensed.

'This is my son,' he said. Kessian raised his head and knew that he felt pride. With it, came guilt.

'I am well aware who he is,' said Khuran. 'As I am well aware of the enemy we face. How old are you, boy?'

'Ten, your Majesty.'

'Ten.' Khuran rolled the word round his tongue. 'Ten. And coddled on the Hill of the Advocate all your life.'

'My King—'

'I am talking.' Khuran rounded on Gorian. 'And I will not be interrupted.'

Kessian found his heart beating fast. This wasn't like when the Advocate got angry. He could see the king's energy map and it was pulsing a dangerous deep red. Gorian's too, but his was spitting because he was trying to control himself and only just doing it. The king had no such doubt.

'When you left Khuran City, you told me you were going to find help. Foolishly, I assumed that help would be in the form of your Ascendant brothers. But you have brought me a ten-year-old child who shrieks and pukes at the sight of blood. How will this help me win the war and take the Conquord? I have put faith in you, Gorian Westfallen. I am not seeing enough to justify it. Speak.'

'You judge too quickly. Age is no barrier to ability and my son has more potential ability than all the other Ascendants put together. He is the only one who can deliver what I have promised. I am the expert in this, not you.'

'And I am King of the Tsardon and you do my bidding.'

'Your success lies in my hands.'

'You think I do not know that?' snapped Khuran. 'Lord of stone, I am warning you, Westfallen. I have mobilised what little remains of my regular army because of my belief in what you can achieve. If you embarrass me, or let me down in even the smallest way, you and your precious little brat will be staked out for the cannibals of the Toursan Lakelands; and not your dead, nor your magic will be able to save you.'

Khuran bent to Kessian and grabbed his face in one hand. Kessian felt terror rise within him and he clamped hard on his bladder and his gut, tensing every muscle inside.

'I do not make idle threats. Fail me and you will be eaten alive.'

'Leave him,' said Gorian.

Khuran let Kessian go. He straightened up. 'Introduce him to your friends. See he understands what is expected. See he understands what he must do if you and he are to live. Go.'

Gorian put an arm on Kessian's shoulder and turned him away towards the dead. When they had walked beyond earshot, he spoke.

'I am proud of you, Kessian. You were very brave. Don't let him scare you.'

'I don't want to be eaten alive.' Kessian's skin was crawling.

'No stake can hold me. No army can beat me. Stay by me and you will be safe always. Khuran is a good king but he is an arrogant one. He has reigned for too long and he is complacent. We will do as he says and bow to him for now but remember, all useful things eventually wear out. Come on. The Dead Lords are anxious to make your acquaintance.'

Chapter Fourteen

859th cycle of God, 24th day of Genasrise

Jhered didn't need to be an Ascendant to feel the mood in Yllin-Qvist. Years before and on the run with all four young Ascendants, he had witnessed simple joy, ancient knowledge and innocent curiosity. Now, blank suspicion and a cold depression swamped the beautiful mountain-valley village the moment he and his people emerged from the tunnels. They made their way down to the river-run grass and farmlands studded with smooth stone houses.

Many of the young faces had no idea what they witnessed but those of more certain memory knew what they represented; the confirmation of the deepest fears harboured by the Karku over countless generations. There had been no question that all Jhered's two hundred would be taken through the tunnels in contradiction of their cautious ways. Another fact not lost on the Exchequer.

He told his people to wait in the cold sunshine near the tunnel mouth while he, Harkov and Mirron walked into the centre of the village past the gaze of every man, woman and child.

Harban had been alerted to their arrival. They were led to the meeting hall through the depressing spectacle of farmers, herders and miners sharpening inadequate weapons. The hall was almost as Jhered remembered it; flanked by hot spring temples and with smoke billowing from its central chimney. Closer to, though, he saw that the bright murals of mountain, snow and sun had been painted out. Images of darkness, rockfall and the destruction of Kark replaced them, dominated by one depicting a mountain with its peak lying shattered at its feet. He felt Mirron shiver as they walked into the heat of the hall.

'They're resigned to it,' she said. 'They expect it and so it happens. What can you do with belief like that?'

'We are resigned to nothing,' said Harban from beyond the fire and the circles of empty benches. 'But portents are always frozen in image on our walls, good or bad. Come near.'

The three of them walked in. Jhered was glad to be out of the harsh, cold gaze of the villagers. Harban was alone in the hall and he paced slowly from behind the roaring pit as he spoke.

'A strange fate is it not, Exchequer Jhered? That you who would once have been assumed an invasion force and dealt with as such are today guided to our hearts as our only hope of survival.'

It was unlike the Karku to dispense with their ritualistic welcome but Jhered didn't feel any surprise.

'How bad is it?' he asked.

'They are unopposed,' said Harban. 'We are not capable of turning such an enemy. No one will stand before them. They will be at Inthen-Gor in two more days.'

'Two days?' Harkov couldn't help himself. 'It has to be two hundred miles from the Hidrosh Valley, assuming that's where they came in. We have had tunnels to bring us this close. They have had just cliff and ice. How can they move so fast? It's impossible.'

Harban regarded him a moment, taking in the armour and gladius, the pristine red-plumed helmet of the Ascendancy guard tucked under one arm.

'You are a soldier and you understand battle. And if you are with Paul Jhered, you understand it well, I have no doubt. But you do not understand our foe. The Tsardon we can defeat. Not the dead.'

Harkov bristled. 'It is a simple case of mathematics.'

'No, it is not,' snapped Harban. 'Not those you are familiar with. This army does not rest. It does not eat and it does not sleep. It does only its master's bidding and He knows where they must march and what they must take. Your name? I do not know you.'

'Harkov. General of the Ascendancy Guard.'

'And I am Harban-Qvist. You are a friend to Ascendant and Jhered and you have my respect. But you cannot judge this enemy by anything you know. You must see them to understand.'

'So let's do that. Show them to me.'

'Bravery is easy when your enemy is but words and formless fears.'

Jhered put up a hand to stall Harkov's retort.

'It's all right, General,' he said, feeling his own mood soften as he spoke. 'The Karku speak their minds. Seldom is it a personal slur. And of course, in this instance, he is right.'

'But we must see them,' said Mirron, quiet until now. 'We must face them. After all, that's much of why I'm here, isn't it? To stop them. Me.'

The fire roared its energy. Men fell silent.

The entourage of Marcus Gesteris swept in under the Victory Gates and rattled to a stop around the grand fountain and its statue of horses rampant to each principal point of the compass. Herine watched them from the top step of the basilica. There was a sharp taste in her mouth and a disquiet in her mind. She'd had notice of his arrival. Good news dwarfed by potential bad.

'Bring him straight in and clear the public and reserved seating. This is now a closed session,' she said to an aide.

'My Advocate.'

Herine turned to the sound of snapped fingers and terse orders. Guards came to attention. Before she'd reached the uncomfortable throne where she heard petitions from her citizens, the cavernous basilica was emptying. She sat and watched grumbling citizens and haughty members of the Order of Omniscience disperse. It was almost a shame. She'd had a long list of complaints concerning Order activity and Ascendant meddling to deal with. Both Arducius and Felice Koroyan had agreed to be present. Still, another day ...

Herine knew she should probably have conducted this meeting in private chambers and returned later to the business of the day but it never hurt to remind people who was in charge.

'Sit, Senator Gesteris,' said Herine when the one-eyed hero of the Conquord, weary from his voyage, approached. 'The Speaker of the Earth has warmed a place for you. And no doubt one of my aides is already organising some sustenance.'

Gesteris marched to the dais and slapped his right arm into his chest.

'My arm and heart are yours, my Advocate,' he said.

Dust still clung to his boots and cloak though his ceremonial armour was freshly polished and caught the light that washed through the basilica between the columns.

'I do apologise for my appearance,' he continued. 'I have not had the opportunity to change since disembarking.'

'On the contrary, it does you credit.' Herine smiled. 'And I think we can dispense with formalities, you and I. Sit down, Marcus.'

Gesteris sat and blew out his cheeks. 'Thank you, Herine. A good journey but a lengthy one. And we set a fast pace.'

'And how is my son?'

'As brilliant and determined as ever. He'll make a fine Advocate, one day.'

'I hope he still has a Conquord worth the name to govern.' Herine felt a welcome warmth at Gesteris's words. 'I understand not all your news is to our advantage. Worrying messages arrived in advance of you too. I would hear the worst now.'

'Had it not been for Roberto's diplomatic powers—'

'And your genius with numbers no doubt.'

Gesteris inclined his head, '—we would not even know as much as we do now. The Sirraneans have alerted us to a Tsardon force. It's heading due west tracking the southern border of Sirrane. Bound for Gosland.'

'Big enough to hurt us?' Herine's words came out but the blood rushing in her head meant she could barely hear them herself.

'Roberto is already ascertaining their purpose and he'll report as soon as he can. Gosland will be warned well in advance of any invasion.'

'That isn't quite what I asked, was it, Marcus?'

'No,' admitted Gesteris. 'But it is all I have. The Sirraneans weren't forthcoming with the size of the force but they were certain it was threat enough to tell us about it. They know the thinness of our border defence after all.'

'But an incursive force is a long way from one that might topple a country. There's something you're not telling me.'

Gesteris shrugged. 'Intangibles really. I didn't wait for concrete news on numbers. Roberto will supply those as fast as he can. But the manner of the Sirraneans concerned us both. We've got to know them as well as any man alive these past cycles and one thing we've learned is that they demonstrate no urgency or worry about anything unless it is utterly critical. This Tsardon army worried them, no doubt of it.

'That's why Roberto is asking for the Conquord to mobilise. It's why he is going to assume command of the defence at Gosland and finally why I have brought back chemicals for Orin and Rovan to examine. They're a weapon. A powerful one.'

Herine cleared her throat, feeling uncomfortable. 'I cannot mobilise the Conquord, such as it is, based on supposition and a vague understanding of Sirranean emotions. The Senate will never agree. You know that, Marcus. What more can you give me?'

Gesteris chuckled and pulled a letter from a pocket inside his cloak.

'If there's one thing your son knows better than anything else, it is you, Herine. He said this is how you would react. He said you would be right to do so.'

'But you thought you'd test me anyway,' said Herine sharply. 'Clever man, my son.'

Gesteris blushed. 'I am not attempting to test you or waste your time, my Advocate. But there is a point to be made. We have little information on this Tsardon force but the information we have is exactly why we've been striving all these years to gain an alliance with Sirrane. Perhaps there is no threat. But even as a political and diplomatic gesture, a mobilisation, even a limited one, will send the right message to Sirrane and tell the citizens that our allies can really help us.'

'Now that I can understand,' said Herine. 'But there's still a nagging problem, isn't there? Why is it that my son is so worried that he feels he must take charge of the Gosland defences from some very capable soldiers? And so worried that he sends you back with some as yet unnamed powders for my scientists. Why? He's an Ambassador of the Conquord now. He hasn't picked up a sword for a decade.'

'But he always carries it with him. He carries all the trappings of his campaigning past with him.'

Gesteris proffered the letter. Herine waved it away and leaned back in her chair, fighting for a comfortable position.

'Read it for me. I need to think.'

'Of course.' Gesteris nodded and broke the seal on the paper. He unfolded a sheet watermarked with the Del Aglios crest and, Herine could also see, written in Roberto's scrawling hand. '"My dear Mother. If I'm right, poor Marcus has met with your most blank of expressions. And Marcus, I know you are reading this. Whatever my mother says, this is because she has never been able to read my writing and it makes her nervous—"'

Herine laughed out loud and clapped her hands together. Gesteris joined her and she felt the release of a tension she hadn't realised was clogging the atmosphere. She wagged her finger.

'One day, he will out-clever himself. I just hope I'm there to see it.'

'Shall I go on?'

'Please.'

'"I am not going to expound theories for my beliefs. I am not going to try and twist the facts into something they are not. All I am going to do is call upon your faith in me and in my feelings as a son, a man and a soldier. I fought the Tsardon for years. I examined their tactics and their motives as closely as any man. They do nothing merely for show. If they are marching towards Gosland it is for one reason only. And if the Sirraneans believe they have sent an invasion force, I believe it too.

'"Furthermore, if they are advancing on Gosland, they will be doing the same further south. It is their way to attack on multiple fronts. Remember what happened in the wars of a decade ago. They are quick, determined and ferocious. They do not risk themselves unless they believe they can win. We were lucky last time. We will not be so again unless we act now. Mobilise, Mother, I urge you. Bring the legions to ready. Move them to the pressure points that we outlined in the aftermath of war. And look to the south. Look to Atreska and Gestern too. Delay and we will fall. Your son, Roberto."'

Gesteris looked up. He again proffered the letter and this time, Herine took it and stared long and hard at the words. Roberto might have been clever and foreseen everything that had happened in the basilica so far but she had not foreseen this. She had expected numbers and speeds and a timetable. She had expected a clinical assessment. But not this. This plea laced with raw passion.

Herine licked her lips and swallowed the lump in her throat. She could envision him as he wrote it. Her son, Roberto, one of the three citizens hailed as a saviour of the Conquord. Along with Gesteris and Jhered, the men the people loved above all others. Above their Advocate, certainly.

'And yet this does not give me the means to act,' she said.

'Herine?'

Herine shook her head. 'Sorry, Marcus, thinking out loud. I believe him. As God-surrounds-us-all, what else can I do but believe him? But these words are not enough. He sees much. Does he not see that?'

'Of course he does,' said Gesteris gently. 'Just as he, you and I understand the system and the powers for circumventing it.'

'Marcus, I—'

'Please, Herine. I know this appears difficult but in reality, I do not believe it to be so. He is not asking you to go to the Senate with this letter. He is asking you to trust his instinct. Trust his gut and experience. I do.'

'I know what he's asking. And I can see the belief in you. God-embrace-me, it burns in you like a forge. But I know the state of our treasury and I have some information on the feelings of the citizenry. A mobilisation will do two things. It will bankrupt the exchequer and it will poison the minds of the people against the Advocacy.'

'And it will save the Conquord,' said Gesteris.

'Will it?'

'If you trust the beliefs of your son, then you believe that it will. So there is the question, my Advocate. Do you trust your son? Do you trust Roberto Del Aglios?'

Herine felt the heat rise in her face but she stared Gesteris straight in the eye.

'Go and clean up, Marcus. Take your powders to D'Allinnius. And then come back to the palace. I'll be in the genastro garden.'

'Yes, my Advocate.'

'And Marcus? Bring the Marshal General with you.'

Chapter Fifteen

859th cycle of God, 24th day of Genasrise

Mirron had been this way before. Into the mountain where the river plunged from the sunlight of Yllin-Qvist to the dark of rock and the roar of water. She shuddered at the memory. She'd been fourteen at the time and the dreams had never fully left her. This time, though, they would turn left and not right, heading for Inthen-Gor. And they would be the first non-Karku welcomed in to see it. Honour and tragedy combined.

'It is so beautiful,' said Harban. His tone was soft and reverent. 'A great cavern and lake that we call the Eternal Water. At its centre is an island where our ancestors built the Heart Shrine. Both are as vital to us as the air we breathe. They govern all our lives and bind us to the mountains and the air and to all the creatures that walk the paths of the living and the tunnels of the dead.'

'You said the same thing last time,' said Mirron.

'The same words,' he said. 'Always the same. The beauty never changes. Or so we believed.'

Harban's face darkened and Mirron felt the urge to embrace him. But it would have made no difference. They walked on towards the boats that would take them into the mountain. Narrow and sturdy, with oars but also hammer-headed poles for fending them away from the lethal rock walls and roof.

All of them were to go. All two hundred. It would be a relay that would take a day. And while as many as could would be taken by the few boats, the remainder would make the longer and harder trek by foot. Mirron didn't really understand the geography of it all. Up on the mountainside a hundred or so feet above them, ninety soldiers were already entering the pathway. She almost wished she was with them but knew why she wasn't. The walk would take at least a day and the Karku would not risk her of all people not reaching the heart of the mountain before the invaders.

'Ready for this?' asked Jhered, getting into the lead boat and helping her down in front of him.

'No,' she replied.

'Nor me,' he said.

Harban thumped into the centre seat behind them. Two Ascendancy guard followed him and another Karku took up the rear fender. Four similar craft were lined up along the bank. A silence fell, nervous and apprehensive.

'Think how I feel,' muttered Mirron. 'I've done this before.'

'Karku,' called Harban. He spoke more words Mirron could not understand. Quick and thickly accented. Her Karku was not up to translating them. They sounded like a prayer. They were of no comfort.

The boats pushed away from the shore and moved forwards. Warm afternoon sunlight transformed into cold, wet darkness.

Mirron's next scream was lost in the roar of water over rock echoing from the walls that surrounded her; getting closer and closer. Behind her in the bow of the front boat, Jhered had one hand clamped around her waist while his other, like Mirron's, gripped the ropes running along the inside of the gunwale.

She'd tried keeping her head as low as she could but something inside her made her look ahead at what was coming. She didn't know why. Once they had dropped below the tunnel mouth, the darkness had closed in so completely that she knew they would never emerge. They'd plummeted, or so it had felt, into the bowels of the earth. The sides of the boat had shuddered and rumbled. She had caught the odd snatch of a shout and felt the vibrations of the fending poles against walls she could not see.

But slowly, slowly, the world had resolved into looming shadows and grasping, stabbing rock spikes. They had hurtled along the river course at a speed she could sense but didn't want to. The energy trails in the water were fleet beneath them and the knowledge took her breath away. She had been unable to stop the scream when the faint energy of vegetation on the wet rock faces gave dreadful light to her journey.

In front of her, the river bucked and frothed, splashing high up the walls no more than her body's length from the boats at any time.

Above, the tunnel roof was lower than Jhered's height and she could imagine the Exchequer having to crouch low to avoid losing his head. The rock was smoothed where the water ran day by day but above the flow the face was jagged and uneven.

She shrieked and ducked hard. A rock spear lurched out of the roof as they turned a hard left and dove further into the depths of the mountain. Her vision blurred. Water frothed and splashed across her face. Jhered grabbed her harder.

The boat bucked wildly. Harban banged his fender into the left wall to jog them past an eddy that would otherwise drag them onto a razor-sharp face just above the gunwale. Mirron's heart thrashed in her chest. Her stomach turned and she was sick. Again. She needed Ossacer to settle her body but he was a long, long way away, safe in Estorr. And she needed Arducius to tell her the risk was worthwhile.

But as fast as she tried to concentrate on those she loved, another jolt and ripple in the flimsy floor beneath her legs brought her back to her hideous reality. Her ears were full of the roar of water, and her mind with the scattered energies of her shivering body. She felt the fenders rattling against the roof again. They slewed left and sheared past a rock protruding from the river, bleak and menacing.

The timbre of the water changed. The echoing of the river seemed to dull. There was a faint glow growing. Her heart leapt. Surely they were coming to the end. How long they had been travelling she couldn't gauge. Not long but forever. The fenders thudded again into the left hand wall and drove them right. The biting water dragged them down and spat them up. The boat bounced along the surface twice and, quite without warning, the rock ceiling was gone.

So was the river below.

Mirron's scream was joined by those of Jhered and Harkov. For a fleeting moment, the boat hung in the air. And then it fell. Mirron's stomach flipped. There was light around her but she couldn't focus. There was the feeling of great space but she couldn't tell why. The moment was less than the beat of her heart but it hung in the void of her mind.

The boat slapped down onto water once more. Wash fled away to either side and they rocked and settled. It was a while before Mirron realised they were on flat calm and had stopped moving. She sat down hard in the bottom of the boat and let the relief flood over her. Jhered leaned forward and kissed her cheek. The Karku were laughing. The soldiers in the stern were silent.

'Did you enjoy that?' asked Harban. 'The ride of your life?'

'It seemed to last for the whole of it,' said Jhered.

Mirron had a sudden thought and turned to look back the way they had come. Sounds and images were crowding her mind now she was able to think again. They were in an immense cavern. About twenty yards behind, water tumbled from a hole in the wall about five feet from the surface of the lake on which they sat. The Karku had shipped the fenders and dragged out the oars. Already, they were moving away.

As she watched, she sensed a growing presence in the tunnel. A mass of chaotic energy. The second boat punched out of the hole. The cavern echoed with the shouts of Ascendancy guard who ducked reflexively. The Karku steersmen sat still and calm, their fenders high above their heads. Mirron followed the boat as it fell to the water. The occupants sagged much as she had done, the Karku reaching for the oars to move them away and onwards.

'Are you all right, Mirron?' asked Jhered.

'Sort of,' she replied.

Mirron tried to take it all in. The light came from two sources. A greenish, pulsing luminescence from the lichen that covered the rock everywhere she looked, even up to the roof fifty or sixty feet above her. It reflected the light from a host of lanterns set on what she assumed was an island at the centre of the lake.

Now she looked more closely, she could see pathways etched into the cavern's walls and began to understand where the rest of the guard would be travelling. There were other rivers emptying into the lake. Some almost level with its surface, others from so high they reminded her of Genastro Falls in Westfallen. She smiled at the memory. There were other Karku here too. Other boats rowing to and from the island which was some hundreds of yards from them and to which they were steering.

'How big is it?' asked Jhered.

'The lake is three miles across at its broadest. We have entered in the narrows,' said Harban. 'Beyond the island the lake goes on and on it will seem. It's why we call it in your language, the Eternal Water. The first who came here thought it genuinely endless.' Harban pointed around the walls. 'Every settlement in Kark has its path here, whether by boat or on foot. Many join together well before they reach here of course or the roof would look like a sponge.' He laughed at his own joke.

'I think I'd have preferred to walk,' said Mirron.

They rowed quickly across the calm lake and beached on the island, the other boats crunching in by them soon after. The party of Estoreans jumped gratefully to the shore where they stood and looked at one another as if unable to believe they had all survived the trip. Harban was talking to someone and a crowd was gathering. Mirron didn't like the tension she could feel on the air. So many glances cast at them and then at the paths and openings all around them in the vast cavern. She knew what they were thinking. Many gaps to plug. Only one Ascendant. Should Gorian and the dead reach here, they had precious little defence.

The island was curious. It was covered in fine sand and was almost completely flat. At its edges had been built wooden jetties and at its centre, a single stone building had been raised. It looked ancient. It wasn't painted, unlike so much of the building they had seen in the village. On closer inspection, though, its faces were covered in inscriptions. Not a single scrap of rock was free of the language she assumed was Karku and that looked like so much meaningless squiggle.

They were all drawn to it. The building was about five times her height and very broad at its base, covering easily a hundred yards on a side. It was a pyramid of five steps crowned with a single central block on which burned a bright yellow fire. Light flickered from within and she could hear low murmuring.

'No closer,' warned Harban. 'It is forbidden.'

'What is it?' asked Mirron.

'It is the passage from child to maturity,' said Harban.

'What do you mean?' asked Jhered. He was squinting up at the inscribed walls.

Harban exchanged a few words with the Karku who appeared to be guarding or administering the building. They were dressed in plain grey trousers and shirts over which they wore fur waistcoats tied with leather. All had shaven heads and feet and wore a dark stone make-up on their faces. It occurred to Mirron that they must be freezing. There was no warmth in the cavern. The water was ice cold and there was a chill breeze circulating.

Eventually, Harban waved them towards him and he walked away back in the direction of the boats. He was smiling.

'It seems you are most blessed. Further even than I dared assume, even accepting the reasons for your presence here.'

'Why?' asked Harkov.

'Because I am allowed to tell you the reason for this place and the ceremony that you can hear but cannot see.' His expression changed, his eyes glistened. 'It will also explain what it is that Gorian wants to take from here.

Every Karku must take this journey to achieve maturity and be assumed into their tribe.'

'Every Karku comes here?' Mirron looked around. 'It must be strange.'

'Not so,' said Harban. 'They are schooled for it at an early age. There is so much they must learn in so few years. And that is in addition to the knowledge they need just to live in our dangerous land. Too many who do not listen are never found.'

Harban stopped speaking for a while and his face bore an expression of such tragedy that Mirron felt tears coming to her own eyes. Whatever it was, it was personal.

'What is it? What's wrong?' she asked.

'No matter. It is a tale for another day. Perhaps.'

'Tell us about the journey,' said Harkov. 'Where does it begin?'

Harban nodded his thanks.

'At the child's home village. When they are ready, when they have passed thirteen years under the lords of the sky and the light, they must walk inside the mountain and learn the dark for the first time.'

'Or in your case, float down the rapids,' said Mirron.

'Oh no. They walk alone into the mouth of the mountain and are delivered from it into the Eternal Water. Only those with solely dry paths here may walk and they are few and dangerous as your people will testify.'

Mirron looked back to the cascade and screwed up her face. 'They can't do that, Harban. No offence, of course. But they would be killed, wouldn't they?'

Harban smiled. 'To you of course, it must seem a crime to force them to swim the darkness, or walk the narrows. But there are ways. And a single child alone can seek holds on rock that five in a boat can never see. We are one with the mountain. We are born to understand it and in return it provides for us. Not just minerals, but the paths of survival.'

'But some are hurt, surely,' said Jhered.

Harban nodded. Sorrow crossed his face. 'And when one is not yet ready or worthy, the mountain reclaims them. But they must try.'

'A rite of passage,' said Mirron. 'We have nothing like this.'

Harban shrugged. 'You are not Karku.'

'When they reach here, they come to the shrine and speak the inscriptions of Inthen-Gor.' He was pointing at the markings on the building. 'All of them.'

'Presumably pacing round the pyramid and reading as they rise up its levels,' said Harkov, nodding.

'They may refresh themselves by doing so but to be granted onward travel to their maturity, they must recite them all from memory within the shrine.'

'*All* of them?' Every eye was on the building. 'How can they possibly remember them all?'

Harban laughed. 'We do not just teach them how to hold on to smooth rock when they grow. All their language and learning is here. The inscriptions are what guide all our lives. They bring to us all that we see, hear, touch, smell and taste.'

'And there is someone to listen to them, I presume,' said Jhered. 'Check accuracy.'

'There is no higher office in Kark.'

'What happens if they get it wrong?' asked Mirron.

'Then they walk the walls until they are confident once more,' said Harban. 'It is not uncommon. The ceremony is long and difficult. Children are nervous.'

'I'll bet they are,' said Jhered. 'So what would happen if a child rebelled, refused to come here?'

'It can never be,' said Harban, voice quiet. 'Not to walk the path breaks the circle between Karku and mountain. On the walls the inscriptions tell that the mountains would shiver and fall and all Karku would be lost in fire from the earth and the sky. Wind would scour our land to desert and everything we were would become dust.'

Jhered spoke into the awed silence that fell amongst the Estoreans. 'You can see how your words and your beliefs have touched us all. And we are honoured beyond mere speech that you have chosen to bring us here and tell us what you have. But I remain confused. What is it that Gorian can take from here that is so catastrophic?'

'The words a child speaks give strength to the mountain. They feed it. But spoken words are nothing if no one stands to hear and accept them. Gorian wants the Gor-Karkulas. People you would call guardians, I think. They are the guardians of our scriptures and the Heart of the Mountain. They are those blessed with senses beyond those of normal Karku.' Mirron watched Harban's face. It took on the look of a man recalling a warm memory. 'There are six. Young, energetic. At the height of their mental powers with memories so sharp no errant syllable of scripture would escape them. If the Karku had names for gods, these six would bear those names while they guarded our faith, history and destiny.'

Mirron looked towards the shrine and looked again at the energy trails she had assumed were mixtures of heat, light and water. But they weren't so chaotic and in amongst the random energies of the cavern, some pulsed bright and focused. Six of them.

'They're Ascendants,' she breathed.

Harban smiled and relaxed. 'Yes, though not emerged as you and your brothers are. Your Academy would see them as raw potential needing training to release what they have. We see it differently but that hardly matters. They can harbour and amplify energies in a latent fashion just as your son can. That is why Gorian wants them.'

'I don't understand,' said Harkov.

'I do,' said Mirron. 'He took Kessian so he could manage a larger dead army and that is what is attacking Kark even now. But that isn't enough.'

'Even so, six more minds means only so many dead that can be driven by his will, doesn't it?' asked Harkov.

'Yes but every Ascendant can amplify by a massive amount. Join two together and the amplification is multiplied by a factor of ten not two. Link six more . . .'

'If he takes the Gor-Karkulas, the mountain will shiver,' said Harban. 'And the world will fall.'

Jhered turned to Harkov. 'You brought your best tactical minds and here's your battlefield. We cannot afford for the shrine to be breached. Imagine the battle for the Conquord is taking place here. Impress it on your men and I will do the same with mine. If we fail here, we can presume we are lost.

'The enemy are coming. You have a day to prepare.'

Chapter Sixteen

859th cycle of God, 25th day of Genasrise

Herine had never doubted her son. She dreamed of nothing else than to trust him and know he would be proved correct. And so her decision to invoke the executive powers and circumvent the Senate to order a full Conquord mobilisation had been simple. But for the storm of consequence to be quelled she had needed some hard evidence.

And at first light on the day after, she had it in her hand and she felt enriched, though the news was dire. A ship had arrived from Gestern on the morning tide. It told of plague ships hitting the east coast of that great country. Ships flying Tsardon flags. Any doubt of attempted Tsardon invasion was gone now. She would march into the meeting of the Estorean Senate, and later the full meeting at the Solastro Palace, with head high and confidence in her decision complete.

But with her satisfaction came new problems. A coast-wide alert was already being transmitted by messenger south through Estorea and into Caraduk and Easthale. From there, it would be taken along the south of the Conquord. And she knew that ships had sailed for Kester Isle. The Ocetanas fleets patrolling the Tirronean Sea and south around Gestern had to know. No Tsardon ship was to make landfall. No Ocetanas was to board a Tsardon ship. They were to be sent down into the arms of Ocetarus in flames.

'How long did the message take to get here?' asked Arducius.

Herine had come to the Academy to get the very latest news on public opinion and ability emergence. Responses had been a little evasive thus far.

'Seventeen days,' said Herine.

'*Seventeen days?*' Ossacer scratched at his head. 'That's a long time on the sea.'

'Enough to reach a great deal of Conquord coastline,' said Herine.

'Of this I am acutely aware. But I'm also aware that containing plague for such a long time on a ship is extremely difficult. Let's not roll up the Conquord records just yet.'

'But if they have landed, there could be forces of the dead and the living already approaching key cities in Caraduk and Estorea. We could already have lost places like Port Roulent,' said Arducius.

'Is everyone my military adviser now?' Herine's instant frustration lent her tone a sharp edge.

'And Westfallen,' said Ossacer quietly.

His words took the ire from her. 'Look, you two, I understand your concerns and for what it's worth, Westfallen remains the most secure Conquord settlement outside of Estorr and Kester Isle. But more than that, a lot has changed in the last ten years. The messenger service is vastly improved and we would have heard by now if ships had landed. And my senior staff, I like to think, is the best available.

'So let's concentrate on what we three can do right now. Marshal General Kastenas is well aware of every facet of our defence. Admiral Iliev has the navy working so well an undersized cod would have trouble getting through undetected. Now, please, where are we in Estorr? I still see graffiti. I still get complaints from the Order.'

Arducius sighed. 'We can't pretend it's easy out there.'

'Welcome to my world,' said Herine. 'Be specific.'

There were days, Herine considered, when it seemed that everyone she placed in a position of responsibility looked to her for answers. Arducius's expression signified that today might be one of those days.

'At the core, there are two of us and, I would estimate, two thousand Order Readers, Speakers and, of course, Felice Koroyan, in Estorr at the moment. She appears wherever we are. I remember what you said about winning the theological argument and that is what we are trying to do. Yet, while we are in one place talking to people about what we represent, trying to find latent ability and calming anxieties, in a hundred other places, the Chancellor has Readers outside Houses of Masks denouncing us as heretics, morning, noon and night. Not to mention raising fears of Gorian's return.'

'It is the problem Order missionaries have faced for hundreds of cycles in new territories.'

'But this is Estorr. This is home,' said Ossacer.

'Not to the Ascendancy it isn't,' snapped Herine. 'No one said this would be easy. You have my support because I believe in you. What more do you want?'

'Legislation,' said Arducius.

'To do what? Force people to listen and agree with what you say? Make it illegal to disagree with Arducius and Ossacer? God-embrace-me, sometimes I wonder if you two have any sense at all. Have you really not analysed why it is you are struggling?'

A contemplative quiet fell. The two Ascendants looked at each other, something Herine found disconcerting given Ossacer's blindness. There was such passion in those eyes. It was so difficult to believe he really could not see except through the energy trails filling his mind.

'Hard work and belief are not enough,' she said. 'I've had reports on your efforts, of course I have. And no one can fault the hours you put in. But you're trying to change every mind in Estorr at the same time and you will not succeed.'

'It's not that,' said Arducius. 'The problem is that the Order undo all our efforts as soon as we move on. And they have muscle, threats and history as weapons we do not possess.'

Herine breathed in deep. She felt like laughing. 'Of all the people in the world, you should know the lengths the Order are prepared to go to maintain their hold on the citizens' religious hearts. And it doesn't matter that actually, you and I believe in the same God they worship. You are fighting the wrong battle out there. It won't work here like it does in some far-flung corner of Bahkir or Morasia.' She put a hand to her brow. 'Is it me or am I repeating myself here?'

'No, well, perhaps a little,' said Arducius. He smiled. 'And we are eternally grateful for your help, advice and support.'

'I should hope so,' said Herine. 'And you should remember that the Advocate is always right.'

'I never doubt it,' said Ossacer and Herine could see that he had missed the humour. Again.

'That's why you aren't in the cells as Felice demands every day. As do a growing number of my citizens.'

'So what is the Advocate's word about our tactics this morning?' asked Arducius, a twinkle in his eye.

'Undermine your enemy,' said Herine. 'Pull up the corner of the mosaic, don't try to break it in the middle. Do your research. Find the Readers and Speakers who sympathise. Speak to them quietly, bring them together. They are out there somewhere. And if they are scared, protect them. You have the Ascendancy guard. Almost a thousand Conquord professional soldiers. Use them. And next time you speak to the citizens, do it from a House of Masks, not from a fountain.'

Herine leant back in her chair watching them see how it all made sense. How it all seemed so simple. She had Jhered to thank for that. A man for whom most people's lives were unnecessarily complicated.

'You think we should have thought of this for ourselves,' said Ossacer.

Herine raised her eyebrows. 'I think the Academy is unstructured in its approach to everything but teaching. I think you don't use all the facilities and services the Conquord has for its favoured institutions. But I also think you are a very young organisation and running your operation in Westfallen is a world away from becoming a Conquord-wide organisation. You were right when you told me it would take generations. But if your enemy becomes your friend, you will find the path smoother and straighter. The Order has been operating that way for a long time. It's only Felice who believes suppression is a better way.'

'Wrong, isn't she?' said Arducius.

'Some people never learn,' said Herine. 'Don't count yourselves amongst them.'

Ossacer spread his hands suddenly. 'We should talk to Marshal Vasselis, shouldn't we?'

'Congratulations, you're thinking,' said Herine. 'But be careful when you talk to him. Remember what his service to the Ascendancy has cost him. He's not the man you remember from your youth.'

Arducius inclined his head. 'We did try to include him in the work of the Academy. He'd have been the perfect figurehead. He refused. As far as I know, he hasn't left Caraduk, barely left his villa in Cirandon, for years.'

'Well, he gets out a little more than that,' said Herine. 'He's still a functioning and excellent Marshal Defender. But he lost his heir and they can have no more children. He's broken.'

'Then perhaps we should leave him alone,' said Ossacer. 'Let him have peace.'

Herine shook her head. 'Don't do that. He's here in a few days and we're travelling to the Solastro Palace for the Senate meeting together. Talk to him then. Let him decide. He would be further damaged if he felt you thought him useless because of Kovan.'

Still that name brought a tear to the eye of the Ascendants. Another hero of the Conquord. Only seventeen when he gave his life to save Mirron and perhaps the whole Conquord with her. But Arvan Vasselis, his father, had found no glory or comfort in the manner of his death. It was Herine's most enduring sadness. A friend had been stolen from her and replaced with something hollow.

'My Advocate?'

'Yes ... Arducius. Sorry, miles away.'

'We know you didn't come here just to tell us where we're going wrong in Estorr. What do you need from us?'

There was suspicion in Ossacer's blind gaze. And knowledge in his brother's.

'You haven't taken any of the next generation out with you yet, have you?'

'Not blooded them, you mean?' said Ossacer.

'I don't much care which words you use. I'm asking if they've been out with you. If they've demonstrated abilities in public and under pressure.'

Herine stared at Ossacer, knowing he could read her mood, daring him to say more. He was no longer timid, that was for sure. Sometimes, she wished he still hid behind his disability. His eyes displayed a wash of bright colours, then settled to a cool blue.

'No, they haven't been with us. It's risky out there. And until we are certain they can handle the hate and the suspicion they won't come out.'

'Very laudable, and I agree absolutely,' said Herine. 'Until yesterday and this morning. And now I have changed my mind. The Conquord is readying for war, as you are aware. The Ascendancy must also make ready. We may well have need of you. It seems that not only was your friend Harban, the emotional Karku, speaking some sense, the Tsardon are attacking Gosland and Gestern.'

Ossacer's face had gone grey. 'And what exactly is it that you expect us to do, my Advocate?'

'Oh dear,' said Herine, a flush of frustration rushing through her. 'I saw this coming.'

'I'm sorry, I don't follow,' said Ossacer.

'Yes, you damn well do,' said Herine. 'And I expect you to do what the Conquord demands. What the general of your army demands, should you be in the field. And that, be assured, is where I expect you to be. After all, I should think a man who can bring down hillsides, cause hurricanes and raise tidal waves might be quite useful in a fight, don't you?'

'And we will undo everything we have striven so hard to achieve in the last ten years,' said Ossacer.

'Gorian's already doing that for you. We have to fight this threat.'

'I will not conduct a Work that results in death and neither will any of the new generation,' said Ossacer.

'You and they will do as ordered by your commanding officer,' said Herine. She pushed herself to her feet and loomed over Ossacer, who did not flinch. 'People that refuse orders on the battlefield are executed.'

'So be it. But I will go to the embrace of God clear of conscience.'

'And burned,' she said. 'Their ashes scattered to the winds.'

'You cannot scare me, my Advocate. I will not change who I am.'

'Damn you, war changes everything for everyone.' Herine's shout bounced from the stone and glass of the Chancellery. 'Have you so short a memory that you forget that? You have already killed in battle and in doing so saved the Conquord. Your conscience is clear to do so again.'

She turned away and bit her tongue against saying more.

'I think we should all take a breath,' said Arducius quietly. 'Tempers flare when our abilities are discussed in here as they do in the streets of Estorr. Ossacer, we all understand your position but even you might have to step away from it in the depths of war. And my Advocate, if I may, I suspect that you respect and even support Ossacer's stance.'

'Someone else who can read my damn mind,' muttered Herine. 'Am I such an open book?'

'My Advocate?'

She waved her hand. 'Never mind.'

'We will play our part in any conflict should it arise,' said Arducius. Ossacer opened his mouth and was hushed with a touch. 'What that part is will be decided at the time. As for the new generation, Herine, I don't know. They are untried and if war is as close as you think, there will be no time to school them.'

'You were untried and you were fourteen. Three years younger than the next five Ascendants.'

'And we are still paying the price,' said Arducius. 'We will never be free of the nightmares, the sound of the screams and the tumbling of rock. The sucking of water and the scream of wind. We have to live with what we have done. An individual soldier kills or is killed. We stand back and murder thousands.'

'Yes!' Herine smiled, aware the expression was inappropriate. 'And think how many Conquord citizens you save in so doing.'

'You would not think like that if the power was in your body,' said Ossacer. 'One step too far and we are no better than Gorian.'

'And I'm sure Gorian will exercise no restraint whatever.' Herine sucked her top lip. There was such passion in these young men. And such fear. She continued.

'I understand. I do. I do not envy you the weight upon your shoulders, the duty of care to those who follow you. But we all have responsibility to the Conquord and its citizens. Whether you feel it is a blessing or a curse, you have abilities that can make a significant, perhaps critical difference in times of war. I cannot ignore that.'

'As you cannot ignore the aftermath,' said Ossacer. 'I am offended by the assumption that the Ascendants are weapons first and foremost. We are not. We are people like you.'

'Wrong,' said Herine. She sat back down in her chair. 'Firstly, you are not like me or anyone else in this world. You are the first of a new breed of human beings, with all the glory and pain that comes with that. And second, it is your abilities that are the weapons, not you, Ossacer Westfallen. A farmer trains for war. He will be given a sarissa, bow or gladius, depending on his aptitude. That is his weapon.'

'I am not a soldier and I will not kill,' said Ossacer. 'And I will not allow my fellow Ascendants to be used so casually.'

'*Allow?* You are neither Mother of the Ascendancy nor are you Advocate. We will decide what is allowed and what is not.'

'I understand that we must defend ourselves against invaders. I understand the necessity for war. But I live to heal, not to kill.'

'Then be a battlefield surgeon, damn you.' Another shout, another echo. 'And stop wasting my time.' Herine stood and moved towards the door. 'I will say it one more time and you will deal with it in an appropriate way. Should war break out, you and the five will be despatched to the armies, there to do what your commanding officer demands. Failure to do so will result in your execution for cowardice or insubordination. And where will your precious Ascendancy and principles be then?'

She tore open the door and stalked away down the corridor, past the bust of Father Kessian.

'Live in the real world. See what I see.' She let her voice drop. 'Idealists. God deliver me from idealists.'

Roberto Del Aglios had long admitted to himself a certain selfish pleasure in coming to Gosland, despite the reason for his journey. He had sent fast messengers ahead of him and a large welcoming party was waiting for him on the main border crossing. A border crossing bristling with weaponry.

'I knew you wouldn't let me down,' he said quietly.

In all his years travelling to and from Sirrane, he hadn't travelled this way, always taking to the river further north and rowing under the grand arch he was now about to cross. It looked ordinary from the river. From here it was a spectacular and imposing statement of Conquord power.

Seated ten miles south of the Sirranean border, the Gorneon Bridge over the wide, sluggish River Triesk had been a gateway for Conquord legions marching to the invasion of Tsard. The gatehouse on the Tsardon bank of the river was carved with heroic figures of the past and rose forty feet at its highest. Ballistae poked from tower windows, battlements were manned with archers and the huge iron-bound gates, wide enough for a column fifteen men across, were closed against the enemy. Flags flew from six places and statues placed in alcoves adorned the structure, daring any Tsardon to attack.

Those gates rumbled open when Roberto approached. He was welcomed through with cheers and salutes which he returned with a humble nod. The span of the bridge rose in front of him. Behind it, the fortifications on the Gosland bank were formidable. Concrete and stone towers and a fortress that would produce a withering fire on an enemy attempting a crossing. Looming into the sky and glowering down, a barrier that only a fool would attempt to bring down.

It was enough alone to banish any lingering doubts that Roberto might have had about the chances of the small Tsardon force breaching the Conquord borders. Standing in front of the honour guard of shining legionaries were a trio that warmed his heart.

'Damn protocol,' said Roberto, sliding from his horse and striding quickly up the slope. He was aware he was grinning like a fool but more keenly he felt guilt that he had ignored them for so long.

'Hello Roberto.'

'Dahnishev, you sly bastard, what are you doing here?'

Roberto crushed his old friend, the man who had served as his surgeon for so many years on campaign, into a huge embrace. The Goslander miracle-worker. Still going strong.

'Hey, careful of an old man's bones,' grunted Dahnishev.

Roberto laughed. 'You will never grow old.'

And he didn't look it. He must have been pushing eighty and had the appearance of a man thirty years younger. A man Roberto's age. Tall, slender and with that sparkle of genius still in his eyes.

'Anyway. Heard you were coming. Thought you might want a check-up.'

'I may take you up on that,' said Roberto, breaking away. 'That Sirranean food is challenging.'

He moved along the line.

'General Kell.' She proffered a hand but he grabbed her shoulders and kissed her on both cheeks. 'Dina, it has been too long.'

'For me also, Roberto. Wonderful to see you.'

'And finally, if it isn't Pavel Nunan.' The two men clasped hands and Roberto clapped him on the back. 'Fatherhood been good to you, General?'

Nunan chuckled. 'Ask Dina. She's the one that sees me in action.'

'He had a lot to learn,' said Kell. 'He treats the three of them like a little legion. I'm surprised they aren't lined up here in front of you rather than in Estorr with their grandparents.'

'She exaggerates. They may have wooden swords but they also have horses and I can't think where the cavalry influence comes from.'

'A noble calling, and it would have been a pleasure to see them. Later perhaps. But talking of family, where is my little brother? Where is Adranis?'

'Not so little, I can assure you,' said Kell.

She turned and looked along the bridge to where the honour guard stood. She made a beckoning gesture and the lead horseman dismounted and marched towards them. Roberto's heart swelled. Adranis removed his impeccable plumed helmet and swept his cloak over one shoulder to reveal equally perfect armour. His bearing was assured, his pace even. Kell was right, he was not little. Adranis had grown into a powerful figure. Tall, black-haired and with a face that had surely broken hearts already. He kept his expression professionally neutral and came to a stop just behind the two generals. Kell glanced at him and raised her eyebrows.

'At ease, Master Del Aglios, for God's sake.'

Adranis glanced quickly left and right before handing his helmet to an aide and rushing forwards to embrace Roberto. He felt the air burst from his lungs and the emotion surge inside him.

'You make me so proud, Adranis. You honour the name of Del Aglios by the very beating of your heart.'

'Where have you been, Roberto?' Deep and melodic, Adranis's voice sounded in his ear. 'Is Sirrane really so enticing you could not break away until now? Until trouble?'

Roberto pushed back and looked into Adranis's eyes.

'Is that admonishment?' he asked, smiling.

'Maybe a little. I've missed you.'

'But I haven't missed news of you. Mother was right to give you to General Kell, I see. Twenty-seven and Master of Horse for the Bear Claws. You're some rider, I understand.'

Adranis blushed and Roberto almost sobbed at the humility.

'I still have a lot to learn.'

Kell snorted. 'Who from?'

'So you don't think twenty-seven a little young and brash for such a command?' asked Roberto, winking.

Kell met his humour blankly. 'Not in this case. You should see him.'

'Perhaps I will have cause to. Little brother, all I shall say is this. Should I fall, the Conquord has an able deputy to the Advocate.'

Adranis drew in a sharp breath and then gasped. He bit back sudden tears and managed a nod.

'Thank you.'

'Not necessary. You are born to it. I can see it in you instantly.' Roberto clapped him on the shoulder. 'Come on, let's eat and yarn. Don't know about you but I'm famished.'

Chapter Seventeen

859th cycle of God, 25th day of Genasrise

Roberto banged the table and roared with laughter. He sat up on his recliner and drank some sweetened hot wine. On the table around which they all lay, meats, sauces, fruits and breads were still piled high. Servants had been dismissed. Outside, light was fading and the evening was cold. Rain threatened. In the banquet hall, the atmosphere was warm and the fire banked.

'God-take-me-to-my-rest, I had forgotten that,' said Roberto when he could speak again. 'That bloody red Atreskan shield. I can recall it sticking out in the midst of battle like a fire in the night. As if Davarov wasn't obvious in the first place. If I hadn't so much faith in him, it would have terrified me. That was Herolodus Vale, wasn't it?'

'That's right,' said Dahnishev. 'The day Arducius brought the blizzard and Mirron turned the Tsardon catapults to ash.'

'That was some day,' said Roberto, sobering at the naming of the Ascendants.

'Why did he do that?' asked Adranis who had been drinking in the stories of the Tsardon war all afternoon. 'Davarov, I mean. Why did he carry an Atreskan liveried shield? Why did you let him, Roberto?'

'You haven't met him, have you?' said Roberto. Adranis shook his head. 'It is an education. He's one of a kind and Dahnishev will back me up on this. I have never met a man more impassioned about his duty to the Conquord, yet I have also never met a man more immovably cemented to his country of birth. He is the most ardent Atreskan you will ever meet, and he's against some stiff competition as you can imagine.

'It was a difficult combination to command in the early days, but what I had to remember is that his loyalty to the Conquord was unshakeable and he brought all his charges with him on that basis. It meant that I could give him the latitude to express his individuality because in his case, it merely strengthened his belief in me and in us. You don't take a shield from a man like that, just like you don't treat him like any ordinary soldier. If you do, you remove his identity and make him less useful.'

'But that's an open invitation to insubordination,' said Adranis.

'Not so. Not so long as he understands where his boundaries are and his duties and loyalties lie. And Davarov always knew that. Passion wasn't and isn't everything with him. He is clever and charismatic and those are qualities to be encouraged always.'

'Couldn't sing though, could he?' said Dahnishev. 'Remember the road to Neratharn?'

'Remember?' said Roberto, putting his hands to the sides of his head. 'My ears still hurt on cold mornings.' He looked over at Adranis once more. 'But he did sing and it kept us all going when we might have given up. If you find a man like that, don't gag him, give him a platform.'

They'd reminisced for a long time. Too long, really. Roberto felt a little foggy. He fell silent and let the mood quieten. He topped up his goblet with water this time.

'You're thinking we could do with him here,' said Nunan.

'No,' said Roberto. 'I look at what you have here and there is no immediate cause for concern. In any case, he may well have his own problems. Atreska's a mess. It seems always to have been so.'

'So what is coming at us?' asked Kell. 'Your messengers talked about six thousand. Hardly an invasion force.'

'No indeed, but the Tsardon do nothing without reason and the Sirraneans believe something larger is going on. I find it impossible that this is the only action they are taking. We must expect other forces on the move further south, and presumably more coming up in reserve. How they have rebuilt so fast I can't begin to guess but assume they have, that's all that matters.

'For that reason, I have asked the Advocate for a full mobilisation. It's expensive, I know, but the Exchequer is in full flow once more. We can probably just afford it and we can also drive the Tsardon back into their hinterlands for good this time, if we are ready for them. We're well served up here in the north. Gosland has good legion strength and we can call on Dornos and Tundarra, even Phaskar, though they may send to Atreska via Neratharn. What?'

Around the table, the other four were looking at each other, faces suddenly glum.

'You've been away a long time, Roberto. You're missing out on recent events,' said Dahnishev.

'Like what?'

Kell nodded for Adranis to speak.

'Dornos has left the Conquord.'

'They've wh—' Roberto stopped, stunned. He frowned. 'They can't. That's ... that's unbelievable. Bastard traitors. They'll regret it.'

'Will they?' Adranis shook his head. 'Not in the short term. They know we aren't strong enough to impose martial law and we can't afford to invade. Atreska bled us dry a second time. They think they can avoid us altogether if they ally with Omari. And we're hearing reports that Tundarra might go the same way.'

'No better than the rats in their Conquord-built drains,' said Roberto. 'God-embrace-me, I would build a road to Cabrius and flag the Tsardon all the way. And then I'd laugh when the Dornoseans came crawling back for mercy.'

'We all know how you feel,' said Kell. 'It makes us isolated up here. It's half the reason the Bear Claws weren't redeployed further south.'

'But they won't attack,' said Roberto. 'We'll pull Estoreans and loyals out and close the borders, right?'

'Already happening,' said Nunan. 'But it leaves us woefully short of strength should the Tsardon prove to have greater numbers than we suspect.'

'All the more reason for a full mobilisation of what we do have. Has the message reached you from Estorr yet?'

'No,' said Nunan. 'At least, it hadn't when we left Goscapita ten days ago. Your messenger intercepted us on the first leg of a see-and-be-seen tour. All very exciting stuff. The message will break where the river conjoins with the Bysane a hundred and fifty miles south of here. We'll get the news before Gosland's Marshal.'

'Good, because you're in the front line, let's face it. All right, what do we have here?'

'The full legion, 2nd Estorean, the Bear Claws. We have five hundred of the 4th Ala, the Gosland Spear acting as they always do in peacetime, as roving border guards. That gives us five thousand in all but in truth there's little behind us. The Spear are undermanned to the tune of a thousand foot and horse. The 30th Ala, the Firedragons of Gosland, are mainly north on the border with Omari. Still difficult up there. Best to assume we're it if Tundarra sends no one.'

Roberto nodded. 'Good enough. For now at least. Those following me won't get across the bridge and I suspect your onagers can reach bank to bank anyway. No reason why we can't keep them back from the gatehouse even without placing you all on the Tsardon side.'

'The same assessment we made,' said Kell.

'That reminds me. Who's in charge of the legion today?' Roberto smiled. 'Still can't believe our Marshal General consented to this husband-and-wife-on-campaign idea. Actually, I can. Elise Kastenas has a dreadfully romantic heart beneath that sparkling armour of hers. It doesn't really work, does it?'

'We have no complaints,' said Nunan. 'And anyway, it was either have us both here or lose us both from the legions. Simple choice really.'

'Blackmail,' said Roberto.

'Such an ugly word,' said Kell, face cracking. 'We prefer to call it familial negotiation.'

'And one day, I will ask you how you divide the task and keep the legion happy. Or perhaps I'll ask Adranis in private.'

'It's not important right now though, is it?' said Nunan. 'We understand you are assuming command of the Gosland defence forces.'

Roberto felt uncomfortable now it came to it, sitting in front of two such competent people.

'We can work it for mutual benefit,' he said.

'Not at all,' said Nunan. 'To have you as our commanding officer would be an honour. You must assume control. Take a look at Adranis's face if you want to know the effect you'll have on morale.'

'Come on Roberto, don't be bashful.'

'That's you digging the latrines, little brother.'

They all laughed. Roberto refilled and raised his glass. Wine again this time.

'Let us toast the Advocate, the Bear Claws and the inevitable defeat of the Tsardon.'

The Ascendancy guard and the levium soldiers had all brought fuel. Fires were alight all over the cavern, shimmering stars in a tiny firmament. But still it was cold. The chill set in slowly, soaking into the bones and leaching through every muscle. From their vantage point, high up on the south wall of the cavern, looking down over the island and away to the outflow of the lake to the north, Mirron gazed on a sight she knew no Karku had ever expected to see.

Drinking in the warmth of the fire around which she sat with Jhered, Harkov and Harban, Mirron scanned the results of a day's feverish planning. Karku had been flooding into Inthen-Gor the whole time, bringing stories of the advance. Worrying stories because while the Tsardon army was being tracked and harried all the way, the dead had to all intents and purposes disappeared. No scout knew where they were. No Karku brave enough to follow them had come back.

The Karku thronged the island and stood at the opening to every pathway. Boats littered the lake in case they should appear from any stream outflow. And in amongst them stood the two hundred Estoreans giving out advice, conducting training in weapons and tactics. It was a tiny effort given the time but anything might help swing the oncoming battle. The noise of organisation echoed, sometimes painfully, from the scarred rock that enclosed Inthen-Gor.

Mirron tasted the energy. It was fevered, nervous and laden with an inevitability that felt like defeat. By now, the Tsardon would have reached as many entrances to the cavern as they could. The tragedy of the rout of the Karku was happening up there somewhere. Murder, torture and slaughter, with information the prize.

A fear had gripped the Karku, spreading like disease across every mountain and flooding into every valley. For all Harban's words and his strength of will, it was not shared by enough of his countrymen. Their doom was upon them. Mirron could hear it in the way they talked and see it in the way their eyes roved the pathways and entries into the cavern.

Not enough had come here to make the last stand against the dead. Too many had scattered into hiding places deep underground or on ridges no Tsardon or dead walker could reach. What was written was coming to pass and most were just waiting for the end. It made Jhered furious and he had let Harban know often enough this last day. Mirron had winced at some of his words. He didn't understand what underpinned Karku faith. But Harban took it all. Just like now. He was probably the only one looking forward to the battle starting. At least it would get Jhered out of his ear.

'God helps those who help themselves,' said Jhered.

'Your God, perhaps.'

'Yours have not built these mountains on sand. You are strong here, or you should be. But what have you? Two thousand scared rabbits standing on an island, waiting for it to be swamped by a tide of the dead. If three times that number had come, we would win this. Now we cannot be sure.'

'I hear you. Yet what can I do? The path of a Karku is his to choose. When the paths to Inthen-Gor have been traversed and the passage to adulthood is made, our destinies are our own.'

'Right,' said Jhered and he shook his head. 'And you expect me to believe that most of you have chosen to let your society fall and your most sacred place be raped?'

'I expect you to believe that the Karku will do what they believe to be best for those they must protect.'

'And let the mountain fall?' Jhered shot to his feet and took a step perilously close to the edge of the path, spinning round to jab a finger at Harban. 'You say your people are bound to their faith, that it is the centre of their lives. How much more important can it get than to protect this place? Surely, to keep Inthen-Gor intact is to keep their loved ones safe. It's basic mathematics, isn't it? If losing this place is said to be the end of the Karku, then what other choice did any of your bloody free spirits really have to make?'

'I've brought two hundred here prepared to die on your account. What happened to the rest of you?'

'Then go, Exchequer Jhered.' Harban's voice was quite calm, his face betraying no anger. 'Take your people away. If you think this is no longer your fight then I will bear you no ill.'

'Damn you, Harban, you told us it was *everyone's* fight. That's why we dragged ourselves into this freezing tomb. Pity you couldn't sell it as well to the rest of the Karku. People who should know better and have the guts to stand up for their beliefs.'

'Paul, I think you should step away from the edge and sit back down,' said Mirron, who winced every time he moved his feet a fraction closer to a drop into the lake a hundred feet and more below.

Jhered turned his face to her, thought to say something but simply nodded instead.

'No high diving today, you think?' he said, a smile dragging itself on to his face.

'Not in that armour, no,' she replied. 'I've been down to the deeps to save you once before. I don't really fancy a repeat performance.'

'It's cold enough up here,' said Jhered, poking a boot at the fire.

'Here, let me help.'

Mirron took his hands and opened her mind to the chaotic energies of the flames in front of them. She teased open a break in the circuit and let the warmth flood into her and over her. Her skin warmed from the inside and Jhered jerked in surprise when she allowed it to flow through her hands, into his and away into his body. The hard, tense energy lines that pulsed in him began to soften as the heat eased away the cold and his mood.

'That's quite some trick, young lady. Is it tiring?'

'Not at all,' she said. 'Well, a little. I could channel the fire through me directly but it would go out and that wouldn't be much help. So I'm boosting the energies myself. I shouldn't do it for too long.'

'No. We'll have need of all your stamina all too soon, I fear.' He looked across the fire at Harban. 'Sorry, my friend. But you can understand my frustration, can't you?'

Harban nodded. 'I share it. We know why so few are here. Besides those in places so remote the message hasn't even reached them, those that do know are scared. We none of us willingly place ourselves in the path of that which terrifies us. Most of us, anyway.'

'Those who have come will find their place by God should they fall,' said Jhered. 'We must just pray that we are enough.'

The echoes of urgent shouts sounded from all around the cavern. At four entrances to the north, green Conquord signal flags were waved. Jhered was on his feet again, Harkov with him, already barking orders.

The Tsardon were in the passages. They were coming.

'But where in God's world is Gorian,' muttered Mirron.

Abruptly, she felt a slam of rotten nausea that took her breath away. The temperature in the cavern plummeted. Her breath clouded in front of her. The fire sputtered before regaining a little substance. All over the cavern, flames wavered. Some were extinguished. Jhered cut off his next order and crouched by her.

'Mirron, are you all right? What is it?'

'God-surround-me, it feels like a suffocation of decay,' she said. 'He's here. He's close and he's doing something. Something big. I can't—'

The temperature dipped again. Sharply. Dampness on the rocks turned to frost. Cries of disbelief and fear rose to a clamour from the island. Mirron dragged herself to her feet and looked out over the lake.

'Oh dear God-take-me-to-rest,' she breathed.

Ice. From the outflow of the lake it spread like a wave sluicing up a sandy shore. Gorian was turning the lake to ice.

Chapter Eighteen
859th cycle of God, 25th day of Genasrise

'It's a bridge!' Jhered was already running down towards the island to make himself heard. 'He's going to use the lake as a bloody bridge!'

Mirron just stood and stared. Unconsciously, she had taken energy from the fire at her feet to warm her while the ice formed on the walls of Inthen-Gor and marched across the lake. She felt the energy drain around her like it was pulling at her skin, trying to drag it from her bones.

'How can he control this much power?' she whispered. 'How is it possible.'

The lake was vast, the outflow river long and deep. Crusting the whole was a Work that should be beyond the four of them together. She shivered and it had nothing to do with the cold. A paralysis gripped her and she felt helpless but to look at the march of the ice. Hypnotic. It chased the water south to north across the cavern faster than a man could run.

She dragged her eyes round to the island where a swell of noise was growing. Karku and Estorean alike were backing away from the shore. It didn't matter what previous experience they had of the Ascendants, no one had seen the like of this Work. No one. She stared at terrified faces. Those in the front had forgotten their drawn weapons.

Mirron could hear Jhered and Harkov both bellowing for some form of order. Screaming at the defenders to look past the ice rushing across the Eternal Water and to prepare for what was coming after it. But their words were getting lost in the increasing clamour in which panic grew, threatening to explode.

Yet there was a fascination in Mirron that would not be ignored. The sick feeling deep in the pit of her stomach and climbing into her throat told her the dead were very near. She could imagine the dead walking under Gorian's control, moving inexorably forward, just as Harban had told them.

What Mirron had trouble with was how Gorian could control the dead and form ice simultaneously. It shouldn't be possible. Every mote of research in the Ascendancy pantheon said that it couldn't be done.

She couldn't help herself. She reached out to the energy map Gorian was using to drive the ice forwards. It was beautiful, stamped with his personality. He'd always been the most accurate of them all. There were few stray strands of energy. So little flailing at the edges of the map and wasting precious stamina.

Gorian's map of ice was pouring both over and under the lake. It was dark at its centre, and a blindingly bright blue at its edges. She could see immediately what he had done. So simple and so effective. A classic circuit. In another life, Father Kessian would have been proud. He was taking the living energy from the water, draining it through his body and stripping it away to another place. It left the aura of a deep dusas night and without the depth of life to combat it, the water encased in the map froze solid.

Mirron sought on, moving her mind down, far into the outflow tunnel where Gorian had to be and where perhaps her son stood by him. The more her mind probed out, the more concentrated the feeling of nausea became. It churned in her stomach and fogged her thoughts. She gasped and leaned back against a wall, reacting sharply to the frost that covered it, the intense cold shearing straight through her cloak.

Swallowing the saliva that filled her mouth, Mirron opened her mind further. The flat, cold negative energy of the dead, for that's what it was, threatened to swamp her. But there was something else there. Something pure and bright which drew her on. Long before she felt him she knew it was him. Her son. Kessian. Standing among the dead, standing with Gorian whose aura pulsed with power and greed. It was a disturbing life map. Distorted from that which she remembered even that short time ago when he took Kessian. There was a sensuous beguiling purple wreathing the tight map of his body. It was like sickness though it wasn't the normal dull grey.

Instead, she let Kessian's aura fill her. She could almost touch him, feel him. If only there was a way to tell him she was near. Gorian might sense her but Kessian wouldn't and her life map could not form a communication. So close but it felt like a thousand miles apart. She dragged in a sobbing breath.

'I'm here, my love, I'm here,' she said.

A spear of pain drove her to her knees. The purity of Kessian's life map had a dark heart and the most gossamer-thin of paths connecting him to Gorian. Trembling, she sought the reason for the bleakness infecting her son. The truth brought, clarity, fury and horror.

There was a voice nearby though it sounded distant. She hadn't realised she'd gone so far within herself and into the energies that flowed and formed around her in the cavern. She felt herself being shaken. Gently at first but then more roughly. She drew back, shutting out the multitude of colours and lines her mind could see. She focused.

'Mirron.' It was Jhered.

'Paul,' she said. It was little more than a whimper but she remembered the anger and let it lend strength to her voice. 'He's using my son to control the dead. I know what he's doing and I know what he wants here. That bastard is using my son.'

'Then we have to stop him,' said Jhered.

The noise in the cavern was suddenly intense as Mirron's normal senses reopened.

'We—'

'Mirron.' Another shake of her shoulders. Jhered hauled her to her feet and stepped back. 'Later. Concentrate now.'

'What can I do?'

Mirron cast about her. There was panic on the island. She could see Harkov amongst them, standing to the fore and urging steadiness and courage. From out of the outflow they came. The dead. Shambling, slipping, falling and rising. But moving on, never stopping. Coming for the island.

Mirron gaped. The sickness boiled in her throat and the scratching of the ice captured her. A silence spread across the island. Every Karku voice was stilled. Distantly, gorthock could be heard in the tunnels, keeping back the Tsardon. The sound of boot and metal scraped over ice filled Inthen-Gor. The dead spread like flotsam from a wreck washing towards shore.

'What can I do?' she repeated.

Jhered looked at her, demanded her attention. Despite what he was witnessing, he alone seemed to retain control.

'You're an Ascendant. Work your talent.'

'But he'll know I'm here if I act.'

'God-embrace-me, I hope so. He needs scaring off.'

'What can I do?'

Jhered frowned, then pointed. 'It's ice, Mirron. Melt it.'

He turned and ran back down the path away from her. He was shouting at Harkov to bring the Karku to readiness and not to take a backward step. That he'd be with them soon. A boat waited for him.

'Stupid girl,' muttered Mirron, feeling a flush of shame.

Melt the ice. Easy.

There was heat within her, heat from the fire at her feet and from every blaze that still illuminated the cavern, giving shape to the ghastly advance. And her target was everywhere.

'Out in the deep, Mirron.' Jhered's voice floated up to her. 'And care for the dead. Don't burn them. They can still feel the embrace of God.'

'No, Paul,' she said quietly, letting the fire everywhere coalesce and thrum through her body, amplifying with every heartbeat. She moulded the energy, projecting it forwards. 'At the mouth of the beast.'

Heat marked a shimmering line in the air above the Eternal Water's outflow. Below it, the dead disgorged onto the ice plateau, heading for the island. All but invisible, heat washed down in two sheets, like the graceful slow opening of a butterfly's wings. Their edges struck the ice.

The dead moved on oblivious, while beneath their feet their platform was under attack. Steam clouded in the cold air, gouting up from the lake surface. Water poured over their feet. More of them slipped and fell but rose again, unconcerned. Blank. Gorian had done his work well. The ice was deep and solid. Mirron increased the heat, driving the sheets down, widening them too. They covered the whole outflow now and were still growing. The clouds of steam deepened, obscuring much of the dead advance.

She felt herself thrilling to the energy surging through her. So long since she had exercised her ability to such an extent. A jolt told her she'd broken through the crust and into the pure waters of the lake below. There was energy there she could use. Immediately, she released some of the fires in the cavern to regain their strength and pulled on the slumbering power of the Eternal Water.

Mirron felt it wash through her, a mighty force waiting to be tapped. She opened herself to it, relaxed her mind and let the deep blue trails modulate into the harsher lines of her heat construct. They lent intensity to the heat and it fed on the ice, driving it to water and sending more steam into the cavern and down into the outflow.

Fissures and fractures ran across the surface. The weight of the dead amplified the weakening. The result was inevitable. In great swathes, the ice gave way. The dead fell through into the chilling water. Shelves of ice reared up, spilling the helpless, expressionless walkers to splash and flail briefly before their armour dragged them down to the bottom of the lake.

'There to feel once more the embrace of God,' whispered Mirron.

Yet there was still work to do. Across the lake, the ice needed to be melted if Gorian's advance was to be seriously dented. Mirron also needed to find some way to interrupt the work that Kessian was, she prayed, doing unwittingly. And in the shallows, the dead still walked. Splashing in to threaten and engage the Karku, who were led by Harkov. There was something else nagging at her too. Another presence drawing on the lake's energy. Growing stronger.

Harkov saw the great mass of the dead, a thousand and many more, crash into the water and disappear from view. The steam obscured any struggle but not one of them made any sound. He thought he could handle the few that were left.

'Bless you, Mirron,' he said. 'Bless you.'

Around him, some modicum of confidence returned to the scared Karku.

'Stand firm!' he shouted, Harban translating his words. The Karku responded, his own soldiers among them urging courage. 'We have the numbers now. Strike hard. To stop them now is to help them return to God.'

He looked out at the dead still coming at them. He shuddered. Men and women in tattered Conquord livery. Karku in torn furs. Faces were blackened by frostbite, wounds gaped, jaws hung slack. Boils and sores covered pasty flesh. But the cold couldn't mask everything. The closer they came, the more the stink of decay grew, assaulting the nostrils. Resolving from the steam that still rose in clouds from the water and remaining ice came bodies that were literally falling apart. Limbs missing, bone showing through skin that had sloughed away, heads lolling where muscle had withered. Not all. Some, Harkov considered grimly, were fresher.

Harkov swallowed on a dry throat and gripped his gladius and shield tight. He sensed a shuffling around him. The dead were scant yards from them.

'Stand!' he roared. 'You have nowhere to run.'

He raised his shield, took a pace forwards and butted it into the face of a former Conquord legionary. The man raised no defence. The skin split from nose to forehead, revealing pale flesh beneath. Thin blood lined the split. The blow should have knocked him senseless. But he merely staggered back, rebalanced and came straight back in, sword raised.

Harkov paused. Against a fast, living enemy, probably fatal. Here, not so. The dead march was relentless but it was ponderous. What worried Harkov now was not their ability, it was how they would ever be stopped. Harban shouted and the entire Karku line engaged, roaring determination after Harkov's lead. The few archers they had, fired over the front ranks and into those still chest deep in water.

Next to the general, a Karku warrior buried his blade in the chest of a badly mouldering militia man bearing Gesternan insignia. The blow stopped him but only temporarily. And while the Karku tried desperately to drag the blade from his ribs, the Gesternan brought his gladius through waist-high and drove it into exposed gut.

'Dear God-embrace-me,' whispered Harkov.

He struck his enemy, though it was hard to see this victim as an enemy, once more with his shield, pushing him back, buying himself more time. He stared at the blank advance. No flicker of emotion, no recognition of enemy. Nothing. And behind the front rank the next walked on oblivious of the defence, pushing, pressing.

'Harban,' called Harkov. 'Tell your people. No killing blows. Disable them. Bring them down. It's our only chance.'

Harban's voice rose above the growing anxiety, halting the backward step some of the Karku were making. Harkov took a deep breath and faced the rotting legionary one more time.

'May God forgive me for what I must do,' he said.

Harkov changed the angle of his attack and hacked down into the man's unprotected legs at the knee. He felt the blade part flesh and rattle into bone. The leg gave way. Harkov kept his shield high, fending off the falling body. Even as he went down, the Gesternan dead man lashed out, his blade clattering into Harkov's defence.

'Bring them down!' he shouted. 'Go for their legs.'

In the chill mist that blew across the island from Mirron's work on the ice, the Karku and Estoreans got to their grisly work. The silence of the dead was deeply unsettling. Harkov was desperate for a reaction but got none. Passion begets passion and in the carnage that followed, tears mixed with determination in many of the island's defenders. It was hard to fell an opponent who did not have the will to kill you.

The Estoreans led the attack. The dead were slow but implacable. Shields were held firm, in front and above. Harkov found his gladius a difficult weapon for the work it had to perform. The short stabbing blade was unsuited to the hack and chop. But there was no choice. He drove himself into the press of the dead, trying to blank his mind and think only that he was clearing a path.

'Dead wood,' he said to himself. 'They aren't alive, they aren't alive. Send them back to God. To his embrace and to peace.'

Harkov carved his gladius into the hip of a soaking, stinking Karku. He felt the bone shatter and the man was flung sideways into one of his grim companions. Not a sound but the splash as he hit the water right on the shore. His heart might not be beating but Harkov's thundered in his chest. He felt sick. The stench this close to was appalling. Like a five-day-dead horse on a hot solastro battlefield.

Harkov gagged and battered his shield forwards, feeling it connect with armour. He looked over the top. The man in front of him had no eyes. Dear God, he had no eyes and a flap of diseased skin hung down from one cheek, ripped by small teeth. But still he came forward. He held a gladius. He was another Gesternan. Another militia man brought here by foul Ascendant magic.

'Release him from torment,' he muttered. 'Help him.'

He tried to chop down and round at the back of the thigh to cut a hamstring. The man's blade whisked just above his head, clipping the top of his shield. Harkov raised his arm a little more, giving him better defence, and hacked his blade in again. The flesh parted. The man stumbled. Harkov stepped back out of his way, the next blow missing him. The man fell.

Left and right he saw frightened Karku and Ascendancy guard engaged with the dead. Next to him, a Karku screamed his disgust and horror, slashing an axe across in front of his face. It struck the neck of his victim, smashing through leather and bone. The man's head fell from his body. The Karku grunted satisfaction but in the next instant whimpered in fear. The body came on. The man's sword rose and fell blind. The Karku stood helpless, the blade cutting him deeply in the shoulder.

'It can't be,' said Harkov. 'Tell me, God, please.'

It could have been that all of them sensed what Harkov had just seen. But in truth it was the fact that not one of those who had been felled was still. Panic rippled through the defence. The crippled dead were dragging themselves slowly up the beach while those behind them simply walked on and over them if they were in the way.

Harkov could do nothing more. He backed off a pace. He needed time to breathe though he knew there was none.

'Don't break!' he called, his voice perilously close to just that.

But they were. He couldn't deny the fear and the sense of helplessness. And yet at his feet, there were dead who could not threaten them and only a couple of hundred still walked. The rest, the mass, were lost to the bottom of the Eternal Water.

'We can take these down,' he said, hearing Harban shouting what he presumed were similar words.

Jhered's voice behind him gave him fresh heart.

'Send them to the deeps. Stand. You're on an island. Where are you going to go? Harban. Tell them.'

But he didn't wait for Harban to speak. Jhered crashed into the fray right next to Harkov. He'd picked up a long blade from somewhere and had abandoned his shield. He wielded the blade in both hands, sweeping it into the shoulder of one man and then back down into the midriff of another. Both enemies were flung into other dead, making a gap into which Jhered strode.

'They can't hurt you without arms, they can't come at you without legs.'

Harkov moved in behind him, crouching and hacking out with his gladius, feeling it shear into exposed flesh. Karku came in to support them, bringing a remnant of tattered confidence back to the defence. Voices rose again, echoing from the cavern walls and sheeting across the water. Harkov felled another, his gladius chopping into an enemy spine just above the waist.

In front of them, the density of dead was just beginning to lessen. They were tripping over the crawling bodies of those fallen in front of them. Karku, led by Ascendancy guard, were beginning to work the flanks. Harkov heard Harban's voice, loud above the thud of weapon on armour and the sick sound of flesh dividing. The Karku began chanting. It sounded like a prayer but more important, it sounded like victory.

Harkov found himself energised. He surged upright and slammed his shield into the face of a dead Karku brave. The man's head snapped back and he fell backwards, splashing down in front of another who tripped over his body. Harkov smiled.

'Touch the embrace of God. Leave this place.'

Around them, the fires guttered on the island and the pathways above. Harkov felt a rush of warm air. Mirron, surely. A blink before the Work was cast, Harkov smelt the taint. A tongue of flame speared from the mouth of the outflow. For a heartbeat it lit the cavern as it traced across the roof. Harkov shielded his eyes. He didn't see the impact but he heard Mirron scream. Darkness fell.

It was blackness so complete it stole the breath and stilled the tongue in every mouth. Harkov could hear the dead still moving forwards and the panic that swept the island, the whole of Inthen-Gor, was complete and all-consuming.

'Stand!' roared Jhered. 'One pace back and stand.'

There was little he could do. Harkov took his pace and raised his shield. The noise was growing around him. Shouts bounced from the walls, the sound of feet scrabbling on sand and stone came from everywhere. Men were screaming. He heard the wild swishing of blades. People were running, colliding, plunging into the water. Anything to try and escape the stumbling dead menace.

'Harkov?' Jhered's shout nearby was curtailed by his violent exhaling as he was struck by some desperate Karku.

'Behind you, Exchequer. And right.'

Harkov was rocked by a hand placed on his shoulder as a fulcrum. He steadied himself.

'I'm feeling out. Don't put your sword point in my way.'

'It's down,' said Harkov. 'Shield is towards you. Low. I'm crouched.'

'Best place to be. God-around-me. Calm! Calm!' The last a bellow at anyone who might be listening.

There was the faintest luminescence growing in the cavern. Blue-green and gaining slowly. Lichen all over the walls and algae in the lake. Harkov blinked, trying to discern the distance to the dead, aware he couldn't hear their movement over the screaming panic sweeping the island. Another Karku bounced from him on his way to who knew where. In the half light, Harkov saw his eyes; wild and terrified. No coherent thought behind them.

More images swam before him; shapes in the gloom, ghosts in shadow. The pale glint of light in dead eyes. He had expected to feel the dead at his shield by now but it was Jhered's hand that gripped his shield arm.

'They aren't advancing.'

The light grew to a watery green, strengthened a little by the relighting of a few fires behind them at the shrine. As it did, the clamour and the panic died away. Two thousand Karku and two hundred Estorean guard stared out over the Eternal Water. Some Karku began mumbling prayers. Harkov shivered, feeling cold deep inside. Next to him, Jhered's face was set.

The beach was crowded with the dead. Before them, under their feet, those of their like that had fallen, discarded now like grotesque unwanted dolls. Thousands of them. They had spread all around the island as far as Harkov could see before the shrine obscured his view. He was in no doubt they were encircled.

'How?' began Jhered.

The answer was walking from beneath the lake's surface. All those they had thought perished in the deep. Some just breaking surface, heads and eyes above. Others wading chest and thigh deep. Yet more moving to stand with their comrades. Water dripped from them, poured from opened mouths. Cough reflexes sent spasms through bodies but the sound was guttural, sub-human. These were the only sounds that the dead had made.

From the mouth of the outflow, the ice was growing again. More slowly this time. The dead crowded the entrance, waiting their order to march. Harkov glanced up to the passageways and tunnels. All sounds of conflict there had ceased. Not even a gorthock roar punctuated the quiet.

Harkov's heart missed a beat.

'Mirron,' he said. Her place was empty, her fire smoking gently in still air.

Jhered turned to him. 'She can't burn and she can't drown. So long as she survived the impact, she'll be all right.'

'But she can't help us.'

Jhered shook his head. 'No. But who can?'

'What can we do?' asked Harkov.

His mind was filled with images of his family. Dangerous thoughts to harbour right now. He tried to push them away and believe he would survive. He just didn't know how.

'I don't know,' said Jhered. 'Beyond surrender.'

Harkov looked at him sharply. 'You mean that?'

'It is a bitter drink but it might save us for another day if Gorian or whoever is commanding these corpses will listen.'

'You aren't serious. You heard Harban. The mountain will fall.'

'Do you really believe that, General? It is figurative at best. It certainly has no basis in geology or physics. Remember yourself.'

'I didn't believe the dead would walk or that the Ascendants could tame the elements.'

Jhered's smile was brief and without humour.

'Harkov, look around you. Do you think for one moment these Karku have the courage to stand together against this enemy? I can't even vouch for our own people, not if those they are here to help cannot fight.'

'But they have no choice, they have nowhere to run. You said it yourself, this is an island.'

'Speak logic to a panicked man. How far do you get?'

Harkov's response stopped in his throat. In his heart, he knew Jhered was right. And there was that part of him that was already prepared to cling on to any vestige of hope he might see the daylight again. Thoughts of a heroic death faded. What heroism was there dying at the hand of a rotting dead man here in a cold, dark cavern.

The temperature fell away again like it had before. Wind played across the island. The ice fled out ever faster and the dead waiting in the outflow began to walk. The fires guttered. The algae and lichen dimmed. Darkness closed in once more and they heard the dead moving forwards.

The screams and shouts started afresh. The running of feet and the calls for order too. Harkov and Jhered stood their ground trying to pierce a blackness that was so complete that neither could see their hands in front of their faces. The crush and tumult was all behind them. Harkov knew a few Ascendancy guard stood with them but the bulk of the broken defence was swarming in, over and around the shrine.

So it was that Harkov knew the dead had stopped walking after perhaps only a couple of paces. It dawned on the terrified Karku stumbling about in the dark with agonising slowness and it was only then that the shouts of Jhered and Harban began to be heard. The island fell silent once more, bar the whimpering of those too scared to know reason. And they waited.

'You are beaten yet I will be merciful.' The voice was carried easily over ice and water.

'Gorian.' Jhered's gravel whisper made Harkov start, the fury it contained feeling like murder.

Not another sound. How many could understand him was hard to guess. Not many. But enough. And all of them knew a voice of evil when they heard it.

'I will take what I came here to take. You can choose the manner in which that takes place.'

The voice was so calm, so measured. It seemed to float in the air and caress the ear. And beneath it, the sound of countless echoes whispered in countless different tones. Harkov swallowed. He didn't need to see to know that the echoes came from the mouths of the dead.

'You will never take the Heart Shrine!' Harban, from somewhere behind them, voice choked with emotion. 'You will not overcome us.'

'I already have, Harban-Qvist.' Gorian's voice was all around them. 'And I have no desire to take your shrine, just those within it. Give them to me and none of you will be harmed, certainly not your Gor-Karkulas.'

'Take not one more step,' shouted Harban. And then he spoke loud in Karku. His people stirred and muttered their anger. 'We will not let you tear down our mountain while we stand and watch. We would rather die.'

'I can arrange that,' said Gorian, irritation edging his tone. There was a shuffling in the darkness from the dead. Whatever courage Harban had instilled quickly evaporated. 'Do not test me, Harban. We were friends once. It is because of this that I am offering you life in exchange for something I can take anyway.'

'We were never friends, Ascendant.' Harban's voice spoke of a loss of control. 'Karku—!'

'Harban, no!' Jhered's voice bounced from the walls of Inthen-Gor. 'Don't let him tempt you. He isn't bluffing.'

'Well, well, well.' The voice was so cloying, Harkov almost expected to feel Gorian's hand on his shoulder. 'Exchequer Jhered. Still my sister's protector and still failing in that task, I see.'

'You have not harmed her, Gorian.'

'Perhaps just her pride.'

'We've come for Kessian, you know that, don't you, Gorian? And we won't stop hunting you until we get him.'

Gorian was silent for a moment and Harkov thought Jhered might have made an error.

'I expected nothing less. And he is safe and will remain so. He is a great talent, my son. And he is in the right place. But enough, Exchequer. Delay is not helpful for any of us. You can persuade them. You cannot win here. You understand that, just as you understand that every man who dies today merely adds to my strength.'

'Which is why you must be stopped,' said Jhered.

'You cannot,' said Gorian and there was regret in his voice. 'All you can do is bow to me. Harban will tell you that the world will tip and the mountain will fall. I've read the prophecy too. I had someone bring it to me. But it is not the Gor that will fall. The only mountain that will crumble is the Conquord. Think on it as I take what I want and you watch knowing there is nothing you can do to stop me.'

The darkness was oppressive. The stink of cold sweat was everywhere, mixed with the rotten stench of the dead. Harkov had never been in a hopeless situation before but hearing Jhered try to keep himself calm, slowing his breathing and clearing his throat, he had no doubt he was in one now.

'State your demands,' said Jhered.

'No, Exchequer.' Harban was trying to come to them. There was stumbling and cursing and the sound of him being passed almost hand to hand. 'You will not stand over our demise. The Karkulas may not leave Inthen-Gor. I will not allow it.'

Jhered turned and hissed in his direction. 'He will take them anyway. What chance do you think we have? Think, man. Stay alive for the fight to come. Your mountain will not fall. And if it does, Gorian will die right along with it. Think Harban. Order an attack in this blackness and you gain nothing and give Gorian everything. Think.'

The pause was for eternity.

'Gorian?'

'Harban.'

'We will deliver them to you.'

'Wise.'

'But know that you are now the sworn enemy of every Karku. That we will not rest until you are staked out for the gorthock to feast on your dead flesh.'

'If it makes you feel better, I will tell you that I will live in fear.'

'You little bastard,' muttered Jhered, then raised his voice. 'Allow light, Gorian. And call your dead back. Or so help me, we will kill the Karkulas and none of us will have them.'

'We should do that anyway,' said Harkov quietly.

'No,' said Jhered, 'Because it won't stop him, just slow him down. All it will do is rip the heart from the Karku. And the Conquord will need them in the times to come.'

The light began to grow again from the lichen and the algae. A shifting around them told of the dead moving backwards. However on the frozen path from the shrine to the outflow, they stood waiting.

'Give them to me,' said Gorian, voice lessened by distance now the light eased their fear.

Jhered sighed. 'This is the worst day of my life.' He nodded to Harban. 'Do it. And Harban, this isn't the end. You must believe it.'

Harban's voice, faltering and choked, issued the order; into the face of the Karku's silence and tears.

Chapter Nineteen

859th cycle of God, 25th day of Genasrise

'How has he got to be this powerful?' demanded Jhered.

Mirron was still shivering and Jhered was worried about her despite all her talents. She had spent a long time in the water, under the ice that Gorian had created, only breaking through when he had gone and his hold over the elements with him. She had used so much of her inner energy to keep herself warm that now, despite the fire roaring at her feet, she couldn't warm up quickly enough. She was too tired to focus the warming trails through her body. Harkov put another cloak around her shoulders and she smiled up at him. Her clothes had all been burned from her and her hair was scorched. Her lips were blue and her eyes bloodshot.

'I saw it. Just as he struck out at me. But I don't know how he does it. What about my son? You let Kessian go.'

'We couldn't get to him, Mirron. We explained that. Please, I need you to concentrate.' Jhered glanced up at Harkov who raised his eyebrows. 'What did you see?'

Mirron screwed up her eyes and sighed, a melancholy sound that struck Jhered deep in his heart.

'He ...' She stopped and tears pushed out from behind her eyelids. 'He ...'

'Hey, take it easy.'

Jhered sat by her and pulled her into an embrace. She clung to his arm and cried, her sobs filling the cavern and turning the heads of all who remained there. The Karku shared her pain and understood her suffering. The Gor-Karkulas were gone. All but the very brave had left Inthen-Gor.

Jhered didn't think he could feel any lower but if he was honest with himself, the only reason he wasn't joining Mirron in grief was the need to remain strong for her. Everyone else was desolate, inconsolable.

It was only now he understood the desperation of Harban to keep the Gor-Karkulas. The heart of their belief was gone. Taken by a foe they could not touch and they were left with nothing. There were no lights in the Heart Shrine. No fires on its steps. Some stood and stared into the gloomy emptiness; others were clearing the island. It was an instinctive response, no more than that. Only Harban and a few of his closest friends believed anything Jhered had said. The Karku brave was leading a scouting party after Gorian and the dead. Others would follow the Tsardon forces.

None had any doubt that the next target would be the Conquord. The Karku, for what it was worth right now, would ally against the common enemy, hoping against hope that their treasured six would be returned to them alive.

'What will happen to them, do you think?' asked Harkov.

Jhered stroked Mirron's hair and kept her close while she gathered herself. The crying had stopped but still she shivered.

'I dread to think,' said Jhered. 'It won't even cheer them that the mountain will not physically fall, will it?'

'Why not?'

'Because the fact of its survival undermines their beliefs still further. You heard what Harban said before he left. They believe the will of the Gor-Karkulas keeps the roots of the mountain strong. Even he still thinks this place will crumble to dust and he's the most enlightened of them. None of them see the words are figurative. Harban's trying to keep them together, using some story about strength already invested in the roots but it won't wash for long.'

'Not least because he doesn't really believe it.'

'No indeed.'

Harkov rubbed his face. He looked exhausted and had a haunted look that suggested an urgent need to see sunlight again.

'How many did we lose?' asked Jhered.

'None,' said Harkov. 'It is the one blessing of the day. There are some injuries but nothing life-threatening. But it's their morale that really worries me. The nightmares are sure to come. And fear of the next contact with the dead.'

Mirron had relaxed just a little and her shivering was beginning to subside. One of Harkov's soldiers brought over mugs of broth. It was thin but felt like a feast fit for the Advocate.

'We'll have to work with them just like we'll have to work with every Conquord legionary. We need some tactics and weapons against them.' Jhered didn't speak what both of them were thinking. The weapon most likely to be effective was a crime in itself.

Harkov blew out his cheeks. 'Is there any room for debate with the Order, do you suppose?'

'You're joking of course,' said Jhered. 'I can only imagine in my darkest dreams the capital that Felice Koroyan will make of this. The Ascendancy is going to be under serious threat, Gorian has seen to that.'

Mirron moved in Jhered's arms, making herself a little more comfortable.

'You all right in there?' he asked, looking into the folds of her cloak where her face was just visible.

'I want to get out of here,' she said.

'I won't dispute that,' said Jhered. 'Sit up and drink your broth then we'll go. Your people ready, General?'

Harkov smiled. 'After a fashion.'

Mirron moved back into the warmth of the fire and picked up her mug from the ground, sipping gently.

'The question is,' continued Harkov, 'where are we going to go?'

'A good question,' said Jhered. 'And are you able to answer yours, Mirron?'

She nodded. 'I know how he does it though I have no idea how I would do the same. Theory and practice, eh? Always a long way from each other for an Ascendant.'

'Who said that? No, let me guess. Father Kessian.'

Mirron smiled. 'Actually, no, not this time. A different teacher. Hesther. She uses it with all the new emerging talent. Doesn't make any difference, of course, they're still horribly impatient and frustrated.'

'So, expound on this particular theory.'

'Gorian can place his Works elsewhere once they are complete. He can lodge them in the mind of a latent, or presumably emerged, talent so that they run independently of him. That leaves him free to pursue other Works. Kessian, my little Kessian, was keeping the dead walking.'

Mirron swallowed and Jhered could see she was close to breaking again.

'It's all right Mirron. He's an unwitting victim.'

'But the harm it will be doing to him. We have to get to him.'

'And we will,' said Jhered. 'But I'm not with you yet on what Gorian is doing. You're saying Kessian was controlling the dead?'

'No,' said Mirron. 'Gorian was using Kessian's energy to keep them moving and doing his will while he worked on me and the lake. If he wanted to change their task, he'd have to take control of the energy map again. I don't know how he does it. It's like those jugglers that use gossamer cloth. They can keep plenty up at a time by moving from one to another in turn before they hit the ground. He's managed to corrupt Kessian's energies to keep feeding and amplifying into the Work that drives the dead. That's against all we know. Without the control of an Ascendant, a Work will dissipate because the energy map will collapse.'

'And can't Kessian do anything to break the map himself?' asked Harkov.

'You assume he knows it's happening. Or even if he does, that he understands enough to counter what Gorian is doing,' replied Mirron.

'So I wonder where he'll take his dead,' said Jhered. 'Straight through Atreska is favourite unless he plans to push west into Gestern. From the insignia we saw, he's already been there to kill.'

'You're missing the point,' said Mirron. 'He took the Gor-Karkulas to do with them what he did with Kessian. He has seven huge pools of latent energy now.'

'Maybe but it doesn't mean he can attack on any more than one front. Just that he can control larger numbers, no?'

'No, Paul,' said Mirron. She shook her head and Jhered found himself going cold. 'The Work that controls the dead uses the earth. He doesn't have to be next to them to control them. He doesn't have to be anywhere near them if he's good enough and I have no doubt he is. Gorian can control the dead using the Karkulas and Kessian as remote conduits. He can attack on multiple fronts yet be hidden far from any point of conflict. The only way to stop him is to kill him, just like Ossacer said.'

Jhered put a hand over his mouth. 'And if Harban loses him now, we could find ourselves with the whole of Tsard and the Conquord to search for him.'

'Unless I or my brothers can work out a way to trace him through the energy maps he is creating. Find a way to the source so to speak.'

'And can you do that?' asked Harkov.

'I don't know,' said Mirron.

'Drink up,' said Jhered. 'We need to get a message to Harban and then we have to get back to Estorr.'

'Sounding the alarm all the way,' said Harkov.

'Dammit.' Jhered punched the sandy ground. 'Invasion.'

'I'm proud of you today,' said Gorian. 'Really proud.'

The boat was being rowed quickly down the outflow, heading for the sunshine of northern Kark and a quick exit into Tsard, where a rendezvous with King Khuran would take place. Other boats followed, all simple open vessels with a dozen oarsmen, carrying two of the Dead Lords, the six Karku prisoners and Khuran's observers. And what a victory they had seen.

Behind the small flotilla, the dead walked along the narrow banks of the river. Gorian felt exhausted by his labours and it was a source of fascination that Kessian seemed almost unaffected by what must have been a supreme effort. It was the boy's stamina keeping the dead walking.

'You have shown me that you are as talented and powerful as I thought you were when I sensed you in Estorr.'

Kessian shrugged. His face held a sullen look and his cloak was wrapped about him against the cold in the river tunnel. He had said nothing when Gorian planted the energy map in him and told him to hold hard onto the complex shape that looked like a grand tree-root network bounded by thick ropes. Gorian hadn't been sure it would work and the success had surprised and delighted him.

'What's wrong? You have advanced the knowledge of the Ascendancy today.'

'I didn't do anything,' said Kessian. 'And you hurt my mother.'

'I—' Gorian quashed the anger that rose so easily inside him. Kessian had been way down the tunnel, well out of sight of Inthen-Gor. 'How could you possibly know that?'

Kessian frowned and looked up him as if he was stupid. Gorian raised his eyebrows.

'I've *always* been able to feel her if she was close enough. And you wouldn't even let me see her or speak to her. You hurt her. And I might have let your army go and that would have been your fault.'

'But you didn't, did you?'

'Because you would have been angry with me.'

'Perhaps a little.'

Kessian looked at him briefly then turned his head back to staring at the rock wall passing by. Gorian shook his head.

'Why aren't you happy? We won and your mother is barely injured. You know that too, don't you?'

Kessian deigned to nod slightly.

'So what do you have to be down-mouthed about? You're a hero. You helped me win. We went in there and took what we wanted. I told you, that's what the strong do. It's destiny.'

'I didn't have much choice, did I?'

That whine was back in Kessian's voice, going straight through Gorian and setting his teeth on edge.

'What?'

'You didn't ask before you used me. You shouldn't have done that.' Kessian was staring at him now, fearful. And well he might be.

'I beg your pardon?' said Gorian quietly.

'An Ascendant should never do anything against their will. Ossacer said—'

'Ossacer. Bloody Ossacer!' Gorian bunched his fists. 'When will you realise that you are not there any more? You are here, with me. So you do what I say until you learn what is right for yourself. I'm here trying to rid the world of evil and you're whingeing because a blind man thinks we should all be pacifists. Get out.'

'What? No.'

Gorian's face cooled. 'No? Kessian, no one refuses me. You least of all of them. It'll do you good. Give you time to think and put some muscle on those scrawny bones of yours. Go and walk with the dead. I'm keeping them here to teach you anyway. Get out of my sight.'

Kessian gripped the gunwale. 'No, I won't.'

'Oh yes, you will.'

Gorian grabbed his hand and squeezed until Kessian cried out and his grip on the boat loosened. With his other arm he scooped the boy up and dumped him into the river. He screamed as he went under and thrashed when he broke surface. Gorian laughed.

'Walk on the bottom if you can't swim, boy. You can't drown, you're an Ascendant. Enjoy it. Come back when you have something new to tell me.'

Gorian faced front and waved his oarsmen to continue.

*

Before they'd left the island, Harban was back. Jhered's initial keen disappointment turned quickly to respect. The Karku had brought back a prize. One of the dead. A Gesternan. He was unresisting and though he didn't respond to spoken orders, he walked where he was pointed and prodded and stopped when his way was barred.

'How far ahead is Gorian?' asked Jhered while the dead man was taken to the fire where Harkov and Mirron would begin to question him.

'Six miles,' said Harban. 'Or thereabouts. He is on the water. The dead are walking and well behind. That one was easy to pick off. Something that should interest you is this. They didn't hear us and we weren't particularly quiet. And when we took this one, he didn't make a sound and none of those walking right by him made any move. There was no reaction. Just like they didn't know we were there and he was gone.'

Jhered shrugged. 'They probably didn't. Mirron doesn't think they have individual will or thought. Just walking muscle. And rotting muscle at that.'

The dead man was not a pretty sight. Much of his armour was gone. There was a huge gouge in his skull which oozed blood and brain and one of his eyes was missing. But all his limbs were intact and he was a powerful man. He stank.

'I need to get back to my trackers.'

'Yes. And Harban, don't worry about anyone else. Make sure you don't lose Gorian.'

'He will not escape us forever.' Harban looked up to the roof of Inthen-Gor. 'Don't linger here. It isn't safe.'

Jhered smiled and inclined his head. 'We won't. Stay safe, Harban. My arm and heart are yours. We will prevail. Your mountain will not fall.'

'Go to your dead man,' said Harban. 'We are all short of time.'

Jhered walked back the short distance to the fire. Harkov was asking questions. Mirron, a sick look on her face, was trying to probe the dead man's energy map. The odour was rank. Wet rot and mould. The Gesternan was standing, slightly slouched. He was breathing, or so it looked, but there was no other movement.

'So, what have we got?'

'He isn't much of a talker,' said Harkov.

'He doesn't have much of a brain, so we can't be surprised. Does he even recognise that you are talking to him?'

'Not a flicker.'

'I see. Mirron?'

He watched her pull back from the subject and clear her throat.

'Paul, it's horrible.'

'I'm sure. Anything interesting?'

'He is being fed by energies in the ground. But his map is weak and the link to what must be Gorian's overall map is very indistinct. Almost not—' Soundlessly, the man collapsed to the ground, his last breath issuing in a sigh that sounded like relief, '—there at all.'

'Interesting,' said Jhered. 'Pluck a single leaf from the tree and look what happens to it.'

'But we have to assume that in this case, the leaf can be reattached to the tree, should the tree return for it,' said Harkov.

'Or the roots seek it,' said Mirron.

'Still. It is something we didn't know this morning. Mirron?'

'The earth energy sustained him while he was close enough to the mass of the construct. But while it can feed him, so to speak, it obviously can't stop the natural process of decay.'

'Why is that?' asked Jhered.

'Ossacer would know more about this than me. I think it's because although some functions seem to be restarted, the body isn't self-sustaining and others, crucial ones, don't work or don't need to work for him to do what he did.'

'Like what?' Harkov was crouched by the body, closing the eyes.

'No heartbeat.'

Jhered shook his head. 'I've seen enough. This man will return to the embrace of God. See he is interred then let's get out of here. I know it shouldn't bother me but suddenly I don't like the way Harban and the Karku look at the roof of this place.'

Chapter Twenty

859th cycle of God, 30th day of Genasrise

Arducius put his head in his hands. Only twenty days since Mirron had left the Academy and it was already clear who it was that kept the place tight and focused. He'd been away too long, preaching to those whom he had come to save and who would turn their backs on him the moment he left their homes. Wasted time. Wasted years. Because, for all the passive ability he and Ossacer had brought back to Estorr, there was nothing to show for it but growing dissent.

He had to hand it to Felice Koroyan. The Chancellor's disinformation machine was well-oiled and as reliable as one of the Conquord's new scorpion bolt-firers. As accurate too. Now she was certain the Ascendancy wasn't about to go back into the field to pick at the corners of her dominion, she was concentrating all her efforts on Estorr itself.

If latest rumours were believed, then he, Ossacer and possibly even the Advocate herself, were engaged in human experimentation on innocents snatched from the provinces where they would not be missed. Gorian had developed into a monster of nightmare proportions, marching on the homes of the innocent. Truth hid in certain exaggerations.

Looking at the class in front of him, it crossed his mind just briefly that human experimentation was too good for them. The Morasian intake. Twenty of them. Rescued, so he thought, from persecution in their home country. And now staring at him as if he was some kind of jailer-cum-torturer. His translator was sitting alongside him looking decidedly uncomfortable while he tried to persuade the rag-bag of ages and intellects among the men and women in front of him that they were both safe and normal.

Arducius looked down at his red-slashed formal toga to his sandalled feet and took a deep breath. When he looked up the suspicion was hanging in the air like a cobweb just out of reach. He could sense it in all their auras. Flickering tendrils of pale blue and red, eating at the energy in the room, feeding the unease.

'Is it me or is this really difficult to understand?' he asked of them, hearing the translator, a hawk-faced, middle-aged woman called Norita, speak his words in an awkward clicking dialect.

He strode to the door and opened it, startling a clerk who was walking by. He gestured out.

'Here. If any of you feel so inclined, please, take your leave. I'll even pay your passage back home.' He walked back to the centre of the room, leaving the door open. 'But what I really want to do, what all of us here want to do, is help you understand your ability and to make you feel comfortable with what you are.'

Arducius was greeted with silence though it was a little embarrassed this time. He took it as a gossamer-thin sign of progress.

'Are your rooms uncomfortable? Do guards keep you under lock and key? Have any of you been stopped from going anywhere in the city or the public areas of the Hill? No. And you won't be. You're here because we want to help you. We think you are safer here than back in your homes. For now at least. But you are not here against your will. I can only work with people who want to learn. So I say again, anyone who wants to leave, do so.' He jerked a thumb over his shoulder. 'I will not stand in your way.'

Their attention was on the door and some had even relaxed a little. Arducius turned his head and found Hesther in the doorway. Her cheeks were a little red.

'Perhaps I can help,' she said.

'Anything,' said Arducius.

Hesther moved into the room, smiling broadly at the Morasians. She paused when she reached Arducius and dropped her voice.

'And while you might not stand in their way, I'm not so sure the Advocate won't.'

'Why would she? War or no war, these people will never become Ascendants.'

'You know Herine. Always an eye to the far future. It is their grandchildren who interest her.' Hesther cleared her throat and pushed her hands through her greying hair, retying the scarf that kept it out of her face. She smiled at Arducius but the gesture had no comfort in it. 'Anyway, you have a more pressing problem.'

'I do?' Arducius's heart sank still further.

'Ossacer is preaching pacifism.'

'Who to?'

'Who do you think?'

Arducius sighed. 'What am I supposed to do? He's right. We aren't training an army here.'

Hesther's eyes flashed and she grabbed his arm. He was aware that every eye was on them. At least Norita had ceased translating.

'It doesn't matter if he is right or not. The Advocate is asking questions.' She jabbed a finger back out of the room. 'And those five down there *are* being trained for combat whether you, I or Ossacer like it or not.'

'Yes but—'

'But nothing, Ardu. None of them is a Pain Teller. None of them is going to be a healer of the calibre of Ossacer and he should not be telling them otherwise. All that will happen is that if there is a war, they will appear on the battlefield poorly equipped. That cannot be allowed to happen, for all our sakes. I may be the Mother of the Ascendancy but you are its leader in Herine's eyes. She is losing her patience and what with the pressure the Chancellor is beginning to exert, we cannot afford to make an enemy out of her. You do understand.'

'Of course I do.'

'Then prove you're the diplomat we all thought you were way-back-when in Westfallen. Make Ossacer see sense and stop Herine prowling our corridors making the students nervous.'

Arducius broke eye contact and looked away out of the classroom. 'I'll do what I can.'

'Good, in that case we don't have a problem.' Hesther pecked his cheek. 'That was a compliment, Ardu.'

'Oh, right. Thanks.'

He smoothed down his toga and walked away to speak to his brother. Ossacer wasn't far. His favourite classroom was only three doors away. It was converted from the grand office of the Speaker of the Earth and held some spectacular carvings of Kester Isle and Easthale's Dragon Tooth mountains.

The students had just left and he was alone in the room. Arducius could sense the energy of their lesson in the air and hear their excited babble echoing from somewhere nearby. They were good, all of them. Very raw at seventeen but with great potential. Arducius prayed daily that the war would never come. He was not confident the Omniscient was listening.

'Hello, Ardu,' said Ossacer, not looking up.

He was tracing his hands over the carvings on their display tables.

'A good lesson, Ossie?'

'They seemed to like it. Particularly Cygalius. He has a huge future, I think.'

'If he lives to see his eighteenth year,' said Arducius.

Ossacer ignored him. 'These carvings are sublime. The textures and contours hold such colour. It's like not being blind. Just for a moment.'

Arducius smiled. 'Then we should track down the sculptor. Get him to do some commissions for us.'

'I don't think so. Letting go is painful enough as it is.' Ossacer took his hands from the carved stone. 'And then all I am left with are memories and the violent, indistinct world that is energy maps.'

'What's brought on all this introspection?'

'Well, it's either that I'm trying to garner sympathy for my unfortunate plight or that I'm hurriedly trying to avoid what you've come to talk to me about.'

'I see,' said Arducius, feeling awkward. That was another knack Ossacer had.

'I didn't mean to upset Hesther. I would never want to do that.'

'So that was you, was it?'

'And it didn't take a genius to know where she would go next.'

'No indeed. She was very red-faced, really upset. So why did you do it?'

Ossacer moved across the classroom and sat in one of the dozen high-backed chairs that stood on the marble floor.

'Because no one seems to understand that we are simply being used like animals. Trained for a purpose to be cast on to the wheel of war. And with no thought for the future. So I was telling the emerged that they should be honing their healing and growing skills. Everyone has to help the war effort should it come to that and we are clearly best placed to keep men, women, animals and crops alive, fed and watered. I don't want them to wear blood on their hands like we did. Like we still do.'

Arducius worried at his lower lip for a moment before taking the seat next to Ossacer.

'I don't know what to say, Ossie.'

'You could agree with me.' Ossacer smiled and winked.

'You know it isn't as simple as that.' Arducius shifted, uncomfortable. 'We can't afford to make an enemy out of the Advocate. Not now, not ever.'

'So you're prepared to train our Ascendants to murder just to keep her smiling, is that it?'

'God-embrace-me, how many times have we been through this?'

'Not enough, clearly.' Ossacer's smile was a distant memory. He'd tensed and Arducius could see the stress in his life map as shimmering, chaotic clashes of colour. 'Because none of you see what's really happening here.'

'I think you'll find we all understand exactly what's going on,' said Arducius. 'It's just that one of us refuses to accept it.'

'Damn right I refuse.' Ossacer's voice pitched up a level.

'Your trouble is that you think you're untouchable. That you can push Herine as far as you like because you're an Ascendant. All she'll do is stop you teaching and then where will you be?'

'And your trouble is that you let us get used as weapons when we are born to be the opposite. If we all stood up to her, she would have to back down. And she can't stop me teaching.'

'No? You'll have to shout loud to be heard from the cells, Ossacer.'

'She wouldn't do that. She wouldn't dare.'

'God-take-me-to-my-rest!' Arducius slapped the arms of his chair and stood up, walking away a few paces while his temper calmed. 'How can you be so naïve?'

'I am not naïve.'

'Ossie, you think more deeply than the rest of us put together. Your principles are a guiding light for us all. But you mustn't let them blind you to reality. "Dare"? She's the Advocate, she can do anything she likes. And you have to start understanding the way she thinks.'

'Like what?'

Arducius bit his lip to stop himself tearing into Ossacer for his idiot belligerence. 'Like realising that she will do anything to keep the Conquord together. And she will sacrifice anyone who gets in the way of that. She used us in the last war even though she knew it would put her against the Chancellor. And she took us in because she saw our potential in all areas as much as for a reward. If we turn our backs on what she wants now, at her time of greatest need, what do you think she'll do?'

'We must be prepared to die for our beliefs,' said Ossacer evenly.

'But not toss our lives away for stubbornness. The Ascendants must be prepared for what will be demanded of them. What *will* be demanded.'

'I won't have you gag me, Arducius.'

'Then you will not teach, nor have contact with our emerged Ascendants.'

Ossacer gaped. 'You have no right—'

'When I see my brother walking the frayed tightrope I think I have every right,' said Arducius. 'And Hesther will back me. Don't make us do it. I'm not asking you to teach them anything bar Pain Teller skills. Just don't fill their minds with your rhetoric. You will drag us all down.'

'Down?' Ossacer's face betrayed his contempt. 'You can stoop no lower, brother. You're as much the Advocate's lackey as any consort.'

'I only do what is asked of me by my Advocate,' said Arducius carefully.

'And if she asks for lightning to smite our enemies and tempests to purge their blood from the field, you will do that?'

Ossacer was staring at him, his eyes carrying such passion, such ferocity that it was difficult for a moment to remember he was blind. Arducius knew Ossacer would be able to see the certainty in his aura. Still he could barely speak above a whisper.

'If it would keep our enemies from the gates of the Conquord, yes, I would do that.'

'I knew it. Sad to see one so strong driven so weak. Brittle bones, brittle will.'

Arducius started and a felt a wound-like pain in his stomach. Ossacer dropped his gaze.

'I'm sorry, Ardu. I lashed out. I didn't mean it like that.'

'Then how did you mean it, Ossacer?'

'I th—'

'I think you've said enough for one day.' Arducius turned to go but a thought struck him on the way to the door. 'Ossie, you are my best friend, you are my brother and I love you. But some days you test my *affection* sorely. Do you think for one moment in that high-and-mighty head of yours that I would not be crushed inside if I was asked as an Ascendant to kill for the Conquord? Do you think that somehow I escaped the nightmares of what we did in Atreska that day? A lesser evil to perpetuate a greater good is a choice that I will make and so should you.

'You know, I used to hate Gorian when he taunted you about your blindness. But I remember once he said you weren't just blind on the outside but on the inside too. I didn't understand at the time. Now I think he might be right.'

Arducius closed the door firmly behind him and almost walked straight into the man standing immediately outside the classroom.

'Sorry,' he said and stepped back, looking up to see who he'd encountered.

It was a face aged beyond its years. Kindly but broken. He was seventy but looked a hundred. All the thick dark hair was gone, replaced by thinning white wisps. The eyes that used to be brown and all-embracing at one time, were sunk into the skull and lined red. Sleep was clearly an uncertain friend. He was stooped a little and all the power was gone from his frame. Unrecognisable to many. But you couldn't change the base of your aura. No disguise would ever fool an Ascendant.

'Hello, Arducius.'

'My Marshal,' said Arducius, thumping his right arm into his chest. 'It's been too long.'

'You can drop all that nonsense, Ardu,' said Arvan Vasselis. 'It's a long time since I required you to call me Marshal.'

Arducius gestured towards the reception rooms away at the back of the Chancellery. 'Can I offer you some wine and food? There was a pig roast last night and the cold cuts are exceptional.'

'In a moment, perhaps.' There was no real power in Vasselis's voice any more but he retained the same easy pace to his speech which begged interruption, and the natural charisma which forbade it. He nodded at the classroom. 'Did he mean what he said?'

'You overheard our ... discussion, I take it. All of it?'

'I made a career out of overhearing things,' said Vasselis. 'So?'

Arducius moved them a little way from the door.

'Of course he means it, Arvan. You know Ossacer. He can barely breathe for the principles and morals crowding him. He won't turn and it'll cause us trouble. I'll just have to manage him away from Herine as best I can.'

'I see.' Vasselis's face was grim and a chasm of sadness yawned in his eyes. 'An Ascendant should know better. Excuse me a moment.'

Vasselis walked back to the classroom and opened the door. Arducius heard a chair scrape and Ossacer begin to speak. Vasselis did not move from the doorway. He held up a hand.

'My son made a sacrifice that no one had the right to ask of him and the Conquord was saved as a consequence. No one is asking you to die, Ossacer, merely to uphold the meaning of the actions of those who did.'

Vasselis closed the door.

'Wine and pig, I think, young Arducius. Lead the way.'

A single tear ran down his cheek.

Chapter Twenty-One

859th cycle of God, 30th day of Genasrise

'I try not to let it consume me but every day it is harder, not easier. I cannot explain it.'

Vasselis's hand had a slight quiver as he raised his goblet. Arducius had chosen a snug room for them. Just two recliners and a table between walls lined with books The solitary window was closed against the late afternoon cold.

'But your words were well chosen and well said. Ossacer doesn't think widely enough sometimes. You might just have given him something to chew on.'

'Then it was worth my trip.'

'How is Netta?'

Vasselis's shoulders sagged. 'Kovan was our life, the future of our line. When it became clear Netta and I could have no more children, he became unspeakably precious to us. But you can't stand in a young man's way. Still, I never for one moment thought when I sent him away with you that day in Westfallen that it would be the last I ever saw of him. For Netta it is even harder. The heart of our house has stopped beating but she exists there still. I am only here because I will not suffer another to rule over my people.'

'God blesses us while that remains the case.'

'Not every one would agree with you.' Vasselis raised his eyebrows.

Arducius sniffed. 'Let me guess ... are we talking about the Order by any chance?'

'Who else? The public face is all about a Marshal needing a line of succession and that the family ethos of the Order is undermined if a senior figure in the Conquord cannot provide that. But we all know what it's really about. I have to fight my corner hard at the moment,

Ardu, and I don't need Ascendants causing trouble on the Hill. The ripples will rock my boats too.'

'Understood.' Arducius helped himself to a thick pork chop and poured a hot sweet sauce over it. The smell made him salivate. 'So do I take it this is the wrong time to ask you about getting to some of the Order's more radical Speakers and Readers?'

'It is never a bad time to cause Felice Koroyan trouble.' And for a moment, the old Vasselis sparkled. 'That witch needs burning outside her own House of Masks. But I must tread carefully. I cannot deny my position is weaker at home these days. I neglect too many duties, I fear. Koroyan's people never stop searching for those in the Order that helped the Ascendancy flourish. I will put the word out but don't expect names any time soon. People are cautious. Despite the Advocate's support your position with the citizenry remains perilous.'

Arducius had been eating the chop while Vasselis spoke. He swallowed a mouthful and wiped his lips.

'Is there no pressure you can bring to bear on Herine that might see her decide to legislate?'

Vasselis smiled a little sadly. 'It must seem so simple from up here. The trouble is that Herine is already so far out on the limb that it is cracking behind her. Another pace and she will fall. The Chancellor knows it. The lines are drawn between them and they will not move until one or the other can make the decisive statement, bring forth the immutable proof that they are following the true path.'

He leaned back but only for a brief pause.

'Which reminds me. You have time to work on Ossacer with the Advocate away at the Senate. Don't waste it. But watch yourselves these next days. You are vulnerable. Even here on the Hill.'

'Why?'

'Herine and I are travelling to the Solastro Palace at first light tomorrow. Paul Jhered is in Kark and Harkov is with him. You have little senior defence and Felice will know it only too well. Don't give her anything on which to feed. Keep Ossacer quiet about the Advocate's plans for you in the event of war. That is very important.'

'What might she do?'

Vasselis shrugged. 'This is Felice we are talking about. How can any of us possibly know? Now then, one of your chops, I think. Assuming you have left me any.'

*

Roberto Del Aglios stood with his brother Adranis on the gatehouse fort overlooking the Tsardon encampment. Behind them, lights would burn into the early hours of the morning, marking fevered preparations for an attack that some had begun to question would ever come. For the five days since they arrived, the Tsardon had simply ignored them. They had camped about a mile from the bridge and seemed intent on nothing more than hunting and archery contests. But the bizarre nature of this show of strength, if such it was, concerned Roberto.

'I must be missing something very obvious,' he said.

The Tsardon fires were burning brightly. The odd snatch of song drifted to them on a warm evening breeze. The brothers were standing directly above the gate on the artillery platforms, leaning on the forward battlements. Arrows were standing against the stone in wrapped quivers, hundreds of them and with more being made every day. The platform was stacked with onager stones, ballista bolts and pitch barrels ready for firing. The whole place stank of fresh oil and new wood.

'That would be a first,' said Adranis.

'Would that that were true. There must be a point to what they are doing but I'm damned if I can see it. Too long a diplomat, I expect.' Roberto chuckled and looked at Adranis, feeling that flush of pride again. A fine young man, full of energy and the passion of the Conquord. Roberto recognised it very well. 'Come on then, Master Del Aglios, you're a soldier of today's legions. What's your assessment?'

'It's the talk of the barracks,' said Adranis, keeping his gaze outwards. 'It's clear that their current strength is not enough to hurt us. And they've given us time to reinforce and position our artillery exactly where we want it. It's like they want us to be as ready as possible, which cannot be true.'

'So you think they do not intend an attack?'

'That's the betting,' said Adranis.

'So what are they?'

'A distraction, it has to be. We're waiting news from further south about any other Tsardon forces approaching the borders. Nothing so far but it's southern Atreska that should worry us. We're thin down there and the country is in turmoil.'

'Again.' Roberto scratched his head. 'I'm not sure I buy the distraction angle.'

'You have a better suggestion?'

'No. But we are a long way north, and even assuming they wanted to keep the Gosland forces on alert and tied down here it doesn't make a big enough difference. Even if your messengers come back telling you there is a Tsardon army threatening the Atreskan borders as far south as Haroq City, it is no reason to send a few thousand up here merely to keep the Bear Claws busy.'

'Perhaps their intelligence is lacking and they think we are more strongly represented here than we actually are.'

Roberto shook his head. 'This is not a secure border. You can't get an army across unseen but a few scouts? Simple enough. And the Tsardon have many sympathisers here and in Atreska. No ... and we're sure there is no other army moving up in support?'

'Nothing that is going to get here in the next twenty days. Your Sirranean contacts have tracked no one at all and our scouts have uncovered nothing either.'

'So they really might just be there simply to piss us off.'

'You don't believe that, though, do you, Roberto?'

'Indeed not. So I go back to my first statement. We're missing something obvious. I mean, look at them. No artillery, no cavalry. Just a few oxen pulling carts of supplies, and a whole lot of foraging. Unless they're planning to enter an archery team for the Games this solastro, I am at a loss to know what they think they will achieve. Adranis, think about it. They haven't threatened anywhere else. We were already here defending this bridge. It couldn't be much more convenient, could it?'

Roberto looked at Adranis again. He was frowning and itched at his skull just under his green-plumed helmet.

'I don't know what it is you're driving at,' he said.

'If they don't attack in the next few days, I won't be able to justify staying here. What I don't want is for you or anyone else to make assumptions, that's all. This smells all wrong. When the Sirraneans told me they were heading this way, it worried me. It still does and the size of their force and their apparent lack of ambition does nothing to change that.'

'I hear you.'

'Just be careful, that's all. You're a jewel in the Conquord crown. Mother would never forgive me if you perished out here because any of us got careless.'

'I'm not wrapping myself in blankets and hiding, Roberto. I'm a cavalryman and I fight. It's my job just like it was yours.' Adranis had tensed and his jaw jutted proudly.

'I'm not asking you to.' Roberto wrapped an arm around his neck and dragged him close. He lowered his voice. 'Just remember yourself and who you are. Don't throw yourself away on an errant thought. The Tsardon are clever and they will know you stand here. You are a target more than any general. I had to live with that and I may have to again. The Del Aglios line must continue if the Conquord is to remain the dominant force in this world. We have a responsibility. You, me and Tuline.'

Adranis pulled away. 'Tuline?'

'Yes, of course. If we both die in battle, she will be heir. She needs to understand that and I intend to make that point to her.'

'Good luck,' said Adranis. 'She works for the Conquord in name alone. The only thing I hear she is good at is spending the Del Aglios fortune on cloth, art and that bunch of perfumed imbeciles she calls her friends and advisers.'

Roberto laughed. 'It is what little sisters are put here to do, isn't it? Get under your skin and appear to waste everything that comes their way?'

'If that is so, she is peerless.'

'But don't underestimate her, Adranis. She is smart and a sound politician when she has need. There is much of our mother in Tuline and the good folk of the Senate would do well to realise it. I'm looking forward to the meeting at the Solastro Palace even if I attend none of it. I guarantee it will be the most ordered in Conquord history.'

'You think too much of her skill, Roberto. Secretary to the Consul General? Let chaos reign.'

Roberto wagged a finger at his brother. 'You work on memories, Adranis. She may be extravagant and her reputation for certain excesses is something Mother will no doubt discuss with her but in affairs of state, she has grown beyond all recognition.'

'If you say so.'

'I do.'

Roberto let a silence fall between them. He listened instead to the Tsardon voices raised in song, louder than before. Cold trickled down his back. He'd heard this song before. It was no work-party chant or campfire ditty. It was a song of victory.

*

Marcus Gesteris walked into the workshops and offices of Orin D'Allinnius, chief scientist of the Conquord, and all but felt the weight of creation and intelligence on his shoulders. He hadn't often been here; it was not a place for soldiers in his opinion, though what came out of it had been of extraordinary military value on countless occasions.

He could hear the sounds of endeavour as soon as he walked into the small building attached to the administration offices on the Hill. Herine Del Aglios had ordered it built after the last Tsardon wars. Not just so the worth of her scientists was made apparent but because she wanted to keep them secure. The principal reason why looked up and made his halting way across the room as soon as Gesteris's name was announced by the guards.

Gesteris had to force himself not to let his gaze stray to the chalk boards covered by figures, angles and formulae that hung on every wall; nor to wonder what it was in the three workshops that led from the room that required so much heat, shouting and hammering. The forges were stoked today and the air was heavy with sweat and soot.

Instead, he walked towards D'Allinnius, whose cane tapped on the stone-flagged floor and whose occasional gasps of pain escaped his mouth despite his best efforts.

'You're looking well, Orin,' said Gesteris, eating up the distance between them to halt the painful advance.

D'Allinnius stopped and regarded him with his one good eye, his head slightly turned to get best focus. All it served to do was show Gesteris the mess of flesh where Orin's left ear had been and the bald patches on his skull where his hair had been burned away, never to return.

'Idiot liar,' he said, voice whistling through broken and missing teeth. 'It is a decade since that was true.'

'Then sit down and stop trying to prove it.'

D'Allinnius scowled. 'I am quite capable of moving about, Senator. Sitting down will not show you what you are here to see. Come.'

Gesteris inclined his head and followed D'Allinnius towards the smallest of his three workshops. The scientist's brain was still fertile and his thirst for understanding unquenched. But he could not hide his bitterness and no one escaped his bile. Gesteris couldn't blame him. Felice Koroyan, the architect of his condition, still walked free.

D'Allinnius gripped the door handle with his three-fingered left hand

and pulled it down. It was a mercy she had left him his thumbs. She'd probably think of it as an omission. Acrid-smelling air rolled out through the open door. Gesteris walked into a room almost empty but for a sheet of metal which stretched a good ten feet into the air and across the room, and which was bolted to the floor at the near end of the workshop. Three men stood behind it, bent over something at a small table. At the other end of the room, illuminated by a single smoking torch, there was nothing but scorch marks on the walls and a scattering of wood splinters on the floor.

Gesteris raised his eyebrows. 'You've made quick progress, I presume.'

'I would not call you down here to waste your time,' said D'Allinnius. 'I have none myself for pointless pleasantries.'

'I can respect that,' said Gesteris. 'So, what have you discovered?'

D'Allinnius's eye sparkled and he almost smiled. 'This stuff is amazing. Dangerous but amazing. We have a demonstration ready for you. Don't we?'

One of his staff raised his head. 'Whenever you're ready, chief.'

'Now is a good time.'

'Yes, chief.'

Gesteris noticed that the man had no eyebrows. His faced looked red, too, like it had been scrubbed with gravel. He picked up a metal flask and walked it to the far end of the workshop. Meanwhile, the other two picked up a rough wooden carving of a man standing in a corner and walked it down to place it by the flask. It was clearly very heavy.

'This should be good to watch,' said Gesteris.

'That depends on whether you want to keep your other eye, Senator. Best to just listen and then look at the aftermath.'

'It's your demonstration,' said Gesteris.

'So it is. Step to the centre of the barricade.' D'Allinnius raised his voice. 'Set and light the taper at your leisure, Master Lagalius.'

The two statue-carriers returned at a trot, one of them closing the door to the workshop. Both looked excited but a little nervous. After a brief pause, Gesteris heard hurried footsteps and Lagalius reappeared. All three of them placed their hands over their ears, nodding at Gesteris to do likewise.

'It's loud,' said Lagalius.

The detonation came a few moments later. Gesteris, hands clamped to the side of his head, jumped half out of his skin, drawing grins from the scientists. Noise reverberated around the workshop and there was a brief rattling against the metal barricade. Gesteris was aware that the room had darkened. No light came from the other end of the workshop. Even with his ears covered, Gesteris had felt the force of the explosion and his head was ringing. D'Allinnius spoke, his voice sounding muffled.

'Come and see.'

They picked up lanterns from the small table and the five of them walked round the barricade. Gesteris's eyes widened. The wooden dummy was gone. Not merely damaged or broken but gone. Obliterated. Shards of wood covered the floor. Mere splinters really, nothing thicker than his thumb or longer than his arm.

'God-take-me-to-my-rest,' he said, his voice echoing in his head. 'I don't believe it.'

D'Allinnius was resting on his cane, a self-satisfied expression on his scarred face.

'I take it you approve.'

Gesteris gestured, his mind turning over a dozen possibilities. 'How can it be?'

'Come,' said D'Allinnius. 'I'll show you how it works.'

They returned to the office. A thoughtful clerk had left wine and fruit on the desk. Gesteris sat opposite D'Allinnius who sketched as he spoke, an edge of respect in his voice.

'There are two compounds. From the notes that came with them, it was clear very quickly that experimenting with levels of mix would give us a wide range of results. What you saw there represented perhaps one tenth of our supply.'

'Is that all?'

D'Allinnius raised his eyebrows. 'Small quantities make big bangs. What the flame does is ignite one of the compounds, some alloy of phosphorus and magnesium we think. The heat causes a reaction with the other compound, we aren't quite clear what that is yet, creating a spontaneous, violent, and complete combustion. It rips the container to shreds and those shreds plus a mass of expanding energy destroy the target. In this case, the figure. Oak, by the way. Tough wood.'

'Didn't the notes tell you what exactly the compounds are?' asked Gesteris.

'After a fashion. We're searching the libraries for translations though.

It seems the Sirraneans have no Estorean words for some of their metals and minerals.'

Gesteris nodded. 'That does not surprise me. Now don't take this the wrong way but having to light a taper to detonate this mixture would appear to severely limit its battlefield use. Good for bringing down walls, but no good in the front line, I'd say.'

'On the contrary, I am happy you are able to think clearly. We've been working on that and we found something. By accident, as so often is the case. Lagalius has no eyebrows for a good reason. In fact he is fortunate to be alive. We discovered this morning that impact force alone can trigger an explosion. Friction, it seems, is enough for ignition.'

Gesteris felt his face prickling with sudden warmth. 'That means—'

'Yes, Senator. Just imagine. A flask of this set amongst a net of stones and flung from an onager onto the heads of your enemies.' D'Allinnius's hands, clenched together as he began to talk, now pulled apart further and further in time with a rumbling sound he made by rattling phlegm in his throat.

Gesteris felt flushed. He couldn't keep the delight from his voice.

'You can manufacture this stuff, can't you?' he asked.

'I would prefer to discuss the method with my Sirranean counterparts while delivering them the knowledge they will no doubt want from us in return.'

'There may not be time. The Tsardon are already on the move.'

'So I understand. Don't be surprised to hear that we are working every moment on understanding both compounds and modes of manufacture.'

Gesteris stood up. 'Bless you, Orin. May the Omniscient smile upon your every breath.'

D'Allinnius's face darkened immediately. 'There is no God, merely blind faith. I have no time for the Omniscient belief nor the perpetrators of its evil. If you want real faith, look to the current incumbents of the Chancellery. That is our future, not the scriptures of intolerance and repression.'

'We can debate theology another day,' said Gesteris. 'But let me assure you that our future lies in no small part in your capable hands. Crack this one, deliver us this weapon, and your name will shine forever in the pantheon of Conquord heroes.'

D'Allinnius cracked a crooked smile. 'Just make sure my bust is modelled on the face of my youth. I do not wish to still be frightening children long after I am gone.'

Chapter Twenty Two

859th cycle of God, 35th day of Genasrise

'God-take-me but I hate the night watch. Darkness, chill and not even a Tsardon song to hurl abuse at.'

Centurion Charikus looked the few paces along the rampart path to Lissa Helanius. She was a bleater at the best of times. But give her the dog watch on the Gosland border looking out over the bleak plains of Tsard and she was abandoned to misery. He wondered why she'd joined the legions in the first place. Mind you, she could fight. And fire a bow. She should have gone a long way but her mouth always let her down at the wrong moment. Some never learn.

'You know what, Lissa. If they had a gilded leaves for whining at the games, you would be feted on the balcony every time.'

'Well, it's true, sir. Look at us. All lined up here, what, twenty of us on this platform? And for what? To make Ambassador Del Aglios sleep more comfortably in his bed.'

'That's General Del Aglios now, isn't it? And I tell you something, legionary. If Del Aglios wants us up here, it has nothing to do with his beauty sleep and everything to do with something he knows. He's won more battles than you've had lovers, and that's saying something.'

Helanius thought to retort but chuckled instead. 'Very funny, sir. I suppose so. It just doesn't seem worth it. Three people could give enough warning of an approach. There's four maniples on standby under my feet and the onagers are oiled. Let's face it, they aren't coming and this is just a show.'

'We'll see. All I know is, he wants eyes front, not to the side and not dreaming of tea and fires. So I suggest you point yours in the right direction.'

'Sir.' Helanius thrust her hips at him and turned back to the Tsardon night.

Charikus suppressed a laugh, managed to force a frown and shake of the head and followed his own orders. He saw the arrows a heartbeat before they washed over the ramparts and found their way between the crenellations. Far too little time to give a warning. Charikus didn't even have time to shout. He staggered back a pace, saw the shafts protruding from his chest and felt a dragging heavy pain in his throat. He clawed at the wounds, feeling blood gushing over his hands. Dimly, he saw Helanius tipping backwards but perhaps it was he who was falling. He closed his eyes.

And gasped in a breath.

If it was a breath.

Charikus was lying on his back. His mind was jumbled. He couldn't feel his body. But there was something. A rushing through his insides that felt like voices. He was aware that was an odd notion. Voices didn't feel like anything, or they shouldn't. But he couldn't force his mind to think anything. It was like someone had closed a door and he couldn't get in.

Memories bled in. Arrows. Coming from the night and drenching them in death. Them. Those that were with him. Standing. Looking into the dark. Falling. Blood. Charikus closed his eyes. He knew that because the light he saw had gone but he had no sensation.

He felt fear. A swarming anxiety that flooded his muddled mind. But immediately following it came calm. Like a hand on a fevered brow or an arm around the shoulder. The relief cascaded along his spine and filled him from within. He opened his eyes again.

Charikus could see stars above. And gentle cloud moving across the dark sky. Light about him caressed him. He felt warm. A tingling built inside him, building through his back and bringing him sensation in his fingertips and down into his feet. He could feel a breeze on his face.

Charikus opened his mouth and air sighed from his lungs. He would take more in but there was no rush. Serenity suffused him. He knew where he was at last. He felt the embrace around him, supporting him. All of them. Because he could sense them too. Others who had made the journey to a rest that would be spent in glory until the time was right for his return to the earth.

Rise.

Charikus rose. The tingling, more a vibration now, fed through his feet and moved through him, making him complete. Around him, others rose too and he experienced a closeness that tasted like family. He was safe here. He looked about him. He recognised this place. From his memories. Down at his feet, the ground was stained. A moment's sadness. He had died here but now would move forward to the next task set for him.

In front of his eyes, the air seemed to shimmer. He waved a hand in front of him to disperse it but it changed nothing. He saw others doing the same. He recognised them too. Family. A woman stood just a few paces from him. An arrow jutted from her stomach. Another from the side of her neck.

But they were all safe from arrows now. And from pain and from longing and from fear.

Enemies.

Charikus tensed. The woman did the same as if she had heard the same word, sensed the same threat. Charikus drew his gladius. It felt familiar in his hand. God needed him to work in death as he had in life until his cycle came again. That was right and good.

Enemies below. Enemies behind you.

They began moving towards the stairs from the ramparts. Some others came from hidden places and moved across the platform, past the catapults and stones. They would need to be turned if the enemies behind were to be defeated. Some began that task.

Charikus led the rest to the stairs. His people, all as one, sure of purpose. With every pace, his vision cleared a little more and the closeness he felt to the rest, the connection like a rope linking them together, grew stronger, more comforting. He didn't want to be separated from them. Not ever. All of them, touched by God and blessed to do his work beyond the mantle of death.

All that are not you can be made you. Bring them.

Clarity.

Charikus walked down the stairs and inside a room. There was light here. Harsh. It was fires. There was noise too. Movement. Enemies. There were seven with him. And all these enemies had to be made into them all.

Enemies. Your blade will release them.

Of course.

An enemy turned to him. There was a look on his face like he did not believe. It was a look that saw the arrows he had within him. The enemy spoke but the words were indistinct. They were unimportant.

Charikus moved towards the enemy. Those others of him spread to bring other enemies to them. The enemy was shouting. A word kept repeating and he could almost hear it. The enemy was afraid. Charikus would release him from fear.

He raised his gladius. The enemy fell over a chair and sprawled on the ground. In the room the shouting had got very loud, overcoming the muffling of the ears. He heard that word again.

Charikus!

He paused.

Enemy.

He struck.

Adranis awoke with a start. It was a shout that had broken his sleep but he couldn't be sure if he had dreamed it or not. In the bunk next to him, Roberto slept on. There was the experience of countless campaigns and the noises of the army camp. Adranis felt comforted. If the shout had been real, or a warning, Roberto would surely have woken.

He heard it again. It was distant, probably from across the bridge. He couldn't make out the tone. Perhaps the Tsardon were playing one of their games.

Finding himself fully awake, Adranis pushed himself up from his bed and pulled on boots, thick wool toga and cloak. A breath of air might do him good and he was needled by the shout. He closed the door quietly behind him and walked the short distance to a flight of stairs that would take him towards the grand gatehouse balcony overlooking the span of the bridge.

Lanterns and a brazier fire gave the balcony a warm glow. It was not a cold night. Genastro was in full flow in Gosland and he was not alone in welcoming the season of growth after a long, harsh and icy dusas. There were four guards on the balcony, all of them looking out across the bridge towards the forward gatehouse. Lights and fires speckled the concrete and stone. Soldiers moved about on the bridge.

'Everything all right, centurion?' asked Adranis.

The four legionaries snapped to attention. Adranis waved them to ease.

'I think so, sir. There was some shouting over at the border gate but it seems to have subsided.'

'I thought I heard something.'

'Probably a fight over cards or something, sir,' said the centurion. 'All quiet now.'

Indeed it was. Adranis felt a little silly. He'd tried to do the nonchalant enquiry but they all knew he'd hurried up here because something had made him that touch nervous. They didn't know why and neither did he but career soldiers would chat and inevitably he'd be the butt of a few jokes. Roberto always said you should let the rank and file see your human side. Adranis didn't think he meant it in quite this way.

A breeze blew across the bridge and into his face. Almost like someone blowing air directly at him. He frowned. The wind was across them, surely, and directed downstream.

'Did you—?' he began.

The air stilled. Adranis heard a rumbling sound, emanating from beyond the border gate. In moments, the noise had eclipsed his every thought. It became a battering roar. Just before the torches and fires were snuffed out on the border fort, he saw windows and shutters explode outwards, sending lethal splinters down towards the bridge. And what looked like a dark cloud streamed around the gate and surged across the bridge.

'Oh dear God,' muttered Adranis. 'Down! Down!'

He had no idea if the others could hear him. He dropped to the ground, dragging the centurion with him, yelling for the legionaries to take cover. The cloud impacted the fort and gates. It thrashed across the balcony. Adranis covered his head with his hands. He heard a thrumming on castle stone and a beating against wood and marble. Something fell across his legs. He was peppered with dust and what felt like small stones. Wind howled around him. The balcony shook, the very foundations of the castle were rattling and vibrating. Distantly, he thought he could hear screams but he dared not look up into the maelstrom.

It went on and on, a purgatory that he feared would have no end. The dust thickened around him, making him cough. Adranis had to raise his head from the floor of the balcony to avoid choking. His face was raw where particles had scoured him, even here behind cover. His hands, he could just about see, were covered in dust. The lanterns and fire on the balcony had long since been extinguished but the pale moonlight swam through the thick cloud.

The wind dropped. Briefly, grit and dirt fell like rain.

Adranis became aware of several sounds at once. Shouting, alarm, orders and pain. He heard moaning nearby. He dragged himself to his knees, feeling the weight fall from his legs. He felt faint and shook his head to dislodge dirt and what he saw now to be sand. He knew he had to move fast. No doubt the Tsardon would be able to take advantage of the sandstorm, if such it had been, sent on a wind that tasted bitter and rotten.

'Start small, be right,' he said to himself, Roberto's words a comfort. 'Keep calm. Assess the immediate.'

The centurion was moving and looked unhurt. Adranis turned and had to stop himself gasping. The weight on his legs had been one of the legionaries. No one but God could offer him hope now. His face was gone. Scoured clean. His eyes were full of blood and bone showed through the skin around his jaws, nose and brows. The other two legionaries were moving but struggling.

'Centurion?'

'I'm all right, sir. What happened?'

'Let me worry about that. See to your men, those you can help.'

Adranis stood up, feeling his heart thumping hard. He looked out over the balcony. He'd read that when a volcano erupted, the ash covered everything. It was just like this. Every outline was indistinct, almost like it had snowed. There were drifts of dust against the gates and bodies lying on the bridge. Soldiers who had been afforded no warning and no opportunity to find cover.

He looked to his left, and quickly to his right. The towers and artillery platforms were dark, looming shadows. He thought he could make out movement but it was vague. Some people were alive but he was only certain of that because of the screams and shouts. Somewhere, calls for order were being made. A lantern flared in the darkness above and to his right.

Adranis's ears were roaring, his eyes beginning to adjust to the half light and gloom. At his feet, one of the legionaries moaned, deep in agony and barely conscious.

'It's all right,' said the centurion. 'You'll be fine. Help is coming.'

He looked up and caught Adranis's gaze. He shook his head.

'What happened?' he asked.

'A dust storm, I suppose,' said Adranis. 'Never seen anything like it.'

'How can it be?' An edge of panic was in the centurion's voice. 'It came from nowhere. It isn't dry enough. And look. There are stones. Chips of granite. Like someone picked up the road the other side of the gate and threw it at us.'

The centurion was right. It didn't make any sense. Adranis tried not to think too hard about it. The Tsardon were beyond a severely weakened border fort. If they had escaped the storm, they might well seize the opportunity. Security was everything. Adranis looked back over the bridge. There was no light at all in the fort. No braziers on the artillery platform, no lanterns in the rear gatehouse.

'They can't all be dead,' he said. 'Can they?'

Adranis heard a creaking sound, joined by others. Artillery wind-lasses being winched on the border fort platform. He didn't know whether to be relieved or scared. He had to pray it was no more than caution because if the Tsardon chose to attack, they would find the defence not up to the challenge. He, Kell, Nunan and Roberto needed time.

The rear gates were opening onto the bridge. Adranis froze. Within the growing clamour that was overtaking the castle on which he stood, he felt within a well of silence. The echoes of the wind blew around his ears and his skin raged with the sand and grit lodged there. He felt vulnerable but with no will to move a muscle. The gap between the doors yawned wide. People spilled out onto the bridge. His people, Conquord people. Perhaps thirty, running headlong across the span. Looking behind them, shouting for the castle gates to be opened. Consumed with fear.

Adranis waited just for a moment, until the Tsardon emerged after them. He had to be sure. But they didn't come. Instead, behind came more in the livery of the Conquord and the Gosland border militia. Not running, walking. Adranis frowned. Something wasn't right about them and the way they moved. It was a little slow and clumsy, even. He looked back to those rushing towards the castle, approaching the gates, their voices loud and panicked.

He made to speak to the centurion but the onager arms at the fort thudded into their rests. Stones whined into the sky. For a heartbeat, he watched them.

'God-embrace-me,' he breathed, then shouted. 'Cover!'

For the second time, he grabbed the centurion, this time diving through the balcony doorway and tumbling onto the stairs. The stones smashed into the castle. Lumps of masonry and rubble fell, pounding into the balcony and sending clouds of dust into his face. The centurion pushed himself upright, wanting to get back outside. Adranis's voice stopped him.

'You can't help them now. We have to build a defence. Find the castle captain.'

The centurion nodded, confused and scared.

'Centurion. Calm. Do the simple thing. Be right.'

'Yes, sir.' He ran away down the stairs.

Adranis looked after him. From below, orders were bringing some semblance of calm to the castle. He heard the shout for the gates to be opened and, more distantly, horns calling the legion from their beds. They were away two hundred yards and more, camped on open ground. It would be a long and cruel pause before they could be brought to order and marched to the defence.

Adranis knew what he had to do. He took the stairs three at a time, heading for his room. He had to get his armour and helmet on; and he had to find Roberto.

Chapter Twenty-Three

859th cycle of God, 35th day of Genasrise

Roberto's aide was chasing after him with breastplate and helmet. Roberto clattered into Kell's and Nunan's quarters to find them already dressed and strapping on their blades. Horns were blowing in the legion camp. The two generals were grim and angry.

'Dammit but we're in the wrong place,' said Nunan.

'We got complacent,' said Kell.

'It doesn't matter now.' Roberto came to a standstill and let his aide place his breastplate over his head and begin to strap it up. The walls of the castle shuddered under further impacts. Screams echoed in the corridors. 'Bring them up to the clear ground behind the castle. Cavalry free on the flanks. Don't come in, keep a line. Remember you are a legion and bred to fight in open spaces. We can't afford to lose hundreds in hand-to-hand in here. I'd rather lose the castle and hold them later.'

'Yes, General.'

'Dina, Pavel. You're in charge. Don't look to me. Make the decisions.' They nodded. 'Good. Go.'

Roberto turned to his aide and held out his hands. His gloves were thrust on. He took his helmet and placed it on his head, feeling the comforting weight and a rush of memories. His heart beat faster, his body charged. Now he had to face a problem that should have been dealt with a decade ago. He'd smelled this air before and he knew exactly what it meant. The Conquord was about to pay for the mercy of the past.

'Get yourself safe, Herides,' he said to his aide. 'Go to the camp.'

'My place is here by your side,' said Herides. 'It always has been.'

Roberto placed a hand on his shoulder. The man who stared back at him still had the eyes of the one he had taken into his service on the Tsardon battlefield all those years ago. But illness had robbed him of strength and brought a tremble to his limbs.

'I have been a long time out of this armour but I still retain legion papers. You do not and should not place yourself in the path of danger. It is your mind, I need, my friend. Keep it safe.'

'My General,' said Herides.

'Never could call me anything else could you?'

'No other name seemed to fit.'

Roberto headed for the door. Men and women were running past in the direction of the bridge gates. Armour rattled and spears glinted in the light from lanterns being relit across the castle. Herides went right, Roberto left. Coming down the stairs from the balcony, was Adranis. Relief was keen. The two men shared a brief embrace.

'You need your armour,' said Roberto.

'I know. Listen, Roberto. These aren't Tsardon stones hitting us. They've turned the catapults on the platform. We have to assume the Tsardon have taken the fort. Survivors are at our gates and more are behind them but ...'

Roberto looked into his brother's eyes and saw confusion.

'What is it? Come on, anything.'

'The ones following on. Something's wrong with them.'

'And the storm that hit us,' said Roberto, beginning to add it all together. 'It didn't feel natural, did it?'

Adranis shook his head. 'No.'

'That's because it wasn't. Get yourself dressed. Meet me back at the gates. We're going to need your courage, brother. The rogue Ascendant has come to call.'

Roberto ran towards the gates. One had been opened to admit the terrified militia. The doorway was crowded with soldiers. Roberto shouted people from his path and elbowed his way to gain a view. He tried to ignore the words he was hearing and the anxiety that they fed into those guarding the gates.

'Hold all of them, Captain,' he said to the castle's commander. 'We need statements from each and every one.'

'Yes, sir,' she said. 'You heard the ambassador. Take them to the mess hall. Warm drinks and whatever you can find to feed them.'

'The Bear Claws are coming,' said Roberto. 'Let's not think this fight lost.'

Further stones tumbled into the castle structure. Dust and plaster fell.

'This place will stand that all night,' called the captain. 'Hold your stations. Archers to the ramparts.'

Roberto looked out of the open gate. Conquord citizens were moving across the bridge. Behind them, in the fort now blazing with new light, a Tsardon flag was unfurled on the artillery platform. Enemy forces massed in the gateway and crowded every window. At first he thought they were cheering but they weren't.

'Close the gate,' he said. 'Do it now.'

'But sir, we need our people inside,' said the captain. 'There's no danger.'

'No? Did you not hear what those who ran in were saying?'

'But you can't believe that. It's a trick.'

'All I know is that I can see people stuck with arrows walking this way. People who should be dead.' He raised his voice. 'Close the gate.'

Soldiers were looking at the captain and back to him.

'Those are our people.' There was pleading in the captain's voice.

Roberto took another look. Throats were pierced, armour damaged. One had lost a hand, another had a tear across his chest through which his ribs were clearly visible.

'Trust me,' he said quietly. 'And don't make me pull rank. Those are not our people. Not any more. Close the gate.'

The captain looked to her soldiers and nodded. 'Do it,' she said, turning back to Roberto immediately. 'What now, General? We've closed the gates on people we could have saved. You know something. We need to know it too, sir.'

There were better than fifty people around the gates as they clanged shut and bolts were thrown. Every one of them looked at Roberto, anger in their faces. The gates were in the centre of a broad wall and faced into a staging area big enough to hold two thousand legionaries or five hundred cavalry. It was filling up quickly. Stairs led off left up to the gatehouse balcony and right to the artillery platforms. Other doors and stairways studded the walls all the way around, giving access to the rest of the castle.

'Let's form our defence here first,' said Roberto. 'Sarissas and archers in ranks facing the door. Swords to the flanks, ready to use as shock force.'

The captain didn't move for a moment.

'Captain, the Tsardon are coming. We have to hold here until the legion arrives. The stones will soon be hitting those gates and they will not hold forever whatever the strength of the walls. And I fear the Tsardon have more than just artillery backing their assault. Form up and I will speak to you all.'

The captain nodded and began to issue orders. She knew him. They all did. The Conquord's most successful living general. He was relying on that reputation now, more than he ever had. He knew what they were thinking. That he'd left good citizens outside to die. How could he tell them something he dare not believe himself? He needed evidence, testimony. Something to back up the foggy memory of a conversation he'd had with Paul Jhered years ago. The mess hall had plenty of that.

'Thank you, Captain,' he said. 'Your trust will not be wasted. I am sorry to say I can promise you that.'

Roberto took her salute and made for the mess hall. Halfway across the staging area, he saw Adranis emerge from their room, resplendent in his cavalry armour, cloak and helmet.

'Over here,' he said. 'Come and help me talk to the runners you saw. We need quick information.'

'I should get back to the Claws,' said Adranis.

'They'll need to hear it too. Best it comes from one of their own.'

'Hear what?'

'Just bear with me,' said Roberto.

Adranis looked beyond Roberto and straightened in complete surprise. His mouth opened slightly. Simultaneously, silence fell across the yard. Roberto spun on his heel. Walking down both sets of stairs, from the balcony, gate ramparts and artillery platform, were men and women bearing gladiuses and knives. It was a determined walk.

On the ground, people backed away. He heard blades drawn and the whisper of voices.

'That man was dead,' said Adranis. 'I saw him myself. Roberto, *look* at him.'

Roberto looked. Skull bone showed through his torn flesh and blood had dribbled from his eyes to draw lines down his cheeks. Walking beside him, another man, his breastplate drenched in blood and across his throat, a jagged tear. A third came behind them, one hand clamped to his gut. Even as they watched, the entrails slipped from between his fingers and spilled on to the ground, hanging and steaming in the cold air. The man simply removed his hand and carried on walking. But he tripped on his own innards and tumbled sideways.

From the platform and towers, came ten more and shadows above told of others. Roberto could all but taste the fear that swept across the living as they beheld their first, disbelieving sight of the dead. They held ranks but only just, backing away further, leaving an open space at the base of each stairway.

The captain held out her hands for calm. She was standing ahead of her soldiers and in front of the gates. She looked left and right, watching the dead advance. She gasped and moved towards the left-hand stair. The murmuring of the living became louder. Someone urged her to get back. Others were pointing, calling out names. Roberto put out a hand to stop Adranis coming past him.

'Captain,' he said, voice bouncing from the vaulted roof. 'Keep your distance.'

'It's Veralius,' she said, pointing to one of the torn, scarred men moving towards her. 'We have to help them. Look at them.'

'It was Veralius,' said Roberto. 'It isn't now. Just a shell. He should be with God and he is not.'

The dead were on the lower steps. The mass of the defenders were still backing off, leaving open ground of a good ten yards. Adranis and Roberto walked around the side, giving them a view across the space. The captain stood her ground. Roberto could see the fear in her eyes. Her sword was drawn and she continually retightened her grip. She was alone and the dead were moving towards her.

'Veralius,' she said. 'It's me, Jorgia.'

There was no flicker of recognition.

'Back off, Captain,' said Roberto. 'This won't work.'

'Alive or dead, it's still him,' said the captain. 'Veralius, come on. Say something.'

Veralius had a long, savage cut down the left hand side of his head. It had been a killing blow, no question. It had smashed his jaw across his face and his neck was twisted to the side. It should be pumping blood but only the tiniest dribble could be seen. He was slightly ahead of the others but all of them, from both sets of steps, were moving towards the captain. Behind her, her soldiers were urging her to drop back.

'Something wrong with him, Captain. Stand with us.'

'We can take them if we have to.'

'Veralius,' she said again. 'Please. Remember me.'

'He can't,' said Roberto. 'He's dead. Drop back.'

'And do what?' she snapped. 'He's dead already? How do we kill him again? I don't even know what I'm trying to say. How can he be dead?' The last a hoarse whisper.

'Taking their legs off will stop them advancing. And taking their hands off will stop them attacking,' said Adranis. 'They'll never get past a line of sarissas, Captain. Do what the general says.'

'And that's an order,' said Roberto.

The captain looked at them briefly and then back at Veralius. He was only four paces from her, the others right behind him. Blades were raised.

'Captain!' shouted Roberto. 'Back off now.'

'Veralius,' bawled the captain into the face of the dead man. 'Veralius.'

There it was. A pause in his relentless advance. A twitch in the sword arm. His expression didn't change but he didn't strike. He rocked slightly in his stance. The captain smiled.

'Veralius,' she said. 'It's all right.'

Four blades crashed into her unprotected sides, carving deep into her back, neck and arms. She went down in a fountain of blood. Her soldiers roared fury.

'Sarissas!' shouted someone. 'Two to a blade.'

The long weapons were levelled, three ranks deep.

'Archers, fire at will.'

Arrows spat across the short space from those who could get a shot. Forty or fifty striking at the dead who were already on the move. There were only twenty of them but they moved with no fear, just hideous purpose. There was no doubt what they would do when they reached the defensive lines. But they weren't going to get that far.

Shafts thudded home. The dead were pitched from their feet, driven backwards or down to their knees. In moments, they were all preparing to move forward again, spreading more anxiety, more fear.

'Sarissas. Let's pin these bastards to the gates.'

The sarissa men surged forwards, battle cries ripping from their lips. The dead raised no defence. The long, counter-balanced blades found their targets. The team pairs pushed on, angling the blades up, lifting dead from the ground and rushing the yardage to the gates where they pinioned them to the timbers. The cheers were muted. Some had been carried up but dropped. Still they moved. Goslander militia fell on them, hacking and slashing.

Roberto rubbed his gloved hands over his face. More dead were appearing on the stairs. Those impaled on blades still moved, still betrayed no emotion, pain or fear.

'I want this castle swept for them,' ordered Roberto. 'Dismember, decapitate. Stop them anyway you can. We will send them back to the embrace of God.'

While centurions sent teams up the stairways, Roberto turned to Adranis. His brother wore his shock in the brightness of his eyes.

'Get back to the legion. Tell Kell and Nunan what we're up against. There has to be no confusion, no mercy. These citizens are dead and we must not think of them as the people we once knew.'

'Easy to say,' said Adranis.

'We have to stop them and we have to do it now. Here.'

'Who's doing this?'

Roberto spat on the ground. Around them, violence flared. The dead were being sent back to God. It was not pretty and Roberto was aware it was driven by anger at their captain's murder. When the fury subsided, the fear would return.

'Gorian.'

Adranis's frown deepened. 'The Ascendant? Dead, surely.'

'The Sirraneans warned me he was still alive and in Tsard. The evidence suggests they were right. I should never have let him live.'

'Can you be sure it's him?'

'Who else? Jhered once told me Gorian thought the dead had an energy of their own and it seems he was right.' Roberto shook his head. 'Walking dead, foul-smelling storms carrying dust and death. There's no doubt. Just as there is no doubt that the Tsardon are with him and the Conquord is not ready for another invasion. If we don't hold them here, we have little else to offer.'

'The Claws won't fail.'

'I'm counting on that. Go. If we can stop them here, we will. Just be ready unless we can't.'

'Be careful, Roberto.'

Roberto chuckled. 'That's rich, coming from you.'

Onager stones rattled into the gatehouse and the timber of the gates themselves, sending the dead pinned there into a hideous jumping dance, like puppets in a cheap show.

'Let's have them down,' said Roberto. 'Even butchering them is more respectful than this.'

The carving up of the dead had finished and the reanimated corpses lay still once again. Someone had found an Order reader and body parts were being taken away for proper, decent burial. Blood was across the steps and more teams were heading out to the open spaces of the castle to ensure no more of Gorian's bastard creations were lurking, waiting to strike.

Centurions had organised their soldiers quickly and effectively. There was a busy quality to the staging area but Roberto could hear it fading away now the immediate action was done. Shock was settling on the two hundred or so assembled there. Defensive commanders were reorganising the sarissa lines to form up before the doors while the pinned dead were taken down to be dismembered. Roberto found it hard to believe such an order was being followed.

But there were problems of more immediate significance to tackle. He could see in the eyes of every man and woman standing before the now damaged gates that they were wholly unprepared for what might come against them. Tsardon or dead citizens, it hardly mattered. And they had no defence against the pounding of their own artillery. Not one of the pieces ranged across the river was functioning. Roberto knew there would be feverish activity from the engineers but that it would almost certainly prove futile. Gorian's storm had destroyed bindings, cups and ropes.

Roberto walked across the open ground in front of the sarissa line. More stones thudded into the gates. The back of one timber splintered. Iron bindings rattled and nails loosened. One of the centurions came to his shoulder.

'Orders, sir?'

Roberto looked at him. Standing proud but with fear etched into his expression.

'This is senseless,' he said.

'General?'

'We cannot hold them here. When the gates go down, if it is not the dead who kill us, it will be the six thousand Tsardon flooding across the bridge. Don't sacrifice one more life.' Roberto swallowed on a welling desperation. Images flooded his mind and none of them suggested victory. 'The Bear Claws are drawn up behind us. This is their job now. Abandon the castle.'

The centurion stared at him for a moment.

'We can't desert the border,' he said. 'This castle is Gosland. We have a killing ground here, surely. We can pin any number back with arrows and sarissas. The door isn't wide enough for them to gain a bridgehead.'

Roberto managed to smile. 'You're a credit, Centurion, but we are not facing a conventional army. You can't fight the dead with arrows. And they are backed by magic. There is an Ascendant with them.'

The stare became a gape. 'The wind . . .'

'Yes. The wind. And worse will be to come, I'm sure. It may be a killing ground in here but it's also a tunnel to direct his filthy power. Trust me.' Roberto held the centurion's gaze. 'The Claws will destroy them in the open. Their artillery will be out of range. Our cavalry can rip them apart. They have no horses.'

The centurion nodded. 'I'll give the order.'

Chapter Twenty-Four

859th cycle of God, 35th day of Genasrise

Roberto sent the border force through the cavalry drawn up on the Claws' left flank. Kell and Nunan had deployed in classic fashion across the wide open spaces cleared behind the castle. Designed for mass camps, staging and transport for the invasion of Tsard, the ground was on a slight slope down towards the river and also ideal for battle.

The front line of the hastati sarissa phalanx stood a hundred yards from the castle walls and its huge double gates. Between the hastati maniples and the second infantry lines of principes, stood their archers. Equipped with long bows made from Sirranean wood, the archers were well in range of the gates. They were backed by scorpion bolt-firers placed behind the lines of triarii. Gladius maniples flanked the phalanx and wide out, cavalry waited. The whole army was on a slight crescent.

It ought to be a massacre but Roberto couldn't help but be scared for the 2nd legion. Conquord elite they might be but it wasn't the Tsardon that worried him. Standing with the twin generals and waiting for the gates to be thrust open, he was fairly sure that whatever dead remained would be coming through them.

'What we need are stones to squash them,' said Nunan, reading his mind.

'And how is the repair effort going?'

Nunan blew out his cheeks. 'A day. Maybe more. Every rope is frayed, every hinge is clogged. It was a very effective tactic.'

'Then we cannot worry about what we won't have.'

'How many dead are there?' Nunan's enunciation of the word was indicative of the scepticism across the legion.

'As few as thirty, as many as who knows?' said Roberto. 'Just don't underestimate their effect.'

The pounding on the bridge gates had ceased. The Tsardon had begun to appear in castle windows and on the battlements looking out into Gosland. Above the chatter of the legion in the first light of dawn edging into the eastern sky, Roberto could hear the enemy advance and their songs of triumph. A little premature; most of them would have no idea what confronted them immediately outside the castle gates.

'They won't get past the sarissas. We'll do what you did inside. And we'll take the Tsardon force right here and end this.'

'I hope so,' said Roberto. 'It's why we're all standing here.'

'Can I ask you a personal question?'

'You don't need permission, Pavel.'

'I've never seen you scared before,' said Nunan. 'We're five thousand strong here. There are not enough of them to challenge us. What's going on?'

Roberto nodded. 'Through the whole war and the rise of the Ascendants during the last war, you never actually saw them cast, did you? Not until now. That bastard wind. But I saw things I never thought to see. Power that I still don't believe any man or woman should control. And that was when they were young and inexperienced.

'While I assumed Gorian was dead, I was happy enough because the others have grown into responsible individuals. But out there, beyond that castle, stands Gorian and he is not constrained by any thought of morals, the rules of war or respect for man.

'Yes, I am scared. Scared because he has found some way to animate the dead and send our friends against us as killers. But I am also scared by what he has not revealed. This battle is one event in a new war. And beyond it, we must look to hunt him down and kill him.

'But what of the damage he will cause across the Conquord until we do? And who but an Ascendant can really kill an Ascendant. What have we created here, Pavel?'

'Then let us destroy him now. Break this Tsardon force and march into Tsard on the hunt for Gorian.'

Roberto looked at Nunan and couldn't force himself to believe that would be the result. Even less could he explain why.

'Hang on to your courage, General Nunan. You may need it before sun blesses the ground this morning. I know I shouldn't speak this way but you have to guard as best you can against what horror might come through those gates, or around the castle walls. The legion will look to you and Dina. You above all, cannot be seen to flinch.'

Nunan nodded curtly. 'And I will not.'

The gates of the castle blew open and a hurricane struck out.

'Hold! Hold!' Adranis's shout was lost in the gale that emanated directly from the castle gates and howled around its walls.

He was on the left flank, Kell on the right. Horses were nervous, their riders barely keeping them in position. Buffeted by the wind, some had been knocked from their saddles and struggled to remount. The noise was incredible, the dust thick and the main force of the wind blew directly into the exposed maniples of infantry. An invisible, unending wave.

Sarissas were snatched from hands, pivoting up and tumbling away end over end, carving into the ranks behind. Anything loose was ripped off. Shields, swords, helmets, flying backwards to strike mayhem into the maniples and men in their paths. Legionaries were cut and bludgeoned down. Bodies blew and tumbled. Tents and braziers were plucked from the ground and were lost in the dark.

And now the whole legion was flat on its face, braced against the gale. It was impossible to tell which were alive and which wounded or dead. Devastation in moments. But Adranis could not hear the screams, just the roar of the wind. A shout from the throat of God. It bawled at the Bear Claws. Biting, scratching, blinding dust scoured into exposed faces. Gusts strong enough to uproot trees and laced with chill, stinging water rendered the legion all but helpless.

Adranis couldn't see across the line as far as Kell and the right flank cavalry. God-surround-him, he couldn't even see the castle gates any more. He peered into the darkness with slitted eyes, trying to make out anything in the new fall of night. The ordered infantry lines had been literally blown apart and he must be able to react when at last the wind died away.

He had no idea if any of them could hear him. Perhaps the man next to him. Adranis leaned out of his saddle and dragged him close, yelling into his ear.

'We must be ready,' he bellowed into the wind. 'It will be sudden. Pass the message.'

The man nodded. A rending, clattering sound carried out on the wind. Adranis's horse took a nervous pace back. A huge shape barrelled across his vision left to right. An onager. Three of his cavalrymen were swept away by it, gone in a heartbeat and it smeared its way headlong into the hastati lines. His horse reared, threatening to throw him. He clung on to the reins much as he did to his courage.

Adranis fought to control his breathing. There were other onagers still standing on the river bank. He prayed that Roberto was safe. Prayed that the next catapult didn't pick him up and fling him to his death. But there were no more. Like the earlier storm, the hurricane faded like thin cloud before the solastro sun. Dust and misty rain hung in the feeble light. Adranis peered hard towards the castle, certain that the Tsardon would advance. His horse calmed under his hand but to his right, the infantry was in disarray. He had but one choice.

'Claws! Ride for the hastatii. Look to the castle. Sweep and turn!'

He raised his arm high above his head and brought it down, jabbing his heels into his horse's flanks. The animal sprang away, happy to be on the move. His numbers were depleted, perhaps two hundred would follow when the order and intent were seen. He gambled that Kell would think the same.

Adranis directed his horse at a slight angle that would take him in front of the hastatii and towards the castle gates. He had his shield set against enemy arrows and he released the reins to draw his sword, controlling the horse with thighs, knees and heels.

Vision was poor. He could see movement at the castle but it was indistinct, enemies in the dust. Adranis searched the gloom ahead. He could see something, and at the edge of his hearing, there were horns. Kell's cavalry. He smiled. Seemed like for the first time in a long time. They all knew the drill, it was long rehearsed. Admittedly the training grounds were usually well lit but the theory was the same. Buy time, unsettle the opposition.

Adranis felt a rush of adrenaline and pushed his horse on faster. Hornsmen in his detachment saw the oncoming Kell, and sounded the warning and standing order tones. The beat of hoofs sent a glorious shudder up his spine. Hundreds of horses ridden by the Conquord's finest ripped up the ground, closing at a full gallop.

At forty yards distance, Adranis leant in with his left knee, raised his sword and begin to turn. Kell, at the head of her hundreds, mirrored his move. In the midst of chaos and growing despair, it was a drill completed to perfection. Adranis brought his five-wide column alongside Kell's. They drove forty yards towards the castle before breaking left and right to a final blast of horns. Legion cavalry. Discipline, order, victory. Adranis had to stop himself shouting.

Aware of his vulnerability, he sobered and looked right. Tsardon were pouring from the gates to form up into a fighting line. Pikes were already set against a cavalry charge and Adranis would not risk one. He didn't need to. The enemy were already making cautious moves rather than the headlong advance they had surely expected. Bowmen fired down from the castle walls but it was disordered, not threatening.

Adranis switched his gaze ahead. Not fifty yards in front of him and walking at the Claws' far left flank were around thirty figures. The dead. Adranis growled.

'Like my brother said. Time to go back to God.'

He set his shield arm low and his blade for an upward sweep. The dead hadn't seen him or didn't care. They did not flinch nor change their pace. No defence was raised against the mass of horseflesh about to engulf them. The rear of the column wouldn't even know a blow had been struck. These dead would be ploughed under, destroyed. Adranis looked forward to sending the Tsardon his message.

Adranis's horse tossed his head and shudder ran down his flanks. And five yards from the backs of the dead, the animal sheared away sharply towards the enemy lines. Adranis was caught completely by surprise and was flung from the saddle, crashing to the ground and landing heavily on his shield arm, his sword flying from his grip.

Pandemonium consumed him. Horses slewed left and right. Hoofs were dug into the ground, riders catapulted from saddles to land in the midst of the dead. Others ploughed through from behind, unable to stop. Adranis tried to get his shield above his body. A hoof thudded into his back and spun him over. Pain speared through him. His shield arm was broken. Adranis drew up his legs, making himself as small as possible. Another hoof clipped his shield, dragging his broken arm wide. He howled in pain. A third hit the back of one leg behind his knee. He felt a bone crack.

Every hoofbeat travelled through his back, vibrating along his body. He could sense the pace of the gallop drop as the rear of the column saw the trouble ahead and reined in. Adranis could see horses all around him. Someone was shouting his name but in the crush of man and beast, he doubted anyone could see him.

There was movement behind him and horses backed away quickly, leaving him suddenly exposed. He heard nervous whinnies and the unmistakable sound of animals bolting. And away to his left, a roar from the Tsardon lines and a fresh thrumming through the ground sent a barb of fear through him. He had to get up, get away.

Adranis dragged himself to his knees, feeling faint with the pain and with his vision fogging badly. He blinked. There was movement nearby, fallen cavalry trying to gather themselves. There was movement everywhere. Horses stamped and snorted, refusing to move close. More were fleeing back to the Conquord lines. Others, riderless and confused, followed on. The Tsardon were marching quickly across the open ground. To the right, Kell was doing her best to break up the advance. But the Conquord lines were a mess. Onagers had destroyed parts of the formation, precious few sarissas were in evidence and the whole seemed to be shifting, nervous despite horns and flags demanding order and focus.

Worse for Adranis, he and his isolated few riders had drawn the attention of the dead. They had turned, or had been turned, and were moving directly at him. Ten yards and closing. He tried to rise but his left knee collapsed under him and he pitched once again to the dirt.

Fighting to remain conscious, Adranis dragged his shield from his broken arm and leaned on it with his right to drive himself to his feet, favouring his right leg, his left barely touching the ground. Arrows had begun to fall. One of his men, just upright, was struck in the back and fell face forwards.

Tears were on Adranis's cheeks. He turned towards the Conquord lines. He was sixty yards from them and the same from the Tsardon. Soundless, the dead were moving closer. He shivered, heard the shouts from his friends, saw archers and gladius infantry rushing forwards to provide him with cover and began the agonising march to safety.

'I need more skirmishers out there. Get a shield round that cavalry!'

Roberto ran headlong through the devastated lines towards the front. The shock of seeing the cavalry charge break down was still rippling through the ranks. The Tsardon had taken the opportunity and were advancing quickly under a concerted barrage of archer fire. The Claws were responding but in lesser numbers. It was impossible to say how many had died, or how many weapons and shields had been broken or snatched away and flung into the tattered remnants of the camp. The infantry was in disarray. The cavalry had to supply cover while they regrouped. And now they were scattered too.

'Come on, Dina,' he muttered. 'You know what you've got to do.'

Roberto couldn't see Dina Kell's cavalry. He could only pray they were massing for another ride across the enemy lines. Anything to distract and disrupt or the Claws would be overwhelmed. He pushed on through injured men and women, past the wreckage of an onager that had tumbled straight through a gladius hastati maniple before coming to rest in the midst of the principes.

The wind had taken every loose piece of armour and weaponry and flung it into the legionaries behind. Soldiers lay dead and injured, impaled on sarissas, cut by shield and sword, battered by flying helmet. All around him, centurions bellowed for order and to present a front to the Tsardon. The lucky ones began to form up but they would offer little defence.

The carnage was awful and the Tsardon had not made a single strike. Without Kell, without Adranis, the Claws would be routed. Soldiers had broken away from the front of the lines and were running with shields held before them towards the stricken cavalrymen. Archers followed, stopping to send volleys into the approaching Tsardon.

He could see half a dozen cavalrymen trying to outrun the Tsardon and the hideous dead that were closing on them too quickly. All were injured. One was being supported by two others and clearly in a bad way. More legionaries were running towards the dead, trying to buy the cavalry some more time. A pace later, Roberto could see who the stricken man was.

'Oh no,' he whispered. 'Adranis!'

Roberto stopped and snatched a shield from the ground and drew his gladius. The thrashing of his heart threatened to bring him to his knees. Every sound roared in his ears. He raised the shield high and burst through the lines. Arrows were peppering the ground. Conquord archers responded. Tsardon soldiers fell, shields blocked out. At least one of the dead was struck from his feet, only to rise again.

'Adranis!' Roberto saw him raise his head. 'Come on. Faster.'

Other throats took up his call. Adranis and those carrying him picked up their pace. The dead were practically on them. Roberto was twenty yards from them, the most forward legionaries just a few paces from them. Arrows fell again. One of Adranis's supporters was taken through the back of the neck and plunged forwards, bringing the three of them down.

'Force them back,' ordered Roberto, sprinting across the gap, sacrificing his shield defence in the pursuit of speed. 'Archers, knock them down.'

Roberto knew there was desperation in his voice but he couldn't keep the even tone of command. Adranis was struggling to get up again, trying to shake off the grasp of his erstwhile helper. The other cavalryman was already on his feet and facing the dead.

He'd lost his weapon and shield. He had nothing but his hands and feet. He moved towards them, just a couple of paces distant now. He kicked out, pushed and punched. Arrows slammed into dead either side of him, giving him space. But their swords lashed out, carving into his head and sides. He went down in a welter of blood and the dead were past him. Another blade came down.

'Adranis!' screamed Roberto.

His brother sprawled on his face, unmoving. The skirmishers barrelled into the dead, fury lending their strikes raw power. Roberto skidded to a stop by his brother. He dropped his shield, sheathed his sword and fell to his knees. The sword had struck Adranis's back plate and slid down into his lower back. The wound pulsed blood. It was deep and filthy. But he was still breathing. Roberto looked around him for help. There was none forthcoming.

The skirmishers were holding the dead but no more, finding them almost impossible to put down permanently. The Tsardon were closing but Roberto could hear and feel onrushing hoof beats.

Cavalry stormed in front of the Tsardon lines. He heard the clash of weapons and the screams of men and horses. He thrust his arms beneath Adranis's chest and waist and picked him up, blowing at the limp weight.

'Hang on, little brother,' he said. 'Please hang on.'

He ran back through the lines, running between two maniples that pointed the way to the only man who could save Adranis. Roberto thanked God for his one small mercy. The Goslander miracle worker: Surgeon Dahnishev.

Chapter Twenty-Five

859th cycle of God, 35th day of Genasrise

Kell took the cavalry into the flank of the Tsardon advance. They had become over-eager and while the pikes were bristling centrally, without cavalry support of their own, they were vulnerable at the edges. Her riders hacked and slashed their swords at undefended bodies. Horses battered past enemies, trampled through dying men. Arrows flew over her head, rattling on shields or finding their marks.

The horns sounded withdrawal and she dragged at the reins. Her horse came round easily, her move covered by her deputies. It gave her a view of the Bear Claws lines and her heart fell. The few enemy dead had been destroyed. The surviving cavalrymen from Adranis's detachment moved but there was no security in where they had been taken. And Adranis himself was not with them.

As they galloped away, chased off by Tsardon arrows, she leaned into her senior hornsman.

'Take them back in one more time. Right-hand flank. Then I want archer passes across the front of their lines. I'll rejoin you presently.'

'Yes, General.'

Kell galloped away to find Pavel Nunan. Every stride she took made her more and more certain. The Tsardon advance had slowed but it wasn't purely because of her cavalry. They had made enough ground to get their whole force on to the field. And when they did, they would roll over the fractured, plainly demoralised legion.

Behind them, the imperial highway led up a sharp slope between two heavily tree-lined valley sides. Dahnishev had set his emergency triage area there a few days before. Always by the book, Dahnishev, bless him. Set with crag and difficult terrain, it was a place you could retreat a legion into and hold out against a greater number forced to attack upslope. She hoped Nunan was already contemplating it.

She found Pavel in a tide of wounded and dying legionaries. In the half-light, his face was white and full of the shock they all felt. None but Roberto and Dahnishev had ever seen an Ascendant work before on the battlefield and it was a weapon against which there was no defence. Even so, he was marshalling one, manufacturing maniples from across the legion to present some form of front to the Tsardon menace.

'We cannot fight this,' she said, dismounting near him and pulling him to one side. 'Retreat now. Get the legion back into the hills and regroup.'

'The Bear Claws do not run,' said Nunan.

'Oh, Pavel, look around you. When the Tsardon come at us that'll happen whether you wish it or not. And if another Work is used, what then? We've lost a third of our number—'

'More if you count the wounded.'

'—so let's move while we still can in some semblance of order.' She reached out and touched his face. 'The fact that they haven't been routed now says so much about your strength. But we need an Ascendant fighting with us.'

'They're in Estorr, Dina,' said Nunan, his voice a hiss.

'Then we'd better get messages to them quickly or the next thing they see will be the dead marching through the Victory Gates. We have to pull away now. Leave anything that'll slow us and get out fast.'

'I'll not leave them one of our fallen,' said Nunan. 'Don't you see that's exactly what they want?'

'Either that or risk giving them more by moving too slowly.' Kell pointed out towards the castle. 'My cavalry are spread too thin as it is. One break and they will be upon you.'

The wind picked at their cloaks and hair once more. Never had a gentle gust caused such anxiety among professional soldiers. Kell could see some crouch reflexively, awaiting the blast. Nothing came by way of a hurricane. It was far worse than that. A stirring behind the reformed front line and through to the back of the legion. A weary twitch of muscle and the opening of eyes thought shut for good. Kell saw a man covered by his cloak sit up as if plucked to wakefulness by God. The cloak fell from his face and a tiny trickle of blood ran from a wound in his forehead. Those standing near him and hundreds like him, scattered.

Screams and shouts ricocheted across the legion, swelling in intensity, driving terror into every heart. Breaking wills. The Tsardon didn't need to attack. The Ascendant didn't need another gale. The job was done most effectively. The Bear Claws, those that were able, broke and ran.

Kell's mouth fell open. Her horse snorted and backed away, threatening to pull her over. She held the mare, just. Nunan was bawling for order, his shouts lost in the panic.

'They're gone,' shouted Kell into his face. 'Go with them. At least be with those you can.'

She gripped her reins and swung into the saddle.

'Dina, come with me.'

'I'll cover you as best I can, bring the cavalry in from the west. We can't ride near the dead. Go, Pavel.'

'Don't die,' he said.

'It isn't my day for that,' she said. 'And neither is it yours.'

But as she rode away, Dina saw Pavel and a few of his bravest facing their fallen comrades and found no solace in her words.

Roberto ran as hard as he could. Adranis was a dead weight in his hands. Blood was running from the wound. It soaked his brother's clothes and stained Roberto's gauntlets. His heart thudded hard, every beat painful. He had to ignore who it was lay in his arms. Had to avoid panic.

The legion was in tatters. Standards were flying over a few maniples but Roberto had to look at his feet as much as ahead to avoid standing on dead or wounded. He didn't have the strength to be angry, that would come later. This desolation was a crime that had to be avenged. The fact of Adranis in his arms had to be avenged. But first they had to live to turn against the enemy.

Hurrying through what was left of the legion order, faces loomed at him out of the pale, dust-filled darkness. Men and women were screaming. There were those that received help where they lay or were being carried back away from the front but most would get no assistance.

Roberto barely knew where he was running. The line of tents and the temporary stockade that had made up the camp were gone. For the first time, he wondered if he would find any surgeon, let alone

Dahnishev. And if he did, he had no guarantee they would be able to offer any aid.

Behind him, he heard the roar of the Tsardon army, the clash of weapons and the thunder of hoofs. Dina Kell was all that stood between them and slaughter and in the meantime, the Bear Claws had to reorganise. Roberto made it through the chaotic infantry lines, brushing off offers of help. A few tent spars were all that remained of the encampment. A hundred yards behind, he could see tent canvas and wood hanging in the boughs of trees and strewn across the highway. He could see people running across the road and heading up towards the southern crag. Not deserting, looking for a place to stand.

'Dahnishev!' Roberto shouted into the tumult of battering noise. 'Where is my surgeon.'

Someone was running towards him, dodging through legionaries and bodies. Hope flared.

'Hang on, little brother.' Roberto ran on. 'Herides. God-surround-us, we're in a mess.'

Herides looked down on Adranis and his eyes widened. He gasped. 'Master Del Aglios.'

'He's still alive, Herides. Just. I need Dahnishev. Tell me you know where he is.'

Herides nodded. 'I do. He's taken his people up to the crag. Did it the moment the wind dropped off. We were lucky, General. He hadn't unpacked much equipment on the battlefield. It's still in the trunks and they're undamaged.'

'Take me to him.'

'Let me help you, carry him for you.'

'No, Herides. This is my burden.'

Herides nodded. 'Follow me.'

The tenor of the shouting in the legion changed as if chasing them across the road and up the slope towards the crag. Roberto risked a glance around. He could see legionaries scattering from their positions. And in the moonlight, Kell's cavalry circled and pounded again into an exposed Tsardon flank. But the pike blocks were still coming and would find no resistance from the Bear Claws because the dead had awoken in their midst.

Shapes of men and women loomed from the dimness. People were flooding past him, terrified faces snatched by the gloom as they went.

'Stand and face!' roared Nunan, still unwilling to believe this really was a rout.

He'd lost a third of the legion to the enemy. God knew how many more were lying wounded and dying out there. He couldn't contemplate losing the rest to fear.

'Hold your strikes. These are our people.'

Were they?

Nunan's standard was upright and proud unlike too many others, discarded on the field. His extraordinarii were with him. Yet all they could do was watch from their position while the legion, such as it was, disintegrated.

His hornsmen blared for order but the sound was lost in the cacophony consuming the Bear Claws. Estorea's finest. On the field, knots of terrified legionaries were hacking at those they had so recently known as friends, lashing out at anyone who looked suddenly different. The innocent living were surely being sent to bolster the ranks of the dead. Other soldiers stood in mute shock, just staring. The mass, carrying wounded with them if they had the courage left, just ran. Up towards the fires at the crag base.

'We aren't going to form a line here,' said Nunan to his centurion. 'We have to get them all out of here. Take half and get back up the road. Reform there. We have to make a defence before the Tsardon break the cavalry.'

The centurion nodded. His eyes were wide, his face disbelieving.

'Go.'

'Yes, General. What about the – the dead, General?'

Nunan took a breath, unable to fully accept what he was saying. 'Leave the dead to me.'

'Yes, General.' He turned. 'Count off fifteen. You're with me. The rest, protect the general. Get those we can back up the road to me. Move.'

Nunan stared at the battlefield. Hundreds had streamed past him. Hundreds more were lost in themselves on the battlefield. He really had only one option. The Tsardon advance was being severely hampered by Kell driving her cavalry forward and back across their tight, crowded line. It was giving him precious moments but it couldn't last. Attrition and tiredness would both take their toll. Soon enough, the dam would burst.

'Get amongst our people. Give me some order. Wounded away.

Disengage from the dead. You know where to send them. Break up and move fast.'

Nunan ran into the midst of the confusion. The dusty ground was covered in broken equipment, blood and bodies. He had to assume all that still lay there were alive, if only barely. Ahead were a group of thirty infantry, mainly hastatii. Leaderless and confused, floating wreckage. They were facing a knot of the dead twice their number. Nunan felt his heart skip a beat as he breasted through them, shouting them to lower weapons and back away. But they were screaming at each other and at the dead and he had to stand in front of them to get them to notice him

This close it was so easy to see why many had simply run away. How could a man stand against his friend? How could he strike him yet how could he not? None should be made to face the fallen. Yet here they were. Nunan felt his shoulders sag. He knew some of these men and women. Perhaps ...

'You're sure they're dead?' he said. 'They aren't attacking.'

And they weren't. They were just standing, staring. Like they were waiting for something.

'Of course they're dead, General,' said a hastati soldier, barely containing himself. 'Look, it's Darius. I was next to him when he fell. What is this, General? God has turned against us.'

'Not God, just one of his wayward people,' said Nunan and raised his voice. 'Disengage. Get back to the road. Find the extraordinarii.'

'But General, our people.'

'And take wounded with you. These aren't our people.' Nunan shuddered. 'Not any more.'

The hastatii turned and ran. Arrows were falling. The Tsardon advance was gaining ground inch by tortuous inch. Kell's cavalry had split again and rattled into both flanks of the enemy. The dead were beginning to move too. Forming into larger groups, organising into lines.

Nunan stared, hypnotised for a moment. He watched them pick weapons from the ground if they had none. Men and women displaying no pain, fear or understanding. His legionaries with fatal wounds walking as if compelled by some guiding force. Huge sarissa gashes, stove-in helmets, split faces and bodies.

'How can we fight this?' he said. 'What can we do?'

'General?'

He turned to his extraordinarii. 'Nothing. Let's get about our business.'

Kell called the charge and her cavalry struck the rear right flank of the Tsardon. They'd tried to bring pikes to bear but it had served only to weaken the front of the line. Her horse drove through the flimsy defence, its shoulders breasting through shields, bodies flung to the sides as the uncertain defence splintered.

She'd brought her people in on a narrow front, aiming to punch a hole right through to attack the rear of the pike blocks and expose the archers. They represented the biggest danger to the shattered Bear Claws. But she couldn't go on losing people like she was.

Kell brought her sword down on the head of a Tsardon warrior. He crumpled and she was beyond him, striking out right at the next. Yet to her left, three of her riders were taken from their saddles by arrows. The charge lost pace, riderless horses turning to seek escape. Her own archers poured shafts into the lines in front of them. They struck shields, found holes in armour, pierced face and neck or skipped harmlessly over the ground.

She began to turn, seeing more Tsardon reserve running to bolster the flank. She dug her heels into her horse and dodged her way through the press of horseflesh and enemy, charging back into open ground. Kell galloped away fifty yards before pulling up to allow the detachment to fall in around her. Away three hundred yards to the other side of the field, the Tsardon were moving quickly towards the road. The cavalry cover was faltering, outnumbered and being worn down. Horses were tiring and with no cover or relief, the outcome was inevitable.

In the middle of the field, Bear Claws, those that could, were pouring away from the front and up the road, leading to an increased pressure from the Tsardon she was trying to hold back. And the dead. Dear God-surround-her, the dead were forming into a new front line and no one was standing in their way.

'We've got to get round behind them,' a captain shouted in her ear. 'We have to make them turn.'

He was looking at the Tsardon, who outnumbered her cavalry ten to one and rising. There would be no glory this day. The very best they could hope for was for some to survive and buy others the time to take the path up through the crags. It all but brought a tear to her eye. It was a difficult and challenging climb. She and Nunan had been up, not ten days before, for some relaxation and exercise. That had been fun and the views had been spectacular. How the world turned.

'They can slaughter us there. Trap us against the castle and the river bank,' she said. 'All we can do is buy the infantry as much time as possible. We cannot break them here.'

'And should the dead turn on us?' he asked.

'Ride away, Captain. And rendezvous with the legion. Some time today all of us will be standing on our own two feet, shoulder to shoulder with the hastatii, just doing what we can. I'll not put my horses in their way.'

The captain nodded. 'What would you have me do, Master Kell?'

'Take the message across. We are reforming to a single force. Get moving.'

She watched him take two others and ride away and felt her hopes fade into the gloom along with them.

'Dahnishev!' yelled Roberto. 'Dahnishev!'

He was close to breaking. His arms were quivering with exertion. Adranis's wound had not stopped bleeding and it was only the continued flow that convinced Roberto his brother was still alive. Herides was ahead of him, trying to find the surgeon. Heads were turning. People were running towards him. He didn't want any of them.

'Get back to your tasks,' he said, choking on a sob. 'Get me Dahnishev.'

He was running towards the harsh dark rock wall into which a single deep gouge formed a treacherous pathway to its head some three hundred feet above. People were moving inside it. Through the trees that covered the slope, Roberto saw tents being pitched. He saw people carrying baggage, chairing the injured, and tending wounds on makeshift stretchers or just on any patch of clear ground.

So difficult to see. The woodland was dense up here. Worse than further down where he'd been able to move more easily. There was so much mess up here. So many legionaries screaming their pain. Every blade of grass it seemed was covered in blood.

'That Ascendant. Bastard Ascendant,' he muttered. 'You'll pay, Gorian Westfallen. You'll pay.'

'General?'

Roberto looked to his left. A bloodied medic had fallen in next to him.

'Yes?'

'Surgeon Dahnishev is this way.'

Roberto felt a cascade of relief. 'Bless you, my friend.'

'Let me help you.'

'No. Just show me.'

It wasn't far. A small tent, brand new by the looks of its creases, set in the lee of the crag. Soldiers were clearing the ground in front of it and setting up the triage site. Roberto could hear Dahnishev shouting instructions, his voice like a call to prayer. Roberto breasted through the tent flaps, gasping at the smell of blood and bile that struck him. The tent, a square shape, no more than twenty feet on a side, was packed with more wounded than he could quickly count. Dahnishev had an operating table set up in one corner and he was covered to the elbows in blood, which also smeared his face and clothes.

'Clean him up and put him outside. Watch he doesn't die unseen,' said Dahnishev, seeing Roberto's entrance. He hurried round the table and snapped his fingers to an orderly to help him.

'Please, Dahnishev, please. You have to save him.'

'Dear God-embrace-me, Roberto, did you run all this way with him like this?'

'No choice,' gasped Roberto, feeling blood pounding around his head, fogging his thinking.

'It's a miracle he's still alive, then. So we have that in our favour. Get him to the damn table.'

At last, Roberto let his brother go. After hurried scrubbing and the scattering of more sawdust on the floor to soak up the blood where they stood, Dahnishev and the orderly laid Adranis on the table. Dahnishev took a quick look at the wound and breathed in hard.

'Prepare him,' he said to the orderly. 'Clean the wound, get my instruments sterilised. I'll be back soon so don't dawdle. This man is not going to die, do you understand?'

'Yes, Master Dahnishev.'

'Good. Roberto, outside with me.'

Roberto gaped and gestured towards Adranis. 'My brother—'

'Will not die in the next minute and if he does I could never have saved him. Out. And let my people do what they're best at.'

Roberto let himself be brought out into the breaking dawn. The bedlam outside was growing. More and more wounded were coming out of the tree line right in front of the crag.

'I can't cope with all this,' said Dahnishev. 'I lost half my staff in the hurricane.'

'Just save my brother,' said Roberto. 'And not just because he's my brother. He's Master of Horse for this legion.'

'I know, Roberto, I work here too.'

Roberto blinked and looked behind him. 'Got this all pitched fast, didn't you?'

'Never fight without a secondary medical facility ready set up,' said Dahnishev. 'Not when you don't have a stockade.'

'Of course, of course.' Roberto sagged.

'Look, I didn't get you out here to discuss my brilliant planning and vision. I saw what happened out there. I'm hearing the stories now. And all around us, men and women are going to start dying. Do you understand?'

Roberto nodded. 'I know. I thought of nothing else while I carried Adranis up here. I won't have him become one of them.'

'And how do you propose to stop him, should he die?' asked Dahnishev.

Roberto knew the answer to that too. And he knew the consequences. He swallowed and looked up into Dahnishev's hawk face.

'Is the naphtha up here?'

Dahnishev pursed his lips and nodded.

'I had it moved,' he said quietly. 'We couldn't afford to lose it to the Tsardon.'

'No indeed.'

'Can it be countenanced? Even now?'

'What else do we have? The dead are coming this way and we are showing no signs of standing before them. We are, what, fifteen hundred fit legionaries probably, facing the same number of dead backed by six thousand Tsardon. We have to even the odds.'

'Yes, Roberto, but to burn our own ...'

'I know, I know.' Roberto felt sick at the thought. 'It may be pragmatic but it's also the worst crime we can commit. We could do with a word from the wise and a little understanding to smooth the way.'

'He's right over there. Let's make this quick. Your brother needs my urgent attention.'

They walked to where the Order Speaker, Julius Barias, was kneeling by a stricken legionary.

'Speaker Barias,' said Roberto, making the Omniscient-encompassing sign at his chest. 'The Omniscient chose you well.'

Barias inclined his head and rose. 'Thank you, Ambassador. God sets us tasks and demands our strength to complete them. We can but do his work, wherever it occurs.'

'And you have not been found wanting,' said Roberto. 'The Bear Claws are grateful. Walk with us.'

The three of them walked back towards the crag, out of casual earshot.

'I am no more important than any legionary standing with the hastatii,' said Barias. A thought struck him and he took a quick glance about him. 'You have not brought me here merely to thank me. You have an issue you wish to discuss?'

Roberto felt a flash of nerves. He wished they were seated about a table sharing wine and food, anything to relax the situation a little.

'I do. It goes to the heart of our faith. You must know that I would not be bringing this to you if I felt there was any other choice.'

Barias smiled faintly. 'All right. You have me concerned for us all.'

'Good. You should be. There is not a citizen here who has been in a more difficult and deadly position. We face an enemy that flies in the face of God and faith, that uses sickening evil to attain its ends and would see us all marching without life or will to strike down our own families.'

Roberto thought Barias was going to break down. 'Ambassador, I will not sleep or eat for the pain it will cause me. I reach out to the faithful who should be in the embrace of God yet still walk and I cannot help them. And to think the one who perpetrates this crime was one born into the love of God in the Conquord. It tears at my heart.'

'Even though he is an Ascendant?' Roberto raised his eyebrows. 'Surely you don't believe him anything other than heretic, never to feel the embrace of the Omniscient.'

Barias sighed. 'The debate has been more fierce in the ranks of the Order than the Chancellor would have you think. Not all of us can ignore the plain fact that they were central in saving the Conquord and countless numbers of the Omniscient faithful. We must respect that, though their methods and their abilities are a challenge to God.'

'And here is another challenge.' Roberto took a deep breath. 'We cannot suffer Gorian to continue creating an army made up of fallen legionaries. Not here, not anywhere. Our dead must be rendered useless to him.'

'I cannot disagree. And though dismemberment is an abuse, the body may still be buried as complete. This is not a faith issue, it is more a practical issue, surely? There are too many of them though you have my blessing to try.'

Roberto held up his hands. 'You are both ahead of me and behind me, Julius. Please, let me finish. Because dismemberment is not now an option we must consider other methods. The Conquord has long held to the tenet that even an enemy can be converted to the way of the Omniscient and in war, it means that we must treat our enemies as we would our own. But that was before Gorian turned and changed the rules.

'And now we must be able to use the ultimate sanction on friend and enemy alike. And we must have your blessing for that too.'

'For what?'

'Naphtha. Liquid fire. Call it what you will. We have to burn the walking dead.'

Barias staggered back a pace. Roberto would have called it over-dramatic but for the expression on his face. He had blanked with shock. His mouth opened but he couldn't form words.

'Please, Julius, think.' Roberto held out his hands, fingers skywards. 'This is not a blanket tactic. In extremis only.'

Barias was shaking his head, God-surround-him, his whole body was shaking.

'That you can utter these words, these thoughts. And ask me, *me*, for my blessing.'

'I understand your reaction and your feelings,' said Roberto.

'Your words are proof that you understand nothing,' spat Barias. 'To burn the flesh of innocents, to cast their ashes to the demons on the wind and see their cycles on this earth finished forever? To deny them the embrace of God? To speak such words is abhorrent. To carry out such actions a crime that makes you no better than a common murderer.'

'I sympathise,' continued Roberto. 'I really do. But—'

Dahnishev put a hand on his arm. 'Let him speak. Let him explain the problems he has with what you ask of him ... we ask of him.'

'You agree with this heresy?' Barias turned on Dahnishev, his voice beginning to rise in volume.

'I know that unless we stop this harvesting of our innocent dead by Gorian Westfallen, we will all become his slaves. I would rather burn than be sent against my people, devoid of will and denied my rest,' said Dahnishev.

Barias snorted. 'It is not in your gift to choose whether your cycle continues or not. Only God can do that. And you most certainly cannot make that decision for Conquord citizens nor Tsardon invaders. No burning will happen. This conversation is over.'

He turned to go. Roberto grabbed his arm.

'No, it is not,' he said.

Barias looked down at Roberto's hand. 'You will release me, Ambassador Del Aglios. I would never have believed it of you. Your mother is the figurehead of our faith and yet her own son spouts filth. I have to consider what action I will report to the Order concerning what you have just proposed.'

Roberto laughed. He couldn't help himself. He released the Speaker and dismissed him with a wave of the hand.

'Write your report, Julius,' he said. 'Who will deliver it for you?

He turned away.

'It is my duty to make this a matter of record.'

Roberto felt something snap inside him. He rounded on Barias, grabbed his cloak at the collar and drove him back against the crag wall.

'Do you really have no idea what is happening here? Do you really think I care what you write and to whom you entrust it?' He pushed harder. Barias grunted. 'We face annihilation here. A precious few might escape up the crag but the rest will die. And unless we hack or burn them, they will become our enemies. Do you think that is in God's plans? Do your damned scriptures discuss an attack by walking dead who were once his people and torn from his grasp? Because they are coming and we have to defeat them.'

'Now, you listen to me,' said Barias.

'No. You had your say and you chose to insult me. Well now it's my turn. I asked for your blessing but I do not need it. You claim heresy but you do not know how this decision tears me apart. My own brother lies on the edge of death. And I will not let him walk against us. I would burn Adranis rather than see that and know the pain that he would be suffering.'

Roberto let Barias go and the Speaker straightened his clothing.

'The dead have no feeling.'

'No? Then why did the dead man Varelius hesitate when his centurion called his name? Coincidence?'

'I—'

'Get out of my sight, Barias. And do not dare to spread half-truths. This is a desperate situation and any citizen who acts against us will be deemed guilty of treason. My mother is the Advocate, and that makes me number two in the Conquord. I trust I make myself clear.'

'You will be tried for this, Del Aglios,' shouted Barias. 'Your crime will not go unpunished.

He glared at Roberto and walked away along the base of the crag, shaking his head and muttering. Heads across the triage site had turned.

'You wouldn't really have him killed, would you?' asked Dahnishev.

'I don't know,' said Roberto, and found he believed his own words. 'All I do know is that this plague will spread through the Conquord unless we stop it here. And if that means some are sacrificed to the demons, myself and my brother included, then so be it.'

'I stand with you,' said Dahnishev.

'And with a heart as heavy as mine, old friend. I'll give the order to the engineers to open the crates. The dead are not going to wait, are they?'

'And Barias?'

'Barias must make peace with his conscience. As must we all.'

Chapter Twenty-Six

859th cycle of God, 35th day of Genasrise

It was worse stood here than in the chaos of the muster ground. Nunan was at the head of his vastly diminished legion. He had maybe a hundred sarissas and they were stretched across the road and on to the slopes of the valley through which it ran. Gladius infantry guarded the flanks as best they could but it was a woefully thin line. Perhaps twelve hundred but no more.

Yet even that was not what scared him the most. He thought they could hold against the Tsardon regulars for some time. Attacking his flanks through the trees would be difficult and costly, given where he had stationed his meagre number of archers. It was the dead that caused every heart to flutter and every man and woman to question their faith and their will.

They were not far away now and moving at an even pace and in sound order. That made it worse somehow. They maintained their legion discipline. But it was a parody. A line a hundred bodies wide and over ten deep. Some had shields, most did not. There were pockets of sarissas but mainly it was the gladius in hand. At a glance, they might be mistaken for the living and undamaged. But a second look told a completely different story.

Where one marched unhindered, another dragged a leg, limped heavily or swayed as if their balance had been stolen. Hardly a body was fully upright. Dropped shoulders, hunched frames, missing arms, heads hanging to the side or front. And silent. Silent but for the drag of feet over the ground. A dreadful scraping that picked at people's courage.

Nunan drew himself up tall. He was alone in command. Kell was still keeping at bay a Tsardon army lacking in any immediate ambition. It was easy to understand why. Nunan wouldn't have risked wasting his own people either. Their job was being done for them with hideous efficiency.

He could feel the fear and uncertainty in his legion. Standards stood tall but were gripped in sweating hands. The advance of dawn was bringing everyone sights they could never have conceived as night had fallen the previous evening. They were already wavering and the dead were still forty yards distant.

Nunan walked out in front of them and turned. There was precious little noise to quell and his numbers were so slight he could be sure all would hear him.

'Bear Claws. Second legion of Estorr. We know what we must face and it scares us. Out there, coming towards us, people that we all knew. People you will recognise. Friends that lined up next to you until the evil wind blew. It is hard, I know, but these who march towards us now are not those we knew. We saw them die. Hold on to that. That they walk does not make them live. That you do not believe the dead can walk does not make this any less real.

'We have a duty. The Conquord must not be threatened. These dead must be stopped here and then we can deal with the true enemy. But every time you strike, and for every one of our former friends who falls once more, pray that they may find the peace denied them.

'Bear Claws. Fight to free your friends from their thrall. Do it for them, for Estorea and for me!'

The shout of the Bear Claws answered him. He nodded and indicated his centurions, shorn of their Master of Sword, to take command. He moved through the ranks, making eye contact, assuring his people of his belief in them. The orders rang through the army.

'Sarissas to level! Gladius ready flanks. Moving in on my mark. Disabling blows.'

Nunan turned left and trotted quickly up the slope to his left, looking for a vantage point. His thirty extraordinarii joined him there.

'Thank you for your efforts,' he said. 'But now there's more to do. Stand with the legion. Be the strength they need. Even the triarii are scared down there.'

'Yes, General.' The captain saluted, right arm to left breast.

'Discipline. Order. Victory.'

He watched them run away, trying to radiate confidence. Centurions bellowed for solidity. Voices began to rise. First in prayer and then in song. The words bred strength and faith where there had been precious little.

'Omniscient surround me
Protect me
Fill me.
God my master show me
Hold me
Save me.
Estorea is my home
The Conquord cries your name
We stand as one
In your great light
To ever spread your fame.'

The dead simply marched on.

They were thirty yards from the Bear Claw lines. Nunan took his magnifier from his belt sheath and put it to his eye. The light was still poor but it was just good enough to bring him grim detail. Badges hanging from torn cloth. Blood lines showing wounds. Blank expressions. He stopped moving the magnifier.

One was different. He marched at the exact centre of the force and he was not dead. He was Tsardon, head covered in what looked like piercings and tattoos and he was speaking. His lips moved and though he could not be shouting, he was certainly saying something. The dead surely marched to his tune.

'Who …?'

It didn't matter. What mattered was that he was there and that the momentum of the dead march had a metronome. Nunan grabbed his hornsman who was staring at the advance, shivering.

'Sound the advance. Sound the advance now.'

Nunan began to run back towards the rear of the lines. As the horn sounded its single long, repeating tone he shouted for attention from his centurions.

'Break their advance. They want us to stand in fear. Take it to them, Claws. Archers, target the centre. Tsardon commander is centre. Do it, do it now.'

More horns took up the order. The legion began to move. Songs swelled in throats. Arrows began to pepper the centre of the dead line, disrupting its flow. Left and right, the gladius flanks moved in. The dead ignored them, moving on forwards towards the sarissas.

'Engage!' ordered Nunan.

The prayer echoed from the sides of the valley and bounced from the cliff behind. The sarissa infantry lowered their weapons and drove them into defenceless dead. Some of the living cried out at what they were doing. Nunan, following the line in, saw tears on the cheeks of triarii. The flanks of gladius infantry pivoted down their slopes. The Bear Claws moved in. Weapons clashed. Men were screaming.

The dead marched on. Those who encountered sarissas were driven back but did not fall. They walked, they pushed themselves up blades and those who came behind them did the same. Alarm started to filter across the centre of the legion. The Bear Claws' advance stalled almost as soon as it started. The sarissas could not make any more ground. Step by step, the dead forced gaps in their defence. Dead legionaries impaled on the long blades, began to walk up the shafts. And the more the legionaries held their weapons secure, the more they helped those making the grisly walk towards them.

Not knowing what to do, the sarissa infantry began to back away. Centurions roared for them to hold but between each shaft, the dead were closing. The right flank marched into the dead at pace. Nunan heard the crunch of impact. Shields up, the gladius infantry ploughed in. Swords hacked around and over shields. Nunan saw the dead sway inwards. Men and women lost their balance, falling into others who were still facing forwards, not realising for a moment that they were being attacked from three directions.

Nunan's hope rose but it was a brief flicker. Almost immediately, the dead on the flanks began to turn. Feverish strikes from the Claws battered and bludgeoned heads and bodies. Dead with smashed skulls dragged themselves back to their feet and tried to move on. Those with sword arms chopped from their bodies still moved forwards, adding to the weight. The initial push was stopped. Dead filled in behind those pushing back outwards on the flanks. And still they walked up the centre along the sarissa shafts.

To put down any of the dead took so many strikes, so much energy. And now they were beginning to strike back. Nunan had expected the blows of the dead to be directionless but they were not. Dead turned to face their attackers and struck out. Bear Claws were shouting at them to stop, begging them to remember who they had been, calling out names. And while one might falter and drop his sword, another would not.

Standards began to waver. Nunan could see the Claws shift backwards. Dead were on them in the centre. He looked but could not believe, while a man who had walked right up the shaft of a sarissa thrust his blade into the chest of the screaming legionary who held it. He collapsed, dragging his attacker down. But the dead man still tried to move forward. Into the gap came more, trampling over those in their way. Sarissas were dropped from dozens of hands, disrupting the advance further but nothing was stopping it. Gladiuses were drawn. The front rank closed again.

A bellowed order saw a renewed rush into the enemy. Nunan saw soldiers possessed by a frenzy, crashing their swords again and again into the dead that faced them. Bodies were dismembered, heads smashed inside their helmets, legs cut from underneath. The dead began to fall, yet as fast as they did they tried to rise once more. They were not tiring. They had no fear of death or pain. The fury of the assault began to dissipate.

The Claws were creaking. Arrows came overhead but those they struck ignored them, only breaking shafts that obstructed movement. And still the Tsardon commander lived. Nunan could hear him. A lone voice in the silent army.

'We have to get the leader,' shouted Nunan. 'More arrows centre. Press, Claws.'

Horns sounded again. They, like those they commanded, were uncertain, losing heart. But they moved in again anyway. Shields forward to batter a path, swords looking to disable, eyes front and fearful of any strike. No one wanted to become like them and it showed. A timidity was falling on them.

'Nunan!'

The general turned. Roberto Del Aglios was running towards him. Others were with him, carrying crates and a brazier. Engineers. He frowned. Behind him, the cries of his legion reached a new level. The line was under threat. The legion was retreating.

'Hold!' bellowed a centurion. 'Hold.'

'God-surround-me, General, we can't stop them. We can't even contain them.'

'Then help me,' said Roberto. 'We no longer have a choice.'

The crates were placed on the ground, the engineers levering up the lids to reveal straw-packed flasks. Nunan stared down and then up at Roberto.

'You can't mean this,' he said.

'Got a better idea? Some must perish that the rest can live to fight another day.'

'But this isn't just death, this is cycle's end.'

'I know,' said Roberto and Nunan could see the conflict in his face. 'Now will you help me or not? I will throw the first flask.'

Nunan scanned the engineers. They were with him but there was a sheen to their faces that told of the crime they were abetting. And more were running down the road too. Shouting for Roberto to be stopped. The Order.

'What is going on, General?'

'Speaker Barias does not agree with me,' said Roberto.

'I can see his point.'

The orders and shouts of the infantry had an edge of desperation to them. Centurions were looking to Nunan and he was not looking back.

'You have to make a choice,' said Roberto, his tone sharp, voice loud enough to carry to the rear ranks. 'Give them something or watch them fall and join the dead.'

Nunan paused.

'You haven't the time, General,' said Roberto. 'Examine your conscience later. We have to destroy these now before the cavalry is broken and the Tsardon hit us full force. Take the fear from your soldiers.'

Nunan nodded. 'Light the tapers,' he said.

'Yes, General,' said an engineer.

The Order delegation were pounding down the road at a sprint. Roberto glanced in their direction.

'Don't let them divert you.' He beckoned to the engineers. 'Quickly. One for each hand. Pray as you throw.'

Nunan turned to the hornsman. 'Signal disengage.'

The hornsman stared back. 'General?'

'Do it,' snapped Roberto. 'Or the Bear Claws die here and now.'

Tapers were lit. The engineers were ready. Julius Barias and three Order Readers were roaring, their fury understandable but their self-control gone. Nunan felt cold inside. His mind raced, his pulse likewise and he fought to control a shiver in his arms. He nodded at the hornsman and the disengage was sounded. Roberto picked up two flasks and proffered them to the engineer holding the taper.

'May God forgive us this day,' he said.

'May our friends forgive us,' said the engineer.

The disengage was heralded across the line and Nunan heard instant confusion. Centurions were looking to him for explanation. They were going to get one but they weren't going to like it.

'You'd better be right, Roberto,' he said.

'Trust me.'

The legion was moving backwards. It was a controlled move designed to produce a gap of four yards, then ten, quickly and without casualties. But of course the dead weren't like any other army, happy to rest and defend the inevitable arrows. They just moved up and the gap was under pressure.

The engineer lit the fuses on Del Aglios's flasks and those of another two engineers whom he'd convinced to his thinking. Nunan bent to take flasks himself. Del Aglios was moving forward to the back of the line and into it, shouting men from his path. Julius Barias sprinted past yelling his rage. Del Aglios cocked an arm to throw. Barias grabbed it, tore the flask from his hand and threw it away behind him where it smashed on a rock and threw fire over the grass; a sudden flare in the dim light.

Del Aglios turned on him, fuse burning down his second flask.

'Touch me again and you'll feel the flame, Barias.'

'I am an officer of the Omniscient and you will—'

'And I'm a man trying to save my people and my country,' said Del Aglios.

He shoved Barias so hard that the Speaker stumbled and fell backwards and into the arms of his Readers. In the next motion, he'd switched his second flask to his throwing arm and hurled it in a high tumbling arc.

'General, no!'

It was the voice of a centurion. Others joined it and every eye watched the flask. The flame illuminated the clear liquid sloshing within, the upturned faces blanking in realisation. It hadn't even landed before Roberto was shouting for more. But then it did. Cannoning into the helmet of a dead Bear Claw legionary. The naphtha sprayed wide, the flame igniting it as it travelled, sending a sheet of flame that covered twenty.

Four other flasks followed quickly, shattering in the centre of the dead army. The Bear Claws took another pace backwards. The cries of condemnation began to ring out but they were drowned by the shout of the dead. Weapons dropped from every hand, burning or not. Every face turned towards the Bear Claws. Eyes that had been blank registered betrayal. And from the mouths of those aflame came a dreadful keening wail. Within it, Nunan was certain he could hear a scream of 'why?' and the sound tore at his heart and drained his determination.

'No more!' he shouted. 'No more fire. Claws, let's get into them. Save all you can.'

The dead did not raise a hand. In their midst, the single living Tsardon was trapped. The Bear Claws waded back into the attack. They carved and hacked and bludgeoned. Nunan pressed forwards to be seen in the centre of the action, stamping out fires, trying to send the screaming dead back to the embrace of God, trying to save them from the demons on the wind.

But while they did not fight back, the dead had found their voice. The wail had become a howl. It spoke pain and dread. It dredged horror from the deepest recesses of the human mind and flung it at the living who could do nothing but try to scythe the limbs from their former comrades and try to bring them new peace.

Yet on the ground, even those with arms hanging by a thread or with heads crushed in or cut from their necks still tried to move. Nunan felt nausea growing. Around him, men and women could not control themselves, vomiting, calling out for it all to end but knowing it could not.

'Finish the job,' called Nunan. 'We must.'

He stopped talking before his voice broke. In front of him, a dead legionary was a sheet of flame. He battered his shield into the man's body, sending him sprawling backwards. He chopped down, taking the sword arm off at the elbow then dropped to his knees to heap dirt on the burning, writhing body. To roll it over to extinguish the naphtha flames that he himself had thrown.

'I'm sorry. I'm so sorry,' he muttered. 'Forgive me.'

And in the next instant, the dead dropped soundlessly to the ground. Crumpling where they had stood and leaving just one man standing. The tattooed Tsardon commander.

Silence washed across the battlefield. The growing dawn illuminated the smoke-blown carnage. The air stank of burned cloth and flesh. From down the road towards the castle, Nunan could see the surviving cavalry turn and pound up towards him. Prayers were being said in every quarter. And those accusing eyes turned from the dead all around them, fixing on him and Roberto Del Aglios.

'This crime cannot go unpunished,' said Julius Barias from behind him.

Nunan turned to see the speaker moving through the ranks of exhausted, bemused legionaries. Nunan put up a hand to still the voices that rose in support of the Order minister.

'You will wait before coming into the area of combat,' said Nunan.

'This is not combat. This is slaughter. It is murder.'

Nunan stepped up to him and waved legionaries away from them. 'I will not have you cause trouble down here. This is not the time or the place.'

Kell, leading her sweating, tired horses and riders, pulled up around the edge of the battlefield on the slope heading up to the crag. Nunan turned.

'General Kell,' he said and smiled. 'It is good to see you still upright. The Tsardon?'

'Withdrawn,' she said, her gaze and that of every rider on the dead, some still smouldering though legionaries moved among them to do what they could. 'I didn't know why, they almost had us but now ... what happened here?'

'Desecration and heresy happened—'

'Speaker Barias you will be quiet. Remember your place.' He turned back to Kell. 'We'll talk later. Best get your horses seen to at the rear staging area. We've still got work to do here.'

'Are you all right, Pavel?'

Nunan shook his head. 'No one is all right, Dina.' He raised his voice. 'Bear Claws! We must have all our fallen dismembered and buried. You do God's work now and I will be with you. Today, you are all heroes of the Conquord. Today you must honour your comrades and pray for them.'

Barias opened his mouth to speak but Nunan grabbed his cloak.

'And you, Speaker Barias, will do your appointed task in this legion. Spread no dissension. No matter what your feelings we still face six thousand Tsardon and we must not fall before them. Do I make myself clear?'

'General Nunan—'

'Do I make myself clear?'

'Yes, General.'

'Good. Bring the bodies into the trees to bury. I will be with the surgeon, my wife and the ambassador when you are done.'

Nunan turned away and breasted through the legion, which was coming to reluctant order under the insistence of its centurions. He found Roberto already walking back towards the crag, his head hung low, his bearing stooped.

'It had to be done, Pavel,' he said when Nunan hailed him. 'We had no other choice.'

'But what have we started? And where will it end?'

Chapter Twenty-Seven

859th cycle of God, 35th day of Genasrise

Gorian's scream of frustration had brought them all running. He had tried to hide the pain but his head was pounding and he had no idea if he had been successful. In those final moments, he had lost control of them all. Their wills, so easy to subvert, had reasserted themselves in their moment of greatest fear.

It had left Gorian weak, furious and not a little confused. He pushed himself from the chair in his adopted chamber and walked away a few paces, palms to his temples.

'What did they do, Father?' asked Kessian, who had been with him the whole time, supplying the well of power for him to direct the battle. The boy looked none the worse for the shock but then he had merely been a conduit, not the architect.

'They burned them,' he said, disbelieving. 'Omniscient followers threw fire over their own people. They would deny them the embrace of God. That cannot be allowed. They were my people. I made them walk again. They had no right. No right to do that to my people.'

Gorian found his anger lending him new strength. Two Dead Lords stood in front of him now along with the King's son, Rhyn-Khur.

'A weakness, Westfallen?' asked the prince.

'A crime,' said Gorian. 'One that will not go unpunished.'

'Who by, you?' Rhyn-Khur made no attempt to keep the sneer from his voice. 'Lost your army, didn't you? You are weak without them.'

Gorian shook his head. 'Don't make that mistake, Rhyn. Not ever.'

'We should have pressed on. I could have broken their cavalry. Then we would have fallen upon them, destroyed them. Your caution has led us nowhere. We can still win today. They are in disarray. Order the attack.'

'No,' said Gorian. 'We cannot risk it. We already have the victory we need today. We must produce dead under control. What you suggest is not control and they have just shown intent we hadn't foreseen.'

'Perhaps you did not, but nothing they do surprises me or any warrior of Tsard. At heart, they are godless. Quick to turn their backs on their faith if it suits their purposes. That the Ascendancy flourishes is evidence enough. Today merely reinforces that which we already knew.'

'It changes nothing. I must think and I must rest. I must tell our forces in Atreska and Gestern what has happened here and then we must move forward again.'

'Ridiculous,' said Rhyn. 'We should move forwards now. They are in disarray and hiding under a cliff. We must slaughter them now and move on at once.'

'We will do no such thing,' said Gorian quietly. 'They are going nowhere. You can move to surround them but no more. I want them in my way. Undamaged if we can. And with Roberto Del Aglios leading them to battle at the gates of Estorr.'

Rhyn stared at Gorian, hatred undisguised. 'My father made a grave error leaving you in charge here.'

'I'll be sure to let him know. Now leave me. There is much to do and I need my strength.'

'You are incompetent, Gorian Westfallen. My father will see it and command will be mine.'

Gorian laughed. 'Your protestations are pathetic. I am in charge because only I can ensure the victory of our combined forces. No one is about to take command from me. Least of all you, my Prince.'

Rhyn-Khur pointed at him. 'One day, Westfallen. One day.'

He spun on his heel and stalked out of the room. The Dead Lords remained. The chamber was cold. A new fire had been laid but its warmth had not reached all corners. It was a bleak castle, this Conquord structure. Not designed for comfort. But it was strong and functional and that was something not to be dismissed. More than that, it boasted plenty of escape routes for the quick individual, both back into Tsard and into lonely Conquord lands.

'Lord Garanth has been taken alive,' said Gorian.

The Dead Lords registered barely a flicker. They stood side by side in the chamber. They were a fascinating breed. Priest, jailer and executioner. Tsardon with a link to those who had passed from life to death that could neither be denied, nor understood. Gorian was still trying to fathom it. They had energies that no other living person bar an Ascendant exhibited but like passive talents, they used those energies without comprehension.

'Then he must be rescued,' said one, filed front teeth giving a whistle to his words.

'He knows what he must do, Lord Runok.' Runok was a man barely able to string a sentence together. One for whom the tattoo had become more than a badge; it was an obsession. 'He will speak and then he will listen and I will hear.'

'As you wish, my Master.'

Gorian smiled. 'Indeed.'

'You spoke of harvesting dead undamaged,' said the other, Lord Tydiol. 'I do not see how it can be achieved.'

'The edge of a blade or the bite of a rat are only two ways to kill a man. The earth holds many secrets. Tell me. To whom do you pledge your loyalty?'

'To he who commands the dead,' said Tydiol immediately.

'The dead do not answer back. The dead do not question authority and tactics,' said Gorian. 'And soon you will have your reward for your loyalty.'

The two Dead Lords bowed. 'We await your command.'

'A word of advice before you go,' said Gorian. 'Stay off the alcohol tonight. It'll be a little sharp.'

'You are not to blame,' said Dahnishev, his hand on Roberto's shoulder.

Roberto tensed at the touch, hunched and turned away from Adranis for a moment. Dahnishev's hawk-like face, getting old now, filled his vision. Sympathy and strength radiated from it.

'Do you think I can really believe that?' Roberto felt the darkness threaten to swamp him again. 'Can I say that to my mother if he dies?'

'It's the truth, pure and simple. He's a cavalryman and this is a war. He has been struck down trying to save others in his legion. He's a hero and critically, he isn't dead.'

'Not yet,' said Roberto, turning back to his brother.

Adranis was lying on his front with his head turned to the right facing into the surgeon's tent. It was in the lee of the crag below which the remnants of the Bear Claws were spread thinly across the tree-covered ground.

What else they had given up in terms of spirit and will was yet to be seen. The camp was seething with unhappiness at Roberto's actions earlier in the morning. Julius Barias was doing everything he could to stoke the ugly mood and Nunan was finding it difficult to force his legion to make the best of the position they had.

The danger of another Ascendant-fuelled hurricane was real and it had meant the army was not in legion order but dug in and hidden in pockets scattered over a three hundred yard front, a wide arc with flanks guarded by the crag at their backs. The triage site was well-defended and behind it, a secure pathway was being constructed with stake and rope up through the crags. Evacuation would begin as soon as was possible.

Nunan's pressure for high activity had done a great deal to defuse tensions following the use of the naphtha but as midday became mid-afternoon, minds were beginning to turn. The muttering had begun and Roberto felt he was better off out of sight. At least the men around him right now would not judge him too harshly.

'And he won't die if I can help it,' said Dahnishev. 'But don't tell me to earn my reputation, it'll just make me angry.'

Roberto didn't think even the miracle-worker could save Adranis. The dead blade had bitten deep into his lower back. The muscle bands had stopped his intestines spilling out and killing him then and there but the damage was severe. Dahnishev had stitched up what he could but there was internal bleeding he was struggling to stop and if he reopened the wound he risked new infection. Below the bandages, the wound was red and angry. Adranis was running a fever, forcing Dahnishev to give him bigger and bigger doses of white mandrake to still him.

Roberto squeezed out the cold cloth and wiped his brother's face again.

'I'm here, Adranis. And I will never leave your side. Come back to me, little brother. Stand with me and save the Conquord for our mother.'

Dahnishev knelt by the cot and took the cloth from Roberto's hands. 'How much rest have you had?'

'I don't need it. Not much. I can't,' said Roberto.

'Not good enough. You won't help him by making yourself ill. I'm your doctor and I'm telling you to get some. You've been haunting my workspace.'

'I can't leave him.'

'Yes you can. Get outside, go and speak to Nunan and give him a hand up. He needs your help to get us out of this mess. Then go to sleep. If I see you back in here before nightfall, you'll be getting the white mandrake too. Do I make myself clear?' Dahnishev raised a hand. 'Uh-uh. Can't pull rank on me, Roberto. You're a visiting ambassador, technically. And I'm head surgeon for the Bear Claws. Do what I say or I'll have you restrained.'

Roberto sagged. 'You would, wouldn't you?'

'You are one of my oldest friends, Del Aglios. I will not stand by and let you harm yourself.'

Roberto held up his hands and dragged himself to his feet. He felt so weary. Even turning his head felt like he was wearing weights around his neck. His legs ached, his arms and hands shook and he felt sick.

'If anything changes, if he's dying. You will find me.'

'Roberto,' said Dahnishev sharply. 'This is me you're talking to. Trust me, all right?'

'All right. Sorry.'

'So you should be,' said Dahnishev. He put an arm around Roberto's shoulders. 'I will do everything in my considerable power to keep this great man alive.'

'Funny thing,' said Roberto, though he had never felt less like laughing. 'I ran up here, carrying him and cursing the Ascendants. But we could do with Ossacer right now, couldn't we?'

'That we could. But we have to get out of here first.'

'And if we do, can he travel?'

Dahnishev sighed. 'I can't lie to you, Roberto. For him and every injured man, us leaving here presents great risk. There'll be no wagons on top of the crag so we'll have to stretcher him. We're ready to go if it comes to it but some of those lying here and in the other tents won't make it if we do. Pray Adranis isn't one of them.'

Roberto found he couldn't hold back the tears. He gripped Dahnishev's arm. 'I can't let him become one of them. Please, Dahnishev, don't let that happen.'

'With every fibre of my being. Now get out, wipe your eyes and help them. They need you out there.'

'If he dies, I will burn him myself to save him from that bastard out there. Burn him or cut the legs and head from him.'

'I know, Roberto.'

Roberto looked down at Adranis one more time, pushed his fingers along under his eyes and ducked out of the tent. It was quiet but that surely wouldn't last. He thought he understood part of the reason the Tsardon hadn't attacked yet. Not just to rest their men but to let their enemy brood and wonder who would be next dragged from God's embrace to stand again.

Death was no longer the final release.

People saw him emerge into the sunlight. Most turned away. Some stared, not disguising their anger. Others made the Omniscient sign at their chests before moving on. He shook his head and walked left along the crag to the command position, just a sheet of canvas held up on long poles. Nunan and Kell were both standing in the shade looking at maps. Julius Barias was there too. He exchanged a sharp glance with Nunan and said nothing, satisfied for the moment to try to burn holes of guilt in Roberto's forehead.

'That you are able to stand there resplendent in your fury is testament to the wisdom of my actions,' said Roberto. 'Why not go out and tend to the sick. Do your job, like your generals.'

'My job, Ambassador, is to maintain the ethics of my faith and tend to those in strife on the battlefield and away from it. What's yours?'

'To maintain the cohesion of the Conquord at all costs. All costs, Speaker Barias. And ultimately to succeed my mother to the seat of the Advocate. So I might be careful what I said, were I you.'

'A heretic will never ascend the Hill,' said Barias.

'If a blacksmith burns his arm, is he a heretic? If a brazier is spilled and men are injured, is that an act of heresy?'

Barias looked confused. 'Are we debating theology in general or your particular crime?'

'How many of the dead on the battlefield today were reduced to ash and lost to God, Julius?'

Both Kell and Nunan looked up from their maps. Guards on the periphery of the command post turned their heads and adjusted their stances. Barias jutted out his chin.

'Fortune does not make your actions any the less an act against the Omniscient,' he said.

'How many, Speaker Barias? And don't lie to me. I can guess the answer because I saw the entire contact. But humour me and tell me anyway.'

'None,' said Barias evenly.

'None,' repeated Roberto.

'Not this time,' said Barias. 'But what about the time we cannot reach them to put out the flames? Where will your defence be then, eh?'

'Exactly where it is today. That my actions saved hundreds of lives that would otherwise have been lost to the Conquord and to you, Speaker Barias. I would do the same again and take the same risk. And I would and will answer any charges you lay.'

'I will personally see to it.'

Roberto laughed. 'You should go out and infect others with this amazing confidence in your own survival, rather than your odious religious bile. That really would be useful.'

'I don't—'

'Has our situation completely escaped your attention? We have a legion reduced to ... Pavel, how many fit bodies?'

'We have a hundred and ninety-seven cavalry riders, and horses for them to ride. The hastatii are almost non-existent. Principes suffered massive damage. Triarii got off only because they were third rank. But even they have been hit hard. Eleven hundred and eighty-three gladius infantry. One hundred and one sarissa bearers and seventy-four skir-mishers. Our bow total is four hundred-odd. Every other bow is broken or lost.'

Roberto swung back to Barias and raised his eyebrows. 'You understand what that means? It means that if the Tsardon come at us, they will slaughter us. None of us have any idea why they haven't done so already. They might at any moment. Now we'll get as many as we can up the crag and away but it won't be all of us, now will it? And if I am to stand trial it will be in Estorr. And I'll tell you something else. I will be the happiest man in the Conquord to stand in the dock in the basilica and answer your charges from you personally, Julius. Because that will mean a miracle has occurred.

'So, carry on casting your accusations if you like. I'm going to try and save some lives and work out what Gorian and the Tsardon are planning next.'

'And you are little better, General Nunan,' said Barias. 'Unless you denounce him and admit your complicity.'

Nunan spoke over Roberto's shoulder. 'Go and bandage a wound, will you, Julius? I'm sick of your bile and the sound of your voice. I'm with the ambassador.'

Roberto smiled. 'You know, Speaker Barias, I actually agree with your position. And I will have to live with the consequences of my actions for as long as God grants me breath. But you've swallowed too much of the Chancellor's rhetoric. You have to apply the teachings to the battlefield in a different way.'

'Flame is outlawed. There is no other interpretation.'

Roberto threw up his arms. 'You make my point so flawlessly. You should be buried in your scriptures, examining them for reasons why God would allow the dead to walk. New enemy, new tactics required. Please, Julius, work with us. Every dissenting voice weakens us.'

Barias scoffed. 'You have already broken the spine of this legion, Ambassador.'

'Enough,' said Nunan. 'Guardsman Gerus.'

'Yes, sir?'

The guard turned from his station at the edge of the command post.

'Escort the Speaker back to his scriptures. And see that he does nothing but read them. He is to talk to no one until I say otherwise.'

Barias paled.

'I warned you, Julius. This is an army and we are facing an enemy far too powerful for us. I cannot have fragmentation. I must have cohesion. Go.'

Roberto watched the Speaker stalk away along the lee of the crag.

'It doesn't get any easier, does it?' said Roberto. 'But thank you for your support. I know it's a difficult call for you.'

'Not difficult at all, Roberto. But here's the rest of it. The Tsardon have not massed yet but enough are on station to keep us penned in here. We have little food other than what strays into the woods, and even less water. The crag path will not be usable until nightfall, at which time I will start sending people up it. At dawn, when the Tsardon see what we are doing, as they undoubtedly will, they will attack and those of us remaining will be killed. We cannot hope to hold out so we will not be trying.'

'How many can we get up between dusk and dawn, assuming we aren't attacked in the meantime?' asked Roberto.

'It's a tough climb, particularly at night and we cannot afford to light the way or they'll know we're escaping them. Even a fit soldier will take at least half an hour to get up there. It's steep and they'll have to carry their kit and more. Two with a stretcher . . .? Anybody's guess.'

'So what does that mean? How many?'

'With no interruption and just sending up the fit ones and with no accidents, we think we can get between six and eight hundred up during the hours of darkness. Then it's as many as can escape before the Tsardon overrun us.'

Roberto frowned. 'No more?'

'Think about it. We can only send up one at a time and even with minimal gap between each one we won't get more away.'

'But that leaves six hundred plus as, what . . . sacrifices, nothing more,' said Roberto.

'And don't forget surgeons, blacksmiths, engineers, orderlies, medics and five hundred and thirty injured or dying,' said Nunan.

'There has to be another way,' said Roberto.

'This is the best we can do,' said Kell. 'The cavalry will stay and punch a hole in the Tsardon line to give a chance of escape around the crag base to the south but whichever way you look at it, we're going to be leaving some of our people behind.'

Roberto scratched at his forehead. 'Can this be right?'

'So, tell us this,' said Kell, voice flat, face pale with exhaustion. 'Who lives and who dies? Do we send the sick up, knowing they might die on the way back to Estorr, or do we leave them here, helpless victims? Do we send up fit men and women because they are of more use to the cause, or do they stay here because they can buy the sick and wounded a little more time? I am not God, I cannot make that sort of decision.'

Roberto sighed. 'It's a shame the enemy doesn't share your humility.'

'And that's something else. How do we leave it such that those left behind are of no use to Gorian?' asked Nunan.

'We should have run while we had the chance,' said Kell.

'There never was a chance,' said Roberto. 'Don't burden yourself with that. We were in no position to defend ourselves on the run and we couldn't just abandon our wounded and non-combatants. The Tsardon were fitter, more numerous and they had the dead. And the dead wouldn't have rested when we had to. We had to face them sometime. At least today we gave them a bloody nose.'

'But it won't save us, not all of us.'

'No it won't.' Roberto began to shake. 'And it's obvious what we must do isn't it?'

Nunan nodded. 'I'm so sorry, Roberto.'

He couldn't meet Nunan's gaze. 'I need some time alone. And some time with my brother.'

'We'll handle everything from here.'

'Not everything,' said Roberto. 'I need to speak to Dahnishev.'

Roberto walked out of the command position and looked down the slope. It was a beautiful valley. Genastro flowers in bloom, trees in new leaf, burgeoning with energy. Birds everywhere. Life surrounded him. He wiped a tear from his eye and walked back to sit with Adranis. Dahnishev did not attempt to stop him.

Chapter Twenty-Eight

859th cycle of God, 35th day of Genasrise

'Name,' said Nunan.

Roberto translated his words. Adranis had not yet regained consciousness. It was likely now that he never would. Roberto had shed his tears on Dahnishev's shoulder and responded to Nunan's request to help him interrogate the Tsardon commander of the dead. He was a most extraordinary-looking man. Hideous. His whole character was repellent and his face and head tattooed to inspire fear. Black, blue and red, the tattoos formed intricate swirling patterns and symbols. Completely impenetrable.

'Garanth,' replied the Tsardon, showing the filed front teeth that had set Roberto's on edge.

Garanth's hands were bound. He stood before them in the command post, three men around him, hands on gladius hilts but still nervous. He was a huge man, looming almost as high as Paul Jhered. His shoulders were bunched with muscle below his furs and his entire body ran with power. One on one, he would beat any of them easily. Fortunately, he seemed entirely tranquil.

'What are you? A soldier?' asked Nunan.

Garanth chuckled.

'Not a soldier,' he said, his voice a whispered whistle. 'A shepherd. A father.'

Nunan raised his eyebrows. 'You sure about that translation?'

'Absolutely,' said Roberto, though he understood why Nunan had questioned him.

'Not what I was expecting. A shepherd of the dead?'

Garanth inclined his head. 'The path is not always clear. Some have need of light and guidance.'

Nunan massaged his temples with thumb and middle finger. He shook his head.

'But this is a battlefield position?'

Another chuckle.

'The Temples of Khuran are my home.'

'You're a priest.'

'If that definition helps you.'

'So what role do you serve on the battlefield?'

Garanth paused, debating whether to answer.

'I serve my master,' he said eventually.

'That's no help,' replied Nunan. 'I serve mine too. What do you do in service?'

'I guide the dead.'

'You control them?'

'No. They feel me amongst them.'

'Is this helping?' asked Nunan.

'I'm not sure,' said Roberto. 'We'll let the Ascendants work that out when they read the transcript. Mind if I ask a question?'

'Go ahead.' Nunan gestured with a hand and took a sip of water from the goblet on the makeshift map table.

'Who is your master?'

Garanth stared at him for a while, his dark eyes piercing, staring right through Roberto, making him uncomfortable.

'You are Del Aglios,' he said.

'Correct,' said Roberto, stiffening. 'You know me?'

'All of Tsard knows your face and your deeds. Respected enemy. Great prize.'

'I'm flattered but you'll have to catch me first,' said Roberto. 'Answer the question.'

Garanth smiled and those teeth had Roberto feeling at his own with his tongue.

'You expect me to say King Khuran but you worry it is another. My master is he who commands the dead. Who sees the energy we can only feel and who brings fresh hope to all who fall.'

'Gorian,' muttered Roberto. 'And what does he want?'

'As the Karku know and the Sirraneans fear, he wants to tip the world. And he will. You cannot stop him.'

'And what does the King think about all this?'

Garanth shrugged. 'He does not understand. It will cost him as it will you.'

'Tip the world?' asked Nunan.

'Cast down the old powers and install the new,' said Garanth evenly.

'And he intends to do all this with armies of ...' said Roberto, struggling still with apparent reality, '... the dead?'

'Who will stand before them?'

'It passed your notice that we have just defeated your abomination of an army?' said Nunan.

'That army was a tiny drop that will become an ocean across the Conquord. An experiment from which my master will learn.' Garanth closed his eyes. 'It is beyond your conception what awaits you.'

Roberto felt the chill through his body.

'And that is why you are here,' said Nunan. 'To enlighten us.'

Garanth shook his head. 'I think not. My work is done. I go to seek my master.'

'You are going nowhere,' said Nunan.

That smile from Garanth again. 'Not yet.'

He collapsed to the floor. Nunan knelt by him and felt for a pulse.

'He did say he could feel the energies of the dead.'

'Let's hope it brings him no comfort whatever,' said Roberto. 'You need to have him taken away and rendered useless. Pick your method.'

Nunan's smile was grim. 'I think perhaps fire is not the tactful course.'

'Julius will be pleased.'

'Do you believe him?' Nunan stood up from Garanth's body.

'That what we faced today is just the vanguard? What's not to believe? We've seen it with our own eyes. We know the effect even a small force has on elite legionaries. We need that Sirranean powder to be as good as they hinted it was.'

'Where is it?'

'Gesteris took it back to Estorr for analysis.'

'Then someone should get back there and get some.'

Roberto sighed. 'Pavel, we just need to get as many as we can up this crag and away. Gorian's coming and until we can bring the Ascendants and any new weapons into play, I have to agree with our erstwhile friend here. Who will stand against him?'

Nunan's gaze snapped back down to Garanth's body.

'Something wrong?' asked Roberto.
'I could have sworn I saw his eyelids flicker.'

Kessian's head was pounding. It was late in the afternoon and he had only just been allowed to rest. Gorian had called it a great victory, with more to come, but the songs that the Tsardon warriors had sung on the ice fields of Kark were absent here. He knew it was a different army and everything, but all the ones he'd seen looked unhappy. None more so than the prince. Gorian said it was because they hadn't had the chance to use their swords, and Kessian didn't really understand that. He thought they'd be pleased they hadn't had to risk their lives.

Kessian lay in the large room he shared with Gorian. Most of the Tsardon soldiers were outside and the very few most recent dead Gorian had brought back were standing outside too. Kessian had kept them on their feet. That was easy. But no one thanked him for it. And now he was tired. The storms Gorian had created and made him sample had been so painful inside. He knew he had a lot to learn. Gorian had promised to show him.

But right now, Gorian was sleeping across the other side of the room and none of the shouts echoing in the castle would wake him. Kessian couldn't sleep. He found himself sitting by Gorian and staring down at his face. He had hated him when they left Kark. Hated him for humiliating him by throwing him in the water and making him walk with the dead.

Gorian had changed, though, when the sun had begun to warm them. Got so much more friendly and helpful. Happy, even. And Kessian had learned a lot by having to walk with the dead. None of those ones were here now. They'd all been left behind on the Atreskan border with three of the Dead Lords and two of the Gor-Karkulas. Some of them had gone back to the earth and the embrace of God. Gorian had said their work was done but Kessian thought it more likely the smell had got too bad. The worst hadn't been able to grip swords any more and the rot in their skin made them very weak.

Kessian wondered what had happened in Atreska by now. He wasn't quite sure why Gorian had made them go so far north. It was a very long way round to Estorr. But Gorian had wanted to come here, and so he did. Not even the King had made him change his mind and from what he had heard, the King had wanted him to travel through Atreska with the royal party. That left Gorian always arguing with

Rhyn-Khur. There were lots of questions he wanted to ask but Gorian wouldn't wake for a while.

There was something odd about his father's look today. Some discoloration on his skin. Like bruising, only a little green. It was on his neck and temples and a little bit in his cheeks. Kessian reached out a hand to touch it and recoiled. It was hard, like fired clay.

Gorian's eyes opened. Every colour of the rainbow swam across his eyes, settling on a calm pale grey. He smiled.

'You should be sleeping,' he said. 'You worked very hard last night.'

'I'm not tired,' said Kessian, yawning.

'Really? Well, it doesn't matter. Too excited, I expect. See how easy it is to win?'

'I suppose. But not everyone is happy.'

'I can't help that,' said Gorian, sitting up. 'But they'll see.'

The door to the room opened and in came Rhyn-Khur, flanked by four guards. He didn't look happy at all. Kessian sprang up and stood to attention. Gorian just rubbed his eyes.

'Lucky we were both already awake. Are we not worthy of rest despite what we have achieved for you today?'

The prince marched to the centre of the room where he stopped. His men spread out, hands on their sword pommels like always when he was with Gorian.

'You will stand before your prince until you are given leave to sit,' he said.

'I have earned my rest just as I should have earned your respect,' said Gorian. 'Are we not beyond such posturing?'

'You will stand and pay me the respect I demand,' said Rhyn-Khur quietly. 'You forget that you are my father's subject. You swore your allegiance to my family.'

Kessian tried to shrink away but there was nowhere to go. Rhyn-Khur and Gorian stared at each other. The guards fingered their swords hilts. It was like they were waiting for a reason to draw them. After an age, Gorian shook his head, blew out his cheeks and stood.

'If it makes you feel better,' he said.

'At least, now we may speak as equals. Your assumption of superiority is not one I will bear.'

Gorian smiled. 'And now, may I sit?'

'Now we may all sit,' said the prince.

He snapped his fingers and one of his guards brought across a chair.

He sat down and waved Gorian and Kessian to do the same. He smoothed his robes, finespun wool woven with gold braid. His guards stood behind him, fierce-looking men, scarred from battle and wearing the metal helm and brown cloak of the king's royal elite.

'It remains as it did when you walked in, an honour to sit in your presence,' said Gorian.

'You think too much of your position,' said the prince. 'Every man in my army knows you are but one man. Storms and walking dead will not save you from a knife in the night.'

'Oh, my Prince, your father and I got over this a long time ago. We should be friends. We even share the same age.'

Rhyn-Khur ignored what he said. Kessian felt scared. Why it had to be like this every time they spoke, he didn't understand. He thought they ought to be friends too. It would make things much easier.

'You denied my army battle and victory,' said Rhyn-Khur. 'Again. I thought my father had made himself clear in Kark. A Tsardon warrior needs blood on his blade or he feels his steps are wasted. We were ready to drive them away from their dead, scatter them and bolster your foul force. We had a plan.'

'We've been over this already today and anyway, I saw a better one.'

Rhyn-Khur's face darkened. 'I do not agree.'

'What do you mean? It was plainly better.' Gorian stared at him as if he was simple. Kessian sat on his hands to stop them shaking. 'We have forced them into a trap. We can harvest them at will. You won't have to lose a man.'

'You undermined me.' The prince's voice was hard like concrete. 'My men are looking at me like I am no longer in command.'

'That was not my intention.'

'No?' Rhyn-Khur pushed himself up from his chair and loomed over Gorian. 'You strut around here puffed up by your importance and make enemies everywhere you tread. You are pushing me, Gorian Westfallen. And I will be pushed no further. You have not deigned even to report on the advances in Atreska and Gestern. You seek to weaken me by keeping information from me.'

'I merely needed to sleep, my Lord. If I am to march to glory in Estorr, I need my rest.'

Rhyn-Khur raised his eyebrows. 'You? You march to glory? Well, well, well.'

'Words meant to encompass us all,' said Gorian. Kessian could see the frustration boiling within his father. 'We must make the best use of our resources. Your soldiers should be kept for the final battles.'

Rhyn-Khur put a finger to his own chest and barked his words. 'I. I will decide how our resources are used. I will decide when and where my men are entered into combat. I will choose the manner and place of our battles to come. And you. You will do nothing without my express consent. Or you will die, and your son will become my servant and speaker for the dead.'

'And as I fall, so will your chance of breaking the Conquord. Back away, Rhyn, you cannot afford for me to die. This war will be won through fear. Fear of my dead. You know it, I know it. So does your father.'

The prince glanced back at the impassive faces of his guards and gestured towards them.

'I know this. I know that every man of Tsard here is loyal to me and me alone. I know that out there, my warriors do not feel invested. They feel unsettled and I have sympathy for them. They question whether Tsard is being supported by you or supporting you and the dead. To believe, they must know they are the authority. That I am the authority. I stand on Conquord soil. You have done the hardest job for Tsard here, and in Atreska and in Gestern. No, no, say nothing. I know we have triumphed there because your smug ego would have cracked if we had not.

'I suffered you this far but I think you should ask yourself this. Who is it that needs who? And what will I do if my men begin to openly speak against you?'

'They all know I am in command because he does not trust you.'

Rhyn reached for a blade. His men clutched hilts tighter.

'That is a lie you will pay for, Westfallen.'

'You cannot scare me, Rhyn-Khur. For all your words you will not throw away your principal weapon. I will concede that we need each other. I will seek to keep it that way for as long as I possibly can.'

'You are not in sole command and you will not use your Works again until I give you leave. You are one pace from death, Westfallen.'

'And you one pace from failure in the eyes of your father. Now please go. I have to regain my strength or your invasion of the few against the many will fail.' Gorian leaned forward. 'And we do both know that. Don't we?'

'I mean what I say.'

'So you are fond of repeating,' said Gorian. Rhyn-Khur turned to go. 'My Prince? Enjoy the wine tonight. I understand it to be the end of a fine vintage. And don't worry. Tomorrow, you'll be looking on the world with entirely new eyes.'

The prince scowled and left.

'Will you let him attack tomorrow, Father?' asked Kessian.

'In a manner of speaking,' said Gorian. He smiled broadly and placed a hand on Kessian's shoulder, dropping to his haunches in front of him. 'Now I want you to go to sleep. We have a great deal to weary us tomorrow and every day until we each Estorr.'

Kessian felt a thrill of excitement. 'Estorr?'

'Just like I promised you. Didn't I promise you we'd be going to Estorr? We'll be staying here a while but you'll be seeing your mother as soon as I can make it happen.'

Kessian sucked back a sob. 'Thank you, Father, thank you.'

'I told you to trust me. And I haven't lied to you once, have I?'

'No. I'm sorry I doubted you.'

'Your journey is almost complete. But go to sleep now or every other pace will be more difficult.'

Kessian hurried across to his bed, thoughts of his mother, his friends and his sailing boat crowding his mind.

'What are you going to do?' he asked Gorian as he slipped under the blanket.

'I'll show you in the morning. Don't worry, I'll wake you.'

Kessian closed his eyes and slept amidst the comfort of his memories.

General Davarov sat in a high tower in the royal castle of Haroq City and gazed out beyond the city walls to the east and Tsard. And he could not believe his memories nor the sight that was approaching deliberately and inexorably. Each time he looked through the magnifier he shuddered and rubbed at the wound on his shoulder. He'd been the only one standing in the face of them when he'd received it. And had it not been for some of his loyals determining to rescue him he would be just like those in the vanguard of the invasion force marching through Atreska.

Davarov had sent messages back to Estorr. Rumours were already reaching him of huge defeats in Gestern. Atreska once again was a battleground and the only solace was that it would not be one for long. The Tsardon had no interest in occupation. But there was tragedy in that. Because they would fight and kill every Atreskan or Conquord man they could on the way because that was how they would grow their army.

Davarov shook his head. Megan Hanev, his Marshal Defender, was at the Solastro Palace. He was the de facto ruler in her absence. And in less than a day, the forces he had assembled along the border had been humiliated. Slaughtered on one wing and routed into the hunting lands and the central forests on the centre and remaining wing.

The thought that he had never seen anything like it and could never have hoped to defend against it was of no comfort whatever. The notion that he was more scared of this than he had been of overwhelming Tsardon odds ten years before was one he faced with no shame.

He had no idea what to do, barring what was already done. They weren't coming to Haroq City. They were marching a little way to the north and would skirt the capital of Atreska unless attacked.

And Davarov knew he should attack.

'But what would be the point?' he asked.

'Of what, General?' asked his Master of Horse, Cartoganev, looking away from the magnifier. A man who had eschewed the opportunity to command, preferring to keep to the saddle.

'Of attacking them,' he said, gesturing out of the window. 'It is like fighting a flood by pouring water into the river. We get weaker, they get stronger.'

'But we would not be giving up.'

'No, we would not.'

'And there are thousands of Tsardon who I presume do not want to join the walking dead either,' said Cartoganev.

'But we can even the odds by merely keeping our distance. Or at least, not worsen them. I do not know what to do. I am unworthy of command.'

'Nothing is unworthy about you, barring that statement,' said Cartoganev. 'But within it lies a tactic.'

'Go on.'

'We have been watching them, those of us who can bear it, from as close as we dare. They may walk, these dead, and they may fight unless we remove their capacity to do so. But in a most important way, they are clearly still dead. They decay. Every day, they get weaker. It is a slow process but it is definitely happening. We can clear a path for them. Ensure they meet no resistance. And we can try and find the one at the centre of the abomination.'

'I already know who that is. The air on the battlefield stank of rogue Ascendant.'

'Yes, but where is he? Remove him and you take the head from the monster.'

'But one day we must fight or this small army will march uncontested to the gates of Estorr.'

'And every day, we gather strength to place in their path when that day comes. Think, General. Today we are fractured, in twenty days we might not be.'

Davarov smiled at last. 'Aye, and in twenty days, we can have tactics and weapons to combat them. All right, let's get messages to anyone ahead of them north to Gosland, south to Gestern and let's you and I take our legions west ahead of them. We'll do it your way, Master Cartoganev, or we'll perish in the trying.'

Cartoganev nodded.

'One thing.'

'Yes, General?'

'I will not become one of them. If I fall, I want my body burned if it cannot be dismembered. Do I make myself clear?'

The cavalryman sucked on his top lip, frowning. 'Burning? My General, do you know what you're saying?'

'That I would rather end my cycle of life forever than walk against my friends as one of the dead? Yes, I think you could say that I do. Well?'

'Orders are orders,' said Cartoganev.

'Yes. Indeed they are.'

Chapter Twenty-Nine

859th cycle of God, 36th day of Genasrise

Nunan's extraordinarii had formed a ring around the base of the crag path. Thirty of them prepared to keep back as many legionaries as they needed to. A case of naphtha stood behind them out of sight but Nunan had authorised its use if the anger turned to riot. Kell and the cavalry were on horseback and had formed a line in front of them. Down the slope on the front lines, multiple fires burned, to throw the crag base into as much shadow as possible to hide the ascent of the fortunate.

What had begun peacefully as a tap on the shoulder following discussions with centurions had been slowly unpicking as the import of not being chosen sank home in the chill hours of night. Entreaties and desperate pleas had to be ignored. Every man and woman had people who would miss them should they not survive the break-out. But it didn't dampen the personal feelings of betrayal and Nunan was beginning to fear a total breakdown of order. Swords were not as yet unsheathed but the numbers breaking off from their duties on the pickets and in the trees as defence were worrying.

Nunan walked to the line of cavalry. A legionary of the principes was jabbing a finger in his direction and berating Dina. Thirty more stood around him, looking jealously at the lines of those waiting to ascend the crag.

'Oh, and here he comes now,' said the legionary. 'One of the fortunate few, I have no doubt.'

'Fortunate?' said Nunan, moving in front of Kell. 'I would gladly give you the great luck I had being one of those tasked with choosing who ascends and who does not. And yes I am one of those making the climb. My wife, as you will be aware, is not. Explain my fortune, legionary.'

'You have a chance to escape greater than mine. That is your fortune.' The soldier's face was full of anger and desperation. His body so taut his hands shook. 'I am expected to stand and die.'

Nunan nodded. 'Yes. Yes you are. As every time you stand and fight for your country. But that does not mean that you will. You are a Bear Claw. You are Conquord elite. And the Conquord expects you to do your duty. Tell me, when was it your courage failed?'

The man stepped forward a pace. 'My courage will never fail. It is those who run up the crag who you should question. Look inside yourself.'

Nunan drew his gladius. 'You should choose the words you speak to your commanding officer with greater care. I can end your life sooner if that is what you wish. I would prefer for you to stand a hero so that others I have ordered ... ordered, I will repeat ... to climb can do so.' He rested his gladius on the man's breastplate. 'I asked for volunteers to stand in defence. Every soldier in the triarii raised a hand. But I need them if I am to reach Estorr. So I asked again. Your hand did not go up. Not many did. So I had to choose. You were one of those chosen because your centurion believed you strong enough to stand before the Tsardon and not to run until the order. Was your centurion wrong?'

'He was not.'

'Then why are you standing before me, begging for a place in the line?' Nunan let his sword drop. 'We need the Claws to stand more than ever.'

'We should have broken out already. More would live.'

'I will not discuss matters of command with you.'

The legionary gestured over his shoulder.

'No, but you will with Del Aglios the heretic. And we are expected to die for him too.'

Nunan grabbed the man by the throat, surprising him by the move. He coughed and staggered back. Behind Nunan, swords came from scabbards and the cavalry readied.

'We will all die to save the son of the Advocate and you will not say another word. You might be desperate but you will not talk of Roberto Del Aglios in that way again or I will execute you myself.' He turned to his guards. 'Take this man and see he is isolated. He is of no use to the Claws and is dishonourably discharged.'

The legionary spat on the ground at Nunan's feet. Nunan didn't break his gaze.

'And now you will have no weapon with which to defend yourself either. No civilian fights. No civilian makes the ascent.' He shoved the man back. 'Anyone else care to join him?'

Nunan heard footsteps behind him as he watched the crowd begin to lose its ire. A hand was on his shoulder.

'May I?' asked Roberto.

Nunan nodded. Roberto stepped in front of him. He was ashen-faced and red-eyed. His armour, though, was polished, his cloak perfect about his shoulders, gladius at his waist. He walked up and down in front of them, looking each in the eye, daring them to speak.

'Is there anyone any of you can point to and say that you would not lay down your life for them? Is there a one amongst you who truly believes that they should make the ascent instead of one who is already chosen? You know there is not, yet you let your base fear overwhelm you. You are soldiers of the Conquord.

'You feel yourselves doomed but you are not. You have a chance yet when dawn comes. General Kell will take the cavalry and try to punch a hole in the Tsardon lines so that you might escape. It will take luck and courage but you have a chance. While you are contemplating occupying the Tsardon forces, I should tell you what I will be doing. I will be killing my own brother and cutting off his head and legs.' Roberto stopped and Nunan could see him steeling himself not to break down. The silence in front of him was palpable. He continued.

'I will be doing that because he has no chance and because he cannot become one of the walking dead. He has no chance because he, like the hundreds of others for whom the same fate awaits, stood in front of *you* when the hurricane and the dead struck. Adranis Del Aglios, without thought for himself, rode into battle to save you. He will die as a result.

'You want to talk to me about fairness and about chance and choice? I'll be at my brother's side.'

Roberto turned and stalked back through the cavalry line. Nunan faced the crowd but they would not face him. Every eye studied the ground. Nunan cleared his throat but his voice was still gruff when he spoke.

'Get back to your posts.'

*

Gorian awoke to silence. He felt refreshed and ready. His only regret was that he had not been able to act in the depths of night but even for him there was a limit to how much he might do. For Kessian, too. Lord Garanth had been able to channel much useful information before his body had been removed. Some would escape. But not all.

Across the room, the boy still slept. Gorian rose and put his feet on the cold stone floor. The fire in the grate was long dead and the room was chilly. He walked across to Kessian and sat on his bed.

'Today is the beginning of everything I've been dreaming about since I found out you were alive,' he said, stroking the boy's hair. 'Today people will see that what we have done thus far is but preamble and testing. I am ready. And you are ready to stand by my side. Time to wake up to your destiny.'

Gorian teased Kessian's life map open and fed in a gentle heat. Kessian opened his eyes. He didn't recoil like he had done so often in the past when he saw Gorian so close on awakening. Gorian smiled.

'It is a fine morning,' he said.

'It's still dark,' said Kessian.

'Yes. Three hours before dawn but there is much to do. Get yourself up. We need to eat.'

'Yes, Father.' Kessian pushed himself up in his bed and rubbed his eyes with his hands and frowned. He pushed out his mind into the castle. Gorian saw the energy lines probing to discover the cause of his confusion. 'It's so quiet.'

'Yes, it is.'

'Not just noisy quiet. Where is everyone?'

'Awaiting a new future, free of worry,' said Gorian. 'Come. Get dressed and I'll show you.'

Kessian's expression cleared and a little fear was back in his eyes. He got out of his bed and put on his toga, slashed Ascendancy red. The material was looking a little shabby but it still served. He strapped on his sandals. Gorian held out his hand and Kessian took it.

'Don't be frightened. It was always meant to be this way. You know that, don't you?' said Gorian.

The boy nodded. Gorian squeezed his hand to give him strength and comfort, and opened the door. They were on the ground floor of the castle in a room that let directly onto the covered yard. It was currently a makeshift barracks and all the Tsardon not on duty were lying on their cloaks or on straw. Not a one made a sound nor twitched a muscle. Kessian drew close to Gorian.

'You can feel them, can't you?' asked Gorian.

'They are all dead, aren't they?'

'They await me,' replied Gorian, looking upon them as a general might on his waiting army. 'And I will awaken them soon.'

'Why did they die?' asked Kessian. His voice was trembling.

'So they can serve me better. No dissent will lead to a quicker victory. Come with me.'

Gorian led him around the edge of the courtyard. Two men stood outside a room down a short corridor.

'My Lords Runok and Tydiol, I trust you slept well.'

'Very peaceful,' said Tydiol.

'And the prince?'

'He awaits you inside.'

Tydiol pushed open the door and Gorian led Kessian inside. They were in the chambers of the castle commander. Spartan but spacious. In the ante-room, the two Gor-Karkulas were sleeping still. Their chests rose and fell in time with one another. Truly a fascinating group, that Gorian had only just begun to understand. Their power and potential though, he already knew very well.

Rhyn-Khur had demanded they be kept near him. He thought them the key and Gorian was happy to oblige. It kept them quiet and in fear of their lives and that was just fine.

'Wrong pick again, my prince,' said Gorian.

'Father?'

'Nothing,' said Gorian, walking across the ante-room to the bed room and opening the door. 'The prince overlooked you, that's all. He made a lot of mistakes. But not any more.'

Rhyn-Khur looked peaceful enough. He was lying on his back in the large bed, eyes closed and a tinge of blue around his lips. Kessian gasped.

'Him too,' he said.

'It's a lesson on the evils of drink,' said Gorian. He laughed. Not a bad joke, that one. 'They all drank a little wine or ale or spirit and then went to sleep, dreaming of another day. And when they wake, they will see it but not exactly as they thought.'

Kessian withdrew his hand. 'You killed them all.'

'Yes, obviously.' He laughed again. 'You know your namesake used to say that every time one of us said something stupid. But you know why I killed them, don't you?'

Kessian shook his head. 'They weren't doing you any harm.'

'Not yet but soon enough. Come on, Kessian, you heard the prince threaten me yesterday. How long before he carried out his threat and killed you into the bargain? I can't have that. I can't have people disagreeing with me, can I? This way, none of them will go against me. It's quite simple.'

'It's wrong to kill.'

Gorian felt the heat of brief anger. 'This is war,' he snapped. 'People die all the time. Most of these wouldn't make it to Estorr alive. Much better for them they see the white walls and the Hill this way rather than not at all, wouldn't you say?'

He could see and sense Kessian's confusion. The boy had no love of the Tsardon, that was certain. But he still clung on to ideas that did him no favours. There was still a lot of work to do.

'Have you not heard what the Dead Lords have told you?' Gorian continued. 'Death is not the end. It is just another step on a grand path. It comes to us all and most of us cannot choose when that will be. I chose the time for these Tsardon and the prince. What's wrong with that?'

'But what about all the others outside?'

Gorian smiled. 'Ah. Now you're thinking. And you're right. They probably won't be happy. But that's all right too because I have something planned for them.'

He scratched at the hard discoloured skin on his cheek. It had appeared when he'd raised the dead outside the castle yesterday. Kessian watched him.

'What is that?'

'Not everything under the soil is good,' said Gorian. 'It'll go soon enough. And that's part of the lesson. Now, I'm going to wake up these good folk and set them to their work. I'll need you to hold them until the Karkulas are ready. Then I'll show you something new and amazing.'

'When?'

'Good question.' Gorian considered. It should be a time fitting for the event. A time when no one could miss what was happening and marvel at his talent. 'Dawn, I think. Very first light. Now, hold my hand. I have need of you.'

Gorian sat down in a chair facing the bed and the dead prince. Kessian came to his side and sat on the floor. Gorian placed a hand on Kessian's head. The well of the boy's power opened to him and again he marvelled at the sheer enormity of it. Gorian and the other original Ascendants had an energy well that Arducius had once described as a water butt in size with which to amplify the elemental threads they took inside themselves. Kessian's was more akin to an entire reservoir.

When the boy fully understood it, he would be an enormous force in the world. And Gorian wanted him by his side when that happened. For now, though, it meant he had the capacity to sustain Works over very long periods. What was more, he, like the Gor-Karkulas, could do it unconsciously. It was a gift and Gorian was determined to learn the secret one day. There had to be a way to increase the well and thereby increase the potential duration of any Work or indeed its intensity.

Gorian fed calm into his life map and into that of Kessian. He felt the boy relax under the gentle tones while he pushed out with his mind, sampling the energies of the castle. So different than the day before. The chaotic colours and stray lines that characterised hundreds of people living in the same space was gone, replaced by a slumbering calm.

The cold dark of the castle's stone was underpinned by the leviathan power of the earth beneath its foundations and topped by the multiple grey shapes that indicated the bodies of poisoned Tsardon warriors. The Ascendants used to think that grey was the residual colour of lost energy. They were wrong. It merely waited to be re-energised. Reawakened.

To bring life where there was none. Surely a gift for gods.

The ambling energy of the earth was beautiful. Slow-moving browns, shot with the delicate quickness of tiny insect life and the incandescence of plants awaiting their moment to grow or of small mammals about their tasks. He drew on the earth, shuddering as its force entered his body. Under his hand, Kessian gasped. It was pleasure and pain combined. He settled quickly. Gorian and Kessian were part of the circuit of the earth now.

Awakening the dead had proved so simple in the end. The energy map was like a burst of pure fire in its intensity. But it had required plenty of tuning to reach a point where the dead, his people, would walk in great numbers and not be prey to spikes in the energies feeding them.

Gorian constructed the life-giving map. Somewhere in his subconscious the number he was raising was counted. And for each one, a tendril of concentrated energy sought its home. At its base, the shape was a pulsating ball of brilliant blue from which the tendrils emitted. He waited for his construct to settle. He and Kessian might be able to awaken one or two with the power they could direct from themselves; the addition of earth energy and its subsequent amplification gave him everything he needed. The problem was containment.

'Are you ready, Kessian?'

'Yes, Father.'

There was no strain in his voice. So naturally gifted. Such a talent in waiting.

'Then I will allow the earth energy into the reanimation construct. We are bringing back over three thousand. There will be turbulence.'

'I understand.'

'I have no doubt that you do.'

Gorian opened a pathway to the ball of light and let the earth wash in. The energy would have swamped him in moments. To animate so many dead required a huge volume. But with his linked circuit to Kessian he could channel the raw fuel into him too and between them, they controlled and fed the earth into the reanimation. The ball flared, the energy grew exponentially and tore out through the tendrils which thickened and fled away in every direction.

Gorian cried out. His body stiffened and shook. His hand gripped hard on Kessian's head. The boy did not make a sound. Energy was dragged in from across the castle. Fires guttered. The air became charged. Beneath their feet, the stone flags rippled as the earth sought to burst out. He clamped it hard, desperate to maintain control.

He fed more earth energy into the construct, purity mixed with tiny motes of decay. Life was driven through everything that dwelled there. Plants burst to life, roots sought sustenance and then were dead. At the edge of his hearing, a squealing of thousands of rodents and tiny creatures whose life spans were condensed into mere moments by the power flooding through them on its way into the Ascendant wells.

And out it went, multiplied by a factor of ten, a hundred and more. Thrumming through the tendrils that thrashed and sparked. They sought, burrowed and tore, finding paths through the latent energies of the air, each one arrowing to its target, thudding home. Gorian felt every impact as a jolt through his body. He juddered and shook. A scream tore from his lips. Life was pain. Skin on his neck and chest hardened. Kessian grunted and tensed.

The tendrils sought the dormant energy within each Tsardon body. They expanded to encompass each one. Life drilled in, energising, awakening. Eyes snapped open. Breath was gasped into bodies. Confusion spread like a fire on dry grass. And for every body that sustained consciousness once more, the pressure on Gorian eased. The life construct lessened in intensity. He could feed calm through it and into the minds of his subjects.

'Rise,' he said.

And they did. He could feel each one, marvelling at a new chance. Clawing at the life he had given them. He felt fear but he could quash it easily with the promise of release when their job was complete. Each new life fed back into him, the pleasure after the pain had gone. His Work was done. He had created life from death. He passed the construct into Kessian's mind and broke the circuit between them. He closed off the earth. He opened his eyes.

'Have them dress and move them outside,' said Gorian. 'It takes too much energy to sustain them through the stone. They will live easily on the ground out there.'

'Yes, Father.'

Gorian monitored his son. He could sense the movement of his new army. He could see the complex lines that made them what they were. Each one was linked to every other. Each one was linked hard to the earth and the earth gave them the strength to take the next step, to swing the sword. And in his mind, Kessian held the hub of the circuit. Should he let go, it would unravel in a heartbeat and the dead would fall. But he wouldn't. He didn't even know how.

Gorian stood and stretched quivering limbs. He felt at his skin and looked down. Beneath his toga, there was discolouration and small bumps. Pale green and brown or purple. Like fading bruises but covering his entire chest. To create purity you had to filter out the impurity. It would fade. His body would renew. He was an Ascendant. He was master of the elements, not prey to them.

Gorian knew he should be tired but he felt more awake and alive than he ever had in his life. In front of him, Rhyn-Khur got out of his bed and moved to his armour stand. Silently, he began to dress.

Efficient, deliberate moves. Not quite natural, still a puppet. Gorian smiled.

'Enjoy your new life, my Prince,' he said. 'It is the one ordained for you from the moment you joined me.'

He turned to the door back into the ante-chamber.

'Lord Runok!' The dull-witted, tattooed monstrosity walked in. Lord Tydiol followed him. 'Your army awaits you. They will be outside presently.'

'It is my honour to lead them,' said Runok. 'Will a Karkulas hold their key?'

'When it is practicable. Lord Tydiol, soon is the time to create yours.' Gorian began to walk to the door, suddenly desperate to feel fresh air on his face. 'Up there on the road and at the crag. Enough have escaped us while I was resting. It is time the rest fell into line, don't you agree?'

Chapter Thirty

859th cycle of God, 36th day of Genasrise

'He's in no pain,' said Dahnishev.

'No, that's what I'm in,' said Roberto.

'Del Aglios, that is not like you.'

Dawn was close. Hundreds had escaped up the crag path. Others waited and wondered if they would get their chance. Their comrades watched for the first signs the Tsardon had seen them. The cavalry was ready to move. All had their instructions.

Moving among the sick and dying, Dahnishev and his medics with triarii swordsmen were conducting the awful task of putting to death those who had no chance of escape. The sick sound of butchery – of legs to stop them walking, of heads so they were not forced to see as living dead – had punctuated the night in the triage centre. Only a handful were left. The begging of those who felt they deserved a chance when they did not have one would remain in the memories of survivors forever.

'Perhaps it isn't,' said Roberto, cooling his brother's forehead with a wet cloth. 'But I have sat in here or stood outside and searched myself and all I have done; and I find that I am to blame. No matter what you say, I was in charge of the army that Gorian rode in and it was me who allowed himself to be persuaded that Gorian should live. Dear God-forgive-me, Dahnishev, what have I done?'

'Showed mercy, Roberto. Demonstrated you are human, aye and fallible.'

'Others' mistakes do not lead to their brother's deaths. Nor to the toppling of their Conquord.'

There was a burning guilt inside Roberto that he had no desire to quell. Every heartbeat, events of his life played out before his unwilling eyes and every single one was shown to be a waste, because of his actions in that marching camp ten years ago. They had been moving relentlessly towards this doom and their eyes had been firmly shut.

'There is no sense in this bitterness, Roberto,' said Dahnishev quietly.

'What else is left, old friend?'

'Don't make me angry, Roberto. I share your pain but not your hopelessness. What is left is to show that the Conquord will not fall. That you will unite all who are left and strike back victorious.'

Roberto shook his head. 'The future is lying here, though. And it is dying. He is dying. I'm so sorry, Adranis.'

Dahnishev grabbed Roberto's face and turned it to look in his own.

'I won't hear this, Roberto. And I won't have my legion hear it. We need you. Don't let it go. Not now. You didn't give up before and I will die before I let you give up this time. I trust I make myself clear.'

'What are you? My father? Who the hell are you to tell me how to act and feel?'

Dahnishev nodded and withdrew. He stood and walked across the tent to tinker with his instruments, placing them in their leather cases ready for the climb.

'I'm sorry, Dahnishev. That was uncalled for. Forgive me.'

'Time you did what you are here to do, Roberto,' said Dahnishev gruffly. 'The drink you gave him will stop his heart presently. Are you sure you don't want someone else to do it?'

'That would be the final betrayal, wouldn't it? He's my brother.'

Another nod from the old surgeon. 'I'll be outside.'

Roberto watched him go.

'Just you and me now, little brother.' Tears began to fall unchecked down his cheeks. He put a hand inside Adranis's shirt to feel his heartbeat. It was weak and irregular. 'Why did you have to fall, Adranis? It should have been me making the journey first to God's embrace. I should have been there to welcome you. The Omniscient will hold you close.'

Adranis's heart stopped beating. Roberto scooped up his body and held him close, sobbing into his shoulder.

'Goodbye, my brother. The Conquord will weep for you but none so hard as me.'

Roberto clung on for what felt an age. So warm, the body of his brother. So recent, the life departed. And so wrong, what had to be done. Reluctantly, he laid Adranis on his bed and stood back. The axe lay on the ground near him, atop the boards that had to go beneath Adranis's neck and knees.

Roberto stooped to pick up the boards. He lifted up Adranis's head and slipped one board in; raised his legs and placed the other. He stared down at the axe and bitter bile flooded his mouth.

'That it should come to this,' he whispered. 'Gorian Westfallen, I swear on the name of Del Aglios that you will pay for all that you have wrought.'

Roberto knelt to the axe, kissed its blade, prayed for the sharpness of its edge and hefted it in both hands. He stood, shaking, and turned to his brother one last time.

'Forgive me.'

Roberto swung the axe.

Dina Kell heard Roberto's cries of despair. Many among the charnel that had once been the triage area did too. She found she didn't care if the sound of this most appalling of nights had carried to the Tsardon and alerted them in any way. Indeed she wanted them to hear the depths to which Gorian had forced the Estoreans.

She wished now that they had fled this morning before dawn. But she knew there had been no decision possible other than to stay with their injured and try to find a way out. Nunan had done his best, she knew, but it would never be good enough in the eyes of the infantry. So many were dead, butchered and being laid in the mass graves. Side by side and on top of one another. There had been no time or manpower for anything else. Julius Barias was yet more enraged, if that was possible. He hadn't volunteered to stay with those defenders who were to be left behind to run however.

Light was growing though it wasn't yet dawn. At any moment, the Tsardon would see the escape and rush to overwhelm it. They wouldn't find a single Bear Claw standing in their way. The legion had been pulled back as soon as they had fuelled the fires to hide their movements in the deep shadow behind the glare.

Perhaps they could have made the break out in the dead of night but that would have meant fewer getting away up the crag and more risking death at the hands of the Tsardon. Death that would mean hideous new life under Gorian's control. Whichever way you eyed it, the decisions had condemned hundreds to death. She, Nunan and Del Aglios would all have to live with that.

The plan was to ride hard down the cragside and back onto the road where the Tsardon had placed significant defence. They wouldn't expect an all-out assault and should be easily broken. But it was the aftermath that Kell worried about. An army six thousand strong chasing them to Estorr. They would be fast, full of the joy of victory and with the scent of the hunt in their nostrils. She would be leading a few hundred at best. Broken-willed, desolate, beaten.

The only thing that would drive them on would be the desire not to become one of the walking dead. The trouble was of course that the dead would not stop at night. They surely didn't need rest. Kell hoped Roberto had been wrong in that assessment but she didn't think so.

The man himself emerged into the pre-dawn light and the embrace of Surgeon Dahnishev. She saw Dahnishev speak words and Roberto shake his head. Dahnishev nodded to two triarii and the men disappeared inside the tent, appearing shortly afterwards with Adranis's butchered corpse in a blood-soaked blanket. Roberto touched it briefly and laid a sheathed dagger on it before the triarii walked away to the grave.

Kell felt compelled to offer support and walked over. The two men stood silent, side by side. Roberto's eyes shone wet and he was staring away from the grave area and down the slope towards the castle.

'It's dark down there,' he said before she could speak. 'Odd that there is no light or fire glow above the castle.'

His voice was flat but bless the man, he was still thinking straight about their plight.

'Perhaps we'll have more time to get our people away,' she said.

Roberto looked at her as if noticing her for the first time.

'We cannot afford such hope,' he said. 'And you should be by your horse and with your cavalry. Dawn is close.'

'We must get as many away as we can. Are you ready?'

'Yes, Ambassador. But part of my duty is to see you and Pavel on the path up the crag.'

'And you know we have to wait until the Tsardon begin to attack,' said Roberto. He managed a smile. 'After all, the captain is the last man to leave the sinking ship.'

'And so Pavel will be last man up the path. But you are heir to the Advocacy and we have a responsibility to your safety.'

'I've been trying to tell him the same thing,' said Dahnishev.

'So I respectfully request you move to the path now,' said Kell. 'Until you do, I cannot go to my horse.'

Roberto held up his hands. 'All right. All right. But one thing, Dina. You know what you're doing. Every triarii running in your wake knows what to expect. Do not turn round and try to buy the infantry time. We need you and we need your cavalry. You are the ones getting messages south. Information is going to be more valuable than any coin in the Exchequer's coffer.'

'I hear you.'

Above the sound of the last of the legion moving into position, Kell became aware of a rumble in the air. She glanced up but the sky was clear. Roberto had heard it too and was staring back down the slope. She thought she could hear voices too. Shouting. She tensed.

'They're coming,' she said and raised her voice to a practised bellow. 'Move, Bear Claws. Positions. Remember your orders. Go! Go!'

Legionaries began to run. Across at the gravesides, earth was being piled on the bodies by soldiers and Order ministers. Julius Barias, surprisingly, was still there blessing the dead. At the crag path, the lucky few, for whom luck was just running out, crowded onto the steep, treacherous path in tighter numbers.

'Roberto, you have to go,' said Kell. 'Or you won't make it.'

But Roberto wasn't listening to her. The grief he radiated was masked temporarily by confusion. His frown was deep and his eyes searched the downslope. Sunlight crept over the horizon, bathing much of the woodland in new light, leaving patches in heavy shadow. It was a classically beautiful genastro morning.

'There's something wrong,' he said, half to himself. 'Dahnishev, go. Take your people, go now.'

'Roberto . . .'

'Just do it!'

Dahnishev started, looked quickly into Roberto's eyes and gave the order to move. Roberto chewed his lip.

'What is it?' asked Kell.

'Listen to the noise. That's not a battle cry and it's not a system of orders.'

Kell listened. All she could hear was the multiple sound of voices and what had to be running feet. 'I don't—'

'Something's wrong,' repeated Roberto. 'That's not confidence, it's fear.'

'What can they be afraid of?'

Roberto shook his head. 'I don't know. Get to your horse. I think we're running out of time a lot more quickly than we thought.'

Kell still couldn't work out what it was that had worried Roberto but there were others sharing his concern. The last of the triarii were pulling back up the slope now, heading for the break-out muster point. They were being shadowed by archers and many of them were looking back over their shoulders, hurrying their pace. But some were even walking back to see what was going on. The woodland, which had hidden their positions very well, was working against them now, obscuring their view of the road and the castle.

'I don't—'

Kell felt her fear rising. She smelled something on the air. Indefinable. Roberto grabbed her arm.

'Dina. Run!'

Roberto shoved her away from him and made to turn away to the crag path. A series of dull thuds echoed up the slope. Debris was thrown high into the sky above the tree line, floating gently down. It looked like vegetation; leaves, branches and even tree bark. Kell's heart began rattling painfully in her chest. Now she heard what Roberto had known was beginning. There was screaming and it wasn't coming from the Bear Claws.

Every eye had turned to stare. Swords were out of scabbards, held in nervous hands. Clutches of legionaries pointed. Individuals backed away toward the crag. From high up on the crag path, people were shouting, their vantage point giving them the view denied Kell and Roberto.

'It's Gorian,' said Roberto. 'It has to be.'

Chaos descended. Tsardon were running headlong up towards the crag. Not a one of them had a weapon drawn nor cared who was in front of them. Individual Bear Claw legionaries remembered years of training and began to form up where they could find comrades. People were shouting. Kell added her voice but the loudest was Roberto's. For a moment, he was the great general once more.

'Claws. Break. Double to the muster point. Break out, break out. Move!'

His words rolled over them and they reacted. The final few and Kell ran with them. She couldn't afford a glance behind to see what became of her husband and the Advocate's heir. The crag was on her left, just a few paces away, and to her right something was tearing across the ground and it lent speed to her legs. Ahead of it, Tsardon warriors ran for their lives right into the teeth of what should have been a Bear Claw fence of steel. But the Claws were running too, the cavalry ahead of them already charging. Down the slope along the side of the crag to turn left along the road and away.

Churning blackness flooded across the wooded slope faster than a man could easily run. A mist of spores or dust travelled at its crest like spray on a wave. Kell stumbled in her run but could not drag her eyes away to look where she was going. She was in the midst of a knot of legionaries, and ahead of a stream of blacksmiths, Order ministers, medics and other non-combatants responding to the order to run.

There was no discipline in it. As the black wave rolled up the hillside it became a stampede. Ahead of Kell, she could see the dust of the cavalry and hear their shouts. And she could see Tsardon too, abandoning their positions and joining the rush.

In the air back down the slope to Kell's right, a cloud of brown and black was thickening. Every few moments, more of the dull detonations could be heard, more debris thrown up into the sky. She ran harder. Screams reached her ears. Horrible sounds of terror, cut off abruptly. Panic was spreading across the whole hillside. Conquord and Tsardon ran together, allies in fear.

The blackness was gathering pace. Kell could see it clearly now. It ate up the ground and crawled up trees. Trunks rippled, branches vibrated, wood split, hurling sap, bark and leaf high into the sky and setting a rotten stink on the breeze. On the ground, Tsardon warriors were sprinting hard, desperately trying to outrun the wave. She watched it gather in a line of men, swarming up their bodies like tentacles, grabbing them and bearing them down beneath it, shrieks turning to silence. There was a rumble through the earth. Kell could feel the vibrations in her legs.

She was breathing hard. No time to urge others; this charge needed no further impetus. The wave was rushing faster and faster. She streaked along in front of the crag, seeing the darkness racing to cut her off before she reached the road which remained untouched, a haven for them all. Whatever Gorian had done, it only affected living things.

Bear Claws and Tsardon alike were turning left and disappearing from view. With every one that made it, she felt a tiny sense of satisfaction. But she could hear the popping of grass and flowers, and the thuds of splitting trees so close now. And the begging of men reduced to corpses in moments as the hideous diseased rotting cloud engulfed them.

One more glance behind her before the down slope stole her view. She wished she hadn't. Men and women fighting each other to get on to the crag path. A crowd of people reduced to animals, scratching, pulling and biting to survive instead of those who had been friends as dawn broke. The wave and spore-ridden cloud washed against the crag. So many dead in an instant.

Kell dragged in a breath and focused forwards, desperate not to trip and so to die. The wave roared in her ears and hissed in her skull. Closing, closing. She forced more pace into aching legs. Screamed. Twenty yards to go. The black, roiling filth grabbed more victims, destroyed the hillside, ate everything in its path.

Ten yards. The wave cruised along the verge at the roadside. She could smell the foul stench. It stung her eyes and burned in her throat but she would not stop. Five yards. It was going to beat her to the crag base. She took another two paces and jumped, diving forwards. Beneath her, the wave splashed against the bare rock and fell back. Spores and dust kicked into the air. She held her breath. Down she came. Her hands struck gravel. She turned a forward roll across the road and slithered further, hearing her cloak rip and her armour shriek against the hard surface.

The moment she stopped moving she leapt to her feet and turned. The wave was fading. The smell was of rot, disease and death. Stagnant and fetid. She turned her head and vomited onto the road. Her heart was thrashing so hard she thought it would explode up her throat. Her body was shaking with exertion and fear. Her eyes were running with tears, trying to wash away the itching that spread across her whole face. She coughed and spat. Looked round again.

The whole hillside was gone. Dead half-trunks still stood, split open and oozing pulp. The grass was a memory. Nothing moved. Nothing made a sound. But it wouldn't be that way for long. She backed away. There were others on the road with her, standing and staring. Bear Claws and Tsardon alike, all thoughts of friend and foe forgotten.

Down at her feet, a Tsardon warrior was sitting nursing a gash in his left leg. His shoulders were wobbling and he looked up the slope, his mouth open, unable to believe. He turned, sensing Kell's eyes on him. There was fear in him at the sight of her but she just shook her head.

And held out her hand.

The Tsardon took it and hauled himself to his feet.

'Come on,' she said. 'We might fight later but no one deserves to die like this. Let's get you out of here.'

He slung an arm around her shoulder, she one round his waist and the pair of them walked slowly away along the road, neither knowing what might be around the next corner.

Chapter Thirty-One

859th cycle of God, 36th day of Genasrise

Ossacer could find no answers on the Hill. Only the disciples of the Ascendancy strand of the Order could discuss scripture with him, and their allegiance was to the Advocate alone. He didn't need sycophantic interpretation. What he needed was genuine understanding.

For days, he had wrestled with his conscience, feigning illness very effectively, for the most part to keep away from Arducius and the new emerged Ascendants. Every moment he was away from them he wanted to run in and shout for them to stop their folly, to see what was right in front of their faces and refuse to bow and scrape without thought.

But it had become very clear to him in the brief time he had chosen to spend with Arducius that only he, Ossacer, had any sense left in him. The war machine was rolling. And not just in the Ascendancy. He'd been called to examine the elements that made up some explosive powder the Sirraneans had given Marcus Gesteris. Foolishly, he'd taken along Cygalius and the young lad had identified the ingredients in moments. The Advocate's scientists were sourcing and manu-facturing even now, while in the classrooms, Arducius and Hesther taught fire and ice.

There was no one here to preach reflection. Mirron was who-knew-where at the moment. Jhered with her. And Vasselis, who might have had a thing or two to say about engaging in another damaging conflict without proper diplomacy, was away with the Advocate.

All for rumour too. Rumour that the Tsardon were approaching Gosland and Atreska and rumour that Gorian was doing something unspeakable. Actually, Ossacer believed the latter part but it was separate to a war in which the Ascendants were to be merely weapons. An arm of the military. Wrong. So very, very wrong. Only killing Gorian mattered.

Ossacer really felt he had no choice, and his heart was not even heavy when he walked out of the Victory Gates and headed for the only place he knew he would get a proper hearing and an alternative perspective. He understood it was risky. Foolhardy, even. But there were times when the service of the Omniscient transcended personal risk.

He felt like a recalcitrant child with his cloak hood pulled well over his face as he walked the warm streets of Estorr on a breezy but sunny morning. Sneaking by people who had no idea who he was on an errand that all those he called friends would try to stop. Genasrise smelled beautiful. The first flowers were in bloom and the mood was light. Even the scents from the sea were fresh. He expected every rooftop and whitewashed wall would be sparkling in the sun but that was a sight denied him.

Ossacer navigated by the currents of energy in the air and through the cobbled streets. He walked by people if they crowded the way, letting their life maps draw him a picture of what lay before him. No one would have guessed he was blind, nor that he was an Ascendant. One of the more famous people in the Conquord and yet none of them knew he passed. There was some satisfaction in that. And some relief.

The atmosphere in the city was troubled. Demonstrations had come as far as the gates of the Hill on three occasions. The Chancellor had maintained her demands that the Ascendants and their allies be locked away. Graffiti had been daubed on walls across Estorr. Offensive, frightening and unsettling.

His destination villa was enormous. Not just of a scale within a set of similar villas, but massive. Before approaching, Ossacer gauged the mood of the square in which he found himself, walking slowly around, apparently admiring the fountain at its heart. From his reading, he knew what the fountain represented. A tree in full spread, providing nourishment, security and comfort. It looked a bit of a mess to him. The water running through the marble upset the natural harmonies of the sculpture and made the map a chaotic mix of colours. He had been assured it was beautiful though.

Ossacer sniffed. Visual beauty. Another concept consigned to memory. It still left a bitter taste in the mouth. He moved on. The square was busy. It was set in the heart of a luxurious district of Estorr, high up above the harbour and commanding magnificent views it was said. Every villa had extensive buildings and gardens. All had private fountains piping water directly inside and giving their owners even more reason not to mix with the masses.

He could hear building work going on but couldn't quite place it. Roads led from the square in four directions. Down towards the harbour, left and right towards the arena and the Hill respectively and up to where the principal House of Masks dominated the skyline. Not a place for beggars, though of course they had more reason than most to look for succour here.

For a moment, Ossacer questioned his decision. There was no going back once he passed the guards and announced himself at the gate. But he could see no other way. Not if the Ascendancy was to be accepted and not if the Academy was to develop free of its tag as a military training camp.

Ossacer took a deep breath and strode up to the gates, closed against the public. Guards moved to block his path.

'I am sorry but the Chancellor is not able to entertain visitors,' said one in a gentle, almost apologetic voice that took Ossacer by surprise.

'I am sure she will want to speak to me.'

'A lot of people say that,' said the other, humour in his tone. 'And if we believed them all, the Chancellor would never be able to carry out her duties. You can write for an appointment and may be seen in the House of Masks but I have to advise you that the Chancellor's diary is brimming, what with the ongoing Ascendant trouble. I'm sure you understand. Please move on.'

Ossacer couldn't resist the dramatic.

'As I say,' he said, sweeping off his hood and looking up at the guards. 'I am sure she will want to speak to me.'

Both guards stepped back, staring at his eyes. Ossacer was drawing on the energy of trees in the garden and knew that browns and greens would be chasing across them.

'There is no need to be afraid. I am Ossacer Westfallen and I am here to offer help, information and advice in a difficult time for us all.'

He couldn't read their expressions but knew that they were looking at each other.

'Stay,' said one. 'Stand there, don't move.'

'I have no intention of doing otherwise.'

A bell was rung. Presumably it was set into the wall. It was an insistent ring and didn't stop until he heard running feet. The left-hand gate was opened and Ossacer counted four more soldiers approaching. He kept his expression warm though inside his heart had begun to thrash in his chest. No turning back now.

One guard watched him while the others gathered in a whispering huddle. Every energy map was shot through with nerves. Lifelines shimmered. Nearby, plants sampled the change in the atmosphere. If only they knew just how close they really were to nature. Shortly, three men marched towards him. One reached out as if to grab him but pulled back, not wishing to touch him.

'You will come with us.'

'It is all I have been asking for,' said Ossacer. 'Please, you don't need to worry. I am here to make good, not cause trouble.'

'That will be for the Chancellor to decide.'

'Clearly.'

The guards surrounded him but kept at arm's length, walking him quickly between vibrant, pulsing beds of plants and flowers. Ossacer drank in their purity, using it to energise and calm himself. He ran through in his mind the content he wanted to impart. The only unknown was Felice Koroyan herself and whether she would give him the opportunity.

Inside, the villa was cool and quiet. The ceilings were high and Ossacer could sense great open spaces beyond walls and felt the weight of the two storeys above. It made the Ascendancy villa in Westfallen, a place he held in his memory as the grandest barring the palace itself, seem like a tight terrace. They walked thirty paces down a central passageway until he was shown into an ante-room. Two guards came in with him and the door was closed firmly behind him.

Ossacer let the mind map of the room coalesce. He was a little weary from the effort already expended this morning. This level of concentration stretched the mind and he was no longer used to it. He made a mental note to change that.

The room had shuttered windows down one wall and was otherwise clad in wood panelling. He could make out the dark shapes of hanging paintings while beneath his feet was flat, cold black marble. There was a low narrow table in the centre of the room and recliners were placed along its long sides. Ossacer moved to one of them but did not sit. He turned and faced the door, wondering how long he would have to wait.

*

Herine Del Aglios, Advocate of the Estorean Conquord, walked down the centre of the Prima Chamber at the Solastro Palace, fighting to keep her eyes fixed upon her throne at the far end. In so many ways, it was as every time she sat before the Conquord Senate. The light inside sparkled from the white walls. Warmth eased up through the stone flags, pushed by the hypocaust below. The flags of the Conquord territories hung from the ceiling moved lazily; and the grand busts and statues, decked with flowers, gazed regally down on the esteemed assembled company.

And saw what Herine saw. Dozens of empty places on the three tiers of benches.

Marshal Vasselis gave her the tiniest touch in the back when he stopped to take his place among his full delegation. When Herine turned to sit down, she nodded her gratitude and smiled though she felt like raging. Numbers were a third down at best guess. That meant only two hundred facing her.

None were present from Bahkir, where marshal law meant that they had no debating power. The Dornoseans had withdrawn from the Conquord and their absence was not a surprise. But, barring Neratharn and, of course Caraduk and Estorea, no one had sent a full delegation, so far as she could see. Gestern's absence was disappointing and a great surprise. Katrin Mardov needed a good reason for it. And while the Gatherer bench was sparse because of accepted duties, the fact that the Order bench was completely empty was a slur on her authority and position.

'Welcome,' she said, hearing her voice echoing across the chamber. 'The Conquord hierarchy must be astoundingly busy for the attendance here to be so reduced.'

The muttering of conversation had ceased. Her tone had produced the desired effect. Herine paused and stared at them, letting the silence grow to uncomfortable proportions. She put her palms together and brought them to her face such that her two forefingers touched her lips. She waited on as long as she dared before dropping her hands back to the arms of the throne.

'I am not naïve,' she said. 'There is trouble in the Conquord. It has been a struggle to rebuild ourselves, following the war with Tsard. And rumours of new enemy forces approaching our borders are sure to cause anxiety. I understand that and my orders for mobilisation of the legions are specifically designed to counter those concerns and secure our borders.

'But surely the Prima Chamber is the place to debate our issues. The genasrise meeting sets the agenda for the year. I find it difficult to believe, therefore, that problems in your countries, most of you, are so severe that your delegations are small if they are here at all. I notice civil servants in place of at least three Marshal Defenders. I understand my executive orders would have been surprising and no doubt irritating, but that is no excuse for this.

'So you shall not be naïve either. Do not think I will thank you that you have sent a delegation of sorts. I will not debate with juniors, I will merely instruct. Do I make myself clear?'

There was the clearing of throats and a nervous shifting on benches.

'Good. So first, I will hear the state of the legion mobilisation and arrival time at designated muster points. First, I would like to extend my thanks to both the Atreskan and Goslander Marshals for their personal attendance. Despite the immediacy of potential threat, you are here and I am grateful.

'I will thus turn to our somewhat sparse Phaskareen delegation. I am sure I do not know who you are, who represents your Marshal ...'

Herine waited for the man to rise to his feet. He was plainly nervous just as he should be. Middle-aged, balding and in need of exercise. His toga was tied too tightly across his gut and there was a sheen of sweat on his brow.

'I am Consular Secretary Karesidi, my Advocate.'

Herine glanced briefly to her left and scowled at Tuline. This was worse than she had been briefed.

'Consular. Secretary.' Herine clacked her tongue. 'What an honour. I have no doubt you are about to exhort me not to execute the messenger.'

Karesidi's laugh was shrill. Around him on the benches, every other delegate was delighted they were not standing and fearful of when they must.

'It is traditional, my Advocate,' he said.

'A feeble attempt at a joke,' said Herine. 'It is also traditional that when the Conquord Senate is convened, the Conquord Senate turns up.'

Herine's words echoed loud, her voice pitched to make them flinch. She continued.

'So speak the words your puppet-master bids you. I will make my decision on your fate when I have heard them. And I should point out to you, to all of you, that my mind is very much open.'

Herine leaned back in her throne. She looked over to Arvan Vasselis. He displayed the disquiet she felt. Poor Arvan. It never did get better for him. Karesidi coughed and cleared his throat.

'Our accounts and levy dues are with the Gatherer delegation for their examination in accordance with our obligations,' he said. And hesitated, wiping at his brow.

'Oh dear,' said Herine. 'Is that really the extent of the good news?'

'We received the mobilisation orders five days ago via messenger service. I received our response just yesterday. You have demanded that we should mobilise six legions. Three are the standing Phaskareen defence force. Three are from the trained reserve. All six to be full complements of four thousand five hundred citizens, and to be despatched to the Gosland and Atreskan borders.'

Karesidi gulped and Herine went cold.

'We cannot fulfil these demands.'

'Cannot, or will not?' asked Herine.

'As our accounts demonstrate, we are unable to pay for such a force. We are not a rich country and we give all that we can. We consider ourselves loyal to the Conquord.'

'I'm so pleased,' said Herine. The atmosphere in the chamber was taut. Karesidi looked about him for support. No one would meet his eye. 'Lonely, isn't it?'

'If we are to remain valid, useful members of the Conquord, we must first secure our local economy and security. Dornos to the north is no longer a friend. Gosland to the east is under pressure. Our muster has not brought the numbers required to send legions to the defence of the Conquord. Only to protect those interests which deliver the levies to the Exchequer.'

'Cannot, or will not?' repeated Herine.

'Both,' said Karesidi, voice a tiny whisper that filled the chamber.

'I see,' said Herine. 'You feel that to best protect yourself, you should allow the enemy to march uncontested all the way to your borders, is that right?'

'I understand your anger—'

'I very much doubt that, Secretary.'

'We cannot supply numbers that would be useful in the field without stripping our own border defences to the bone.'

'Your border defence is that which Gosland shares with Tsard!' shouted Herine. 'Your border defence is that of the Conquord. Phaskar is not an independent nation, it is a territory of the Conquord. And until today, I thought a loyal one. This. This is treason. Unless you can express a different view. Secretary Karesidi.'

'I—' Karesidi gestured at his papers.

'You are just the messenger. Yes, I know. Here is what is difficult for me to understand. Unlike the Dornoseans, you are not telling me you are withdrawing from the Conquord. Am I correct?'

Karesidi nodded.

'And hence you still expect the protection and the economic, trade, transport and administrative support the Conquord offers. Don't answer that, it is blatantly true. So let me remind you, and hence your gutless Marshal, while he remains your Marshal, that a mobilisation order is not an invitation for debate and negotiation. It is a command from the Advocacy. And you will respond in full.'

Karesidi swallowed. 'My Advocate, I regret that we will not.'

Herine, the clamour of fury suffusing her body, saw Marshal Defender Potharin of Tundarra rise from his position on the front bench in front of Karesidi. He loomed large in the Prima Chamber. Potharin was a very tall old man, Marshal for over fifty years, predating Herine's ascension to the Advocacy. He was well built despite his years, heavy-featured and with a strong voice. Typically Tundarran. She awaited his words.

'My Advocate. Herine. It is with the deepest regret that I inform you that our decision is in accord with that of Phaskar. These are hard times. Difficult times, requiring new tactics and open diplomacy, not aggression.'

He wanted to continue but stopped. Herine was aware she was swaying where she stood. Tuline took a pace towards her but Herine waved her away. She sat down heavily and took in a deep breath, trying to clear her mind. Just to her left, Vasselis was gaping at Potharin. Herine felt as if she had been stabbed. God-surround-her, she had been.

'*Tundarra* would let the Tsardon march across Gosland? Gosland whose people stood in defiance of the Tsardon to keep Tundarra free of invasion?' She pointed a finger at Potharin. 'I will send your most famous son to discuss this with you, Potharin. A son whose father's name is carved on the Victory Gates in Estorr.'

'Not even Paul Jhered could change this decision. It is the only one available to us. Don't make this difficult, my Advocate, please. We all know the forces on the Gosland border are not big enough to threaten us. But we have all heard the rumours circulating about what faces Atreska and what has already happened in Gestern. We cannot face them down on three fronts with any hope of success. We must negotiate.'

'I do not negotiate with invaders, just as I do not with traitors. The Conquord is a military might. The Conquord will fight.'

Potharin's expression held a deep regret.

'Then the Conquord is failing,' he said quietly.

Herine jerked in her throne. She looked away from Potharin and to the Gatherer delegation.

'Clear the Prima Chamber,' she said. 'And summon the Advocacy guard to secure the person of the Advocate.'

She gazed out at the ranks of delegates, sitting in mute shock at her words.

'We'll see who is failing. And then we'll see who survives the reckoning. The Senate is dissolved. Get out.'

Chapter Thirty-Two

859th cycle of God, 36th day of Genasrise

'Ossacer Westfallen,' said Felice Koroyan, rolling his name around her tongue. 'The fly seeks mercy from the spider. The enemy walks into the halls of the righteous, seeking redemption.'

'I am neither fly, nor enemy of the Omniscient, Chancellor,' said Ossacer quietly. He knew he'd have to ride out a level of provocation. It was just a question of time. 'Not today. I never have been. I have never wanted to be.'

Koroyan closed the door to the room and walked in a few paces. She didn't approach too close and made no attempt to sit down. Nor did she motion for Ossacer to make himself comfortable.

'You were born my enemy. And with every breath you take you become more so. With every action, you taint the face of God the Omniscient.' Koroyan made the encompassing gesture of the Omniscient over her chest. 'Your presence here is an affront to every citizen in the Conquord.'

She was a powerful figure. Ossacer hadn't really considered it before. She had come into the room alone, utterly confident in herself despite the potential danger in which she placed herself. And she filled the room with her presence. Ossacer couldn't help but be impressed. Her aura pulsed strength. It was deep green, shot with modulating browns, and it touched walls, floor and expanded well beyond, connecting to everyone and everything beyond her current space.

If only she knew how beautiful it looked. How absolutely right it was that she was the head of the Order. All for reasons she would dismiss and consider heresy.

'I have only ever sought to do God's work on this earth. Blessed by my talents and mindful of my responsibility. And I am here in that capacity today.'

'Responsibility.' The Chancellor shook her head and jabbed a finger out of the door. 'Gorian is out there and his version of responsibility means we face invasion.'

'That is Gorian. It is not me. It is not the rest of us.'

'You are the most consummate of deceivers. Even more so than your bastard brother because you use silence and your apparent disability to garner sympathy. It is mind control. I should have you killed and burned where you stand.'

'And I will not stop you.' Ossacer put his hands down by his sides. 'But first, I ask you to hear me.'

The Chancellor smiled and threw up her hands.

'Of course, why not?' She walked towards a recliner and sat down, leaning against an end cushion. 'After all, I am but the Chancellor of the Order of the Omniscient. What else could I possibly desire other than to chatter with my mortal enemies?'

She linked her fingers in prim fashion and placed them in her lap. Ossacer so nearly lost his temper.

'I would have thought your most profound desire would be to protect your devotees from threat, death and the ending of their cycles under God.'

'I have many duties,' said the Chancellor. 'More than you could possibly imagine.'

'Then let me help you stop an inevitable conflict becoming a horrific slaughter where friend and enemy alike will be destroyed with no chance of ever feeling the embrace of God.'

Koroyan waved a hand impatiently. 'War is a necessity. If the Tsardon come at us their destruction is on the conscience of their priests. It does not concern me how they make peace with their false gods.'

'If the rumours are true, if the knowledge I have and the path I have foreseen it will take prove accurate, then most of those who come at us will not be Tsardon. They will be Conquord citizens, ripped from the clutches of God and sent back to shatter the Conquord they once loved.'

The Chancellor laughed. 'You know, it is funny, it really is. The Advocate is forever warning me about my supposedly over-dramatic delivery. Presumably she welcomes yours. Still, at least you have my attention. All I need now is to understand what on God's good earth you are talking about. So speak, Ossacer Westfallen. And then we shall discuss your particular crimes.'

Ossacer nodded. She couldn't keep him here against his will. Perhaps she didn't realise that. She could shoot him dead with arrows but if she chose to imprison him, it would prove a mistake.

'It is quite simple, though you may not choose to believe me. Gorian, we believe, has found a way to reanimate the dead and send them against us.'

'Wait wait stop!' The Chancellor shot to her feet. 'What is this poison? Even for an Ascendant, that statement is an admission of ultimate guilt. You can raise the dead? You want me to believe that?'

Ossacer felt nerves surfacing once again and his stomach turned over. 'I want you to believe that there are rumours, substantiated by witnesses I have spoken to, that Gorian can do this. Not us, Gorian. We, the real Ascendants, are sworn to stop him. We have to kill him.'

'Well there we can agree.' Koroyan walked around the room, shaking her head. 'What ... I can't ...' Eventually she stopped walking and gathered herself. 'Gorian can make the dead walk?'

'So we believe.'

'Right. Stop there. This is heresy of the most heinous kind.'

'I agree—'

'Silence,' she spat. 'How can I believe this? I woke to this morning and drank in the beauty of God's earth and scant hours later you walk in and tell me there is a rot at large that seeks to steal God's people from him. It is preposterous. Why should I believe you? And why should I not just have you put to death here and now. Never mind your latest utterance. I have twenty years of crimes on the books with which to condemn you.'

'Why would I come here, to your house, merely to spout lies and put my life at risk?'

The Chancellor considered that and inclined her head. The anger seemed to drain from her. She returned to the recliner and sat.

'Why must we meddle? The Omniscient provides all that we need every day we draw breath. And when we die, our reward for a life of faith is to know the embrace of our God until He decides we should return to do His work once more. You. You Ascendants, more than any damned scientist, seek to undermine that. And yet you still claim faith.'

'I need your help,' said Ossacer quietly. 'Judge me, judge us, another day.'

'Help?' There were tears in the Chancellor's eyes. 'You would destroy my faith and that of millions and you ask for *my* help? What would you have me do, Ossacer?'

Ossacer was confused. The anger he understood. This was most unexpected.

'Help us not to make the situation worse. You have the ear of the citizenry. They need to know that the Ascendants and the scientists are being pressured into using explosion and fire to bring down our enemies. I cannot countenance it. I will do nothing that harms another person, I will only help and heal. For that I am barred from the classroom. The public can stop us burning the Conquord dead. Stop us scattering their ashes to the wind like convicted murderers denied the continuance of their cycles. Help us find Gorian. They won't believe me. They will believe you.'

The Chancellor's expression cleared.

'Go back to the Hill and make your peace with God. Despite your words, I cannot believe we share the same one. But you, I can at least respect for the possession of a conscience. You think you are clever, coming here. That this will somehow change my view of the Ascendancy and its place in this world. That perhaps I might even forgive you.

'But you are mistaken, Ossacer. You have seen in this room the depth of my belief and my despair. And now you will see the depth of my anger. Go. And if you take my advice, you will remove yourself from this life before the flames find you.'

'What are they doing to me? To our Conquord?'

Herine could hear the pleading in her voice but no longer cared. She had retired to her private reception rooms in the Prima Chamber. Guards stood on every door, while the Gatherers were working through the accounts submitted by Phaskar and Tundarra. And with Herine were Tuline and Arvan Vasselis. It didn't matter if she cried in front of either of them.

'They are frightened, Herine,' said Vasselis. 'They do what we all do, look to their own.'

'I don't.' Herine beat her chest. 'My own is the whole Conquord. And so is theirs. Have I taught them nothing? Has my family really been stitching together a cloak of lies to cover the thoughts of traitors? Estorea has given them everything they have today. Now they turn and I do not even know why. Ten years ago I would have understood.

But today, the threat is as much rumour as it is substance.'

'They simply aren't ready, or don't think they are,' said Vasselis. 'They believe their enemies are beginning to close in and they have lost f—'

She gazed at him.

'You can say it, Arvan. Faith. Where did I go wrong? Are the Ascendants to blame?'

'Why would you think that?' asked Vasselis.

'Because if there is one point when history sees my rule slip, it will be when I welcomed them in and made them a part of the Advocacy, despite the religious confusion it caused.'

'I disagree. Tsard came back before we were ready. Had they waited another two years, there would be no such questions. Don't kill yourself over things you cannot change. Think on what you can. There are states loyal to you. We've had representations from Avarn, Neratharn, Gosland and Atreska in this past hour. We are still strong.' Vasselis gripped her arm. In his eyes, there was a flicker of the past.

'But where is Gestern? Where is Katrin Mardov?'

'We all know Katrin. None of her travelling delegation have arrived. It can only be something has delayed her. Pray that it is not what we fear is coming.'

Herine nodded. 'Damn them. Can you believe Tundarra? Potharin is like an uncle. Or he was. He is sworn protector of Roberto. And he's betrayed us.'

'It is difficult to comprehend,' agreed Vasselis.

'Isn't it just. And he, Dornos, Phaskar, Morasia ... they will all come to understand their error. I want every loyal Conquord official out of those countries and back in Estorr at the soonest. I want borders closed. I want trade halted. I want them to understand what isolation from the Conquord means. I will bankrupt them all. Break them.'

'You can't do that, Mother,' said Tuline.

Herine drained her goblet of wine. 'Can't I?'

'No,' said Tuline.

Herine blinked. She looked at her daughter. Tall, compared to Herine. A little plain, too. But slender and regal, with those piercing dark eyes that all the Del Aglios women possessed. The red veil fell from Herine's eyes. A shudder ran through her. She frowned.

'Why can't I?'

Tuline smoothed down her toga, stood up and walked to a set of shelves near the table around which they sat. She returned with a thick sheaf of papers.

'This is why,' she said, dropping them on the table. A dull thud rattled the crockery.

'I'm not going to do the thing you want me to,' said Herine. 'Just tell me and don't make a meal of it.'

'I was getting reports and rumours as soon as the mobilisation orders went out. The standing delegates here at the palace, the Tundarrans, Phaskareen and Morasians in particular were making disgruntled noises. But there was an arrogance about them. They were talking together and you didn't need to hear what they said to know their collective state of mind.'

Tuline began to spread out the papers.

'This is detail, and I don't think it is exhaustive, of every contract we have with the rebel states, if I can term them that.'

'It is a more polite term than I would choose but it will serve,' said Herine.

She was staring at her daughter with new eyes and when she caught Vasselis's gaze, he raised his eyebrows and she smiled, feeling a growing pride. Tuline kept her head down, looking at the contracts.

'We have deals for iron and steel from Morasia. The finest horse breeders beyond Caraduk and Estorea are all in Phaskar, as you know. We buy a lot of horses from them. Tundarran timber and cloth is the best outside of Sirrane. Their leather goods are pretty good too. Then there are the arable fields of northern Phaskar, the livestock drivers of the Tundarran plains and the—'

'All right, all right, I get it,' said Herine. 'But I will not deny you your moment of glory, dear daughter, so say it.'

'What?'

The look of innocence on Tuline's face was comical.

'Just say what it was you were going to.'

'If we are going to fight and win the coming war, we cannot break off trading or diplomatic relations with these people. And they know it.'

Herine threw up her hands. 'So how the hell am I going to satisfy my anger and lust for revenge?'

It was a moment before Tuline realised she was joking and burst out laughing.

'Well I don't know, Mother. I said we couldn't break off relations.

I didn't say we had to make it easy. They may know we need them. But we know that they need us too. Right now, this is a unity of desperation.'

'There's something else too,' said Vasselis. 'Diminished though we may be temporarily, the Conquord commands an awful lot more muscle than they do, even should they combine, which they won't. We could, if we wanted, invade any one of them and they could not stand before us.'

'But we won't do that,' said Herine. 'Come on.'

'They don't know that. And there's no harm in dropping hints of a questionable accuracy, now is there?' Vasselis smiled. 'Enough to gorge your anger on?'

'For now,' said Herine. 'And thank you, Arvan.'

'And just think,' said Tuline. 'The rebels are gambling on a lengthy conflict leaving us committed along two thousand miles of borders with Tsard. Consider where it leaves us if we can win this war quickly.'

'Tuline, you have grown today more than in any other day of your life on this earth. I have always been proud you are my daughter but today, you have proved my faith in you and that is a greater gift than you know.'

Tuline blushed and Herine leaned across to plant a kiss on her forehead.

'Orders, my Advocate?' asked Vasselis.

'Get me an aggregate of what we do have, where it is and where it is going. I need it for dawn tomorrow when we three are all leaving to return to Estorr, where we will meet our Marshal General and, with any luck, Paul Jhered carrying Gorian's head on a plate.

'Let's win this war quickly, eh? I've got revenge to consider.'

Chapter Thirty-Three

859th cycle of God, 36th day of Genasrise

'Julius!' Roberto's voice echoed across the bleak face of the crag. 'Hang on. Don't fall now. Don't let go. The Omniscient will give you strength.'

Julius Barias was weakening. His position was difficult and draining. Roberto's fingers, hands and feet were on fire but he knew he could hang on. Julius was clinging to the crag face across the path from Roberto. Both men were fifteen feet from the ground. When the wave of disease or whatever it was, had washed up the slope and the panic around the crag path had dissolved into bloodshed, he had yelled for any who would hear him to climb the rock.

Ten or more had followed his lead. Three had fallen back and had died choking on spores and filth. He and Julius had clung on and climbed as far as they could. The other five, Dahnishev and four medics, had been far more fortunate, finding a ledge and secure foot and handholds. They waited twenty feet above and to Roberto's right. Roberto had refused their offers of help.

The scene at the base of the path and up inside it had been dreadful. It would live with Roberto for the rest of his life. Experienced legionaries chopping down their comrades and scrambling over their bodies to get to the path. Hauling off those already on the ropes to clear a space for themselves. Only one voice had tried to maintain order. Pavel Nunan. Roberto had seen him engulfed by his own legionaries.

And then the wave had struck them all. It had washed over those trapped on the ground and grabbed up higher and higher on the path, consuming men and women who were crammed together as they tried to get away. But the Work could not jump the gap between living and dead. It did not climb the bare rock. Silence had fallen broken only by the desperate scrambling of the survivors higher up the path.

The shouts of those on the crag reached them a little later, exhorting them to hold on, that help would come. That had been two hours ago and it had become clear to Roberto that there was not enough rope to lower down to them and he had forbidden them to descend the path to use the rope still set there.

'I can't,' said Julius, desperate and terrified.

'You can,' said Roberto. 'Yes, you can. Remember how you want me tried by you in the presence of the Advocate? Remember that? Use it, Julius. Don't you give up.'

Roberto had his face flat against the rock. He looked across the path and at the Speaker. Julius was staring at him, not knowing what to think or say.

'It doesn't matter now,' he said eventually.

'It does if it keeps you hanging on there. They'll move on soon and then we can move. Want to stop me burning more of your flock? Then hang on.'

Julius smiled, laughed. It was an incongruous expression and sound. 'You're provoking me.'

'Trying to,' said Roberto. 'Anger gives strength and determination.'

'I've misjudged you,' he said.

'I doubt it, Julius. My position hasn't changed. Neither has yours.' Roberto flexed a cramping finger. He dare not move his feet. The crack into which he'd pressed his toes was tiny and dusty. Slippery. 'But right now, we need every man and woman to live. That includes you and me. Don't become one of them, Julius, or I'll want to burn you too.'

The dead were walking across the ruined ground. The rising stench was eye-watering, appalling. It was like something five days dead in the heat. Rank odours floated from the rotten ground. Flies had begun to gather. Tsardon and Conquord dead gathered as they rose. Those Roberto had managed to glimpse were covered in boils and sores and with a sickly green tinge to their skins. When they exhaled, clouds of spores spewed out.

Ever since they had begun to rise, Roberto had been praying they would move off. The black mat of the Work had long since faded. He felt sure the ground would be safe. But right now, to drop there would be to die. Every dead man or woman had sword and shield in hand.

And there was an order to what they did. They were forming up at the base of the crag where the ground was clear.

So far they hadn't thought to climb the rope up the crag path. Perhaps the dead could only be given a single, simple instruction. Either the whole force would attempt the climb or none of them would. Roberto didn't think Gorian would waste his time. Thousands of dead were gathering along the line of the crag, silent but for the sporadic chink of metal on metal. They waited. Roberto was worried about why. He feared one of the living coming to move among them. While the dead had not looked above the horizontal, no living man could fail to see the helpless few Conquord citizens trapped on the crag.

Julius was speaking again. Roberto looked at him and his heart fell. The Speaker was leaning out from the wall, looking down at the dead mustering there. What Roberto had first heard was a muttered prayer but now his voice was rising. Roberto didn't like the way it was going.

'Turn away from the path of evil. Lie back down. Feel the embrace of God again. This is not your cycle renewed. Join me in praying for those who walk with you. Let me walk among you and show you the way to the Omniscient's bosom. He who commands you is not God but man. Set your will against him. Stop him. I will help you. I will come down to you.'

'Julius. Don't even think about it.'

'They have to listen to me, Ambassador.' Julius's voice was choked. 'Look at them. Confused. Alone even though they stand in a crowd. I cannot save myself while so many are abandoned.'

'Julius, look at me. Please.'

The Speaker turned his head. His eyes were gone, unfocused. They darted everywhere. His breathing was furious and his face held an expression that burned with righteous action.

'No one will save those who do not try to save another,' said Julius.

'You don't understand. They will not hear you. They will try to kill you. Make you one of them.'

'I have to try.'

'Save it for those who can hear you.'

'They will hear me,' said Julius.

He let go his hands.

'No!'

Julius Barias dropped to the ground, landing lightly and rolling to avoid hurting his legs. He was no more than three feet from the nearest dead man. Above Roberto, Dahnishev and his medics were shouting, urging the Speaker back to the crag path, and their cries were joined by echoes from above. Roberto clung on and watched.

The dead ignored him and initially, Julius ignored them too. His eye had been caught by something else away to the left. Gorian's army continued to muster and at last, began to march away down the slope towards the road. They were clearing from below Roberto. It was as ordered as it was repulsive. And it least it gave Julius a ghost of a chance of survival.

The Speaker was kneeling near the freshly filled graves. Roberto strained to look. There was a shimmer in the air over them. Either that or Roberto had some tick in his eye because it looked like the earth was moving. Julius spread his arms wide and spoke words that Roberto didn't quite catch. A hand sprang from the earth, grasping at the air, and Roberto all but lost his grip. He felt a wave of nausea roll over him. Julius cried out too and began to shout.

'O God, the Omniscient, let your people rest. Blessed by your servant, they should be safe in your embrace and yet still they move. Do not punish them further for their misfortune. They come to you damaged of body but whole in will. God the Omniscient, I beseech you.'

The whole grave was rippling now as if the dead below responded directly to Julius. Headless corpses but still Gorian had given them life again. They were useless to him and yet he tormented them. Though surely they could feel nothing, the violation of their rest was enraging Julius. Roberto felt the same way.

Adranis ...

Roberto began to move down the crag face. Dahnishev was shouting at him to stop but he wouldn't hear. The dead had moved from below him and even had they not it would have made no difference.

'Roberto. Stay where you are.'

'My brother!' he shouted, voice catching in his throat. 'That bastard has brought my brother back.'

'No, Roberto,' called Dahnishev. 'It is not. It is just flesh made to move. Your brother is gone. Hear your own words. Please.'

'My brother,' he repeated and dropped the last few feet to the ground.

He ran towards the graves. Julius was praying now. Roberto slid down next to him, making the Omniscient symbol at his chest. Across this grave and the others further right, the fresh piled soil vibrated. Roberto could see a dozen arms and parts of torsos that had broken through the shallow layer covering them.

'Keep going, Julius,' he said. 'Please give them rest. Give my brother rest.'

'They can't hear me, Ambassador. I have begged them to lie still and seek our Lord but they won't. I don't understand.' He looked at Roberto. Tears stained his face. 'What are you doing down here?'

There was renewed shouting. Dahnishev again. Roberto saw him waving and pointing away in the direction of the road.

'Saving you, I think. The dead are coming back.'

'I can help them. They will listen because they can see.'

'You will do no such thing.'

But Julius was already up and moving. Back along the base of the crag. Roberto strode after him. He drew his gladius and felt totally vulnerable. Armour but no shield. Moving back up the rise, Roberto could see thirty or more of the dead heading towards them. They would reach the crag path before the dead but Julius was not interested in a climb. A small unit of dead, acting independently of the mass.

Roberto frowned. 'How is that possible?'

'Faithful of the Omniscient. Come to me.' Julius had his arms outstretched. 'Pray with me. Turn back from your path.'

'Julius, stop,' said Roberto. 'This is madness.'

And it was. Dahnishev was bawling at him from his ledge above the action. The rest of his medics wanted Roberto to climb the crag path. The dead were ten yards beyond it. Julius was marching towards them, blind to the risk, lost in his belief.

'They will kill you. You can't help them.'

'The Omniscient's arms will always be open to you. I know you believe. The voice in your head is not your God.'

'Julius!' roared Roberto.

He stopped. Julius was not listening. Roberto stood at the base of the crag path. The Speaker was a few paces ahead and a few more from the advancing dead. The sight of them did not deter him. Within his madness he had courage at least. The dead were focused on Julius while others still moved across the slope to join the mass heading for the road.

Roberto found the scene surreal. In this lifeless landscape, standing on the sludge of rotten grass among the debris of trees destroyed, he watched dead people, blistered and green-hued, stride towards a man who wanted to save them. They might even be aware of that but a compulsion within them took the compassion from their eyes. Each had a sword. Many had shields. Conquord men were at the head but in the group, Tsardon walked too. Roberto's mind screamed at him to get up the path while he still could but a stronger force forbade him move.

Julius had stopped walking now. His head was held high and he spoke directly to them. He was praying for them, speaking the names of those he recognised, willing them to stop and see. But they just kept walking. A blade slashed out. Julius leapt backwards, the edge missing his stomach by a hair. His voice did not falter. Indeed it strengthened. The dead began to close around him in an arc. They would surround him. Cut him down.

'Back off, Julius. Don't throw your life away,' said Roberto, moving towards him once more, meaning to grab him and pull him bodily from his own demise.

Another blade stabbed at Julius, and another. One caught his arm, cutting through cloth and into flesh. The other whistled just above his head. Julius stumbled backwards, slipped and fell. Roberto ran the few paces to him. The dead were on them. He hacked at the nearest leg, chopping deep into flesh. The legionary fell sideways, catching another and bringing her down. The march was disrupted for a heartbeat. Roberto grabbed Julius's uninjured arm and hauled him backwards towards the crag path.

'Julius, get up, get up.'

Julius turned his head to Roberto, displaying a face from which the veil of confusion had been lifted. Now he was blank with fear.

'I don't—'

'Up!'

Roberto was still dragging him over the slick ground. The dead advanced at their even pace. The man whom Roberto had chopped down could not walk but dragged himself across the ground, still intent on his perverse duty. Julius was trying to get to his feet but couldn't get them under him.

'Up, Speaker Barias.' Roberto wrapped an arm around his chest and hauled him to his feet, half choking him as his arm slipped up to the Speaker's neck. 'And climb. Don't look back.'

Roberto pushed him towards the path and stepped up to face the dead. He ducked a slash and kicked the feet from under his attacker. Keeping himself moving forwards, he stayed in a crouch and turned his body in hard, shoulder impacting with a second dead. The woman overbalanced, fell backwards. Roberto threw himself to the right. A sword struck the ground next to his left foot. He rolled further. The dead turned to face him. An idea spawned.

He got to his feet and backed away, heading down the slope towards the castle. Slowly.

'That's it,' he said. 'This way. Come this way. Just a few paces.'

Julius had made it to the cliff path and was watching. Roberto could see that not all the dead had taken his bait. If this really meant independent thought, the Conquord was in even more trouble than Roberto had feared.

'Climb, Julius.'

Roberto couldn't afford to draw the dead away very far. Down the slope he could see hundreds more had gathered. All were Tsardon. And on the road, yet more. From this distance he couldn't see if they were living or dead but the fact that there was no noise coming from them; no rank and file chatter, no songs and no shouted orders left him in little doubt. He shook his head, unable to fully conceive the magnitude of Gorian's crime.

He began to circle back towards the crag. He'd only strayed ten yards from it. He glanced at the path. Julius wasn't climbing. He was backing away towards the writhing graves.

'No! Idiot. Go up, it's your only chance.'

Roberto broke into a run. The dead tracked his movement. But from the back of their party, others broke off to close the gap to the crag path. Julius had stopped again. His head turned this way and that.

'Up! Climb the bloody path. God-surround-me, climb.'

It was too late. Roberto slid to a stop by Julius. The first of the dead had reached the path. Others were joining him. Those that Roberto had led away were coming back. Still more were heading back up from the road. And as Roberto looked on, his heart fell. They dead began to climb. He rammed his sword back into its scabbard.

'Congratulations, Julius, I think you've killed us both.'

'They wouldn't listen,' he said. 'They couldn't hear me.'

Roberto grabbed his shoulders. The dead closed in on them.

'I told you. I tried to tell you but you wouldn't listen. They are lost to you, don't you get it?' He shook Julius, got some reaction at least. 'Come on. Only one way to go now.'

He turned Julius and began to run him down the crag towards the river, not sure quite what he'd do when they got there. Dahnishev was still shouting at him. The surgeon and his team were trapped now. No way down, no way up. Roberto stopped and turned.

'Then you're like me, Dahnishev! You'll have to wait until they're gone. Pray, old friend, that we see each other again.'

Roberto shoved Julius in the back and made him move again.

'That I should be stuck with you of all people,' he said. 'You'd better make yourself useful or so help me, I will leave you behind.'

'Where are we going?' asked Julius, breathing hard as they ran.

'Back to Estorr. What else is there? And don't worry about your damned lost flock. Because I can promise you that you'll see them all again at the gates of the Hill. Now run. Can you swim?'

'I ... yes, I can.'

'Good, because I doubt anyone left a boat moored down at the river bank and I am not about to knock on the castle gates and ask for one.'

Trying not to think too hard about his predicament, Roberto ran from the dead, ran from the legion, ran for his life.

Chapter Thirty-Four

859th cycle of God, 36th day of Genasrise

Gorian fell back on the bed and his hand came away from Kessian's shoulder. The Gor-Karkulas relaxed.

'Keep the path closed to them. And the road. They won't get far.'

'I think we lost them,' said Kessian.

'But we learned so much,' said Gorian. 'Just look what we can make our people do.'

'But it costs a lot of energy to split them so small,' said Kessian.

'Yes it does. Yet there are times it might be necessary.'

'It makes them weak, the ones we split away.'

'But we can return them to the mass and there be strong again.' Gorian rubbed his face and sat up. He stared at Kessian. 'You felt this all by yourself?'

Kessian nodded.

'You learn fast.' Gorian fell back on the bed again. 'I'm exhausted and I still have to contact Atreska and Gestern. Kessian, go out with the Karkulas and my Lords Tydiol and Runok. We have to track the enemy.'

'What about that man you want?'

'We have him trapped,' said Gorian. 'Now go on. Our people need their leaders. I'll join you later. Don't go far. I don't think our trapped enemy has plans to run. They'll want to watch us, so keep out of sight.'

Silence grew as their footsteps died away. Gorian felt he could sleep for three days but his work was not yet done. The excitement of raising six thousand, and the realisation of the power they gained from being among so many of their kind was still with him. The ability to split their tasks if only temporarily. And the thrill of the brief chase for Del Aglios who had revealed himself through the eyes of one of his own legionaries so recently taken to stand by Gorian.

'And I will get you, Del Aglios.'

If Gorian was honest with himself, he felt quite ill, not just exhausted. A consequence of the dark energies he had sent up the slope. Another wonderful result, another successful experiment harvesting so many undamaged dead. But there was residue in him that he was fighting off. He laughed to himself, wishing just for a moment that he was Ossacer and could dismiss disease on an instant. He would work it out. Later. Other matters were more pressing.

Gorian settled himself and let the energy maps coalesce in his mind's eye. Thousands upon thousands of gossamer threads emanated from his body and fled away to every point of the compass. Thick knots of slowly pulsing energies led to Kessian and through him to the two Gor-Karkulas. Here rested the structures that were the Works keeping the dead animated. They were intense orbs of incandescent blue from which the individual strands that linked to each dead writhed away.

Those energy lines that tracked away through earth and under sea to more distant places were those that interested Gorian now. These were barely visible filaments but still one existed between Gorian and each one of the dead walking and fighting for him in Atreska and Gestern. The Gor-Karkulas merely boosted his own strength. He could feel them, his dead, and if he concentrated, he could channel his thoughts. His greatest discovery had been the ability to maintain these links without conscious, constant thought. It was the beauty of the earth; the greatest rumbling circuit of them all.

Gorian breathed deep and pushed out along these distance lines. Fed by the slumbering muscle of the earth itself, those extraordinary powers that fed earthquake and volcano; using amplification points along the way where the energy concentrated and leading to the lights that represented the Gor-Karkulas travelling with the Tsardon, the Dead Lords and his people.

Without Kessian by him, he was too tired to go further than his chosen Karkulas but he could at least use the Karku priest.

'I am here,' he said.

Gorian felt a ripple back through the lifelines. It was a reflexive defence. The Karkulas couldn't know how to respond proactively but he was uncomfortable with Gorian's intrusion into his life map nonetheless. They had been quelled very quickly, these Karku. Having promised resistance to all Gorian and King Khuran desired, they understood almost immediately that Gorian could use them whether or not they gave consent.

They had threatened to starve themselves but the Tsardon had demonstrated a willingness to force-feed and Gorian had been happy to call their bluff. The Karkulas feared him, he knew that. They could sense the power within the Ascendant even if they did not fully understand it. And he let them know he understood the implications of their deaths on the whole of Karku society. In return for their compliance he had promised them their safety and ultimate return to the Heart Shrine.

For the moment the Karkulas were acquiescent. They hated Gorian but he could live with that. He was used to it.

The Karkulas couldn't respond directly through the energy map but he could speak. Gorian heard the words (or those of the people speaking to the priest) through the Karku's ears. Again, the understanding had been so simple to come by in the end. In the same way that Ossacer used life energies against the blankness of stone to draw a mind map of the world to counter his blindness, so it was possible to interpret the modulations of energy in the ear and reproduce them as sound in his own. It was the same with his remote sight.

'What do you want?' said the Karkulas.

It would always give Gorian a thrill. It had to be five hundred miles as the crow flew to the army of Tsardon and dead marching through Atreska. More than fifteen hundred miles between him and the devastation in Gestern that was quickly approaching the capital city of Skiona and the principal port of Portbrial. That was for later.

'I will speak with Lord Hasheth,' said Gorian. 'And you will open your eyes. Don't forget that though I am a long way from you, I can still hurt you.'

The world slowly swam into view. It revealed a stark picture of the march, most resembling a child's painting. Colours brightly drawn, shaped with hard edges. The Karkulas was sitting in an open cart, facing backwards over open ground. He was unbound, surrounded by Tsardon. He moved his head quickly from side to side, giving Gorian uncomfortable blurring images. He responded, feeding cold through the lines of the earth.

'I do not need all six of you,' said Gorian. 'Face forward, keep your head still and get me Hasheth.'

Gorian heard the Karkulas ask for Hasheth to be brought to him.

He didn't hear the response. The Karkulas turned, making sure to move his head quickly and bounce his body around. Gorian chose to remain silent this time. Ahead of him, the Tsardon army were in a loose marching column. They were travelling across the wide open spaces of Atreska, heading for the border with Neratharn. The dead would be a fair distance in front of the living. The Tsardon warriors were openly hostile to the dead, only Khuran keeping them in check. Two Dead Lords and two Karkulas marshalled the dead in rotation. Hasheth, the preferred, was soon in Gorian's vision, climbing into the front of the ox-cart.

'My Master,' he said.

'You still move well?'

'The King has set a healthy pace,' replied Hasheth. 'And there is still no resistance though we are tracked and observed.'

'And my people?'

'Well enough. Your efforts maintain them in better condition than those on the snows of Kark but there is attrition. We need to harvest more.'

Gorian chuckled. 'The Atreskans have done what the Gesterners did not. But I do not see the Neratharnese simply opening their gates, do you?'

'No, Master,' said Hasheth. 'Your progress is assured?'

'I have been forced to bring forward the plan but we remain strong and are chasing down the remainder of the opposition. They are broken.'

He felt Hasheth's hesitation rather than saw it. Nuances were lost in the vision afforded him.

'The prince?'

'Is content and whole,' said Gorian.

'I understand. We await your instructions.'

'No need for anything precipitate before Neratharn. The King and the Tsardon must have their time on the battlefield. A warrior must feel flesh beneath his blade.'

The soldiers around the wagon grunted approval. Hasheth nodded his head.

'I hear you,' he said.

'Good. Relate our success to the King. Assure him of my allegiance. We are unstoppable. I will speak with you again tomorrow.'

Gorian broke connection. He would have sat up but a wave of

tiredness swept over him and his stomach turned over. Gestern would have to wait. He needed to rest.

The panic had subsided, the running had stopped and a bizarre altered reality had fallen on the survivors of the wave of disease that had consumed so many. Most of the cavalry had survived and the majority of them were in a dense block across the road about a mile from the crag and in clear sight of any enemies coming at them from the castle. Scouts had already been despatched. They would not stop all day and had been tasked to make contact with the force travelling on the slopes high above them that led into the Farian Mountains.

Kell had remained on the road. Not thirty yards away, the surviving Tsardon were gathered. They were leaderless and confused. Kell knew how they felt. Following the escape, when it became clear that quite suddenly, they were outnumbered and amongst two hundred Conquord horsemen and a similar number of angry legionaries, the Tsardon had grown suspicious.

There had been scuffles and enemies who had helped each other away were separated and the sides drawn up again. But Kell had no intention whatever of attacking them and she was sure the Tsardon felt the same. She stood by her horse as did the rest of her riders and she waited.

'No taunts, no breaking of ranks,' she said, voice echoing against the rock to their right as they faced the Tsardon. 'Remember our role is to protect our infantry and non-combatants.'

Kell turned her head at the sound of a throat being cleared.

'Yes, Captain?'

'Fine words,' he said quietly. 'But they won't buy it. Tsardon on our soil. What are you going to do?'

Kell shook her head. 'Tricky. Can't send them back or they'll only end up dead, we assume. And actually, I'm rather interested to find out what their scouts have to say.'

'If they choose to tell us.'

'I don't think they'll consider they have a choice.'

Kell wasn't kept waiting long. She saw Tsardon warriors run back into the midst of their group, two hundred and fifty-odd at a rough count. There was talking that became shouting, finger pointing and pushing and shoving. Eventually, a decision was made and a man separated himself from his comrades and walked towards the Conquord cavalry. Kell gave the reins of her horse to her captain and went out to meet him.

'Keep watching. If I'm attacked, ride them down.'

'Yes, General.'

Kell stopped after a dozen paces and waited for the Tsardon warrior to come to her. He was quite senior by his insignia, probably a prosentor. His armour was scratched from his hurried escape and his expression was uncertain. His face was unshaven, his long hair gathered in a pony tail. He was a big man but he had no confidence in his step.

'I am Prosentor Ruthrar of the Tsardon kingdom, a commander of the north-eastern armies.' His Estorean was passable. Better than her Tsardon, certainly.

'I am General Dina Kell, second Estorean, the Bear Claws. And you are on Conquord territory. What is it you want?'

Kell was aware that not a sound was coming from her people. She could imagine them straining for any hint of what was being discussed.

'Passage south,' he said. 'In exchange for information.'

Kell raised her eyebrows. 'Why don't you simply turn round? We will not stop you returning to Tsard.'

'That is the information.'

Kell shook her head. 'He's killed everyone, hasn't he? Friend and foe alike.'

'It seems we are all his foes now.'

'And you are short on friends. Seems you chose poorly, doesn't it?'

Kell could find no satisfaction in the turn of events. It could easily make matters worse, not better. And despite the fact the man before her was an enemy, she found she had sympathy for him as a soldier. She had never experienced the cold grip of betrayal and seeing him, she didn't ever want to.

'We must unite against a common enemy.'

Her sympathy evaporated. 'You brought him here. You gave him the manpower to make his perverted dreams a reality.'

The prosentor inclined his head. 'You will have no love for my people. But you were one who helped an injured Tsardon from the road. You do understand.'

'I understand that no man should suffer the fate of the walking dead. And I do not blame a conscript for the decisions of his superiors. But here I have two hundred and fifty of a nation who we have been fighting for over fifteen years. And you want passage to where?'

Ruthrar smiled. 'We both have a problem and at heart, they are similar. I want passage to a place where I can contact my king and tell him what has befallen his son and six thousand of his warriors.'

'Well, that's honest at least,' said Kell. 'And where is your king?'

'Marching through Atreska.'

Kell raised her eyebrows. 'You know that for sure? I am aware of a considerable defence on the Atreskan border and significant legion presence. We have only just retaken Atreska. We will not give it back.'

Ruthrar made to respond and Kell didn't like the expression on his face. It was almost apologetic and it was unsettling. But there were raised voices behind him. He raised his hand, nodded his head and didn't respond to her statement.

'We must all move. Lord Westfallen's army is close and marching. We will not turn back to them. We do not want to fight you to get away but we will if you force us. Please, General. A stand-off will not help us. Any dead add to the enemy strength.'

'How far back are they?'

'In your measures, less than half a mile. They are moving slowly but . . .'

Kell had no choice.

'Then we go. Can you ride?'

'I am from the southern steppes.'

'Good. Your warriors will march ahead of my cavalry. You will ride with me. You still have much to tell me. If any of your people break, we will ride them down. You may retain your weapons only because we have no way to carry them and I will leave nothing behind. But you will consider yourselves my prisoners. Is that clear?'

Ruthrar nodded. 'But some of my people should shadow the enemy.'

'Not a chance. My riders will do that.'

'I understand.'

'Then let's move. The dead will not wait.'

Roberto sat with his head in his hands and listened to the dead march away. The vibration through the ground had been sickening and frightening. He'd had to stop Julius calling out and had quickly moved them to rocky ground overlooking the sluggish river, out of sight of both castle and slope. The once-verdant ground where they'd stopped initially on escaping the dead was rotting. Gorian had used all its life force in creating his disease. Quite the most repellent use of Ascendant power barring raising the dead, and Roberto had seen more than most. He couldn't shake the vision of the writhing in the grave. His brother, tormented in death.

'What will we do now?' asked Julius.

It was barely mid-morning and Roberto felt he had already lived a lifetime today. He wanted to sleep but he knew he wouldn't escape the visions there. He wanted to shout his fury and impotence to act. He wanted to dig his brother up and find him whole and alive. And he wanted to punch Speaker Julius Barias so hard that he could never speak again.

Roberto stared at Julius. The Speaker was sitting slightly below him and gazing into the river. He was streaked with mud and the filth of the rotten hillside and there was a trail of blood coming from a cut on his left shoulder.

'Why did you do it?'

'Do what?' Julius turned to him.

'Drop down like that. Try to save the irredeemable. What possessed you?'

'A good minister never abandons his faithful,' said Julius. 'No matter the risk. Why did you do what you did?'

'You know what, I have absolutely no idea. Had I really thought about it, I don't suppose I would have bothered. Oh, sorry, was that not the reaction you were looking for? I suppose I could have said something glib like "a good heir to the Advocate never abandons his Order ministers, whatever the risk" but frankly, in your case that would be a lie.

'You'll be sitting there thinking me immature and embittered I expect and that's fine by me. I've just lost my brother. I have just seen Pavel Nunan engulfed by a tide of disease, die and then drag himself back to his feet and march away, now my enemy. I've just seen an army of the dead march into my mother's Conquord and I'm stuck with the last person on God's good earth that I would choose to be with in a crisis; a man who wants me tried and burned.

'You want to know what's next? Well, at nightfall, I'm going to snoop around that castle to see if I can find anything useful. A boat seems the most useful thing. I am then going to make my way as quickly as possible back to Estorr while warning every one I meet about what is coming at them. You can come with me if you can keep up, and if you keep quiet. But if you put my life at risk one more time,

I will not hesitate to cut you down and leave you to rot, do I make myself clear?

'You might have enjoyed the protection of Kell and Nunan and the Bear Claws until you jumped in to try and spare the dead but just in case you're in any doubt, Nunan now walks with the dead and Kell's fate is as yet unknown. Out here it's just you and me, and I don't notice a sword at your belt.'

Julius said nothing and by the look on his face, he wasn't about to.

'Good,' said Roberto. 'Stay scared and you might just stay alive. Just follow my lead.'

Julius frowned. 'You're scared too?'

'Never more so.'

Chapter Thirty-Five

859th cycle of God, 37th day of Genasrise

They had managed to scratch together a few hours of broken sleep, taking it in turns to watch the river and, if they had a mind, the approach to the castle. Roberto watched more than he slept. Adranis wouldn't leave him. He was so close and his smile invaded every dream. And each time Roberto began to return the smile he saw it was fixed to a decapitated head and lying on the blood-stained ground.

Barias had been plagued by nightmares too, or perhaps he was just wrestling with his conscience in his sleep. Roberto thought several times about leaving him and going on alone, but knew it would be unwise. Two was better than one when you had nothing. No water, no food and precious little in the way of hope. Marooned the wrong side of the invading army.

Well before dawn, and having observed no light whatever, Roberto and Julius walked along the river's edge to the castle, keeping just above the steep bank. The dank rotten ground masked their footsteps and they skirted along the side of the road, hugging the shadows of castle out-buildings to bring them right to the main rear gates which stood wide open.

The night was full of sound. The river under the bridge, slapping echoes against the concrete piles. The wind mourning through myriad shattered openings where timbers, glass and coverings had been torn away by the hurricane. The flat smack of a door in its frame. Curious that the place didn't stink of death given what Roberto suspected had happened here. No rot on the stone flags.

The castle was plainly abandoned but it shouldn't have been. Tsardon should have remained to guard the escape route, man the onagers that stood on the gate fort across the bridge and probably above him on the castle's artillery platform. No supply organisation had been put into place with this perfect building as its administrative hub.

But then, Gorian was no soldier and it was even more clear, if clarity was needed, that no soldiers were alive to tell him how to go about his invasion. The thought should have brought Roberto some comfort but there was none to be had. Why did he have need of a supply chain when the dead marched on the power of his Work. Puzzling out how might give them the edge they needed to beat him but Roberto needed an Ascendant for that. Meanwhile, anything he could find here would have to do.

Roberto made to walk inside but felt Barias's hand on his shoulder.

'You're sure? You don't even have your gladius drawn.'

'There's no one here, Julius. Just you and me and the scene of a mass murder.'

'We might find food and drink here, then.'

'Entirely likely. You coming?'

Barias nodded and Roberto stepped in through the huge gates. The assembly yard was enfolded in darkness. Roberto kept to the left-hand wall and traced his hand along it until he found a doorway. The wide open space of the yard loomed cold and full of dread memories to his right. As his eyes began adjusting to the dark, he could make out shapes on the ground. Not bodies. Clothing and equipment perhaps.

Roberto fumbled for the door. It had been his and Adranis's room. There were lantern brackets either side of it and unless they had been moved, a flint, steel and oiled tapers atop a low wooden shelf just inside. He listened for any sounds coming from within before unlatching the door and pushing it inwards. There was a low creak and Roberto shivered in spite of himself. The room was dark. It smelled of recent occupation; ash, soap and sweat.

Roberto felt to the side of the door, unwilling to go in. The dark inside held a malevolent quality. Gorian had been here, maybe even slept here. Roberto's hand closed on what he was looking for, sitting in a tray.

'Good,' he said.

He placed the tray on the ground and quickly sorted out the equipment. Lighting fires in the dark was something he'd learned in the legions and a tiny smile crossed his lips. Like most, he'd cut himself on the flint, scraped skin and managed to burn his fingertips. Not this time. The taper flared very bright in the dark. The lanterns were still hanging on their hooks. He lit them both and handed one to Julius.

'Well, if there's anyone else here, they'll know where to come, won't they?'

Roberto raised his lantern and looked into the assembly yard. As far as the light went, there were pieces of clothing, blankets, sections of armour and backpacks scattered across the floor. There were jugs, plates, goblets and the stains of old food and drink.

'Hungry, Julius?'

'Starving.'

'Well, the kitchens were well stocked when we left and I suspect they still are. Something tells me the dead don't need a great deal in the way of supplies.'

He raised his eyebrows at Julius, who nodded, gaze flickering over the scene. It was as if they'd just got up and marched away. In a way, of course, they had done just that but not under their own wills. Roberto led the way across the yard. The lantern light illuminated more debris abandoned on the ground. Very little of any use but Roberto looked for a good backpack and blankets that looked in any way clean. He directed Julius to do the same and by the time they'd reached the refectory, Julius held both lanterns and Roberto had an armload of equipment to sift. He dumped it on the end of the first long table. There were three dozen tables, covered in jugs, plates and rough cutlery.

Roberto wandered over to the serving tables that stood right outside the kitchens, the door to which stood open. Tapped barrels rested in racks and a huge upright water butt on the floor was still half full. There was a goblet on the table, sitting by several stained, empty iron cauldrons. He swept it up and turned the tap on the nearest cask. Dark liquid flowed out. He sniffed it.

'Hmm. Well, they knew their wine, anyway. This, if I'm not mistaken, is a Dornosean red. Better with water and a little honey in my opinion but right now, it'll be like balm in my throat.'

He tipped the goblet to Julius who still held both lanterns and raised it to his lips. A movement to his right caught his eye. The man came from the kitchen, shouting. He dived straight across the serving tables, his arms and upper body collided with Roberto, bearing them both to the floor, his legs dragged through the cauldrons, knocking two over and down with a booming clang that reverberated about the walls.

'No, don't drink it, don't drink it,' shouted the man.

The goblet was long gone. Roberto shoved the man back, slithered away from him and grabbed at his gladius. Julius had backed away too.

'It's how he did it.' The man was holding up both hands in a placating gesture. 'He poisoned them all.'

He was not Tsardon, this man, though he wore similar clothing. His body was short, his limbs long, and his feet were bare but covered in thick hair. The hands that reached out were immensely strong. Roberto relaxed just a little but kept his sword out in front of him while he got up.

'You're Karku,' he said.

'Yes.'

'What are you doing here?'

The Karku studied Roberto before answering, looking at his armour, sword and cloak.

'I am trailing Gorian Westfallen. Looking for a chance to strike at him and his bastard son. They took that belonging to the Karku and we will have it back.'

'Then we are friends,' said Roberto. He sheathed his sword. 'And I think we have a great deal to talk about. I am Roberto Del Aglios.'

'The heir to the Ascendancy. I am Harban-Qvist. We share a friend in Paul Jhered.'

Roberto smiled. 'Now there's a man we could do with at the moment. But first things first. Are we safe here?'

Harban nodded. 'The last of them left before midnight. Gorian was with them. I couldn't get close.'

Roberto pulled out a bench and sat down, gesturing Julius to do the same.

'Speaker Julius Barias,' he said by way of introduction.

Harban inclined his head. 'There is much work for your kind to do.'

'Yes, there is,' said Julius, with a glance at Roberto.

'This is the most peculiar situation,' said Roberto. 'So much has happened in the last few days and yet I feel I have missed the most important events. I'm stuck in a cold castle and the world is passing me by to the south. I would never think to see a Karku this far north. It gives me a chill that there is much more and much worse than I already understand.'

'I will tell you everything I know,' said Harban. 'But first, I have found clean water and untainted food. You're hungry?'

'Never more so,' said Julius.

It was plain but it was delicious. Bread and cold sauces, honey and some dried meat washed down with cold water.

'You mentioned Gorian's son. This some Tsardon brat, is it?' asked Roberto.

Harban looked at him as if to check that he really was joking. 'Much has passed you by. Gorian's son is Kessian, whom he took from under the noses of the Advocate and the Ascendancy.'

Roberto nearly choked on his bread. 'Impossible.'

Harban raised his eyebrows. 'Not so. The two of them will bring about the tipping of the world. Paul Jhered knows. The Ascendants know.'

'All right,' said Roberto, raising a hand. 'But all I know is that the Sirraneans said the Tsardon were coming this way and so it has proved. I suspected more attacks further south. What has happened?'

'Your Conquord is failing,' said Harban. 'And with it will go Kark, and eventually even Sirrane. Gorian took the six Gor-Karkulas from Inthen-Gor. With them, he can control vast armies of the dead in as many places as he has them. Two travel with him from here. Two march through Atreska with the King of Tsard. Two more will be with the Tsardon in Gestern which is become a walking grave. Plague ships seek out fresh ports to kill more of your soldiers. Soon the dead will be rising all around Estorea. I warned them but they wouldn't listen. And now we will all pay the price.'

'You're saying more than one dead army is attacking us?' said Julius.

'So that's how he does it.' Roberto drained his goblet. 'He uses them to help him do his work. Like commanders on a distant battlefield. What are they, latent Ascendants?'

'You know a lot about this,' said Harban.

'It's my job to know. I'll be in charge one day. Then we'll see change on the Hill.'

'What do you mean, Ambassador?' asked Julius.

'Nothing. Forget it. Harban, let's say for a moment that I accept Gorian can manage armies over thousands of miles of land, and I know better than to dismiss it out of hand, no matter how preposterous it sounds. But Atreska is full of Conquord legions. One of my most trusted friends commands the armies. What happened here cannot happen there because no Ascendant was present to make a hurricane. They won't break through, not just sword on sword.'

'You had better pray your friend is still among the living then, Roberto Del Aglios. Because I know the border is already overrun and the dead are marching to Neratharn. It is why more Tsardon went there. He can make a huge host in Atreska.'

Roberto rubbed his hand over his head, unwilling to believe Davarov had been beaten on his own border. 'So why, if what you say is true, did Gorian come so far north? The main force and the King of Tsard are both in Atreska. What is he doing up here?'

'It is because here, killing the king's son did not carry so much risk.'

'What? Rhyn-Khur was here?'

Harban nodded. 'Gorian doesn't want to topple the Conquord as a subject of King Khuran. Our writings are quite clear on the matter. He wants it for himself.'

Roberto held up his hands once more. 'All right. All right. Let's go back. I'm getting lost in some of this, I think. Tell me everything you know. Tell me what Paul Jhered is doing in all this, what the Ascendants and my mother said when you spoke to them and what is going on in Gestern, if you know that. Tell me which Karku writings you are referring to, and what exactly it is they say.'

So Harban did and when he was done, Roberto felt the cold of despair like he had in the wars of a decade past. At least he knew what had to be done. The trouble was, no one was in the right place to do it.

Twenty miles south and west along the highway that led south along river and mountainside, Dina Kell had also heard words that had turned her remaining hopes to so much ash. The Tsardon prosentor could have been lying but the look in his eyes told her every word he spoke was the truth. Three armies made up of Tsardon and dead and all heading through the Conquord, bound for Estorr and the gates of the Advocate's palace. Three armies who could communicate over vast distances because of Gorian and some kind of Karku priest. She didn't begin to understand but then, neither did the prosentor know how. He just knew that they did.

Ruthrar feared for his king much as Kell feared for her husband and her Advocate. Ruthrar did not think Gorian's mass murder was an act of spite or vengeance but a plan to rule in Estorr himself. And that meant King Khuran's days were numbered and that he would live only while he remained useful.

From the little Ruthrar knew about Atreska, the Tsardon and dead were marching freely across the country because no one would stand in their way. As for Gestern, the country was already as good as lost, so Ruthrar said. The dead there were massing in ports and awaiting ships to carry them across the Tirronean Sea.

And no one knew they were coming. Not one beacon had been lit if Ruthrar was to be believed. There was still a hint of pride in his voice when he spoke. An invasion supremely planned and executed. But within it, a sense of wrong that he couldn't be putting on, because Kell was sure he didn't realise he was doing it.

'So what would you want to do, in an ideal situation?' she asked him.

'Find my king in Atreska. Warn him. Take our people from the Karkulas and capture the Dead Lords.'

'You think Gorian could pull this disease trick from so far away?'

Ruthrar shrugged. 'Who knows what he can do. There may be other means, I don't know. But I must warn my king.'

'I understand,' said Kell. 'But there's the problem. I have to report back to Estorr and I'm not about to let you out of my sight on Conquord territory.'

'The risk is worse if my king walks willingly to his death.'

'And Estorr will fall if no one realises what is coming at them.' Kell leaned back against a tree. 'Look, Ruthrar, for what it's worth, I think I believe you. But before I agree to go with you to the Neratharn border, I have to be certain my messages will get to Estorr and be treated with the gravity they deserve. If everything you say is true then the Bear Claws, what's left of them, will be best placed at the Neratharn walls anyway. We have some time before we have to make a decision and we've other problems to sort out before then, not least what's coming behind us. We can't let them march on unwatched.'

'General?'

Kell looked up. 'Captain Dolius.'

'Permission to order the march on.'

'We've had our hour already, have we?'

'Yes, General.'

Kell nodded. 'Permission granted. And Captain. We won't have to do this for long. We'll lose them eventually, surely. They are already five miles adrift. I mean to increase that. Make sure everyone knows that.'

Dolius smiled. 'We'd march and rest this way forever if it meant not becoming like them.'

The dead might have been well behind but Kell could feel the menace of their march nonetheless. That and the two hours double-time march, one hour rest she intended keeping up for at least two days were the only constants they had. They were learning about the dead and their limitations and their one-paced march was one she intended to exploit.

Kell pushed herself to her feet and turned to Ruthrar. Dolius's order rang out around the small camp.

'Thank you, Prosentor,' she said.

'For what?'

'For your honesty in fear. In another life, we might have been friends.'

Ruthrar inclined his head, got up and brushed himself down.

'Such is war. Those on the front line carry only the hate their masters seed in their minds. We bear the Conquord legionary no personal malice but we hate your Advocate. She gave the invasion order. We're only fighting to preserve our way of life, just like you are.

'Your Advocate's decision to go to war fifteen years ago haunts us to this day. It's why we're standing here now. Let us not allow a second tragedy to happen because we once were enemies. We cannot afford our past to taint our decisions now or Gorian will win.'

Kell stared at him. His face was mostly hidden by the dark but his eyes were shining.

'I hear you, Prosentor. But the wounds of yesterday remain raw. Come on, let's ride.'

Chapter Thirty-Six

859th cycle of God, 37th day of Genasrise

Paul Jhered switched his gaze from left bank to right, and wondered whether the storm would have broken across Kirriev Harbour before their ship arrived. He had no idea what they would find there. The *Hark's Arrow* should be in the Gatherer berth but that was by no means certain. People were flooding towards the port and, he had to presume, every port on Gestern's western seaboard, looking for an escape from the dead marching unhindered across their country.

At least their small vessel was travelling quickly. Mirron, despite bouts of sickness, had managed to place a stiff wind behind them. It gave the oarsmen in the two ranks of thirty a breather and moved them on past the myriad vessels threatening to clog the River Tokarok.

Any warnings he could have sent south to Skiona and Marshal Defender Katrin Mardov would have been woefully late. The Tsardon invasion, backed by Gorian's hideous power, had overtaken this great country and all that was left now was to flee and try to find somewhere else to hold out and fight. Jhered bit his lip when he thought of Mardov. Perhaps she was one of the refugees running for their lives but he doubted it. Too much courage to turn and flee. The sad fact was that she was more likely to be marching behind the wave of Gesternans as one of the dead.

Part of him almost respected the perverse genius behind the invasion. In the early part of their voyage from Ceskas they had seen walking dead that were not soldiers. They didn't have to be. Fear had been the key weapon and anyone able to hold a weapon and walk with the dead was enough to turn the living on their heels.

So strange to see this beautiful country pushed to such extremes. The mountains still stood proud, the growth of genasrise was unhindered where the dead had not journeyed but the beauty was blemished by smoke and flame. In every direction, the evidence of fire was obvious. Smoke rose to blot the sky, buildings were gutted and the stink of ash was in the air. Panic had taken Gestern, fuelled by rumour and later by the sick knowledge that reality had not been exaggerated.

The wind in the sail began to drop. Behind Jhered, the captain of the trading vessel they'd hired for the river trip to Ceskas and back called the oarsmen to order. Blades dipped and the boat picked up its lost speed. Jhered was standing on the port rail and Mirron joined him there. She was pale, tired and looked sick. It wasn't just the sea sickness that had always plagued her. She could feel the disease in the ground and through the air. What Gorian was doing, from wherever he was, took strength from her.

The two of them stood together and looked forward. Kirriev Harbour was close. An hour away. Boats of all shapes and sizes thronged the river and Harkov had already brought the Ascendancy guard and Gatherer cloaks to readiness. Bows were strung, just in case.

'You mustn't hurt anyone,' said Mirron.

'Not if there is any other choice. But what we know and what you have within you are things we cannot sacrifice for the weakness of mercy. Not today. You have to get back to Estorr. I will order the fight if I must but pray it doesn't come to that, all right?'

Jhered reached out and ran a finger along her chin. She tried to smile.

'What will we find in Kirriev Harbour?' she asked.

'Panic and chaos at best,' said Jhered. 'Be ready because it isn't going to be pretty.'

'What do you mean?'

'No one is your friend when they feel you might live at their expense.'

Mirron drew into him. 'Will we make it?'

Jhered shrugged. 'We have to.'

Every oar-stroke deepened Jhered's concern. The numbers of refugees grew. Thousands of people, some carrying a few possessions, some with carts laden down, all heading for the coast and a boat out of the country. They must know that there could never be enough for them all. Some had clearly made the judgement early. He saw men and women wading out into the shallows, babies and small children held high above their heads, imploring those on the river to help them.

Still more were swimming out, trying to grab on to the sides of any craft that came too close. He saw a low, overcrowded rowing boat rock violently and capsize. The river was full of noise. He even heard the clash of weapons.

'This is madness,' said the skipper, coming to his shoulder.

'We just have to get past it. Keep to the centre of the channel.'

'Yes, Exchequer.'

Every craft was beginning to do the same. A clamour was growing. Where one desperate man went, hundreds would follow. There was a thrashing in the shallows. His men and the Ascendancy guard were shouting for reason and order and were not going to inspire either. Arrows had started to fly from both shore and some of the larger craft. There were collisions, the crunch of timbers breaking. There were screams and there was anger.

Jhered shook his head.

'See what I mean?'

Mirron only nodded. 'What can we do?'

'Nothing. Nothing at all. We're already a target, look.'

He pointed to where a few small craft were turning ahead and heading for them. All had either one small sail or a couple of pairs of oars. Just river fishing boats but crammed with people wanting a way out.

'Exchequer?'

Jhered looked round. The captain, back on the tiller, had seen them too. His hand was unsteady on the tiller. He was not a naval man.

'Hold your course,' said Jhered. 'Don't deviate, whatever happens.'

'But we'll run them down.'

'If they get in our way we cannot help it. Up your speed if you can. We cannot afford to falter.'

'Yes, sir,' said the captain, but his unhappiness was plain.

'Mirron, stay in the centre of the boat and keep down. Better still, go below.'

'What are you going to do?'

'See if I can get some of these idiots out of our path.'

Jhered ran forward along the crowded deck. He moved his people aside and stood at the prow. The merchant vessel was low and wide, designed for heavy transport on calm water. It would be easy enough to board were it not for the two hundred soldiers lining the rails. Not that that would stop some trying.

'Let's shout this together,' he said to those next to him. 'I'll keep it simple. Listen and join in. Not that I think it'll make any difference.'

'Yes, Lord Jhered.'

'Clear the channel,' he shouted, cupping his hands around his mouth to try and get some projection. 'We will not stop and we will run you down. You have been warned.'

Other voices joined his as he repeated the message over and over. Smaller craft still came at them, individual swimmers too, in the fast-flowing river. Jhered had no idea what they thought they'd achieve. Their boat wasn't even going to sea. That wasn't the point of course. They saw soldiers, they saw security.

Closing in on the first flimsy-looking fishing boat, every guardsman was shouting and waving them aside. Someone stood up in the little craft, crossing his arms backwards and forwards, calling them to stop and bring his family on board. Jhered went cold. They were all in there with him. A woman, four or five children. An elderly man. Two dogs.

'Clear the channel!' he bellowed. 'Move, move.'

But he wasn't going anywhere. The sail was down, the oars shipped, just drifting slowly and gently to port.

'Damn you, you idiot,' muttered Jhered. He turned back and shouted. 'Captain. Hard to starboard. Hard to starboard. Now. Ship oars.'

The order was relayed. The captain leant on the tiller. Below, a multiple rattle as the oars drew in. Jhered hung over the port rail, watching the small boat pass. He wanted to shout at the man, vent his fury but he could not. He and his whole family were staring up at the shadow of the merchantman looming over them so close, turning slowly away.

'Get into the mountains,' called Jhered. 'Find the Karku. There's no escape from Kirriev.'

The fishing boat, rocking in the wake of its larger cousin, was swept away aft. Oars tucked into the water once more. The captain brought the ship back to the centre of the channel. Jhered took up his place in the prow, ready to shout more from their path.

'A close call, my Exchequer,' said one of his Gatherers.

'Too close,' said Jhered. 'But next time, no mercy. We cannot afford it. I just wish I'd take my own advice sometimes.'

'I'm sorry, my Lord?'

'Nothing.' Jhered took a deep breath. 'Nothing.'

The approach to the riverside dock was worse than Jhered feared. There was no landing space anywhere. Craft were moored in such density that it probably wasn't necessary. People crammed the dockside and he could see them streaming in on the approaching roads. It was anyone's guess what was happening on the sea port side but given the mass going nowhere here, things were bleak at best.

'Where did they all come from?' asked Mirron, coming to stand with him.

The *Hark's Arrow* had slowed and was marking gentle time towards the riverside dock.

'It's hard to believe there are this many in Gestern, isn't it?' said Jhered. 'But never mind them. We've got a bigger problem.'

He pointed towards the massive sea gates that led into the seaport. Vast concrete aprons had been built out into the river to support them and the buildings surrounding them. They were monstrous pieces of work. Over a hundred feet each in width and sixty feet high where they swept up to meet each other in the centre, forged of rods of iron thicker than a man, and set with the shapes of mountains and creatures of the deeps.

They were designed to keep invaders out but not the tide. A monument to Gesternan expertise in metal working and engineering. The gate posts on which they hung were more akin to small castles. And each supported an artillery platform. Heavy ballistae and onagers sat upon them and no one would fail to notice the barrels of pitch that burned alongside them.

The gates were closed.

In front of them was the only open space. A calm patch of water in shadow and on which the odd piece of debris floated. Mirron pointed it out.

'More like an exclusion zone,' said Jhered. 'I fear the ballistae have been in action today and they will be again, no doubt. Where's my apprentice appros? Paulites, where are you?'

'Here, my Lord Exchequer.'

Jhered looked down on the young woman. He liked her in the same way he had liked Appros Menas, the strong woman Gorian had murdered and for whom he still had to pay. Paulites was bright-eyed and clever, quick rather than strong, and a particularly fine archer, though longbows were a problem for her. Great mathematician too.

One who should have gone far, except Jhered had no confidence in any of them surviving too much longer.

'Do you have the flag?' he asked. 'You did bring it with you, didn't you?'

'And your seal, my Lord. Respectfully, you told me that if I ever replied in the negative to that question, you would strip skin from my back and paint the Gatherer symbol on it as a replacement.'

Jhered nodded. 'I do have some recollection ...'

'Paul, how could you?'

Mirron's face had gone a shade whiter, if that were possible. He spread his arms.

'The message got through, didn't it? And now it might just help us out of this mess.'

Paulites hauled the flag out of her backpack. It was the spare from the *Hark's Arrow*. She held it out reverently.

'Well, I don't want it, Appros. Take it to the mast and get it raised.'

'Yes, Exchequer.'

'What are you going to do?' asked Mirron.

'I'm going to knock on the door and present my credentials,' said Jhered. 'In a manner of speaking.'

The Gatherer flag, the Del Aglios white horse crest enclosed in a circle headed by clasping hands, certainly brought them new attention. Their approach had been seen by many and Jhered had been keen that his soldiers were visible. Confirmation as to their identity brought them space as well as more pleas for help. Jhered could do nothing but ignore them.

The captain brought them gently to a stop in the centre of the gates and perhaps ten yards from them. The tide was coming in and the oarsmen kept up a slow stroke to keep them on station. Jhered cleared people from around him so that he could be seen. He waited. Eventually, a uniformed man walked out along the walkway atop of the gates, stopping at their high point and leaning over, arms resting on the iron frame.

'I am not used to being kept waiting,' said Jhered. 'Open the gates; my ship awaits me at its berth.'

'Naturally it does,' said the man, his voice echoing over the water. 'As do the ships of everyone here. Our dock must be a thing of wonder that stretches from here to Portbrial.'

'What's your name and rank and that of your commanding officer?' demanded Jhered.

'I don't really need to tell you that. But you sure need to tell me who you are if you think I'm going to let you through rather than sink you where you lie.'

Jhered took a good long look at the Gatherer flag before turning back to face the gateman.

'This ship is under the command of the Gatherers.'

'I'm sure it is. Lucky you found a flag in the bilges too, just to make it true. And I have no doubt that you are Exchequer Paul Jhered, just happening through with a hundred cloaks.'

'That is correct. I'll have my portrait sent to you so you don't repeat the error. Open the gates.'

The gateman frowned but found himself again very quickly. 'Every trick in the book has been tried these last couple of days. You could be anyone, you and your hired blades.'

'That is true. But I remain Jhered. Send your commander out here on a pilot skiff and I will show him my seal. I will also be asking him whose orders closed these gates against innocent citizens of the Conquord.'

'It was by order of the Marshal Defender.'

Jhered looked away just for a moment. 'Now you are making me angry. Katrin Mardov is a personal friend. That makes you a liar. And we Gatherers, we hate liars.'

'Hate who you like. I'm this side, you are that side. Back off or I'll have you sunk.'

Jhered gestured and thirty bows were raised and trained on the gateman.

'You will never live to give the order. Now, do the right thing and open the gate. You are a Gesternan, a Conquord loyal. I know you are scared but this ends here.'

The gateman had ducked down so that only his head was showing. It was a target plenty big enough. Particularly for Paulites.

'That's the problem, you see. This port's under what you might call local control now. Can't trust anyone from what I've heard and some have seen. Dead people walking. Boats full of plague rats. Kirriev is full. We can't take anyone else and all the ships have sailed. Tsardon are coming. You need to find another way home.'

'I don't have time for this,' muttered Jhered. 'This bastard would serve up everyone here to the dead and the Tsardon to save his own filthy skin.'

'I could warm the gates up a little,' said Mirron.

Jhered paused. 'How much do you have left right now? Enough to destroy the artillery as well?'

'Easily,' said Mirron.

'All right.' Jhered turned his attention back to the gateman. 'I'll give you one last chance. Open the gates or I shall open them for you.'

The gateman laughed. 'Oh really? Tell you what, *Exchequer*, I'll give you one last chance. Back off or I sink you. Can't say fairer than that.'

Jhered signalled for the skipper to back-water and the vessel began to move away from the gates. The gateman applauded and laughed again, joined by some of his artillerymen who poked their heads over the protective high walls. Jhered smiled and waved.

'A pity you won't live to tell your children about this,' he said.

He swung away and faced down the ship.

'I thought everyone knew your face,' said Mirron. 'You keep on saying so.'

A titter ran through those who had overheard her words.

'And normally, I'd be happy that someone didn't. Today though, marks a big exception ... Right, Captain! Hold your station at the edge of the exclusion zone. Paulites, I give you command of the archers. I want that bastard resembling a hedgehog and cursing my name as he drops to the water. And I need you to keep artilleryman heads down. Go to it. Mirron, quickest way to open the gates? Knowing that the channel is not deep and we don't want them falling in and obstructing our path.'

Mirron thought for a moment and looked away to the gates and their supports, the artillery and the smoking barrels.

'I need fire here too, right by me to get good focus. If I get this right, you won't have to worry about the artillery either.'

'And if you get it wrong?'

'Then we'll be ramming the gates.'

'And what is it you're going to do?'

She gestured at the gates. Her eyes sparkled and she smiled broadly. 'They're metal, Exchequer Jhered. I'm going to melt them.'

Chapter Thirty-Seven

859th cycle of God, 37th day of Genasrise

Mirron was going to use the path of least resistance, so she said. That meant the air, and it also meant she had to sit up front with no one in between her and her target. Jhered didn't like it but she had assured him nothing would get their range before it was gone.

'And we all know better than to question an Ascendant,' he said.

'We do?' asked the captain.

'Yes, trust me like I trust them. You haven't seen one in action. Just keep the oars going and don't flinch on the tiller. Steady as she goes.'

'Very well, Exchequer.'

'On my mark.' He hurried forward. 'Mirron, you ready?'

He had to stand a few feet away. The heat from the three fire barrels was intense. Through the haze, she didn't look like she was breaking into a sweat, though she might need new clothes after she was done.

'The map is almost complete. I can feel the fires around me and I can sense those on the tower posts. Ohhh.'

'What is it?'

'It's been a while since I tried to amplify so much, that's all. I am ready.'

Mirron was breathing hard. Jhered knew she would be bearing down on a fire construct she was barely able to contain. Soon she would have to release it or let it dissipate harmlessly into the air. Feeding raw fire energies in would catalyse the map and then all she had to do was give it a target. Apparently. Try as he might, Jhered couldn't penetrate the ways of an Ascendant. And despite the regard in which he held the three of them, he couldn't help but feel that they were a step too far on the evolutionary road. As for the rest of them, he didn't know and hence didn't trust them. Gorian was just a bastard murderer who needed putting to death. To Jhered he was barely human, let alone an Ascendant.

Jhered signalled the captain, who gave the order to dip oars. The ship moved forward. His archers were on station, shafts nocked and ready. He stood behind Mirron. Far enough away not to get burned but near enough to drag her away should she get hit. The captain was shaking his head.

'Trust me,' mouthed Jhered and faced front.

Their move back toward the gates had brought instant response. A few men with bows had run onto the gates themselves and the artillery was moving, tracking them, waiting for best shot. Jhered heard Mirron mutter something. It sounded like 'stand back'.

The fire barrels roared. The pitch inside glowed an intense deep red. Flame swarmed inside the lips, coiling and spitting. It settled momentarily. Jhered saw Mirron draw breath in the pause before spears of fire rose from each barrel and plunged into her body. Gatherer archers backed further away. Bows were lowered, the Omniscient invoked.

Mirron juddered inside a sheath of fire. Her arms were outstretched and shaking violently. She glowed in the fire that engulfed her, drawing in its energy, shaping it within her. A mist formed above her, smoke billowed around her. Her body stiffened.

Jhered watched her skin rippling under the flames. Mirron's fingers pointed out towards the gate towers. Heat washed across the deck. A baking stillness descended. Just for a heartbeat. The ship's oars dipped, water rippled around the blades. The pace drum sounded. Shouts echoed from the gates. Mirron struck. The barrel fires roared. Columns of superheated air rushed from Mirron's arms and hands, clouds of coiling steam marking their passage. They crossed the space in an instant.

Jhered's jaw dropped.

The barrels on the gate towers exploded. Metal shards tore through man and machine. Flame hung in the air like the talons of some great bird. In front of him, Mirron began to close her arms. He could barely see her through the smoke and fire wreathing her, channelling through her and out over the shortening space.

The claws of flame pounced on the artillery and the stone of the towers, scorching the latter black and reducing the former to ash in moments. No man up there could possibly have survived. With the speed of a galloping horse, the heat surged into the iron gates, driving away loose dust as it raced across the span from both sides.

Steam began to rise from the river below. Men on the gates screamed as their clothes smouldered and ignited. They dropped, flaming tears, into the water. The gates began to glow a dull red. The river beneath them boiled. The heat came across Jhered in waves. His brow burst out in sweat. The last of the gatemen, who had had his hands seared to the metal, dropped away. No need for archers. All of them had fallen back, staring at the Ascendant. Jhered could feel the awe and the fear.

Quickly the gates went from their dull red through a deep tone to a bright, glaring crimson. Great rending sounds split the day. Joints broke. Rivets melted and popped. Clouds of steam and smoke belched out along the waterline. The river seethed with the first of the drips of yellow-brown molten metal as Mirron's Work gorged on the metal at an extraordinary rate.

What began as a trickle became a thunderous torrent. Right across the failing structure, the iron reached melting point. Lower struts could no longer support the upper weight. The gates collapsed. Glowing yellow metal struck the water, turning to hot slag and sinking away out of sight. Bubbles thrashed on the surface of the river. Steam as dense as the worst Estorr sea fog rose from the impact.

The ship drove on. Jhered was aware of shouting from all around him now the sounds of destruction were lessened. The gate towers were black. Stone had crumbled and torn at the gate hinges. People on either bank were pointing or running away, confusion generating bedlam. The ship's drum beat on. The craft pierced the steam and the bubbling water. Jhered felt the slightest of grazes as the keel scraped across cooling metal.

For a moment, Mirron was obscured from his sight and when the ship broke through the cloud and into the sea dock, she was slumped in front of the smoking but extinguished barrels of pitch fire.

'Water!' shouted Jhered.

Sailors had been waiting. Buckets of sea water washed across the prow of the ship, coiling barrels, scorched decking and splashing over Mirron's naked body. Jhered hurried forwards, unhitched his cloak and threw it over her, crouching beside her.

'Dear God-surround-me, Mirron but that was some show. Are you all right.'

Mirron looked up at him and nodded. Her hair was scorched away but her skin looked glowing, like the fire was still there beneath it. She radiated health, though her eyes were tired and there were crow's feet at their edges.

'I used the last of it to renew me. How did I do?'

Jhered smiled. 'You look beautiful, even in your baldness.'

Mirron brought a hand up and felt her head. 'Damn. Thought I'd worked out how to save that. I'll grow some more when I'm rested.'

'Never mind. Let's get you away from the prow and into some new clothes.'

Mirron looked around her. Jhered knew she was sampling the energies.

'People are angry,' she said. 'Will we get away?'

Jhered stood up with her and held her to him while he took in the dock. It was crowded with people but it was silent as had been the case in the past when the shock of an Ascendant Work settled on those who had seen it. But while every berth was full, the channel to the inlet was open and largely empty. Moored under a cliff face and far from the attentions of even the most desperate of refugees, was the *Hark's Arrow*.

Their ship was already turning towards her, the captain seeing her early.

'Yes, we'll get away,' said Jhered. 'You've done a wonderful job.'

'People died,' said Mirron. 'I killed them.'

'You can't blame yourself,' he said. 'They chose their path and we were forced to choose ours.'

'Ossacer will be angry.'

'Ossacer is always angry.'

Mirron didn't laugh. Instead she stiffened and looked away to the south. A whimper escaped her lips.

'Just in time,' she said.

'What do you mean?' asked Jhered.

There was distant screaming.

'The dead have reached Kirriev.'

Fifty Ascendancy guard now barred the entrance to the Academy buildings. The heavy doors were shut and bolted behind them.

'Take him to the Chancellery. Lay him on the recliner in front of the fire,' said Hesther. 'Ossacer! Damn it where is he? Ossacer!'

The Academy echoed to the sounds of alarm and frightened action. Hesther could still not believe it herself but she had seen it with her own eyes. The guards carrying the stricken young Ascendant hurried along the corridor past the busts of Chancellors gone by. That of Felice Koroyan caught Hesther's eye. She felt a surge of fury she was unable to contain. Hesther was ninety years old now. Perhaps she should have known better but at that moment, all the frustrations of the past few days boiled out of control.

While the guards moved on, she stopped in front of the bust. She spat on it, watching her spittle run down that arrogant bitch's nose. It wasn't enough. Hesther placed a hand on the statue's forehead and pushed, hard. The bust toppled backwards and crashed to the floor. That nose broke off. The neck cracked and the forehead sheared. Fragments of marble scattered across the corridor.

'That might not have been the wisest move.'

She swung round. It was Arducius.

'Think I care? And where have you been? Didn't you see it coming?'

'Who do you think caused all that dust that masked your escape? Come on, Hesther, now is not the time for questions like that. We were all taken by surprise.'

'Where is Ossacer?'

Arducius shrugged and took her arm, hurrying her along the corridor towards the Chancellery where the boy had been taken inside by the guards.

'How's Cygalius?' he asked.

Hesther shook her head and put a hand over her mouth. The scene replayed in front of her eyes and she felt physically sick.

'I don't know,' she said, swallowing back a sob. 'It all happened so fast.'

And so it had. The act of what she had thought was mercy for a poor man having a heart attack in the basilica. The deliberate attack. The fists, the feet and the knives. All so fast that the guards could not save Cygalius from massive injuries. The shouting and the roaring in her ears as she tried to drag people away. The thundering of feet as palace soldiers had flooded the basilica. The dust that had sprung up in the courtyard and funnelled around the fountain. Running feet. Pursuit. Choking sounds. All on such a perfect genasrise day. All from nothing but hideously premeditated. The satisfied sneer on Felice Koroyan's face.

'Where did they all come from?' demanded Arducius.

'Where they always come from,' snapped Hesther. 'It was a petition day. The Hill is full of citizens. It's open. She, that bitch, she used it.'

They reached the Chancellery and Hesther saw Ossacer was already in there. His face was white but his blind eyes swam with complex colours. There was a sheen of sweat on his brow and he knelt beside poor Cygalius, waving the guards back.

'Hot water and clean linen,' he said. He laid his hands on the boy. 'Dear God-surround-me, what have I done?'

Hesther frowned but ignored the words. So much was said in confusion that made no sense. Instead, she looked at Cygalius. Just seventeen. Just trying to do his best and use his skills to save a dying man. And now look at him. His Ascendancy toga was dark with his blood. His face was battered. His nose, mouth and ears all bled. There was more running down from his scalp under his beautiful brown hair.

'Do you need me, Ossie?' asked Arducius.

Ossacer nodded. 'I'll need everything I can get. He's a mess. Eight stab wounds. Skull fracture, broken ribs and jaw. Compressed cheek fracture. Bruising everywhere. Omniscient save us but it was animals did this.'

'No, just the Chancellor's lackeys,' said Hesther.

'Like I said,' said Ossacer. 'What a fool I am. What a fool.'

Under his hands, Cygalius moaned. Blood ran anew from his shattered mouth.

'Shh,' said Arducius. 'Calm.'

He placed his hands on the boy too and at once, his body relaxed.

'Thanks,' said Ossacer. 'I'll need your stamina to save him, though.'

'Can you do it?' asked Arducius.

Ossacer looked at him and the expression on his face was guilt and fear. 'I have to. This is all my fault.'

'Don't be stupid,' said Arducius. 'Just do everything you can. Tell me what you want of me.'

'All right,' said Ossacer. 'First we have to stop all the internal bleeding.'

Hesther couldn't watch. She walked over to a window and looked out across the courtyard to the basilica. Calm was beginning to descend on the scene. The basilica itself was all but clear though she could see some people moving about in it. The Leader of the Estorean Senate,

Lorim Aurelius was standing on the steps surrounded by guards. He had been taking petitions in the Advocate's stead. An old but strong and competent administrator, he was shaking like a leaf.

Down in the courtyard and around the fountain, hundreds of palace guard were herding a still angry mob out of the Victory Gates to where thousands more were standing, waving flags, banners and shouting chants. Marcus Gesteris walked with the soldiers, lending his considerable presence and authority to the evacuation. Marshal General Elise Kastenas was with him. Both had been in the basilica answering questions on the invasion, calming fears that had risen with the lighting of beacons across the Conquord and visible to Estorr's citizens.

The orchestrated demonstration, attack and subsequent semi-riot had been planned terribly well. None of them had seen it coming. Crowds walking under the Omniscient banner had been patrolling the streets for days now. No Ascendant had been allowed to leave the gates. The Chancellor had worked hard on the rumours and intelligence reaching the city and had whipped a good part of the citizenry, mainly the poor and the dispossessed, into an effective disruptive force.

But they had stayed away from the Hill. Until today, that was. Today had been well chosen. Petitions without the Advocate. So much of the senior government absent. And it had been so easy to plant murderous, violent elements in the basilica. Indeed it seemed to Hesther that most of the audience had been given specific roles. She wanted to look in the eyes of the man who had staged the fake heart attack. She wanted him to see what he had done.

A bitter taste rose in her throat. There was the Chancellor. Standing by Aurelius and shaking her head as if she too could not believe the scenes that had so recently overtaken the Estorean seat of government. She was talking with the senator. Her arms were moving and her hands gesturing. More than once, she pointed to the Chancellery.

Hesther became aware that people were chanting the Chancellor's name. They had stopped moving toward the Victory Gates on seeing her emerge from the basilica. There was even a move back against the press of guardsmen. The atmosphere changed. From angry pointing to fevered excitement.

The Chancellor held up her hands and the crowd fell silent. There was pushing and shoving as people struggled to hear what she was saying. Hesther looked quickly at her window. It was sealed and the distance was too great for Koroyan's words to be carried in. Hesther wasn't sure she wanted to hear the lies anyway.

'Treacherous bitch,' she said. 'Someone needs to get to Aurelius. Tell him what really happened.'

'What really happened?' asked Arducius.

Hesther turned from the window briefly. He was watching her. Ossacer was working. One hand was on Arducius's head, the other feeding his healing genius into Cygalius's broken body.

'She tricked us, Ardu. She arranged the whole thing. She wanted a victim and she knew how to get one. Anything you like, she hoped it was Ossacer who came to help but Cygalius certainly didn't disappoint her.'

'You think she would do that? Even her?'

'There is nothing of which she is incapable. Just ask Orin D'Allinnius. God-embrace-me, just trawl your own memories of Westfallen. You think it's coincidence this happened while the Advocate was away?'

Arducius shook his head. 'Not really. But even so, the mood of the city has been angry ever since first reports came from Atreska and Gestern about the invasion. Lit beacons and battle flags make for scared citizens.'

'Yes, and she's brilliant at harnessing high feelings and bending them to her own ends. The fear of the Omniscient's wrath on them all is far more powerful than the Advocate's potential retribution on any individuals.'

'Even so, this is a Tsardon invasion. And you'd think with news of Gorian leaking out, they'd want us to help, not hound us and beat us.'

'You'd think,' said Hesther. 'But you'd be naïve if you did. Sometimes I wonder if you ever listened to what Herine said about the Chancellor. Or to me. She doesn't have reason and logic, she has religion. And she is frightened of losing her power to you. Wake up, Ardu. This is only the beginning.'

'Can you keep it down?' said Ossacer. 'It's hard enough without you two chattering on.'

'How is he?' asked Hesther.

'With time, I think I can save him.'

Hesther looked back to the window and her relief fell flat.

'Be as quick as you can, Ossie. We've got visitors coming.'

'It's her, isn't it?' he said.

'Who else?' Hesther shook her head. 'Who else?'

Chapter Thirty-Eight

859th cycle of God, 37th day of Genasrise

The chanting continued unabated. Though the Victory Gates were closed and the whole palace complex was ringed, inside and out, by Ascendancy and palace guard, the crowd had thickened, not dispersed. Koroyan had what she wanted. The ear of the Senate and the will of the citizenry.

'You can hear what they're shouting, can't you?' said Arducius. 'How has this got out?'

Ossacer looked at his feet. He was exhausted but his heart clamoured for attention and would give him no peace. He thought he might have saved Cygalius but it was really too soon to tell. And if the boy died, the blame would sit squarely with him. He, Arducius and Hesther were sitting with the other four emerged Ascendants of the tenth strand. All seventeen and all very scared. They were in the Chancellery, which had been cleaned of blood. Cygalius was in the care of the surgeons now and safe from further harm.

Felice Koroyan and Senate leader Aurelius were having a heated discussion in a chamber just inside the main doors of the Academy. Soldiers of the Armour of God had arrived to ensure her safety and were outside in the courtyard. Arducius reckoned them more likely to be jailers than personal guards.

'I told her,' whispered Ossacer. 'I told her because you wouldn't listen to me and I had to stop you preaching violence.'

He didn't need to use the trails to know that they were all staring at him. He could feel the weight of their anger and their surprise like multiple slaps in the face. He didn't expect them to understand or sympathise at this stage but they had to know nonetheless.

'You idiot,' breathed Arducius eventually. 'What possessed you?'

Ossacer looked up and let Arducius's outline trace in the brightness of the room. Unfocused blobs of yellow and red around his brother represented other people. But Arducius had gone that horrible calm pulsing deep green he always did when he was beyond furious and had reached a detached calm the other side.

'I wanted her to know that we weren't all evil like Gorian. That we would be a force for good. We all know there has to be death in war but if we deal it out, it just gives her ammunition to beat us with later.'

'Unlike what you've done now, of course,' said Arducius. 'I don't believe this. I might wish to see the best in everyone, even her, but I wouldn't go to her and bleat out our plans. You had no business, no right.'

'Neither did you, agreeing that we should be used as battlefield weapons.'

A tinge of red had entered Ardu's map now. 'I will not go over this again. I will not remind you what Marshal Vasselis said to you and later to me. I love you for your morals and your principles but I hate you for what you have done to us now. You have betrayed us to Koroyan.'

Ossacer started and began to protest.

'Well, what would you call it?' said Hesther, her voice full of fire. 'You might as well have given her the key to the Chancellery again and a knife with which to kill us all.'

'What exactly did you tell her?' asked Arducius. 'And don't leave out a single detail.'

Ossacer told them all. He tried to apologise but he could see the lack of forgiveness in the maps of all six of them. He couldn't really blame them. He wanted to tell them he knew how stupid he had been, how acting in frustration and anger had been wrong but it would have done no good. He had acted like a petulant child and brought the house down on top of them all.

Arducius's voice remained quiet and under control. Ossacer shuddered as he spoke.

'You told her Gorian could animate the dead, her Omniscient dead, and expected her to react rationally? You told her we were planning to burn and blow up our enemies, and hence her Omniscient dead, and expected her to understand and provide you with her religious support?' Arducius shook his head and put a hand over his mouth. 'I am lost for words to describe your stupidity.'

'I know ...'

'Cygalius is—' began another of the Ascendants.

'I know!' shouted Ossacer. 'Mina, I know. I only wanted us to act in peace and I have brought down violence instead. Believe me, nothing you can say will make me feel any worse. I will go out and face her.'

'Oh, Ossacer, you don't understand,' said Hesther. 'Cygalius was just a sideshow for Koroyan. She was there to denounce you. She had a petition, and what she wanted more than that was a live example of an Ascendant trying to bring back from the rightful embrace of God, one whose time had come.'

'But it wasn't—'

'Dammit, Ossacer, it doesn't matter what it was or wasn't!' Hesther slammed her hand down on the arm of her chair and stood up. Her map was flaring. She might have been old but her energy was still that of a much younger woman. 'She had a room full of her faithful and proved what she believes to be an act of heresy right there in front of them. It doesn't even matter that the man was faking. The point is, Cygalius was ready to save him, using means that she deems against the Omniscient.'

Ossacer shrugged. 'I taught him. I will face the charge.'

'Ossie, you are missing the point,' said Arducius. 'That was a way in.'

He broke off. There were footsteps approaching the Chancellery. Guards opened the door and Aurelius entered. Koroyan had chosen not to accompany him. It was a tiny mercy. Everyone rose to their feet but Aurelius waved them back down with a weary hand and sat himself on a high-backed chair. He had a piece of parchment and he held it up.

'I can't deny this,' he said. 'It is put together exactly as the law allows and has been presented in public forum with the requisite number of signatures of the citizenry.'

'What is it?' asked Arducius, though the tone of his voice suggested he already knew.

'I had better read it to you,' said Aurelius. 'It concerns you all and the entire Academy.'

Ossacer put his head in his hands. Finally, he thought he understood. Though it was worse even than his new-found comprehension had suggested.

'"I, Felice Koroyan, Chancellor of the Order of Omniscience and speaker of the faithful citizenry of the Conquord do hereby accuse the under-named, whom I shall group as the Ascendants, of heresy against the Omniscient in two principal counts. In that of using means granted only to God to prolong life that God has deemed complete. And in that of planning to use fire and explosion to destroy innocent citizens of the Conquord on the battlefield, so ending their cycles forever.

'"Furthermore, I accuse the organisation known as the Ascendancy Academy, formerly, the Ascendancy Echelon, of allowing to be born and nurtured, one who would wrest from death those of the faithful rightly gone to the embrace of God, and use them for purposes other than those which God allows. This too, is a heresy against the Omniscient.

'"Furthermore, on proving the above cases, and securing verdicts and punishments commensurate with the crimes, I further accuse the Advocate, Herine Del Aglios, of dereliction of her appointed duty as divine representative of the Omniscient on this earth. The proving of the former condemns the Advocate to guilt in this matter. I will thereupon issue orders for her removal from the office of the Advocacy whenceforth she too will stand trial for heresy.

'"We, the undersigned, do hereby give notice of this intent under the laws of the Omniscient and demand proceedings are begun immediately."

'The list of names is there for you all to read if you have a mind.' Aurelius sighed. 'She further moves that your trial is for the good of the people and cites today's disturbances as reason for your immediate detention in the cells. I refused that demand but I cannot refuse any others. You may all consider yourselves under arrest. No one leaves this building. I am sorry.'

'This is preposterous,' said Ossacer. 'She can't do this. The Advocate will not allow her to get away with it.'

'Ossacer, the Advocate is not here. She is not due back until the forty-sixth genasrise. That's nine days from now.' Aurelius shrugged. 'And in matters of heresy, trials are held at the earliest instance. You have until dawn on the fortieth, three days from now, to prepare your defence. I will make anyone available to you that you think you need.'

'But she can't,' continued Ossacer, feeling his panic rising, threatening to overwhelm him. He coughed and sensed the sickness within it. 'Surely the Advocate is a witness for us.'

'You're the one so proud of living by the rules. Well, now we're all going to have to suffer that with you.' Arducius's words held painful venom. 'Senator Aurelius *is* the Advocate in the eyes of the law because she has placed him in that position for matters not able to await her return. Like this one. So congratulations. In a few days's time, you might not only have managed to get us all put to death, you might also have managed to remove the most successful dynasty the Conquord has seen at the time it can least afford to lose it.

'With friends like you, eh, Ossie? Gorian will be delighted that you have removed us from his path.'

Arducius got up and strode out of the room.

'I'm sorry,' said Ossacer.

'Sorry gets us nowhere just now,' said Hesther. 'And while you may not be able to burn, I most certainly can and I do not intend to. So let's get to work. We have no Advocate, no Jhered, no Vasselis. Barely any allies at all. Get thinking, Ossacer, and I will calm down Arducius for you.' Hesther came and sat by him, put an arm around his shoulder.

'You only acted for the good of the Ascendancy because that's the way you always act,' she said. 'And Ardu will come to see that. But if we get out of this one, and I have little confidence that we will, you are going to have to start seeing what the world is really like. Man cannot live by high morals alone.'

They all left him alone after that; Hesther, Aurelius and the young Ascendants. Left him to ponder and find a dark corner of his mind in which to dwell.

'Do you believe it, Mother? All this about the Tsardon, the dead and Gorian Westfallen?'

The carriage rattled along the road around Solastro Lake on its way to its namesake port, and a boat south and east along the River Solas. Rain had arrived as it often did in this lush green land surrounded by mountains.

Herine Del Aglios had had little sleep. Messages had been reaching the palace. Little more than rumour really but beacon fires had been lit, flags were flying atop watch towers on high peaks and the Conquord, such as it remained, was in a state of agitation. It was amazing how fast rumours spread. Birds flew, people shouted to each other across valleys, horses galloped until they dropped, and there was the delightful desire of the common citizen to be the first to pass on news to as many as he could.

It meant that little trust could be placed in the words that finally reached her ears. Unless, that is, you had prior knowledge. There was talk of walking dead and of Ascendant treachery. The latter no doubt a lie peddled by the Chancellor but backed by unfortunate truth. Goslanders had reported the movement of a Tsardon force towards their border.

Herine already knew that a significant force was camped on Atreska's border because Megan Hanev had seen it for herself before travelling to Solastro. Rumours hinted it had invaded. Megan felt that unlikely, given General Davarov's position in front of it, but the words in Roberto's letter kept on repeating themselves. No smoke without fire.

And there was talk of plague sweeping Gestern. Katrin Mardov's absence from the Conquord Senate was already a deep concern. This rumour added to it, particularly when mixed with the Karku man Harban's assertions of experimentation just inside the Karku border with Gestern.

'Absolutely, I do,' said Herine. 'You were young when the Ascendants first came to such extraordinary prominence. Your memories are probably a little dim on the subject. But I have lived with them and their development very closely this past decade. They think Gorian is a threat. They believe this walking-dead theory has credence. Your brother is concerned about Tsardon invasion and I am far too long in the tooth to do anything other than respond to his fears.

'But that's not the issue, is it, my love? It's those papers in your hand that we have to deliver to Elise Kastenas and then see if she can make them into some form of coherent defence.'

Tuline was clutching the leather bag containing latest definite legion strengths as if her life was tied to it.

'You know, you could put it down,' said Herine. 'I won't try and steal them, I promise.'

Tuline smiled and laid the bag on the seat beside her. Both of them knew it would be back in her hands soon enough.

'I don't understand,' said Tuline. 'Shouldn't we just be making the decisions here? We aren't going to get back to Estorr for nine or ten days. Won't it be too late?'

'We'd better hope not or we might encounter the enemy before we reach the Hill.' She patted Tuline's hands indulgently. 'No. What you need to understand is the length of time it takes any army to march across a country or cross any sea. You also need to understand what our legions' standing orders mean.'

'Yes, but so many of them aren't even turning up.'

'No.' Herine felt the betrayal bite once more. 'And that is another reason we must be careful. Not only do we have fewer legions for the defence of the Conquord, we also have to watch our backs, I'm afraid. And we need to know where to place our forces once we have beaten back the Tsardon and whatever this menace of the dead really turns out to be.'

'Oh.' Tuline reached out and grabbed the bag again.

'But we're amongst friends at the moment,' said Herine. 'So don't worry. When we get back to Estorr, we'll have all the latest messages and news from the territories and we and the Marshal General can make some informed decisions.'

'Will you be sending the Ascendants out to fight?'

'Wherever Gorian is, they are first on the roster sheet, believe me.'

'And what happens when we beat the Tsardon? We seem to have enemies all around us now. The Conquord was so great and now it's broken.'

Herine picked up her daughter's chin and turned her head so their eyes met. Tuline had tears in her eyes, and a single one dripped down her cheek. Herine wiped it away. There was so much of her in her daughter. Tuline, whom she'd thought would be fit for nothing in government, and yet who had proved herself so passionate and capable. A wonderful daughter to complement two wonderful sons. Roberto would be with Adranis now in Gosland. That border was as secure as it would ever get. She had her best people in all the right places. And Jhered to welcome her with accurate information when she returned home. It was a comforting thought. She smiled.

'We are not so weak. The heart of the Conquord still beats strong and you have to keep on believing that. The Del Aglios way is to remain positive as well as realistic. We have been betrayed by those we thought of as friends but that doesn't mean that whole countries have turned against us. Just individuals. And individuals can be replaced.

'Our loss of Dornos, Tundarra, Phaskar, and the martial law in Bahkir ... it's all only temporary. People are scared and they have turned away from us rather than turning to us for help. And that is deeply disappointing. But as Atreska discovered, so shall they.

'What belongs to the Conquord is only ever mislaid, and never lost. We always find what is ours and we always, always keep it. No matter how long it takes.'

Chapter Thirty-Nine

859th cycle of God, 40th day of Genasrise

The whole trial was to be conducted to the backdrop of anti-Ascendant chants and shouts from beyond the Victory Gates. News of the event had spread to every corner of the city and beyond. Citizens thronged every street, every alley way and every open space on the approaches to the palace complex, waiting for news.

Already, there had been ugly scenes. Pro-Ascendants had staged a counter-demonstration, denouncing the Chancellor. People had died as a result. It had left the mood charged and aggressive. Every palace and Ascendancy guardsman, every Estorean garrison legionary and even every member of the Conquord navy, the Ocetanas, in port had been pressed into service.

Inside the basilica, the noise was deafening as the Ascendants and the Academy hierarchy were brought in to sit in three rows of seats to one side of the throne. Opposite, sat the Chancellor, with the Speakers of Winds and Oceans. In the throne sat Aurelius. To his left, the Speaker of the Earth, to his right the Speaker of Fire.

The trial was under the jurisdiction of the Order of Omniscience, as were all matters of faith and heresy. It was fortunate that Aurelius was a strong man and determined to take his place in the stead of the Advocate, spokesman for the Prime Speaker of the Omniscient in her absence.

Even so, Arducius tasted injustice on the air. The public benches were packed with the great and the good of Estorr. Merchants, Order ministers, senior soldiers, Conquord administrators. But the Chancellor had ensured a good number of ordinary citizens were present to shout their hatred and vent their spleen.

Surrounding them and covering the courtyard, the palace guard were an imposing presence. No chance of summary justice the way Koroyan would doubtless have preferred, but none of escape either. The will of the people would ever be stronger than the fear of the Ascendants. As it should be.

Arducius sat with Ossacer on the front bench. Hesther Naravny, Mother of the Ascendancy, was to his right. Her sister, Meera, Gorian's mother, sat to Ossacer's left. Behind them, the four fit members of the tenth strand. Scared teenagers. And in the third rank, three twelve-year-olds. The eleventh strand. Emerged so very recently and plainly confused by all that surrounded them. They were flanked by two more members of the old Echelon, Gwythen Terol and Andreas Koll. Poor Andreas, one hundred and four. His service to God should not be called into question at this late stage.

Arducius thought it fortunate that the ancient Willem Geste, well into his mid-one hundred and thirties, was in Westfallen and far beyond the clutches of the Chancellor. Every day they waited the call to travel back for his ceremony at the House of Masks. But God had use for him yet, it seemed, limited though it must be.

'It doesn't look promising,' said Arducius, his voice a whisper in Hesther's ear. 'This is hardly a judge-split that favours our continued cycles, is it?'

'But we are not without allies. Aurelius is smart. And this is a time we should all be thankful that the military considers you a powerful weapon. No verdict will be given without due diligence of prosecution or defence.'

'But they will find against us.'

'In all probability. But it is then our allies will stand or turn. Appeals, objections. Anything to delay sentence until Herine returns. The Chancellor knows all this, of course. Now we'll see who's the better at playing the game.'

'We're wasting time,' said Arducius. 'We lose training and Gorian gets closer.'

'And we must waste as much more time as we can.' Hesther managed a smile. 'A paradox indeed. Just keep your brother's spirits up. You might hate him this morning but we need him.'

Arducius nodded. 'We spoke last night.'

'Good.'

'Hesther, I cannot see Orin.'

'He'll be here.'

'He should be here now.'

'He'll be here.' Hesther looked out into the basilica. Like Arducius, she could see the empty place next to Marcus Gesteris. 'Probably doesn't want to show his hand too early.'

Arducius was not comforted by the explanation. They needed all the help they could get.

Aurelius stood. The basilica fell silent. Outside, the singing and chanting echoed through the columns and into the roof. Across the stage, Koroyan smiled. Arducius shuddered. Memories of Westfallen's forum and murder crowded his mind.

'The charges have been posted and read. The trial for heresy will begin and every rule and law of its conduct will be followed to the letter.' Aurelius stared hard at the Chancellor. 'I will not allow hearsay. Nor will I allow fabrication and exaggeration. Any who speak without express permission will be excluded from the basilica. Any in the public benches who feel the need to shout for one side or the other should think again. I will not hesitate to clear the chamber if I feel it necessary.

'Let us not forget who is in charge here despite the seniority of those involved in the proceedings.' Aurelius tapped his chest. 'I am in charge here. My honoured Speakers of Fire and Earth will join me in final judgement but in all other matters, I stand as sole arbiter. I trust that is clear to all present. Chancellor, proceed.'

Aurelius sat down. Koroyan shared brief words with her Speakers before standing. She was, as always, an imposing and charismatic figure. Her energy map was alive and densely interconnected with the world around her and everything the Omniscient gave to His people. She wore a formal toga, slashed green for the Advocacy, and braided gold and purple for the seniority of her position within the Order. On her greying head sat a tiara of interwoven leaves and roots, centred by a sun motif.

She smiled at the Ascendancy benches. It was such a warm gesture that even Arducius felt himself swayed. It suffused her map with gentle green and slow pulsing blue. She had a mastery that she could only guess at. Surely it was not a genuine emotion she displayed yet her life map spoke otherwise. It was love and it was forgiveness.

'I do not set out each morning to hate anyone. No one who opens their eyes on a God-blessed morning can have such darkness in their hearts. The joy the Omniscient offers us with every breath sweeps away such notions. We are all free under the gaze of God to go about our lives as He deems we should. And in return He gives us this bountiful world in which to live.

'Yet within this beautiful simplicity there is darkness and there is evil. If there were not, then I could disband the Armour of God, could I not?'

A titter ran around the rear benches. Arducius saw smiles on most faces. But by no means all.

'It is my job to ensure that such evil does not persist to taint the work of the Omniscient or turn the heads of his faithful. And I fear that many heads have been turned by the evil of the Ascendancy. Senior heads. For more than ten years, crimes against the Omniscient have gone unpunished, and indeed have been indulged by those whose position surely forbids them to do so.

'But, I am not going to stand here and read out that list. After all, we all need our rest tonight, do we not?'

Another titter and a few calls of agreement, hushed quickly.

'I do have it with me though, so if pressed ...' The Chancellor indicated behind her. 'What I am going to do is keep this very simple, but first I am going to answer a question that will be on the minds of all here present. Do I hate those who commit heresy? Is it this that drives me to seek their destruction, because destruction is what awaits the guilty.'

She turned back to the Ascendancy benches and delivered that smile again. Arducius fought hard not to believe what she said next.

'No. Of course I don't. Hate has no place in the heart of any minister of the Omniscient. What I feel, as do my fellow Speakers and Readers, is pity. Pity that any should have been turned from the path to follow evil. Pity that there is anyone in this world who seeks to destroy the work of God.

'But I live in the real world so I understand that there will always be those who will set their wills against the Omniscient and seek to undermine Him for their own ends. So it is not for me that I seek out this evil and determine to destroy it. It is for every faithful citizen who awakes to the same beauty I do every morning.

'I understand that destruction is the only way because those who choose heresy cannot be brought back into the embrace of God. They must stand as markers to those who are faltering that the Omniscient is the only way. Not hate, pity. And I weep for every one of them who burns, as does my God.'

The Chancellor paused. Within his heaving sense of injustice, Arducius found time to admire her and even understand her just a little more. He had certainly just gained an education as to why she remained so powerful and so popular, even though shorn of the support of the Advocate. That she would end with the majority of the public on her side was not in question. Aurelius was the key. He, Marcus Gesteris and Elise Kastenas.

'So, as I said, simplicity. I do not need to prove a vast number of individual crimes. On their own, many might not be considered heresy. Indeed some might argue that taking back a life from God to be some form of mercy. I tire of such debate. No. I can prove far more conclusively, that these Ascendants and their backers are heretics by the words of one of their own.'

Arducius nudged Ossacer. 'Here it comes, Ossie. Be careful.'

'Ossacer Westfallen, you will stand,' demanded the Chancellor.

Ossacer did so. Wearing his Ascendancy toga and with his hair cut short, he looked every inch the respectable citizen. He clasped his hands in front of him.

'Ossacer. May I call you Ossacer? It is informal but familiar.'

'It is my name,' said Ossacer.

'Did you or did you not state to me that Gorian Westfallen, previously thought dead, is able to raise the dead? To wrest the faithful from the arms of God and impel them to his will?'

'I did.'

A ripple of conversation and revulsion fled around the basilica. Aurelius raised a hand to still it. Arducius watched Marcus Gesteris rise and excuse himself.

'And did you not tell me that to counter this apparent threat, your brother Arducius and the rest of the Academy were training in, Works, is it? Works of fire in order to destroy these faithful?'

'I did.'

'Is not the threat of the use of fire to destroy an innocent of the Omniscient a heresy against the faith?'

'It is written thus.'

The Chancellor spread her hands wide. 'The case is proven. Surely?'

'You are asking me?' said Ossacer.

'Naturally.'

'Of course it isn't proven,' said Ossacer. 'Only the feeble-minded would believe so.'

To her credit, the Chancellor did not flinch despite clearly expecting a less vehement response.

'Are you sure that is what you believe? You did come to me to ask me to stop what you yourself described as a crime, did you not?'

'I did.'

'Then surely, you agree that the crime is one of heresy because to burn or threaten to burn is such a crime.'

'The problem, Chancellor Koroyan, is that you claim simplicity but we all know the world is not that simple or every legion commander would be facing similar charges every time they dipped a stone or an arrowhead in burning pitch. I asked for your help by calling on people's—'

'Enough. I have heard enough.'

'I am merely answering your question for the assembled company,' said Ossacer. He made to continue but the Chancellor turned to Aurelius.

'Senator, order his silence.'

But Aurelius shook his head. Arducius smiled.

'I think not. Or at least not yet. As I mentioned in my opening address, I will decide what is allowed and what is not. When I feel the question is answered, I will call it so. Continue, Ossacer Westfallen.'

Ossacer inclined his head. 'Thank you, Senator. I did visit the Chancellor to stop what I would describe as a crime before it was committed. The Chancellor was invited to win an argument on theological grounds that would have seen the use of any form of flame or explosive by Conquord armies outlawed. This is because the use of such puts the faithful in the front line at inevitable risk. The fact that in the enemy front line we might face, should the rumours be true, our own dead walking against us merely heightens that risk.

'No Conquord commander stands with us, accused of this particular heresy. On the battlefield, use of fire is currently sanctioned by her own Order. I disagree with it but it is so. Hence, no crime of heresy has been committed by any Ascendant, merely one of ethics.'

Aurelius held up his hand for silence, having heard far more than was necessary. The Chancellor was incandescent.

'Perhaps you should read out your list of charges after all, Chancellor,' said Aurelius. 'Unless you wish to pursue this line further.'

*

Orin D'Allinnius ordered that the door to the laboratories be unbolted and had his guard stand outside until Marcus Gesteris left. He didn't get out of his chair. His back and legs were agony today and there was a crawling sensation where his missing ear had been. He laid down his quill when Gesteris reached him, not wanting the senator to see the tremble in his hands.

'Sit down, Marcus. Come to see our progress?'

'That was one reason,' said Gesteris, taking the proffered seat.

D'Allinnius cleared a space of papers and two flasks and signalled for herb tea.

'I didn't realise you were coming or I'd have organised something a little more fitting.'

'Tea will be fine,' said Gesteris. 'And you knew full well I'd be coming.'

'But not the exact time.'

'Where the hell have you been? There is one empty seat in the front row and it has your name on it. We need you there. They need you there.'

D'Allinnius sucked his lip and looked away. Gesteris couldn't miss the trembling in his hands now. He put them in his lap and wrung them together. He felt cold though the office was hot.

'I cannot go out there,' he said, voice a hoarse whisper. 'I will not.'

'Koroyan has got to you, hasn't she?'

'She got to me ten years ago,' snapped D'Allinnius.

He could still feel the pain like it was fresh and see her smile as the hammers fell on his joints and his face, the knives ripped at his skin and the flame ate at his balls.

'Today. She got to you today, didn't she?'

'I have too few allies here,' said D'Allinnius, fighting to keep his tone steady. 'No Advocate, no Jhered and no Harkov. They can speak for me.'

'Yes, but as you so rightly point out they are not here and the trial will not wait for them.' Gesteris reached out a friendly hand. 'You are no coward, Orin. No one who knows you could accuse you of that. But we have a real chance of discrediting the Chancellor here.'

'I know. I know. And so does she. Why do you think I've got all these guards outside my door? If I appear and get questioned she'll have me killed.'

'And if she wins and the Ascendancy and Advocate fall, what then? Think she'll come by here and thank you?'

D'Allinnius started. He couldn't gather his thoughts. The smell of his burning flesh was in his nostrils again. The ball of the hammer on his mouth and cheeks so cold and crushing.

'I cannot,' he whispered.

'Orin, she is out there now, telling the court that to threaten to burn is a heresy. You are the one man alive who can denounce her for the same actions. Please, Orin. We have to beat her now or we never will.'

But D'Allinnius could only shake his head. Gesteris's words sank into his mind, each one lifting the fear further into his consciousness.

'Orin? You like the Ascendants, remember? These are friends, these are allies. Do you think they'll let any harm come to you if you speak?'

'How... H- h-how can I face her again?' he managed and then he broke and the tears stung his eyes. 'She will hurt me again and I can already feel the pain, Marcus. She only has to look at me and my courage will fail. I am a coward. I cannot stand before her. She will make me look a fraud. Please don't make me face her.'

D'Allinnius's head was pounding. The pain ached through all the old wounds of his face. He felt Gesteris's arm wrap around him and draw him close. D'Allinnius lost himself in the man's strength.

'I'm so sorry, Orin, I had no idea.'

D'Allinnius pulled back and found a little composure. 'You know what it's like to be faced with a memory you prayed was buried. You told me about the blade that took your eye. How it stings every time the thought rises unbidden. The man is long gone who did it to you. But she, she is out there, not a hundred yards from where I sit. I dare not move.'

He clutched at one of the flasks he had moved.

'Your explosive powder.'

'Yes. And she will taste it if she tries to take me.'

Gesteris raised his eyebrows. 'Really? Then bring it with you Orin. Take it everywhere with you. A man must feel secure, after all.'

'No civilian may take a weapon into the basilica,' said Orin.

'It won't be in your scabbard, Orin. And it won't be in your boot or up your arm. It will be in full view in your hands. It is, after all, just a bit of powder.'

Gesteris winked.

Chapter Forty

859th cycle of God, 40th day of Genasrise

'But you did save the boy's life,' said the Chancellor.

'I did,' said Ossacer.

His turn again, and this time they were in a far more difficult position. It was a tricky point of Order law and the verdict of heresy was by no means certain, but Aurelius had let it go too far. Now there was no coming back.

'And you did this without recourse to any accepted medical practice.'

'I do not need accepted medical practices.'

'Really? So what do you need?'

'My hands, the strength of my mind and the grace of God to do my work,' said Ossacer.

'The grace of God? You assume you have that? Such arrogance. Explain to us how, with just your hands and the power of your mind, you managed to save a child who was clearly dying of a disease that has no cure.'

Ossacer sighed. 'We all have energy maps ... lifelines that are the encapsulation of our being. I can see these energies. All Ascendants can. Where there is damage to that map, the colours are altered. What I do is channel some of my own energy into the altered map to put it back as it should be. That's as simple as I can make it.'

The Chancellor was silent for a time.

'Only God can chose to bring back someone whom He has called to His embrace. We can only ease that passing. A surgeon who uses instruments or medicines is using the gifts of God and might save someone whom God has not called, someone whom it is possible to save. What you assume is the power of God. That is heresy.'

'No,' said Ossacer. 'What we have are gifts—'

'You will not respond,' said Aurelius. 'That was statement, not question.'

'No,' said the Chancellor. 'Let him speak. He will merely cement his guilt.'

Aurelius shrugged and indicated that Ossacer continue.

'All we use is the gifts God has given us. Nothing more. Like a skilled rider or surgeon, we can do no more than our ability lets us do. That is gift, not assumption.'

The Chancellor nodded. 'Good. Ossacer, sit. Arducius, a final few questions.'

Arducius rose to his feet.

'Arducius. We are old sparring partners, you and I. The length and breadth of the Conquord. I told you that one day we would stand under independent judgement.'

'If that is what you call this,' said Arducius.

'I do. I am sorry you feel the need to question the impartiality of the honoured triumvirate of judges.' She waited for Arducius to respond but he did not. One mistake was enough. 'Tell me. Without recourse to weapon or even touch, you could kill every man and woman in this basilica, couldn't you?'

'That is a difficult question to answer.'

'Just yes or no will do,' said Koroyan.

'It's not as simple as—'

'Yes or no.'

'I'm sorry but—'

'Arducius,' said Aurelius. 'You will answer the question.'

Arducius felt flustered and a little hot all of a sudden. He glanced down at Hesther. She gave a minute shrug.

'Technically, yes. But—'

'Thank you, Arducius.' Koroyan delivered that smile again but this time it was to the assembled audience and the judges. 'How is irrelevant. The possibility is shocking and terrifying, I think you will agree.'

Koroyan waved Arducius down and he sat heavily. The explanation, the mitigation, was on his lips. The time to give it was missed. By the time the defence came round, it might already be too late and this angle was not even in their strategy. The Chancellor had not finished.

'The reality is that I could have begun and ended there,' she said. 'But you need to know the depth of the crime that is being committed even by allowing these Ascendants to draw breath and their Academy to continue its research into these God-like powers. Not God-given, God-like.

'Let us make no mistake. God alone can bring death to people through the use of the elements. It is His way of demonstrating wrath or of bringing back to his embrace those who should no longer walk the earth. The scriptures are clear on this. So how can it be that mere mortals assume such powers. Arducius would have told you that it would take time to kill you all but that is not the point. The reality is that he could have done many things. Bring a wind to knock down the basilica. Drive roots so hard through the foundations that the structure collapsed. He could bring lightning from a clear sky to scorch you, or bring rain so hard it washed you into the harbour. He could pick any one of you and snuff out your life by accelerating your ageing.'

She stopped and a look of nausea passed across her face.

'*Accelerating your ageing.* Think about it. And these people walk our streets and pretend to dispense health and favour? Who knows what damage they really cause to all they purport to heal. Who knows the damage they do to God's earth by their casual use of His elements, His world.

'By any reasonable measure, whether scientific or religious, this kind of power is evil in the hands of men. Men are arrogant if they believe it will not corrupt them. Gorian Westfallen demonstrates that the Ascendants cannot be trusted to use their assumed power wisely. Only God the Omniscient has the wisdom and the clarity, the purity, to wield such forces. Any man who thinks he can do the same is adopting the role of God.

'That is heresy by example and definition. I—'

The Chancellor broke off her oration. Arducius followed her gaze to the source of the tapping noise that had interrupted her flow. He smiled for the first time. Walking across from the right of the basilica was Marcus Gesteris. With him, leaning heavily on a cane in one hand and holding a flask in the other, was Orin D'Allinnius.

The scientist looked frightened and in pain as he approached. His face was pale and a sheen of sweat clung to it. But his bearing was as proud as he could muster and his eyes did not flinch when they met Koroyan's. Arducius did not miss the look of pure hate that passed across her face. So brief but undeniable.

She looked away quickly and stared hard at her team. The Speaker of Winds shrugged; the Speaker of the Oceans shook his head. The Chancellor spared Gesteris a cold glance before turning to Aurelius, speaking over the tap of D'Allinnius's cane.

'The charge of the threat to use fire to burn the faithful is dropped,' she said. The words dragged from her lips. 'The heresy of assumption of God-like powers stands.'

Aurelius nodded. The corners of his mouth twitched very slightly.

'You have more to say, Chancellor Koroyan?'

For the first time in the proceedings, the Chancellor looked nervous, unsure. She didn't reply for a time, choosing to watch every tortuous step D'Allinnius took as if willing him to fall each time he placed a foot. But with Gesteris beside him, a look of triumph on his face, that was not going to happen. The pair of them sat down amidst a flurry of conversation from the benches. Few, if any, knew the significance. But all understood that Koroyan's retraction of a principal allegation was no coincidence.

'Chancellor Koroyan?'

She tore her gaze from D'Allinnius, let it pass meaningfully over someone in the audience Arducius couldn't see, and let it come to rest on Arducius and Ossacer.

'A man may not tinker with the elements, bring life where there should be none or take life on a whim of will. These are the gifts of God, and God alone. The Ascendants are heretics by the fact of birth and I put it to the court that they, and the complicity of the Academy that sit by them or hide in their little town, all be put to death for this most heinous of crimes against the Omniscient.

'My case, my honoured judges, is irrefutable.'

Koroyan sat down. She jutted out her chin and set her stare on the Ascendants opposite her as if daring herself to look back at the scientist who had come so close to undermining her by his very entrance.

Aurelius spoke briefly to his fellow judges, coming to a decision quickly.

'There will be no recess. Facts must be kept in mind and fresh. Mother Naravny, your defence of the charge of heresy.'

Ossacer and Hesther both leaned in over Arducius so that the three of them could speak.

'Which way do we go?' asked Hesther.

'She's proven very little,' said Ossacer. 'And nothing that hasn't been sanctioned by the Advocate. Her central plank is gone because D'Allinnius will counter-charge her. I say we go short and simple. Don't attack her. List benefits, responsibility and reference every murderer when you talk about Gorian.'

'I agree,' said Arducius. 'She's relying on evidence very much in the public domain already. And already accepted by many. This is a pure theological debate in many respects now. Are our abilities gifts of God or taken from God? We can argue that angle.'

'Who should argue it? Me?' Hesther indicated herself.

'Yes,' said Arducius. 'More sympathy for the older woman.'

'Damn cheek.'

'Damn true,' said Ossacer. 'And you know you speak better than us. Less emotion, more reason.'

'Call on us if you need us.' Arducius laid a hand on her arm.

'You can absolutely count on that.'

Hesther Naravny, Mother of the Ascendancy, stood to give the speech that would determine the fate of them all. Arducius felt perversely calm. He sat back and sampled the energies in the basilica. The Chancellor had done a satisfactory job in turning up the emotions of the citizens. There was anxiety out there, based on her assertions of his ability to kill them all from where he sat. Hesther would ease their fears.

'Senator Aurelius, honoured Speakers of Fire and Earth, I will be brief because, as the Chancellor said, this really is a very simple subject. Evil. Heresy. We all think we know what these words mean. But do we? Do we apply them properly? What is evil? The use of abilities granted at birth or the denial of that use that costs a child his life?

'The Chancellor speaks of our Ascendants as heretics because they can save lives, cure disease in animal and field, and bring rain to parched land without use of accepted techniques. Is it just me or is that simply laughable? Let me quote to you from the scriptures of the Omniscient.

'"... the body is inviolate. Illness and injury to the body are the work of God in his mystery. Disease, should it afflict a man, is part of the Omniscient's plan and he should not fear it but celebrate the fact that he is being tested or that he is to be taken back to the embrace of God. Interference by another is against the will of God and is a heresy."'

Hesther spread her arms wide.

'The Order of the Omniscient used to fear the medical man, the surgeon and the scientist. They used to burn them because their practices were not accepted. Presumably, the Chancellor would not take an infusion should she catch a cold, nor suffer the knife should she break a rib. All part of God's plan? Where do you draw the line. If the land is parched, is that part of God's plan? If it is cold, is that part of God's plan, to test our mettle?'

Hesther had the audience tittering much as Koroyan had done.

'It is no laughing matter. Presumably the Chancellor would not touch a vegetable that had been grown in an irrigated field. Nor would she ever set foot in a room warmed by a hypocaust. You understand my point. We are discussing method, not faith and heresy. The world moves on. The more we learn, the more we can do.

'I ask you a simple question. Is it heretical to save a life, water a field or warm a room, however it is done? Of course not. Hence the Ascendants are not heretics. However, they can be evil. We accept that, just as any man or woman born into the grace of the Omniscient can be evil. To condemn us for the tragedy that is Gorian Westfallen is as ridiculous as burning a mother because her son falls to thievery or murder.

'We do not know why the Chancellor, and through her the Order, is so determined to extinguish the potential for good that is the Ascendancy. We have ever offered ourselves to the Order as faithful servants, ready to use our abilities to strengthen the will of God, never to undermine it.

'We serve the Omniscient. We are His children, as is every one in this basilica. We could never, never seek to supplant Him, assume ourselves His equal or His superior. The very thought is abhorrent, sickening. Should that ever happen, I will light the fires myself.'

Hesther bowed to the judges and to the audience.

'I have said all I need to. You must decide.'

She sat down and Arducius put an arm around her shoulders.

'Short, sweet, simple and sure,' he said, aware that the atmosphere in the basilica had calmed. The conversation was measured, the debate lively and the citizens unsure on which side to fall. Arducius was surprised. 'You've moved the people.'

'Yes, but two of our judges are Koroyan loyals. Reason has little to do with this verdict, far more on what follows.'

Arducius felt his heart fall. Hesther was right, of course. He had harboured brief thoughts of pronouncements of innocence. He turned to speak to the benches.

'Remember, everyone, whatever the verdict, do not react. We all know that this is not the end. Guilty does not mean death, just as innocence does not mean acceptance. Humility and bearing. Remember who you are.'

On the dais, the judges were in close conference, their backs to the basilica. They were taking their time; shadows moved with the sun. Aurelius was tense, his movements agitated and angry. The Speakers were quite the opposite. Across the stage, the Chancellor sat in smug satisfaction, her Speakers talking with her, congratulating her on the job well done.

Arducius let his eyes wander over the audience. He met D'Allinnius's gaze and nodded his appreciation. The scientist barely acknowledged him. He fidgeted with the flask in his lap, his eyes flickering continually to the Chancellor. Beside him, Gesteris watched the judges speaking. His expression was carefully neutral. Marshal General Kastenas was less still. Her arms were folded and she was noting the positions of various people in the audience. Arducius wondered if she anticipated trouble or whether she was counting allies.

Aurelius turned back to the basilica. Instant quiet fell. Arducius's heart began to pound hard in his chest and heat rose in his face. He could barely control himself, trying to force cool energies over his lifelines. His words about not reacting seemed hollow suddenly. Up there, someone was about to pronounce whether he should live or die. Now there was an assumption of God-like powers. Arducius almost laughed but he caught the expression on Aurelius's face.

'A verdict has been reached. On the count of heresy on the assumption of God-like bearing and powers, the Ascendants are found guilty. On the count of and allowing to be born and to be nurtured, etcetera, the Academy is found guilty. The charge against the Advocate shall be deferred until the Advocate can respond in person.'

The basilica filled with noise. Arducius let it wash over him. He felt no surprise at the verdict. The sound of wind filled his mind. Whether it was the rushing of blood in his veins or the morass of voices, some angry, some cheering, he couldn't tell. He heard music too, but from nowhere. He looked over at Aurelius. The Chancellor was standing in front of him. She was still not happy about something. The clamour in the audience swelled and subsided. Nothing of any focus penetrated Arducius's senses. The wind and music faded.

Arducius felt proud. Not a flicker on the Academy benches. No plea for mercy, no howls of protest. The Chancellor was looking at them again. She was smiling but this time there was no love or forgiveness.

'Speak your sentence, Senator Aurelius,' she said. 'The Advocate can wait.'

'First, I must ask if you, the accuser, are demanding that the sentence be that as set down in the statutes for the crime of heresy.'

'What else?' said Koroyan. 'Heretics burn.'

Further hush in the basilica. The drama of pronouncement. Arducius felt removed from it all.

'The sentence for heresy is death by burning on all counts, ashes to be scattered to the devils on the wind, a warning to the faithless,' said Aurelius. 'Subject to appeal, sentences to be carried out as dusk marks the sky, and in the order in which the charges were laid.'

The Chancellor lifted her chin, unable or unwilling to disguise the triumph.

'The evil shall forever fall before the Omniscient and I am the Chancellor of God.'

'However.'

Just one word but it fell on the audience, on the Ascendants and on the Chancellor like crystal glass on rock, shattering and covering everything. The Chancellor spun round, daring Aurelius to speak. His fellow judges, recently so satisfied, did likewise. Aurelius was happy to oblige.

'The burning of a heretic must take place while they still live, such that they can see the devils even while they speak their words of confession and contrition. So it is written in law and scripture. But there is a problem, isn't there? An Ascendant is impervious to flame. Their statements of confession would be lengthy indeed.'

The Chancellor's stare strangled any laughter at birth.

'Then we behead them before burning them,' she said. 'I see no problem.'

'But then you are not the presiding authority and I am.' Aurelius stood. 'Sit down, Chancellor, I am speaking.'

'This is ridiculous. You are creating—'

'Sit. Down.'

Aurelius was indeed a strong man. There were not many who would face down Felice Koroyan in full fury. He held her stare while she backed off, not so much as blinking. And all the while, hope began to beat in Arducius where there had been none.

'Good,' said Aurelius. 'There is only one legal punishment on the statutes for heresy. It cannot be carried out on the Ascendants. Hence, until there is a revision to the law, they cannot be executed for this crime.'

'Then revise the law,' grated Koroyan.

Aurelius smiled in deliberate mimicry.

'A lengthy process, even if I were not otherwise engaged in the multifarious tasks of government and were desperate to make such a change. It is a matter that must first go before a full meeting of the Speakers of Scripture and Order Law, is it not? Requiring a statutory notice of amendment and agenda specifying thirty days' notice of the meeting. Unless I forget my teachings. I am an old man, after all.'

Aurelius pitched his voice low enough that not everyone in the basilica could possibly hear him.

'When you choose to enter my world, Chancellor, you need to do your homework more thoroughly. I have forgotten more of the administrative complexities of the Conquord and its faith than you will ever learn. You will never beat me in the basilica.'

Aurelius banged a gavel on the arm of his chair.

'The verdict stands but the sentence cannot currently be passed. As spokesman for the Advocate, it is my responsibility to make an interim judgement. This I have made. It is that the Ascendants and the Academy personnel be kept under house arrest in the Academy buildings until such times as their sentence can be carried out, appeals heard or the case is reviewed.'

The Chancellor was back on her feet. 'The final insult! You would keep these heretics in the halls of the Omniscient in the heart of the Conquord? Your incompetence and complicity will see you brought to justice yourself.'

The basilica erupted. Everyone was off their benches. Fists were raised, shouts were deafening. Palace guards came to ready and moved in. A line of soldiers ran across the front of the stage, spears levelled. Arducius saw Elise, Gesteris and D'Allinnius excuse themselves, move through the guards and exit quietly. Aurelius had kept his trump card very close to his chest. A wise man as well as a strong man.

More guards were mounting the stage to give Aurelius security and to guide the Ascendants to their extremely comfortable prison. A line of Advocacy guards stood across the Chancellor's path, stopping her reaching either of them, but Arducius could see her pointing and hear her enraged declamations. Aurelius cupped a hand and said something to her. Arducius didn't catch it. He looked to Ossacer who he knew would have been following the exchange and had far better hearing than he.

'What did he say?'

'He was just reminding the Chancellor that the Advocate is due home shortly.'

'Bet that pleased her.'

'I think she just threatened to kill him.'

'And ...?'

'Aurelius said he would add it to his full report on proceedings.'

Arducius chuckled. 'Tough bastard.'

'Brave,' said Ossacer. 'And wonderful. Ardu, I'm so sorry I've put you all through this. It was not my intent.'

'You know, Ossie, it's just possible you've actually done us all a favour. Come on, let's go and get something to eat.'

Chapter Forty-One

859th cycle of God, 41st day of Genasrise

The palace complex was quiet. The riots had been brief and broken up with typically overwhelming force by legionaries, palace guards and mounted Gatherers under the command of Elise Kastenas. Trouble still rumbled on in the centre of the city but it was nothing the militia couldn't handle. The Victory Gates were closed, the public excluded until tomorrow and Senator Aurelius was happy with his day's work.

He walked to his rooms, chatting to an adviser and in the company of four Ascendancy guardsmen. Closing the door behind him, rattling the bolt across and hearing the guards stand at ease outside, Aurelius let himself relax. There was a fire in the grate, warming his reception room. Shutters were closed and lanterns gave the room a warm light.

Aurelius was too tired to sit and read. Having written the report of the trial throughout the afternoon and evening, he was fuzzy with detail. An infusion of strong herbs and a gentle incense burn would bring him the rest he required. His servants had already anticipated what he really wanted. He could smell the aroma of beech and orange. A steaming jug rested on a salver just outside his bedchamber. He filled a goblet, took a deep breath and a sip and pushed open the door.

His bed looked wonderfully inviting. It was only five hours until dawn and Felice Koroyan had promised hers would be the first face he saw on welcoming the new day. He had no doubt she would keep her word.

'The time for sleep is long past.'

Aurelius dropped his goblet and backed away into the reception room. At the same time, he heard swords clashing outside. His door shuddered under an impact and burst inwards. Armour of God soldiers ran in. Aurelius backed away towards his shuttered windows, fear constricting his throat.

'How did you get in here?'

'Don't be a fool, Aurelius,' said Koroyan, walking out into the lantern light, more soldiers crowding around her. 'The Chancellor of the Order has friends absolutely everywhere. And they are never more vocal than when the Advocate is away from the Hill.'

'You're here to kill me,' said Aurelius, cursing himself for his quivering voice.

'Very perceptive of you,' said Koroyan, still moving towards him. He came up against the wall. 'Small wonder the Advocate made you her deputy.'

'Don't do it. Don't make the mistake.' Aurelius clawed his mind for a way out. 'The trial is recorded. Nothing can be changed. Process will continue. Killing me will make no difference.'

There were men either side of Aurelius now and ringing the Chancellor three deep. Under their helmets, he saw blind zeal and knew he was lost. A steady drip caught his attention and he looked down to his right. The man closest to him had blood dripping from his gladius.

'You must be old indeed to be so wrong. For one thing, your lifeless body returning to the embrace of God will give me enormous pleasure. Undeserved but that is not for me to decide. Perverse is the grace of God, don't you think? Once you and your craven staff are out of the way, I can dispense the justice the people demand.'

'You can't ...' began Aurelius.

'Count up, Aurelius. Advocate away; you, shall we say, incapacitated and Jhered absent with another heretic. Unless I am mistaken, that leaves me at the top of the tree, doesn't it?'

'The Advocate will return soon. The military are with the Ascendants. Your authority will be brief. I am sad I will not be there to witness your demise.'

The Chancellor shook her head. 'Oh, Aurelius. And to think I used to actually respect the sharpness of your mind. Even this afternoon, I had to admit you beat me on a point of law. But you haven't seen it all unravel, have you?'

She reached out and stroked his face. He turned away but she grabbed his chin and he wasn't strong enough to deny her. Their eyes met.

'The Advocate will come back but she will be too late, I'm afraid. Poor woman, deluded and distracted by the evil Ascendancy she took to her bosom. She will, of course, be arrested by my officers to stand trial on the charge you deferred before your "unfortunate" death.

'I've waited a long time for a catalyst to bring the citizens behind me. And the military will have no choice but to bend their knee to me. They are, after all, servants of the Conquord as are we all. Thank you, Aurelius, for the part you played in my succession to power.'

Aurelius struggled in her grip and shook his head loose. Armour of God soldiers grabbed his arms and held them down at his sides.

'The legions are mobilised. The Tsardon are coming, backed by Gorian's Ascendant power and the marching dead. Kill the only people capable of standing before him and you kill yourself.'

The Chancellor laughed. 'Do you think I really believe that feeble lie? Rumours designed to scare the faithful into accepting the Ascendants as saviours. There are no marching dead. Gorian Westfallen is almost certainly dead and rotting on an Atreskan field. And the Tsardon? They can come. And I will speak with them. And if they do not listen, I will destroy them, faithless heathens.'

She shook her head and made the Omniscient symbol over her chest. 'Poor, poor Aurelius. Blessed are you who go now to the embrace of God the Omniscient. Your cycle on this earth, this time, is complete.'

The Chancellor bowed her head. Aurelius closed his eyes. He didn't want to see the sword coming.

Ossacer and Arducius ran through the long dark corridors of the Academy. Fighting echoed on the floors below but chasing past a window, Arducius could see that the Victory Gates remained closed. There had been no alarm yet that the Academy was under attack. The barracks beyond the gates appeared dark.

'Get the eleventh-stranders, Ossie. Tenth should be in the safe room. I'll bring the twelfth to you.'

'See you there.'

The brothers split at an intersection. Arducius raced down a long corridor, his sandals slapping off the marble. He ran past ranks of doors, each letting into small rooms once populated by visiting Order ministers and now used to interview new potentials if they were used at all. Further down the corniced corridor, decked with paintings of Order hierarchy of ages past, they'd knocked together several rooms to form dormitories. One used to house the tenth strand until they were granted their own rooms on turning sixteen. Another, the eight children of the fledgling twelfth strand. Little ones, only seven years old.

In this distant corner of the vast, sprawling Academy, the noise of conflict was little more than dim echo. There was no noise either from behind the dormitory door. Arducius had no time for delicacy. He pushed open the door. Shutters were pinned partway back to let in the cool of night. Colonnaded alcoves and shelves were filled with books, rammed in after an instruction to tidy up. The gentle sound of breathing filled the air.

'Up, up, up!' shouted Arducius, slapping his hand on the door. 'It's Arducius. Come on. Up.'

Three of them jerked awake. He heard one cry out. In the darkness there was confusion and alarm. He hadn't lit a lantern. He didn't want the enemy to track his progress if he could avoid it. Questions came at him but he couldn't tell from who.

'No time to dress. Grab your togas and follow me. Dress later. Come on. Genna, Delius, Julius, Paul. Wake up.'

'What is it?'

'Trouble in the Academy. Remember what we spoke about and what we have to do?' Arducius crouched down now, getting to their eye level and calming them. 'Who can tell me?'

'We have to be quiet and go to the safe room.'

'Excellent. Don't be scared. We'll be all right. But hurry. Come on. Drop that book, Garrell.'

The children were crowding into the doorway. Someone was crying.

'Come on, now,' said Arducius. 'Don't cry. I'm here with you and I won't let anything happen to you. Follow me to the back stairs. All right? Everyone ready?'

Nods and yeses had him smile.

'Good. Come on then, and remember ...' He put a finger to his lips.

Holding Genna's hand, for the poor little girl was shaking and barely awake, he walked quickly back down the corridor to the intersection where he had left Ossacer. He turned left and hurried towards the back stairs. Servants' stairs. They stood behind a grand oak door and were rough underfoot with unfinished walls hemming them in as they spiralled down a central column.

Arducius pushed open the door. A shout echoed up from the floor below. There was a clash of swords and running feet. The children bunched. One let out a scream.

'Shhh,' said Arducius. 'Please. They don't know where we are and they're going away.'

He looked over them all. So small. So innocent. His anger flared but he quashed it and instead, forced calm into his lifelines.

'Come here. All hold hands.'

They did and he gripped Genna's hand a little harder. Their energy maps were revealed to him. Taut and too bright. Blue, yellow and red clashed as they tried to deal with the shock. Arducius bled his calm across them all. He saw them begin to breathe a little easier and the brightness fade from them.

'Good. Good. That's it. Now we need to be very quiet on the stairs. And you might see things you don't like. Trust me. It isn't far now.'

Their eyes were wide in the dark but he thought he had them. He led them into the stairwell. No light came from below. No shadow. Arducius didn't need light. The blank grey of stone was the backdrop against which tiny motes of loose energy fluttered in the airflow. But below there was a concentration of dim red and brown. He thought it was on the ground floor and it was certainly a person. And outside the door to the stairs. The drab brown of worked wood formed a barrier to his energy sight.

'Come on,' he whispered.

Step by tiny step, they moved downwards, heading for the cellars where the safe room was located. Built of steel and stone, and with an entrance covered by wine racks, it was big enough for the whole Academy. Provisioned and ventilated, they thought it might even survive the destruction of the entire building. A fine idea but they had to get there first.

Arducius kept his focus on the human energy map below. It was moving. The sounds of fighting were growing louder. The morass of energies out in the main halls of the Academy were chaotic. Light and fire, gathered masses signifying groups of men. Impossible to know if they were friend or foe.

Sweat was creeping down the back of his neck. The hand in his was twitching and hot. He looked back up the stairs as they turned the corner that would bring them down behind the door and the single figure outside it. Arducius put his finger to his lips again. Every head nodded. Every little body was pressed against the outside wall. There was a feeble light feeding down from above. Moonlight, he thought. Enough for them to see by.

Closer to the door, Arducius could see that there was another energy map. Another man. But sitting down. No. Slouched, slumped against the wall. And the energies were dimming. Bleeding away. He froze. Someone else was walking towards the doorway. Voices. He couldn't make out what they were saying but they were both men.

The door opened. There was a rustle on the stairs behind him. A helmeted head appeared. If he looked up, he'd see Arducius but not the children who were that bit further back round the corner of the central pile. He let Genna's hand go. He could feel all the children cringing into as small shapes as they could muster. One slip of a foot and they would all be discovered. Arducius sampled the gentle movement in the air, ventilation in the stairway. It would be enough. He let the map of wind form in his mind.

Below him, the soldier looked to his right where the stairs went down towards the cellar and complete darkness.

'Been down there?' asked the soldier.

'No,' replied the other. 'Not yet anyway.'

'Keep an ear out.'

'Yes, sir.'

The soldier looked up. Arducius released his Work. The slight air energies in the stairwell channelled though his body, amplifying into a blast of wind that picked the soldier up and threw him out of the doorway. Armour shrieked as it scored across the marble floor of the corridor outside. Arducius kept the wind blowing and marched down the stairs.

'Children, run. Down to the cellar. Don't look back.'

He moved into the doorway. The soldier was lying prostrate, unable to rise. He was shouting. Of his companion, there was no sign. The body of the Ascendancy guard was slumped to Arducius's right. A slick of blood ran away across the floor, picked at by the howling wind and spattered on a nearby wall and door. The children ran behind him, shouting and screaming on their way down into the dark of the cellar. They were safe but they had been seen. Arducius knew what he had to do.

A sharp point jabbed in to his neck, right below his ear.

'Lose it, devil boy,' said a voice. The point pushed harder, breaking the skin. 'Or sentence is carried out here and now.'

Arducius let the Work dissipate. The howling subsided. The other soldier got up, dusted down his skirts and breastplate, rearranged his Armour of God cloak and walked towards him. Arducius held his head high.

'You come with us. The Chancellor wants to see you. We'll come back for the brats.' The soldier stood right in front of him. He was a centurion. There was blood on his gladius. 'Very impressive trick. Pity it'll be your last, eh?'

'It won't be, and you'll never know it's coming,' said Arducius. 'Murderer.'

The man frowned and took off his helmet. He was greying and short-haired, eyes hard and full of hate.

'I don't recall asking you to speak, devil boy.'

His helmet connected with the side of Arducius's head. He was conscious long enough to fear for his bones when he hit the ground.

When Arducius opened his eyes it was to see Ossacer's face looking above him. There were hands on his head and a throbbing pain that dissipated quickly. He smiled but Ossacer's expression bade him drop it.

'Don't,' he said quietly. 'Had to fix you, but pretend you're hurt, all right? They'd kill me if they knew what I'd done.'

Arducius frowned. He felt fine. A blow to his head that Ossacer had plainly eased but apart from that. He looked down his body. His toga was smeared red. He started.

'Don't worry, Ardu. It isn't yours. You fell on a victim of our glorious Chancellor.' Ossacer raised his eyebrows. 'Broke your arm, dear brother. And a couple of fingers. You really should let me investigate how to fix that brittleness.'

Arducius shook his head. 'Keeps me careful.'

Memory swam back into his mind.

'A bit late now, anyway. You didn't make it to the safe room either? Where are we?'

'Chancellery,' said Ossacer. 'Why don't you sit up. Remember your head hurts.'

Arducius was lying on a recliner in front of the cold fireplace. He put an arm on its back and helped himself up, Ossacer's hands on his shoulders pushing him. The Chancellery was ablaze with light. And it was crowded. Arducius's heart fell.

The eleventh-strand trio were there, sitting on a recliner at right angles to his, staring at their feet. Two of the tenth strand as well, Cygalius who was in no condition to run and big Bryn, named for the old dear departed blacksmith of Westfallen and just as strong. No doubt he had stayed with his brother. Brave but foolish, but still he stood over the prone Cygalius, daring anyone to try and hurt him. Andreas and Meera were with them too, sitting on high-backed chairs pushed together so Meera could put an arm round the old man's shoulders.

All of them were surrounded by Armour of God soldiers. They ringed the Chancellery and had bows or swords ready. They stood at a safe distance and they watched. Ossacer and Arducius kept their voices low.

'What about the others?' asked Arducius.

'You know more than me,' said Ossacer.

'The little ones made it. I didn't see anyone else.'

'Let's hope the rest of the tenth made it down there too. Haven't seen Hesther either. If she's made it, we still have some hope.'

'They know where the twelfth went,' said Arducius. 'They saw when they caught me.'

'There's still time,' said Ossacer. 'We're never helpless.'

Arducius nodded at the watchful guards. 'Yes but we can't beat this many. Not you, me and Bryn together.'

'And you're wondering why we aren't already dead.'

'The thought had occurred.'

'I think we have the Chancellor to thank for that. We're public enemies, don't forget. She'll want to make the execution a piece of theatre.'

'That is not a comforting image.'

'No but it does give us more opportunity.'

The door to the Chancellery opened. Felice Koroyan walked in.

'Act one?' said Arducius.

Ossacer nodded.

The Chancellor walked slowly around her captives, appraising each of them in turn and completing her circuit in front of Ossacer and Arducius.

'Well, Ossacer, you said you wanted to take tea with me in the Chancellery and now it seems we have our opportunity. Not quite as you envisaged, I expect, but it really is the best I can do.' She smiled indulgently and cast her gaze quickly around the room. 'I missed this place. One in which to entertain, to contemplate matters of faith and to discuss the propagation of the Omniscient among the peoples of the Conquord. And you left it just as I left it. How kind.'

'Like I also said, we are but tenants. We were always happy to return your buildings to you and join you under the grace of God,' replied Ossacer.

Koroyan's expression took on disgust. 'You will join no one under the grace of God the Omniscient. Whatever foul idols you worship have no place here. And your presence has tainted this place. I shall probably have to knock it down to be free of the filth of your habitation.'

She gestured back down the corridor through the doors. The bust of Ardol Kessian lay smashed on the floor.

'I have already begun the process.'

'Did you see yours?' asked Bryn, turning heads. 'Hesther accidentally shoved it off its stand and we thought we'd leave it there. It looks far better without a nose, don't you think?'

The Chancellor had tensed but she didn't move. 'Have your fun, little boy. But remember that I will survive for the sculptor to remake my likeness. All that will be left of you, your Academy and your whole sick history will be in the memories of the few we will hunt to extinction. You are finished. Your pyres are built outside in the courtyard. The executioner's block awaits you before the flames carry your bodies to ashes.

'The late Senator Aurelius was wrong, I am afraid. There are many ways for heretics to die. Yours shall be in front of the city when dawn lights the day and the Omniscient shines upon me and the faithful.'

Arducius didn't even feel scared and he knew why. Instead, an all-pervading sadness and waste obscured everything else for him. He sighed and rubbed at his temple where Ossacer hadn't quite removed all the pain and bruising.

'The wheel turns full circle, doesn't it, Felice?' he said.

She narrowed her eyes. She always did when he used her first name. 'All our lives are a cycle, Arducius.'

'And you still choose force and murder to achieve your ends when all you ever had to do was listen and understand. You will murder us too but you should do so knowing we were never a threat to your authority. We grew up loving you. It's what the faithful do.'

'Perhaps neither of us ever changes our methods,' said Koroyan, her voice gentle, almost friendly. 'You still peddle your lies. Lies that are so convincing, so plausible that I almost believe them myself. But enough of this idle chatter. Our time for debate is done. Tell me, where are your other bastard creations and Hesther Naravny, mother of all this evil?'

Arducius was confused. 'Surely you know?'

'Clearly not,' snapped the Chancellor. 'We know some of the brats went down to the cellars and I know there is no way out of there. But we cannot find them just at present. I will know where they are.'

'Not from me,' said Arducius. 'Not from any of us.'

'Don't make me hurt you.'

Arducius laughed in her face, enjoying the fury that rose there.

'You cannot hurt an Ascendant like that. Do you not know we can all dampen our pain reflex and any of us can do the same for the Echelon and you'd never know we were doing it. Threaten something real. We are already going to die, after all.'

Koroyan shrugged. 'Very well.' Her eyes scanned the room briefly, falling on Ikedemus, an eleventh-strander. A Pain Teller in the mould of Ossacer. 'That one.'

Ikedemus yelped as he was hauled backwards from the recliner. The soldier, a massive man with huge arms, wrapped him under the neck and held him off the ground. Ikedemus kicked again and again but to no effect. Koroyan walked towards him, drawing a long slim-bladed knife from his belt. He kicked and struggled harder, crying out for help.

'None can come,' said Koroyan. 'Now you know where they are, don't you? Tell me and I will sheathe my knife.'

'Say nothing, Ikedemus,' said Ossacer. 'Keep calm, you'll be all right.'

'Hurt him and I hurt you,' warned Arducius.

Two dozen bows were flexed the next instant.

'I don't think so. One move and you all die right here, right now.'

'That might just be preferable,' said Arducius.

'If you think so, move on me.' Koroyan turned back to Ikedemus who had calmed and who returned her stare evenly. 'Now. Ikedemus. One more chance. Where are they?'

She toyed with the knife in front of his face. The boy said nothing. The Chancellor blew out her cheeks and shook her head. She had lost none of her speed and accuracy with the knife. She put one hand hard on the boy's right leg just above the knee and slashed the blade very deep right at the top of his thigh. He jerked with the pain. Blood quickly stained his toga and pulsed from the gash.

'Femoral artery, isn't it Ossacer?' she said. 'Watch him bleed to death. Or tell me what I want to know and I will let you fix him for the pyre.'

Ikedemus was trembling and quaking. He was jerking in the grip of the soldier, tears falling down his face. His mouth opened, imploring them to help but he would not cry out. Ossacer stood up.

'Calm, Ikedemus. You know what to do but you must be calm.'

'Stop this charade, Felice,' said Arducius. 'It'll get you nowhere.'

'I disagree,' said Koroyan. 'He's just the first, believe me.'

'It will take you the rest of the night,' said Arducius.

'*I* have all the time I need.'

Arducius smiled. 'You just don't know what you're dealing with.'

Koroyan followed his gaze. Ikedemus had stopped struggling. His eyes were closed. The blood had stopped flowing. Koroyan grabbed away his toga. The cut was still there but looked healthy and days healed. Arducius saw her tense. She stepped back a pace.

'Try and stem this, you Godless little bastard!'

She plunged the knife into Ikedemus's chest with such force that the blade went straight through his heart and out of his back, its point screaming on the soldier's breastplate. The soldier dropped the boy, and jumped back, staring at the Chancellor. Ikedemus slumped to the floor. Blood flushed from the wound. He spasmed and was still.

The Chancellor turned back to Arducius. Her eyes were wild, lost in fury.

'Tell me where they are or as God surrounds me, I will do to each of you what I did to that little brat.'

'This has gone far enough,' said Andreas Koll.

Arducius spun round, still numb from what he had just witnessed. Andreas was standing, supported by Meera. He had tears on his cheeks and his face was terribly pale. The memories of a decade ago on the forum oratory in Westfallen tumbled through Arducius's mind. That time it had been Father Kessian who spoke. Another frail old man. And if Koroyan preyed on Andreas too, she would not escape him. Not this time.

'Yes, I quite agree,' said the Chancellor, knife still held to stab, her breath coming in gasps.

'Even your own people struggle with what you have just done. You have just murdered a twelve-year-old boy.'

'I passed sentence on a heretic,' she said quickly. 'And all my people know that.'

She looked around the Chancellery and Arducius could see her emotions begin to drain. Andreas was right. Bows had been lowered, sword points too. Armour of God soldiers were staring at her or at poor Ikedemus lying in a pool of his own blood. Far from help now but far from pain and fear also.

Koroyan glared at her soldiers.

'Remember your God and your enemy. Remember the price of our failure.'

Ossacer had slumped back down on to the recliner. He had his head in his hands. Arducius knew why but no one could blame him, not for this. Bryn looked ready to pounce but Meera had a free hand and it grasped one of his, keeping him in check.

'What now, Felice?' asked Arducius. 'Who's next. Me? Ossie? Someone more helpless is normally your style, isn't it?'

Meera hissed at him to be quiet. He couldn't see the point. It struck him then that, famously, Arvan Vasselis once deserted Westfallen rather than defend it against overwhelming numbers of the Armour of God. He had saved the whole village by doing it because he believed heroism was not necessarily about dying for a cause but in making the right decisions that brought your people new hope. Arducius hadn't understood when first he read about it. Now, though, he did. He nodded at Meera and mouthed an apology.

Koroyan was on the move. She walked past Arducius and Ossacer and stood by Cygalius. Putting the knife point to his throat.

'This helpless enough for you, Arducius?'

Bryn growled and shook off Meera's hand.

'Threatening your best friend, am I?' Koroyan smiled sweetly. 'Then tell me what I want to know or watch him judder and die like the other one.'

'Bryn,' said Arducius sharply. 'Don't say a word.'

'If you touch him ...'

'Yes I know, Bryn, you'll hurt me. But not as much as the arrows will hurt you. Last chance.' She pressed the knifepoint in. Blood ran down Cygalius's neck. The unconscious boy swallowed reflexively.

'Felice, Andreas is right. Stop it now,' said Arducius. 'What do you want us to prove? That we are all willing to die to keep our friends safe? We will do it. And all you get is more blood on your hands. More enemies.'

Koroyan turned her head to Arducius and he could see that the burning was back in her eyes.

'I will tear this place apart brick by brick to find them. If you are alive or dead to see me do it makes no difference to me.'

'Think, Felice. Think what you are doing. You, Felice Koroyan, Chancellor of the Order of Omniscience. A woman more steeped in faith and love for this earth than any other that draws breath. And you are holding a knife to the throat of an unconscious youth. Heretic or not in your eyes, he remains just that. If you must execute him at dawn with us all, then you must. Verdict has been given, sentence has been passed. We all live on borrowed time in here. But for now, show him the mercy of the Omniscient. Don't murder him where he lies.'

Arducius thought she might remove the knife. Her mouth moved a little, gauging his words. The corners of her eyes twitched ever so slightly. Her face softened. Silence grew in the Chancellery, allowing the sounds of shouting to reach them from outside on the courtyard. Pyre-builders about their task.

Koroyan rammed the knife home. Blood spurted from Cygalius's throat. Meera screamed. Ossacer was shouting 'No!' and Andreas fell back in his chair, a trail of blood on his face. He was blinking, gone in shock. Bryn launched himself at the Chancellor. There was the multiple sound of bowstrings. Bryn was struck three times, his body tossed in the air and dumped on top of Cygalius. The Chancellery descended into shouts and threats. The doors thundered open. Bright light washed in. Heat followed. The Armour of God soldiers bunched and moved away.

Arducius turned. Mirron was aflame. She stood behind a huge figure that was thrown into shadow, her whole body spitting fire. Gouts churned from her fingertips, licking out at the soldiers, pushing them further and further away. Beside him, Felice Koroyan straightened and dropped the knife. The figure spoke.

'What in the name of my God the Omniscient, and my mistress the Advocate, is happening on the Hill?'

He walked out of the shadow and into the light.

Chapter Forty-Two

859th cycle of God, 41st day of Genasrise

'Anyone so much as touches a weapon, burn them, Mirron.'

'It would be my pleasure.'

Gatherers and Ascendancy guards were sprinting down the corridor towards them. Paul Jhered marched deeper into the room. His gladius was out. He grabbed the nearest soldier by the throat and held his sword at eye level.

'Want to threaten me? Drop your damn weapon.'

The blade clattered on the ground. Jhered moved on.

'You? Or you?'

He paced in front of them, his presence utterly overwhelming. He seemed even taller than before, bigger somehow. His face held that dreadful calm of the man entirely prepared to back up his words with action.

'Any of you want to take me on? Didn't think so. Drop them. All of them.'

Weapons clattered down on the marble. Jhered turned from them. Arducius wasn't sure if they were more scared of him or of Mirron who stood naked and glaring at them through the flames that covered her. She looked so powerful, so beautiful. Gatherer cloaks swarmed into the room. When every weapon was down, she let the Work drop. An Ascendancy guard covered her with a cloak.

Arducius watched Jhered pace into the centre of the Chancellery. He took in everything. Andreas and Meera, who were hugging each other. Ossacer, who was coughing as if his lungs would explode. The bodies of Ikedemus, Cygalius and Bryn. The terrified eleventh-stranders, just two of them now, standing in expanding puddles and stained togas.

And lastly at Felice Koroyan.

Jhered towered over her, his eyes piercing her, reaching the darkest recesses of her being. His stare was unwavering and he held it until it was Felice who flinched and looked away.

'What have you done, Felice?' he whispered. 'I see it but I don't believe it.'

'These people are convicted heretics—' began a soldier.

Jhered turned and pointed his sword. 'Shut. Up.'

'I am carrying out sentence,' said Koroyan.

Jhered sighed. He sheathed his gladius, it was clean and free of blood, took off a glove and dug in the corners of his eyes with thumb and forefinger.

'Didn't remember I was due back, did you? If the weather had been with us, I'd have been in port a day ago.' He was standing so close to Koroyan she could go nowhere, backed as she was against a recliner. 'Perhaps the Omniscient delayed me so I could witness this ... whatever it is. Murder? Treachery? This is no sentence for heresy I am aware of.'

'There was a trial yesterday,' said Koroyan, finding a little courage. 'The Ascendants and the whole Academy were found guilty of heresy and sentenced accordingly.'

'Really? You manufactured a trial, too? I must discuss the proceedings with Senator Aurelius. Perhaps he can explain to me why sentence involves slaughtering children in the Chancellery.'

'I think you might find that difficult,' said Arducius. He realised his heart was still thundering in his chest. His focus had narrowed right down and all he could really see were Jhered and Koroyan now. 'I think she visited him before she came here.'

'Sit down, Ardu,' said Jhered gently. 'Before you fall. It's all right, I know what happened to Aurelius. I'm just sorry I couldn't save everyone. What about the others?'

'Safe,' said Arducius.

He sat on the recliner. Jhered's invitation had broken the line keeping him upright. He felt so tired. Ossacer was wheezing next to him. He looked as white as Arducius felt.

'Good.' Jhered turned back to the Chancellor. 'I don't want to speak to you any further tonight. The list of charges that will be raised against you is going to be the work of several days, Felice, or so it seems to me.'

'Bring them to me at the Principal House. I look forward to them.'

'You have got to be joking. You are not going anywhere. You and every member of the Armour of God inside the walls of the complex is under arrest and will be held in the cells. All of you on charges of murder.'

'You can't arrest me, I am the Chancellor of the Order of Omniscience. You have no authority here.' Koroyan drew herself up, chin pointing, arrogance returned.

'Want to bet? I know who you are but you have forgotten who I am. Head of palace security. Want to see my badge of office?' Jhered leaned in, their noses all but touched.

'You were retained as the Exchequer.'

'I'm doubling up as a favour to the Advocate. Take them. And Felice. Not another word.'

Arducius watched palace guardsmen enter and take the Armour of God soldiers and the Chancellor away. Heads were bowed and not one of them raised objection. The ring of their shoes faded away. Mirron ran into the room and hugged both Ossacer and Arducius. The three of them clung to each other.

'I thought you were all gone for sure,' said Mirron.

'Touch and go,' said Ossacer.

'Lucky Felice likes the sound of her own voice,' said Arducius.

'And the feel of a knife in her hand,' said Jhered.

The three Ascendants broke their embrace. Jhered was standing over Cygalius. Two Ascendancy guards had lifted Bryn's body from him. His toga was red and soaking. Not a hint of white.

'You weren't talking, were you?' Jhered walked over to Ikedemus. He knelt and gave his throat a cursory press. 'Think it was the right decision?' He nodded and guards stooped to pick up the body and take it out of the Chancellery and away to the medics and morgue. 'Well?'

'We had to buy as much time as we could,' said Arducius. 'She was going to kill us all anyway. Any chance that others could escape we had to take.'

'What will happen to her?' asked Mirron.

Jhered shrugged. He was flat, emotionless. Drained. Arducius knew how he felt.

'I don't know, I really don't. I'd like to tell you that she'd be tried along with her thugs, found guilty and executed. The Omniscient knows there is evidence enough to convict a hundred Chancellors. But she is who she is. And out in the city, there is no doubt she holds sway. We had to break through organised demonstrations and near-riots. Couldn't get any sense out of anyone. When you get yourselves together I need to know exactly what's been going on. All I can guarantee you right now is that we cannot afford this. Not with what we've seen and heard.'

Arducius looked round at Mirron. Her face had taken on a haunted look like she'd just woken from a particularly bleak nightmare.

'You didn't find Kessian, did you?'

Mirron couldn't answer him. Tears spilled down her face and she crumpled back into his arms.

'We found him all right,' said Jhered. 'And that bastard Gorian. But there was nothing we could do to stop him.'

'Stop what?' asked Ossacer. 'It's true, isn't it? The walking dead.'

'He's building armies out there,' said Jhered and shivered at the memory. 'He's able to manage forces over great distances. He can make dead soldiers fight for him. Gestern is already gone. Unless the Ocetanas can stop them, they'll sail here and take Estorr too. The whole mainland, if they want. I don't know how to stop him. God-surround-me, we don't even know where he is.'

'We've got a few ideas for seek-and-destroy,' said Arducius. 'Felice may not believe it but we've had no choice. And some explosive powder has come from Sirrane. It's powerful stuff.'

'Really?' Jhered brightened. 'Being able to blow them up from a distance would be a mighty weapon.'

'Orin D'Allinnius is fine-tuning it and he's started manufacturing, I think,' said Arducius. 'And we—'

But Jhered had stopped listening. He shot to his feet and ran from the Chancellery, shouting men to him, shouting others to guard the Ascendants.

'What's got into him?' asked Arducius.

'I hope it's not what I think it is,' said Ossacer quietly.

At least she hadn't left him alive this time. There had been an end to the suffering. Eventually. Jhered was almost pleased. He stood at the door to the workshops, unwilling to step inside for a while. He was cold with rage. This was worse than looking around the Academy. There he had seen things he could at least comprehend. Religious outrage made flesh.

Here it was brutal revenge that had been a decade in the making. And it hadn't been quick. Orin D'Allinnius, the most brilliant scientific mind in the Conquord, had been strung up between two roof beams in the centre of his office. He had been beaten, his head a mass of bruising and blood, his lower jaw smashed across his face such that every cry of pain would have brought fresh agony. He had been partially burned and disembowelled. Great threads of intestines hung from his body and spread across the ground under his feet inside a pool of drying blood.

Orin's face was slack, his eyes mercifully closed. Jhered wondered why Koroyan hadn't gone the whole way and reduced him to ashes. His cycle would continue. The Chancellor's should not.

Jhered swallowed hard against the sight and smell. He walked across the floor and drew his gladius. He cut at a rope. Orin's body swung down to the left and smeared across the floor with a sick thud and swish. He hung by the other rope, spinning slowly.

'Sorry, Orin,' whispered Jhered. 'Sorry I wasn't here to save you.'

Jhered cut the second rope and tried to cushion Orin's final fall. He laid his head gently on the blood-slicked stone flags. A noise at the door made him look up.

'Marcus,' said Jhered. 'God-surround-me but it's good to see you at least have escaped this. What are you doing in Estorr? I thought you to be in Sirrane.'

Gesteris walked into the room, single eye burning as it stared at D'Allinnius's mutilated body.

'Roberto sent me back with information,' he said gesturing vaguely. 'I've been here for some time. I was meeting with Elise Kastenas for much of the night. Just got a message that there had been trouble in the palace. Who ...?'

But Gesteris knew who. He ran to one laboratory after another, throwing open the doors and looking in. Furnaces were still alight but there was no other sound. When he returned, his face was pale and grey.

'She's killed them all,' he said.

'They were manufacturing a powder.' Jhered stood up and stepped out of the blood and over intestines to get close to Gesteris. 'An explosive. We need it.'

Gesteris nodded. 'I brought the materials back from Sirrane. They obviously thought we'd need it. All the powder we can find is all that we'll have. This was the dedicated team. They were working day and night. We might find a couple who were off duty but Orin hadn't even started formalising the procedure. Nothing will be written down.'

Jhered put a hand to his mouth. 'She might have killed us all.'

'What do you mean? Paul?'

Jhered couldn't answer him for a moment. Visions cluttered his mind. Of him doing to Koroyan what she had done to poor Orin. Of legions of the dead marching through the Victory Gates. Gorian sitting on the throne. He felt a hand on his arm and came back to himself.

'You've been out there, Paul. What have you seen?'

'Everything is true. Gorian, the dead, the Tsardon. God-embrace-me, Marcus, but the things I have seen.' Jhered shivered. 'Anyone killed, Gorian raises to fight again. They have no fear or will. They don't suffer pain. We couldn't stand against them. Gestern is already lost. They don't even have beacons alight. The dead are coming here and no one even knows it yet.'

'Walk with me,' said Gesteris. 'Let's get out of here, let the medics clear up. Elise came with me. She's at the Academy.'

Jhered nodded and the two men left the workshops, heading back towards the Academy buildings. Jhered felt numb now. The rage had left him and something else had settled on him instead. It was unfamiliar and it muddled his thoughts. Gesteris put it into words for him.

'There's shock on you,' he said. 'All that you've seen ... It's one thing to deal with it at the time, quite another to relate it, bring it back to the front of your mind. Stick to simple facts. How many are coming through Gestern?'

Jhered stifled a laugh. 'That's the problem. I don't know. We saw thousands in Kark. But by the time they reach the western coast of Gestern how many might have fallen to decay and how many might have been added to the ranks is impossible to tell. Gorian has used plague as well as blades to get his army. And the Tsardon are backing him. If they can make passage to our eastern shoreline, I'm not sure we can stop them.'

The palace was quiet now. Academy and palace guards were at every door and were on the walls and patrolling the grounds. Noise filtered up from the city. Rioting was still going on. Fires marked the night. The slap of feet on cobbles was the only regular sound from within the walls as surgeons and soldiers did what they could to help the injured and give respectability to the dead.

'We can signal the Ocetanas,' said Gesteris. 'The invasion beacons are lit and our defences will be prepared. The Ocenii squadron will not let a single ship make land here.'

Jhered paused at the door to the Academy. A guardsman held it open for them.

'Why did Roberto send you back here?' Fresh anxiety was flowing in Jhered. A realisation that he did not want to face. 'Why did the Sirraneans give you the powder? What do they know?'

Gesteris took his arm and they walked inside. The door closed behind them. Inside, the corridors were bright with lantern light. Bodies had been moved but blood still marked floor, wall, bust and painting.

'Roberto went to the Gosland border because the Sirraneans said a Tsardon force was headed there. We are pretty sure others were moving towards Atreska too. We'll be all right. We have sound defence in both places, great men will be in charge. I think you need to calm down.'

'And I think you need to understand what we are facing here. This is not some simple invasion by an enemy we know. You cannot kill what is already dead.' Jhered shuddered afresh. 'Marcus, I have tried to fight them. I have struck my gladius through the heart of a walking dead man and he came at me again and again. Everything we know about warfare, about legions and phalanx, archer and gladius. It's all useless.'

'Paul, come on—'

'Listen to me, Marcus! Think. If we fight them one on one, every man of ours they kill swells their ranks. We have to stop them moving because they move day and night. Catapult, fire and Ascendant. That's all we have.' Jhered walked on towards the Chancellery. 'Pray the Advocate gets back soon. We have to know the Conquord strength of arms and we absolutely have to find Gorian. We encountered him once and we couldn't kill him. But he is the key.

'This is terrifying, Marcus, believe me. Because he can control dead armies on three fronts, have no doubt about that. And that bitch Koroyan has managed to kill at least four of our weapons and murdered our best mind.'

'But if they really are coming on three fronts, we don't have the strength of artillery, we don't have the Ascendant numbers and we certainly won't have enough powder. How can we stop them?' asked Gesteris.

'Exactly. If we can't find and kill Gorian, we are lost. And the sand in the timer is running very low.'

Chapter Forty-Three

859th cycle of God, 42nd day of Genasrise

General Dina Kell reached her decision and despatched fast riders to connect with the Conquord messenger service. She sent six. Each with the same message, each to find their quickest route to Estorr to deliver the news that might bring Ascendants into the field quickly enough to save the Conquord.

She had agonised for days while she and Prosentor Ruthrar talked and her people became more and more despondent. The dead were following and they did not pause in their pursuit. She couldn't make enough distance between them to put them off the scent, if that were even possible.

Conquord legionary and Tsardon warrior alike were blistered and exhausted, but at least the animosity was fading. One thing was becoming very clear to them all. Gorian did not recognise the difference between them. To him, all of them were potential recruits to the army of the dead. Conflict between them was a pointless exercise that only strengthened Gorian's hand.

The Tsardon were no longer the enemy.

But while there was no hostility, there was no real trust either. The two groups maintained their distance and Conquord soldiers still guarded their erstwhile foe at every rest break. None should be allowed to forget that this was Conquord territory.

'How long before we reach the Atreskan border?' asked Ruthrar.

He was riding beside Kell as he had done these past four days. His Estorean had improved from their constant conversation and Kell could not help but warm to him. Just a soldier doing what his rulers demanded of him. And now cast adrift. She had searched for subterfuge within him and had found none. He had been open about the Tsardon forces he knew were marching on the Conquord and he had never once asked the questions about the Conquord defences she half expected. The only conclusion Kell could realistically reach was that his first assertion, that he be allowed to warn his king of the danger Gorian presented, was an honest one.

'Thirty days at least. And that assumes we don't have to slow because of the condition of our infantries. It's not the worst country but we won't have highway all the way. We may find river transport but don't trust to the possibility. It's a hard march ahead.'

'And then?'

Kell shrugged. 'And then I release you and your men back into Atreska to warn your king and I stand with my people to defend our backs as well as our fronts. My prayer is that Khuran listens to you.'

'He will listen.'

'You sound so sure.'

'The evidence he can hear from any one of those under my command. And he will know from where I have come. You should ride with me to meet him.'

Kell shook her head. 'No. My duty will be at the fortifications. The dead will be at our heels. We'll need you to bring them down ahead while I deal with those behind.'

'I understand.' Ruthrar looked at her. His was a keen mind and he sensed in her something she was trying to keep hidden. 'What of your people who escaped up the cliff side? Roberto Del Aglios was with you, wasn't he?'

'He was.'

'And your husband. A hero of the battle of the Gaws.'

Kell bit her lip and let her gaze fall to her horse's mane. She tried to keep him out of her thoughts but he crowded in every time she closed her eyes. So hard to believe that he had fallen. But so hard to believe he had escaped, or Roberto. The filth and disease had been rushing towards them and they had not made the path before she had been forced away. She had lost sight of them both. What would she tell their children if he had become one of the dead? What can you tell a small boy who idolises his father and believes him invincible. Or a daughter who delights at her father's smile and wants to follow him into the legions, as a surgeon to rival Dahnishev.

'Dahnishev ...' she said, closing her mouth abruptly.

'General?'

'Three great men were at those cliffs when Gorian did what he did.

I cannot afford to believe any of them survived.' She frowned. 'How did you know about my husband?'

'It would be disrespectful of me to speak further. I can only join you in hoping he and Del Aglios survived. They will be useful in the days to come.'

'We agree there. But tell me. I will not take offence.'

Ruthrar paused to consider how he should frame his words. 'A couple are married and in charge of an elite Conquord legion. It was news that spread through the whole kingdom of Tsard.'

'Really?' Kell managed to laugh. 'I had no idea my fame was so far-flung.'

'I'm sorry it is so, now I have met you. We thought it a weakness of your Advocate's leadership. An experiment that had to fail.' Ruthrar gave a rueful smile. 'There were many jokes coined about it. You can imagine ...'

'And I have heard them all. But it worked, Ruthrar. I promise you that. Or it did until Gorian came back.'

Ruthrar nodded. 'I have no doubt, General. No doubt whatever.'

Gorian clutched at his sides as the pain swept him again. He laid a heavy hand on Kessian's shoulder and the boy staggered beneath it but did not buckle. His head pounded and his legs were stiff. Ahead, the dead marching around Lord Tydiol faltered a step before regaining their rhythm. Tydiol looked round and his face did not mask his concern. Gorian waved that he was all right.

'Why don't you go back on the cart, Father?' asked Kessian.

'A commander should not rest while his troops march,' said Gorian. 'I'm fine. I'm fine.'

He and Kessian were walking alone some thirty yards behind the dead of Tydiol and Runok. They had kept their forces going admirably and the Karkulas had not let him down. The priest was on the cart, one they had found at a farm they had overrun and now pulled by the farmer, his three sons and four others. Their deaths had given Gorian new ideas.

While he could not rely on horses or oxen, he did not have to waste the strength of his fighting force on mundanity. It would be wise to arrive at their next battle with more than just strength of arms. Artillery perhaps. And maybe a front line of those who could not fight but would sap the wills of the enemy. Was it not the duty of gods to use their subjects wisely and to bring into the fold those best suited to each task?

Hasfort was at the southern end of the Tharn Marches. A place renowned for engineering excellence. A place among others that the Conquord relied upon for its onagers, ballistae and scorpions. A place to increase his strength and versatility. The few hundreds in front of them right now could wait. Gorian knew where they were going.

'Father, please. You need to rest.'

Gorian looked down at him. His expression was not all sympathy and concern.

'You think you see weakness, boy, but you do not. The effort to control such forces is tiring, even for one such as me. You and the Karku, you have no conception. But I feel them, I feel my people. Each and every one as if he is joined to me by a thread I cannot break. I am the tree and my roots are everywhere through this earth. My people, they are the new shoots that spring from the ground. I make the ground feed them and they worship me for my care.

'So do not think me weak, Kessian. I am stronger than you can imagine. But with strength sometimes comes pain.'

Kessian's face was blank.

'Young minds can never understand the workings of gods.'

'But you aren't a god, Father. You're an Ascendant.'

'Not a god to you, perhaps, but then, you are my son. But to them, to the dead given new life, how else do you think I appear to them?'

'You don't look well, Father,' said Kessian. 'Your face. It's all blotchy and rough.'

Gorian felt his left cheek and smiled. He felt the skin protest as it moved, almost creaking.

'I am close to this earth. Is it not right that I take on new skin? The Ascendant will always become that which he loves if he chooses. I choose the strength of wood and the power of earth. It becomes me as fire becomes your mother.'

'You won't hurt her, will you?'

'I could never hurt her,' said Gorian. 'I want us to be the family we should always have been. It's one of the reasons I am doing all this. For you and for her. Now, I think I might travel on the cart. Help me back there, will you?'

'Yes, Father.'

Kessian seemed a little breathless. Perhaps it was the dream of uniting under his mother and father. What a world it would be under the control of the first family of true Ascendants. Majesty and deity, empire without end. It was enough to set Gorian's heart fluttering in his chest.

He let Kessian help him onto the back of the cart and then sent the boy away to walk with Lord Tydiol and learn more about the dead under his control. If he was to become general of his own force one day soon, he had to understand the nuances of energy that kept each individual working within the mass and how each fed off the others to make the whole stronger.

'Why don't you let me help you, Father?'

'How can you help me?'

'Let me raise animals to pull the carts. Ease the burden on you.'

'No,' said Gorian, his tone startling Kessian. 'You cannot trust an animal. And you cannot waste your energy on mere beasts. Men are our army and they are our workforce and muscle. Never forget that.'

Gorian winced as he drew his legs up. The pain had been getting steadily worse since dawn. He drew up the hem of his shabby-looking toga and tensed. From the top of his boots to the middle of his thighs, the skin was discoloured. Brown and thickly veined. In places, he could feel that it was as dry as bark. In others, it felt brittle like dead leaves.

He pushed the material back down, aware that the smell of his legs was not entirely wholesome either. But then, neither was the earth itself. Mould and rot sat by vital soil and new growth. One could feed the other and so it would be within him. He remembered a time when he would regenerate almost on a whim. Those skills seemed difficult to recall now.

Gorian lay back for a moment. His body wasn't important. The well of his mind would keep it in the basic condition needed to do his Work. He could feel the thousands of lines emanating from him, channelling through Kessian and the Gor-Karkulas to be amplified again before reaching the dead. All were linked to him as all the living were linked to the Omniscient through the earth.

Along the coast of Gestern, they were mustering in their thousands. It was his most successful force. Everywhere, the Conquord had tried to hold them back and resistance had brought them to him. They would wait now, feeding from the earth under their feet, keeping them fresh for the difficult journey to come. Many would fall but enough would survive.

And they would fall on Caraduk, Estorea and Easthale like a wave washing up a tidal river. Unstoppable by man, only by god.

Only one place would remain free, because everyone had to keep something of their former selves pure and real. Gorian had chosen home.

In Atreska, they marched without opposition and had sought out those they could attack. It had been only moderately successful and Gorian had to remain satisfied that King Khuran and his twelve thousand marched behind the dead. Their actions had brought new subjects to the fold and with them came the artillery Gorian had demanded be scavenged and stolen.

Yet it worried him that the Atreskan defenders had chosen their course of no resistance. He thought to meet them all at the border with Neratharn but was uncertain of their numbers. He needed a way to ensure his subjects, who had so far endured the long march from the Tsardon border, had the strength left to breach those defences. Too many were falling, decay taking them. There had to be a way to boost their hold on life.

And of course, there was. The dead fed off the slumbering power of the earth as did the vegetation that sprang up with such enthusiasm now genastro was in full voice. Beautiful new life surrounded his subjects, taunting them as slowly they faded, the rot in their bodies eventually overcoming his grip on them. Earth was solid, unquenchable energy. Vegetation was bright light in comparison, its energies those of renewal and of hope. Energies he could give to his people.

Gorian relaxed and felt some of his pain begin to ebb. So simple, he used himself as first recipient. Around the cart as it moved along the grass track towards Hasfort, the green shoots and new flowers, fruit buds and leaves withered and crinkled, giving up their life, bringing them to an early dusas. Gorian let his body map take in the energy, feeling it suffuse him, roar through him like the rush of fire through dry straw.

He played the shape out through the thousands of lines to his subjects, god giving health to his faithful, and knew his benevolence toward them would have no end and that they would worship him for it.

The Gor-Karkulas in the wagons of the Tsardon King jerked as energy flooded through them and away out to the dead marching through

Atreska. Great swathes of grass on the gently waving plains stiffened and discoloured, turning brown and crumbling to little more than dust. Tsardon warriors shouted and cursed, hurrying away from the dead as the circle of destruction expanded out.

King Khuran stood his ground and watched the grass die as it passed under his feet and away for fifty, a hundred, two hundred yards before slowing and stopping. The dead force responded. They stood taller. Feet that had dragged were picked up again. The sick stench of their decay lessened and it seemed that a whisper of health issued from their lips. A cry of new hope.

He turned to his aides.

'What is he doing now?'

'The point is, Julius, that unless we stop this bastard in whatever way we can, you won't have a damned flock to minister. I fail to see why that is so difficult to understand.'

Three days in a small, single-masted, single oar-paired boat and Roberto was ready to kill. The only thing that stopped him was that the object of his urge was the man he had risked his own life to save. The argument was circular and endlessly frustrating. They hadn't come to blows yet but that was mainly due to the calming influence of Harban-Qvist who would gently, or not so gently, remind them of the task in hand.

They had to reach Neratharn and the Gaws before the dead swamped the defences and they had to get messages to Estorr about the threat from the north and east. They needed Ascendants to help unpick the damage one of their own was causing.

'But there must be another way, barring the use of fire.'

'And just say, for the sake of argument, that there isn't? And just say, for the sake of my sanity that we haven't been down this particular dead-end before?'

'Another way must be found,' said Julius.

Roberto looked up at the sail and trimmed the tiller position a little to keep it taut. They'd been lucky with wind direction so far but it had been the source of another argument when Harban had suggested that God was helping them get to their destination by sending wind to the sail. It wasn't quite the way Julius saw things. As usual.

'All right,' said Roberto. 'And this is my final offer. Let's go to a completely theoretical world. And in that world, let's postulate that the use of fire is the only way to ensure the security of the mass of citizens of the Conquord. Every other way has been thought of, tried and discarded. Does it not make sense that in that instance ... Wait, let me finish, Julius, and please, try to prise open your mind just a little to let the air in. Does it not make sense in those unique circumstances to accept that the sacrificing of a relatively few is better than ultimately sacrificing pretty much everyone? Remembering of course that unless you use fire, the dead cannot be stopped.'

'The ending of the cycle of an innocent is not the right of any man on this earth,' said Julius carefully.

'I have accepted that from the moment we stepped on to this boat. Answer the question.'

'I have.'

'So, what you're telling me is that you would rather see the entire Conquord of Omniscient faithful fall under the death walk of Gorian Westfallen than see a single innocent burned to prevent that from happening. In fact, that you yourself would rather become one of the walking dead, thereby denying you your right to find God's embrace, rather than burn even one poor unfortunate who is already in that position.'

'I am saying that we cannot resort to evil to rid the world of evil.'

'You really are a fucking idiot aren't you?'

Barias winced. 'All I do is uphold the tenets of my faith.'

Roberto flapped a hand at him. 'You really don't get it. The rules have changed. Gorian has seen to that. You have to adapt. You have to move forward. And you have to make the hard choices that benefit the mass at the expense of the unfortunate.'

'True faith will turn them from their path,' said Julius, smiling indulgently.

'Right. Like it did at the base of the crag? As I recall, I saved your life that day. Where would your faith have got you if I hadn't been so stupid, eh?'

'I am just one man. Bring Order ministers to bear in numbers and the power of our wills will take the desire to walk from the dead and they will fall into God's embrace once more.'

Roberto looked skywards. Cloud was overhead, the wind blowing along beneath it.

'Well, it can't be sunstroke.'

'What can't?'

'The reason for you talking such utter nonsense. But why should I care? Actually, you've just cheered me up, now I come to think about it. Let's do it your way absolutely. We'll round up all the Order ministers that are willing, plus the Chancellor, and we'll wave you goodbye at the Gaws gate. You can go and do your faith thing and when you're all dead there'll be no miserable whining to stop soldiers like me doing what must be done to save the Conquord and its people.'

Roberto laughed and pulled in the main sheet a little. Guilty satisfaction rolled over him.

'I will be happy to walk before the dead with my fellow believers at my sides,' said Julius but there was no conviction in his voice.

'Don't make me laugh again, Barias, my sides are already hurting. You don't have the guts and what is more, you know you will die. You know it. Deny that and I'll throw you over the side.'

'Your arguments are puerile and childlike,' said Barias.

'Really? Or just simple and pragmatic? Julius, I am happy to call your bluff when the dead are within earshot. Push me and I'll do it. But do me this one favour first. See what comes at us from wherever it comes. Look inside yourself first before letting your pride get you killed.

'The thing is, we don't have to like each other and that is comforting. But after this is over, the survivors will need the Order like never before. They'll need people like you. You might be a fucking idiot, Julius, but at least you've got faith.'

Chapter Forty-Four

859th cycle of God, 46th day of Genasrise

Herine Del Aglios didn't come by sea for the final part of her journey back to Estorr. A bird had reached her. The message was brief but it had been signed by Jhered and that was enough. She came in by the River Havel, arriving under cover of darkness in the private marina deep in the valleys to the west of Estorr, thereby coming back to the Hill almost completely unobserved.

She'd spent the last two days gnawing at her fingers while all the while Vasselis and Tuline had tried to calm her. Times of war leading to greater security precautions. The Advocate being able to take no risks. Assassins could be anywhere. Etcetera. But she knew some form of calamity had struck Estorr. She knew Jhered too well for there to be any other explanation.

Nothing had prepared her for what she had heard when her entourage had swept in under the Victory Gates in the early hours of the morning. It explained the reason for the many fires she had seen down in the city. At one point she thought perhaps the invaders were already in Estorr but had dismissed that as the anxiety of a tired mind. Now she wished it were true. At least your declared enemy was one you could understand.

The enemy that had unveiled itself within the walls of the palace complex was one whose defeat was difficult if not impossible to achieve and certainly not while maintaining the support of the citizenry. Herine had met Jhered as she descended from her carriage. She recalled the rage drowning her as they walked to her private chambers in the palace. She had wanted to go straight to the cells then and there but Jhered had made her freshen herself after her journey, change from her dusty clothes into a formal toga and her Advocate's circlet; and then sit down with a goblet of hot, unsweetened wine.

He was still there now, with her in her least favourite reception chamber, prowling while they waited. Herine watched him. He walked out onto the balcony that looked down over the harbour of Estorr and the unrest that flared there every night. He walked the circumference of the large room with its half columns decorating the walls, its bust-filled alcoves and its paintings of great generals and Advocates.

Jhered paused by that of his grandfather and nodded solemnly at the dour visage, no doubt apologising for the state of the Conquord. He glanced up at the deep green silk sheets that hung from the ceiling, covering a mosaic of Omniscient glories that Herine had never liked. He walked back into the centre of the room and stood across the table from where she sat, ignoring the recliner at his back.

'Are you ready?' he asked.

'I've been ready ever since I got out of my carriage, Paul. Now I'm just marking time while you wear dents in my marble.'

'She's not even contrite,' he said.

'She's never contrite.'

'But she's never committed such serious crimes before. Herine, she wanted to depose you and install herself. And she very nearly succeeded. If I'd been a little later, if the Ascendants had given in to her ...'

'What the Ascendants did, or one of them, I'll deal with later. You already have my eternal gratitude.' Herine held up a hand. She smiled at him, his face getting craggy with middle age and the lines around his eyes deep with his concern for her and the Conquord. He could still make her feel warm and secure merely by his presence. 'I know why you're telling me this and I will not let her goad me, I promise. But I have to meet her alone. Stand outside the door by all means but this is something I have to face as the lonely ageing Advocate, all right?'

Jhered nodded and finally, he sat down.

'I remain unsure why, Herine. She's a murderer, she has committed treason and she must burn. Just put her on public trial. It's the only way to calm the city.'

'Come on, Paul. Felice and I have been friends in the past. She has done magnificent work for the Conquord in her time. I've known her for decades. I know what she's done is unforgivable but still I feel I owe her one last chance to explain herself to me in private. Gain some redemption.'

'What will you say?' he asked.

Herine sagged. 'Oh, dear Omniscient, I don't know. What do you say to Chancellor Koroyan?'

'Lonely Advocate ...' Jhered tried a smile but it didn't come off.

'You know you haven't even asked me about the Solastro Palace senate meeting,' said Herine.

She stared at him again and understood the extent of the horrors he had seen in the palace. It took a great deal to shake up Paul Jhered.

'And you haven't asked me about Kark and Gestern. But one thing at a time, eh?'

Herine shook her head. 'Not exactly. You need to find Arvan Vasselis and my daughter at the earliest opportunity. Sit with Marcus Gesteris and Elise Kastenas. And maybe Arducius.'

'What happened?'

'Half the Conquord decided not to send troops but defend their own petty borders.' Herine could feel herself flushing at the memory. 'What's in Neratharn, Gosland and Atreska right now is pretty much all they'll be getting.'

Jhered sneered. 'Don't tell me, Phaskar has been listening to Dornos.'

'And Tundarra, Paul. I'm sorry.'

The colour drained from Jhered's face. He stood abruptly and turned away, catching sight of his grandfather's portrait. He cleared his throat and swallowed. When he turned she thought she could see his eyes glistening but it might have been a trick of the lantern light.

'I'll have them send in the Chancellor,' he said. 'Be careful.'

Jhered bowed and turned to leave.

'Paul.' He looked back at her. 'One thing at a time, eh? Let's clear up this mess then take back what is ours.'

He stood still for a moment before nodding fractionally and marching from the room. Herine sighed and leaned back into her recliner. She snapped her fingers for a servant to refill her goblet but of course they had all been dismissed already. She wondered instead how she should appear when the Chancellor walked in.

It was perennially difficult to predict what would disarm Felice Koroyan. And perhaps now was not the time for such games. Herine stood and walked across to her balcony. Dawn was coming but fires still burned away at the early hours of the morning. A picture of the continuing trouble sparked in the Chancellor's name. It would do perfectly.

There was a knock on the door at the far end of the chamber. Herine did not turn when she heard the door open.

'Chancellor Koroyan, my Advocate,' said a guard.

Herine waved a hand to acknowledge him. The door closed again. Herine heard the Chancellor's sandalled feet whispering across the marble floor.

'Isn't Estorr resplendent as dawn breaks,' said Herine when she guessed Koroyan was just a few paces away. 'The twinkling lights of the dock, the myriad patter of fountain pools, the white of our walls catching the sun's first rays. The rioters' fires destroying proud buildings that have stood for hundreds of years.'

Herine turned. The Chancellor looked exhausted. There were streaks of dirt on her toga. The odd bit of straw was caught in hair that was dishevelled and needed a wash. And there was a look to her face that suggested minimal food and water.

'Your new quarters not to your liking?' asked Herine. 'I know you would have preferred these surroundings, perhaps my bedchamber and certainly my throne, but I'm afraid a cell is the best I can do for you at the moment.'

The Chancellor chose not to respond. There was caution in her eyes but her bearing still bespoke pride. Injustice burned from her face. Herine shook her head.

'Unbelievable. I have you on five counts of murder, not counting guardsmen in the line of duty. I have you on treason. I may even have you on heresy but I have to look at the statutes for what it means when someone, anyone, attempts to supplant the appointed representative of the Omniscient on this earth. I would have respected you just a little had you stuck to the code of law which poor Aurelius felt it his duty to abide by.

'But that's the trouble with bullies and zealots, isn't it? Things don't go their way and they resort immediately to base methods. I'm surprised you have nothing to say. After all, you clearly feel you have done nothing wrong.'

'It matters little what I say. You will bounce me through court and have me executed anyway.'

'Seems to be all the rage round here at the moment, doesn't it?' Herine took a pace forward. 'How dare you lecture me on the process of law. My officers, like poor Senator Aurelius, carried out their duties exactly as they should, don't you think?'

'Aurelius didn't see the true picture.'

'Oh, he saw it all too clearly. And that was his real problem, wasn't it? And what about Orin D'Allinnius? What didn't he see?'

'That science cannot be allowed to create destruction of the Omniscient faithful.'

Herine gaped, she couldn't help herself. 'I cannot believe my own ears. Have we just marched back five hundred years? Not even you can really hold to the ancient scriptures. This is progress. To keep the faithful, we must have the means to defend them. And if that means explosive powders, then I'm all for it. And if it means the Ascendants too, then that is our future. Not yours, not now. But mine and every citizen's walking the Conquord this day.'

'You can't see it, Herine, but I can and so can the citizenry. The Ascendants are evil. One came to me and admitted as much. Another makes the dead walk, so I am told. What more must they do to convince you? I had no choice.'

'No choice?' Herine barked a laugh. 'Do you think I am grossly stupid? You waited your chance and you took it. Lucky for the Conquord you failed. Lucky for me, Aurelius wasn't the weak man you thought him.'

'If you think that, then yes, you are stupid. The Ascendants are a plague and they must be arrested, tried and burned.'

The light was back in Koroyan's eyes. She was standing tall and her voice was gaining strength.

'You would have me arrest the only people capable of saving the Conquord? When did you lose your reason, Felice? You have no idea what is happening on our borders. I have. The plague is one of the walking dead and the Ascendants can stop it.'

The Chancellor shook her head. A strand of straw fell to the ground. 'And what then? You hand them power of that magnitude and then expect them to return to their Academy and play their research games again? They will demand more influence over you, over the Order, over everyone. And you do not have the strength to stop them. One day they will rule in Estorr. You just don't see it yet.'

'I trust them, Felice. I trust them far more than I can ever trust you, that is sure.'

'Then you are an enemy of the Conquord and I denounce you.'

Herine went cold. 'I beg your pardon?'

'They are an evil set against the will of God.' The Chancellor was shouting. She jabbed her finger at Herine, declaiming as if from the Principal House of Masks. 'And if you unleash them to do their work then you join them in that evil and you become an enemy of all you claim to support.'

'I am trying to save them, damn you!' Herine shouted back at her, coming closer still. 'I have always said that I will do anything to keep the Conquord together. This is not evil, it is just action.'

'Enemy.' Spittle was flying from Koroyan's mouth. Her face was red, flushed with her passion. 'Every day, the Conquord fractures more. Territories desert you. People turn from you. You are the Advocate of a failing empire and the Ascendants play you for a fool every day, just waiting. Turn back.'

'To what? To you? To your murders and your torture? You and your thugs are tearing the credibility of the Order to shreds. I am about to put that right.'

'You cannot silence me. You are not my Advocate. You are a heretic, you are evil. Once more, I denounce you.'

Herine's hand came round fast and hard. Her open palm caught the Chancellor flush on the cheek and followed through, finishing behind her head. The Chancellor's head snapped to the right. She stumbled back. Her sandal slipped on the marble floor and she fell backwards. The base of her skull caught the corner of the bust of Herine's father. Herine heard a snap. The Chancellor collapsed to the floor, twitched briefly and lay still.

Herine's hand was ringing with the force of the slap. She stared at the Chancellor. There was a knocking sound. The door.

'Stay out,' she called, forcing a little calm into her voice. 'Everything's all right. Just a little accident.'

She knelt by Koroyan. The Chancellor's head lay at an ugly angle, the rest of her body lay in a heap. Herine was quivering all over.

'Oh no. Oh no.' She repeated the words over and over again. She reached out a hand and moved a strand of hair from the Chancellor's face. 'Please, no.'

Herine swallowed hard. Tears threatened. Her heart was pounding wildly. She felt cold. Sweat broke out all over her body. She stared at her guilty palm, trying to still the stinging that would not stop. She rubbed at her lips, they were so dry. She let out a huge sob and forced her mouth closed again.

The door was thrust open. She looked up straight into the eyes of

Paul Jhered. He took one glance, barked at guards to stay out and closed the door behind him. He walked over. Herine met his eyes again and in them was such sadness it tore at her will.

'Oh, Paul. What have I done?'

Chapter Forty-Five

859th cycle of God, 46th day of Genasrise

Paul Jhered knelt down and felt for a pulse at the Chancellor's neck. He had no real need to but he had to be sure. Her neck was broken. Snapped clean. The exposed cheek was red from an impact. He glanced up at the bust, saw blood on the marble at its base and the picture filled in quickly.

Herine had slumped back against the wall and was staring at him, beseeching him to tell her what he couldn't. He simply shook his head.

'It was an accident,' she said, her voice trembling and choked. 'She slipped when I hit her. She fell ... she fell hard.'

'Shh. Shh. It's all right, Herine. Try and be calm. We'll deal with it.'

'How?' Herine's eyes were desperate. 'I've killed her. I've never killed anyone before.'

'I know, I know.'

Jhered moved round and sat by her. He put an arm around her shoulders and pulled her to him. Her head lay on his chest. Breath heaved in and out of her body in great pained gasps but she was too shocked to cry for now. That would come later. The guilt of the first person you kill never leaves you. Jhered knew that. But the real tragedy was that for everyone else you kill, that guilt is never as acute. He prayed Herine would never learn that particular lesson as he and the Chancellor both had.

'What do we do now?' Herine's voice was tiny and frightened.

'I'll think of something,' he replied. 'Don't you worry about it.'

Jhered hadn't thought the situation could get any worse but here was a total disaster. He hadn't even got as far as asking for Vasselis's whereabouts before he'd decided he should remain on station. He'd hurried back and could hear the shouting through the walls and echoing out over the balcony well before he reached the door. He'd run but he'd been too late to avert calamity. Again.

'We have to tell the citizens. Something they'll believe. This can't get out.'

Herine was starting to think again but she hadn't grasped what she'd done or its consequences. Jhered knew that whatever they told the Omniscient faithful, they would believe another story. They would see the hand of the Ascendants in this. The rest of the Order ministry would see to that. Jhered knew he should tell Herine that, get her walking the path of reality.

'It won't,' he said instead. 'Everything will be fine.'

'Liar.'

She raised her head and looked at him. The pain was there but the panic was clearing away.

'Good,' he said. 'Right. I need you to stay here while I go and get things organised. It's an accident, all right? It's all we can say. Don't let anyone in until I return.'

'I don't want to look at her, Paul.'

'Then don't. Come on, get up. Lie down on the recliner and let's top up your wine.'

'I'm a murderer,' she said as they walked the few paces to the centre of the room. 'I should burn.'

'Don't talk like that,' said Jhered sharply. 'It won't help. Did you mean to kill her? No. Accident, Herine. Think nothing else.'

'She's still dead.'

'Yes. She even escaped public trial and burning. Almost like she wanted it to happen.'

Jhered tried to smile at his vain attempt at humour but saw Herine take it on board. She nodded.

'She did, you know. She'd never allow herself to be burned and her ashes scattered. She was looking for a way out.'

'But perhaps not quite like this, eh?'

'She knew she was going to die. She told me.'

'Just sit down. I'll fill your goblet.'

Jhered's fledgling hope that Herine had clawed her way back to reason died. Her voice was distant, unconnected. He knew he shouldn't leave her but he had no other choice. He poured more wine into her goblet and handed it to her. She would have dropped it but he closed both her hands around it. She clutched it hard.

'She escaped us again, didn't she?'

'In a manner of speaking.' Jhered straightened. 'Don't leave this room. Do you understand? Herine?'

She nodded eventually.

'I'll bring help and then I'll take you to your daughter. You'll be all right?'

'Of course,' she said. 'I am the Advocate.'

'Yes, you are the Advocate. Hang on to that. I'll be back.'

Outside the room, Jhered paused only to explain to the guards the penalty for going inside. There had been an accident, he said, but the Advocate was safe. Once out of sight on the stairs, down to and through the gardens and across the square to the Academy, he ran like he hadn't for thirty years. He was sure Vasselis would be with the Ascendants. It was where the Marshal always went when he arrived at the palace. And if he was lucky, he would find everyone else he wanted there too, despite the early hour.

Jhered tried hard to focus his thoughts so he could deliver the news coherently but the same line thundered through his head. The Advocate had killed the Chancellor. And as a result, at the exact worst moment in the Conquord's history, there was going to be trouble in the City like they'd never seen before.

'We should be celebrating, not worrying about what a few Order ministers might say on the steps of their Houses of Masks,' said Ossacer the moment Jhered told them all the news.

They were all awake. In truth, sleep had been difficult to come by. The corridors still echoed to the memories of fear and the Chancellery held the taint of blood on the air. It would probably never be scrubbed away. It was uncomfortable but the Ascendants refused to give up their central meeting place.

The arrival of the Advocate along with Vasselis and Tuline had sparked an immediate gathering of the senior military and the Ascendancy. Marcus Gesteris, Arvan Vasselis and Elise Kastenas were sitting along one side of a table with a man whom a rare stroke of pure fortune had brought into port. Admiral Karl Iliev, Prime Sea Lord of the Ocetanas these days but still Squadron Leader of the Ocenii Squadron. Largely because no one had the guts to tell him he shouldn't still row with the Conquord's elite marines.

On the other side of the table, Arducius, Ossacer, Mirron and

Hesther Naravny. All of them had a couple of hours on Jhered in terms of the numbers and discussions. But his news had just dropped an onager stone on the maps, diagrams and sheets of figures.

'That's something coming from the man with the most rigid personal ethical system in the Conquord,' said Jhered.

'There are exceptions to every rule,' said Ossacer quietly. 'She betrayed us. She got what she deserved.'

Jhered sighed. 'I'll say this just once for everyone's benefit. Ossacer, your going to the Chancellor and bleating about the rights and wrongs of your work for God is directly responsible for the situation we now face.'

'I—'

'Shut up, I am talking.' It was so hard to stare down Ossacer. He fixed you with those blind eyes full of passion. Jhered did it this time, though. 'You misunderstood her fatally. You're lucky to be alive. Others were not so fortunate. And I expect you to make recompense for your stupidity.'

An uncomfortable silence fell across the table. Ossacer had blushed crimson and was staring down at his papers. Vasselis was looking at him without sympathy. Iliev had a smile on his face. No one else betrayed too much. Jhered sat down at the head of the table.

'However, I agree that she got what she deserved. But not the manner of her death. And what it means is that we have to factor in Ascendant and Academy security. There are two legions of the Armour of God in or around Estorr. The citizens are already against you and the Order will keep that passion fired.'

'You think we should leave the city?' asked Arducius.

'And go where?' responded Elise Kastenas. 'There are only three of you capable of battlefield work. Which front would you like to defend?'

'The one Gorian is attacking,' said Ossacer. 'It's the only choice.'

'It isn't that simple,' said Mirron. 'He doesn't have to be present to keep the dead attacking. That means we don't know where he is.'

'Except that Harban was following him north and not west,' said Jhered.

'What information do we have on movements in Atreska and Gosland?' asked Jhered.

'Very little,' said Gesteris. 'Rumours of reverses in Atreska, nothing from Gosland. All we know is that twelve thousand were on the border, being watched by Davarov and half that approached Gosland where Roberto would have been waiting.'

'Neither force will hold,' said Jhered. 'Not without Ascendants and masses of artillery. I sent Harkov through Atreska. He should be back soon if he's coming at all.'

'Sorry, Paul.'

'Yes, Elise?'

'You're so sure border defences will fail? Mirron has been trying to explain but apparently spent much of her time, well, incapacitated.'

'Under the ice, yes.' Jhered smiled. 'And yes, I'm sure. I spent plenty of time thinking about it. All you have to do is create a few dead, be it by disease or arrow or whatever, in amongst your enemy force. Then wake them up and get them swinging blades against people who in the first place, won't be expecting it and in the second, can't stop you without cutting off your legs.'

'Sounds to me like you need a whole new way of fighting,' said Iliev. 'I can sink their ships like I always could. And I don't have much of a problem with fire, either. Not like the legions tied to the Order Speakers who march with you. If you take my advice, you'll leave them at home or gag them and then just do what is necessary with everything you have. In the end, we are all soldiers and we kill to keep our lands safe. Our methods cannot concern us because if they do, we will fail.'

'You cannot afford to think like that,' said Ossacer.

'Give me strength,' said Arducius. 'Ossie, it's too late for that, isn't it?'

'Is it? You're all talking disaster and we actually have no idea whether the threat is big enough to actually harm us. Except Paul and Mirron, none of us have actually seen anything or heard any concrete news.'

'So we wait until one of Gorian's dead taps us on the shoulder and introduces himself?' asked Arducius. 'You read the reports of the last war. Elise's predecessor nearly cost us the Conquord by doing nothing much until it was almost too late.'

'Took my words,' said Kastenas. 'But Ossacer is right. We know dates of enemy arrivals on our borders so we also know worst-case progress. We know Gestern is compromised but we have seen no ships threatening us and the Octanas are patrolling.'

'None will make landfall on our eastern seaboard,' said Iliev.

Jhered believed him utterly. 'Good to hear. And keep the Isle secure. If they get in there . . .'

'They will not.'

'We do have time to counteract land forces at present,' continued Kastenas. 'I am prepared to wait until we hear accurate reports but we have to be prepared to move. That means you three Ascendants need to have your bags packed. Marcus and Paul need to have the powder cased to take out into the field. Sorry, Paul, but I have to repeat this. Because we have lost the support of Tundarra and Phaskar as well as Dornos, our main focus has to be the Neratharn-Atreska border. We can move anywhere from there and it is there I want the muster.'

'No horses,' said Jhered.

'Pardon?'

'They'll run. The Karku gorthock would not face the dead. There is no reason to expect any animal to do so. God-surround-me, precious few men and women will.'

'I can't run legions without cavalry, Paul, be serious.'

'Trust me, we have to find other ways to fight because a gladius in the throat won't stop them either. Focus your thoughts there and warn the generals. They can throw out all the rules and everything they've ever learned. They have to stop them because they can't kill them.'

'Build the walls high and pour burning tar over the edges,' said Iliev.

'It's a good start,' said Vasselis. 'But as Paul indicated, that won't stop the enemy within.'

'We'll do that,' said Ossacer. 'By getting Gorian.'

'So you keep saying.' Jhered spread his hands. 'Time for action.'

Ossacer stood up. 'You want recompense from me? Just watch.'

He started for the door but stopped short, cocking his head.

'What is it Ossie?' asked Mirron.

'Not sure.' He opened the door. 'Sounds like bells or something.'

'Too early for dawn watch,' said Jhered.

'Coming from the harbour,' said Ossacer. 'I can see the vibrations through the air.'

'I can't—' said Kastenas.

Iliev put a hand on her arm. 'I hear it.' He frowned. 'That cannot be right.'

'What is it?' asked Ossacer. 'What does it mean?'

'Shipwreck,' said Iliev. 'Flotsam in the harbour.'

*

They only needed the one horse.

'You really can't ride? I thought you were joking,' said Jhered, heaving himself up into the saddle in the palace paddocks.

Iliev looked at him askance, his deep set eyes piercing. He swung up behind Jhered, his powerful frame thumping down. The horse steadied himself.

'What use do I have for riding, Exchequer Jhered?'

'Fair enough but hang on. It'll be uncomfortable.'

Jhered put his heels to the stallion's flanks. They'd had the same immediate hunch. Whoever had rung the bells, accurately or not, was calling them down to the harbour. There were some answers washing in on the morning tide, they could feel it.

On the gallop through heavily patrolled predawn streets, Jhered had time to consider what an extraordinary sight they must have made. The Exchequer of the Conquord and the Prime Sea Lord of the Ocetanas on a borrowed cavalry stallion ripping along the cobbles of Estorr to the harbour. Curious times.

If only the citizens knew the other half of the rumours the Order had fed them. They wouldn't just be off the streets, they'd be hammering up the barricades.

'How did we ever get to this?' muttered Jhered.

'Some things are a lifetime in the making,' replied Iliev, catching his words.

The hoof beats echoed against wall and shutter. Early tradespeople were moving stock down to the forums. Wagon wheels rattled, hinges and timbers protested under their burdens. Nearer the harbour, the city was coming to life again. It would be another anxious day. Many would try and live and work as normal but always with an eye on where trouble might flare, where the effigies would be burned and declamations made. Estorr was deeply unsettled and it was a situation certain to worsen.

Quite a crowd was gathered on the dockside. Several hundred workers had abandoned cargo nets, blocks and tackle and warehouse floors. Every eye was on the harbour, its dark waters lit by multiple lanterns held by harbour officials on a dozen longboats. They were in a ring around something.

Jhered and Iliev dismounted, handed the horse's reins to a harbour guard and pushed their way to the front of the growing throng. Jhered didn't have to shout people aside. The word that he was among them was enough to see them make passage for him.

'Does this always happen for you?' asked Iliev.

'Sometimes, being me does have its benefits,' admitted Jhered.

'Too many people here.' Iliev hunched his shoulders. 'I can't understand how you can live in a place like this.'

'The sea calling you back, is it, Karl?'

'Ocetarus never ceases his song and the lords and ladies of the ocean beckon me each morning.'

They reached the dockside. It was mainly clear of ships. Most had left on the evening tide last night. More would take their place, sailing in as the sun blessed the white walls and red slates of Estorr. At first, Jhered couldn't make out what it was the pilot longboats were surrounding.

'What do you have there?' he called, his voice carrying over the ambient noise of the crowd, amplified by the calm harbour waters. A lantern was raised and swung in his direction.

'Who speaks?'

'Exchequer Jhered. Is that Master Stertius behind that lantern?'

'Exchequer, praise Ocetarus you are here. We have just sent messages to the Hill, asking for you,' said the harbour master.

Jhered glanced at Iliev who was chewing his lip. 'Why?'

The crowd had gone silent and Stertius realised it. He ordered his longboat make the short row back to the dockside and he invited both men to join him. They rowed back to the circle.

'When the shipwreck bells were rung, we did what we always do, get boats in the water and surround whatever is floating in. Can't afford disease. We've kept him off the wall so far but we didn't need to. He won't get out of the boat and it'll sink before long. Says he'll only talk to you. I think he's delirious.'

'Who?'

The longboat rowed into position and the answer was revealed. In the centre of the ring, a battered rowing boat sat low on the water. It was without any of its three sets of oars. Gunwales were splintered, the tiller was missing and water sloshed under the benches, collecting in the hull.

One man lay sprawled across the stern, dead probably. A second sat hunched on the centre bench, his shoulders shaking with cold, fever or emotion. Probably all three by the state of him. The remnants of a cloak were about his shoulders. His toga was filthy brown and torn at the chest and waist. A gladius hilt jutted from the scabbard still belted on. His hands, gripping the gunwales, were red and bleeding.

'Get me over there,' said Jhered.

'My Lord Exchequer —'

'I know the risks, Master Stertius. Get me over there.'

In a few gentle strokes, they were alongside the sinking boat.

'Want me with you, Paul?' asked Iliev.

'I think you'll need to hear what he has to say if he makes any sense at all.'

With oarsmen holding the two craft together, Iliev and Jhered stepped across into the bow of the boat, sandals splashing into the chill water. The man raised his head to look at them. The first thing he did was burst into floods of tears. Jhered moved to him and pulled him into an embrace.

'It's over now, General,' he said. 'Come on, you're safe now.'

'Who is it?' hissed Iliev.

'Harkov, General of the Ascendancy guard. A very good man. This does not look promising.'

Harkov pulled back and looked at Jhered as if for the first time. He wiped tears from a face streaked with days-old blood and dirt. He was cut and bruised. His lips were thick and dry, his cheeks and eyes sunken. A leather bottle thumped onto the bench next to Jhered. Water. Harkov saw it and grabbed it, drinking furiously, spilling more than went down his throat. Fresh tears ran down his face. He dropped the bottle, wiped fingers across his mouth and stared at Jhered again.

'Exchequer, is it you?'

His voice was a rattling croak. Jhered could see his whole body was shaking. There was an impenetrable shadow behind his eyes, like his mind was shrouded.

'What's happened to you,' breathed Jhered.

'It is you, isn't it?'

'Yes, Harkov, it's me, Paul Jhered. You're home now.'

Harkov collapsed into Jhered's arms again, heaving great sobs. Jhered held the man's head to his chest, stroking his salt-crusted, matted hair to try and calm him. His cries were the only sound on the harbour now. Iliev came into Jhered's line of sight.

'We need to know what happened,' he said. 'Where he's come from.'

'I know. Give me a moment. Give him a moment.'

Eventually, Harkov calmed and Jhered eased him away, keeping hold of his shoulders. A fine soldier, a brave man, one of the bravest Jhered had met. And reduced to a shivering, terrified husk.

'Harkov, can you hear me?' Harkov nodded. His eyes, wild and blood red, searched Jhered's face. 'Can you remember what happened? Can you tell me?'

'How can there be so many? How can they have got so far?'

'Take your time, Harkov. One step at a time. From the beginning. You remember I asked you to go through Atreska.'

'Byscar. I was going to Byscar. All my men ...'

'It's all right. Byscar, yes. To deliver warnings. To get a ship to bring you back to Estorr. Home, where you are now.'

'Harban went to Gosland,' he said abruptly.

Jhered paused to take that in. 'Never mind for now. Focus. What happened to you. Harkov, we need to know, then I can take you to your wife and family.'

It didn't seem to register. Harkov was silent for a time, searching his broken mind.

'Harban went to Gosland. Gorian went there so Harban went there. So why are there so many of them after me here?'

'Paul ...' Iliev raised his eyebrows. 'We're getting nowhere.'

'We're doing the best we can,' said Jhered sharply. 'His eyes are gone. He barely knows where he is. Think you can do any better?'

Harkov grabbed at Jhered's sleeves. 'They marched up from Gestern. So many and they never stopped marching. The land died behind them. We had to run.' He began to rock on the bench. 'We had to run but they just followed us like dogs on a scent. We led them straight to Byscar. We couldn't stop them, we couldn't stand before them please, please, please.'

'Calm, Harkov.' Jhered kept his tone gentle. 'That's it. Take as long as you need. How many came from Gestern?'

'I couldn't count!' It was a choked shout. 'So many. Thousands. And on the boat we took ...'

Harkov began to gesture, making a snake movement with his right hand and arm.

'We hugged the coast. We tried to see into the north. Too close, too close.'

Jhered shook his head. 'What do you mean, too close?'

'A man died on the ship. Should have thrown him over then and there but we thought we were safe to say the rites of the sea on him. I went to sleep and when I awoke the dead were all over the ship.' Harkov squeezed his eyes shut at the memories and when he opened them, they were clear and full of madness. He shouted. 'I couldn't hide. I couldn't run. Five of us jumped into a boat. They came after us. We fought so long. Every time we pushed one over he swam back. Hours and hours trying to lose them but they just swam. Swam.'

His voice cracked again. He made swimming motions and his face creased.

'The ship. What happened to the ship?' asked Iliev.

'The dead are everywhere!' roared Harkov. 'They are on the sea and they swarm the land. We cannot stop them. We will all be like them. Paul, please keep them from me.'

Harkov crumpled. Jhered held him up above the water sloshing in the boat. He looked past Iliev to the longboats around them and beyond to the silence of the dockside.

'I think just about everyone heard that, don't you?'

Chapter Forty-Six

859th cycle of God, 46th day of Genasrise

Word of Harkov's outburst on the dock was travelling almost as fast as Jhered's horse. It could never have been contained but the shockwave was going to have a dramatic effect on the city. Confirmation of the Order's words. The dead were marching and sailing across the Conquord.

Jhered was riding with a group of ten surrounding a cart on which Harkov lay. He'd been given white mandrake and was sleeping for now. Jhered would never forget the dreadful haunting look in his eyes or the desperation to be free of the memories of his recent past.

Iliev had stayed on the dockside. He'd returned to his ship and was already ordering preparations to sail on the turn of the tide. Somewhere in the north Tirronean, a ship carrying the dead was sailing under a Conquord flag. For now Jhered had no real idea how far they could get. All intelligence so far suggested that small numbers of dead would wither quickly and on the sea that process would surely be hastened.

Mirron had said that the dead were fed directly through the earth. And the seabed was far below and they would be separated from the water by the ship's timbers. Perhaps it was those timbers that fed them now. But even so, Jhered couldn't understand how Gorian could possibly feel a single dead body and bring it back to wreak such damage on an individual vessel. Even with a Gor-Karkulas walking the shore Harkov had been sailing beside, it didn't seem credible.

The Ascendants were waiting for him when he returned.

'I think the problem is that we don't really know what he is capable of,' said Mirron when Jhered had related all Harkov's disjointed words. 'Perhaps he can feel every single one that dies.'

'I just don't see it,' said Jhered. 'How can he possibly do that? How can he know that someone has died and hence reanimate him? Our best guess is that he's hundreds of miles north, somewhere in Gosland. This happened on the Atreskan coast.'

'I don't think he does know,' said Arducius. 'I think that whenever a conflict occurs, he is informed through the Gor-Karkulas and then he creates the animation Work. It will cover a reasonable area for sure. You might well find that he was raising dead in that part of Atreska and Harkov's ship just got caught in the net, so to speak.'

Jhered nodded. 'Makes sense.'

'Does it really matter?' asked Kastenas. 'What it means is that a force far bigger than we thought is heading north and west, presumably to the Neratharn border. It could be that Davarov was wiped out completely and has been harvested by Gorian. It could be another force altogether. The point is that we need the Ascendants on that border if we are to halt them. The walls are high, wide and strong. It will take the dead a long time to breach them.'

'Agreed,' said Jhered. He looked across to the Ascendants. 'All right?'

Arducius and Mirron nodded. Ossacer shrugged.

'We have to try and take out these Gor-Karkulas,' said Ossacer. 'Not kill them but stop them working for Gorian. Not only will that reduce his strength but it'll give us a clearer indication of where he is. At the moment, I'd guess that if we tried to find him through the energies in the earth, we'd be confused by the centres of power that the Karkulas represent.'

'You want to narrow the field,' said Gesteris. 'Nice idea but how will you get close?'

'I have absolutely no idea.'

'Right.' Jhered clapped his hands together. 'We have a plan of sorts. Elise, I need you to give me as much strength as you can to defend the Hill. We need the Ascendants, plus you and me out of here on a Gatherer ship. We can follow Iliev out on the tide. Marcus, I'd like you to stay here to oversee the defence of the Hill with Arvan Vasselis.'

'Whatever you wish of me,' said Gesteris. 'You're sure we'll come under threat?'

Jhered shrugged. 'I don't know but we cannot risk it. The Armour of God may not get here, the citizens may not batter down the Victory Gates, but if the Ocetanas fail out there on the ocean, the dead will, unless we prepare. Keep your powder close and keep every catapult working.'

'It'll be good to don my armour once again,' said Gesteris. His single eye shone.

'Let's not forget we are all a good deal older and slower than before,' said Jhered. 'So, one last thing. Any word from Arvan about Herine and the Chancellor?'

Elise shook her head. 'We're still waiting.'

'Well we can't wait any more. Let's get him back here. And the Advocate too. She needs to be briefed and we need to show her our unswerving support.'

The order was given and a guard hurried off to the palace.

'Anything else while we're waiting?' asked Jhered.

'What about the other Ascendants? The young strands.' Hesther was showing the strain of shouldering all their fear and uncertainty.

'It's your decision ultimately, but I'd say they were safest here. There'll be plenty of military muscle and the Advocate will be in residence. Going to somewhere like Westfallen, I don't think we can guarantee that level of security,' said Kastenas.

Jhered nodded. 'I'd back that. And there's a duty to perform too. There are still three surviving tenth-stranders. Three emerged seventeen-year-olds who need to understand they may be called to action. Not against the people but in extremis, against the dead.'

'Then one of us should stay to organise them,' said Arducius.

'No. Ultimately, you have to find and kill Gorian. Nothing else is more important. So you have to be near to where he is, it's as simple as that.'

'And we have to get back my son from him,' said Mirron. 'I need you Ardu, Ossie. I can't do it without you. He's too powerful.'

'We'll save him, Mirron, I promise,' said Jhered.

Mirron smiled. 'I know we will. But every day without him feels more like I've lost him forever.'

'Mislaid, dear Mirron. Not lost. And we always find the things we mislay.'

Mirron punched Ossacer's arm. 'Thanks, Ossie.'

'Will they be able to do it, do you think? The tenth strand?' Gesteris was scratching at the wound beneath his eye patch. 'They are untried, are they not? All of us, with your gracious exception Mother Naravny, have experienced the terror of battle and know how hard it is not to turn and run. If the dead are marching on the gates and our citizens are begging for help, will they be able to stand up?'

'We've taught them all we can,' said Arducius. 'We've given them pressure situations in which to work and they've performed well. And now they have something to hang onto. They are angry as well as scared by what happened in the Academy. And they are determined not to let anyone threaten them again. Will that translate to the ability to stop the dead at the gates? I don't know. All I do know is that we performed when we had to, and I believe they will too.'

'Well said, Arducius,' said Ossacer. 'Fantastic that we have trained our new Ascendants to understand how to take life.'

Jhered put his head in his hands. His sigh was long and loud and it was enough to still any thoughts of further comment.

'And perhaps we should all remain quiet until the Advocate arrives. Give ourselves time to consider what we will say and how we will behave.'

'Stop treating me like a child, Paul,' said Ossacer.

'You know the common response to that, don't you, Ossie?'

There was little more conversation until the Advocate arrived. Herine being ushered into the Chancellery was something of a relief but the expression on her face was a bleak reminder of what had happened in the palace just a couple of hours earlier. She was still largely blank, the shock had settled hard on her, but her eyes were bright. It was a slightly calmer version of poor Harkov who was with the doctors now and being tended by his wife.

Jhered realised they were all staring at her. It was very difficult not to. Herine was readying to speak, aware no one else was going to break the deadlock.

'Are none of you going to welcome your new murderer?' she said.

'Come on, Herine, sit down,' said Hesther. 'No one is thinking that.'

'Really?'

'Really,' said Mirron.

'I have no problem with what happened,' said Ossacer.

Jhered drew sharp breath but Herine chose to smile and take a seat.

'It has not been a good night. Support is thin on the ground, so thank you, Ossacer. I will never really understand you but I know what you're trying to say.'

Vasselis moved to sit beside her.

'How did it go?' Jhered asked of him.

'As well as it could. The body is with the surgeons and will be released to the Order shortly. We are going to collect the Speakers of Earth, Oceans and Winds and will bring them here to explain the situation.'

'And the Armour of God?'

Vasselis nodded. 'Prime Sword Vennegoor may accompany them.'

'He doesn't need an explanation, he needs a warning,' said Elise. 'The Armour of God needs to be elsewhere, defending its citizens.'

'Dream away, Elise. Trying and burning Felice would have caused enough trouble. There is little doubt that her being killed while under arrest is going to cause considerably more.' Herine looked over at Jhered and inclined her head. 'Thank you for indulging me earlier. I think I can handle the reality now.'

'And the reality is it was an accident but one which will have dire consequences,' said Jhered. 'But we have a plan. I urge you not to release the body until we have our defences in place and the Ascendants away from here.'

'What are you going to say, Herine?' asked Hesther.

'The truth,' she replied.

'I'm not sure that's entirely wise,' said Jhered. 'Your direct involve-ment—'

'Will get out whether we like it or not. Let's meet this thing head on.'

Jhered shook his head. 'Perhaps you can't handle the reality. Herine, think. What happens if the Order and the citizenry know you brought about her death? Arvan, you don't agree with this plan, do you?'

'I am but a Marshal Defender who makes his points and ultimately follows orders.'

'And your point was . . .'

'That this would be a disastrous course of action.'

Jhered turned back to the Advocate. 'Herine, please? This is most unwise. I agree it'll come out but we need to manage when as best we can. I presume you've used the guards outside your door to move the body?'

Vasselis nodded. 'The fewer who see the better. We took her straight to the surgeons. She's blanked off. We weren't seen on the way down so only we few, plus two guards and one surgeon, know anything has happened.'

'I know what you're going to say, Paul,' said Herine.

'And it makes perfect sense. Keep the lid on it. We have it under control. Why should anyone know the truth of where and how she died? There isn't a mark on her. The slap mark will have faded. She could have had the same accident in her cell.'

'I can't live with this lie,' said Herine. 'I won't. If I am to face my people over this, then it must be with no more guilt than I must already carry for what I have done.'

'You did nothing,' said Jhered, voice little more than a hiss. 'You slapped her across the face and as you can imagine, there are many of us who would have loved to stand in the queue to do the same. She slipped, she fell badly and she was killed. You did not kill her.'

'I set her death in motion.'

'No,' said Ossacer. 'She did that herself.'

'And this is the rule of universal balance, is it, Ossacer?' said Herine.

'If you place yourself in danger through your own actions, you have to accept the consequences,' said Ossacer. 'I learned to live with what I did.'

'Quite, but the Chancellor does not have that luxury, does she?' said Herine. 'It is me who has to learn to live with what I have done.'

'Yes.' Ossacer continued. Jhered had the hunch to let him. 'Yes, you do, and you will, my Advocate. But announcing what people will see as your guilt from the throne of the basilica will not help that. It won't help any of us and it won't help the Conquord.'

Ossacer paused and a smile crossed his lips.

'Something funny?' Herine did not twitch a muscle.

'No, my Advocate. But a thought struck me. I'll make you a deal. If you promise not to speak the whole truth just yet, I promise not to complain ever again about being sent to the battlefield.'

All eyes fell on Herine again. Jhered couldn't penetrate her expression. She was eyeing Ossacer closely.

'You are a cheeky bastard, Ossacer Westfallen,' she said.

'The blind must develop other talents.'

'Cheeky bastard,' she repeated. 'But sometimes your twittering produces moments of clarity and sense. You have a deal.'

Jhered caught Ossacer's eye and his face cracked into a grin. 'And now, may we get to the job in hand and start saving our Conquord?'

'I think so.' Herine stood. 'You have my permission to do what must be done both here and wherever you choose to make your stand. I'm tired. I need to lie down and endure my nightmares. Just one thing, though, Paul and all of you. I have two sons out there facing the dead and whatever else Gorian throws at them. I want them both back here safe. Do I make myself clear?'

Jhered nodded. 'We'll bring them home for you, my Advocate. That I promise.'

The middle of another long day. The furnaces burned day and night. The blacksmith's hammer accompanied him to sleep and brought him to wakefulness. Carts of best Tundarran and Sirranean wood trundled in at all hours from the north-east and north-west. They were even hacking into the local stocks, unseasoned or not, just to the north-west and also in the Calern and Porbanii forests a little further afield. The Lothiun mountains that stretched away a few hundred miles north provided good quality minerals and metal ores when Kark and Gestern deliveries were poor like they were now.

Sometimes, Lucius Moralius, Hasfort's Master Engineer, hated the fact that he had been born and bred in Hasfort. Even more so that he'd followed his father into the service of the Conquord. And yet more so that he'd shown an aptitude for the science of artillery and the organisation of men.

And he knew for certain that most of the citizens of this once beautiful riverside town hated the fact that over the past forty years, it had become little more than a production line for Conquord war machinery. In his lifetime of forty-five years, he'd seen the fishing and craft industries submerged beneath a tide of industry. The watermills and forges had grown by a factor of ten and not one of them turned out anything much, barring weaponry, armour and artillery. And besides the farmers who fed the populace and the administrators who kept the books balanced for Paul Jhered, there was precious little other employment.

It had made Hasfort ugly. The open fields were lost behind the walls that protected the town from invaders, should that remote possibility ever become a reality. The sky was smudged with smoke and the air tasted of peat and ash.

Lucius strapped his leather apron on over his lightweight woollen toga, waved his family goodbye and walked the short distance from his small house to the east side of the town where most of the industry was located. Saws agitated his already brittle mood, the ringing of hammer on metal went straight though his head this afternoon and the shouting of men spawned a pain behind his eyes.

'Bastard Tsardon,' he muttered. 'Bastard mobilisation.'

It wouldn't have been so bad but for the fact that they had been in the middle of a massive refit of the artillery for five legions. Ballistae, scorpions and the new sled-mounted field onagers had crammed the yards. When the orders had come through and the flags flown from the messenger towers, the already exhausting timetable had been thrown into confusion. The assumed attrition rate of artillery in an open conflict had to be factored in and dozens of new pieces had to be planned, materials sourced, and then built. All in fifty days.

Moralius shook his head. They would do it because he had never failed to deliver and that was a proud record. But the complaints of the ordinary citizen deprived of sleep and forced to work double shifts were getting as loud as the hammers. As if he wasn't doing it himself too. God-embrace-him but he was doing more than any of them. They could all sleep or bathe whenever they were off-duty. Moralius had to plan further. He had to tick boxes, organise rotas, sign supply contracts. A million little jobs.

He realised he was stamping his feet on the walk and he consciously lightened his step and took the glower off his face. That would never do. He paused as if to refasten the straps on his forge boots and let the warm breeze play over his face. He was standing on the approach to the forges and yards, not three hundred yards from the eastern gate and walls.

The tenements and houses he was passing were mired in grime and needed a wash and a lick of paint. When the fifty days were up, he'd make sure that happened. Recompense needed to be swift and appreciable in Hasfort. He couldn't afford dissension.

Moralius nodded at a group of men walking by on the way home from their shifts or more likely straight for a goblet of ale or wine. It made him thirsty just thinking about it. They were covered in soot and sweat and their shambling frames spoke of the tiredness he felt in himself.

'Good day?' he asked.

'Same as every other day,' said one. The group slowed but didn't stop. 'Except it looks like you'll need to crack the whip a bit harder, sir.'

Moralius frowned. 'Oh? Why?'

'Dust cloud to the north-east. Reckon your Gosland orders might need fulfilling a few days early.'

'That can't be.' Moralius scowled, trying to remember the timetable. It wasn't hard. It was practically imprinted on his brain. 'The Bear Claws refits aren't ready for another six days. And the new ballistae not for another ten. That was the agreement.'

The man shrugged. 'I'm sure, sir. But there's a dust cloud just the same. Could be a trader trail but more likely it's the wagons and cavalry of the second legion we reckon, come to get their gear.'

'Fine.' Moralius sighed. 'I'll see what I can do, I suppose. Thanks for the news.'

'We'll be back if you need us, sir,' said the man, a blacksmith by the look of him. Young man. New on the job.

Moralius chuckled despite his mood. 'I'm sure that won't be necessary but I appreciate your offer. What's your name?'

'Barodov,' he said. 'From Atreska originally.'

'Thank you, Barodov, all of you. I appreciate your efforts. Now go and drink and rest. I guess I'd better head for the walls and take a look, hadn't I?'

Barodov grinned, a flash of white from a filthy face. 'If you put the magnifier backwards, they'll look further away.'

The group of men laughed. So did Moralius.

'Sound advice.'

Moralius hurried to the east gate. Stairs there took him up the side of the gate and onto the rampart. It was largely empty but for the standing guard. One of them was looking at the approaching lot, whoever they were. Moralius could see the cloud clearly enough. A brown smudge floating above the southern edges of the Tharn Marches.

Like as not they'd followed the highway down the river and were coming in on the secondary road that led directly to the east gate. Strange they weren't using the river system all the way but perhaps transport was in short supply. Like everything else.

One of the guardsmen saw him approach and the trio turned and came to attention. He waved them to ease.

'How far away, do you think?'

'Not far, sir,' said one, handing him the magnifier. 'Half a day. They're only just beyond the first rises, I think.'

'You have sent out scouts. We aren't going to find this is an invasion force, are we?'

'Yes sir. And no, sir, it isn't. Our scouts have seen legion standards and a number of carts. Looks like they're coming on foot.'

Moralius shook his head and put the magnifier to his eye, smiling as he did. The dust cloud looked very close. The guard was right. The Bear Claws weren't far away.

'Ah well,' he said, handing the magnifier back and feeling a little irritable. 'Better go and see how much we can actually give them.'

Moralius tutted all his way back down to the ground and into the artillery yards. The open spaces were crowded with pieces. Mighty onagers lay in their component parts while workmen shaved at wood, reworked hinges and refreshed ropes. Ballistae, scorpions and more onagers stood in finished ranks, their surfaces gleaming with fresh oil, their metalwork polished to a shine.

To his left, the lumber yards were stacked high. The Sirraneans were, if nothing else, very prompt with their deliveries and word had it that prices might be coming down, due to some form of alliance struck by Roberto Del Aglios. That would please the Exchequer. The Gatherers always grumbled about raw material prices. They'd go on grumbling about metal and mineral prices though. It was a long way to Hasfort from Kark and nowhere provided better quality.

Smoke belched from the eight furnaces, casting soot and acrid odours into the otherwise clear sky. Ahead, a group of men were hammering bolts into the side of an onager base. The steel sled was next to the wooden frame, back to the sky and on supports, being beaten into shape.

Moralius headed for the site office, hoping to find good news of progress since his shift had ended only five hours previously. He felt the weight of exhaustion begin to settle on him even before he reached the door. He needed water and a few moments of relative peace. A couple of engineers glanced at him and then away again as he put his hand on the doorknob. Anxiety was not something he liked to see in his people's faces. He opened the door, walked in and closed it behind him. The shutters were still across the windows and the din was muted. It was almost blissful.

The office was not big. Every plank of free wall space was covered in parchments showing the progression of their multitude of jobs. The single desk was impeccably tidy just as he had left it. Mess was not to be tolerated. Moralius could lay his hands on any figure in a matter of moments. It was a while before he noticed the man sitting in his chair, reading the shift reports.

'Can I help you?' he asked.

While he was used to having people waiting for him when he went into his office, they weren't normally treating the place as their own. The man looked up. He had some form of bizarre colouring on his face. Green and brown, arranged a little like tree bark.

'I think you can help me a very great deal,' said the man, and colours swam across his eyes.

Chapter Forty-Seven

859th cycle of God, 46th day of Genasrise

There was screaming coming from beyond the yards. Moralius barely registered it but even in his confusion, he could hear the hammers and saws falling silent one after another, to be replaced by the shouts of men, the tolling of bells and the running of feet.

'Sounds to me like you're under attack,' said the man, an Ascendant to judge from his eyes. His tone was frighteningly calm.

The dread that filled Moralius was like nothing he had experienced before. He backed away towards the door, fumbling for the handle behind him. The Ascendant watched him, nodding.

'Good idea. Get your people on the streets. Fight back at the invaders.'

'Invaders.'

'Presumably.'

The Ascendant gestured towards the outside and the town where the screams and shouts were punctuated now by the sound of weapons clashing and the bawling of orders. The air was heavy with fear. Moralius couldn't think straight. Couldn't think at all. None of it made sense. The Bear Claws were coming to get their artillery. Who could possibly be attacking them. River raiders hadn't been seen for twenty-five years. No Tsardon had ever got this far, not even a decade ago when they were marching free across great swathes of the Conquord.

'Who?' he said, his head thick, his mouth unwilling to move.

The Ascendant rose from his chair. 'Go and look.'

Moralius nodded. 'Go and look. You are here to help?'

'That depends on your point of view.' The Ascendant waved his hand. 'Go.'

Moralius opened the door, ran outside and felt a wave break

over him. His mind cleared. He looked back at the office. The door was closed again. He couldn't remember if he really had seen and spoken to an Ascendant but one thing was sure: Hasfort was under attack.

Engineers ran for the yard gates, heading for their homes and families, their weapons. Legion guards were moving to close the gates. Forty or fifty of them, spears held vertical. Moralius could see smoke from north-west of the town. Maybe the invaders had come from the forest. He began to run too. His wife, his children, were out there without him.

'The west, muster to the west!' Moralius turned at the sound of Captain Lakarov, the garrison commander's voice. 'Close the East Gate. Riders to the Bear Claws.'

A pair of horsemen galloped through the gate and it was swung shut. Moralius fell in beside the commander, both men running towards the east-gate barracks a few hundred yards away. Bells were ringing across the town. Already, citizens were flooding back up the main street from the forum and basilica. More and more smoke smudged the skyline.

'Where did they come from?' shouted Moralius.

'I have no idea. I was waiting for the Claws outriders,' replied Lakarov. 'Go to your family. Stay inside.'

'Like hell,' said Moralius. 'The engineers do not cower behind the skirts of their mothers.'

Lakarov smiled. 'Good. Find me, stand with me.'

Moralius split away to the right and headed down his narrow cobbled street. There was panic spilling from the tight lines of terraced houses. Children crying, men and women shouting at each other. Doors and shutters slamming. Moralius ran in through his front door, tearing off his apron. In the bright light spilling through the open shutters at the back, he saw his wife and children standing in the centre of the room, waiting. His son held out his gladius for him. Eight years old but with the Moralius chin jutted forward proudly.

Moralius knelt and took the scabbarded weapon from him and crushed him into a hug.

'Look after your mother until I get back, Lucas.'

'I will, father.'

He mussed the boy's brown hair and stood. He bowed his head and let Maria place his breastplate on his shoulders. She began to strap it up while he belted on his sword.

'Keep quiet and keep the back way open,' said Moralius. 'They won't know the alleys.'

'Just don't let them get this far,' said Maria.

'They won't get past the forum.'

'Sounds like they're already inside the walls.'

Moralius kissed her. 'Lakarov trained us for this. We always thought he was playing at soldiers. We'll all be kissing his feet when this is done.'

'Come back to me,' said Maria.

'Always.'

Moralius ran back out of the door and heard it thump shut behind him. The bar was pushed across. He nodded to himself and set off towards the forum. The streets were crowded with people. Lakarov would be pleased. Nearly all of them were following his standing orders.

Stretcher parties were moving to their positions. Every man and woman trained in the gladius, bow or spear seemed to be heading towards the conflict, there to find a legion captain or centurion to place them. Twenty youths trotted past him, each carrying a bucket. They looked scared but determined.

At the head of his street, Moralius glanced back towards the yards. The gates weren't yet closed. He frowned but had no time to find out why. Lakarov would have his plans. Perhaps they were to act as a fall back point should the town be lost. It didn't matter now. A little further down the road, the barracks was emptying. Moralius ran to join them. Grim-faced legionaries in shining armour and carrying weapons unsheathed, greeted him.

Lakarov was at their head.

'We will form our line at the second marker. Secure the forum. Move at a run. Go.'

The legion militia set off. Three hundred here, bolstered by reserve from the citizenry. Another three hundred at the west-gate barracks. Their steady footfall rang from the buildings on the way down to the forum. Others fell in with them. More engineers, carpenters, black-smiths. Hasfort had a proud population. Never mind their personal feelings about the change in their town, it was theirs and they would die to keep it that way.

Moralius saw the young blacksmith Barodov among them. The humour of a little earlier was gone from his face, replaced by anger. Moralius ran to him, fell in beside him.

'No rest, eh, Barodov?'

'The wine will be sweeter when I put my bloody sword on the table next to my goblet,' he said.

'No heroics. We don't even know how many there are.'

The street widened out around Hasfort's central fountain, affording them all a view down a gentle slope into the forum. It had been cleared of stalls and already on station were armed traders, stretcher and bucket chain parties, doctors and surgeons. Some of Hasfort's own artillery was rolling into the eastern end of the forum. Just a couple of scorpions and ballistae so far. Lakarov wouldn't allow heavy artillery to be used in his town. Moralius found himself wondering why the onagers on the wall mounts hadn't been used when the invaders first appeared.

He ran around the fountain and followed the legion militia into the forum. At a barked command, they broke into their defensive line. Like a reverse battle formation, gladius to the centre, spears to the flanks, able to turn in or defend approach routes left and right into the forum.

Moralius felt the dread return and knew he shouldn't be this scared. He could see fighting beyond the forum in the streets closer to the west gate. Or he thought it was fighting. The din of voices and weapons had an odd ring to it. He trotted right to get a better view and his fear grew. Walking down the side of the forum, as if out for a stroll in the sunshine, was the Ascendant. He was with them at least. Perhaps it was about time he did something to help, do one of those things they were reputed to be able to do to break enemy armies.

The Ascendant turned and smiled, sending a shiver through Moralius, like the first ice of dusas. The Ascendant spread his arms and spoke, his voice seeming to carry over the forum, echoing from ahead like it issued from a thousand mouths.

'Come forward, my people, and welcome into your embrace all those you see before you. Join the march that will turn the world and bring the new order to power.'

Across the forum, the march faltered. Legionaries looked to one another, grasping for confirmation that they had heard confusing words carried on the thick accents of others they could not see. As if the words had formed in the air spontaneously. None of them had seen the Ascendant speak. Moralius found himself walking towards him.

'Who are you?' he said.

'I am Gorian. I am the bringer of a new truth and a new glory. Behold my people.'

'Your ...?'

A scream taken up by a hundred mouths gripped his heart. People were flooding into the forum. They were not falling back. They were running. Running for their lives and howling in a terror that shook his body where he stood. No one was moving forward now. Lakarov could not find the words to shout an order. It was inhuman, the sound of the citizens of Hasfort. Reacting to what, he had no desire to see. But he could not move to hide either. Strength drained from him.

Behind the fleeing citizens, legion militia retreated in some form of order. Not all could contain themselves but enough moved back into the forum with their weapons still towards the enemy to stop a rout. Moralius gaped at what came after them.

'Tsardon,' he breathed, knowing it was impossible.

'Move up to support!' yelled Lakarov, finding his voice. 'Ready scorpions, ready ballistae.'

The militia moved forward again. Citizens, reserve guard, still yelling words Moralius could not understand, ran past. One man, his eyes wide, his mind a wasteland ran close enough to hear.

'Dead,' he was shouting. 'Dead.'

Just over and over. Moralius felt his eyes dragged back to the Ascendant. He was still smiling.

'Steady,' ordered Lakarov, marching at the head of his garrison. 'Standing firm. We can turn these.'

The Tsardon moved into the forum. Moralius looked left and right. Citizens were running along the parallel streets. Tsardon were spilling wide into the town. Moralius could see the mass of the enemy at the entrance to the forum. It was a dense movement but quiet. There were none of the battle songs they were associated with. Moralius's dread deepened. The retreat of the west garrison was not stopping.

Lakarov had seen it too. 'Hold the second marker.'

But they didn't. Anxious looks over their shoulders told of a desire to keep on moving back.

'Hold!' bellowed Lakarov. 'We will support you.'

'Come, my people. Fear no thrust. Bring them to me.'

The Ascendant's words sprang from the mouths of every Tsardon approaching across the sun-drenched forum. There was a ripple among the defenders. Again, the advance to the defensive position faltered. One or two broke off from the retreat and ran.

Moralius felt compelled to move forwards. From the corner of his eye he could see the Ascendant doing the same, matching him stride for stride. Beyond him, Tsardon were moving to surround them, marching steadily up the side roads. All sound of conflict had ceased now. The only shouts were those of people scared beyond reason and he didn't know why.

The Tsardon were close now. Forty yards or so away across the forum. Moralius could hear a buzzing noise above the anxious calls of legion militia and the orders of Lakarov. His voice was wavering now. Moralius felt a hand on his arm. Barodov.

'Something's very wrong here.'

'You think so?' snapped Moralius. 'Sorry.'

'We should retreat.'

'To where?'

Both men still moved forwards. Edging now rather than marching. Some of the other reserve were with them, managing to ignore the escaping militia and the cloying atmosphere that had descended on the forum.

'There is nowhere to go,' said Lakarov, voice unconvincing. 'Do not let them take your homes. Stop them here.'

The Tsardon closed. Flies. It was flies all around them. Buzzing clouds settling on faces and arms. They looked sick, the Tsardon. Tinged green, or pale, white like ... Moralius shook his head. It was a ploy. A tactic to scare them.

'They're just men!' he found himself shouting. 'Drive them back into the forest.'

He ran. He attacked. Him, Moralius the Master Engineer. And he brought the militia and the reserve with him. He pulled his gladius from its scabbard and led the charge into the Tsardon who made no reaction whatsoever. He crossed the gap. The buzzing of flies grew louder. He was aware of a sick, rotten stench. The first enemy was in front of him. He raised no defence.

Moralius felt anger supplant his fear. He drove his blade straight into the Tsardon's gut. The warrior took a pace back under the force of the blow but otherwise did not flinch. Blood flowed over the blade but he did not cry out. Moralius stared at his blade and then up at his enemy. His anger evaporated. The dread clutched him. The Tsardon was looking at him with a single eye. The other had been eaten away by some form of mould. Green sores were across his face and through a massive tear in his chest that went through leather, cloth and flesh he could see bone. And a slowly beating heart.

Moralius let his sword go and jumped backwards. A scream left his lips. He had touched rot and disease. The blood on his hand stung him as it found its way into small cuts on his fingers. The Tsardon and all his fellows walked on. The brief Conquord riposte had ceased almost the moment it had begun. The enemy raised their swords now. Moralius's victim ignored the blood pumping from the wound, ignored the gladius that hung from his stomach. He struck downwards. Moralius screamed again and dived backwards. The blade missed him. Just.

The defence crumbled to nothing. Militia turned to flee, weapons falling from their hands. But the Tsardon were coming in from every entrance now. They were trapped. Four hundred militia and reserve crowded the centre of the forum. Men were crying. Some were trying to hack their way clear but the advance of the enemy had become a flood. There had to be thousands of them. Moralius couldn't focus on anything. The pounding in his hand grew and his vision fogged.

Someone was by him, whispering into his ear. And with every whispered word the Tsardon spoke as one. The stench of death mixed with those of shit and urine. Moralius's heart was a ball of pain in his chest. He knew he was crying.

'The pain will cease. And when you awake your family will be all around you.'

Moralius blinked. Tsardon swords rose and fell. Legion militia died beneath them. Barodov pitched to the floor of the forum, a savage cut across his face. Moralius looked round. The Ascendant was inches from him, those eyes firing into his face. Blue chased orange to a flat grey. The sounds of screaming echoed away to a soft muting.

The Ascendant was holding out his hand. Moralius saw his salvation; a way back to his wife and son. He choked on words of thanks and grasped the hand. Ice flowed over the thumping pain in his fingers, palm and wrist.

'Come,' said the Ascendant. 'Be my Master Engineer, Lucius Moralius.'

Warmth flooded him after the ice. Comforting, loving. Moralius nodded.

'Anything,' he heard himself say. 'I'll do anything.'

The Ascendant's face hardened but still he smiled.

'I know you will. As will you all.'

Chapter Forty-Eight
859th cycle of God, 46th day of Genasrise

'Will my brother find the embrace of God, Julius?'

Barias looked at him from the stern of the boat. Roberto and Harban were sitting beside each other, rowing. The wind had died to almost nothing. Roberto's hands were blistered. Barias's were covered in strips of bloodied cloth. Harban seemed completely impervious. His palms were tough from years of climbing the mountains of Kark. And he was indefatigable. It was fortunate indeed that they had come across him in the border castle.

'Is this some new avenue into the questioning of my faith, Ambassador?'

Barias still had bruises from the one time they had actually come to blows, fading now but his left cheek was still a little puffy. Roberto flexed his own jaw. Barias might have been just an Order Speaker but he could pack a punch.

'No,' said Roberto. 'I'm tired of arguing, Julius. And I'm tired of hate. You can still think I should burn for my crimes if you like. I don't care. But every day I pray for my brother who lies beneath the ruined earth back there. I remember the writhing of the corpses under the soil and I fear that he will not feel the touch of the Omniscient. Hate me but love him, Julius. Will he make it?'

Barias straightened in his seat and his expression softened.

'Look at the land, Ambassador,' he said. 'It is and will always be beautiful.'

And so it was. They were moving downriver, tracking the Neratharnese border. In the distance south they could just pick out the mountains that the namesake River Kalde would skirt on its way to Lake Iyre and the Gaws, where Roberto hoped to find the defence that would save the Conquord. Gosland was lost in mist to the north and surrounding them, the Tharn Marches were slowly giving way to the stunning lowlands of the plain. River-run countryside bursting with life. Small hamlets, individual farmsteads and river towns stood deserted, victims of the long loss of Atreska. There must have been so much hope that citizens would return to this fertile land with the retaking of the jewel country. Now, Roberto wondered if anyone would ever dare set foot here again.

They had seen no one in days. No one at all. It was a chilling reminder of the effects of conflict and even more so, perhaps, of the passage of Gorian. Not that he could have extended his hand here so quickly from the north. But from the south there was no clue. If he had done in Atreska what they had seen at the crags, there was really no telling what state the place would be in. Roberto could easily be rowing them to their deaths.

'We can agree on that, Julius.'

'But there is evil within it. We know this because we have seen it in Gosland, and our nightmares will never fade. Yet I believe that purity will out. Whether we live or die in whatever is to come. Those like your poor brother Adranis will feed the earth with the essence of themselves and return it to its pure state. So will he find his way to the embrace of my God.'

Roberto nodded. It was imagery in which he could readily find comfort.

'So Adranis's work is not yet done,' he said.

'And it will never be so. His cycle will surely endure and he will perform the will of the Omniscient from where he lies until he is required to walk the earth once more.'

'That is fitting. It is right,' said Roberto. 'Thank you, Julius. It was troubling me.'

'It's good to know that at least one of your troubles can be eased by reference to the true scriptures.'

Harban cleared his throat noisily. Roberto smiled and looked over his shoulder.

'Don't worry. We're done arguing.' He turned back. 'Isn't that right, Speaker Barias?'

'When the issues are settled, then we will be done. Until then, we are merely pausing to gather our thoughts. However, that pause may be one of considerable length.'

The three of them chuckled.

'To the ends of the earth and the peak of the mountain,' said Harban. 'Your faith is fascinating even though I do not share it.'

'We should talk at greater length,' said Barias. 'I feel sure I could convince you.'

'Not even if you spoke at me until your dying breath. Like you, I am on a quest that lies at the heart of my faith. We share goals but not reasons. Gorian must die. For you that means your Conquord will be spared. For me, it means that the mountain will not fall. I will return my Gor-Karkulas to Inthen-Gor. For you it means nothing, for us it is salvation. You cannot deflect me. I walk to a beat so ancient even the eldest mountains cannot remember its beginning.'

Roberto watched Barias debate with himself if he should take up the challenge. But it had been a long few days. They were all sore and tired. Minds as well as bodies. Nine days on this river and that. And probably another nine to go. More if the wind didn't turn in their favour. Food was not plentiful but Harban was a deft hunter and Roberto's bow skill hadn't diminished, even if the Tsardon weapon he used was ill balanced.

So Julius elected to keep his own counsel for now, though the frown on his face was not something Roberto cared for overmuch.

'What's on your mind?' he asked.

'The same thing that worries you though you choose not to let it surface. Your brother's memory has been so powerful until now, it has dominated you.'

'I think you'd better elaborate,' said Roberto.

Adranis's smile flashed in his mind, giving credence to Barias's words.

'The river is too empty. The land as well. You can sense it if you let yourself,' said Julius. 'It should frighten you.'

'I'm not with you.'

'Last night, you and Harban walked a good two miles before finding a pair of rabbits for our bellies. When was the last time you heard the sound of a bird? It's not possible, or it shouldn't be. Genastro is in full force. The land is glorious with colour and plant life. But the animals are gone.'

'Animals sense the coming of disaster before men,' said Harban. 'They are closer to the earth than we are.'

Roberto felt as if a veil had been dragged from his face.

'And the men are gone too. No travellers taking advantage of empty villages. No riders in the distance.' He stopped rowing and turned to face Harban. 'And no other boats. Not one in nine days.'

'What does it mean?' asked Julius. 'We've seen no beacons, no flags, no nothing. It's like we're alone in this country.'

'It means none would even run here. It means that Gorian is surely attacking through Atreska too, just as we feared, and all who escape him are fleeing south. And it means that no one knows what is coming at them from the north because we are the first messengers.'

Roberto sighed and rolled his words around inside his mind.

'So if Dina Kell chooses to go south to Estorr but Gorian turns to Neratharn and beats the walkers from the crags there ...' said Julius.

'Aye,' said Roberto. 'It means the Neratharn border will be attacked from the rear while all her defence is looking the other way.'

'Perhaps we should row faster,' said Harban.

Roberto took up the oars. 'And pray for wind, Julius. Pray hard, and may our God listen to you.'

King Khuran felt the first shiver of genuine fear and knew then that he might well have made a colossal error. The marching was done for the day. For the campaign, it had been a good one. They had cornered and slaughtered four hundred legionaries from the army that had disintegrated on the Tsardon border all those long days ago. Gorian had reawakened them and now they and their four artillery pieces marched with the Tsardon invasion force.

'But that's just it, isn't it?'

Khuran stared at the dark swathes of dead vegetation that had given the dead their impetus for the day. In the evening gloom, he could still see the dust on the horizon that signalled a supporting army he hadn't even known was coming, heading their way. They had marched north from Gestern. The Dead Lord in command had visited him that afternoon on the march. Lord Jaresh. A particularly odious specimen, who had been delighted to tell him that so many were awaiting ship in Gestern that these new thousands could join the march on Neratharn.

'Your Majesty?'

Khuran had been taking a hot herbal infusion outside his tent before making his evening inspection. His senior aide, Prosentor Kreysun, brother of the fallen hero of Herolodus Vale, was with him as always.

'Is this truly a Tsardon invasion or are we merely spectators. Whores following the trail of the greater power, looking for scraps cast from the table. Do I look to you as if I am in command?'

Kreysun reacted a moment too quickly.

'Your men are behind you to whatever end, my King.'

Khuran nodded. 'You should become a diplomat, old friend. That is not quite the question I asked. I'll be more blunt. What, by the lords of sky and stars, do I think I'm doing here?'

'Overseeing the fall of the Conquord.'

This time, Khuran laughed. 'Now that I cannot refute. But who do you think will ascend the throne on the Hill when the Advocate is cast down? Not I, I think. Nor my son, if only I was spared to speak to him.'

Kreysun was silent for a moment.

'You can speak freely to me, Kreysun,' said Khuran. 'My days of lopping the heads off those who speak out are long gone. Besides, if I do that, I'll still be watching you march tomorrow, won't I?'

'Not a pretty sight, my King.'

'You were never comfortable on the march, even with a head on your shoulders.' Khuran felt a little more at peace. 'Come inside. We need some privacy.'

The two men sat on cushions in the centre of the huge pavilion tent. Khuran's netted bed stood to the left, his dining table to the right. His armour and weapons were on stands to the rear. He dismissed his servants and bade Kreysun talk quietly.

'Gorian does not need us,' said Khuran. 'That has occurred to you, I trust?'

Kreysun inclined his head. 'But I am not as sure as you. Should we turn? Should Rhyn-Khur turn, and should our forces in Gestern not agree to transport the dead, then Gorian has no backing.'

'But he already has what he needs, does he not? There are three thousand ahead of us. Enough to scare away ten times their number. There are five thousand coming from Gestern. *Five.* I fear there is no one left alive in that country. He has pushed them all to the coast and murdered them there, surely. He has the Karkulas and he has the Dead Lords as his eyes and ears. What happens, Prosentor, when he decides we are no longer an asset? He can kill us in our sleep and he is a thousand miles away. At a stroke, he can add almost twelve thousand to his army.'

'You think he will attempt that?'

'It is just a matter of time. Why do you think the Dead Lords march with a hand on the wagons of the Gor-Karkulas. Speak. What are your fears.'

'My King, you have given me new ones to ponder on. Our warriors are unhappy. They too speak of feeling like the train behind the glorious army. We raid and we fight where we can but this is not battle. It is to Gorian's design. No one speaks out against you but surely in their hearts, they question our purpose. We are a warrior race, subservient to no one. Yet—'

He stopped and looked at Khuran. The king was neither surprised nor angry to hear what he had to say. He had been a fool and he knew it. That was where his anger lay.

'Yet we march to the tune of Gorian Westfallen. One man from the heart of the Conquord, who frightens us all because he can do what we cannot,' said Khuran.

Kreysun raised his goblet. 'He was so plausible.'

'We were too happy to bite at anything that might give us the edge and the ability to strike first at the great enemy. Now I wonder if we are not walking behind the true enemy of us all. Death used to mean glory in the annals of legend, a seat by the Lord of the Sky. A spirit on the wind, free forever. Now? It means what Gorian wishes it to mean. If I were a Tsardon warrior blade now, that might make me wonder if I should fight at all.'

'There is no secret the warriors are fearful of dying in this war. So far, he has not seen fit to raise our own to walk with us but I agree with you, that situation might change.'

Khuran drained his infusion and plucked up the copper pot for a refill.

'Yet what choice do we have but to follow him? If we turn away, we throw away what remains our best chance of ultimate victory. If we remove the Karkulas and Dead Lords we weaken ourselves beyond hope of victory.'

Kreysun nodded. 'We have no choice but to stay. One day, we will encounter the rest of the Ascendants and they too can kill from a considerable distance. And Gorian remains just one man ...'

Khuran raised his goblet to toast his friend. 'And that is the weakness of us all. We will talk to our warriors but quietly. There is a time and a place to make a stand and fight the decisive battle. That time may not be nearly as close as we think. The gates to Neratharn are a place where we can lose this war but where we cannot win it. The gates of Estorr are an entirely different place.'

'And Gorian?'

'Leave him to think he has us tamed. Even he cannot look everywhere at once. His weaknesses are easily exposed. All we will ever need is the briefest element of surprise.'

'Be vigilant, my King. A thousand miles away he may be but dangerous he remains.'

Khuran spread his arms wide. 'Kreysun, my friend, how do you think I have remained King of Tsard for so long.'

They clashed goblets and laughed again. A mistake it had been, a fool he was, but he was still at the table, and tables were for turning.

'Paul. Go.'

'My place is here. I am the head of your security.'

'Yes. And I feel my security is best served by you sailing with the Ascendants and winning me a battle or two.'

'You can hear the riots from here. How long before the Speakers arrive to demand audience with the Chancellor, only for you to tell them she is dead?'

'Long enough for you to leave. Have you seen the protection I've got out there? If any more come in I'll have to share my bath with them. God-surround-me, I hope we can feed them all.'

Laughter.

'If I am standing with you, we are stronger.'

'No, it means we are four old people rather than three. Take-me-to-my-rest, Paul, do I really need three ex-soldiers grizzling about how best to save the Advocate's skin? Two is quite enough. Arvan and Marcus are entirely capable. You are still a field officer in your heart and you know it. Now leave before I have you thrown on the boat in an embarrassing fashion.'

Jhered woke again. He was sweating again too. How many times had he replayed it in his dreams? Why wouldn't it rest?

'I've forgotten something,' he muttered. 'Something critical.'

'No you haven't.'

The voice from the gloom of his tiny cabin startled him. He peered at the single chair.

'What are you doing in here?'

'Watching over you,' said Mirron. 'You were shouting out. Making the crew nervous.'

'Like hell.'

'All right but you were shouting out.'

Jhered sat up in the bed. 'What have I missed. What have we missed?'

'We've done everything we can. Iliev has signalled the fleet about the threat and what to do. The flagships have been on station ever since the executive mobilisation order went out. The net is too tight. The Ocenii are hunting. And he's sailing to Kester Isle to bring out the reserve.'

'We're on the fastest ship. Your ship. We have nothing to do but rest until we reach Neratharn. Estorr is in good hands. We have legions to the north, south and west, waiting for the warning signs. I know it scares you to be away but not even a mouse is getting into the palace to threaten the Advocate. We're covered and we have a job to do. We need to sleep and we need to plan our Work.'

Mirron moved to the bed and kissed his cheek. 'And you need to relax or we'll wish you hadn't come.'

'My mother used to do that,' said Jhered. 'Kiss my cheek when I'd had a nightmare.'

'Does it work when I do it?'

Jhered shook his head. 'No, because this is no nightmare. This is a message and I will not ignore it. There's something we've overlooked. I would stake my reputation on it.'

Mirron frowned. 'That bad?'

'Yes. That bad. Now if you don't mind, I need to go over it another hundred times until the truth pops out.'

'You won't find anything.'

Mirron got up and moved to the door.

'I hope you're right.'

But when she had gone, Jhered lay back down, knowing that she was not.

Chapter Forty-Nine

859th cycle of God, 47th day of Genasrise

Arvan Vasselis felt an overwhelming sense of sadness. How fragile, the bonds of power. How slender the knife-edge on which order balanced. How disappointing that the stability and acceptance for which they had worked so hard these last ten years had been washed away so effortlessly.

'My son died saving you, you ungrateful bastards,' he muttered, turning from the balcony and back into the state rooms.

None of the others had heard him. The state rooms were grand and huge and all were well out of earshot. The palace's principal function suite was set out over the palace doors and facing over the courtyard and fountain to the Victory Gate. From that balcony, Herine addressed the citizenry, bestowed honours and entertained the more important heads of state.

Today, they awaited the Speakers of Oceans, Earth and Winds. The Chancellor's body lay in full honour in the centre of the room beneath the vaulted ceiling and its fresco of the battle of Karthack Gorge. She rested on a high table covered with pristine white sheets and with pillows for her head. Flowers of red, yellow and blue were laid at her head and feet.

The Chancellor had been washed and her face made up to hide the pallor of death. She wore her formal robes with her favoured gold circlet on her head. She appeared serene, resplendent, her face no more to scowl, to show contempt, to sneer or to disdain. Vasselis did not lament her passing, only the consequences. He walked across the mosaic-laid apron that separated the balcony approach from the rest of the room and down the single step.

Order ministers sat heads bowed and silent at the four corners of the compass. They represented the four principal elements and were her guard until she was interred to find the embrace of God. They wore grey robes, their heads were shaven and their hands covered in delicate white gloves.

Herine Del Aglios and Marcus Gesteris stood together to the right of the table. Conversation had long since dried up. Herine, altogether stunning in formal toga, gilded-leaf tiara, gold-braided hair and gold sandals, appeared calm though it was forced. Gesteris, armour and weaponry polished, cloak about his shoulders and green-plumed helmet under his arms, appeared as if he had never left his military career, so well did the accoutrements still suit him.

Hesther Naravny hadn't concerned herself with covering her anger or contempt. Her greying flame-red hair matched the fire in her eyes. Her Ascendancy-slashed toga and stola were direct challenges, insults to the Order dignitaries they awaited.

Vasselis walked over to her and she put an arm through his. The two of them turned away from the Chancellor to the blue sky and noise outside and above the gates of the Hill.

'Pretty ugly out there,' said Vasselis.

'Pretty ugly in here, too,' said Hesther, bringing a shush from the Advocate.

'Just go along with it for now,' said Vasselis.

'With what? You were not there, Arvan. You did not see the blood and the bodies of young people slaughtered by her hand. This is a charade. She should be ashes on the wind, not lying here awaiting the melancholy and grief of those innocent of the faith who do not know her for the child murderer I know her to be. You will excuse me if I find it hard to appear polite and deferential.'

The nearest Order member raised her head and speared Hesther with a baleful look. Hesther met the challenge calmly. Herine crossed the short space and took Hesther's other arm.

'Fresh air,' she said.

The three of them walked out on to the balcony. Flags hung from its balustrades. Early genastro blooms stood in display on four plinths adding a beautiful scent to the air. Ivy was woven through the stonework. Whatever Herine had been about to say withered on her lips. She gripped the balcony rail ands gaped while those outside who could see her howled and bayed. The noise swelled as the knowledge was passed on.

'The city must be empty,' breathed Herine.

Through the courtyard packed with soldiers, to the walls bristling with spears; to the five hundred cavalry on the apron beyond the gates standing behind the full sarissa phalanx, she stared at her citizens. Tens of thousands covering the apron in front of the infantry, crammed in along every approach road, hanging from tree, building and sitting on rooftop. Swaying, jostling and shouting.

The placards carried insult and declamation. But what hurt were the effigies hanging from pole and chain. Some bore Ascendancy colours, others the green slash and gold head and feet of the Advocacy.

'Don't they understand?'

'Unfortunately, they understand only too well,' said Vasselis. 'They understand the dead are coming and that the legions can't stop them. Only God. And their God denounces both you and the Ascendancy.'

Hesther tugged her arms free of them both.

'Still want me to play happy academy?'

Herine stepped away from the balcony and moved back inside, anxious to be away from the mob and to let tempers subside.

'When did it grow so huge?'

'It's been like that since news of the Chancellor's death leaked out,' said Hesther. 'The Order has orchestrated this, make no mistake. And we are handing them a martyred Chancellor. You can condemn her and sentence her retrospectively, why will you not consider that?'

'And then what?' hissed Herine. 'They all go meekly to their homes?'

'You think they will go when the Chancellor is handed back?'

Herine shook her head. 'But at least it will divert them.'

'Let's wait to see the mood of the Speakers,' said Vasselis. 'Until then, please, all of us, do what Paul wanted and keep our story straight and ourselves even-handed. Hesther?'

'Best I say nothing, then,' she said.

'Probably.'

'They're in the complex, I take it?' said the Advocate.

'They were at the head of the mob,' said Vasselis.

'Then let's have them in here without further delay.' Herine nodded at Gesteris and turned to Hesther. 'Check my hair.'

Hesther moved a strand or two from her face. 'There. Perfect.'

'Thank you, Mother Naravny. Stand behind me, won't you? I need your strength.'

Gesteris opened the grand double doors at the far end of the state room. He retreated quickly to stand with his allies. The Advocate had chosen to stand on the single step and could see the Speakers come in past the table carrying the Chancellor. Vasselis stationed himself to her right, Hesther her left. Gesteris took up station at Vasselis's shoulder.

Without a Chancellor at the head of the Order, the Prime Speakers were dressed as befitted the leaders of the elements. Vasselis had always found it gaudy. Like a male bird preening and displaying for a mate. Their robes were brightly embroidered with imagery of earth, or ocean or sky. Bright colours, voluminous material. All had shaven their heads in deference and the new growth of hair symbolised the renewing of a cycle under God.

With their personal entourages, they poured into the state room. In moments, the sound of their sandals on marble was eclipsed by that of their grief. Wailing and crying, shouting prayers and quoting scriptures. They draped themselves across the Chancellor. Kissed her feet, fingers and cheeks. Their faces were crumpled like discarded parchment. Tears rolled unchecked. Whole bodies shook.

'Give me strength,' muttered Hesther.

The vaguely nauseating display went on for an eternity. Herine did not move a muscle, waiting for them to finish. Vasselis wondered what was really going through their minds. No doubt they were stricken by their first view of the dead Chancellor but they, and their absent colleague, the Speaker of Fire, would all be vying for ascension to the Chancellery.

And tradition dictated that the appointment would be made by the incumbent Advocate.

'My Speakers, your grief honours your Chancellor as it honours the Order of Omniscient. Felice Koroyan is a loss to us all.'

Herine had chosen a lull in the weeping to make herself heard. Their entourages retreated and the three Speakers straightened. Smoothing robes and dabbing puffy eyes, they approached the step. None of them was particularly tall and each was forced to angle his face to see the Advocate. Vasselis suppressed a chuckle. She had set her back to the sun too. She never missed a trick.

'My Advocate,' said the Speaker of Winds, a narrow-faced, narrow-minded old man. His voice was clogged from his outpouring of emotion. 'Our beloved Chancellor is dead. Nothing can change that.'

'Well now, that's an interesting debate, isn't it?' said Herine. 'Given what is on our borders.'

Vasselis stiffened but Winds ignored her.

'Nothing can change that. Our only succour is that she goes to the embrace of the Omniscient, there to feel His glory for eternity. But we must put aside our personal grief. The faithful need answers.'

'And is that why you brought so many of them with you today?' asked Herine. 'Winds, I am happy to entertain you and your colleagues at any time but I will not submit to the pressure of the mob. We will talk but first you must disperse your crowd.'

'They are here of their own free will,' said the Speaker of the Earth, rounder and shorter than Winds, but possessed of a sharp mind. Vasselis once thought he would make a fine Chancellor. 'We guide, we do not coerce.'

'Oh, come on, Earth. Every House of Masks must be shuttered and dark. Every Armour of God barrack bunk must be empty. Guidance with an iron hand pointing the way.'

'Their Chancellor has been murdered,' said Earth. 'They will not disperse until the guilty are brought before the court, tried and sentenced.'

'So we have a problem,' said Herine. 'The Chancellor was not murdered. She was the victim of a tragic accident, nothing more.'

Winds scoffed. 'Accident. She came here in full health to do the work of the Omniscient. The Ascendancy finally revealed itself for the abomination we always knew it was. She is arrested and while in your custody, she has an *accident*? None but an imbecile would believe such lies. It is clear that she has been killed by one or all of your Ascendants. It is them you must arrest. They have blood on their hands. We demand their immediate restraint.'

Herine laid a hand on Hesther's arm to stop her response. She walked off the step and stood toe-to-toe with Winds.

'Since you are unaware of the law, I will enlighten you.' Herine's voice was quiet and measured. Vasselis shivered and he wasn't even the target. 'I can do that because I make the laws. To arrest, I need suspicion. And there is no suspicion. No Ascendant is to blame.

'If you want me to demonstrate suspicion, evidence and guilt, I will take you on a tour of the Academy where the blood still stains the rugs and whose stench still haunts the air. I will show you children whose beds are wet every night because of the nightmares they will suffer all their lives. I will bring before you fifty citizens who could point at the person responsible for the only murders to have occurred on the Hill in fifteen years. And shall I tell you a secret?'

Herine put her mouth to Winds' ear and spoke in a stage whisper. 'She's lying right behind you.'

Winds started and his face reddened. Beside him, both Earth and Oceans gasped. All three began to protest, their voices loud and brackish. Herine stepped back and spoke again and her voice demanded their immediate silence.

'And finally, I will take you to the cells where your Armour of God thugs await their trial for complicity. All have confessed. And if I have to, I will have them repeat those confessions in public. Is that really what you want?'

'Lies,' hissed Winds. 'Terror will gain you any compliance you demand.'

'Well, you should know,' said Hesther.

'Do not talk to me,' spat Winds. 'Vermin of the Ascendancy.'

'Silence!' Herine's body had tensed. 'I will say this to the three of you. You seek to unsettle me and you are not good enough. Neither was Felice Koroyan. There will be no immediate appointment of Chancellor. None of you has yet demonstrated worth.

'Estorr and the Conquord does not have the time nor the patience for conflict between us. Take your Chancellor. Give her the burial you feel she deserves. No one from the Hill will be attending. You are fortunate we are not giving her to you in an urn.

'And one final thing. I know what you have been doing in my capital city. Ascendancy sympathisers beaten, tortured, murdered. I have some of the survivors here. That will stop. We are at war and whether you believe it or not, the only certain weapon we have is the Ascendancy and those within it who are utterly dedicated to saving the Conquord and your worthless skins. I need my citizens working together. I need their eyes to be looking out for enemies and their hands doing the work their Conquord demands. If you do not disperse your mob, I will use mine to disperse it for you.'

Herine smiled sweetly. 'Am I clear?'

General Davarov of the Atreskan legions had gathered three legions to him by the time he reached the major fishing port of Tharuby on the northern coast of the Tirronean Sea. It was a better return than he dared hope, following the debacle on the Tsardon border. Almost twelve thousand infantry, cavalry and significant artillery.

The latter he had sent on ahead. Some he had managed to put on ships for transport to the Gaws. Infantry went on in support, cavalry covered the ground north, south and north-west. Every day they brought back more and more worrying reports. The dead were being gathered from a widening arc. But at least they marched in their armies. There was no such thing as a dead scout nor dead cavalry rider.

It was small comfort.

Atreska was a country in chaos. Davarov's orders not to attack the dead or the Tsardon had been largely adhered to but it had led to a flood of refugees as well as soldiers heading west to Neratharn. Messengers had been sent there to try and give some advance warning for the ground to be prepared but it was going to be very difficult.

On leaving Tharuby, Davarov would split his legions, staggering their journeys north and west to try and maintain supply. The fishing port itself was heaving at the seams and his arrival had provoked panic, not calm. He would be advising evacuation but not necessarily to Neratharn.

One thing he could be glad about was his decision to bring civil administrators with him on his journey. Even so, the situation was terribly confused. He was sitting in the basilica with Cartoganev, the praetor of Tharuby and the three legates he had borrowed from Haroq City.

'At the moment we have two principal forces. The Tsardon-backed force about five days behind us and fifty miles north of us. And we have the new force heading north, from Gestern by the livery that has been identified.'

Cartoganev placed markers on a map. Davarov had given him the task of gathering information on friend and foe alike. His cavalry was stretched and tired but still took to the roads every day on relay-messaging and reconnaissance missions. It had left Davarov himself free to try and marshal the mass of refugees that trailed the army and to whom he felt personal responsibility. Free to search for fighting tactics that might be effective. He had come up with a few but the most effective were also the most unpalatable.

'How far back is the second force?' he asked.

Cartoganev placed a marker on the map. Davarov hissed air between his teeth.

'They don't pause,' said Cartoganev. 'They march night and day.

They'll be able to join with the first force in a day should they wish.'

'The only good news is that unless they abandon the Tsardon living, they'll have to slow down.'

'Thank the Omniscient for the Tsardon, right?' said Cartoganev, eyes sparkling.

Davarov chuckled.

'They're the best ally we have until we reach the border.' He turned to his legates. 'Refugees and food?'

There was a shuffling of parchments and the lead spoke up.

'Our attempts to record the name and origin of every man, woman and child who has joined the main exodus is ongoing. We have recorded thirty-five thousand names and more join every day. We suspect there are upwards of forty-five thousand displaced people marching with us. We have managed to persuade some to turn back but most are simply too scared. Why would they march where the army does not?'

'But the great plains are vast and we know the dead have not deviated,' said Davarov. 'We can't feed or water this many, can we?'

The legate shook his head. Davarov felt for him. He'd enlisted a small army of acting administrators to help him but still he barely slept. He had sprouted grey hairs and he was only thirty-seven.

'We haven't a hope of doing so. We've looked at operating feeding stations but we cannot buy or requisition enough supplies to make the slightest dent. People are having to fend for themselves.'

'How?'

The legate shook his head again. 'I don't know. All we can do is advise them not to travel with us when we take their names. We tell them we have no food, water or medical supplies. We are saying that the central plains are the safest place with the enemy moving towards Neratharn. We are not getting that message through. And we have another problem. Disease.'

Davarov sighed. It had just been a matter of time.

'The last thing we want is people dropping dead of hunger, thirst or disease and then rising again.' He kneaded his temples, feeling the pressure going. 'Any thoughts?'

'One,' said Cartoganev. 'From everything we've seen so far, the dead awakened are almost exclusively soldiers. We've seen no real evidence that ordinary citizens are being targeted in significant numbers. Even so, disease could spread to the army. How about delaying tactics?'

'I don't think so. The artillery is too far away now. Turning it would be a waste. I still say that we must range everything we have at them on the walls of the Jewelled Barrier. If they come through that, then we have our field tactics to try. By that time, I'll be happy to try anything.'

Davarov smiled but didn't feel any warmth from it. He knew what he should do but it was as unpalatable as trying to reduce the dead to ashes to stop them. He needed Megan Hanev with him but the new Marshal Defender would almost certainly not return to Atreska until this trouble was done. That left him as the most senior Conquord loyal confirmed alive.

'Praetor Juliov, anything to add?'

The praetor was pale. She was a timid woman and the very rumour of marching dead had terrified her. The arrival of Davarov and tens of thousands of refugees had merely confirmed her fears and she had let her town slip away from her.

'Every ship is gone,' she said. 'Stolen or hired for murderous rates. No one brings in fish. Food stocks are very low. Many have fled west. I cannot help you.'

Davarov cleared his throat. 'I see. But try this. Talk to your people. Make them see because it is the truth. The fight is moving west. The dead do not cover much of our great country and they can be skirted easily. If your citizens run, then make it be east into the plains. Go yourself. I promise you it is the best place for you.'

Juliov nodded. 'I'll try.'

'It's all I ever ask.'

'So, General, orders?' Cartoganev gathered his papers.

Davarov sighed. 'Who would be me?'

'Ah, but who would you otherwise be?'

'Good point. Roberto Del Aglios, I think. Then I'd be wearing a toga and standing in a Sirranean tree-house or whatever they are, talking wood and treaties.'

'But you're not.'

'No, I'm not. So this is what we must do. The army must make all speed to Neratharn now. I want at least four days to prepare. We will force-march. The refugees must be broken up if we can make it happen. This is where you come in Cartoganev. Cavalry can't operate on the battlefields to come. You need to keep up your information gathering but I want you to find volunteer units ... a hundred strong at best, to offer to take refugees away into the plains. The legates can help you carve up the followers as best we can. Any that choose to stay must know they are not going to be protected any more. We cannot wait for them.

'We aren't going to be able to support them anywhere else. They'll go if they're made to feel protected. What do you say?'

Cartoganev shrugged. 'Orders are orders.'

Davarov nodded. 'That they are.'

But even as the meeting broke up, Davarov wondered whether his abandonment of his people was really the way to save them, or an act of self-preservation. One thing was sure, he wasn't going to sleep well that night.

Chapter Fifty

859th cycle of God, 53rd day of Genasrise

The winds and the tides had been kind to Prime Sea Lord, Admiral Karl Iliev. His oarsmen had worked hard when the breeze had slackened at all and he had made an average nine knots on the journey south to Kester Isle. He was so much happier on the sea. Too long in port made him nauseous. Out here, the mind was free to think in a way that was impossible in a stuffy office on the Hill. But he still couldn't get the cries of young Harkov from his mind. He heard them on the breeze, the mouths of gulls and in the creak of timbers.

The *Ocetarus,* flagship of the fleet, was in supreme working order. A marker against which every other vessel in the Ocetanas needed to feel measured. He had received confirmation of the orders he had sent out on leaving Estorr harbour and that meant his flag- and bird-lines were working at acceptable efficiency. He had seen no unidentified vessels and was encouraged that the patrol pattern of the fleet in the eastern sea was apparently very tight. No ship carrying the dead would pass the Ocetanas while he remained on deck.

Iliev stood in the prow as he always did on approaching the Isle. The Lances of Ocetarus had slid by to the north, great spears of rock reaching high into the sky, magnificent natural monuments to the glory of the god of the sea. The one true god. Ahead of him, the bleak rock walls of the Isle rose from the morning mists and sea spray. Waves were beating hard against its base.

Through his magnifier, Iliev could see the dual flags of Conquord and navy flying from every watch tower. Welcoming him home. Home. The palace and city of the Isle. The miles of rock-hewn corridor. The bleak beauty and the peace. The battering of the elements that were like the kiss of life itself. And from where he would order the salvation of the Conquord before heading out to sea once more, this time as Squadron Leader of the Ocenii.

By midday and with the Isle towering above him, casting its shadow across the ocean, his joy at first sight had disappeared, replaced by nagging anxiety. No bells had sounded to mark his approach. The flag of the sea lords had not been unfurled to hang from the sea gates, heralding his presence. It meant no one was on the forward towers. No one was standing in the artillery shelters north and looking out to sea. And no one had been through the western sea gates in four hours.

That could not be right. Harkov's words resounded in his head. He gripped the prow rail hard, pushing back a shiver. No one could take Kester Isle. No invasion force no matter how large could hope to fly its flags on her towers. It was impossible. Unless, of course, the gates were opened because the harbour masters thought they were admitting friends. Iliev strode to the stern to stand by the tiller man.

'Lower sail. Oars to ready. Steady fifteen stroke. Oar master, when you are ready. Execute.'

'Yes, my Lord.'

'Tiller, nudge us out a way. Let's come at the sea gate head on.'

The tiller man nodded and moved the tiller away from him. The ship began to turn. Riggers swarmed across the deck. The sail descended and was tied against the mast. A grim silence fell across the ship. Eyes roved over the mass of rock dominating their horizon. Nothing moved. Not even a bird could be seen flitting about the eddies. The sound of sea on rock and beneath the hull rang loud.

Iliev turned his body to watch the northern tip of the Isle go by, revealing to them the first western sea gate and harbour. Inside the wall, the masts of ships could be seen, bobbing in the swell. Glancing upwards, he could feel the quiet. This close, two hundred yards from the Isle, they should be able to hear shouts from inside, the sound of work in the dry docks and there should have been traffic in and out of the gates.

Iliev glanced back at the tiller man. He was looking nervous. He licked dry lips.

'Keep a steady hand,' said Iliev. 'Turn in. Gently now.'

The sea gate was standing open when they breasted the edge of the harbour wall. Four spiked corsairs were tied up along the north wall. Two biremes were with them. He could see no one on board. Inside the dock, deep in the bedrock of the Isle, all was night. No lights could be seen pushing back the darkness.

The *Ocetarus* came about and moved towards the harbour. Iliev stayed by the tiller. Riggers and Ocenii squad marines moved to the prow.

'Tell me what you see,' called Iliev. 'Oars slowing, ten stroke.'

'What has happened, my Lord?' asked the tiller man.

'Prepare yourself, son,' said Iliev. 'Nothing good can explain this silence.'

Down on the deck, lanterns were being lit. The ship moved slowly past the harbour walls and into the relative calm within. The dark gates loomed above them. Set into the rock walls, the double iron gates pointed out to sea. Great works of Conquord engineering designed to withstand the fiercest bombardment. But they weren't fully open.

'There's a sail up inside,' shouted one of the marines at the prow. 'Trireme. Identification not possible, sir.'

'A sail up? Are you sure?'

'Yes, my Lord. No doubt.'

Iliev pondered a moment. 'Take us in,' he said.

'My Lord?'

'It's all right, son. Set us at our regular berth. Prow first. And listen for my orders.'

'Yes, my Lord.'

Iliev set off along the length of the ship. 'Ocenii, to the prow. Armed and ready. All of you, keep your eyes open. Assume anything that moves is an enemy. Where's my aide and where are my knives?'

'Coming, my Lord.'

A man detached himself from the group at the prow and hurried down the fore steps and out of sight. Iliev joined Ocenii marines as the ship moved under the rock wall and through the gates. Squad seven. His squad. Their corsair was suspended under the stern between tiller and timbers. All triremes sailed with a squad now. All had been adapted to carry the fast assault craft. How glad he was that he had his men with him.

'Trierarch Kashilli.'

'Yes, skipper.'

The huge Ocenii marine turned to him. Dark-skinned and tattooed, he loomed over them all. His hair was jet black and he kept it tied and braided at the nape of his neck. A single ring was through his left nostril. Iliev didn't approve of jewellery but Kashilli was a proven marine and he didn't interfere with the personal superstitions of his best killers.

'Disembark and hold passage four south. Check the lift status.'

'Yes, skipper,' he said. His large brown eyes studied Iliev. 'You think the dead are here, don't you?'

'What else is there to think? Just remember what I told you about Jhered's encounters. If a man does not respond. If he is dull of face, appears injured or diseased, then he is our enemy. Move to disable. Legs, heads and arms. Tell the squad.'

'Done, skipper.'

'And pass this word also. If the Isle is taken, we must raise the quarantine flags. If I fall, take it on. Someone has to make it to all the towers across the Isle.'

Kashilli turned back and began barking instructions to the squad while weapons were checked and strapped on. Thirty-six men ready to retake their home for the whole of the Ocetanas. Iliev's aide reappeared with his light leather breastplate, dual short swords and knife belt.

'Is there naphtha aboard?' Iliev asked.

'Only in the bellows and pipes, my lord. Nothing hand held.'

'We'll bring as much back as we can. Kashilli, you hear that?'

'Aye, skipper. It's in the dry stores first level above the docks. We'll liberate it.'

'Good.' Iliev raised his voice. 'Crew of the *Ocetarus*. Be ready to leave fast on my order or the order of any Ocenii, should I fall. Ready the bellows, keep the pipes trained on the dockside. Let no one on board you suspect is no longer your friend. Ocenii, to me.'

The ship was inside the dock now. Iliev could feel the vast space where upwards of eighty triremes could be berthed comfortably. It felt empty, which was of some comfort. The single Conquord trireme they could see, sail still up and slapping slack against the mast was dark and quiet like the cavern. The tiller man angled the ship into the berth.

'I need room for oars port and starboard. Not too close to the angle, there.'

'Yes, my Lord.'

The lanterns forward lit the harbour wall. Iliev could see a lone body sprawled with his leg dangling over the edge. His back was bloody, his clothing torn. Iliev frowned. He was an Ocetanas and he had not been reawakened.

'Ocenii, I have seen a brave man reduced to madness by the walking dead. Remember yourselves and remember your training. Look to each other. You have brothers either side of you. See to it that none fall, only to rise and walk against you. Are we ready?'

A roar greeted his question.

'Then I commend all our bodies to Ocetarus. May He bless our work and give us the strength to reclaim our land for Him. Bring torches. When we are done, we will burn the bodies.'

The ship nudged the harbour wall. On a command from Kashilli, the Ocenii swarmed up and over the prow rail, jumping the short distance to the land or running along the ramming spike. Their feet slapped loud on the stone. They split into two groups. The first headed left and out of sight but for their lanterns, making for passage four south. Kashilli led them. Iliev took the second group. Moving directly ahead down the wide approach that led to the dockside from the lift stations.

They ran past trolleys and small carts stowed to the sides of the passage, waiting cargo and supplies that would not be coming. Iliev leapt three more bodies on the way. He paused at the fourth, waving the squad onto their target. This man was no marine, no sailor. His clothing was that of a legionary. Insignia of the twentieth ala, the Stone Fists of Gestern.

'Dear Ocetarus, save us. The dead are crossing the ocean.'

Any lingering hopes that this was all the result of an outbreak of disease were gone. Iliev took to his feet and caught his squad by the lift stations. Splintered wood, broken tackle and cut rope littered the bare rock.

'They tried to slow them, skipper,' said a marine.

'But we must assume they found a way. Come on. Passage four. It's been a while since we've done the long run up there.' Iliev turned and led them back to the harbour side. He shouted information over to the ship on his way past. 'Kashilli?'

'Skipper.'

The marine resolved himself from the gloom at the passage head. His men were already inside it.

'Report.'

'Bodies scattered up the passage as far as we've gone. I'm securing the dry stores. Looks like everyone went up to the plateau and the palace.'

'Right. Change of plan. When the dry stores are secured, pick four to maintain guard while the ship's crew take everything they can lay their hands on. The rest of us, up the passage but let's not make this a competition. Any one up there is either dead, walking dead, or very well hidden by now.'

'Yes skipper, these bodies are stiff. This didn't happen just now.'

'But just now is when we'll finish it.'

The long, steep slope of passage four led directly into the cellars of the Ocetanas Palace that ran below the hypocausts. It was a cold, dark walk and Iliev wanted squad seven to arrive ready to fight. They walked silently and quickly. Steady pace, regular breathing. He could feel their apprehension, he shared it.

'If it talks, it's still alive,' he said. 'Let us not kill those who have done so well to survive.'

'If there are any,' muttered Kashilli.

'Indeed.'

The few bodies were long behind them now. Any who had escaped this far had probably made it to other defensive positions. Doors should be shut and bolted. So many places to hide in the palace. Iliev brightened momentarily. Of the two thousand odd who lived and worked here, some must surely have survived.

The cellars had been a battle ground. Dozens of bodies lay amongst the wine jugs, the crates and the stacked pottery, tiles and blocks of marble all stored there. It didn't take long to see how the fight had gone. Arrows had come from the two sets of doors at the opposite end of the cellars to the passage but they hadn't stopped the advance. Shafts lay on the ground. Others stuck in some numbers from bodies that had been hacked apart.

Iliev could almost feel the desperation in the defenders as they realised their attackers would not stop. Would not lie down. When a thrust to the heart was of no use, what would a man think? Ocetanas lay amongst them. About twenty were here. And ahead, the doors had been chopped open.

'Read this, Ocenii,' he whispered. 'When you strike you must be quick. Hamstrings, knees, ankles. Our swords may not dismember. Any of you good with axe or longer blade, help yourself. Plenty here.'

A couple of the marine oarsmen took him up on his invitation. One hefted a wood axe in both hands. Another picked up the curved blade of a Tsardon. Iliev raised his eyebrows. He led them through the doors. Light was beginning to filter down. Ahead of them, a stairway led between the hypocaust vents and up into the palace proper. Kitchens and storerooms were before them.

It was quiet up here too. He bade them leave their lanterns behind. All of them knew this place. It was the centre of their lives. He paused.

'I feel as you feel. Use your anger at this desecration, for silence is desecration here. Feel no pity. Strike without mercy.'

'Skipper,' came the hushed response.

'Kashilli. Go along the eastern wall. Raise the flags. I'll take the western.'

'Aye, skipper. Skipper? The rosters and placements?'

Iliev felt a rush of cold through him. 'I'll bring them. Good thought. Let's go, Ocenii.'

They split at the grand dining hall. It was laid for a feast. Crockery sparkled under polish, cutlery shone. Candelabra stood along every table. Chairs were decked with individual colours. Ready for the celebration of light, the end of the Quietening for another cycle. A feast that would have to wait.

Iliev took his men and ran out to the right, across the inner courtyard and up the stairs to the admiralty offices. Not a man, not a body. Just quiet. The paintings looked down on the emptiness, the rugs muffled their footsteps. The cool of the marble calmed their nerves.

Iliev waved a marine forwards to open the admiralty doors. He glanced around the landing that overlooked the courtyard and fountain. Ranks of closed doors. Nothing moved. Nothing made a sound. The doors swung silently open. Amidst the papers stacked on tables, the models of vessels and the tapestries of Ocetarus, bodies. Men and women he knew. Some still carried the terror of their deaths. Blood matted the rugs. The place stank. Flies had already found the corpses.

The squad ran in. Doors to ante-rooms were thrown open. His own office was tidy and empty of life or death. There were papers spread on his desk. He moved around to look at them. He sank into his chair, picked up one or two. The rosters. Positions of ships. Manpower. Destinations and resupply rotas.

'I didn't leave these out like this,' he whispered.

'All clear in the admiralty, skipper.'

Iliev looked up and nodded. 'Take the squad up to the palace towers. Hang the flags. You know where they're stored. Every tower. Don't miss one. Keep your eyes open.'

'And you, skipper?'

'I'll be up presently. I don't think there's anyone here.'

The marine nodded, dubious. 'I won't pass that on.'

'Don't. And go. I'll pack this up.'

'Aye, skipper.'

Shouting for the squad, the marine trotted back out to the landing. The stairs up to the roof and towers were next to the admiralty doors. Soon, he could hear footsteps going up and crossing the space above him. Iliev tried to think. This didn't ring right. Someone had been here looking at his papers. There was purpose here. This was not merely an attack of the dead to harvest more bodies.

So the fact they had found no one was confusing. Surely the enemy would take these papers. They held such key information for anyone wanting to avoid the fleet. Or indeed to find it. Iliev shivered. If you'd come all this way, you would not leave behind what you came for. He was wrong. They were here. Somewhere.

Iliev stood up and drew his short blades. Shouting came to him from above. A single scream. The door to his office swung open.

Chapter Fifty-One

859th cycle of God, 53rd day of Genasrise

That the man did not expect him to be there was almost comically apparent. He had walked five paces into the office before drawing up short and beginning to move backwards. Others were at the door. This first man was alive. The rest were not.

'Looking for something?' asked Iliev.

The man spat an insult. He was Tsardon. Head shaved and covered in tattoos. His teeth were sharpened at the front and he wore heavy furs over dark leather armour as if the land was still gripped by dusas. He drew a mace from his belt and hefted it in his left hand. But he was confused. He became aware of the sounds from above.

'That's right, I'm not alone,' said Iliev.

He came around the table. The Tsardon backed off another pace towards the door. Dead moved in behind him. Six of them. Iliev came on.

'Who—?'

'This is *my* office,' said Iliev.

'Too late for you,' said the Tsardon, his accent thick. 'We already swarm the sea.'

'Not as late as it is for you,' said Iliev.

He ran at the Tsardon who raised his mace. He was no soldier. Iliev ducked the flailing blow and rose, slashing one blade across the man's thighs, the other into his face, letting his anger give him power. He roared the name of God. The Tsardon cried out and pitched backwards.

The dead behind him shuddered but came on, walking around the Tsardon who was yelling something in his own language now, through his pain.

'Come on,' said Iliev. 'Scare me.'

The dead came in. Gesternans, or they used to be. Just legionaries.

Gladius bearers. Four still had their shields on their arms. All bore wounds and sores. Their skin was discoloured, armour and clothing torn and in need of repair. One walked dragging his left leg behind him. They stared at him, eyes blank but he could have sworn something flashed inside them just for a heartbeat. He couldn't worry about it now. The sounds of fighting intensified above his head. He needed to get to his men.

Iliev rushed forwards. He didn't expect them to flinch but he knew he had the edge of speed. And he did not fear them. Swords and shields were raised in front of him. Iliev stepped smartly to his left, planted his foot and round-housed the right-most soldier. Their balance was poor. The dead man toppled over to his left and fell, upsetting another two. Iliev pounced on the fallen man, slashing his blades across his hamstrings, cutting as deep as he could.

Iliev drove to his feet. The dead were turning to surround him. He buried one blade to the hilt in the thigh of his next target, dragging it clear, chopping down hard on the wrist with his other. The hand went limp, sword clattering to the ground. He was standing now. He butted the dead man in the forehead. The man staggered back. Iliev helped him on his way, pushing him hard in the chest. He collected two others and fell back through the door.

Iliev dropped to his haunches. A blade whipped over his head. He balanced and swept out a foot, tripping a walking dead who crashed to the ground. Iliev bounced and dropped with his knee in the small of the Gesternan's back. He felt bone give. Iliev rolled aside and came to his feet. Two were down, unable to rise. A third had no weapon but came on. The Tsardon was trying to rise. Blood poured from his face and down his legs from the cut at his waist. He was in a bad way.

Iliev waited for the dead to move in on him. Again he dropped to his haunches. He hacked his blades in from left and right, catching the back of an enemy's knees. Joints collapsed and the man fell. Iliev sprang back out of his way. Three more walking, three down but still trying to move in on him, impelled by what, he couldn't begin to imagine.

The dead were slow. Too slow for the Ocenii. Iliev ran at them again. There was space behind them. He dropped and rolled, bowling one aside. He came up quickly, delivering multiple strikes to the rear of calves, ankles, driving deep to snip hamstrings. The dead staggered on a pace before they began to turn. Iliev grabbed the Tsardon by the arm and dragged him out of the office. He howled in pain. Iliev dropped him and closed the door, turning the lock.

'Time enough,' he said. 'You. Tell me what I want to know.'

'You know enough. That you are finished.'

'Do I look finished to you?' Iliev knelt and grabbed him by the collars of his furs. They stank. The man's eyes began to roll back in his head. 'He speaks through you, I know he does. Can you hear me, you bastard? The Isle is mine again. And I am coming for you, burning and sinking every ship you have taken on the way. Fear me. Fear the Ocenii.'

Iliev dropped the Tsardon back to the ground. He was still breathing but it was ragged. The cut to his waist was deep and he was bleeding to death. Iliev got up, unlocked the doors and kicked them open. The dead faced him.

'Gentlemen, I'll be needing my papers,' he said.

And he closed the doors behind him.

'Hammers and axes!' roared Kashilli. He smashed his fist into the face of a dead man and pitched him over the cliff wall to tumble two thousand feet over rock and into water. 'If just one of you bastards gets away from here, tell them we need more hammers and axes.'

The flags were flying on the eastern turrets of the Ocetanas Palace. Kashilli had led his squad onto the walkway and wall that marked the length of the Isle's inhabited area. It had watch towers every mile. Four in all. And the same along the western edge where Iliev should be emerging. One flag was raised on the skipper's side and they were fighting hard, he could see that at a glance.

And a glance was all he could spare. The dead had boiled up the stairway from the first watch tower and rushed them down the path. More had emerged from nowhere behind them as if on some prearranged signal. He had lost three good men. Now it was his turn. Ocenii with axes were at their rear. He was at the head, a wood axe gripped in one big hand.

'Keep moving forwards. Don't let them stall us.'

Three abreast they stood despite the risk of injuring each other. Kashilli on the outside, swinging his axe in. Twenty dead stood in front of them. There were more, many more on the lawns and in the gardens below. Most weren't moving but some were bunching and walking towards the steps.

Kashilli battered his axe into the side of a dead man. He felt the ribcage shatter. Kashilli growled and kept the swing going. Heaving the dead off balance.

'Push them over! Go, go.'

The other two turned and helped the dead on. Three more tumbling, this time into the gardens. They'd be back. Kashilli had a moment's space. He grabbed the axe in both hands and swept it low and very fast. The blade carved through the legs of a Gesternan dead and deep into the knee of the second. The one fell, scrabbling with his hands. The other collapsed forwards. Kashilli barrelled into him, shoving him backwards into others. One fell from the path. Gone without a scream to the mercy of Ocetarus.

It gave him an idea.

'Stand back. Follow in my wake. Heave them over. Cut at the legs.' He grasped the axe firmly. 'I want that tower. There's oil and wood to be had there.'

Kashilli stared over the blade at the dead. They were coming on again. Two abreast but clumsy. Some behind walking faster than the damaged ahead. It gave them a stumbling, undisciplined look. But effective enough because they showed no emotion or distress from the horrific wounds some of them carried. It was bad work but someone had to dish it out.

'I will deliver you to mercy,' he said and shouted to clear his mind. 'Ocetarus awaits you.'

The dead in front of him had one eye and half a face. Brain oozed from cracks in his skull. Kashilli sheared his axe through the unfortunate's neck, catapulting him into the wall. His head flew out over the ocean, the body spasmed but did not fall. It tried to move but the legs would not coordinate.

Kashilli did not pause to let the fear grab him. He swung the axe back and forth, each time taking a pace or a half. He turned the blade a quarter, electing to use it as a flat edge, beating a path.

'Get them off our path,' he called. 'Move.'

Dead blades swung at him. He ducked, jerked back. Another nicked the axe shaft. A third clipped the top of his gauntleted hands. Kashilli yelled out. The cut was deep. He gripped harder. Blood pulsed down inside the glove. He struck again. A dead was crushed against the low wall. He could hear his men surging in behind him. The sick crunch of bones being broken. The odd silence as a writhing, grasping dead was thrown out over the rock.

'Keep on coming.' Kashilli spat in their faces. 'Fear the Ocenii.'

Kashilli took another pace. The axe caught a dead under his arm as he readied to swing his own weapon. He careered left. Kashilli paced forwards, kicked out and up, snapping the man's head and sending him teetering on the wall. Behind Kashilli, hands sent the dead back to God.

The big Ocenii spat blood from his mouth. It tasted sour. It was cold and thick. Another sweep of his axe. Another. And the way was clear. Below him. More dead grouped to head for the stairs up to the watch tower. Kashilli growled and ran ahead. The Ocenii behind him chanted victory and pushed harder, opening a gap between them and those dead who pursued them.

'Get fire down those stairs to the gardens. Keep them back.'

Kashilli charged up the stairs. Magnifiers lay on the single table. The stove and brazier sat under canvas. Beneath the small table, on which sat three tin mugs and a water pan, was a wooden chest carved with eels and seaweed. He threw open the lid, sorted through the flags and found what he was looking for. It was the largest flag the Ocetanas possessed. Blood red and with a white circle dead centre. It was crossed black on the diagonal. Quarantine.

'Get this up the pole,' he said, thrusting it at the nearest Ocenii. 'Five stay and guard our backs, keep the fires going. The rest, with me. There's a lot of running still to do.'

Away across the great gardens, fire leapt into the sky. Kashilli looked over. The flames came from the palace doors and tumbled down a set of steps, scattering dead who thought to ascend. Ocenii were running towards the first watch tower. Kashilli waved. It was returned. Satisfied, he ducked his head and forced his way back down the stairs past his own men.

'One down, three to go. Let's go, squad seven.'

Iliev packed his parchments and charts into leather tubes and stowed them in a leather satchel that he slung over his shoulder so it hung down his back, leaving his arms free. Two of the dead in his office still twitched. They had weakened quickly under his assault. Breaking the spine of one had seen him collapse. He still moved feebly, hands clutching at the rug on which he lay, trying to pull himself forwards.

Iliev knelt by him. Those eyes bored into his. They showed no pain, no recognition. Blood dribbled and bubbled from his mouth. He said nothing. Iliev picked up his chin and examined the face. He had died of disease, not injury, this one. There were sores across his cheeks and eating into his eyes.

'Bitter's Plague ate you, my friend. But why won't you die now? Why won't you stop?'

Iliev let the head drop and walked to the window looking out over the back of the palace. The gardens held hundreds of dead. Where they'd come from, he had no idea. Cover was good. Hedges, trees. Easy enough to conceal yourself if you knew how. But that indicated some form of sentience beyond the single apparent desire to kill.

Something gave them direction. Or someone.

Beneath the dead standing outside, the vegetation was blackened. Wherever they moved, so that blackening continued. Iliev looked instead at the wall pathways. His squad and Kashilli's were both making good progress. Almost at the second watch tower now. Dead tracked them along the ground but didn't climb up the steps until the last moment.

Iliev looked back at his victims. Only one moved now. He had inched closer to Iliev.

'Don't like the stone so much, do you?' he said. 'Interesting.'

He walked past the dead and back out into the main rooms of the admiralty. The Tsardon still lay there. Blood was on his lips too and not just from the cut on his face. Iliev stood over him.

'Nicked a lung, did I? Well, such is the price you pay.' He shifted to his other foot, leaving his right free. 'It's you, isn't it? It's you that keeps them focused. Keeps them standing, maybe. Let's see, shall we?'

Iliev's right foot stamped down on the Tsardon's neck, crushing his windpipe. The tattooed man thrashed briefly, clawed at his throat and then was still. Iliev cocked his head, listening.

The fighting continued.

Gorian sat back hard against the side of the wagon as it jumped and jolted on a poor section of road. He felt like he'd been punched. And he felt loss. They would stand and move for a while but there was too little for them there. They would fall soon enough. He took his hand from Kessian's head and the boy relaxed but looked round, concern on his face.

'What happened, Father? Who were they?'

'I told you not to piggy-back the energy trails,' said Gorian, impressed again at the boy's ability nonetheless. 'You should be concentrating on keeping our people here walking and well.'

'I did that too.'

Gorian had no doubt that he did. He smiled briefly.

'I shall have to watch you, shan't I, Kessian? Never too young to be the pretender, eh?'

Kessian's frown merely deepened. 'I don't understand.'

'Good,' said Gorian.

He rubbed his hands over the hard green and brown skin of his face. It had got a little worse these past few days. So much to do, keeping the advance going. The sea was the hardest place. Energy everywhere but every person one step removed from it. He was lucky to have got them through the stone of the isle and onto the grasslands atop it.

But it hadn't been enough. That idiot Kathich had wanted too much time. And he hadn't been watching like Gorian had told him. Gorian growled deep in his throat. That boot coming down was an insult too far.

'Who were they, Father?'

'Enemies. And they took what I needed.'

'Were they the Ocenii, Father? Like Arducius was always talking about?'

'But even they will learn to fear me.'

'It isn't what that man said.'

'I know what he said,' snapped Gorian and Kessian flinched. 'Just leave me alone. I need to think.'

So much was going so right. But he was alone. If only Mirron had come to help him bear the burden. Kessian was still too young; the Karkulas remained reluctant conduits and the Dead Lords could only hold the complete attention of the dead if Gorian was there to help them personally. It was hardly worth the effort. But it would have been. Should have been.

Gorian thumped the side of the wagon and looked out. The Gaws at Neratharn were next. Once the Tsardon king had orchestrated throwing them down he would join his son, marching under Gorian's banner. The living were almost beyond their uses. Most of them.

'I can help you,' said Kessian.

'Not now, boy. I'm tired.'

'Then let me take this day on my own,' said Kessian. 'We only march. Don't look over me. See what the rest are doing. Help the ones on the sea to find what you want.'

Perhaps the boy did understand after all. Gorian gazed down on him and saw him shrink away a little. But then, a rest from being linked to every one of his subjects might not be a bad idea. Little harm could come to them out here. Still a long way from Neratharn. And he needed to find more new ways to keep his subjects from simply dropping where they stood. Decay was becoming a real problem.

'You really think you can do it?'

Kessian nodded. 'I can, Father. Please let me show you. And you might be able to rest more when I do. Perhaps the green will go away. It scares me that it is on you.'

'It is nothing to fear. It is the touch of the earth upon God, remember that. All right then. You try and hold them. Use the Karkulas as much as you need to. And if you are struggling, tell me. I won't be angry. Just don't let any of them fall. Then I would be angry. Raising is so much more draining than maintaining.'

'I won't let you down, Father.'

'See that you don't.'

Transferring overall control of the Work to Kessian was technically easy but it felt like handing over a helpless child to a clumsy adult. The Work sat in Kessian's consciousness with great comfort and Gorian watched as the boy, surely not consciously at all times, adapted to take on the new load.

Simultaneously, Gorian felt a great release of energy. He let it surge through him and he became more alive, more awake, than he had been in days. It cleared his mind. Kessian sighed and sat back against his cushion.

'Are you secure, Kessian?'

'Yes Father, but it is a weight.'

'Then consider how much more I bear on my own and be happy. I'll stay beside you, in case you need me.'

'Thank you, Father.'

Gorian smiled again but his mind was already far away. South to the Tirronean Sea. South to Estorr and beyond. The Ocenii were on the water and waiting for his people. He had to find ways to stop that. Only one Karkulas with them but four Dead Lords. It would have to suffice.

But first he had to be sure of something. He traced back north along the energy lines. The world lay like a map before him. The thick grey masses were the dead on Gestern's shores and sailing across the sea as fast as vessels could be brought to them. The slow deep brown and blue energies of the ocean that he used and refocused to bring life to those inside the timbers of triremes. They weakened every day they were afloat. It drained him to keep them going, drained the Karkulas too.

North of Estorr and sailing towards Neratharn was a light so bright and so closed to him that it could only be one thing. The energy web that linked him to the dead picked it up and played it back to him. Strength set deep in the elements of the earth. Unwavering. A danger sign but one that surged through him with an orgasmic force.

No longer did they hide in the palace, awaiting their doom. They were coming for him.

'So much the better,' he said.

And he fell deep into himself and mulled over things that only Gods could understand.

Chapter Fifty-Two
859th cycle of God, 53rd day of Genasrise

Estorr burned.

Marshal General Elise Kastenas rode out of the Victory Gates and down the cleared path through the crowds that had barely thinned over the last seven days. With her went two hundred cavalry and twenty wagons. The sun was hot in the afternoon and the city basked. Late genasrise was a magnificent season but none paused to look at the beauty all around them.

One route had been established between the palace and the dock. Lines of infantry behind wooden barriers and carrying shields and truncheons, gladiuses sheathed, held back crowds that lined the way. The cordon was established from the gates, all the way along the processional drive towards the arena, down the slope of the Del Aglios Way, skirting the forum, through a maze of narrow streets and out in front of the harbour barracks.

The narrower roads were simply closed to all traffic and only the pavements of the wider ways were left available. This latter because paralysing the city for those few still keen to go about their business was not an option, and because Herine Del Aglios still believed in the necessity for free demonstration.

Her patience, though, was wearing extremely thin.

'And she hasn't even ridden out here,' said Elise. 'Shields!'

The order passed quickly down the four abreast column. The barrage of rotten fruit, vegetables and fish flew out over the infantry line. Horses skittered, cavalry spat filth from their mouths. Cheers rang out when a direct hit was made on helm or face. And there was worse. Elise could smell it. She turned in her saddle and looked back. Two cavalrymen right behind her were wiping shit from their faces.

Ahead, flimsy sacks were thrown into their path and at the head of the column, impacting wetly and spreading red across the road.

'Blood of the Chancellor!'

'Advocate murderers!'

Elise did the only thing she could reasonably do and upped her pace.

'Canter,' she ordered.

The column followed her lead gratefully. Shouts, taunts and hoots, even a few cheers, followed them along the processional. She kept her bearing proud and her face calm despite the emotions boiling inside. At the turning downhill into the guts of the city, she saw that the road name had been hacked away from the wall. Only the 'A' of Aglios remained. The statue which had carried the name had been defaced.

Through the tight streets, they endured water and slops from windows above their heads. Endless detritus slapped on shield, breast-plate and horse. Placards were thrust in their faces. Messages that had been vaguely humorous in the first couple of days were now painted bold and red and were extremely direct.

Burn the Advocate.

Del Aglios wears God's blood.

Ascendants will be ashes.

The Order must rule.

The Conquord is finished.

Elise could see the smoke and flames more clearly now. The violence had been contained in the harbour quarter to a large extent. Fears of the dead arriving by ship and flooding the city from the seaboard had sparked vicious rioting. Citizens had been killed, palace guards among them. It had forced much of the first Estorean legion to secure the docks and pen the rioters into an area of warehousing and slums already dubbed the Corpse Quarter. There the Advocate had been happy to let them destroy as much as they wished. No one else was allowed access. She hoped the fury would burn itself out, meta-phorically and literally. Looking at the dozens of fires within the square half mile, Elise doubted it would happen any time soon.

And time was something that appeared to be in short supply. Industry had ground to a standstill. Order agitators had organised attacks on armouries and weapons manufacturers, denying supply to the legions, stopping deliveries to the field. A great deal of damage had been done before the areas were secured. The water supply to the palace had been disrupted, food deliveries were attacked and robbed.

All vital supplies were now guarded and secured. Pipes had been repaired and well stations guarded by archer and sarissa alike. But it had forced a dangerous thinning of the defence. The Armour of God, of course, knew it. They hadn't moved yet but it was surely just a matter of time. To do so would declare open rebellion and without a figurehead, even their ageing Prime Sword, Horst Vennegoor, would not take a chance.

Elise and her cavalry rode through the harbour security cordon and rattled to a stop on the wide apron that led away from the dockside. So far, the dock remained working and most of its employees still turned up. Many lived there, knowing that to go back to their houses meant intimidation. A stream of men and women with buckets and cloths ran up to help clean away the filth from rider and horse alike.

Dismounting, Elise nodded her thanks and strode to Harbour Master Stertius who waited by his offices. The harbour was open but was eerily quiet for the middle of the day, barring a hum from the dockside itself. Ships awaited goods that were not forthcoming from the city. And inward trade was piled up with nowhere to go. The forum was closed to merchants, transformed into a makeshift centre for the organisation of dissent; and the roads out of the city were blocked by demonstrators in more places than the Advocacy could properly cover.

'Marshal General, I'm honoured.'

'Master Stertius, the Advocate wishes to convey her personal thanks for your continued loyalty. And I needed to ride out here. Sometimes, the guiding hand must see at first hand what has only been reported.'

'Brave,' said Stertius.

Elise shrugged. 'Not really. The mood is ugly but they won't attack an armoured column.'

'Not yet.'

'What do you mean?' Elise didn't like the look on the master's face.

'Hold on a moment.' Stertius snapped his fingers and a man came trotting over. 'Let's get those wagons loaded and turned. And find the cavalry something to eat and drink if they feel clean enough.'

He gestured for Elise to walk with him and she fell into step as they walked across the apron and out on to the dockside. It was heaving with ships and sailors. They lounged on deck or sat on the concrete sides playing dice, cards or just talking. The atmosphere wasn't unpleasant but it was plainly discontented.

'I'm a couple of days from closing the harbour to new traffic,' said Stertius. 'Every ship here is empty. No one will leave because to do so is ruin. But staying here means they cannot pay their crews and it won't be too long before trouble flares. We've enough food and drink for a while but it won't last.'

'You can't even get them to sail a couple of days north to Vettorum? Trade will be fine there.'

'But it's not Estorr, Marshal. The prices are not as keen. We can't force them away and most have unloaded. It's expensive to reload and profits are already squeezed. Yet that isn't why most won't actually go, though they won't openly admit it.'

'Ah,' Elise said.

'They're a superstitious lot. And we've had refugees in here the past couple of days as you know. The dead are on the sea. You think a sailor not in the Ocetanas has any interest in joining them?'

They walked on along the dock. Stertius paused to speak to reassure people that Elise's presence was evidence of a determination to ease the situation and ensure security. Elise related Karl Iliev's plans and the fact the entire fleet was at sea and patrolling was of both interest and comfort.

Stertius kept the smile on his face until they had walked the entire length of the dock to one of the harbour-mouth castles. There, he let it drop and Elise felt a tightness in her throat while they climbed the stairs to the artillery positions on the roof. The onagers were gleaming. Engineers were all over them, tightening, replacing, oiling.

Harbour guards saluted Elise but there was no pleasure in the greetings. Each and every one of them appeared strained. Scared, even. Stertius still didn't speak. Up on the flagpole, the green flag signifying message received was fluttering in the sea breeze. Stertius handed her a magnifier and pointed her towards a ship in the deep water, well outside of the harbour and casual sight.

Elise found it after a few moments flitting across open expanses of sea. She let the magnifier track up the mast to where two flags were flying. One, the mark of the Ocetanas. The other, the red, white and black crossed flag of quarantine. Elise lowered the magnifier and looked at Stertius.

'Kester Isle is lost?' she said, not believing it.

'Compromised at least. It was where Admiral Iliev was travelling. He could have reached there this morning. This is no trick. That ship out there will have received flagged, coded confirmation. They may not still be there but the dead have invaded Kester Isle. And every ship that comes into the harbour from now on will know it.'

'Dammit,' said Elise, knowing it was a totally inadequate response. 'I need to get back to the Advocate.'

'Yes, you do. I will not carry the flag because it will signal panic in the city.' Stertius mopped his brow. 'But I'm not going to be able to contain the news. The citizens will believe the sea defences compromised.'

'But it's a long way from that,' protested Elise.

'Absolutely true but then, the Ascendants didn't murder the Chancellor, did they? Think that matters? I get the mood of the city every day, Marshal, trust me. The Order can change it if they wish. We cannot.'

'All right. What will happen?'

Stertius smiled ruefully and gestured at the harbour mouth.

'This is the biggest hole in the city walls and two defensive forts are not going to be seen as enough. People aren't going to hang around to see if the dead can get in, they're going to head for anywhere they think is more secure. Many, maybe the majority, will either barricade themselves in their homes or run into the hills.

'But the Order are behind all this, Marshal. And they will get in the ears of everyone willing to hear. Right now, the citizens don't believe there is an invasion threat worth the name because the Order tells them there isn't. But with the simplest of nudges on their part, that could be made to change and we will all know where the most secure place in Estorr is, don't we?'

Elise swallowed on a dry throat.

'Can't you stop ships coming in? Keep the harbour closed?'

'I'll keep the secret as long as I can. But in the end, I cannot deny refugees landfall. Here, yes, on the fishing beaches north and south, no. Word will reach the citizenry. Look around you. All these men know. One loose word ...'

'How long do we have?'

'Better to tell the Advocate it is imminent. Could be an hour, could be five days. I have no real control, Marshal Kastenas. The next knock on her door might be the city populace wanting to come in and hide.'

'Then we should open the gates and let them in,' said Herine.

'What?' Vasselis gaped. 'I'm sorry, my Advocate but that is tantamount to suicide. For you, for me, for the Ascendancy.'

'I am sorry, Arvan but what are we if not the defenders of the citizenry?'

The basilica stage fell silent. Vasselis sat with Elise Kastenas and Marcus Gesteris on the benches normally reserved for Order dignitaries. Behind them, the business of administering the crisis went on unabated.

'And that is what we are doing. The navy is at sea, the armies are preparing at Neratharn. And the seat of government must remain secure.' Vasselis ignored the Advocate's sigh. 'And who will you let in and who will you exclude? Please, don't even entertain the possibility. The best defence of this city is to mobilise the citizenry on our side in support of the emergency measures we've so far been unable to implement.'

'So I should just lock them out and let them die.'

Vasselis's worries about Herine gained intensity. She was given to considering grand gestures to appease the citizenry. But she didn't ever walk the palace walls. She didn't understand the mood.

'No, my Advocate, you should be allowed to effectively defend the city. That means persuading the Order to cease their stupidity and encourage the people to back us through the crisis. It means an orderly evacuation of the city.'

Gesteris stood. 'One thing we aren't considering. I respect Master Stertius as we all do. But he is making some pretty bold assumptions. We have upwards of two thousand guards and legionaries defending this palace. Unless the Armour of God wheel artillery up here, they simply won't be able to get in unless we open the gates and let them.'

'Yes, Marcus, and that is what Herine seems to be considering.'

'Arvan, Marcus, thank you and sit down,' said Herine. 'I hear you. Many things may or may not occur and we must be prepared for a number of eventualities. So I will do what you ask, Arvan. And I will speak to the Council of Speakers. Bring them to me. And if they refuse to listen we will take further steps to clear the streets and empty the city.'

Vasselis kept his mouth closed to avoid gaping. Gesteris and Kastenas both reacted but kept their calm.

'You wanted to say something, Arvan?'

'If I may, I feel you are sending out conflicting messages. A moment ago you wanted to open the gates for everyone. Now you want to clear the streets if you don't get what you want from the Order.'

Herine shrugged. 'Can I not change my mind on hearing advice from my most trusted friends?'

'Of course, my Advocate, but—'

'I hear you and I consider that we have been on the defensive too long. Let those who will not help perish under the swords of the dead. Let those who would still clamour at my gates feel my anger.'

'That's not quite what I—'

'Be quiet, Marshal Vasselis.' Vasselis started. Gesteris stared at him and his expression said everything. 'I will talk to the Council but I will be issuing demands and not negotiating. I shall be doing it in private. I expect you all to back your Advocate without question. Marshal Vasselis, should I give the signal, I want the Ascendants to earn their keep this day. The streets must be cleaned of dissent. A little rain might be appropriate. Dismissed, all of you.'

Evening and the three tenth-strand Ascendants stood in a shadowed tower overlooking the crowds, their fires, torches and effigies. The sun was dipping behind the western hills, casting a glorious radiance across the torn city. Vasselis and Hesther had thought it prudent to bring the Ascendants here to see their target, for such it was almost certain to be. They'd left the shouting coming from the basilica offices where the Advocate was with the Council of Speakers. It was a debate only going one way.

The apprehension in the tower was palpable. Vasselis was by no means convinced that the trio could deliver what the Advocate would inevitably demand. They still bore the grief of the loss of Cygalius and Bryn. Now these young people, Mina and Yola, the sisters, and Petrevius, the brother, were about to personally incur the wrath of Estorr's angry populace.

'Seen enough?' asked Hesther. 'Wind and rain. Sleet and hail if you can do it. We need to extinguish the fires and force them all back to their homes.'

'But there are so many,' said Mina. She was a stick-thin child and her bony hands gripped each other. 'Hundreds of yards square and that's just what we can see.'

'Can you do it?' asked Vasselis.

'Should we?' asked Petrevius.

He was tall and slender. A gentle giant, Hesther said, but like them all, chock full of very individual principle.

'That's dangerous talk right now,' warned Vasselis. 'You've had Ossacer in your ear too much, young man. I'll answer your question. Yes, you should because the Advocate demands it and you are sworn to serve her.'

'But—'

'No buts. To serve is not always to agree. Now answer my question. Can you do it? We aren't asking you to kill anyone, just soak them and scare them a little.'

Petrevius sighed. 'Yes, we can do it. We can use the fountain pool.'

'About time we washed the filth from the streets,' said Yola. 'We've spent too long not fighting back.'

She tossed back her long brown hair and stared at Vasselis, dark eyes steady in her plain face.

Vasselis raised his eyebrows. 'But you will be working together in harmony, right?'

'We don't all listen to Ossacer,' said Yola. 'Petre knows my feelings, I know his. Doesn't change anything. Except I'll be leading this Work, won't I, my brother?'

Petrevius said nothing but his face flushed. He was the Wind Harker of the trio, Yola principally a Land Warden.

'Are you sure?' asked Hesther.

'We're sure,' said Yola.

A guard cleared his throat. 'They're leaving the basilica.'

Vasselis turned to look. The four Speakers were striding down the steps and heading past the fountain. He could see Herine framed in the light of the basilica. She stood very tall and very proud. There was no need for a message.

'Time to play,' said Yola.

Vasselis watched them walk down the steps and out into the courtyard. The Ascendants walked in a tight group with Hesther a few paces behind them. They talked and gestured as they went. The courtyard was largely clear. Much of the reserve was deployed elsewhere. Vasselis would have liked them back.

The Speakers approached around the opposite side of the grand fountain, its rearing horses lit by lanterns and candles. Hesther tried to guide them away but Yola led them on a collision course. She walked slowly by them, staring right into their faces. Vasselis couldn't see the Speakers' expressions but he heard the echoes of words, the trading of insults. He cleared his throat to cover a smile.

'Cheeky little minx,' he said.

'Arvan.'

Vasselis swung round. 'Marcus, where do you spring from?'

'I've been walking the walls,' said the one-eyed senator. 'Come see what I see.'

With a final glance at the fountain, where the Ascendants were kneeling to prepare, all three in the fountain bowl for maximum contact, Vasselis allowed himself to be led down the short stairs on to the rampart. Out of earshot, he presumed.

'What do you see?' asked Gesteris, gesturing out over the demonstrators.

It was relatively quiet at the moment. The citizens were waiting for news of the council's meeting with the Advocate.

'Look, I know where this is going, Marcus.'

'She is making a huge mistake. She'll bring the Armour of God against us.'

'I know,' hissed Vasselis. 'But we must stand behind her, now more than at any other time.'

Marcus shook his head. 'You are her closest friend with Jhered absent. She trusts you, she'll listen to you. If you run you can stop her now.'

'I agree with you. And yet I find myself asking; is it a bad thing that the citizenry are given a live demonstration of Ascendant power?'

'Yes!' Gesteris spat the word out. 'Of course it is. Perhaps Herine is not the only one with muddied thoughts. We cannot throw away all the efforts of the last ten years. Painstaking effort to get acceptance. Endless promises that no Ascendant will ever use a destructive Work on the Omniscient faithful.'

'What would you have me do, Marcus? Look behind you.'

Marcus did. And he saw what Vasselis saw. In the fountain, water sluiced up over and around the Ascendants. The Advocate stood with them. She spoke briefly to Hesther and then signalled the Victory Gates. Centurions without passed orders by flag. And every legionary and cavalryman delivered the same warning.

'Disperse. Disperse immediately. By order of the Advocate, the palace approach is to be cleared. Move now or you will be moved.'

But the people did not understand. Their initial surprise at the announcement turned to jeers and a barrage of soft missiles as the legionaries and cavalry began to back off towards the gates, spreading around the base of the walls as they had been ordered. Citizens came over the wooden barriers. In ones and twos and then in a flood, breaking them as they came. They filled in the apron and advanced. Not in a hurry, they were wary.

'Too late,' said Vasselis. 'Pray this doesn't go wrong, Marcus.'

The beautiful evening sky began to darken.

Chapter Fifty-Three

859th cycle of God, 53rd day of Genasrise

Clouds boiled into the once-clear air. A column of water turning to mist speared up from the fountain, amplified a hundredfold by the Ascendants. Vasselis had to grab at the rampart rail as a wind sucked inwards over the wall, energy howling into the Work.

Moment by moment, the clouds darkened and spread so fast the eye could not track their speed. Low, a thousand feet or less, they swarmed from the palace and hung over the apron and well beyond like a predatory bird ready to strike. There was a swirl at their centre and the whole turned slowly about this axis.

Vasselis could feel the power within the Work. It pressed on him like a weight, crushing at his chest, forcing him to gasp for breath.

'They'd better not get this wrong,' said Gesteris, rasping.

The legionaries and guards delivered their warning again. Some had heeded it this time, taking in the lowering, brooding cloud above them, and had turned on their heels. But most stood. Vasselis could see Order ministers and Armour of God soldiers amongst them. Cajoling people, exhorting them to resist and to pray. Many knelt, one hand crablike to the ground, the other to the sky.

The first drops of rain began to fall. Wind began to drive into the centre of the cloud from every direction and blow down on the apron, still packed with thousands of citizens. Quickly, the rain thickened, became spears thundering down, bouncing from the cobbles. Thunder crackled inside the cloud. The wind whistled over buildings, picked up debris and hurled it at the crowds.

At the margins, citizens broke away in larger numbers, seeking shelter anywhere they could get it. Below Vasselis, the Conquord military bunched closer to the wall and held on to each other. On the walls, he and Gesteris were getting drenched but neither felt able to move. Both men clung harder to the rail, buffeted by the wind that was strengthening at an alarming rate.

Abruptly, the cloud deepened and spread, sending the worst of the deluge over the palace. A sheet of light flared inside the dark mass. The coil tightened and spun faster. A tongue licked down, almost touching the ground. Citizens were beginning to run in large numbers. The job was close to being done. Vasselis, his eyes stinging from the rain that thrashed over his helmet and beat into his eyes on the teeth of the gale, turned, looked and knew he had to get to Hesther and the Ascendants.

Yola screamed with excitement as the energy coursed through her. The fountain water surrounded her, surrounded them all. Its clean energies soaked into her and through into the pooled well of their power. There it grew exponentially and flooded out into the Work that refocused it into cloud, storm and thence back into water as hard, relentless rain.

She could sense the citizens below the cloud beginning to break and run. Their quick energies were like motes of light in the morass of pulsing deep reds and blues that powered the weather Work. White bloomed inside it, reported back down the energy lines and shook them all.

'What was that?' yelled Petre.

The rain was hammering so hard on them now, on the fountain above and fizzing into the fountain pool that she could barely hear him.

'It's too big.' Mina's voice was a wail.

'It's all right, we can hold it.'

Yola saw that the Work was steady but that more energy than they had planned was feeding in. Not from the fountain, from the Work itself. Arducius had warned them about this once. The Work feeding itself. Another flash. And a sucking at their energy as if the Work was trying to break free.

'Hold it, hold it!' Yola was shrieking.

'Where did the lightning come from?' Petre sounded scared. 'There shouldn't be lightning.'

'Take some energy out of the Work,' said Mina. 'It's getting too big for us.'

'No, hold it.'

But Yola wasn't really sure they could. The wind blasted around inside the palace courtyard and she could sense it howling away across the open apron and rushing down into the city. The sky was filling and filling. There was another flash and the cloud dipped and touched the earth.

Vasselis could barely move. If he let his grip go, he'd be thrown from the rampart. The wind seemed to be straight in his face, whichever way he turned. People were scattering from the apron now. Someone was trying to haul open the Victory Gates to let the legionaries in but they would fail. The wind sucked them into their frames and rattled them there, shaking the whole triumphant arch.

The rain was so hard it hurt the face and hands. The crowd was packing towards the exits to the apron. Wind buffeted them, hurled them into one another. Fighting was breaking out at the edges, people trying to hide themselves in the mass. The cloud darkened and deepened a second time. Lightning flared again and again across the sky and up into the heavens.

'We have to stop them,' yelled Vasselis at Gesteris.

Gesteris scowled. 'What did I warn you about, Vasselis? Think this will fix anything?

His words were snatched from his mouth and Vasselis only just caught them.

'Later. We have to get down there.'

Gesteris nodded and the two men came together, using each other as shields. They inched towards the watch tower, moving hand over slow hand along the rail. Every step brought the risk of a fall to the courtyard. Rain sluiced along the rampart and poured over the edge. The wind screamed to a new height and the cloud spiralled. It seemed to have slowed but the colour was a malevolent deep grey.

Without warning, it spat down. All the way this time. A tongue, a coil of cloud spinning hard. It touched the ground and spun directly into the back of the crowd.

'Oh dear God-surround-me,' said Vasselis. 'Come on!'

People were hurled aside. The column of wind scoured straight through them. They were like dolls, scattering from a tantrum, impelled by a massive hand. Impacting buildings, smearing across the cobbles or sucked high into the cloud before being ejected, slapped away by the vengeful hand of God.

'Hesther!' shouted Vasselis, though there was no possibility of her hearing him. 'Hesther, stop them!'

He waved wildly with one hand but had to grab hold quickly as the wind threatened to pluck him from the rampart. The twisting coil of cloud changed direction, heading for the open spaces of the processional road to the arena. Citizens scattered before it, those who saw it and chose the right direction.

But hundreds were caught within its spitting, grabbing compass. Roof slates were plucked from buildings and hurled as deadly missiles in every direction. Gesteris dragged Vasselis below the parapet. They felt impacts and heard shattering against the wall.

Down here there was relative calm. Vasselis crawled towards the watch tower. Above the howling of the wind, he thought he could hear the screams of men and women. There was the rumble of falling stone. He crawled up the few stairs and made the shelter of the tower. It was shaking. Slates were ripping from its roof and shattering on the cobbles of the courtyard.

Vasselis looked down at the fountain. The Ascendants were shuddering. The water covered them. From the sky, rain was attracted to them, spewing onto them like it came from pipes in the sky. Hesther was near them, clutching onto the fountain side. Vasselis could see she was talking to them, shouting at them.

Back outside, the apron was empty of people. The column of cloud had turned left and was heading down towards the forum and the dock. The strength of the wind lessened. Vasselis ran for the stairs and braced himself against the outside of the spiral as he raced down.

He burst out into the courtyard. The Ascendants all fell sideways into the fountain. The rain ceased. Up in the sky, the cloud rumbled. One fork of lightning struck down at them. It impacted the fountain statue. The top of the rearing horses triumphant exploded. Shards of stone flashed out. Something whistled past Vasselis's ear, he turned and saw it shatter on the inside wall. Slowly, slowly, the crack in the statue widened. Two of the horses fell gently sideways, tumbling into the fountain, opposite the Ascendants.

Their Work had spared them. It would not be the same outside the gates.

The cloud cleared as quickly as it had come. The evening light returned to the city. The wind died to nothing, leaving just a roaring in the ears as a reminder. Vasselis turned and ran back towards the gate. Gesteris was already ordering them open. Vasselis came to his shoulder and waited.

The gates rumbled open, straining on damaged hinges. They looked out on to a soaking arena of carnage and destruction. Soldiers still in possession of their wits ran out to try and help who they could. The majority looked to their officers for direction or pushed past Vasselis and Gesteris on their way back inside the palace.

Vasselis walked out. He gave up trying to count the bodies strewn across the apron. The sound of crying had overtaken that of the wind. Buildings along the processional road had been torn open. Stunned citizens walked and staggered amongst the fallen. People were screaming for help, sobbing in their pain.

He felt sick. Ordinary citizens bent and twisted in unnatural positions. He counted eight hanging from the upper floors of ruined buildings, hurled there by the force of the wind. Bits of clothing covered the ground. Shattered tiles crunched underfoot. The setting red sun made the whole rain-soaked apron appear covered in blood.

Right outside the palace of the Advocate. He put his hand across his mouth and knelt by the first victim he came across. A man. Middle-aged. Lifeless. Blood had dribbled from his mouth and his body was canted at an angle from his legs; his back snapped clean.

'May the Omniscient take you to His embrace. I am sorry.'

'Sorry.' Gesteris scoffed. 'Too late, Vasselis. Way too late. I might as well have hurled my stock of powder over the walls. At least it would have been quick.'

Vasselis stood. He could see the Advocate coming towards them. He touched Gesteris on the arm and the senator turned, hissing in a breath. She was white with shock. Both her hands clutched at her mouth and she walked unsteadily, as if she might fall.

'I only wanted to send them home,' she said, lost. Tears were on her cheeks, her hair matted with the rain, her clothes soaked. 'I only wanted to scare them away.'

Gesteris stalked up to her. 'There is no justification for this. None. This is slaughter. And all they were doing was throwing fruit. I can no longer stand by you, my Advocate. I will not.'

Gesteris swept his helmet from his head, dropped it on the ground at her feet and walked back into the palace grounds. Herine sagged to her knees and began to cry.

And Vasselis stood and watched, unable to offer her any comfort.

*

No trumpets or horns heralded the first day of genasfall. No celebration, no prayers and no feast. Bear Claw and Tsardon helped each other to move as fast as they could but still the dead were catching them.

Hope had flared when their scouts first reported the splitting of the dead force and the change of direction. But it was brief. Those same scouts reported the sacking of Hasfort, the theft of artillery and the strengthening of the dead. All the while, Kell had rested her exhausted legion and the erstwhile prisoners. She had to shadow the enemy. She should have attacked them but there was no realistic chance of success. Civilian losses were inevitable until they could mount a defence of a scale and solidity that might stop the dead advance.

After leaving Hasfort, the dead had turned south and east. They moved back onto the trail that would eventually take them south down the western side of the Kalde Mountains and bring them onto the approaches to the Gaws. And they upped their pace. Not by much but then it didn't have to be. The dead barely paused, let alone stopped, and the living were flagging in front of them.

What had been twelve miles became ten, eight and five. Now it was barely two. And with another ten days of walking before they reached the questionable haven of the Neratharn border fortifications, the famous Jewelled Barrier, Kell knew they would be overtaken. She walked beside her horse with a limping Ruthrar who had, like her, put a crippled warrior aboard. No one was to be left behind.

Every foot was shredded and covered in blisters. Every leg roared protest. Every shoulder sagged under the weight of supporting those who by rights should be lying flat on their backs for five days to regain some strength at least. But they could not. The relentless advance of the dead kept even the most damaged legionary walking if there was no horse to ride. Fear was a prime motivator. Yet the horses too were beginning to fail.

'Is there something else we could have done?' said Kell. 'Turn from their path, let them continue to Neratharn. Should we have attacked them at Hasfort? Look at the artillery they've taken.'

'No,' said Ruthrar. 'You cannot afford to think that way. Attacking at Hasfort would have been suicide. They are chasing us, Dina. We all believe that. Better we lead them to an army rather than to some helpless city further south.'

Kell nodded. 'I know you're right.'

'But even so, we cannot outrun them.'

'It seems ridiculous, doesn't it?' said Kell. 'The dead are making no more than two miles an hour and yet they are closer and closer to our footprints.'

Ruthrar winced with every step he took. 'Perhaps not even that pace. But it adds up to forty miles in every day. No man, no horse can match that for long. We have achieved more than I imagined.'

'But it isn't going to be enough, is it? We aren't going to make it to Neratharn. Not like this. They'll be on us in two days. Three at the outside.'

'How far short are we?'

'Does it matter?'

'Of course it matters,' said Ruthrar. 'Because some of us have to make it to the border to speak to my king and to your people. Your cavalry should ride away. Make distance enough before their horses drop. Take another path.'

'Leaving the rest of us to stand in their way and die?'

'That is unworthy of you, General,' said Ruthrar.

Kell felt the sting of guilt. 'I'm sorry. But I look around at what we have become and I am proud to be a part of it. Twenty days ago we would have cheerfully killed each other. Now Tsardon supports Estorean in common purpose and we are stronger as a result. To divide our force is to throw that away.'

'I don't think so,' said Ruthrar. 'It will test it but you will see that all walking and riding here know what is at stake should we fail to reach Neratharn and warn off my king. He marches with twelve thousand Tsardon warriors. They need to be fighting with the Conquord, not against you. Only then do we have a chance of success.'

Kell nodded. 'Then we will come to a parting of the ways. Because I will not ride away from my people and you must.'

'Another will travel in my stead.'

'You are the senior voice,' said Kell. 'None here doubt your courage and your desire but I will not risk our message not being heard by King Khuran and by whoever it is that leads the Neratharn defence. Pray Davarov has survived. At least then the Conquord will not turn and run.'

'I would be honoured to fight beside him.'

'So would we all.' Kell and Ruthrar stared at each other. And she felt sad that their friendship was to be so brief. 'Well? What will you do?'

'Speak to my warriors. As you must speak to your people.'

'I have a better idea. Double time for another hour and let's stop and speak to all of them together.'

'You know that standing in front of the dead will barely give them pause. We are four hundred and fifty, they are six thousand and more.'

Kell smiled. 'That is not my intention.'

There was no protest when she ordered them to increase their pace. And she kept them there for as long as she dared. There was something keenly satisfying about knowing distance was being put between them and their enemy. Even though all knew it was temporary.

When she brought them to a halt it was on the top of a rise, a foothill of the Kalde Mountains. They could all look back and see the dead. Thousands marching across the open ground leaving a trail of blackness behind them. It looked like death and the stench of them carried on the breeze even up here.

She made sure everyone saw them. The carts pulled by dead men. The artillery pushed by the dead and heaved by the dead. Tsardon and Conquord dead. She shuddered, thinking of who might be marching as part of this dread foe. With the horses being tended by cavalrymen already appraised of what would transpire, Ruthrar and Kell gathered their forces together and spoke as one. Two voices delivering the same message in languages that none who heard them would ever have thought to be spoken in unity, even friendship.

'I look on you and I am more proud to be a Bear Claw today than at the scene of any victory of our glorious past,' said Kell.

Only the wind and Ruthrar's words competed with her. Claw stood with Tsardon warrior. It seemed churlish to separate them. Her people stood a little taller, some at the expense of their own pain. She waved them down.

'Sit. Please, this is not the time for formality. It is the time we have feared and now must face. Any chance to rest must be taken and this is our last.' She took a deep breath. 'None of you is stupid and none of you is blind. The dead are catching us. As we are, we cannot outrun them all the way to Neratharn. And we must see our messages and our desires communicated there. If we do not, all of this we have achieved will be in vain.

'So we must ask one more thing of you. And that is to turn and fight. Not to win, because we cannot. And not to sacrifice yourselves for nothing, which would be unforgivable. But to disable and to weaken. To give those that must fight after us a better chance to win.

'Some will go on. Twenty riders taking a string of spare horses to give them the chance they need. Ten Conquord, ten Tsardon. I will stand and fight with you. Prosentor Ruthrar must, as you all now know, deliver our message and stop the pointless shedding of more blood that will only give strength to our foe.'

Not a sound. Not a voice raised in objection. Only a weary acceptance of fate mingled with relief that the running had ended; and that the chance to deal out some small revenge was upon them.

'You know what comes at us. And it will roll over us if we stand in a line before it. So we shall not. Let us challenge the dead. We know they will fight as they did when they lived. In line, disciplined. So we will skirmish. Get amongst them. Target their artillery pieces and their wagons. Do what damage we can, while we still stand. Stop them in their tracks. Even for a short time. Make those who impel them think again. Make the dead themselves confused. For such we have also seen. Shout the names of those you recognise. And do not seek to kill. Disable.

'If each one of you fells two of the enemy before falling yourself, then we will have reduced them.'

She paused. Ruthrar still spoke and his men were wearing the same expressions as Kell's.

'We are all afraid. We dread ending up as one of them. But all we can hope for now is that those who come after us will send us back to the embrace of God one day. And we can pray that somewhere within us, if we are to be the walking dead of tomorrow, we can fight back. Make our wills stronger than those who make us walk and fight.

'I go to my death with you. I go to my death believing that one day I will face my friends and be able to lower my blade, not raise it. Make that your oath and no longer fear your fate.

'Are you with me?'

The dead would surely have heard the roar rolling down the hill.

Chapter Fifty-Four

859th cycle of God, 1st day of Genasfall

'If you see Pavel Nunan ...' said Kell.

'I will tell him that I have ridden with his wife and she is the bravest, most honourable soldier it is been my fortune to meet. That he must be proud and that if our peoples are ever to forge peace, then she, Dina Kell, must go down in history as the one who took the first step.'

Kell blushed. 'I was going to say, make sure he looks after the children and don't stop them joining the legions but you can add what you like, of course.'

Ruthrar bellowed a laugh and hugged her suddenly. She could do nothing but hug him back. When he released her, he had to wipe his eyes and she wasn't sure if the laughter had turned to tears or if they were as a result of his mirth.

'And I will never forget your modesty or the calm voice of your command. My next born daughter will carry your name.'

'That is greater honour than I deserve,' she said. 'Now go. The dead are at the base of the hill and we're trying to give you some breathing space.'

He bowed and turned, shouting his riders to him.

'Dolius?' Kell called. 'A word.'

'General Kell.'

'Keep him safe. If we get through this, by which I mean, the Conquord, we need him to be alive. I'm sick of fighting the Tsardon, Captain. If I am to give anything to you after I am gone, let it be that thought. We need another path. The Conquord has to seek peace with these people. Think what we can achieve together.'

'It has been an honour to serve.'

'Likewise, Captain. Get going.'

Kell knew she was being profound, pompous even. But when could you say these things if not in the hours before your death? The standing army, four hundred and thirty-seven Tsardon warriors, Conquord legionaries and Conquord cavalry, watched the lines of horses go, led by the twenty who would carry the story to Neratharn and beyond.

The dead had indeed reached the base of the hill. More accurately, it was the rise between two hills. The only place to march an army. The hundred horses and skilled riders even now cantering away could go where artillery could not. Kell was confident they would not be caught.

The first time they had faced the dead, in darkness and with the shock of the knowledge consuming them all, there had been such fear. This time, it was not so. She felt determination around her. A willingness to embrace their fate. How long that would continue when contact was made was anybody's guess. Kell would use it for as long as it lasted.

She signalled them to move to their starting positions and they began to spread around the rise up which the dead were coming. They had shown no recognition that the Conquord was waiting for them. Tsardon and Conquord dead marched in close column seven wide. The artillery and few wagons were surrounded by dead and more dead came after. Thousands more.

Kell wished they had naphtha. Anything to make decent fire. Artillery was so vulnerable on the move. It was a strange reality they faced. She had supported Roberto's decision to use fire to disrupt the dead advancing on them outside the castle. But now, knowing she would see those she knew, knowing she was almost certain to join their ranks, she could think of no bigger crime. Yet one she would willingly commit, or suffer as victim.

Below them, the dead were finally beginning to react. There was some ponderous movement, a spreading of the ranks. Some looked to climb the steeper sides of the upslope against those spreading above them. Others hemmed in around wagons and artillery.

It was time. Kell drew her sword. She'd dropped her buckler, meaning to use her blade two-handed. She nodded left and right. Horns were sounded and answered.

'Good luck everyone,' she said. 'Keep your friends close. And remember. Those you face are not the living as you knew them. They are the dead and we must return them to God's embrace. Let's go.'

As a plan it was little more than hopes and dreams stitched together.

Untried, unlikely to succeed. But then they were facing a force that outnumbered them by as much as fifteen to one and who didn't feel pain or fear. The joint Conquord and Tsardon forces advanced as quickly as they could. No one ran. Mainly they trotted as best they could, ignoring the pain and knowing it would all be over soon enough.

Kell walked with those heading for the front line. Hers was a vital task and that which was taking the greatest initial risk.

'Keep with me. Break only on my order.'

A hundred Conquord were with her. Ten abreast. A single maniple attacking the front of a full legion and more. Ahead, the dead were moving with greater purpose but still with the air of direction by an incompetent. Kell held her sword in front of her, making and remaking her grip.

The breeze washed over her, travelling uphill. With it came the sick stench of death and disease. It was rot and it was the odour of a fetid swamp and an animal, torn asunder and laid out in the heat for ten days. It was shocking and it caught in the nostrils and stuck in the throat. It clung in the lungs and stung the eyes. Kell blinked away the tears fogging her vision.

The dead closed with her, broadening their attack front. Tsardon and Conquord like those around her but in their lines, the dead were barely distinguishable. Twenty days of decay. And despite what Gorian could do to slow it, the decay was having its effect. Limbs hung useless. Skin sloughed from faces. Muscle withered taking strength from legs and forcing eyes to close. Control of movement slackened. But it would not be enough to save the living this time.

Kell spat, trying to rid herself of the taste that threatened to make her vomit. She focused on the first rank of the dead. She assessed the gaps between them and the open spaces around their left and right flanks. There were so many coming against them. Relentless and implacable.

She could see armour now. Conquord insignia. The plumed helmets of centurions. The green shields of her legionaries, now smothered in mud and filth. She could see their breath clouding in the air above them. Spores on the wind. Death and disease sweeping towards them.

'Strength!' she called. 'Strength. Stay with me.'

Her soldiers did not falter. Not yet at least. They came closer to the dead. Grey- and green- tinged skin was visible. The flesh of every nose seemed gone. Lips were slack and black with rot. Hair hung limp.

Sores and splits were on every face and on exposed hands and legs. Oozing with sickness, mould and maggots.

Despite her words, seasoned legionaries from the triarii and principes were gasping as they recognised some in the ranks through the disguise of decay. People were starting to shout out names. Yelling for their former friends to drop their weapons, to stop and lie down. Kell looked for a face she knew. Someone whom she could turn. And she found him. And the strength disappeared from her legs and she collapsed to her knees, pointing.

'Pavel!' she screamed. 'Pavel! Why did nobody tell me?'

She heaved in breath. The dead came on and her people were faltering, hearing her lose her mind. A hand grasped her shoulder, tried to drag her to her feet.

'General, we can't stop now, please.'

She couldn't see who it was through the tears and the fog that had descended in front of her reason. She opened her mouth and screamed again.

'Why didn't someone tell me he was gone!'

'Come on, General. It isn't him. Send him back to God. Give him rest.'

'NO!' Kell threw off the hand. 'Don't you touch him, you bastards. Don't you make him stop.'

Kell drove herself back to her feet and started to run. Straight at him. Straight at Pavel Nunan whose face was perfect. Who walked towards her to tell her it was all right. That she was safe and they would return to Estorr and their lives together with their children. All she had to do was throw her arms around him and bring him back to her. She did hear other voices but she ignored them. There was only one thing that needed doing. One thing that stood between them and victory.

'He's alive,' she said. 'Alive.'

Pavel could see her. Of course he could. They were barely twenty paces apart. He was marching towards her, head held high, helmet proud, plume ruffling in the wind. It was the portrait that would be hung on the walls of their villa. The one generations would see and know the glory of their family. Kell dropped her sword and pumped her arms harder. A smile broke on her face. Sobs of joy from her throat.

An impact threw her sideways down and to the right. She cried out, struck the ground and rolled once. Hands grabbed her and dragged her backwards. She knew she was thrashing and screaming but she couldn't break free. They let her go and someone was kneeling in front of her. Kell recognised him. He couldn't be here.

'Let me go to him.'

'No. You will remember what you said. These are not our friends. They are not our soldiers and they are not our loved ones.'

Kell's sword was thrust back into her hands. She looked down on it. She screwed her eyes shut and reality cascaded through her mind. She heard fighting.

'Ruthrar, what are you doing here?' she asked, opening her eyes and grabbing his hand to be pulled upright.

He was standing between her and the dead who were so close she could almost touch them. But they were dead. All of them.

'Dolius thought you might see him. I had to come back in case you did.'

'I've let them down,' she said, unable to believe what had possessed her. 'I've let them all down.'

'Join them now,' said Ruthrar. 'There is still time.'

'Ruthrar, if I see you again, I will cut you down.'

The Tsardon prosentor smiled and stepped aside.

'Bless you,' she said. 'Bless you, my friend. Now run and ride. Don't fail.'

Ruthrar ran and Kell screamed once more. But this time not in despair. She could see her people deep in combat. The plan had worked better than she could have hoped. Rather than tackle them head on, the living had changed direction at the last minute, running along the face of the dead line, ducking through gaps and down the flanks.

Tsardon and Conquord soldiers were pouring down towards the artillery from the left and right. And the dead had not the speed to react. They had moved on, slashing at empty air, marching up the deserted slope. Only Kell stood right in front of them.

'I'm so sorry, Pavel,' she said. 'I cannot send you back to God. But I can hurt the man who did this to you.'

Kell turned and ran right. Slowly but surely, the dead were made to stop and turn. She heard screams from within the mass as her people were overwhelmed. And she heard orders and warnings barked in Tsardon and Estorean. The smell was almost overpowering but she put it from her mind.

A sword sliced the air in front of her. She put hers in its path reflexively, feeling the enemy blade sheer away. Sparks flew from the contact. Dead, grey faces were turning towards her while she ran beside them. Some were slow, their legs dragging on the heavy ground. Under their feet, all was mire and sludge.

Kell ran away a few paces up the slope right. The centre of the dead column was in chaos. The march had broken form and it appeared some dead were acting under different orders to others. They collided, bumped each other, staggered and even fell, unable to adapt to what was happening amongst them.

Meanwhile, her people were taking full advantage. Kell joined in, angling towards dead legionaries still with their backs to her. Sword in both hands she hacked deep into a pair of exposed thighs. The dead fell. She darted away again, another sword threatening her. A dead moved out, bringing others with it. Kell dodged around them, beating their ponderous movements easily. She chopped down hard on a sword arm, almost taking it off. The blade fell from fingers deprived of any strength but the man still advanced.

Kell retreated a pace. Abruptly, the chaos resolved. Like someone had cast a heavy blanket over grass blowing in the wind. The dead came about in multiple directions, facing their foe on all fronts.

'Dammit.'

Kell darted down the right-hand side. Men who had been making hay in the centre were engulfed by the new order. The dead were moving more quickly, more surely.

'Get the artillery,' yelled Kell. 'Bring it down.'

The two dozen and more pieces were a hundred yards from her. She found herself running at a steeper and steeper angle on the slopes above the path as dead spilled outwards, looking to cut off the living. A Tsardon ahead of her was felled by a spear jabbing out, taking him by surprise and skewering his ribcage.

Kell stamped on the spear, breaking its shaft. The dead dragged back the bladeless haft. Kell took one pace towards him and slashed her blade across his exposed neck. His head rolled backwards and hung down his back. He walked on two paces, and stumbled backwards, balance gone, but still he prodded out with the haft as he went.

Kell shuddered. The grey of their faces and the quiet of their assault blended in front of her. Impossible to think of them as people now. The stench of their decay reminded her what they really were. She ran harder. Blisters in her boots were split and bleeding. She risked a glance behind. The numbers of living were decreasing rapidly. Ahead, some had reached an onager. She saw the arm shoot into its stay and then topple sideways as ropes were cut, bolts beaten aside. Dead swarmed up the frame, taking those so briefly on board.

Two men fell in beside her.

'We're losing it, General,' said one. 'Some are running.'

'Join them if you will. I'm taking at least one of those catapults with me.'

'It's why we're here.'

'Good. The Omniscient will remember you.'

They guarded her left. Thumping in boot and blade, battering shields in, forcing a path. Kell watched three more groups attacking artillery, onagers and ballistae at the head of the column where the defence had been thinned. Mainly Tsardon with a sprinkling of Conquord legionaries.

'Move in!' she said. 'Let's get ourselves with our friends.'

In between them and the first wooden frame was a four-deep line of dead, some of whom were already looking to clear the artillery. It gave her the chance she wanted. Moving in between the two legionaries, she battered her blade into the face of a Tsardon dead and shouldered him aside. She ducked a flailing sword and cut deep into the body of a second man. Rotting entrails boiled out of the cut. Kell gagged and jumped the uncoiling mess as it struck the ground. Her move forward took her directly into the body of a third dead whose blade was raised above his head, poised to strike. He was pushed backwards and the hand carrying the sword was cut from his arm from above.

Hands reached down and she was dragged onto the onager frame. Kell turned immediately and lashed out a kick into the head of a dead threatening one of the two legionaries still on the ground.

'Take those in the yoke. Let's stop this thing moving.'

She ran forwards. Dragging the onager were vulnerable dead. She dropped to the ground between the two ranks. Like flaying at corn she struck again and again. The edge of her sword ran through leather boot, bare skin and greaves. Dead collapsed forwards and backwards. She divided foot from ankle, slashed hamstring and ruined the backs of knees. The onager lost forward momentum. The dead who fell began to turn, looking to bring her to the earth with them.

'Down!' yelled someone.

Kell ducked her head. The onager arm sprang upwards, sending a shuddering vibration into the frame. She jumped up, grabbed the rope binding the arm to the frame and hauled herself back on to the body of the piece. No pause. Kell joined two others slicing at the ropes and brackets. Along the line of the frame, ten men stood, keeping back the press of dead. Behind them, the next onager in line collided with them, giving them a path backwards.

With a final cut, the onager arm was released and fell to the left, crushing dead beneath its weight, its cup caving in the skull of an ex-Tsardon warrior.

'Back, back.'

Kell led her three along the frame of the first ruined catapult and across to the yoke spar of the second. She ignored the dead dragging it, focusing on those beginning to crowd in greater numbers around its rear. Other dead were climbing on to the third, forming a solid defence. She put one foot on the frame and kicked out with her other, boot connecting with a chest. With a sick crunch, her toecap went straight through the ribcage. The dead man began to fall backwards.

'Shit,' she rasped.

Kell's foot was stuck. She windmilled her arms, sword more of a risk to her own than her enemies, and leaned backwards. A hand grabbed her and her foot came clear. She sat down hard. No time to rest. The dead were clawing at her. She hacked at fingers and heads even as she scrabbled to her feet. Behind her a sword took one of her people in the calf. He screamed and dropped. Four other blades came down on him and he slumped from the frame.

'Come on, let's break this one. Just keep them off. Forget taking them down.'

Kell ran down the length of the frame. A dead climbed on, others behind him. He stared at her, eyes dim, jaw slack, face grey and with the skin peeling away from the features. Kell swallowed her revulsion. He took a pace forwards and struck out with his gladius. Kell ducked. The blade swished above her head, taking the dead off balance. Kell came up and shoved him hard in the back, sending him sprawling on to others below.

Two Tsardon ran past her and launched a frenzied attack on the dead beginning to swarm the back of the onager. Blow after blow anywhere. Head, shoulders, arms, legs. Blood spattered. Kell seized her chance. She turned and struck down on the rope holding the onager arm flat. It divided beneath her blade. The arm pivoted upwards.

'Brace!' she yelled.

The windlass unwound. The arm whipped past her face and thwacked into the stay. The onager bounced in its sled. The living had gripped on, the dead were unseated. The two Tsardon ahead of her drove their attack in again. Kell looked backwards. Conquord and Tsardon chopped at the bindings, bringing the arm crashing down right.

More dead were crushed. But the press was becoming difficult to defend. Hands grasped at feet, looking to bring the living over the side of the artillery pieces and into the mass.

'Get away from the edges!' yelled Kell. 'Move back. Next piece.'

Ahead, one of the Tsardon fell. Hands clutched at his ankles. His countryman turned from his newest attacker to chop repeatedly at the grasping dead. A blade came in from the side. Kell lunged out, deflected it. Conquord and Tsardon eyes met. He nodded. Waved her on.

Kell backed up three paces, ran and jumped the short gap to the next onager yoke. Three pieces down, her people were all over a pair of ballistae but the dead had filled in around them. They didn't have long. She moved along the yoke spar. The onager was covered with enemies. Kell paused and licked her lips.

She stood in a sea of dead. On an island about to be washed clean by the tide. It was extraordinary. They seethed around the artillery. Every one of them able to walk had turned. Their march was halted while they dealt with the enemy in their midst. The living were like a cancer in them. One that had to be excised.

Hands were grabbing at her legs. She barely looked, sweeping her blade down beside her leg, feeling it slice through palm and finger. Kell stepped on to the frame of the sled. Others were with her. A Tsardon man pushed past her and into the attack, using his considerable weight to knock dead off the onager. Two Conquord legionaries followed him. Shields ahead of them, bludgeoning, shovelling and heaving to make space.

The ballistae shafts ahead splintered under the battering of her people. They got no further. Shrieking, they were taken. Dragged from the broken wood and put to death. Kell sent a silent prayer but knew God was not listening. Not out here. She moved onto the frame.

The soldiers were coming up against a dense mass of the enemy.

They crowded the onager sled and pressed in on all sides. The Tsardon man took a blade under his ribcage. He was spun around. Blood jetted from his mouth. Even in death, he retained the courage and the presence of mind to nod at her. Kell returned the gesture. An image of Pavel appeared in front of her. Not whole and smiling, but rotting with dull eyes and face covered in boils and sores. Maggots hanging from him.

Kell's calm broke. She strode into the space vacated by the Tsardon. Her sword came down again and again on the head of a dead man wearing the insignia of the Hasfort militia. The man was knocked back. She balanced and thudded a kick into his midriff. He flew back, taking two others off the back of the onager with him.

'Get the cup stays,' said Kell. 'I'm going back for the bindings.'

'Yes, General.'

Their voices carried easily and clear over the silence of the dead. Kell shuddered. She turned. Dead were gathering on the onager again. She ran at them, shouldering one aside, sweeping her blade through the legs of another. Sick smells of decay covered her. Clouds of spores erupted from the mouth of a man whose throat she slashed open. A kick out shattered the kneecap of a man who had once been an engineer. His dull eyes met hers while he toppled sideways and off the machine.

'General!'

Kell stepped smartly a pace left. The onager arm swept up. It caught two of the dead, hurling them dozens of yards into the heaving mass surrounding the artillery. She turned to congratulate her men but they were gone, submerged beneath the tide. Kell whipped in three quick cuts while hands tried to dislodge her and more dead climbed aboard. Her sharp blade parted the rope. Another piece down, another onager arm trapping dead beneath it, crushing bodies, taking them from the fight.

Kell raised her head and looked about her. She was alone. Her people either dead or fled. She squared her shoulders. Along the slope a man and a boy were walking. No more then fifty yards away but so far out of her reach as to be like distant memories. Their faces were pink with health. Or at least the boy's was. The man walked a little unsteadily, his hand on the boy's shoulder. Other men walked behind. Three of them. Tsardon by their clothes but not warriors.

Kell felt a sword bite into her calf. She stumbled forward but did not fall. Too late to fight back. Too late to do anything more than she had done. The living enemy were looking at her. She raised her sword and pointed its tip to the man resting on the boy.

'You are marked,' she said, knowing he would hear her. No other noise obstructed her. 'And you will be brought down.'

Another blade jabbed in under her breastplate. Searing heat and pain flooded her body. Kell shuddered, feeling the blood rushing from her. She weakened, struggling to maintain her balance.

'Join me,' said the man. 'Walk with us. Rejoice.'

'I will never walk with you,' said Kell.

Enough strength was left. She hefted her blade in one hand, stretched out her right leg, and swept her sword through her ankle. With the darkness closing, she prayed it would be enough.

'I hear you, Pavel,' she said. 'I'm here.'

Chapter Fifty-Five
859th cycle of God, 1st day of Genasfall

Three hundred and fifty-eight had died. Twice that number had been injured and that was the number the palace doctors knew about. How many had taken their wounds to be tended in the city was anybody's guess. It had been a devastating Work. All Vasselis had left was to regret it hadn't been seen on the battlefield.

The days following the disaster had been entirely predictable. Gesteris, while removing his support from the Advocate, had nevertheless worked tirelessly with Elise Kastenas to make the palace complex a fortress. Onagers now occupied the courtyard and the gardens ringing the palace inside the walls. Ballistae and scorpions had been brought out of storage and moved to the walls and towers, places he had never thought to see them. Guards, legionaries and militia had been drilled in defensive tactics.

It would take an army to threaten the Advocate and all those within the walls.

And the Armour of God was massed outside. Whether this was brinkmanship or genuine threat wasn't clear. But it was certainly ugly, and it was certainly a siege.

Vasselis was in the state rooms. He seemed to spend a lot of his time there now. The view over the Victory Gates was peerless, though how hollow that title was now after what had happened in their shadow. The space within had been converted to an administration area for the rationing of food and water and he had placed himself in charge of this delicate area.

Estorr was lost. The Advocacy had no control. The Order was in charge. The citizenry had not reappeared at the gates to vent their rage at what had occurred. Fear saw to that. But they had taken their anger out all over the city. Rioting went unchecked for three days before the Order had stepped in this morning to direct the people into less damaging protest and action. But they hadn't begun the evacuation Vasselis had begged them to organise. They still didn't, or wouldn't, believe and the citizens were in their thrall.

He and Gesteris had watched from the high rooms of the palace as every business and enterprise close to the Advocacy went up in flames. The Advocate's few supporters in the city had been driven out, had run to the Hill or been killed. It was no more than a witch hunt and they had been powerless to stop it.

Only in the hours immediately following the disastrous Work had any loyals been into the city proper. With Herine incapable or unwilling to make any more decisions, the military minds had stepped in and brought to the Hill everything they could think of and easily find. Provisions, weapons, vulnerable people, city guard. Every single empty vessel the palace possessed had been filled with water. Because as Gesteris had correctly predicted, on this first afternoon of genasfall, the water supply to the palace was cut off.

In the Academy, all was quiet. The Ascendants had not emerged from there since the fateful evening. Petrevius and Mina were inconsolable. Yola was defiant and Vasselis did not like the echoes he saw in her. Hesther was furious with Herine for what she had ordered, and confused by how it had gone so spectacularly wrong. Vasselis knew how she felt.

In the whole damned mess, the only continuing blessing was that the quarantine flags were still hidden from the citizenry. Their anger had no edge of panic. The rioters' fires had been extinguished and the Order had imposed itself effectively if not even-handedly or indeed in the right direction. Vasselis was uncomfortably aware that could change at any moment. What the reaction would be he shuddered to think.

The doors opened behind him and eight heads turned to see the Advocate walk shakily into the room, supported by Tuline. Both of them looked exhausted. Herine looked very ill and despite his anger, Vasselis felt worried by that. The seven administrators bent their heads back to their plans and rotas. Vasselis waited for the two women to walk around the grand table and up the step to the balcony.

'Is there anyone here who still supports me?'

Herine's voice was rasping, her breath wheezing. Her eyes were bloodshot and there was a tremor to her body most evident in her fingers and lips. Tuline's eyes echoed her desperation and helplessness.

'God-surround-me, Herine, look at you,' said Vasselis.

He cast around and saw a chair. He dragged it to the balcony edge but Herine waved it away.

'I am not a total invalid, Arvan,' she said. 'Well?'

There was still strength in her eyes but it was fading. Vasselis sighed. She had aged a decade in three days and the ramifications of her orders lay upon her like a blanket of stone.

'What do you want me to say, Herine? Everyone within these walls still believes in the Advocacy and they will fight to the last to preserve it from destruction by the Order.'

'That isn't quite what I asked you, is it?'

'It's the best answer you're going to get right now.'

Herine looked away but nodded her acceptance. Vasselis could still find no sympathy inside himself for her. He was surprised by that but could not deny it. He was sure he should have been stronger in his defence but in the cold light of day, she had gone against every tenet of her own rule. The Advocate had attacked her own people. And though she would never have wished for the results of that decision, she had made it and had to face the consequences. She had ignored her advisers.

'I am lost,' she said quite suddenly. She felt for the chair and sat in it, Tuline helping her down. 'I cannot survive this, Arvan. It is over.'

'I think that is a great assumption, my Advocate,' he said. 'A hard blow, yes, but your achievements outweigh your mistakes.'

'Do they? Do they really? And what do you suppose my legacy will be when the history of my rule is written? That I held back the Tsardon tide, brought Dornos, Atreska and Bahkir into the Conquord? That I presided over the greatest growth of wealth the Conquord had ever seen? Or that I, Herine Del Aglios, lost my grip and slaughtered hundreds outside the gates of my own house. That I embraced those that the majority of my people and the rulers of my faith knew to be evil and that I unleashed that evil on them in petty revenge.'

Herine looked so thin, sitting there. Her vitality was gone. Her face was hollow and the dark patches under her eyes reached down into her cheeks.

'I do not deserve to rule this great Conquord,' she said. The tears began to fall down her cheeks. 'I am not worthy of the love of my citizens. I am not worthy of any who yet stand beside me.'

Vasselis knelt before her, putting his arms on those of the chair in which she sat.

'Yes, you have done wrong,' he said. 'Is that what you want to hear? You have made a monumental mistake and the citizens of this city are angry and bitter and denounce your name. This is a setback of enormous proportions. But you are Herine Del Aglios. The Advocate of the Estorean Conquord. And you will not, no, may not, give up.

'Out there beyond the walls they choose not to believe it but we know the threat approaching the Conquord. We know his name and we must not buckle. We must not let our guard slip again. Your sons are out there defending all of this. You, the Order, the citizens of this city and the whole Conquord. And though I might be furious with you, Herine. Though I might not even know how I feel about you today, you are still my Advocate. And I, Arvan Vasselis, stand with the Advocacy and I will not turn away. I will not.'

Herine put a hand on his cheek. His beard was thick on his jaw, it needed trimming.

'Dear Arvan. Never flinching. Always facing. Why are you not sitting on the throne?'

'Because I have no line of succession. And because I am sworn to the Del Aglios dynasty. I have no desire to rule the Conquord.'

'But you have ability. Your people in Caraduk love you. The Conquord would love you too.'

'It will never happen. Roberto will follow you and if I am still alive, I will swear my oath to him too.'

Herine smiled. 'I wish my son were here.'

Vasselis stood up, biting his tongue from agreeing with her. He walked away a few paces. Tuline followed him.

'God-embrace-me, but I am glad she has you,' said Vasselis. 'You have the Del Aglios strength within you and I didn't always feel that way.'

Tuline was beautiful in her mother's image. Pearl-white toga, hair gathered and pinned on her head, decorated with threads of gold and revealing her delicate swan neck. Her eyes sparkled with passion. Even now at the edge of the precipice, she chose to maintain the aura of authority and that was no easy act. Inside, she must be crushed.

'You must help her,' said Tuline 'I don't like the way she speaks sometimes. Just now even. It's like someone else is inhabiting her body.'

Vasselis glanced at Herine. She was gazing out over the edge of the balcony, her chin just above the ledge. She wouldn't be able to see much. Probably just as well.

'What would you have me do?' he asked and gestured out beyond the walls. 'Look at this. This is where power lies if they choose to use it.'

Tuline looked. Two legions of the Armour of God were surrounding the palace. They could see infantry and cavalry on the apron. Artillery stood further down the processional road. Archers were gathered behind the front lines. It was in every way, allowing for the constrictions of space, a classic deployment. Horst Vennegoor knew his battles well. He had fought in many and lost none with the Conquord legions.

'They should be out there defending the Conquord from its enemies,' said Tuline.

Vasselis sighed. Something else he'd been doing a great deal of lately. 'Tuline, that is precisely what they believe they are doing.'

The *Ocetarus* made good headway with a strong wind at their stern. On the deck, Kashilli was taking the Ocenii squad through their paces with a curious array of weapons. Gone were gladius and short sword or long knife. Gone were bucklers and round shields. In their place, sledgehammers, blacksmith's hammers, wood axes and two executioner's blades from the Ocetarus palace museum.

When the dead had eventually fallen, Iliev had ordered them all burned in the gardens. The huge pyre had thrown a choking black cloud of ash into the air, smudging the sky and visible for hundreds of miles in every direction. It gave credence to the quarantine flags flying from every post and he hoped it sent a signal to enemies that they were far from finished. One day, he would be back to declare the Isle clear. One day, when all the dead were gracing the bottom of the ocean.

Iliev had joined with three other triremes patrolling the northern tip of the Isle, and the Lances of Ocetarus. Flags and birds brought news of Tsardon sails along hundreds of miles of Gesternan coastline. Refugees were sailing in large numbers from Byscar still and each boat had to be checked and cleared for passage to the east coast of Estorea or further south to Caraduk.

The net was tight but it was stretched. Iliev was aware that a single large fleet might pierce the defence but he was also confident that his signalling would give him enough warning. Standing orders and positions around key harbours on the western edge of the Tirronean Sea were well known. He was in the hands of his Trierarchs and captains now.

The *Ocetanas* led the quartet of boats, all of which had the spiked corsairs of the Ocenii squadron slung at their sterns, in pursuit of three trireme sails. They were closing fast. The skippers of the target vessels were making poor use of the wind and he could see the dip and raise of oars fighting the sail. They looked like ships under the control of the incompetent. And as far as Iliev was concerned, that made them enemies. Dead enemies.

They were a mile ahead. Decision time. The flagship had the pipe and bellows fitted to her stern to disgorge naphtha onto enemy vessels. But their supply was limited. Iliev didn't want to waste it on scattered enemies with the spectre of a fleet of the dead still looming large in his mind. On the other hand, an experiment to investigate the reaction of the dead to fire on board might prove invaluable.

Iliev looked down the deck. Kashilli roared with laughter. He had a sledgehammer in his hands and battered it into the barricade they'd built from old timbers and two empty barrels. The hammer went straight through. Kashilli grunted his satisfaction.

'Bring me some dead, skipper,' he called, seeing Iliev watching.

Decision made. Iliev turned to the flagship's captain.

'Signal the patrol. Ocenii to the water. Triremes to stand off. And let's keep our bellows ready, eh? Just in case.'

'Yes, Admiral.'

'Kashilli! Squad seven to the stern. Gentle swell, marines to the tiller. Spike up.'

'Seven!' bellowed Kashilli, his voice carrying to the birds flying high overhead. 'You heard the skipper. Move.'

Ocenii squad seven hefted weapons and ran to the stern. Sailors on the corsair's fastenings released ropes and braced against tackle gearing.

'Straight on,' said Iliev. 'Starting positions, don't dip the spike.'

Iliev watched them swarm down the ladder and onto the corsair that rocked gently between its ropes. Iliev turned to the sailors taking the strain on deck.

'Easy descent on my order.'

'Yes, Admiral.'

Iliev nodded at the captain and went last down the ladder, taking his place with the marines in the stern, his hands already on the tiller.

'Lower away.'

The spiked corsair slid smoothly towards the water. The arm of the ship's tiller swept away to Iliev's right, the captain already turning to give them escape away to starboard the moment they hit the water. All oars were at the vertical, ready for deployment. Tried and tested, they could do this at fifteen knots, under full oar speed.

The boat hit the water. The bow line was loosened. Hands gripped the stern hooks of the trireme. The corsair's bow swung out. The stern line was loosened. .

'Ready starboard oars. Let's get out of the wake.'

Hands pulled the corsair out from the stern of the trireme.

'Starboard oars. Down, and dip, single stroke. Let go the ship.'

The corsair swung away from the hull, past the tiller and out into open water. Iliev held the tiller in.

'All oars dip. Moving to thirty stroke easy. Let's get to work.'

The crew of the flagship cheered them on as they powered past it and away after the dead ships. Iliev had time to rest on two thoughts as they closed the gap hard and fast, his crew fresh and pulling hard. First, that three dead ships alone was a curious thing to find, given what they thought they knew about how the dead were held together and the strength of the mass. And second, that live Ocenii action had become a rare beast.

'Forty stroke if you can fancy it. Been a long time, eh, seven?'

'We hear you, skipper.'

Kashilli led the marines down the centre of the corsair, setting the spike lower in the water, balancing the hull and facilitating raw speed. The huge soldier roared on the oarsmen. Taunting their laxity, sneering at their pace.

'Too much rest and the flab flaps under your arms, you bastards. Look at you. I could do better on my own. Come on, give me your oars.'

They responded, the strokeman driving them towards the forty stroke.

'First one on deck gets a free crack at Kashilli, the man with technique so poor he can sink a single scull on a mill pond.'

A cheer went up. Kashilli's laughter carried across the open water. Iliev aimed the corsair at the frontmost vessel.

'Minimum fuss on contact,' he said. 'Secure the hatches. Remove the deckhands. Flame and smoke. Meanwhile, enjoy the fight, seven. We're back in the water.'

Another cheer. The corsair hummed over the water, chopping through the slight swell. The oars dipped, pulled, rose and returned. Ahead, the dead ships were making no more than five knots. Sails spilled wind, oars clashed and interfered. It was a pathetic display. Maybe the dead could still fight. Iliev was happy that at least they couldn't claim to be mariners. The corsair was making in excess of twenty knots now and was still increasing speed.

'Hear that, skipper?'

'Hear what, Kash?'

'Exactly. No pace drum. No wonder, skipper.'

Iliev shook his head. Seven's corsair drew alongside and past the hindmost enemy trireme. Iliev and the marines scanned the deck. Underhanded. Tiller and a sprinkling of deckhands. And none of them looked at the Ocenii powering past them. Every oar was in the water. An unknown number of dead would be gathered below decks, waiting for landfall.

Iliev turned and signalled the corsair of squad three, indicating they attack this vessel. Beyond the second, similarly crewed trireme, he signalled in squads nine and eleven.

'Our turn next, seven. Concentrate. Oars, we are fifty strokes out and closing. Stern impact. You know the drill. I'll count us in. Ready Kashilli?'

'I was born ready, skipper.'

'Born stupid,' said an oarsman.

'Hey, who stands up and who breaks their back driving this tub?' asked Kashilli. 'Me, stupid?'

The six marines punched the air.

'Steady and quiet now,' said Iliev. 'Here we go.'

The corsair hummed on. Iliev steered away and round, bringing the ramming spike to bear on the stern quarter, just aft of the last oar position.

'Final approach,' said Iliev. 'Counting from ten. Tapers alight. Marines to the ropes. Ladders free. Five and down. Crouch, marines. Brace, brace. Two, one.'

Iliev dropped to his haunches and gripped the guide ropes. Oars came out of the water. The corsair slammed into the hull of the enemy trireme. Kashilli was up an instant later, using the momentum. A ladder slapped against the hull. Hammer in one hand, he raced up and jumped onto the deck. Iliev heard him challenging the dead to bring him down if they could.

'Go. Let's get up there. I want this turned round before they even know they are hit.'

Marines and oarsmen stormed up the ladder. A second ladder struck the enemy hull. Four oarsmen would remain. Keeping dead from the gaping hole the spike had bored in the hull, keeping the corsair balanced and water flowing into the enemy ship. Iliev, last up the ladder as always, took hand axe and blacksmith's hammer from his belt.

Across the far side of the ship, Kashilli smashed his hammer into the face of a dead sailor. The man was hurled backwards and down. Kashilli cycled the hammer, a twig in his hands, took two paces and crushed the man's hips and spine. Blood spouted up. Deck timbers groaned beneath the blow.

Teams were running fore and aft, clearing paths to the hatches. Iliev ran forward, overtaking the fire and nail team, joining the weaponsmen. A Gesternan sailor came at him, clothes just so many rags but his insignia still on his chest, in his hands a boathook. His face was a mass of small scars like scratches. Puncture wounds covered his hands and neck.

Iliev watched him pull back the hook to swing. He darted in and slapped his hammer into the man's temple. The dead sprawled forwards. Iliev jumped and landed knees first in the man's back, hearing ribs break beneath his weight. Iliev chopped his axe down at the man's legs and lower spine. Three quick blows and his legs stopped moving.

Iliev rolled away. His men were at the aft hatch. A taper was at the fuse of a flask of naphtha. The hatch was hauled away. Down went the flask. There was a whoosh as the flask shattered and spread flame across the oar deck. Animal squealing filled the air.

'Rats!' shouted a nailsman.

'Shit,' said Iliev, breaking into a run back towards the corsair. 'Nail them down. Get off, get off. Plague ship. Move!'

He ran to the rail. The oarsmen sat ready.

'Push away. Plague ship. Stand off five yards, we'll come to you.'

Iliev turned. Kashilli struck down at the deck. A rat was smeared beneath his hammer.

'Off,' he yelled. 'Now. Off the ship. Corsair to starboard. Drop weapons you can't swim with. Go. Kash, go.'

Ocenii squad seven ran for the rails and hurled themselves over the side. Multiple splashes greeted his ears. Iliev checked them all over the side. A few rats had made it to the deck. Most were perishing in the fires below but by no means all. From the oar holes they spilled, desperate to escape the flames. And he heard the keening wails of men. Dead men. A desperate sound dredging at his heart.

'May Ocetarus take you to his breast. Rest now.'

Iliev ran to the stern and dived over the side. The water was freezing. The sun took a long time to warm the waters in the deeps. Iliev swam away ten strokes before turning and tucking his weapons back into his belt, treading water as he watched. Squad seven all swam back, clearing the stern of the ship and to escape the rats.

He could see the corsair curve away from the burning trireme and head back in to pick up the squad. Only two were on the oars. The other two stood with bows, shooting into the water. Behind, the other two enemy triremes were well ablaze. But on the deck of one, an Ocenii squad had been caught by the rats. Iliev could see them carving and stamping. And all he could do was pray no one was bitten. He cursed himself for a fool that he had missed the possibility.

Three ships alone, heading directly for Estorr harbour. Never an invasion force. The conclusion should have been obvious.

Iliev heard voices behind him. He turned in the water. The *Ocetarus* was nearing. He had been seen. A scrambling net was dropped down the side. Oars were positioned for use as hand- and footholds. Iliev swam to his ship and hurried up on to deck, waving away the towel he was offered.

He ran to the bow. Mission accomplished but at what cost? The three plague ships would never make port but every squad man would have to be minutely examined. Any scratch, any bite and they would be quarantined. Any confirmed plague and their fate was sealed. No sailor would infect his mates. A weighted belt was the quickest way to the bosom of Ocetarus, glory in the deeps.

'Admiral?'

'Yes Captain.'

The captain joined him at the bow, looking over the spike at the corsairs picking up marines from the water. Iliev saw Kashilli surge aboard, hearing him whoop his pleasure at the fight. The hammer was still in his hand.

'You'll need to see this but you won't like it.'

Iliev turned and took the magnifier from his captain's hand. 'Step away, Captain. I haven't been checked for bites yet. Where am I looking?'

'South south east. On the water.'

Iliev put the magnifier to his eye and looked. His search was brief.

'Oh dear Ocetarus save us and keep us.'

The sea was thick with sails. Hundreds of them. He lowered the magnifier.

'Flag the fleet. Relate position, speed and direction. Every ship is to come off station. Ignore every other vessel. The dead are sailing for Estorr.'

Chapter Fifty-Six

859th cycle of God, 5th day of Genasfall

There were many reasons why General Davarov might have shivered when he saw the border fortifications on the Neratharn-Atreska border between the Gaws mountain range and Lake Iyre. The grand border walls and fort Atreskans called the Jewelled Barrier. It could have been that the steady stream of refugees he'd travelled past on the way here had resolved itself into a desperate clamouring camp outside the fortifications while those inside tried to process all who wanted passage. And he knew there were many thousands more to come.

It might have been that on his journey here from Tharuby, the reports from his trackers and scouts had made for increasingly depressing reading. The enemy strength had grown steadily. Scattered forces had been caught by the relentless march. The Tsardon had raided far and wide, taking town garrisons, stealing artillery and, latterly, harvesting any able bodied man or woman who had stood before them with sword, hoe or pitch fork.

It might have been that this place represented the last real hope of stopping the growing Tsardon and dead army from sweeping south to Estorr by land. And though it was a mighty structure, it was in reality, a very thin line against an enemy that to his knowledge, no one had yet been able to dent, let alone turn away.

Davarov had been present when much of the barrier was going up. It was twenty-five miles long, starting from the lake edge and finishing high up in the foothills of the Gaws themselves. Fifty feet high and forty feet thick. Able to take artillery at any point. Ramparts and battlements were an archer's dream. Oil runs could cover almost the entire face of the wall in flame.

It was a statement from its roots to the tip of its flagpoles. It was a dazzling white, scrubbed every week. And in its centre, the triple gates reared up inside a single gate fort that contained a killing ground that sent shivers through the backs of Conquord greats when they rode beneath it.

Davarov loved the gate fort. Though technically on Neratharn territory, it was built to Atreskan design. Animal carvings adorned its towers. Atreskan heroes decorated its concrete walls, alcoves and gates. The words across the gate frames were oaths of loyalty to the great country, the jewel of the Conquord. It was the gateway to the old Conquord and a welcome to the new.

Flags flew from its turrets and from two hundred masts set along the walls either side. The engineers had said that no artillery could breach gate or walls. Davarov never truly entertained the prospect that this boast would be put to the test. For what it was worth, he agreed with them.

Yet none of this was why he shivered when he approached. Memories were more powerful for Davarov than any present reality. And his memories would forever be of the forced march across Atreska a decade ago. The darkest time in the Conquord's history when only the strength of Roberto Del Aglios's will kept his army going and persuaded them they could turn the Tsardon back, send them scurrying back to their holes.

Davarov had never thought that he might return here knowing he had to fight. Looking at the rolling plains covered in the desperate mass of frightened people, he could recall so vividly the ruin of the land that had come in the wake of the Tsardon forces. The exhausted Conquord forces had marched the last few hundred yards across frozen ground covered in blood and bodies and the discarded detritus of men. And so he shivered at the prospect and wished the world was other than it was.

Cartoganev had ridden on ahead and had been at the Jewelled Barrier for half a day, assessing the incumbent strength and talking to the senior soldiers about exactly what they faced. The arrival of Davarov and his legions on their staggered march had raised the hopes of those marooned outside and the great main gates were opened to accept them. Cheering saw them through into the vast staging area behind and the gates swung shut on the displaced and the hopeless.

Davarov handed over control of the legions to his masters of sword and horse. He watched the beginning of their march away to their camp grounds and trotted away up one of the long concrete slopes leading to the walls and fort. Cartoganev would be in the administrative buildings on the ground but Davarov wanted to make a quick assessment himself before getting accurate numbers.

Taking salutes from everyone he passed, Davarov walked to the highest point of the barrier, the artillery platform above the gate fort. It was more than half empty. There was space for thirty onagers here. Only ten stood facing into Atreska and four of them were in pieces. Far away to the east, dust covered the horizon. Enemies and refugees moving towards him. Thousand upon thousand. For all those they had managed to turn back to run into the great plains, too many had chosen to take the risk of hanging on to the cloaks of the legions.

Davarov turned a slow circle. The barrier walls and their flag masts were resplendent in the afternoon sun. The whitewash reflected brightly out over Atreska and the metal and wooden rails were clean and polished. Guards patrolled as far as he could see in either direction. Carts rattled along the roads built atop the walls, moving supplies, water and ammunition between watch towers. Concrete slopes led up to the walls every half a mile. All were busy with traffic. And in perhaps half of the positions available, artillery stood.

Behind the walls on Neratharnese territory, the vast cleared land stretched away out of sight. Along the length of the wall and for some four miles back into Neratharn, the land was managed to accommodate legion tents. Permanent buildings, barracks, administration, baths, cells, storerooms, stables and forges were away about a mile behind the walls. Directly beneath the walls, there was nothing. Cleared for troops, cavalry and artillery.

Davarov could see line upon line of tents. A temporary city was growing up. But the vast majority were refugees; the displaced with nowhere else to go, waiting to be found new places to live until the war was over. He saw legion standards in a concentration to his left, away to the south-west. And towards them marched his legions. Yet the ground should have been thick with soldiers. The sound of horses and hammers should have been a brutal assault on his ears this long after mobilisation was declared.

Davarov scowled and began to make his way to the administration centre.

'Where the hell is everybody?'

The business of making the Jewelled Barrier ready was moving at a pace Davarov could respect. People ebbed and flowed about him, intent on their tasks, scurrying hither and thither. There appeared to be urgency but no anxiety. Refugees would have brought myriad horror stories with them but it was only the idle hand that shook in fear.

Down on the ground, he crossed the main road that led through the gates and away through the camps and into Neratharn. He walked quickly to the two-storey structure which formed the hub of the permanent structures. Very pretty it was too. Built on the lines of a classic Estorean villa, it boasted colonnaded entrances, formal gardens and even a fountain. He presumed water was fed from Lake Iyre. He raised his eyebrows and blew out his cheeks. That must have been a pipe system long in the laying.

Guards at the walls to the compound thumped right fists into their chests. Davarov responded in kind, swept off his red-plumed helmet and strode into the cool of the villa. It was plain inside. The practical hand of the soldier had prevailed over the creative voice of the artist. The floor was bare stone, the walls likewise. Doors were heavy plain wood and the busts of military heroes were looking out from alcoves. Davarov approved. He wasn't one for fuss. Not in a military building.

He was directed to an open set of double doors on his left. They let in to a tactical room built for the purpose. Open shutters let in the light of the day and illuminated walls were covered with rosters and maps. Sloped tables carried more information, pinned down with miniature standards. The centre of the room was dominated by a huge table with a hole in its centre big enough to accommodate three men.

Upon it was a relief map of the Jewelled Barrier and the approaches from Neratharn and Atreska. Every single building was included. Tent symbols covered open areas. Rivers were marked and each hill and rise was to scale. Soldiers and civilians worked on the map, adding tentage and legion standard markers, pushing artillery into position. Around the walls, figures were written and rewritten as new information came in about troop and refugee numbers.

The door guard called attention and every one of the thirty plus in the room turned to Davarov. Cartoganev was at the table. He saluted and smiled but both were brief.

'We've got a problem, haven't we?' said Davarov, striding in and waving everyone back to their tasks. 'This place is crowded but not with soldiers.'

Cartoganev nodded. 'None are coming from Tundarra and Dornos. The Phaskareen too have turned their backs.'

'Gosland?' Davarov contained himself until he heard everything.

'Rumours of trouble up there but the Bear Claws are on station. Other Gosland legions are extracting themselves from Dornos still. They can guard our backs but nothing more.'

'Neratharn?'

'Full complement already here. The Avarnese are marching to the Estorean coast.'

'So what we have here is all we're going to get,' said Davarov.

'It looks that way.'

'And where is all the artillery?'

'Hasfort, for the most part,' said Cartoganev. 'It should be on its way. Most of it will reach us before the Tsardon and dead get here. That's about ten days from now.'

'Dare I ask about the Ascendants?'

'No word. I am told the sky and the Gaws are scanned for birds and flag messages constantly but so far, nothing. We can assume they will be sent here because Estorr will have worked out by now where the focus of the attack will come.' Cartoganev shrugged. 'We just don't know when.'

'Beautiful,' said Davarov. 'But we can only worry about what we have, not what we don't. We have a maximum of ten days before the enemy reach us. Let's get to work.'

Herine Del Aglios didn't say much to anyone and hadn't done for four days. She kept herself in her rooms, refusing entrance to anyone barring Vasselis and Tuline, both of whom were beginning to feel the strain of her undeniably failing leadership. So it was that Vasselis met the full Council of Speakers alone.

The sun blessed Estorr but it was a joyless warmth. With the siege in its fifth day, tempers inside the palace complex were shortening. Rationing had been harsh from day one, despite the apparent bounty all could see around them. Vasselis had no choice because he had no idea how long they would have to sit it out. At least in front of him was a chance to negotiate.

They sat in the palace itself, in one of the Advocate's favourite reception chambers. At the highest point of the palace, it was flooded with light and filled with images of Estorr's glory. Vasselis had chosen here because he wanted Herine to talk with the Council. Tuline was with her now, trying to convince her it was a sound idea. Vasselis did not trust to hope.

'I am pleased you have chosen to come,' he said once all five of them were seated around a circular table bathed in warm sunshine from open shutters surrounding them.

'The bounty of your table is somewhat lacking,' said Winds.

'Perhaps if you had come here on the first day rather than the fifth, I might have been able to spare you something. As it is ...'

Earth smiled indulgently. 'It is a situation simple to ease.'

'In your mind, I am sure that is true,' said Vasselis.

Earth sniffed. 'Does perfume run short too?'

'No, my Lord Earth, merely water for bathing. We have plenty to drink and enough to eat for some considerable time.'

'But this is surely a ridiculous circumstance to have brought upon ourselves,' said Oceans. 'The Armour of God impelled to lay siege to the palace of the Advocate? How have we allowed ourselves to reach this state?'

'I suspect there are two schools of thought on that subject,' said Vasselis carefully. 'But we aren't here to debate that. All we have to find is a resolution to the crisis. We all acknowledge it is disastrous to Estorr and the Conquord that it should continue. Mistakes have been made on both sides, we must come to a compromise that allows us to get on with the business of saving the Conquord from invasion. And Estorr must be evacuated.'

'*Mistakes?*' Fire leaned across the table. She was an imposing woman, very much in the mould of the late Chancellor. Narrow-faced, with eyes that sunk through a man like a dagger through flesh. 'Mass murder has been committed by order of the Advocate and conducted by the Ascendants in this palace. She and they must be handed over to us for trial in public court. That is our position and it will not change.'

Vasselis spread his hands and let a smile play on his lips. 'I expected nothing less of you, of course. But you must expect me to say that I cannot accede to that demand. If a trial is to be conducted it must be by due process, not under duress as would be the case currently. Lift the siege and we will discuss the situation in open forum.'

Winds shook his head. 'We do not need to negotiate and you are in no position to demand that we do. Hand over the guilty or the siege will stand.'

'Let's not become aggressive,' said Vasselis. 'None inside this palace wished for the recent events to have taken place. The murders of innocents within and without these walls. The death of Felice Koroyan. None of us is blameless.'

'There is no stain on our hands,' said Winds.

'The siege cannot continue,' said Vasselis. 'You risk the whole of Estorr. You know what is coming.'

'We know the rumours shouted by the lone madman in the harbour. Easy enough to quell the citizens' fears on that score. And we know the lies an Ascendant will tell to save his skin. Really, Marshal, this will not do.' Earth was shaking his head. 'How many new ships were commissioned in the wake of the Tsardon invasion? Are we to believe that some fleet of the dead is about to enter Estorr harbour and therefore that our navy is incompetent to act in our defence? They are an arm of the Advocacy and the flags they fly and the words they pass are designed for a single purpose.

'But we are in charge of the hearts of the citizens of Estorr. And they are not as timid as you think, and nor are their minds so feeble as you would hope.'

Vasselis straightened. 'You are seriously telling me that you do not believe the Conquord to be under threat? And you are telling our people that the rumours of the dead walking are lies we have concocted to keep them in line? Every day the city remains populated, the risk increases. You must believe that. Maintain the siege if you must but please get the citizens out of the city. The dead *are* coming.'

Winds waved a hand. 'Oh, we're sure there are some border disputes with the Tsardon but when aren't there? But we will not let you use fear to drive the citizenry to follow your agenda.'

'No,' said Vasselis, throwing up his hands. 'We'll leave that to the Order.'

'It is the sort of reaction we expect from an Ascendant sympathiser.' Winds scoffed. 'We are we talking to you. Where is the Advocate?'

'Here.'

Vasselis turned. Herine stood in the doorway, Tuline next to her. Winds gasped, he couldn't help it. Vasselis was aware of others of the Council drawing in sharp breaths. He pushed back his chair and rose.

His heart pealed in his chest. His love for the Advocate, submerged beneath his anger, resurfaced.

'God-embrace-me, Herine,' he said.

She walked unsteadily towards them. Her hair was unkempt, lying lank down her back and around her neck. Her eyes red and painful. She wore no make-up and her face held a sick pallor. Her toga was stained. Her hands clutched at a roll of parchment, her nails bitten to the quick. She shrugged off Vasselis's attentions and pushed Tuline's hand from her shoulder. She took in the Council of Speakers and frowned. Vasselis thought she was about to burst into tears.

'It is not acceptable that this city and this Conquord tears itself apart,' said Herine, her voice trembling, robbed of its characteristic strength. 'I will not accept the citizens of Estorr being kept from truth and justice. I will not have them exposed to the risk of death. Crimes have gone unpunished. That cannot be allowed to go on.'

'Herine,' warned Vasselis.

The Advocate looked full at him for the first time since she had walked in. Her eyes brimmed with tears and she smiled.

'I have something for you, Arvan,' she said.

She held out the parchment and Vasselis took it. Herine kissed his cheek.

'You always were the most loyal of all my Marshals,' she said.

A chill stole across Vasselis. He caught Tuline's confused expression.

'Herine, what's going on?'

'The citizens need a ruler they can trust. A strong Estorean whom they will follow into whatever is to come. The future of the Conquord must be in safe hands and people must know that those who rule them are accountable for their crimes. They must see that demonstrated, Arvan.'

'Herine, nothing rash. I won't have you make yourself a scapegoat,' said Vasselis. 'I think you are not quite yourself.'

Herine favoured him with another dazzling smile.

'Rash? No. I have thought of nothing else for days. And I am not a scapegoat, I am guilty, Arvan. Aren't I? I am responsible and the Ascendants must be spared because they have done nothing but follow my orders.' She put a hand on Vasselis's arm and clutched hard. 'You do understand that, don't you?'

Vasselis began to speak but she shushed him.

'I know you do. And I know you will make them all see. Don't make the mistakes I made, Arvan. Keep my Conquord safe until my son returns.'

'I, yes, I will but—' Vasselis paused. 'I don't understand.'

'Yes you do, dear Arvan. Yes you do.' She leant in and kissed his cheek again, whispering one word. 'Goodbye.'

'G—?'

Herine let go his arm, strode purposefully to the window overlooking the courtyard and cast herself out.

Chapter Fifty-Seven

859th cycle of God, 5th day of Genasfall

Tuline's scream would live with Vasselis to his dying day. After making a half move to the window, she had turned and fled from the room, her cries echoing from the walls and stairwells. Vasselis set off after her, pausing at the door. The Council of Speakers hadn't moved. They were staring at one another, speechless.

'Now you have what you want, just go,' said Vasselis.

'This is what none of us want,' said Earth quietly.

Vasselis nodded.

'Lift the siege,' he said. 'See the damage this conflict has caused. One last time, evacuate the city. Feel the tragedy that has been sparked here today.'

He chased Tuline down the stairs. Four storeys in all, praying hope against hope that Herine might have survived. Vasselis could not begin to comprehend what had possessed her to jump. Too many hours spent brooding alone or the weight of new guilt; neither would have snapped the mind of the Herine Del Aglios he knew.

Tumult was rising in the palace as he raced through the colonnaded gardens full of the happy chirping of birds. Shouts echoed through the corridors. From a side passage burst the palace's senior doctor and three orderlies. Vasselis joined them in barging their way through soldiers on the steps of the palace craning their heads for a view.

He yelled at people to move from their path and a space opened up before them, a natural circle that none would breach. Tuline's repeated screams reached deep within him. He forced his way through the last of the vultures that had gathered so quickly.

'Mother! Mother!'

Tuline had the Advocate in her arms, Herine's head buried in her chest. Herine's arms hung limp, her hands brushing the cobbles of the courtyard. Vasselis could see blood there and, looking up into the faces of the Council of Speakers now gathered, the true distance of her fall. So high and she had dropped without making a sound.

Vasselis glared at the front line of the gawping crowd, silent but for the shuffling of feet.

'Haven't you got somewhere else to be?' he growled. 'You. Get me sheets, blankets, whatever. Something to make privacy for the Advocate and her doctors. The rest of you. Dare not look on her. Dare not pretend to feel her daughter's pain. My pain.'

Vasselis choked on his last words and turned away. He led the doctor and orderlies over to Tuline and knelt beside her, unable to do anything else but put an arm around her neck.

'Let her rest,' he said quietly. 'Set her down.'

'No!' wailed Tuline. 'Please don't let this be true. Please.'

'It's over for her now,' whispered Vasselis. 'Your mother is at peace. She will go to the embrace of God, there to sit with your ancestors until her time is called again.'

Tuline was weeping. She hugged Herine harder, swaying slightly. Vasselis could not halt the tears that began to fall down his cheeks. The doctor knelt down behind the Advocate and gently, slowly, took her from Tuline's final embrace. Legionaries ran into the circle and quickly deployed sheets, holding them up in a shelter around the scene, tactfully placing themselves on the outside and looking away.

Vasselis sank back to sit on the cobbles, and drew up his knees, clutching them fiercely while he watched the doctor lay Herine Del Aglios, Advocate of the Estorean Conquord, on the ground. Blood matted her hair but her face was unspoiled, her eyes closed. There was peace about her. A silence that spread from her body and across the courtyard, quietening voices, staying footsteps, stilling the palace.

The doctor felt for a pulse as she had to, turned to look at Vasselis.

'The Advocate is dead, Marshal Vasselis.'

Tuline just sat and stared, desolate. Vasselis nodded, put his head on his knees and let the sobbing take him. His mind blanked with sorrow and he cried long and hard, not caring who heard him, hoping they did and knowing what it was the Conquord had lost. When he raised his head it was in response to a squeeze of his shoulder and the sound of someone squatting down before him.

'Oh, Marcus, what have we become?' he said.

Vasselis wiped tears from his eyes and found he was still clutching the parchment Herine had given him. He unrolled it while the doctor and orderlies tended to Herine's body, covering her with fresh sheets ready to take her to the morgue. One of them tried to comfort Tuline who was unmoving, a statue. She had seen something no daughter should ever have to witness.

Vasselis bent his head to the parchment and read. It was written in Herine's hand. Steady and clear, quite at odds with her bearing just before her death.

My dear Arvan,

There comes a time in the life of us all when we must be accountable for our actions. There are moments that define us, shape us and those we love and those we rule. Times when our enemies press, that we make decisions that raise us to the stature of Gods or cast us down beyond his sight.

And when those times come, those who rule must atone for the mistakes that cost the lives of the innocent. I have reached that time and I am unworthy.

Do not grieve for me, Arvan, serve me after my death as you did during my life. Remember me for our love and friendship and for all the good that we achieved for our great Conquord. Forget what you see this day and make your first step on the path to restoring Estorr to her appointed destiny.

This I ask of you, Marshal Defender Vasselis, as my final wish and order. Rule the Conquord until my son returns to Estorr. Keep all that we have built safe from those who would tear it down. Do this for me, Arvan. You are the only one here I can trust. And look after Tuline as your own. I fear she will not understand.

Your Advocate and your friend,

Herine Del Aglios.

'Neither do I, Herine,' he whispered. 'And nor do any of us.'

'Any of us what?' asked Gesteris.

'Understand, Marcus.'

Gesteris pushed himself back to his feet and held out a hand which Vasselis took.

'She's left you in charge?'

'Yes,' said Vasselis, gazing down at the parchment. 'Until Roberto gets back.'

'A sound choice. You can count on my total support and that of the Senate, such as might be out there in the city. The army too will be behind you, Arvan.'

'We need them,' said Vasselis. 'All of them. This has gone on long enough, Marcus. I won't let this situation bring our city down. This siege has to end and it has to end very soon.'

'Any ideas.'

Vasselis brightened just for a moment. 'One or two. Herine wouldn't have liked them but you might. Come on. We need to talk to Elise. But first I need to make the Council of Speakers agree to conduct our Advocate's burial. I'll see you in the Academy as soon as I can.'

Gesteris thumped his right fist into his chest.

'My arm and heart are yours, Marshal Vasselis,' he said.

'Marcus, I am more thankful to hear that than you can know.'

By Roberto's reckoning it was the tenth of genasfall. Their boat was not far from Lake Iyre, not far from the wall and gates of the Jewelled Barrier. The three of them were exhausted, bruised, blistered and aching all over. Too little wind. They'd had to row too much and the River Kalde had a good flow to it this close to the lake, and all in the wrong direction.

Even Harban had begun to suffer though he didn't look like the others. Roberto's breastplate and weapons were stowed in the bow and were safe from harm but everything else he wore, his shirts, skirts and boots, were filthy and torn. Speaker Barias was no better and the sickness that had gripped him the last couple of days gave his face a deathly pallor. Roberto had seen in him then the first signs of fear. That he might die and find he was wrong about so many things.

There had been no time to debate it, no energy either. Harban's sharp eyes had picked out riders cresting the low line of hills that ran up to the Kalde Mountains and all the way down to the lake. They were heading for the river bridge a couple of miles north of the lake's outflow, or he presumed they were. It had to be survivors of the Bear Claws. Roberto had demanded one last effort and they had rowed themselves to the lonely old bridge and waited, hands and feet in the cold water in glorious respite.

The riders were only a mile or so away when Roberto got his first good look at them. They counted twenty and lines of spare horses, thirty in all. He saw Bear Claw cavalry livery and he saw Tsardon armour and faces. All survivors of Gorian's crime. Somehow it didn't surprise him at all to see them together. Indeed it gave him a tiny measure of hope.

Roberto, Harban and Julius stood on the bridge in full sight of the approaching riders. Roberto waved them to a halt, gazing over them as they pulled up. Shuddering horses, riders on the point of collapse. Tsardon and Conquord in equal numbers.

'Ambassador Del Aglios,' said a man Roberto recognised as Dolius. He was gasping in breath. 'We thought you surely lost. Speaker Barias too.'

'Amazing stories of escape will have to wait. What of Kell and Dahnishev? Nunan is gone, I know. What of the dead? Where are they?'

Dolius signalled and the twenty of them dismounted. Roberto watched them grouping together, Tsardon and Estorean, as friends. He nodded to the lead Tsardon. A prosentor.

'Kell is dead and will walk as one of them. Nunan too walks with the enemy. About Dahnishev and the rest of the crag-runners, we don't know. We sent scouts to find them but they picked up no trace. And in the end we had to run as hard as we could to keep ahead of the dead.' Dolius stepped forward. 'He killed them all. Conquord and Tsardon alike. He has artillery and engineers, taken from Hasfort. Kell and four hundred soldiers sacrificed themselves to give us the room to escape and warn you. And to get Prosentor Ruthrar to the king. The dead are scant days behind us and only because they slowed after we attacked. I—'

Roberto held up his hands. 'Hold on, hold on. Some I know, some I don't. The king? Khuran?'

Ruthrar nodded. 'My king marches through Atreska to death and not to glory. I must speak with him.'

'We will all go to Neratharn. But first, we will sit and you will tell me all that you know.'

Davarov was waiting for the scout reports. He had seen the smudge on the western horizon denoting an approaching force and assumed it to be either Neratharnese reservists or his artillery from the yards of Hasfort. Either would have been very welcome. But there was always lingering doubt. No refugees had come in from the west which was encouraging but he couldn't help but feel a twinge of anxiety.

It was probably nothing. More likely his ongoing irritation at the state of preparations at the Jewelled Barrier. There were simply too many displaced citizens to cope with and the Tsardon force backed by the dead would be on them in something like six days. Right now he could maintain the slow move through the gates once processing was done but sooner or later, he'd have to throw them open and let the flood roll over him.

'General?'

He groaned and looked up from the relief map table where he was studying the latest muster times following the morning's rehearsal.

'Give me strength and peace from interruption. Yes, Centurion, what is it? And please don't tell me it has anything to do with catering for the refugees. We've been through this. If they don't like the foraging round here, or the prices of those bastard traders, then they can up sticks and go. It is a big Conquord and it's mostly empty.'

The centurion was nodding his head furiously. 'Yes, sir, and no, it isn't that.'

'Well? You want to tell me how it is it took the Rogue Spears an hour to get from their camp to the walls this morning?'

'Yes, sir.'

'I'm all ears.'

'We did not receive the order at the allotted time, sir. I've been through the communication chain and our papers were delivered late.'

'That isn't possible,' said Davarov. 'I despatched all the riders at precisely the same time. I do not believe yours got lost on the way. It is only a mile and a half across open ground.'

'Yes, sir,' said the centurion. 'But the horse stepped on an animal trap in the undergrowth. One left there by, well, refugees. The rider had to run the rest of the way and he was injured in the fall. The horse is lame.'

Davarov glared at an aide shifting nervously on the opposite side of the table.

'Did we not issue an edict regarding trapping within the camp boundaries?' he growled.

The woman blushed scarlet. 'Yes, General.'

'Then why am I plagued by this stupidity? I have an army of dead people marching this way and yet some within my walls are trying to create more. I have had enough of this.' Davarov slapped the map and unsettled figures and markers. 'Sorry.'

'Trapping is good within the camps,' said the aide. 'Animals come in after scraps. I know it's not an excuse but—'

'Damn right, it's not an excuse!' thundered Davarov and all heads turned his way. 'Now you're all listening I think it time we understood one or two things. This is not a game. We are not drawing this map just to keep ourselves busy. I do not issue edicts just to fluff my ego. I will throw from the walls the next citizen who lays a trap inside the grounds. They want our protection, they need to start respecting my authority.

'I —'

There was a loud knock on the doors, which opened on the same instant. Davarov clenched his fists.

'If you are not Roberto fucking Del Aglios, you had better have a—'

He stopped, unable to quite believe what had stepped across his threshold. Or rather, who.

'You've got a problem, old friend. Half of your artillery is facing the wrong way and you're missing a whole wall.'

'Hello, Roberto. Looks to me like you could do with a bath.'

Chapter Fifty-Eight

859th cycle of God, 10th day of Genasfall

'I am so sorry, Roberto. He was a fine young man. Every Conquord citizen will grieve.'

'None more so than my mother.'

Roberto and Davarov walked the walls of the Jewelled Barrier. Their presence together had lifted the mood of the entire facility. Davarov had admitted that the knowledge of the approaching dead was beginning to wear at the nerves of soldier and civilian alike. He wore it like guilt, like failure.

'Atreska failed you,' said Davarov.

'Say that one more time and you're going over the wall,' said Roberto. 'The fact you are standing here gives the Conquord hope. Knowing the dead had taken the border, I feared you would be walking with the enemy.'

'It is only because I ran that I am standing here.'

Roberto stopped and faced Davarov. 'Between bathing, changing, having my armour polished and my boots repaired, I took the opportunity to talk to one or two people. Your story and theirs don't quite match. Big Atreskan bastard. If there's one thing I hate more than cowards, it's modest heroes. And God-surround-me we are going to need heroes in the days to come.'

'I don't think we have enough strength here,' said Davarov. 'Numbers don't enter into it. Spirit, belief, faith. These are in short supply.'

'Even with Them here?'

Davarov shrugged. 'You said it yourself. They spawn as much suspicion as they do hope. Every refugee has a story to tell. Things they've seen, things they've heard. The Neratharnese here are yet to face the dead. We have, you have, and the result is that we have both been driven hundreds of miles in front of them because we have no idea how to stop them.'

'Had, Davarov. Had no idea.'

'Roberto, come on, take the veil from your eyes. Two hundred artillery pieces, three Ascendants. Twenty-five miles of wall here, no defence at all the other side. If they fight smart, like they did on my border and in Gosland, they will breach us.'

'We outnumber them,' said Roberto.

'Today, yes. Tomorrow? Who knows. We hoped they would decay and fall, they did not. We hoped we could keep the path clear in front of them, they caught us all the same. Roberto, they have destroyed the 2nd legion. *The Bear Claws.* Gone bar maybe a few hundred still lost in the mountains to the north.' Davarov shook his head. 'I will stand until they drag me down. Until the last onager is overrun. But I have people with me who know the depths of the terror they experienced on the Tsardon border. Will they stand this time? Not if there is no hope.'

'Then we must give them hope,' said Roberto. 'We have new weapons. We have you and we have me. We must exude nothing but confidence.'

Davarov smiled. 'I'm looking down on my country, Roberto. And I want it back.'

'And we have Ruthrar.'

Davarov's smile disappeared. 'Weapon or spy?'

'You've spoken to Dolius, Davarov, what do you think?'

'I think that the Tsardon have been treacherous bastards on my doorstep for fifteen years and too often inside the houses of my countrymen. You cannot ask me to trust a Tsardon, not even one with the reputation of this Ruthrar. And don't forget it's a reputation quickly earned. How would you behave if you found yourself marooned like him and his people?'

'People who fought and died alongside Conquord loyals trying to disrupt Gorian's advance.'

Davarov sighed. 'I'm a cynic, I know.'

'Worse than Dahnishev.'

'But I have reason. Letting him ride out to talk to Khuran, if he really is with them, just gives them information. And what are you really hoping to achieve? No Tsardon is ever going to stand on these walls.'

'That is not what I want,' said Roberto. 'We just don't want them fighting with the dead. It has to be worth the risk. Think about it, what information can he really give Khuran that the king couldn't deduce for himself?'

'It's your decision, Roberto. Part of me wants to string up Ruthrar as a warning. The other wants to push him out of the gates and let him do his worst. I don't know.'

'I hear you, Davarov. How long before the Tsardon get here?'

'Five days, maybe less.' Davarov jerked his thumb over his shoulder. 'And Gorian will be in striking distance tomorrow.'

'But he won't attack.'

'No, I don't suppose he will. Not if this long distance communication he is supposed to have is true.'

'Harban has no doubt.'

'Now there's an odd one,' said Davarov.

Roberto smiled. 'Can't disagree with you there. He says almost nothing. Just that what he does say carries such authority.'

'And what does he have to say about all this?'

'He wants us to go and snatch the Gor-Karkulas.'

'Easier to kill them,' said Davarov.

'Not if we want to keep the Karku as friends.' Roberto sighed. 'He's right of course. Take them and we reduce Gorian's strength dramatically. But getting to them through the dead. Got to be almost impossible.'

Davarov nodded. 'Let's try the things we know first. Let him reveal his hand. It's the Neratharn side we have to worry about. No one, dead or alive, is coming through these walls in a hurry. Roberto?'

'Yes?'

'You're avoiding them, aren't you?'

Roberto felt his throat tighten. 'Blame me?'

'No. But I think the big tall one is starting to get a complex.'

'Jhered has a complex about everything.'

'Come and say hello, why don't you?' said Davarov.

Roberto shrugged and felt the touch of nerves. 'All right. Let's get it over with.'

Arducius watched Jhered greet Roberto Del Aglios and could feel the grief in the energy lines that flowed from the pair of them. He stayed back in the barracks canteen, sitting on a bench with Mirron and

Ossacer. They were all tired after the voyage. Mirron was still a little sick despite Ossacer's ministrations and Arducius was sure it was more than just sea sickness this time. From the look in Mirron's eyes, she knew it too. God-surround-him, they all did. Gorian was near and he drove his dead before him. The facts lay heavy in the lines of the earth. Tortured and twisted everywhere, coiled as if trying to escape their fate.

The two old friends talked for some time in whispered tones before Roberto nodded, smiled sadly and walked towards them. Behind him, Jhered turned to them, gave them a meaningful look and fell to his own thoughts, a hand over chin and mouth.

Arducius stood up, his brother and sister with him. The three of them saluted him but he waved it away with a dismissive gesture. Ossacer was tense. Arducius knew why. It was all over Roberto's life map as well as in his eyes and his bearing. He was stricken with grief but boiling around it was anger, directed their way.

'Ambassador Del Aglios, we had not thought to see you here,' said Arducius, having to say something.

'No,' said Roberto. 'Thirty-five days ago I would have been surprised myself. But one of your kin has changed all that and we are all the lesser for it. Small wonder you are treated with suspicion here, at best.'

'I don't understand,' said Arducius.

'My brother, Adranis, is a victim of the evil of Gorian Westfallen and I hold the Ascendancy responsible.'

Mirron gasped. 'Ambassador, I cannot tell you how sorry I am to hear that.'

'Your brother was a great man,' said Ossacer.

'Yes, he was,' said Roberto. 'And had I not decapitated and mutilated him myself, he would be a great man walking with your bastard brother as one of the dead.'

Arducius swallowed. He would have backed off a pace but for the bench at the back of his legs.

'We are as disgusted by Gorian's use of his abilities as any man,' said Arducius. 'Our aim has always been—'

'Quiet!' snapped Roberto and the three of them jumped in unison. 'I have not come here to discuss the aims or otherwise of the Ascendancy my mother is far too happy to keep so close. My aim on arriving here was to demand your presence and for that reason alone, I am happy you are here.

'But let me get one thing straight. Every day, I regret a little more, the fact that I listened to you and did not order the killing of Gorian. My brother is dead because of my stupidity and so are countless thousands of others. So we will not be sitting at the same table and we are not going to be friends, do I make myself clear?

'You are here to destroy that abomination and all his bastard creations. That is all you are here to do and you will take your orders directly from either myself, or General Davarov. You will question nothing and I expect you to sacrifice your lives if that's what it takes.

'Ossacer what is wrong with you?'

Roberto glared at him with an intensity that would have withered a weaker man.

'We are here to help. And we are all saddened that your brother is dead. But please, do not hold the entire Ascendancy to account for the actions of one man. You have to accept that Ascendants are here with the same rights under God as any man.'

'I have to accept nothing,' spat Roberto. 'The very potential in you for this evil sickens me to my stomach. There is no redemption for you, merely appeasement. One day, I will be Advocate and will preside on the Hill. Do not assume for one moment that I will necessarily allow your work to proceed.

'Now get out of my sight and get to work on beating this enemy. I do not expect to have to speak to you again.'

Roberto stood daring them to utter another word. Jhered hissed through his teeth and Mirron led them all away. Ossacer opened his mouth but Jhered's expression gave him pause. None of them spoke until they were outside under the sun.

'How dare he speak to us like that,' said Ossacer. 'We have come in good faith to help.'

Jhered stopped and turned on him. 'Listen to me, Ossacer, and listen well. All of you. For all the support you enjoy back in Estorr, out here it looks like only I will stand up for you. Roberto is broken but his mind is clear enough. Do not cross him. The Ascendancy stands on the edge of a knife and to either side lies disaster. You fight now not merely to win today but for your very survival. Make me proud and make him think again. Because if you can't, it matters little how many you save here. When we get back home, you will be finished.'

*

'Hatred is as fragile as love,' said Vasselis. 'I wonder if she knew that.'

'I wonder what would have happened had the Chancellor still been alive.'

'Instead they are buried side-by-side under the lawn of the Omniscient, Marcus.'

'And do we take any comfort from that?'

The two old soldiers rode together along the processional road, returning from the Principal House of Masks. The first legion was with them. The palace guard was a cloak about them. The Armour of God were an honour guard along the entire route. Across the city, the flags were lowered. Bells sounded flat notes. Horns played the marches of death. A melancholy symphony.

'The anger will return,' said Vasselis. 'We need to make the most of this opportunity while it exists. Get people moving out now the Advocate is with God.'

Marcus Gesteris nodded at the carriage behind which they rode. 'You know the thing that really lifts my heart in all this? Tuline has seen the love that the citizens had for her mother. Her last days were dark but Herine was a magnificent ruler. Their lives have been enriched through her Advocacy and they remembered that at the end.'

Vasselis nodded. 'It should tell us a lot. That the will of the people isn't represented purely by the Order.'

'But two legions of the Armour are very persuasive.'

'They have always known how to still dissenting voices.'

The carriage, covered and curtained to hide Tuline's tears, rattled under the Victory Gates. The sun beamed upon the palace but it could not disguise the fact that the city, aflame only five days ago, was hollow, empty and heartbroken. When he examined his mind, Vasselis was not surprised at the reaction but his relief had hidden that from him.

The fury of the citizenry had melted away, swept aside by a tide of shock and grief. Only a day after Herine's death, the siege had been lifted and the Council of Speakers had sat down with Vasselis and Tuline to discuss arrangements for an interment befitting the Advocate of the Estorean Conquord and the appointed representative of the Omniscient on earth.

The cynical side of Vasselis suggested to him that this was merely a ploy, that the Order was only doing as it did so well and reading the mood of the people, using it to increase their trust. They would find out if that was true in the coming days. But the spectre of an ignominious end to the rule of Herine Del Aglios had been avoided and for that, the Order was to be commended.

Vasselis and Gesteris rode through the gates and into the courtyard. Stable boys ran to them to take the horses' reins and help the men dismount. The carriage had moved on to the steps of the palace. Vasselis saw Tuline descend the steps and hurry inside, out of sight.

'You know we should flag the news,' said Gesteris. 'The beacons should all be black-smoked.'

'I can't do that,' said Vasselis. 'We have to maintain the illusion of cohesion here. Think of the effect announcing the death of the Advocate would have on already scared forces out there. When we hear of victory or otherwise at Neratharn, then we will black-smoke.'

'And what about Roberto? That man is the Advocate but he does not know it.'

'Better he doesn't. Enough on his shoulders already.'

'I'm not sure he would see it that way.'

'I can't help that, Marcus. I have to do what I think is right. Roberto will understand.'

Gesteris turned at the sound of another carriage trundling over the cobbles into the courtyard. Vasselis looked past his shoulder. The sigils of the Omniscient adorned it. Each panel was painted in the bright colours of the elements.

'They didn't waste much time,' said Gesteris.

'Want a small wager on what they will want to discuss?'

Gesteris chuckled and the pair of them moved to greet the Council as they descended the carriage step.

'It's not much of a wager if we both pick the same winner,' he said.

Vasselis drew in breath and stamped a welcoming expression on to his face. The courtyard was filling with infantry. A detachment of cavalry cantered under the grand arch. He noted that the Armour of God had remained without.

'My lords of the Council of Speakers, welcome,' he said. 'And I feel I speak for all here on the Hill and throughout the City and indeed the wider Conquord when I commend you for an interment that was honest, sympathetic, reverent and altogether fitting. It warms my heart and I thank you.'

Beside him, Gesteris was nodding his approval. Winds inclined his head in acknowledgement.

'The Omniscient will make His judgement. For our faithful, the crimes of the Advocate were far outweighed by her achievements. As ministers of the Order, we can but reflect how the people feel.'

'And what about your personal views?' asked Gesteris gruffly.

Earth, Oceans and Fire clustered behind Winds, who continued.

'The Advocate was destroyed by guilt. And her demise, though surprising in its manner, was an inevitable consequence of her actions. However, there is a cold wind now at the heights of power where once there was a consistent barrier. And the architects of the malaise gripping this City are still at large.'

Vasselis felt his mood cool and hope begin to shred.

'Come,' he said. 'Sit with us and talk. The Advocate has opened the door on possibility. Let us not fall back into old animosity.'

Winds smiled rather sadly and shook his head.

'There is no need, Marshal Vasselis. The head of the beast is taken. The body must now die. We will take the Ascendants with us now and should you refuse, we will be sending the Armour of God to collect them and this time there will be no siege.'

'You would attack the palace?' asked Vasselis, unable to believe what he had just heard. 'You would drag the citizens, your faithful, into pointless conflict, nay dangerous conflict. I will state one more time, we are under threat of invasion. We must not waste lives. The Armour of God must defend the city. The citizens must leave.'

Winds scoffed and Vasselis stiffened. Gesteris growled and bunched his fists at his side.

'There is no invasion. There is no threat. There is only denial of evil. And your repetitive demands are wearing on our nerves.'

Across the city the tenor of the horns and bells changed. Harsh, fast, repetitive tones, echoing across the rooftops. Winds gaped and looked into the sky as if challenging more lies.

'No invasion?' said Gesteris, having to shout as the clamour gained in volume, filling the air. He stepped into Winds and grabbed the collars of his cloak. 'Does that sound like peace to you?'

Winds was gaping. 'It can't be. It was lies.'

Vasselis stepped between them, pushed Gesteris gently away.

'No, Winds, it wasn't. And your refusal to believe has cost the Advocate her mind and then her life. It has torn this city apart and that is the last thing we could afford. Now I want to see Horst Vennegoor in front of me inside the hour. Because, whatever you believe, the dead really are coming. And it sounds to me as though the Ocetanas might not be able to stop them. And don't forget to apologise to every citizen you see on your way. Seems to me you might just have killed them all.'

Chapter Fifty-Nine

859th cycle of God, 10th day of Genasfall

'Pump bellows.'

The *Ocetarus* rowed alongside the enemy vessel. The drum beat out a murderous rhythm. Below decks, the oarsmen sang to keep themselves focused. They could not afford to drop the pace now. Iliev looked up at the mast. The sail was furled against it but the pennant was flying straight back along the vessel, pointing at the stern.

'Fire!' he ordered.

Along the deck of the enemy ship, Tsardon sailors lined the rail, firing bows across the short space. They rattled off the shields set to defend the bellows and pipes on the *Ocetarus*'s stern. Iliev's skipper twitched his hand on the tiller, watching for movements to cause collision.

The jet of naphtha was ignited. A spear of flame roared out from the stern of the Conquord flagship and played from stern to bow of the Tsardon trireme as they passed.

'Starboard heave,' ordered Iliev.

The skipper pulled hard on the tiller, veering away from the enemy. Tsardon sailors were aflame. Fires engulfed the entire starboard side. There was chaos on the oar deck. Naphtha fed along oars. There was a clashing and the ship slewed to port. Iliev could hear screams. The bellows could project the naphtha almost forty feet. He wished they could hit mast and sail but this would do.

Panic had taken a hold. He could hear the strange keening sound, the wailing of the dead crammed where they were in the hold. It was a hideous sound and Iliev regretted the fate of every innocent man who had to suffer to keep the Conquord safe. The enemy vessel was in trouble. And water only fed the flames. The naphtha ate deep into the timbers and burned very hot. The fire reached high into the sky and fizzed on the waterline.

Iliev said a prayer for all those being taken to the bosom of Ocetarus. But it was nowhere near enough. He turned forward. Ocenii squadron corsairs streaked across the water from twenty base triremes. Squad seven was on the water, tracking them and waiting for Iliev to join them. He watched squad fourteen strike low in the bow of a trireme a few hundred yards away to starboard. The Tsardon vessel shuddered across the water. Moments later, another squad impacted its stern.

Yet they were the few against the many. Iliev cursed again. They had been looking in the wrong place. He'd known they would need a fleet to bring the dead across the Tirronean. The Tsardon would have to sail around the southern tip of Gestern to do it. Should have.

But they had been out-thought. Gestern was full of the willing muscle of the dead. There was no resistance in that fair country. So the Tsardon had not risked encountering the Ocetanas and the Ocenii where the Gildenean Sea met the Tirronean. They had dismantled their ships and marched them across Gestern. An extraordinary feat. Possible only because of the sheer numbers of dead the enemy used as passive muscle. And by the time the truth was known, two hundred ships were coming from the length of the western seaboard. Too many for the Ocetanas to take.

Whatever they did, some of the dead would make landfall.

Iliev could see the white walls and red slates of Estorr in the far distance. Two days before they knew the horror of the dead. The only hope that the thirty vessels Iliev had gathered to him had was that they had sunk those containing the Gor-Karkulas. It was a game of chance and it was not one they would know they had won until the Tsardon turned back or the ships landed to disgorge nothing.

Tsardon sails stained the horizon and blotted out the beauty of the ocean. In amongst them, Conquord vessels taken from Kester Isle. The reserve Iliev had gone to get but which he had found already taken. The enemy had kept them hidden until now though he didn't know how.

Iliev wracked his brains, thinking of what he might have done differently. But there was nothing. No preparation he could have made would have eased the burden on his heart now. He had flagged the invasion warning and seen the response communicated back by the fleet. At least Estorr knew they were coming.

'Skipper!'

Iliev turned and looked down over the port bow. Kashilli was standing at the tiller on his corsair.

'Kashilli, how goes it out there?'

'Stop nagging yourself like a bad wife and come and see. Enemy to be sunk. Hammers to be swung.'

Iliev nodded. 'Back off to the stern. I'll join you.'

Iliev trotted back down the ship, pausing at the skipper. 'Keep tracking them down. Keep those bellows going. Any dead that falls is a good dead.'

'Yes, Admiral.'

Iliev smiled. 'We can only do what Octetarus allows us, Captain. The call is out and we have answered. Remember that. Fight. And watch for the Ocenii. Strike centre. We'll move out a half mile.'

Iliev stepped on to the stern rail and dived into the sea, feeling the cold embrace him and the hand of Ocetarus caress him. He commended his body to his god and broke surface. Kashilli's shout turned him in the right direction and he struck out. There was damage to be done.

'I can feel her,' said Kessian. 'She's practically just around the corner. Why can't we go to her?'

'Quiet!' Gorian's shout only worsened his headache and exacerbated his fatigue. 'Stop your whining. Don't you realise we are not ready?'

'Why not? Everyone is there. Arducius and Ossacer are there too. Even that man we were looking for before.'

'Yes, and none of them will understand what I have become. Or what you have become. You know they all hate me.'

'I could go to her. Bring her to you and we can be together just like you said.'

'No.'

Gorian groped for the right words but they would not come. The concentration of energies was flooding his mind. The sheer density of it threatened to swamp even him. Everything bar keeping his people whole and walking forwards seemed such a massive effort.

The proximity of the Gor-Karkulas and his second army marching with Khuran had reached a critical point and the well of power he had so close to him was vast. It told him his tactics were right. Once the two armies were joined, the forces he could bring to bear through four of the Karkulas would be simply unstoppable. The energies beneath the earth thrummed as he sucked on their life forces.

Above, where the living still roamed, hoping to defeat him, some would sense it. And they would hate it. Kessian had sampled this bleeding into the complex map Gorian had created, an unconscious attempt to right what they felt was wrong. That was how Kessian knew so much about who was on the wall, damn him.

'How does it feel, my siblings?' he whispered. 'To know that I am here but to be so helpless. To yearn for my blood but to be so fearful of the power I possess.'

'What are you talking about?'

Gorian came back to himself.

'You are like a tick in my ear, boy. Go. Leave me. Prepare. Our enemies will use foul method to try and defeat us. Our people must be strong. They must not lie down. Do you understand?'

'Yes, Father.'

Gorian watched Kessian disappear into the glade of trees where he had placed himself, there to find those he was sworn to command. Kessian had learned hard lessons about control of late and now he was ready.

Gorian smiled. The sun reached him through new leaves and the grass beneath him was wholesome and healthy. It was an oasis where his people would not walk. A place of simple beauty he wanted to leave untouched. Tomorrow, his armies would be one and his power increased tenfold. Tomorrow, he could begin the march to Estorr and the throne would be empty and waiting for him when, in glory, he arrived.

The fear was palpable. It settled on the Jewelled Barrier like a heavy dew, cloying and grasping. The refugees who had thought themselves safe behind the barrier now found themselves on a new frontline with nowhere to go. Everywhere Arducius walked, he could hear crying and praying. It was eerie. There were hundreds of fires alight across the camp sites, throwing tents and people into deep shadow between them. The sounds of their distress rose with the flames. Their hopes, like the flames, tattered on the breeze.

All that stood between them and Gorian's thousands of dead were three Ascendants. Two legions were present also, standing on a wide front, but they were there only as a lure. They were what Gorian wanted. The balance of the Conquord forces was stationed on the barrier itself, watching the dead approach across the plains. They would be within striking distance in less than a day. The Tsardon still followed them. It was yet to be seen whether Ruthrar's mission would prove successful or whether he was the spy Davarov clearly thought him to be.

The Ascendants walked to the frontline through the stink of the refugee camp. Disease was breaking out. Inevitable but deeply worrying. Arducius felt that Gorian would have enough on his plate fighting the battle that was to come. But should he see the dead in the Conquord midst, he could cause havoc. Roberto had insisted that any who die be mutilated beyond his use but it was naïve to believe that all in the sprawling camp, some fifty thousand in number, would listen to that order. Bodies would be there, concealed, buried whole.

'They'd do better rushing the dead when they come,' said Ossacer. 'Fifty thousand against, what, eight thousand or so? No contest.'

'And will you be the man first to attack a walking corpse?' asked Arducius. 'They do not have the will. Feel the fear. Taste it.'

'Anyway, he will not try and rush in. He'll do what Davarov and Roberto said was done on the other borders,' said Mirron. 'Plant some dead in the defence.'

'Then we have to move the refugees,' said Ossacer. 'I don't know about you but I can sense the sickness here. It is spreading fast. Diphtheria, mainly. Bad sanitation, too little food and clean water.'

'And where will they go? There's a city of them out there. If they start to run it'll be a stampede. No wonder Davarov has the Rogue Spears circling them.'

Arducius indicated the line of picket fires within which the entirety of the Spears infantry stood. A thin line of defence whichever way you looked at it. Ossacer was right of course, they should have been moved. Some had taken the chance to run south when first news of the enemy approach this side of the wall was given. Most, though, felt they should stay within the net of the army. Arducius wondered how many of them regretted that decision now. By the feel of the atmosphere, most of them.

The Ascendants carried on walking. Past the lines of artillery, past the resting army and out onto the open ground of Neratharn. Out there, only a couple of miles away, Gorian waited. They were as certain as they could be that he was out there. The direction of the sick energies running under the earth that dragged at their stamina and infected small corners of their minds told them that.

'It's so dark out there,' said Mirron. 'So bleak.'

She knelt on the ground and placed her palms on it, seeking clues. Arducius and Ossacer joined her, opening their minds as one and delving deep into the earth. Nausea boiled up through them. Deep below was a perversion of everything they had come to believe. A negative energy. The elements of death, disease and decay.

So powerful. Gorian had seen it. The universal constant. Every living thing is prey to it and, ultimately, falls victim to it. As far as they could feel to the east and the west, it dominated the endless slow-moving energies of the earth, tainting them with a sick greyness that was death in all but name.

'Is he there too, Mirron?' asked Ossacer.

'I don't know,' she replied through a sigh that brought a lump to the throat. 'I'm not even sure I can feel him any more, even if he is out there. His energy is so distant, like a dream.'

'You must believe, Mirron. Don't let him go, not for one moment, or he might truly be lost to you.'

'I try so hard, Ardu, I really do. But Gorian blots out all else. His essence is all around us. It is in the air and running through the ground like a river in flood. How can we beat it. How can we hold this back?'

Arducius rubbed his hands together and stood up.

'We don't,' he said. 'He's too powerful for that and the dead energy map is so vast. I still don't know how he does it, do you?'

'This path is thankfully closed to us,' said Ossacer. 'It doesn't make any sense. What do you have in mind?'

'What else do you think Gorian has left when he is in control of all the dead? Not much in my opinion. I suggest we give him something to think about. It'll take much of the night to get it right and make it happen with the pace we'll need.'

'Something on the wind, Ardu?' asked Ossacer.

Arducius nodded. 'Will you help us, Ossie?'

'We're only killing him and putting the dead back to rest, right?'

'Only that.'

Ossacer nodded and his eyes swam orange to calm green.

'I am with you, Ardu.'

'What day is it after tomorrow?' asked Mirron suddenly.

Arducius smiled. 'Twelfth genasfall.'

'Father Kessian's birthday,' said Ossacer.

'A fitting day for the end to all this evil,' said Arducius. 'Remember we are one and we will always be one. Let's get to work.'

Khuran's rage would surely be heard on the walls of the barrier. Prosentors Kreysun and Ruthrar were powerless to stop him. He roared his grief. His armour was scattered all over the tent. Cushions, canvas, blanket and clothing were shredded and slit. Feathers clouded the air. The bed was reduced to splinters.

Khuran's blade was sharp and Ruthrar had felt its edge across his arm when he tried for the first time to calm his king. The wound bled freely but he ignored it. Khuran stood in the centre of his ruined pavilion tent, his breath heaving in and out, his sword in one hand, a broken chair leg in the other. His eyes were aflame, his face was red and his head twitched from side to side as he cast about for something else on which to vent his fury.

The only things left whole were Kreysun and Ruthrar.

'My King, please, you will awaken the army, put fear in them.'

Khuran focused on Kreysun and Ruthrar felt the power of his gaze. Kreysun was trying desperately to hold himself together, not break his stare.

'Then they should be scared,' said Khuran, his voice like two rocks ground together. 'They should fear for their lives.'

'It is time to sheathe your sword, my king,' said Kreysun gently, holding out his hands.

Khuran lashed out and Kreysun snatched back. The blade missed his fingertips by a hair.

'He killed my son!' Khuran's bellow carried clear across the camp, surely. 'I want that bastard's heart on a platter. I want his eyes to stare at me in terror for what he has done to me. Get out of my way.'

Khuran made to shove past Kreysun but the prosentor stood his ground. Khuran backed up a pace, raised his sword to strike.

'Out of my way!'

He struck down. Ruthrar was ready. He dived in, got both hands on the king's sword arm and bore him down to the ground. Kreysun pounced on his other arm, trying to stop the flailing chair leg from beating out Ruthrar's brains. The king glared at them both in turn. He was spitting, incandescent, and he had the strength of three men. His legs thrashed, his body convulsed and his neck bulged with his corded muscle.

'I will have both your lives for this. Get off me. Guards! To the king. I am attacked.'

'No, Khuran,' shouted Kreysun. 'You must be calm. You cannot get him. He is too far from you.'

Guards had run into the tent.

'Let me at him. I want him now. Get your bastard hands off me.'

Khuran's struggles intensified. Ruthrar could barely keep his sword arm down, such was the strength of his fury. He turned to the four guards just standing, gawping.

'Make your choice,' he said. 'Help us calm him or take us from him.'

'Westfallen, I am coming for you. Do you hear me you bastard?'

The guards moved in.

'We mean him no harm,' said Kreysun. 'One of you, get his sword. He's going to kill himself or someone else before long.'

Khuran's face was puffed like it would explode. His eyes bulged from their sockets. 'I. Want. Him. Dead.'

'Please my King, you must calm yourself,' said Kreysun, trying to catch his gaze, a gaze that had long since not seen any reason. 'Khuran. My friend, my King. Listen to me. Listen.'

The guards could hear Kreysun's tone. They trusted him. Ruthrar sensed them come to a decision. The right one. One moved to each hand, prising open the king's grip to divest him of his weapons. The other two sat on his legs, forcing him to calm though his torso still bucked and twisted.

With a guard kneeling on each wrist, Kreysun let go the king's arm and took the poor man's face in his hands. He fought the strength in that bull neck to bring his eyes around.

'Khuran. Your rage and your grief. Both are felt by us all. And the Tsardon will extract their revenge on Gorian Westfallen for the murder of your son. But it cannot be tonight. Khuran, do you hear me?'

Ruthrar could see that Khuran's face had cleared. His eyes lost their madness and he frowned. Tears poured down the sides of his face.

'He has taken my own from me,' whispered Khuran and his voice was desperate and alone. 'My line is ended. Who will rule when I am gone. My son. My beautiful son.'

'We have no choice but to go on,' said Kreysun. 'Westfallen is beyond the walls. Remember what we spoke about.'

Khuran nodded.

'Use the dead to beat the Conquord. Let them make the breach in the wall that will bring us to Gorian. Then we can strike. Whatever Ruthrar says, we cannot trust the Conquord. One worthy dead general is of no use to us.'

'Leave me,' said Khuran.

'What will we tell your warriors?' asked Kreysun. 'They will all have heard your grief.'

'Tell them the fact but not the manner. But tell them this also. When the dead assault the walls, we will stand by. Not one of my people is to perish in the assault. The first blood spilled by a Tsardon will be that spilled by me and it shall be the blood of Gorian Westfallen. This is my solemn oath.'

Kreysun knew he shouldn't but he could not help himself. The dead camp was quiet, its stench extraordinary. He imagined disease entering his body through every orifice, every cut. His eyes smarted, his nose itched and his throat was tight. But there was no other choice.

Right in the centre of the camp, the open wagon stood. Surrounded by dead, packed ten deep. Kreysun strode towards it. A figure detached himself from the mass and the mass turned to watch him walk.

'Hasheth.'

'Kreysun.' Hasheth smiled, the points of his teeth gleamed. 'Commotion in the ranks. Is there a problem my Lord Gorian should be made aware of?'

Kreysun spat on the ground between Hasheth's feet.

'The King knows all. Your King. It is time you and your filth decided who it is that you serve.'

Hasheth laughed and the sound was echoed by hundreds of mouths in a foul whisper. Kreysun shivered.

'No, Prosentor. I decided a long time ago who I serve. It is you who must make that choice. But make it quickly. Dawn and glory are not far away.'

Chapter Sixty

859th cycle of God, 12th day of Genasfall

'Keep your heads down and your eyes front!' bawled Davarov. 'I don't want a single one of you dying on me, is that clear?'

Davarov's words were carried along the crest of the Jewelled Barrier and relayed to those mustered beneath the great wall. Pitch fires burned along its length. Catapult arms were drawn back. Bows were strung. Arrowheads and stones were ready for dipping and painting in flame. The powder Jhered assured Davarov would cause great destruction was in metal flasks set among nets of stones that would be set on fire and shot over the walls. Crates of flasks were roped below the battlements on the fort roof.

The answering calls, the flags and the punching of the air spoke that the message was clear.

'The dead come to fight us but they will not climb this wall. Do not let them have clear sight of you. For every one of you that falls brings more strength to our enemy. Look to your friends, your brothers. You know what you must do. And do not look back into Neratharn. For there, the greatest powers known to man are ranged against our enemy. I believe in the Ascendants. I have seen them work. And they will not let the dead take our people from us.'

Davarov stopped and looked out over the Atreskan plains from his position on the gate walls. Issuing across the last mile, they came, leaving a trail of darkness behind them. Advancing in a line that stretched for over three miles, the dead. Thousands upon thousands of them. Fear blew in on the breeze mixed with the stink of decay. And silence rolled before them. The frames of artillery moved on the horizon.

'You cannot give in to your nightmares. The sun shines upon us. The Omniscient will bless us this day. The Lords of Sky and Stars look down upon you. Today the world will be placed back in balance. The dead will lie beneath the ground and only the living will walk the surface. You will play your part, all of you.

'For Atreska, for Neratharn, for Estorea and for me!'

Davarov held his sword high, the heavy long blade catching the sun. How odd it felt in his hand. How ungainly. But he had practised enough. The sarissa bladesmen too, the axe-wielders and the hammer infantry. So little time in reality to prepare for a war unlike any they had fought before.

'Reap this crop for me,' he said quietly as the roars of his legionaries flowed across him. 'Slash and burn.'

'A fine speech,' said Roberto.

Davarov smiled. 'Well, I listened to you enough times, something was bound to rub off.'

'Brevity at least.'

'You're going to stand with me?' Davarov's smile faded, seeing the haunted look in Roberto's eyes. 'You don't think you should be across the other side?'

Roberto shook his head. 'I cannot go there. I cannot watch them. Jhered will see it through, him and your field commanders. Dammit, Davarov, you know part of me almost wants them to fail. To be swept away and killed, leaving the victory for the legions as it should be. A world without the blight of this magic.'

'But it's what we have,' said Davarov. 'And without them, there will be no victory, you know that.'

'I'm not so sure.'

'Yes you are, Roberto.'

'They aren't here on these walls, are they? And do you think the dead will make a breach?'

Davarov scoffed. 'Hardly.'

'Well, then.'

'But there is no wall behind us besides the one they build with their Works. You have to want them to succeed.'

'I want the Conquord to succeed. Not quite the same thing.'

Davarov shrugged. 'Have it your own way, Roberto.'

The sky above was a peerless blue. But over the Gaws and the foothills above Lake Iyre, clouds were building. Black and ominous, tall and churning. The wind picked up pace, swirling around them. Quiet fell across the barrier and all that could be heard above the beginning of the Ascendant Work was the crying, wailing and shouting of tens of thousands of displaced citizens, trapped by the dead and by their own fear.

'Well,' said Davarov. 'Here we go.'

Mirron could see them through the trails in the air, through the ground and in the starkness against the living landscape. The dead were like holes in the elements. A shifting greyness that fed through the ground, turning the slow energy of earth and the quick shapes of animal and vegetation to nothing.

They were coming on two different fronts. Gorian must have known the Ascendants were going to attack the open side and his forces moved several miles apart. Jhered, on Arducius's advice, moved the artillery to cover one force, leaving the Ascendants to contain and destroy the other. Both enemy forces if they could.

'You'd better be right about this,' said Jhered. 'Big open spaces behind us if you get it wrong.'

'We won't,' said Mirron.

Jhered chuckled. 'I bet you won't at that.'

Arducius was already deep into the first section of the Work. He was building deep, tall thunderheads above Lake Iyre and the Gaws, drawing on the geographical features to boost their density and size. A barrel of water had been brought to stand beside him and he used it in conjunction with the lively genastro growth energies to catalyse his efforts.

'Mirron, I need you,' he said, voice distant and showing strain.

'What do you need?'

'Strengthen the energy lines to the cloud bases. I think . . .' he trailed away for a moment. 'Ossie, he's found the construct. Keep him back.'

Mirron blew hard as she joined Arducius in his Work, lending him her strength and the well of her ability. She channelled quickly, drawing in water from the barrel, feeling it flow over her body, projecting out the fast blue lines into Arducius's thick trunk construct, flowing north and south.

She could feel Gorian there. He was attacking the periphery of the trunks. Spears of cold rushed under the earth, frost burst through the topsoil. Mirron shivered as the freezing energy flowed over her. The water surrounding her crackled.

'Ossie,' snapped Ardu. 'Quick.'

'I'm here,' said Ossacer.

Mirron felt his warmth as though he had thrown a blanket around her shoulders. The water and the earth warmed. Mirron could see Ossacer's effect. A sheath of health covering the trunks, keeping back the cold. Mirron opened an eye. Ossacer was shaking, his hands buried deep in the ground. Breath clouded in the air around him. Moisture condensed from the air, gathering in a mist about his body.

'Ossie,' she said. 'Don't use yourself.'

'Only way,' whispered Ossie. 'Can't draw on your sources and the ground around us is dying.'

He was right. Gorian's riposte was taking the life from the earth. Deep below and rising, snuffing out root and insect, beginning to claw at the shallow-rooted plants.

'Push back,' said Arducius. 'Hold him away.'

Mirron could feel the pressure Gorian was exerting. How he was doing it escaped her. Thousands of dead were marching on them and even with the Gor-Karkulas and her son as amplifiers, he surely couldn't keep this up for long. Too much drawing on his mind.

She could feel the thrumming of feet as the army of the dead approached, dragging their artillery with them. They were closing at a double march, Gorian hoping to be upon them before Arducius was ready. She could see them as an amorphous grey mass against the sky and the trees that filled in behind them. The sickness they wore like armour was a thick mat in the air, shrouding the useful energies, dampening them, denying them to the Ascendants.

'Quickly, Ardu,' said Ossacer.

Mirron refocused on the trunks of Ardu's Work. They were humming with barely suppressed energy, dragging in more and more of her and him, exhausting the water in the barrel. But the circuit was complete. The clouds, a mass of spitting yellow and red energy more like fire than anything else, were billowing across the sky, bringing a premature dimness to the day. Inside them, thunder growled and lightning sheared. They spiralled thousands of feet up, spreading faster almost than the eye could see.

'Nearly there, Ossie. Hold on.'

Mirron hoped he could. Gorian's attack on her brother was fierce and relentless. Like he knew it was Ossacer holding him at bay. The cold was deep and abiding, like the harshest dusas on the highest Karku peak. Ossacer was fighting it with everything he had. He poured health and healing energies into a shield about him. Gorian's construct had changed. Where there had been spears of cold, now it was a solid cloak, pounding at Ossacer, driving the strength from him.

'Ardu,' he gasped and Mirron saw the blue on his lips.

Somewhere in the distance could be heard the thud of catapults. Arducius had to hurry. The dead were on them and the living trapped in the camps behind them were beginning to scream.

'Release!'

Davarov chopped his hand down and his flag and hornsmen relayed the command. Along the line of the walls and from the space behind, a hundred catapults sang. Onagers, ballistae and scorpions. Arms slinging forwards, thudding into stays. Great bows projecting thick bolts or fist-sized stones.

From the onagers, stones smeared in pitch flamed away into the air, trailing smoke and ash. Davarov followed their trajectory out over the plain, crashing down three hundred yards into Atreska and on to the mass of the enemy. It was all he could do not to turn away. Ballistae rounds punched holes in walking dead, picking them up and casting them back into the midst of the march. Onager stones plunged down, battering great rents in the lines, rolling on through body after body, scattering pitch in their wake. The earth was churned to mud as other stones ploughed in short or sailed long, sending up huge divots and spatters, muddying the sky.

The march did not stutter. Flaming corpses lay on the ground. Men with arms and legs torn from their bodies tried to claw and haul themselves on, driven on by the shout in their heads that would not let them rest. The sounds of windlasses cranking filled the air.

Davarov could see a wagon drawn up well out of range. It was surrounded by dead and sat about a hundred yards in front of the Tsardon forces who showed no signs of attacking. Their few pieces of artillery were moving forwards. But while they were not attacking the Conquord yet, they were not attacking the dead either.

'Chancers,' muttered Davarov. 'I knew we couldn't trust you.'

Onagers were primed. Powder flask and stone nets were loaded into ten of them. The ballistae and scorpions sang again. Dead were skewered but rose and came on. Gesternan and Atreskan legionaries with rotting faces, torn clothing, rusting armour and massive wounds pulled themselves to their feet and moved on. Davarov shuddered.

Even at this distance, holes the size of his head could be seen in men's chests and stomachs. Entrails were dragged behind stumbling, sliding bodies.

The powder catapults fired.

Every eye followed the trajectory. Every other action ceased. Davarov held his breath. The dead came on. Three hundred yards and closing. The first of the nets came down towards the rear of the lines. The dead dropped like corn under a mighty scythe. Fragments of stone scattered from the impact zone. Bodies were shredded, torn to pieces, utterly destroyed. Fifty, a hundred, more. It was impossible to tell. A heartbeat later the sound of the detonation. Davarov ducked reflexively. Stone chips rattled on the Jewelled Barrier.

Net after net fell. Only one missed its target. The remaining eight struck home. The battlefield was covered in smoke, ash, flame and dust. Blood smeared the ground. The dead, dismembered, lay scattered. Debris was everywhere over an area of four hundred yards. None walked there bar the odd staggering corpse, injured beyond recognition as a man. One moved though the whole side of his body had been torn away from shoulder to hip.

In the centre of the devastation and spreading out, a keening, haunting wail filled the air. Screams of men aflame. Dead men, knowing their fate at the end. Bodies thrashed on the earth. Parts of men, rendered flesh, had scattered hundreds of yards in every direction.

And yet, to the south towards the Gaws and to the north away towards the lake, still they came. Without fear and without pause. Davarov cursed.

'You cannot break their will,' said Roberto. 'You can only destroy them one by bloody one.'

Davarov nodded.

'Turn the catapults! Track the incoming. Fire at will.'

Dead were walking with bow, ladder and spear in hand. Soon, the former would be within range of the walls. And that could not be allowed to happen.

Kessian sat in the sunshine in a quiet part of the glade. He could feel all of those men under his command. His soldiers. His father's people, that his father had entrusted to him. And he would not let Gorian down, not like he almost had the time before. Then he had panicked, he knew that now. And the things he had wanted his men to do, they hadn't. Many had fallen and some artillery too. Father had been very angry and taken command. He had won that fight.

It was so easy when he had his toys. They always did what he said. Father said it was the same and so this time he was going to make them do just what he wanted and nothing else. Inside his mind, the Work was a bright, beautiful ball of light. It fizzed and jumped and was warm. Thousands of lines trailed away from it, went through the ground and then up into the body of each man. Four thousand, his father had said. Or thereabouts.

'March,' he said.

And they did. It made it easier if he tapped out the time with his hands. They put their feet down to his rhythm. He looked through the eyes of them all. It gave him such a view. Lines and lines of enemy soldiers. Standing and waiting with their shields ahead of them. Their onagers and their ballistae. More toys to knock down.

Kessian would send his men in amongst them. Bring them to his father. Make them see what everyone should see. He smiled. His mother would be so proud of him when she knew.

Kessian's soldiers marched with purpose. His artillery was moving into range. Above, the sky was getting very dark and he could hear the wind building up too. He was close to the enemy now. The Dead Lord in the middle of his men was keeping them in close order but it was Kessian who made them fight. His father said they could do it without the Dead Lords but that they made it easier. Kessian thought they weren't worthy. They should become Gorian's people too.

Ahead, he heard sounds and saw movement. The arms of the artillery rose up. Black marks studded the sky. Others were like balls of fire. They came closer and closer.

'Don't be scared,' he said. 'You'll be all right.'

Stones thundered into the front of his people. Red smeared his vision. Nearby, he thought he could hear his father shouting angrily. But next, all he could feel was pain. Pain through the energy lines. He cried out but there was no one near to help him.

His men juddered where they were but he would not let them stop.

'March on. Enemy ahead. Make the stones stop falling.'

Jhered had wrapped his cloak around Ossacer but the Ascendant was failing quickly. His extremities were blue. He was shaking. There was frost in his hair and eyelashes. But still he clung on, doing whatever it was Arducius asked of him.

For his part, Arducius was lost in a sheen of water. It sluiced around him and Mirron; swirling, jumping and thickening. Above them, the cloud was angry, a dark grey, almost black. Illuminated by the flickering of lightning. Deep within, the bass rumble of thunder was a portent of the violence contained in the Work.

Jhered shuddered. The air felt heavy and still. The wind that had arisen had died away, focused up into the mass of the mighty thunderhead that stretched for miles and miles, reaching out to join with its brother, heading in from the Gaws. The power they were calling upon was something beyond his comprehension. What he did understand was that they had to use it soon. The dead were only a hundred yards away and the artillery had stopped within range.

'Mirron, below the ground,' said Arducius.

'What?'

'Magnetic ores. Deep down, below the dead energies.'

Mirron drew in breath. Jhered frowned.

'Yes,' she said. 'We can make a circuit.'

'What?' asked Ossacer, his voice coming from a place deep within himself, dredging from his fading energies. 'Be quick, Ardu, please, he's going to break me.'

'Just a moment,' said Mirron. She glanced up at Jhered, smiling her thanks at his attempts to help Ossacer. 'Magnetic storm.'

'Ready,' said Arducius.

'Ready,' said Mirron. 'We're aligned.'

Arducius held out his arms and brought them together. The two thunderheads collided. Light flashed within. A massive crack ricocheted across the barrier, the camps and the open ground. A single spear of lightning rattled down from the cloud. It struck a spear tip. The dead carrying the spear was ripped apart, body shredding, spattering blood and filth.

Jhered leapt back a pace. He stared at Arducius. The Ascendant's hands came together briefly.

'Here we go,' he said. 'Brace yourselves.'

Arducius separated his hands. The cloud tore asunder. Rain disgorged, ripping into the earth. And the lightning. Dear God-surround-him, the lightning struck. Like a thousand, ten thousand, spears thrown from the sky it came. Crossing the gap between sky and ground in a heartbeat. Dead were shorn in two. They were detonated, obliterated. Smoke and ash funnelled into the sky. A hissing of rain turned instantly to steam. A thumping sound as of a million feet running on dry ground.

Jhered backed off. He couldn't help it. The violence was like nothing he had ever witnessed. The destruction, the noise. Bodies cast high, high in the sky. Flaming corpses sent skidding away in every direction. Body parts, innards, scorched to nothing in instants. Catapult frames exploded. Burning wood splinters sent high into the sky. And the lightning did not stop. Pounding down, ripping up the ground, driving holes deep into the earth. It sparked from armour, shivered swords and incinerated clothing and flesh.

Away to the second front, the artillery had stopped firing. But it wasn't because they had stopped to stare. It was because there was nothing left to shoot at. Nothing at all.

'It's over,' shouted Jhered. 'Ardu, it's over. Stop for God's sake. Stop!'

Mirron had heard him and laid a hand on Arducius's shoulder. The brittle-boned Ascendant drew his hands back to himself and laid them on his chest. The lightning ceased and the clouds tattered, cleared and dissolved to nothing. The last of the rain fell. The water surrounding him and Mirron dropped to the ground to leak away into the earth.

Jhered looked forwards. Smoke was a barrier across the battlefield. And when it cleared, Jhered swallowed and felt the chill of all he had just witnessed. Not a thing moved. Nothing. The dead had been destroyed. Conquord men and women reduced to ash or scorched beyond any recognition. Gone in heartbeats. All that was left was smoke clinging to the ground and flame where a scrap of clothing or plank of wood still burned.

Ossacer slid to one side and lay on the ground, gasping and shivering, pulling Jhered's cloak to him. Arducius and Mirron were hugging each other. Mirron was crying and Arducius was trying to comfort her. But Jhered could see the shock on his face and the mark of regret in his eyes.

'It had to be done,' he was saying. 'It had to be done.'

And behind them in the refugee camp and away to the legions gathered as witnesses, the cheers of the saved began to swell.

Chapter Sixty-One

859th cycle of God, 12th day of Genasfall

'Get these people away from the docks. Into the west quarter and beyond.'

Tsardon sails crowded the horizon. In amongst them, Ocetanas triremes and Ocenii corsairs were causing mayhem. Fire and smoke billowed into the clear sky. Yet their best would not stop the enemy reaching Estorr's harbour. There were simply too many of them.

Vasselis dragged his horse to a stop in a sea of citizens and soldiers clogging the approaches to the harbour. The movement of artillery was tortuously slow. The provision of ammunition, most of which had been removed by the Armour of God for their siege on the palace, was lacking. The muster of the legions and the Armour was being hampered by a populace desperate to ensure their property was safeguarded and to escape the menace of the dead. Estorr had descended once more into chaos.

'Where is Vennegoor?' demanded Vasselis.

'He left an hour ago, Marshal,' said a centurion within earshot.

He was an old soldier, triarii from the wars ten years ago, now in the militia and hoping for a quiet retirement. No such luck.

'Why?'

'He didn't say, sir.'

'I bet he didn't.' Vasselis cast about him. 'Can we not at least get people moving back into the city, to the forums?'

'We've got people wanting to get to their boats and ships. Traders and merchants looking for the quick way out. Plenty of paying passengers not willing to leave the dockside in case their ride goes without them. And the other thousands you see here? God-surround-me, but I don't know. Chancers, thieves and the curious I expect.'

Vasselis turned his horse to look at the throng. The militia and some of the Armour of God had established a perimeter barring entrance to the harbour side itself but the marshalling yards without were crammed with people. The principal routes to and from the dock were crowded with too many. The noise was unbearable. Shouting jostling and fighting broke out every heartbeat. Orders to evacuate west were being largely ignored.

'The price you pay for following the Order,' he muttered. 'Idiots. Do they still really not believe what is coming at them?'

'Master Stertius was looking for you, Marshal,' said the centurion.

'Him and the rest of Estorr. All right. Who's in charge of the city-side soldiers?'

'Marshal Defender Kastenas is riding between us and the harbour-side defence, Marshal. I'm the voice here, though.'

'Then I'm glad I found you. What's your name, Centurion?'

'Milius, Marshal.'

'Keep your standard close, we'll need you when the enemy land. I can see you're lacking in numbers but we need to get a path through this mob up to the central forum. I've got six onagers coming down from the Hill and I can't get them through. Where is the second legion, Armour of God? Vennegoor promised they would be here.'

Milius sucked his lip. 'Want the opinion of the common soldier?'

Vasselis sighed. 'I'm not going to like it but go on.'

'Heading west, Marshal. Running into the hills because they know they cannot defeat this enemy by faith alone and they are fearful of how the citizens will view them.'

Vasselis nodded. 'You're probably right. Running away into the open spaces they denied their own faithful. Well, let's keep the ones we have here. Let me through. Stertius is at the south fort?'

'Yes, Marshal.'

Milius motioned for the legionaries behind him to make a space. Someone grabbed at Vasselis's ankle. He looked down into the face of a merchant, rich by his clothes and jewellery, who had broken from the press and run across the short space between citizen and legionary.

'I am Olivius Nulius and I demand access to my property which is currently moored just beyond your line of thugs, Marshal Vasselis. You are the de facto ruler of this city. Do something about it.'

'When the Armour of God laid siege to the palace, I begged them to evacuate the city. They would not listen. And where were you, I wonder? Demanding the rightful ruler be allowed to rule or standing in a cheering mob looking to make money out of misfortune? Well, now it's too late. You should have run when you had the chance.

'My line of thugs is here to stop morons like you getting in the way of the defence of this city. There is no escape through the harbour. The Tsardon and their army are right outside. I warn you now, get yourself and your friends away from the dock, the approaches and clear the streets.'

'You are obstructing a citizen going about his lawful business,' said Nulius, gaining the ear of many standing nearby.

Vasselis leaned out of his saddle. 'Nulius, I will say this quietly because I do not wish to humiliate you. I see the fear in your eyes. You know what is coming and you would seek to escape, run like the coward you undoubtedly are, no doubt making a huge profit in the process. I am prepared to sacrifice my life here on this dock today. All you have to do is sacrifice your ship. And that is what you will do. I am protecting the citizens and I am shamed that you are one of them. Now take your hand off my ankle or I will cut it off for you.'

Vasselis spurred his horse and galloped onto the harbour side. Here at least there was organisation and there was control. Scorpions and ballistae lined the wall. Every berth had been filled with ships, two and three deep where possible. And each one of them had been coated in lantern oil, dry straw and anything else easily combustible. Pitch barrels stood by the artillery pieces. Archers and slingers were on station. When the dead landed, there was going to be a fire that would surely reach to the skies and the bed of the ocean. It was the best defence they had.

Vasselis made quick progress to the south fort from which the invasion flags flew alongside the Kester Isle quarantine sheet. A depressing message for any who looked on it. He left his horse with a handler looking after twenty others in the entrance yard of the fort and ran up the wide shallow concrete slope that led to the roof.

Here, the quiet was at odds with the rumble of noise from the marshalling yards and beyond. Vasselis looked back over the city, up the wide streets angling up to the hill and saw his onagers still a long way back. Skittish cavalry horses tried to make a path for the ox-drawn wagons but the press of people moving in every direction was a barricade as solid as rock. One thing the Advocacy loyals couldn't afford was more innocent citizens dying.

The fort was in a state of readiness that gave him some hope. Out here, eight onagers stood. Ballistae sat between them, sighted through the battlements. Below, other artillery positions held more bolt and stone firers. Pitch barrels burned. Crews waited. Flagmen passed signals to and from the north fort across the other side of the harbour.

Vasselis could see Stertius and Kastenas in discussion at the wall overlooking the harbour mouth. He joined them.

'It's madness down there. God-embrace-me but the Order did a great job persuading people there was no dead menace.'

'They're going to find out the hard way that they're wrong,' said Kastenas. 'We don't have enough infantry, artillery or archers in any position apart from right here.'

'Well, that's something, Elise,' said Vasselis.

'Not really, Marshal,' said Stertius, handing him a magnifier. 'The dead have already landed to the south and the north. They'll be at the walls in less than an hour.'

Vasselis looked through the magnifier. Across the city and through a gap between rises in the land, he could see sails and the odd keel high up on the beach.

'But the gates are closed, yes?'

'Of course,' said Elise. 'But the dead are carrying ladders and we have no strength there. The Armour of God have not responded to your orders. Vennegoor is nowhere to be seen and if you can show me an Order minister, any Order minister, I'll swim to the north fort and back in my armour and cloak.'

'I heard as much,' said Vasselis. He handed Stertius back the magnifier. 'Where are they?'

Elise made a gesture that encompassed the whole city. 'At every House of Masks. They aren't running, they're protecting their Readers, Speakers, whoever. I have a report here that says they are going to use their faith to turn back the dead.'

Vasselis took his green-plumed helmet from his head and thought about dashing his forehead against the stone of the crenellations.

'A collective leaving of the senses,' he said. 'Stupid bastards. We *need* their muscle. Doesn't Vennegoor see it? He might be a zealot but he's still a soldier.'

Elise shrugged. 'They're scared. They don't want to face it, is all I can think of to explain it. Those from the Armour who are with us are the few with any guts in either legion. Others have already run from the west gates under the pretext of evacuating the faithful who want to go.'

Vasselis held up his hands.

'All right, let's forget them. For now. What's coming through the harbour mouth?'

Vasselis looked for himself while Stertius replied. He didn't need a magnifier. Fifty, sixty or more Tsardon vessels. They were well ahead of the Ocetanas of whom Vasselis could count only eight with three corsairs in the water. The first enemies were within half a mile of the onagers ranged behind him. Not long now.

'What happened to them all?' he asked.

'Remember what Arducius said?' said Elise. 'The dead only need to get one or two sailors on a Conquord ship and if Gorian is reanimating, it could cost dearly.'

'Iliev?'

'He's still out there,' said Stertius. 'The *Ocetarus* is sailing and squad seven is on the water. Kashilli is an unmissable figure.'

'Who?'

'Trierarch of Iliev's corsair,' said Stertius. 'We could use him on shore. Fearless and brutal.'

'Could do with ten thousand of him,' said Vasselis.

From the north fort, a signal was being flagged. And way beyond the din in the yards below, the unmistakable sound of a catapult firing. Its dull thud carried across rooftop and water. The effect was instantaneous. A quiet began to descend on the city. The thud was repeated again and again.

Reality at last, coupled with the first shouts of panic and alarm.

'Let's hope your explosive powder works like you say it does,' said Elise.

The report of a detonation sounded across the city. An alien crack that turned every head, quietening the crowd. Vasselis smiled ruefully.

'A successful test, I'd say. Time to act. Time to pray.'

Davarov had had to shout at artillery crews to keep firing, keep looking ahead into Atreska though it was hard enough to keep himself focused. Roberto and the Karku man, Harban standing with him on the gate fort had long since abandoned looking at the enemy attacking the walls and were gazing back behind them into Neratharn.

The sky had darkened and there had been extraordinary noise like the falling of a mountain. Light had seared across the field behind him and he, like every man and woman on the walls, had turned to look, shudder and give thanks they were not beneath the onslaught out beyond the refugee camp.

East across the walls, the dead were still coming. For every fifty obliterated by stone or the powder that Davarov was still using, if sparingly, another hundred made it that much closer. Bowmen were in range and firing, so far without success. But it was the ladders that concerned him. Just a few dead on the walls and the ripple could spread like disease.

Still the Tsardon had not moved into the attack. Their artillery was stationary and out of range.

'Wait on, you bastards,' said Davarov. 'You, I can take at my leisure.'

Confidence was growing in the defence. The sky behind him cleared abruptly and the sun poured on to the camps and open grounds behind the barrier. Davarov turned at the sound of cheering, swelling in volume and carrying all the way to the walls from the western lines some three miles away. Tens of thousands of voices, most of whom could not have seen what happened on the ground but knew victory when they heard it.

'I don't believe it,' he said.

'Believe it,' said Roberto. 'You know what they're capable of.'

Davarov smiled and enveloped Roberto in a huge bear hug. 'Don't you know what this means? We're going to win. This lot will never get over our walls now. The momentum is with us. It's all but over.'

But Roberto didn't smile or return his embrace. Davarov let him go and stood back.

'What is it, Roberto?'

'Until every dead is returned to the earth. Until Gorian's head is on a platter in front of me, it is not over.'

Cheering had begun to spread along the walls too. Davarov turned to deliver a rebuke that would drown out all their voices but instead he felt more like joining in. The dead weren't advancing any more. And while artillery rounds still fell amongst them they merely stood as if waiting for the inevitable.

'We've done it,' said Davarov, feeling relief flood him. 'We've surely done it, Roberto, look.'

And Roberto did. Only he shook his head.

'Keep firing. Something's not right. I can feel it.'

Davarov's mood deserted him. If there was one thing he'd learned in all his years' service to Roberto Del Aglios, it was that when he had one of those feelings, it was time to worry.

Gorian felt them go, all of them. One by one and then in torrents. Each one left a gossamer thread to trail like a loose nerve ending. They flailed and shrivelled and the pain worsened until it was like ten thousand needle points deep in his heart and mind.

He screamed long and loud. The dead surrounding him and the Gor-Karkulas shuddered where they stood or sat. His agony fed through every energy line he controlled. He felt as if he was on fire. His eyes ached so hard he wanted to expel them from his body. His heart pounded, rattling his ribs. His legs lost all of their strength and he staggered against the side of the wagon. He put his hands to his head and screamed again.

Ahead of Gorian, it was over. His people. Those who loved and trusted him, whom he had brought to him. All were gone. Snatched from him by Them. He had tried to thwart them but he could not combat all three at once. Another swathe of pain washed over him and he gasped and clutched at his stomach. He dropped to his knees, exhaustion sweeping over him.

'Kessian!' he called, his mouth full of blood. He spat it out. His insides were wrecked. He had invested too much. 'Kessian.'

Across the wall, his people awaited his next command. South on the beaches and docks of Estorr, they moved without him for now but the Karkulas would not be able to hold the Work indefinitely without his input. He had to find strength and stamina from somewhere.

'Kessian.'

Nothing more than a half-growl this time. Gorian coughed up and spat another clot of blood from his throat. He picked up his head. He could hear the shouts and cheers on the wind. It enraged him, brought sharpness to his mind. He gripped the side of the wagon and hauled himself to his feet.

'Father? Father!' Kessian ran to him, wrapped arms around him and tried to hold him up. 'What happened? Where did all the soldiers go? It hurt, Father. You're hurt.'

'But it fades. We must avenge our people.'

'But we have no one,' said Kessian. 'Only these few. The Dead Lords are gone too.'

'We have me and you,' said Gorian. 'And that will be enough.'

'What will we do?'

'We will make the land fit for my people and they shall see it and they shall love it as they love me. Stand in front of me.'

Gorian looked at the Gor-Karkulas, both of whom were eyeing him with that mixture of hatred and disdain that he had come to loathe.

'I don't need you any more,' he said. 'You may go.'

The few remaining dead parted from the wagon. Gorian didn't wait to see if the Karkulas went or not. It hardly mattered. He placed both his hands on Kessian's head. He focused all of his hate, his malice and his jealousy on the land that surrounded him. He poured in all of the wrongs that had been committed against him. And with it the will to rule, to succeed where the others would always fail. Everything that had been denied him reared up in his mind and he fed it down.

Grass grew into twisted dark stalks, spiralling up their bodies. He felt the shoots pierce his body but the blood would not flow. Not this time. The energy he drew from himself, Kessian and the land he fed down the shoots. More and more thickened and joined themselves to him. And with this purity of circuit, with no waste of energy whatever, he drove the Work that would make them all realise who he was.

'I am become the earth,' he said and his voice was like the rumble of lava beneath a sleeping volcano. 'I am become the earth and the earth shall be mine.'

'Keep back, give them room,' shouted Jhered.

Refugees and soldiers were pouring towards the Ascendants all lying prone on the ground, tired but not spent, wrinkled but not aged. Yet saddened, all three of them. Jhered knew how they felt, Mirron was sure. He stood protectively over them. Mirron was watching him alternately looking down and then away to wave his arms.

'Give them space. God-surround-me, they need to rest and breathe,' he said, his voice almost drowned by the roar of noise and the drumming of thousands of feet on the packed earth.

Mirron clutched at Arducius and the two of them moved to Ossacer, feeding warmth into him.

'I felt him,' stammered Ossacer. 'He was all over me, inside me. It was like darkness and plague. So much bile and hatred. We must get him. Before he regains his strength.'

'We have taken his strength from him,' said Mirron. 'Feel the earth. Feel it relax.'

Ossacer was shaking his head where he lay. He was still shivering, Jhered's cloak about him. Out on the field, charred skeletons collapsed into ember and dust, the heat still belching up into the air.

'Where is he?' asked Jhered. He had persuaded the crowds to back off and in truth, it appeared their desire to hug their saviours began to dissipate the nearer they came. 'We cannot let him get away or this will happen again.'

'He's out there,' said Arducius, moving to a sitting position and brushing wet hair from his face. 'Not far. A mile, maybe two.'

'I'll have riders and scouts sent out,' said Jhered. 'We'll find him and then you can deal with him.'

'It won't be that easy,' said Ossacer. 'It's never that easy with Gorian.'

Mirron turned her head to the west. Gorian was there somewhere. And her son. He had to be. Lost and alone, thoughts filled with the words of his father no doubt. Evil words designed to turn his head.

'Where are you, Kessian,' she whispered. 'Please be safe.'

Arms were about her shoulders. Arducius and Ossacer were with her.

'He'll be all right,' said Arducius. 'He – unh!'

Arducius leapt up as if he'd been burned, shaking the hand that had been resting on the ground.

'Ardu?' said Mirron.

But the answer was there in every fibre of her being. A rolling, vast sickness in the ground far beneath her. It flipped her stomach, bringing vomit into her throat. Beside her, Ossacer turned his head and threw up. Arducius was clutching his temples, his face drawn in pain. Fog threatened to obscure Mirron's every cogent thought.

'Oh dear God-surround-us,' she managed.

'Mirron?' Jhered's voice cut through to her.

'Something happening,' she said. 'Something growing.'

Mirron fought her nausea, fought the sounds of strangled agony coming from Arducius and the constant retching of Ossacer. Both had expended so much more than her during the Work. She sought down to the sickness where it lurked like an animal waiting to pounce. And beyond it, to the strong lines of energy that fed it, no, that were feeding something else. Mirron knew her heart was beating hard. Gorian might sense her, be able to attack her like he had Ossacer.

There was nothing, though. No ripples in the energies that surrounded whatever Gorian was doing. He had created the sickness deep down while the earth above remained healthy and slow. And having done so, he was using the sickness to drive his central Work. Gorian didn't know she was probing his use of the energies. Or he didn't react if he did. She was able to follow the structure of the Work. Back. Back into the open land where the grass and the trees grew. Back to . . .

Mirron opened her eyes, unable to put into words what she had just seen. There was something she could say, though.

'Run,' she said.

'What?' asked Jhered.

Mirron flew to her feet and tried to drag Ossacer up with her.

'Run!'

Chapter Sixty-Two

859th cycle of God, 12th day of Genasfall

'What are we running from?' Jhered shouted at Mirron.

He didn't think she would reply. Her face was blank and white. But whatever she had seen in the energy trails below the earth, it had frightened her beyond her wits.

'Mirron. Stop, stop.'

They were creating pandemonium among the refugees who were still clustered about them. Arducius and Ossacer were both dragging some way behind, neither sure what was happening, both trying to determine the source and scale of the threat. Ordinary people had begun to bunch and run back towards the Jewelled Barrier, or head north or south to get to their tents, their families or just away from they knew not what.

Jhered caught one of Mirron's arms and made her stop and face him. He grabbed both her shoulders.

'Mirron!'

She jerked and stared at him. Her whole body was shaking. There was a froth on her lips and in her eyes, such fear that it all but took the heart of him.

'Mirron!'

'He has poisoned the earth,' she said. 'It is coming. Through the air and across the land. We have to run.'

'Run where?'

She shook her head and a single tear fell. 'I don't think it really matters.'

Jhered turned towards the open ground west. He heard a rumbling in the distance. It was low and it sent a vibration through the ground beneath his feet, soft at first but growing in intensity by the heartbeat. Mirron wanted to break away to run again but he held her firm.

'Then it's too late to run. You must think of something. You and Ossacer and Arducius. You must.'

'You don't understand,' said Mirron, voice quavering. 'It's too big. It will swallow him. And it will swallow us.'

The rumble was audible to everyone. Refugee and soldier alike turned to the west. There was nothing to see for a moment, bar a shimmering in the air like a heat haze on the horizon. No one moved for a time. It could be an army approaching but no intelligence suggested any other enemy forces within a thousand miles. The mood was still one of victory but Mirron's move to run had dropped confusion into the midst. It was a dangerous state. Fifty thousand refugees. If they ran, there was nowhere really to go.

Jhered blinked. He thought he'd seen the land ripple on a front as far as his eye could pick up in either direction. Mirron's fear loomed in his memory but still he didn't want to believe. A judder rattled through the ground under his feet and people began to shout. There was another, violent this time. Jhered staggered. Ossacer fell. Like several thousand in the mass of refugees. People were screaming now and some had turned to run.

Jhered was still holding Mirron's hands. She squeezed them and he looked down at her.

'I'm sorry,' she said. 'It wasn't enough.'

'Never be sorry for doing everything you possibly could.'

Another shudder through the earth. Cracks appeared in the top soil. The vibration went on and on. Jhered dropped into a crouch while the earth spat dust at him, cracks widened enough to put his fist in. The refugees' belief collapsed. They ran but it was immediately clear that Mirron was right. There was nowhere to go that they would make in time.

The horizon rippled again and then it was coming at them, faster than a galloping horse. The hand of God had shoved the earth. A wave thundered towards the camps, the buildings, the Jewelled Barrier and everyone who stood on, in or around them. It raced north and south too, disappearing quickly out of sight but for its trail of destruction.

In front of the wave, the earth trembled before exploding up ten, fifteen feet and more. Trees tumbled aside, rocks were hurled into the air, plants scattered and dust and debris spewed ahead. Jhered just stood and stared. The Ascendants were around him, talking, shouting over the din.

A breeze kicked up ahead of the earth front and upon it came the sick stench of disease. Steam was rising behind the wave, a dense mist coiling and deepening. The first animals began to run past Jhered's legs. Rats, mice, rabbits, all tearing to nowhere. Birds were in the sky, scattering to every point of the compass.

The series of quakes under their feet continued unabated. Jhered was knocked to the ground by the latest. He tumbled to his left, rolled and came back to his haunches. The sound of the approaching wave was like a scream of vengeance atop the roar of ten thousand gorthock scenting prey.

Jhered's heart hammered in his chest. There was no escaping this. The foul reek was causing his eyes to run. Dust was clouding in the air and washing over them. He could see vegetation turned to sludge and pulp as the wave passed, sucking everything into its body and casting it behind, rotten and long dead.

Gorian was killing everything. Jhered could only feel sad. A boy with such potential but fatally flawed. And he had rewarded mercy with hatred. He had become everything that those who despised the Ascendancy had feared. A monster capable of destruction on a scale no man should control.

But this was not control. This was surely the act of a man beyond reason.

The wave was almost on them. Only fifty yards away. They were alone. An oasis of humanity, deserted by everyone who had thought to thank them so recently. Bedlam behind as refugees and the legions tried to escape was matched by the unnatural roaring drone and scream of the approaching earth wave. Booms were thudding beneath their feet, rocks snapped by the force of the Work and shoved upwards, breaking the surface of the earth, spearing up like new sentinels, fingers up to the sky.

Jhered pulled himself up. Standing to accept what was about to engulf him. The steam, mist and dust were choking him. He would not fall. Defiant in death as he was in life. His final prayer was that the Ascendants lived to fight the enemy. The one enemy not merely the Conquord but the entire world was facing. Gorian Westfallen. Jhered commended his body to the embrace of the Omniscient.

The wave towered above him, blotting out the light. He was hurled from his feet, rolled in darkness. Tossed like a model ship in a hurricane, like being batted from hand to hand by God. He would have cried out but he dare not breathe. Somewhere, a warmth stretched out its welcoming embrace.

Jhered breasted the top of the wave and was dumped in a seething rotting mass behind it. He rolled over and over, his body coated with rotting sludge. It got into his mouth, up his nose and filled his ears. Only when he stopped moving did he dare to open his eyes and wonder how it was he remained alive. There could only be one reason.

He pulled himself from the cloying filth, shook his head, spat out nauseating mulch and ejected mud from his nostrils. The wave was rumbling on, heading undimmed towards the barrier, dampening the screams of the helpless about to be engulfed.

Jhered looked around. Everywhere behind the wave was devastated, returned to swamp and decay. He staggered a few paces back towards the wall. His head was pounding, a sledgehammer at the back of his skull. He swallowed, coughed and vomited. He wiped at the dirt over his face, clearing his eyes.

There. It had to be them. He began to run. A shambling, stumbling run. Rot sucked at his boots with every pace.

'Mirron,' he gargled. He coughed and spat again. 'Arducius.'

They were lying together in a still embrace. Barely recognisable for the slime coating them. Brown, green and steaming grime. One or other of them moved. Picked up a head and looked to the left. Jhered followed the gaze. Kneeling up, arms outstretched, was Ossacer. He was swaying, covered like all of them but his eyes were open, staring sightlessly towards them.

Mirron scrambled to her feet, helping Arducius up. He had to hang from her and when she moved towards Ossacer he dragged a leg and cried out. Jhered renewed his efforts, running harder the last few paces to Ardu and Mirron. He grabbed Arducius's free arm and heaved it around his neck, taking the weight from his broken leg.

'Ossie?' shouted Mirron. Ossacer did not respond. 'Ossie! Hang on. Please hang on.'

Questions were tumbling through Jhered's mind. The wave had struck the camps. Tents tumbled, shredded and rotted. The massed screams of the terrified were cut off as the wave crashed through them. Jhered had to look away. So much humanity swept up, taken in and massacred. Rolled over, turned to corpses in moments. He shivered, a sick feeling beginning to rise.

Mirron and Arducius still called out Ossacer's name. Jhered knew he had saved them all but would never understand how. The Pain Teller to end all Pain Tellers. Protecting them from the rot, the disease and death. The three of them scrabbled over to Ossacer, four living people in this blasted land.

Mirron and Arducius sank down by Ossacer. He sensed them somehow and fell gently sideways into Mirron's arms.

'I saved you,' he said. 'I did it.'

Jhered could see his skin was terribly weathered and cracked. His hair had grown a foot and a half and was straggling and grey-white. His face was that of a man Andreas Koll's age and his fingers, his limbs, were no more than skin and bone. He clawed at Mirron's sleeve with long-nailed hands. He was fighting for breath.

'Oh, Ossie, what did you do?' she whispered, smoothing his hair, holding him close.

Arducius was kneeling by him, hands on him, probing at the life forces within.

'Don't,' said Ossacer, opening his eyes. They were dull, grey hued with tiny sparks of blue at their centres around pin hole pupils. 'Nothing else to use. Nothing else was alive. Only had myself.'

Ossacer coughed and his whole body seemed to rattle with the force of it.

'We can fix you,' said Arducius. 'We can fix anything. Just don't let go.'

'No. You can't.' Ossacer wheezed a breath. Jhered bit his lip. 'Need all your energy for Gorian. You have to stop him.'

A colossal impact reverberated across the ruined plains. Multiple cracking and rumbling echoes rolled over them. And above the tumult of falling rock, the sound of a thousand voices, raised in helpless prayer to the Omniscient who had turned His back this day. Jhered snapped a glance away east. He could see nothing but dust, steam and mist. So many friends. So many fine people.

'What was that?' asked Arducius.

'The wall,' said Jhered. The tightness of his throat denied anything but a hoarse whisper. 'Best assume it's just us against him now. Ossacer's right. We can't afford to lose this one or that wave might just go on forever.'

'I'm not leaving Ossacer here,' said Mirron. 'We can't.'

'I have no intention of doing anything of the kind,' said Jhered. 'I'll carry him. You support Arducius. And Mirron, Ardu. Do whatever you can to sense Gorian. We're already out of time. We've already lost too many.'

Mirron helped Arducius up. Arducius gasped at the pain from his leg. He was white with it and a sheen of sweat stood out from his filthy brow. Jhered knelt, scooped Ossacer into his arms and stood.

'You didn't get any lighter, did you?' he said.

Ossacer said nothing. His breathing was ragged and his head lolled against Jhered's shoulder. He turned to head west, not really knowing precisely where to go. From their backs came a sucking sound. Like the ocean dragging over sand and shells but intensified, slow and malevolent. Like the first breath of evil.

Jhered turned with his burden and looked back over the landscape. The sludge stretched as far as he could see. Distantly, the wave front still travelled outwards, the plume of steam its crest. And nearer, at the edge of the camps, movement. Jhered swallowed and took a pace back.

'Oh no.'

Hands reached to the sky. Heads rose from the slime. Bodies, dripping with filth hauled themselves upright to stand on unsteady legs. Refugees, soldiers. And larger shapes too a little more distant. Horses. Up they came. Thousands. Tens of thousands. And as one, they turned and began to walk west. Their shambling march, the uncoordinated movement of arm and leg. The hanging of a head to one side or other. All of it told Jhered everything he had to know and feared to see.

He turned and began to walk quickly over the slippery terrain.

'Ardu, Mirron. Let's walk. And don't look back.'

'Why not?' said Ardu, looking.

Jhered had to slow immediately. Arducius could barely put one foot in front of the other.

'Because the dead are coming. All of them.'

Cheers died in throats. Men whose spears and swords had punched upwards into the air in celebration let them drop to hang limp at their sides. The dead outside the walls had not moved but the songs of victory from the camps and beyond had ceased. A rumbling had filled the air. The foundations of the barrier had shaken very slightly and the screaming had begun.

Roberto ran to the back of the gate fort and looked through one of the mounted magnifiers positioned there. He moved it up to the horizon and then slowly back down, scanning left and right in a gentle sweep. What he saw chilled him to his bones despite the warm genastro sun. People running. A stampede of humanity with all sense of control and discipline gone. Legionaries pushed aside slower citizens. Refugees clambered over any who fell. All had forgotten anything but the primal urge for self-preservation. Faces were contorted. People screaming as they ran, dragging in fresh breath and screaming again. He saw a man tumble and be submerged beneath a tide of others too terrified to stoop and help him.

Man descended to animal. And Roberto could not find it in his heart to blame a single one of them. For behind them the earth had risen and was charging at them. From horizon to horizon it spread. It would crash against the roots of the Gaws. It would thunder through the foothills and into Lake Iyre. And it would drive straight through every single living thing between it and the Jewelled Barrier.

'Not again, God-surround-me, not again.' Roberto dropped to his knees, placed one hand on the stone and the other fingers spread pointed to the sky. 'Dear God the Omniscient, saviour and loved of all your faithful. Deliver us from this fate. Show us a path to victory that may keep your earth safe for your children.'

A shockwave ran through the fort. Soldiers stumbled. Everything shook. Onagers juddered across the roof. Loose stones rolled. Roberto stood again. The earth wave, higher than two men, eclipsed the western horizon. Clouds and dirt clogged the sky above it. It crashed through man and beast, unstoppable. Roberto turned and ran back to where Davarov and Harban were clinging to battlements while the shudder subsided.

'Hang on to anything you can,' he shouted. 'Whatever happens, do not let go. Don't fall to the ground when this things hits us. Down there is death. Up here we might just live.'

'It is as the prophecy foretold,' said Harban. 'He will shiver the mountains and topple the world. Him and his spawn.'

'That may be but right now, we have to survive what's coming at us,' said Roberto. 'Pass the word to any who have time and the will to hear it. If you want to live, cling on to the rock.'

They didn't have to shout people to the walls. A flood tide of soldiers and civilians was already racing up the concrete slopes. Flagmen were waving the command to get to the walls anyway. Davarov, his bellow managing to carry over the din of panic, was roaring people up. He barked at anyone within earshot to attach themselves any way they could to the barrier. Torch brackets, rope around crenellations, human chains. Anything.

Roberto cast around for a place to secure himself. Bound in a net and held fast against the forward battlements were two crates. He raised his eyebrows and ran for them. Another tremor shook the fort. He pitched forwards. On the roof behind him, onager stones rolled. Engineers dived and leapt the ambling projectiles. Pitch barrels fell, spilling flame and heat across the concrete and stone. He heard screaming, cut off abruptly. The net and its contents had not shifted. It would have to do.

Roberto clawed his way towards them, grabbed the net and fumbled at his sword belt with the other hand. The tremor subsided. Roberto passed the belt through the net, its half inch rope strong and fresh, and refastened it such that his back was to the crates. He looked left. Davarov, his huge arms wrapped around a bolted torch bracket, a rope from his waist to the metal as well, could still smile.

'Hey Roberto!' he called. 'What a way to go. A wall of earth is coming and you attach yourself to the most explosive compound in the Conquord.'

Something broke in Roberto then. The well of his grief ran dry for a moment and every trial, everything that was to come, diminished. Just for a few heartbeats. He howled with laughter and patted the crates. He had to shout over the roaring rumble of the wave and the juddering of the fort and wall that grated stone against stone.

'Hey Davarov! See you on the other side. And you know what? If we survive, these little beauties might just come in handy.'

From his position, Roberto could see over the open left-hand side of the fort and down into the compound. His laughter cramped in his throat and he prayed for the cycles of all those about to die. Down on the ground, the seething mass of humanity had stalled. Below him the great gates were closed and he could hear futile pounding on the timbers. Too many people crammed into the space to allow them to open inwards as they must. It would have been pointless anyway. The wave would surely catch them and the fort needed the strength of the closed portals if it was to have a better chance of standing after the wave had passed.

People were still moving up the slopes. Heaving masses, slowed almost to a standstill. Hands grasped as feet stumbled. Men and women fell from the sides on to the heads of those pinned to the walls themselves with no hope of climbing to questionable safety.

The roof of the fort began to fill. Legionaries taking the lead of their engineers and clinging on to whatever they could find. Camaraderie blossomed. The raw recruit and the triarii veteran beckoned each other into embrace. Armour and belt straps were held in death grips. More and more spilled onto the roof. And through the mess of limbs and bodies, people crowding into Roberto's left and right, hanging like him on to the net, he saw one familiar face.

'Julius!' Miraculously, the Speaker heard him and turned. His jaw dropped and he shouldered his way to Roberto. 'Get yourself in here, you bastard. Hang on tight.'

'Surprised you want me to live through this.'

'Like I said before, we all need to live. Even fucking idiots like you.'

Barias grinned briefly and wrapped his arms through the net. Plenty of people were on it. Roberto hoped it would be strong enough to hold them all.

Screams intensified from below. The juddering of the fort made seeing anything difficult but it couldn't obscure the sight of the wave washing through the administration buildings and overwhelming every man and woman who had crowded in, on or around it. The surge of noise sent a shooting pain into his head. The rumble of the wave became a roar. The steam and dust buffeted up and over the back wall of the fort. It swallowed them up in its choking stench.

The earth wave struck the Jewelled Barrier.

Roberto was aware that he and everyone around him was calling, screaming and shouting. Oaths and prayers or just emptying the lungs. The world shook and shuddered, turned on its side and back again. Leapt high and fell. Roberto tried to look but all he got were jumbled images. They were enough.

People falling, hurled like dolls against wall, man and onager. The onagers themselves, slithering sideways and crushing screaming engineers against battlements that crumbled and threatened to fall. Other engines tipped sideways, sliding and crashing to the ground. Onager stones rumbled across the roof. Pitch spewed everywhere. The wheel of an artillery frame attached to shattered timbers flew across the fort, smashing into people scant inches from Roberto, dashing skulls to fragments, smearing bodies.

A great rending crack ricocheted through the stone beneath him. A dozen others followed it. The fort lurched. Roberto's body was shaking so hard he had to close his eyes for a moment. He heard stone tumbling in torrents. The flat crack of snapping timbers reached him. He opened his eyes.

A rent pulled wide open right along the centre of the fort, passing directly under him. Soldiers, pulled free of their moorings, slid across the fort and followed pitch fire, artillery fragments and projectiles, tumbling to the ground below. The whole right side of the fort sagged outwards over the barrier wall running north to the Lake Iyre. Roberto half slid over the rent but the rope of the net held him, legs dangling over the carnage below.

Bodies covered in stone. Filth spreading from the wave. It passed directly beneath him, a shivering, rumbling unnatural ripple of death and destruction. It burst through the great gates. Battlements crumbled, sheared and fell. Sections of the wall surged up to the sky, thumped back down and toppled outwards into Atreska. People by the hundred were tossed aside, falling back onto concrete or into the fetid rot below.

Of the people who had gripped the net, only four remained. Julius was one of them. He was hanging by his hands over the shattered fort, the whole right side of which was rubble and spears of timber. The rest of it, gone to crush those on the wall beneath it. Blood smeared every surface.

'Hang on, Julius,' said Roberto.

'I will this time, Ambassador.'

'You do that.'

Cracks and rumbles echoed north and south. Sections of the Jewelled Barrier collapsed on themselves, fell in and out. Dust clouds carried on a stinking breeze clogged Roberto's eyes and mouth. He coughed, hawked phlegm from his throat and spat. Stones and shards of rock tumbled and pattered. The noise began to subside. The wave rumbled out into Atreska. And above it, the screams of the wounded and dying, the cries of the terrified and the prayers of Julius Barias.

Roberto glanced to his left. This side of the fort had remained intact though skewed at an angle down and back into the compound where nothing remained but sludge covering the bodies of the thousand upon thousand slaughtered there. Legionaries and engineers still covered the battlements, laughing and crying in relief if they had the wit to make any sound at all.

And Davarov. Davarov was still there. The torch bracket hung by one bolt but he was still there and through the dust covering his deeply tanned face, Roberto could see a grim smile. He couldn't see Harban for the moment. The Karku was too smart a mountaineer to have fallen, though.

Roberto fumbled for the belt buckle, loosened it and pulled himself to his feet. He knelt and grasped one of Barias's arms. Julius turned towards him and with a nod, Roberto hauled him up. Julius clawed and pulled with his free hand until he was once again on the stone, dragging in huge breaths.

'Thank you, Ambassador.'

'The pleasure is all mine,' said Roberto.

He stood and looked out into Atreska. The wave carried on. It swept through the dead standing there, felling them all and engulfing the wagon of the Gor-Karkulas. Roberto frowned. Beyond them, the Tsardon, as if they had been waiting, roared and charged. Roberto wiped at his face, too weary to be scared.

'Bastards,' muttered Davarov now beside him. 'I told you we couldn't trust them.'

'I don't think it matters all that much, Davarov,' said Roberto and he pointed out into the plains, ruined more and more with every passing heartbeat. 'The wave isn't stopping.'

Davarov grunted and pointed down at the ground close to the ruined walls where hundreds of Conquord citizens had been hurled.

'No. And the dead aren't staying dead, either.'

Chapter Sixty-Three
859th cycle of God, 12th day of Genasfall

The dead were flooding into the harbour. The dual fort artillery thudded and sounded. Flaming onager stones, ballista stones and scorpion shafts poured onto the fleet, sixty and more strong crowding the harbour mouth. The fire was withering. Ships were driven into their neighbours by the force of onager strikes. Timbers holed and shattered. Masts were splintered. Sails fell into the water, acting as drag anchors, pulling ships off course. Tsardon and dead were dragged to the bosom of Ocetarus in their hundreds.

Yet still enough got through the bombardment. Inside, the harbour was a wall of flame and smoke. Heat radiated out beyond the walls and into the ocean. Iliev was at the tiller of Ocenii squad seven's corsair. Kashilli rode the spike low. His oarsmen made almost forty stroke. They'd been doing it much of the day.

Out to sea, the Conquord triremes battered at the laggards of the Tsardon fleet. Half a dozen enemy ships were burning, sinking fast. Three squads were in the water wreaking havoc among the stragglers. Others had chased north and south to combat the dead landing on the beaches and heading for the city walls.

Iliev turned them away from the harbour mouth and made for the blank sea-facing wall of the south fort. Atop it, he could see engineers and harbour guards working furiously to prime catapults. Smoke from the barrels of pitch that would be burning low by now, obscured much of its roof.

'Easing back, twenty stroke. Heading into fort shadow and calm water. Time to climb, marines.'

At sight of the approaching corsair, rope ladders were flung from the roof. Escape ladders on another day. They fell to just a couple of feet from the gentle swell. Iliev brought the corsair in spike first.

Kashilli ran out along it, grabbed the nearest ladder and hauled, balancing his weight to swing the corsair in. Oarsmen raised and stowed their blades.

'Let's be having you,' said Kashilli. 'I'm not holding onto this thing purely for my health.'

Squad seven attacked the climb, moving up hand over hand, swift dark marks against the bright white-painted stone of the fortress. Iliev watched them go. Not a one of them had fallen since Kester Isle. Not a one had been victim of Bitter's Plague.

'Let's remember our brothers less fortunate,' he called up. 'Every dead we drop is tiny recompense. There's a lot of dead to go before we achieve balance in the eyes of Ocetarus.'

Iliev and Kashilli took the ladders last. Kashilli had tied off the corsair and had his sledgehammer rammed in his belt at the back. The shaft bounced off his legs with every move up.

'Don't much care for dry land, skipper,' he said. 'But where the enemy go ...'

'The Ocenii follow. And we make our own sea of bad blood.'

Kashilli smiled at him. It was an old Ocenii saying, and it was a long time since it had been made reality.

Breasting the crenellations, Iliev could feel the heat of the burning docks hit him like a heavy slap in the face. He blew out his cheeks and dropped to the roof. Every man came to attention and he waved them away.

'You have better things to do. Carry on.'

Iliev and Kashilli strode to the harbour-side wall to join Master Stertius and Marshal Vasselis. They looked over the side. Iliev barely recognised the scene as Estorr's docks. He caught Kashilli's expression and raised his eyebrows.

'Admiral Iliev,' said Vasselis. 'Well met, even if the manner of your arrival was a little, unorthodox.'

'We'd have rowed in the front door but I see you have it barred against the odd intruder,' said Iliev.

A dense cloud of black smoke and ash was building in the sky overhead, fed by the flames of what had to be two hundred and more ships moored sometimes three deep along the dockside. They made an impenetrable barrier which the dead would not cross. But the fires would soon begin to burn out as ships' hulls were breached and sank.

The Tsardon ships already inside the harbour were standing off the dockside, waiting. Living Tsardon sailors were trying to douse some of the blazes as best they could but the dead just waited. And all the while, scorpions and ballistae were knocking them down, holing their craft. Target practice. The dead, though, unless broken in the lower back or with legs pulped, simply got up again and retook their places.

Forty enemy ships were there as time fled away to the moment when they could assault the shore. Tsardon not engaged in fire duties were arcing arrows over the burning defence. Men were getting injured. Some would be getting killed. Iliev chewed his lip, knowing it was just a matter of time before they would rise once more.

The catapults on the forts sang again. Stones and bolts flew out into the harbour mouth. A Tsardon trireme was struck amidships, just above the second oar rank. The flaming onager stone smashed through timber and man. Oars jerked up or were splintered, shivered in their blocks. The whole ship moved sideways. A gout of water spewed from the hole; the stone had pierced the hull. Smoke and flame could be seen within.

Before long, whoever could make it past the forts would have done so and Stertius would have to reposition his artillery. This phase of the fight for Estorr was almost at an end. The next was soon to begin. Kashilli hefted his sledgehammer in his hand. It was a gesture full of meaning but if any missed it, the growl in his throat was confirmation enough. Iliev nodded.

'The docks are full of infantry but will they stand?' he said. 'They do not have the right weapons to combat the dead.'

'There is nowhere for them to run,' said Stertius. 'The dead are at the walls north and south. They have ladders and they have no fear. But we should be able to hold them there. If the city is not to be overrun we have to.'

'Braver men than either of us have quailed before the walking dead,' said Iliev. 'Reason alone will not keep them standing. We have had some success. I will lead the ground defence.'

Vasselis whistled in a breath. 'Your place is here, Admiral. Directing battle. We need your experience.'

Iliev shook his head. 'I am Ocenii. Experience is nothing today. Courage is everything. That and Kashilli's hammer.'

'Then may the Omniscient smile upon you. For he surely turned from us the moment the first fire was lit and the first innocent dead was reduced to ashes.'

'I don't care if your God smiles upon me or not. And you have done what you had to do to save your city. Any true God will praise you, not damn you for that.' Iliev turned to Stertius. 'Bring your artillery round now. Take down as many as you can. Fire is vital. They will walk the harbour bed to the steps unless they are no more than flames on the deck.'

'Yes, Admiral.'

'Kashilli? Let's have seven with us. We have work to do.'

'Skipper,' acknowledged Kashilli. 'Squad seven! Rest time is over. To the gangway. Double time. Axes and hammers, you bastards, axes and hammers.'

Iliev saw the look in Vasselis's eyes. 'Join us, Marshal. You have skill with the blade. I used to watch you at the Games.'

'My days in the arena are long past as, I fear, is my speed and my eye.'

'So be it. But it is the only place to be. Out there, where the blood runs and the enemy fall at your feet.'

'Ocetarus will keep you, Karl Iliev. And you'll find Elise and Marcus down there somewhere. I think both share your opinion.'

Iliev nodded and the need to feel dead bone crush beneath his hammer surged through him.

'The Advocate chooses her advisers well.'

'She did,' said Vasselis and he looked away, down to the ground. 'You do not know that she is dead, do you?'

Iliev started. 'What?'

'Many are the deeds that will be retold,' said Vasselis. 'Dedicate yours to her memory. Win this for her, Karl. And when it is over, find me and I will tell you what really happened. Anything you hear on the streets is a falsehood.'

'I will not let this City fall to the dead,' said Iliev.

'Then the Advocate's death will not have been in vain.'

Hesther was in the Chancellery with the tenth-strand survivors. Yola, Mina and Petrevius. The youngsters of the eleventh and the little ones of the twelfth strand were already in the safe room in the cellar. Meera and Andreas were looking after them, telling them stories and feeding them sweet foods and drinks. Down there it was quiet and it was as much for that reason as for security that they were there, far from the sounds of invasion.

The palace was secured. Vasselis and Gesteris had seen to that, leaving a good strength of guards and artillery to keep back the dead should the outer defences fall. It was the place where the last battle would be fought if it came to that. The look in Vasselis's eyes when he left told her that he had no real confidence they would live to see out the day.

With two city gates under attack, frightened citizens had few places to go. Those deciding the Hill was the safest bet were outside the Victory gates now, demanding entrance. That time might come. But it was not yet.

The Conquord was on the brink of disaster. The Advocate was dead. No one knew if her first two heirs, Roberto and Adranis were alive or even where they were. The first Ascendants were in Neratharn along with the Exchequer. Only Tuline remained in Estorr and she was lost to grief. Vasselis was holding the threads together but forces were striving to drag them from his grasp every moment.

And despite all this, sitting in the bizarre peace of the Chancellery with shouting and violence muted behind the shutters, Hesther Naravny, Mother of the Ascendancy could only think that these tenth-stranders were acting out scenes from her past in Westfallen. Something like that anyway, because she was damned sure she'd seen all these characters before.

'They wanted to kill us a couple of days ago,' said Yola. 'Now they come here wanting sanctuary. Let them die.'

'What a fantastic outlook on life. You must be so proud.' said Petrevius.

'Meaning?'

'Meaning they were angry because me, you and Mina managed to kill hundreds of their friends. Surely we should be extending the olive branch. Doing everything we can to help them. Put them on our side.'

'Ar ...' Hesther put a hand to her mouth. 'I'm sorry, I mean Petrevius is right. When this is over, we will need acceptance all over again. They might forget the violent breaking of a demonstration. They won't forget friends sacrificed to the dead because the Ascendancy kept the gates closed on them.'

'But they don't deserve it,' said Yola, her face was flushed and angry. 'If they had believed in us from the start, none of this would have happened. It's them who should be saying sorry to us.'

'Don't be an idiot, Yola,' said Petrevius. 'Most of them were just following what the Order told them to follow. But the Chancellor is dead now too, so we can start again.'

'You're the naïve one, Petre. It'll be like before with Ardu and the rest. They'll love us for a day and then they'll turn against us.'

'So what do you suggest?' asked Hesther. 'Our path is not littered with choices, is it?'

'Not everyone hates us,' said Yola. 'Let the rest die and keep those who feel for us.'

'And you'll be the one to choose, will you?' Petrevius was unable to stay seated any longer. 'Who gave you the right to decide who lives and who dies?'

'I'm not choosing. Except to do nothing.'

'Oh, Yola.' Hesther sighed. It was the sigh of disappointment and the sharp-tongued seventeen-year-old still reacted to it. 'You've lived here all your life and you haven't learned a thing. You have to win arguments. Herine will be turning in God's embrace hearing your words.'

'Look where it got her,' said Yola. 'For all the arguments she might have won, she lost the biggest of them all and now she is dead. We have to go our own way. Be strong for those who love us and want us. Not for those fickle ones who hammer on the gates pretending to forgive us.'

'Then let's do that,' said Mina, speaking for the first time. Her voice was tiny. She was struggling badly with what they had done. 'There are people out there standing willing to die for people like us. Let's help them.'

Hesther smiled. 'And how will you do that? I thought you were refusing to work anything that might hurt people.'

'Yola knows something.'

'Shut up, Mina, I told you not to say anything.'

'Well I don't always listen to everything you say. Anyway, this is important.'

Hesther stared at Yola until she could not help but blush. 'Well?'

'A Land Warden feels things in the ground. Things that other Ascendants can't. Even the best.'

'It was me told you that, wasn't it?' said Hesther.

Yola nodded. 'When I was wondering why things came to me through my feet, or so it seemed.'

'And what have you felt?'

'The dead. Now they are close, if I push out with my mind, I can sense them. Or rather I can sense the lack of life energy, but it's still moving, if you see what I mean.'

Hesther straightened. 'I have felt it too but I didn't really know what it meant. Go on.'

'Well, beneath the earth something in the base energies is changed. The slow-moving gentle powers we love so much, Land Wardens like us? They are altered.'

'She thinks it's what drives the dead, makes them move,' said Mina.

Hesther opened her mouth then covered it with a hand, hoping. Hoping.

'And can you do something with it?' she asked.

Yola nodded. 'I think so.'

'What, child?'

'I can interrupt it, I think. Or make it so the changed energies can't advance. Like a barricade or something. If it works it'll make the dead stop.'

Hope kindled inside Hesther. Real hope they would escape all this.

'Over how wide an area can you project this work? The City?'

'No,' said Yola. 'Too big. But on the palace, I can. This is home, I understand how the energies work here.'

'Are you sure it will stop them?'

Petrevius shrugged. 'We don't know. But there's only one way to find out, isn't there?'

Hesther thought hard. 'I really need to know how confident you are about this.'

'Why?'

'Because I know what you're thinking. You're thinking that if the dead break through, you can protect the palace, at least for a time. But I'm thinking that when Marshal Vasselis and Elise Kastenas hear about this, they'll have another thought. And that's that they can bring all the dead here, and you can beat them at the walls. So that's what I need to know before I send out a message. Can you really do this, Yola?'

The walls of the Jewelled Barrier were broken. By what manner of means, Khuran hardly cared. He sent his warriors on the charge to finish the job. He would walk behind them to come upon Gorian

Westfallen and dash his head from his neck with a single blow. Such was the fate of murderers of the Khur dynasty.

Eager to feel flesh beneath their blades and see the blood of their enemies smear the ground of the Conquord, twelve thousand Tsardon warriors charged towards the cloven stone. The mighty structure, the Conquord's greatest folly, torn down by a single man.

Khuran, sword over his shoulder, saw the earth shove the concrete and stone aside as if it was paper. And he saw it cross the open space towards the dead.

'Get the Gor-Karkulas. I will own them.'

His shout rang out over the rear lines of his men and was no doubt passed quickly among those who would compete for the prize. Khuran even managed a smile. Those who sought to best him were always too late to see their error. It could not be done. He would take new wives, have more sons. Rhyn-Khur had been a great prince and would be mourned, but his death could not be allowed to be the epitaph of the Khurs.

The rolling wall of earth and mist rumbled outwards, shaking the ground beneath his feet. He stumbled slightly, placing a hand on Kreysun's shoulder for brief support. A chink of uncertainty opened within him. He paused in his march. The wall reached the dead and engulfed them and the Gor-Karkulas. The triumphant roars of the Tsardon stuttered. Voices fell silent. Behind the wall, in the void, nothing seemed to move. Victory was theirs yet Gorian's devilry still came on.

The front lines of his warriors faltered, coming to a halt. The ground shook, heaved and split. As far as he could see, north and south, the wall moved at him. A great land wave. By the time his men had turned to begin their escape, it was already too late. Perhaps it always had been.

Khuran looked briefly over his shoulder at the wide open spaces of the Atreskan Great Plains at his back. Nowhere to run. Nowhere to go. Nothing to do but stand. Kreysun turned and grabbed his arm.

'Go, my King, you must run!'

'Run? I will face my death. It will not claw me down a coward.'

Khuran, King of Tsard turned to his doom.

'And with such acts, do we understand our own folly,' said Kreysun.

The land wave crested above his head.

Chapter Sixty-Four

859th cycle of God, 12th day of Genasfall

'We have to stop. Please, Paul just for a moment.'

A mile. Perhaps less. That was all they'd made. Tortuously slow but the one feeling the pain was Arducius. Every pace over the bleak, dead swamp was a new agony for him. His broken leg dragged through the sticky slime, bumping over boulders hiding beneath the surface. He moved with a hopping motion under Mirron's support and though he didn't complain once, the sounds that escaped his lips were truly awful to hear.

But they could not afford to slow any further. Blanking the eastern horizon and closing in their inexorable way came the tens of thousands of dead that Gorian had created with his wave. Their movements slow and deliberate, silent and efficient. They were no more than three hundred yards behind now. And all heading for the same small space.

They had crested a rise in the ground and there, less than a mile away, an oasis of life and health. A glade of trees and waving grass. Perhaps an acre in all. They could see figures moving within it. Probably more of the dead. But Gorian was in there too. Jhered didn't need an Ascendant to divine that. He prayed Kessian was there too and alive, but he wasn't holding his breath. The rank stench that bubbled up from below his feet made him wish he was.

Mirron's voice cut through Jhered's carefully laid thoughts. He had been trying to ignore everything but placing one foot in front of the other while Ossacer, a heavy burden in his arms, coughed and wheezed, scaring Jhered that each latest breath would be his last.

'All right. A moment, no more.'

Jhered crouched and let the ground take Ossacer's weight. Jhered's arms were beset by a constant ache and cramp. He stretched them and groaned as the blood flowed into the crushed nooks and crannies of his muscles. Mirron helped Arducius down. He lay flat on his back in the mire, not caring what it held. It wasn't deep here, only an inch or so but right there at its surface, the reek had to be overpowering. He seemed not to notice.

'Not just your leg, is it, Ardu?' said Jhered gently.

The young man managed to move his head from side to side. He drew in a breath and flinched.

'Ribs?' suggested Jhered.

'Yes,' gasped Arducius, his words a little slurred. 'My right arm too, at the wrist. Always was weak, that one.'

Arducius managed to smile and Jhered sat in awe of his courage, wondering where he dredged it from when everything was surely lost. Two crippled Ascendants out of three attempting to face the world's most destructive power. Not promising.

'Anything else, dare I ask?'

'Whole lot of bruising deep down. Bleeding inside, I expect. I think I might have broken a cheekbone. Hard to say, that side of my face is numb.' Arducius pushed himself up on his good arm. 'I know what you're thinking, Paul. I can still Work.'

'I can help him.' Ossacer's voice was dry and cracked, barely more than a croak. 'Let me touch him.'

'Don't let him touch me,' said Arducius. 'Ossie, don't be stupid. Keep what you have for you.'

'Too late for me, Ardu. Let me heal. It's what I do. It's all I do.'

Jhered looked down at him and saw the teenager he had first taken into the wild.

'No one under my command ever gives up,' he said. 'It is not too late. If it were, I would not be carrying you. Do you understand?'

Ossacer drew back his lips. 'Yes, sir, General, sir.'

He tried to move his arm to approximate a salute but it didn't come off. Jhered shook his head.

'If I had half the strength and courage of you two, you three, I would be able to carry the lot of you.' Jhered looked back to the east. 'But now we have to move. And we can't stop until Gorian is dead. Either that or we join as his ... disciples, or whatever you want to call them.'

'Slaves,' said Arducius, holding up his good arm for Mirron to take and help him to his feet. His foot.

'Better term,' said Jhered. 'Come on, Ossie. Let's be having you.'

They set off again. Jhered's arms were immediately on fire and he could only imagine how Arducius must feel. The escaping whimpers told him enough. The dead had closed the gap by half and were making better ground than the four living bodies. Jhered estimated their speed at a little over a mile an hour, so the dead were doing something like double that. He had a moment of clarity, as if looking down over the scene. The crippled chased by the dead. The slow pursuing the slower. Whatever the outcome, Harban had surely been right; the world had turned on its head.

Down the slope they travelled, all of them desiring the flat ground on the approach to the glade, where the camber of the land put less stress on their muscles and bones. Their ears were filled with the sound of the dead walking. Forty or fifty thousand pairs of feet dragging through the thick sludge which sucked and grabbed. It was an unearthly sound.

In his dreams, Jhered had always heard Armageddon accompanied by thunder and the battering sounds of pure power and energy. But this, this dredging scrape was worse. He tried to blot out what it meant. The sheer number of people Gorian had slaughtered. But as they approached he found he couldn't. He wanted to turn and apologise to them all, one by one.

Perhaps it was right that they closed on those whose mercy had let Gorian live. Here they were, all of them alone in the wilderness. Perhaps they deserved to die for what they had done ten years ago. A tear fell on to his cheek. So much innocent waste. Such an insult to the Omniscient.

'No point in blaming yourself, Paul,' said Ossacer.

Jhered started and looked down at him. Those sightless eyes were boring into his body, seeing everything. He appeared very slightly recovered.

'But what a mess we have made of our world,' said Jhered. 'All these people, taken from the earth before their time and denied the embrace of God. How can I not blame myself?'

'Because mercy is the greatest act a man can perform,' said Ossacer. He coughed and a little blood spattered Jhered's cloak.

'Don't talk, rest.'

Ossacer's hand grabbed Jhered's arm just for a moment. 'It is what the recipient of that mercy chose to do that shaped the world. Who are we to judge who does and does not deserve another chance?'

Jhered let another tear fall but he nodded. A new determination grew within him. It lent strength to his legs and his arms. And brought belief to his mind.

'Well, we're judging now,' said Jhered. 'And I find Gorian wanting. Mirron, Ardu, faster. We owe it to all who follow in our footsteps.'

Ossacer smiled and closed his eyes.

Roberto cut the rope net away from the crates and dug his gladius blade in to lever open the nailed-down lid. Davarov was next to him, bawling orders at the few hundred whom they could see on the broken, angled, crumbling walls of the Jewelled Barrier. North and south, lost in the distance, they could hope that some survived but they were not facing what was coming at the gaping rent where the gates had been. Not a single catapult was still standing.

There were plenty of places where the dead could walk straight through and into Neratharn. And there were thousands of them to do it. The original Gesternan and Atreskan dead who had survived the Conquord bombardment were up and walking again. Many carried new injuries but swords and spears were in perhaps a thousand hands. Those many thousands of Conquord dead caught under the wall and in the camps and compound when the wave struck were walking away west and could be ignored.

Behind him, though, was the major problem. The Tsardon army. Roberto found it hard to believe that any had escaped and that meant around twelve thousand new dead. Fresh dead without the problems of decay and only those of injuries sustained during their very recent demise.

It should have been hopeless but for two things. First, Davarov didn't understand the term and had already engendered a fighting spirit in his few remaining legionaries. And second, through a mounted magnifier that had survived the destruction of the barrier, Roberto had seen a handful of figures making their slow and obviously painful way up a rise and away towards where he had to pray Gorian was based. The broad back and imposing figure of Jhered had been unmistakable and the other three had to be the Ascendants, all surviving the wave by some Work or other.

Roberto couldn't help but feel bitter about their survival while having to be simultaneously thankful. He might hate all they stood for but he had to want them to succeed. And quickly.

'Up to the roof and the standing causeway!' bellowed Davarov. 'To the General. One force, one defence. Move.'

Roberto prised off the lid and grabbed at the first metal flasks. He handed one to Harban and another to Davarov. Harban had appeared from the front of the fort. Davarov thought him fallen but he'd found foot- and handholds in the cracking stone more than adequate to ensure his survival. He was completely unharmed but an anger burned in him that would not be tamed. Those he had come to save had died out there. Two of them.

'Feel the weight and heft,' said Roberto. 'This stuff goes up on impact so throw hard.'

Davarov nodded and bounced the flask in his huge hand. Roberto held out his to stop him.

'Carefully, old friend. Drop it and this ends here and now.'

The dead moved in. Arrows and some spears were being thrown at those closing to almost spitting distance but it was a futile exercise. The dead did not stop for such wounds. The Tsardon were almost within bow range too. Roberto stared at the sea of dead and tried to believe he could survive this. He searched the faces for Khuran or Ruthrar but could see neither of them. Ruthrar's mission had been in vain and it saddened Roberto. He had believed in the intelligent prosentor who had ridden to what had turned out to be his death. They could have done with his muscle up here.

Soldiers were gathering on the half of the fort roof still standing. The steps up to it were cracked but had not fallen and its stability had kept the wall standing for another forty yards north. South, it was a gaping mess where no one moved. Below them, dead Conquord legionaries were picking themselves up and moving off west. Shambling, clinging onto weapons with broken hands, pulling themselves over razor-sharp debris if they could not walk. Tragic sights in every direction. It was best not to look, nor to think.

Roberto felt a hand on his shoulder and turned from the scenes.

'Want to give me one of those?'

'What are you going to do, Julius, drop it on my head?' Roberto chuckled and passed him a flask. 'Send them back to God, Speaker Barias.'

'As many as I can.'

Barias was in a state of shock and the dust still covering his face accentuated his condition, but his eyes were focused and that was good enough.

'I might even end up being glad I saved you,' said Roberto. 'I'll put in a good word with my mother when we get back. So long as you don't still want me burned.'

'Perhaps a clean slate is a good place to start,' said Barias.

Roberto nodded, smiling. 'I can live with that.'

'Roberto.'

Davarov's voice held surprise. Roberto looked out into Atreska. The dead had stopped. The tide had ceased to flow in. They stood ten yards from the walls now, stretched back a hundred, and north and south, covered many hundreds more.

'The odds aren't too great,' said Roberto.

Davarov bounced his flask again. 'We can even it up a little.'

'Wait for them to move.'

Soldiers lined the wall, the steps and the causeway. More stood the other side of fallen stone with rock and spear in hand. Anything that might keep the dead at bay when they came. Abruptly, the face of every fallen man and woman turned towards the fort. Mired in slime, cut and damaged but staring right up at the roof. Mouths opened.

'Del Aglios.'

Roberto stumbled back and sat down hard, clutching his flask to him. His name, from ten thousand dead mouths. It shuddered through him like the wave through the stone of the barrier.

'What in the Omniscient's glory was that?' he said.

'Del Aglios.'

The words ripped through him, tearing the heart from him. The living let slip their courage just a little. Roberto got shakily to his feet and looked out over the mass of the dead. Their faces still towards him. Roberto breathed in deeply, dragging his will back within him. Yet still he could not shake that sound from his mind.

'That bastard,' he said. 'He can see me through their eyes. How can he do that? He can see me.'

'Yeah? Well here's something else for him to have a look at.' Davarov cocked his arm and hurled his flask down on the dead. 'Swallow that, you gutless bastard.'

The flask struck an Atreskan breastplate and exploded. Shards of metal carved through the surrounding dead. The force of the explosion battered out in an oval, shearing dead from their feet, tearing limbs from bodies, decapitating. Rending flesh. Thirty disappeared in a welter of blood, shattered armour, skin and bone.

'Conquord!' roared Davarov. 'Let them come and hack them down.'

Julius and Harban launched their flasks. Behind Roberto, an engineer was trying to relight a pitch barrel that smouldered on. Detonations rattled debris against the broken walls. Roberto hurled his flask down. Dead were obliterated in the force of the blast.

'If you want me, Gorian, you'll have to come up and get me.' Roberto bent down to the crate to grab another flask. 'Let's use these while we still can.'

The dead moved forwards.

'It's up to you, Paul. Again.'

Ocenii squad seven held the dock at the base of the south fort. When the fires had died, the dead had moved to shore across charred planking, or landed from Tsardon vessels driving through choking smoke to strike the dock. The fort artillery pounded down on the enemy within the harbour, battering triremes to the bottom of the dock. Hundreds had perished in flames but still they came and the courage of the ordinary soldier was beginning to falter.

More ships were coming through the harbour mouth. Dead who had gone down with their ships were beginning to emerge and climb the metal ladders that littered the sheer wall of the harbour side. Sights none had thought to see. For some it was too much. As many turned to run as the dead who forced their way on to dry land. Hundreds.

Kashilli lifted up a dead and broke his back across his knee. He threw the corpse aside, picked up his hammer and brought it down on top of a dead skull. The head disappeared in a spatter of bone and gore. The body jerked and twitched, driven to the ground under the sheer force of the blow. Kashilli kicked the body into the water. Thirty more were coming to take his place.

'Come on then.' He beckoned them to him. 'One or all, it makes no odds to me.'

Next to him, Iliev was a counterpoint to Kashilli's brutal strength. He balanced and pivoted, planting a kick into the midriff of a Gesternan militia man. He was catapulted backwards, taking two more with him to fall back into the water. In the half pace of space he had, Iliev moved, dropped low and whipped his blacksmith's hammer into the knees of the next dead, smashing one kneecap. The dead crumpled on the broken limb. Iliev darted back and brought his axe down on the dead's lower back, sending his legs into brief spasm before they were still.

A gasp ran the length and breadth of the dock. Iliev paused to take stock. Every single one of the dead had stopped moving, frozen in their next act. Kashilli laughed and crushed his hammer into the side of one and through the back of another who had stumbled. He made to move into the pack of standing dead but Iliev's shout stalled him.

Iliev stared into the eyes of the dead in front of him. They peered from a face thirty days decayed. Flesh had rotted on his face. Maggots crawled in his skin. The smell of him was eye-watering but Iliev had grown used to that. Those eyes should be hollow spaces but remained. And they showed Iliev a moment's confusion followed by a lifetime of pain.

The dead's mouth opened. And his voice was joined by all the others in a juddering shout. Bodies jerked and shuddered. Mould burst out on their bodies, ran the length of their legs and began to bleed into the concrete of the harbour.

'Back, back!' ordered Iliev.

Squad seven responded. Out in the harbour, the sounds of timbers creaking dragged his attention to the enemy ships. He heard splintering but for a moment, could see nothing.

'There!'

Kashilli was pointing to where green had sprouted on the hull of a trireme rammed on the harbour. It raced across timber and deck, clawed up mast and over sail. The canvas dripped, rotted to nothing in an instant. Everything the mould and moss touched decayed. Ships began to sink, to break apart. The squealing of nails pulling out of wood echoed across the harbour.

There was a scattering of cheers but Iliev knew this was not victory.

'This is a weapon. Back. Back off fast.'

He glanced to his left along the harbour. A dead reached out and gripped the arm of a distracted legionary. Mould and disease poured over his body, engulfing him in a cloying mass of sick green and brown. He screamed until the mould reached his mouth, eyes and covered his heart. And then he turned on his friends.

'Go, go!' said Iliev, urging them back towards the fort. 'Don't let them touch you.'

Iliev felt fear. For perhaps the first time in his life. It was an ugly, uncomfortable emotion. Legionaries and harbour guard were dying under rampant disease. The dockside was clearing, those who had seen the new attack not pausing to wonder if they could combat it. Panic moved faster than the mould. There was a stampede out through the yards and into the streets beyond. The sounds of fighting and dying had been replaced by the harsh sounds of terror and the drumming of thousands of feet.

Squad seven stormed into the castle courtyard and up the slope towards the roof. Iliev ran in behind them barking at scared guardsmen to close the gates, an order they were only too happy to follow. The Ocenii spilled onto the roof. The artillery had fallen silent. Iliev joined Vasselis and Stertius at the wall overlooking the harbour. The wall was crowded with engineers and guards. None could find a word. None acknowledged his arrival.

It was a scene from the worst images painted by the Order's artists depicting a world fallen from the Omniscient's grace. The water had been reduced to a muddy pool of rotten timber and algae, spreading slowly out of the harbour mouth. A fine mist of spores rose from whatever had sprung up there.

Dead men were still pulling themselves up the ladders and on to the docks where hundred upon hundred now stood unmolested. No artillery could reach them there. From their feet, the mould spread out slowly, never reaching too far ahead. But far enough that only a sarissa would be long enough to do damage. They were leaving the dockside which was tainted an unhealthy green. It covered cobbles, grew along cracks and extended its fingers a short distance up the outside of the fort.

Ahead of them, the living ran to they knew not where. Flags were waving at the north and south gates. Both were breached. Iliev did not raise a flicker of surprise. Civilian and soldier poured away from the dead. They would not stand. The battle was as good as lost.

'We have to get to the palace,' said Vasselis.

Iliev turned to him, saw the paper in his hand. 'Why?'

'Because that's where the young Ascendants are. And Hesther says they have a plan.'

'There's no escape,' said Stertius, gesturing to the putrefaction on the dock. 'Touch that and you're history.'

Kashilli was already moving to the sea wall. Iliev saw him and gestured Vasselis and Stertius to walk with squad seven.

'Lucky I've got a boat then, isn't it?'

Chapter Sixty-Five

859th cycle of God, 12th day of Genasfall

'Forty stroke constant, Ocenii. Like you're outrunning a tidal wave.'

Iliev's orders carried over the flowing strokes of seven's oarsmen. Marines in harmony and in a desperate rush. They had pushed away from the fort into clear water, beaten a route around a narrow headland and were powering into the south beach where the dead had landed. It wasn't a place you could land an invasion fleet but a small force had all the room they needed. Not a man moved on any of the twelve ships canted over on the coast. Gangplanks were empty, decks clear. Sails flapped idly in a gentle breeze. The sand and pebbles were clear of mould. Iliev had thought they might be.

Sitting aft with him, Stertius and Vasselis gripped hard to the gunwales. Kashilli was taking great heart from their discomfort. A spiked corsair in full flow was a sight to behold and an exciting but very unstable place to be. The two landborn were in awe of the speed and in fear of their lives. And Kashilli moved his marines up and down the centre to give the corsair a little slap and roll before Iliev told him to stow it.

Even in the face of annihilation, Kashilli was unbowed. He stood at the prow now, one foot on the spike and his fist pumping the air, daring the dead to come to him and face him. Dead or alive, it was not something Iliev would willingly choose to do.

'Hard up the beach, skipper,' urged Kashilli. 'Let's hit it running.'

Iliev looked down on Vasselis who had gone a shade paler, if that was possible.

'I think not on this occasion, Kashilli. Soft landing. Back to fifteen stroke, lift on my command.'

'Aye, skipper,' said the stroke.

The corsair began to slow. Kashilli moved away from the spike as it settled naturally closer to the waterline.

'Would have been an experience, Marshal,' he said.

'And probably my last, Trierarch Kashilli. But thank you for the offer.'

'Ship oars,' said Iliev.

The thirteen sets came to the vertical. The corsair ground up the beach, juddering to a halt just a little too fast for the landborn's comfort.

'Marines, let's stow and run,' ordered Kashilli. 'Guard our guests and watch for the sludge.'

'How far to the hill from here?' asked Iliev.

The squad dispersed into a defensive curve, eyes on the path away and the silent enemy ships.

'Two miles, no more. This is the closest gate,' said Vasselis. 'But we don't want to take the main streets or we'll be knee-deep in Kashilli's sludge. Any ideas?'

'I was born here,' said Stertius. 'I'll get us there in front of them all if I can.'

'Good. Can you both run?' Vasselis and Stertius nodded affirmation of Iliev's question. 'Then let's move. Kashilli, on the harbour master's instructions. Let's double it and more until I tell you to stop.'

They ran up and away from the beach, following the path the dead had taken. A straight line up to the gates. Here the slaughter had been fierce indeed. Scattered remains of dead lay in a wide arc around the gates. Victims of flaming stones and bolts and of Gesteris's wonder powder, now apparently spent or in very short supply. Dozens had been dismembered here but enough had survived and when the mould weapon was deployed, they had simply rotted the gates.

Only the great iron and steel bands and hinges remained. The timbers were nothing but detritus on the packed ground. The catapults were all silent now, sentinels overlooking a disaster they had been unable to avert. The squad ran in. The mould was gone, just as it was gone from the main street up towards the forum. Just as Iliev had guessed.

'It doesn't last,' he said. 'And it travels in front of them. Stertius, which way?'

Stertius pointed left and they ran up an incline inside the walls. Here, in a street packed with empty buildings and flapping shutters, the noise towards the centre of the city was dulled. The stench, though, was not, and evidence of the flood tide of invading and newly created dead was everywhere. How many faithful had been taken and turned towards the palace, the place that was surely the dead's target.

'We must be following the Gor-Karkulas,' said Vasselis. He was barely out of breath. An ageing man but a fit man. He needed to be. 'If we can find one, take him out, then we can seriously restrict them.'

'Not going to be easy,' said Iliev. 'Just look at all this.'

They'd turned right up a narrow tenement street that led to a small square containing a fountain. The evidence of discarded life was everywhere. Buckets lay on the ground. Hats, bags, dolls, food. The paraphernalia of the citizen. Dropped because it was no longer needed. And the fountain still contained algae.

Stertius directed them around the main forum, away from the heart of the invasion. Noise of the dead march and the flight of Estorr's populace came from ahead and right. And it was moving away left, west towards the only gate that had not been attacked.

'Best place for them,' said Iliev. 'Keep moving, Ocenii.'

Estorr was built in a series of rings, with central spokes spearing out from the dock. Even with Stertius's knowledge of the city, they had to cross a main highway. It led out to the west gate and it was full of terrified people still running at full tilt though the dead were long behind, making their slow advance, in no hurry.

Squad seven and their guests were in a tiny side street. No mould and no death had walked here. Not yet. But the terraces were all empty, their occupants joining the headlong rush out of the city. It was a seething mass ahead. Iliev shivered in spite of himself. All it would take was the touch of one dead hand.

'Kashilli? Make a path. Seven, in his boot prints. Mind our guests.'

'Already as good as done, skipper.'

Kashilli and two others, hammers held horizontally across their chests, barged into the crowd, shouting people aside. There was anger, screaming and punches were thrown. Iliev led Stertius and Vasselis after him. The rest of the squad filling in, trying to keep the path open.

Kashilli was a bull. He snorted, put his head down and heaved forward, the shaft of his hammer connecting with arm, midriff, rib and head. Iliev could hear the protests building as they made halfway.

'Then move!' bellowed Kashilli. 'Ocenii sailing here. Move, I said, are you deaf as well as stupid?'

Iliev felt their rate of progress increase. He nodded his satisfaction. To his right and down the hill, they'd brought the street to a halt. To the left, a gap was beginning to appear.

'Run round the outside, Marshal, Master Stertius. We'll hold them. Ocenii, your right hands, press in and keep moving.'

The crowd at the front were letting them go, seeing their insignia in addition to Kashilli's bulk. The squad moved freely. The crowd began to edge around their rear. A scream from growing thousands of mouths travelled up from the base of the hill, near the exit from the forum approach road. Iliev looked again.

The crowd were bunching, rushing. It was a wave and its crest was misted with spores and spattered with green mould. In front of it, the living crowd surged. Squad seven's marines stood no chance of holding it back. Kashilli and a few others had reached the other side of the road.

'Fight your way,' called Iliev. 'Buddy up and move.'

The squad's path was washed away by the weight of people fuelled by a rightful panic. Iliev dived forwards, got in between Stertius and Vasselis and pushed them headlong into Kashilli's arms.

'Get them away up the street. Sludge coming.'

'The squad,' said Kashilli.

'I'll get them. Go.'

Iliev turned back. People were whipping past his vision. Looking deep into the crowd, he could see squad members struggling against the tide of humanity trying to sweep them away west. He pulled in one, two, and another two, sent them a street west to see if any were carried further up.

The screaming had intensified. The sludge was coming. How hollow the half-joke was now. Iliev took another look. An arm flailed into the street, low down. Iliev crouched and pulled. The marine came shooting through. People fell over him, and others over them. More tried to climb the piling bodies or run round them, jamming the street.

Iliev saw another squad member inching around the squirming, shrieking pile, three deep and struggling. He beckoned with his hand, made to take a pace out but the marine grabbed him hard, sending them both sprawling backwards. The mould engulfed the street and spattered over the alley walls. Iliev scrabbled backwards still further. He got to his feet, cursed and spat.

'How many more have died,' he said. He put out a hand to the marine, who took it and jumped back to his feet. 'But thank you. You saved my life.'

Instant quiet had overtaken the main street at which they stared. Corpses covered in the stinking fetid mould were strewn everywhere, clawed down to their deaths even as they thought they might escape.

'They're moving,' said the marine.

'Then so must we. Let's see who we have left and get to the Hill.'

They turned and ran, dead eyes following them away. Iliev counted on the run up to the processional avenue. Stertius planned to take them through the parks and come down to the palace gates at the last moment along the processional approach at the junction with Del Aglios Way. It would be their moment of greatest risk.

The noise in the city was startling. No one could be unaware of the manner of the death that stalked them all and the timbre of the shouting and calling was genuinely unsettling, even for hardened veterans like the Ocenii. Iliev had lost seven of his squad and it could have been much worse. He prayed to Ocetarus that he wouldn't have to face them and the thought lent him greater determination.

The remaining twenty-six and the two Estoreans ran towards a growing clamour. Although they had expected citizens to be in front of the gates demanding entrance, they hadn't expected the sheer weight. People had stormed up Del Aglios Way, pouring on to the apron in front of the Victory Gates. They were still coming down the processional approach in droves. The gates stood open and citizens were funnelling inside, yelled on by guards on the gatehouse. Enterprising guardsmen had dropped ropes and ladders down the sides of the walls in dozens of places. Knots of people gathered under them, waiting their chance to climb.

'Straight through, Kashilli,' said Iliev. 'They're going to have to close the Victory Gates and we need that understood.'

'Aye, skipper.'

Kashilli began shouting long before he encountered the edge of the crowd that was swirling and moving as people sought to find the quickest way through the gates.

'Ocenii squad coming through. Stand aside. Stand aside for your Marshal and your Prime Sea Lord. Stand aside.'

Bless the conditioned reaction of the ordinary citizen. People prepared to beat each other to death for a final chance of life melted aside. Citizens tapped each other on the shoulder, indicated the charging Kashilli and his charges and a path began to open up towards the corner of the left-hand gate. Whether it was the sight of him that did it or the words he was shouting, Iliev didn't much care. All he knew was that they were within twenty yards before their momentum dissipated and the hammer was waved and used as a crowbar.

Iliev tried to maintain some sense of civility and order. He did not seek to push, using his hand to gesture people aside from this path.

'The Marshal has crucial information that will turn the fight. Clear a path and give yourself the chance to live.'

The press of humanity closed in around them and they were carried left and right in front of the gates. Citizens were hoping to be swept inside in their wake. Kashilli was hollering at the gate guards for assistance. Their movement had stalled completely.

'Kashilli. Let's move on!' shouted Iliev. 'Time's wasting.'

Kashilli heard him above the roar of the crowd and the stamping of thousands of feet, the clamouring for admittance to sanctuary. There was desperation in the air. Word was filtering forwards that the dead were closing in. Iliev was surprised the rot wasn't spreading already.

Belatedly, a line of guards with shields and spears appeared and forged a space across a short area of the gate and outwards. It was enough. They hailed the squad inside and herded them towards the fountain. Behind, citizens continued to flood in. Vasselis was with a guard, demanding the gates be closed and the citizens sent away into the parks. Iliev joined the call. The dead were coming to the palace. Here was not the safe place people assumed. The rot might bring the gates down but any time they could buy had to be worth it.

Inside the courtyard, the mood was ugly and angry. It was packed with citizens. Palace guard were trying to shepherd people away towards the basilica, the Academy, the legion and Ocetanas headquarters, the palace; anywhere that kept the courtyard on the move. It was a battle they were losing.

Iliev could see why. There were people on the fountain. Ascendants hanging on to the shattered remains of the horses rampant statue. Standing in the fountain pool. Whatever it was they were planning, the water was to be their fuel, or that was how Iliev understood them to work.

But the citizens who had got inside to demand sanctuary were also looking for someone to blame. The Ascendancy, as so often, was the scapegoat. A triple line of Ascendancy guard ringed the fountain. Spears were levelled, shields placed, and so far they were keeping the crowd back. Iliev could see furious, frightened citizens pointing, drawing fingers across their throats. Chanting. It was the road to a breakdown of order.

'Kashilli, let's get there. Squad seven with me. Our guests are safe.'

'I hear you, skipper.'

Kashilli the bull swayed and shoved his way through the gathering mob. Three Ascendants stood there with the brave old woman, Hesther Naravny. And her face was fierce enough alone to keep most of them at bay. He could just about hear her shouts. That the Ascendants were their only hope, their only chance of salvation. But the mob had other ideas. Iliev caught the gist of the chanting as he shouldered on. He passed a young man punching the air to the rhythm.

'The dead want the damned. Give the dead the damned.'

Iliev grabbed the man's shoulder.

'Stop. Singing. Now.'

The man focused on him. Just an ordinary citizen but so full of hate powered by fear. And something else.

'They are the enemy. Isn't it obvious why the dead are here?' The man looked him up and down. 'I wouldn't expect you to understand. Establishment man.'

The man turned away to continue chanting. Iliev stepped in front of him and felled him with a punch to the jaw.

'Yes, I'm an Establishment man but not an ignorant bastard.' Iliev turned and began to shout. 'Still your mouths. Still them or die at the hands of those you thought your brothers. Silence for the Ascendants.'

But all it did was fuel the chants further. Men were edging closer to the shield ring. Iliev spat on the ground, caught Kashilli's eye and nodded him on. Kashilli battered people aside with no thought to the injuries he might cause. And by the time the focus of the mob was on him to stop him, he was through the spear line and up on the side of the fountain, balancing there like he would on the corsair spike.

Kashilli really was massive. Iliev had seen him so often the fact had escaped him. He towered above them on the lip, hefting his hammer, glaring at them until the noise diminished by a hair.

'Come on then!' he bellowed over them, stilling a hundred voices at a stroke. 'You want the Ascendants? Come and get them. All I promise you is that the first of you up here feels my hammer through their chest.'

Kashilli held the hammer by the end of its shaft and held it outstretched, letting it track across the crowd. His arm was ramrod straight, solid as a mast and the muscles bulged.

'So,' growled Kashilli as the noise fell away. 'Which one of you bastards wants to go first?'

Iliev licked his lips and scanned the crowd. No takers. No surprise. He moved towards the fountain and no one stood in his way. The guards let him through and he joined Kashilli on the fountain lip. Below him, the face of a frightened girl looked up at him and Kashilli, admiration in her wide eyes.

'What's your name, young lady?' asked Iliev.

'Yola, my Lord.'

Kashilli smiled down at her too. 'Do what you have to do, little Yola. No one will hurt you now.'

From the gates, panicked citizens bunched and spilled inside. The gates, which had been closing slowly, slapped open once more, timbers rattling against the marble of the arch. People poured into the courtyard. Iliev bit his lip. Whatever these Ascendants were going to do, they needed to do it quickly.

Chapter Sixty-Six

859th cycle of God, 12th day of Genasfall

A line of dead appeared from under the outer boughs of the glade. Not many. Ten in plain view, spreading in a thin line and walking a couple of paces into the mire. Above, the sun shone down on the tiny oasis of life, the place for which the living and the dead were all groping.

Behind the crippled Ascendant group, the dead had closed in on all sides. Arducius was barely able to move. His shattered leg was black and blue with bleeding under the skin. He said he was still able to work but Jhered wasn't so sure. Ossacer had said the same thing, after all, and Ossacer was only vaguely conscious right now.

The three of them staggered the last hundred yards to the glade. There was no escape behind. The game would finish here. Either Gorian would die or they would all join the ranks of the dead. Jhered looked at the few dead ahead of them, a sense of foreboding upon him. Only their faces remained hidden in shadow. They stood absolutely still and silent, waiting with gladius or knife. They were in various states of decay. From the freshly harvested to the forty-day rotten. Clothes clean but for smears of blood, or grey, torn and mouldering from within.

The line of dead moved out a pace and Jhered's heart broke.

'Oh, Gorian, you bastard,' he whispered.

He stopped. With the army behind him less than fifty yards from their backs and the dead in front only ten paces away, he couldn't find the will to take another step.

'Jhered,' said the ten dead. 'Jhered.'

His name shivered through him, a knife in his gut.

'Turn away,' he said to them, voice clogging. 'Please.'

Mirron was at his side.

'We have to destroy them to move on. Quickly,' she said.

'I can't. I know them. My friends are standing there. The King of Tsard's son is standing there.'

Jhered shook his head and squeezed his eyes shut for a moment. Opening them, the scene was the same. No dream. Dina Kell. Pavel Nunan. Dahnishev. Dahnishev who Roberto thought had escaped was there, lifeless but upright. He had a long scalpel in his hands. Jhered choked back a sob. Such a waste. Such a crime.

'I cannot strike them down,' he said.

'No, but I can,' said Mirron. 'Turn away if you must.'

'Use my energy,' said Arducius, wheezing a breath into his tortured lungs. 'And be quick. Trouble behind.'

The rumble of the approaching army of dead refugees and soldiers obscured the breeze rustling the trees. Mirron nodded. Jhered wanted to look away but found he could not. It would be a dishonour.

'I am sorry,' he said, 'that your ends should be thus. Your memories will never be allowed to die.'

Heat blossomed to Jhered's right. He took Ossacer a pace left. Fire washed out in a sheet, drenching the dead, the loved dead, standing there. Jhered forced himself to look on while they burned. Thrashing and screaming where they stood as if alive and knowing their fate. The keening wail that spoke of the comprehension of eternal destruction. An end to cycles under God. The denial of His embrace.

The fire raged out from Mirron's body, consuming them, the heat like a furnace setting light to trees, scorching bark and leaf black. Tears were on Jhered's cheeks. The bodies dropped to the ground, ash and dust in the embers. He looked past them and into the glade. A shout of fury echoed through the branches.

'You're next, Westfallen.'

Jhered marched into the glade, Ossacer tight to his chest. Mirron and Arducius, smoking and smouldering still, came after him. Clothes and hair were burned away. Their faces bore a terrible weight. Not the guilt at what they had done, but the understanding of what lay directly ahead. They could feel it through the earth and the air the moment they set foot on unspoiled ground. Jhered could see it draining them with every passing heartbeat.

The glade was silent now but for the rustling of leaves and the whisper of the breeze over lush grass. All that was needed to make this the perfect genastro stroll were the songs of birds. And Gorian's dead body at Jhered's feet. Mirron and Arducius were struggling with the effects of whatever they were sampling. Ossacer was moving too, coming out of his deep exhaustion, dragged back to consciousness by the simmering evil in front of him.

Mirron gasped in a breath. 'Kessian.'

She began to hurry, Arducius crying out in pain as he was dragged too fast over the ground. She paid him no heed, moving quickly towards a circle of light in the centre of the glade.

'Mirron!' said Jhered and picked up his pace too though his body was screaming at him to stop.

'He's here. He's here. He's—'

Jhered ran. Shouldering under the low branches, protecting Ossacer's face from stray twigs. He burst into the circle of light. It was a small clearing in which a wagon stood. Two bodies lay in it. Karku. Impossible to tell if they were alive or not. And next to it, something . . .

'Hello, Mirron, my darling,' it said. 'You have come back to me.'

Mirron dropped Arducius to the ground, put her hands to her face and began to scream.

It was a sea and it would engulf them and drown them, but not before they had rescued as many of the dead as possible for a return to God's embrace. Davarov stood at the head of the stairs leading back down to the causeway. His long sword felt sublime in his hands. Like in the old days before the Conquord came and taught them a new way to fight. Sharp and heavy, bludgeoning power with an edge to carve the stone from a mountain side.

He crashed it through the shoulder of a dead, carving through mouldy leather armour, through rotting flesh and brittle bones. Davarov roared into the face of the Tsardon corpse. His blade sheared all the way through, exiting at the dead's hip and continuing down to take the leg from another. The body collapsed, spilling stinking entrails back down the stairs.

Davarov kicked the legs after it. The other dead had fallen sideways, partially blocking the way. Davarov backed up a pace, watching the dead slither and fall on the slick ground. Like a dozen times before, he could draw breath until they smeared the blood and guts dry. Then they would come again.

'Duck!'

Davarov ducked. Roberto threw another flask over his head and onto the stairs, about halfway down. The explosive smacked onto a helmet. The detonation ripped through bodies in all directions. Gore peppered Davarov's face. Ten and more dead had been ripped to pieces by the blast, leaving a hole painted in blood and blackened flesh. There was a crack in the stairs. The concrete, weakened by the earth wave, was failing and the powder was widening the fracture. Dead moved to fill the space.

'How many more, Roberto?'

Davarov looked back over his shoulder. Roberto was standing in front of the crate of flasks. Behind him, the thinning line of Conquord legionaries and engineers fought for their lives, driven on by the fear of becoming the walking dead. Like Davarov, they faced Tsardon warriors covered head to toe in slime, killed by the passage of the wave and the touch of the killing ground. Disease had taken their bodies and Gorian had made them walk again. They were strong, these dead. Fresh. The word was bitter in Davarov's mind.

The dead tried to scale everywhere they could. Their ladders had been reduced to rotten waste by the wave but they climbed fallen stone and grasped with their fingers on the shattered roof to try and get at the living they were so desperate to convert. Impelled by pure evil.

And for the hundreds who lost hands and fingers to the blades of the Conquord, others came. And they had started to pile stone on stone, creating slopes of broken rock up which they came. Closer and closer, until at last they could wield blades. Davarov thought they could keep those back until fatigue took them. It was at the stairs where their greatest risk lay. He and the remarkable Harban-Qvist, along with twenty others, worked in relays with long swords or axes to keep the way blocked. But it could not go on forever.

'Roberto?'

'Four,' he said. 'Not many.'

'But maybe enough. Target the same place you dropped the last one. The stair is weakening.'

Dead had trampled their fallen aside and scraped the gore from their path by the attrition of boot falls alone. They came on again. Harban stepped in front of them, axe in hand. His strong legs and short body allowed him to crouch and swing through on a horizontal at waist height. He used the blade flat as often as he did its edge.

Davarov watched him swipe a dead clean off the stairs and back into the teeming mass. On the return, the blade bit deep into the hip of another, crippling him. He fell forwards. Harban stepped back a half pace and crushed his skull. He lifted the axe from the still moving body, stepped in again, butted the boss into the face of a third and brought the blade back down again on his victim's lower back, smashing his spine.

It was so quiet. It gave the battle an unearthly feeling. Ten thousand dead and more all intent on a single purpose and not one making a sound. Only when the pitch fire hit them did they scream and it was a sound that would live with Davarov to his grave. Only on the roof of the broken fort did the living still hold sway and their voices and the thud of their weapons were unnaturally loud in the blasted land.

Harban ducked a swinging sword, came up and kicked straight out. The dead, off-balance, tumbled down the stairs, taking four others with him. A moment's pause.

'Roberto!'

Roberto stepped to the side, took aim and threw his flask. The explosion ripped into stone, armour and bone. The fort shuddered briefly. The gap had widened. A foot now, right across the stairs about halfway to the causeway. Dead were flung from the centre of the detonation, tumbling bodies, torn in half or shredded. Blood misted in the air. The long snakes of entrails whipped and splattered.

'Good shot,' said Davarov. 'Let's go again. Harban, my turn.'

'As you wish, General,' said the Karku.

'Oh, I wish. I certainly wish.' Davarov walked to the head of the stairs and hefted his blade. 'Come on, Tsardon bastards. The only way is up. And the Exchequer is another pace closer to his quarry.'

Davarov heard Roberto's muttered words.

'He'd better be.'

Jhered had laid Ossacer down. Mirron was still inconsolable, though the Exchequer was trying his best. Arducius propped himself up on his good arm and looked but barely believed. It *was* Gorian and it was Kessian too. Mirron had seen that it was and her outstretched hands, where she sat in a heap almost within touching distance, were heart-rending to witness.

Gorian was behind Kessian and they were both standing. Arducius could just about see their faces, their eyes particularly. But that was almost all. From their bodies, covering them almost completely, sprouted roots. Narrow twists and thick, healthy, woody stems. From their temples, their cheeks, and into the tops of their heads a living net of vegetation came and went. It speared into the ground around them, surely pierced every part of them and formed a thick cloak about them. Leaves sprouted even as Arducius watched, and small flowers budded and bloomed.

The earth had grown into and through them. Arducius tried hard to pierce the life map that Gorian had created but it was impenetrable, barring a slow, green and brown pulsing energy. The earth energy but twisted somehow. Arducius couldn't even tell whether in the course of creating the wave, Gorian had meant this to happen or whether it was pure consequence. All he thought he could tell was that Gorian and Kessian were completely interlinked to the earth and the life it spawned.

'Gorian,' said Mirron, speaking through her heaving, desperate breaths. 'Please, let him go. Let my son go.'

'I cannot do that,' said Gorian, his voice soft and melodic, carrying the gentle timbre of nature's beauty. It was beguiling. 'We have chosen a different path. Join with us.'

'Cannot,' spat Jhered. 'Then we will take him.'

Jhered was fast. The years had not diminished his speed and the rage boiling bright within him gave him more. He rose from Mirron, blade in hand, and hacked it into the thick twines of root covering Gorian's neck. Kessian shrieked. The blade bounced from the roots and out of Jhered's grasp, leaving barely a scratch. Gorian laughed.

'You do not understand, Exchequer,' he said. 'You cannot kill the earth. And I am the earth, and the earth is me. And all that walk upon it, all that grows from it, and all who lie beneath it, are mine.'

Jhered took a pace back and glanced about him. People crowded around the edge of the clearing. The dead, staring silently on. Arducius could feel the mass of them growing increasingly dense as they arrived. The weight of their grey, lifeless energy, the energy that Gorian had first sampled and that Arducius still did not understand, overwhelmed the force of nature. Leaves began to wither, bark to curl and discolour. Grass to blacken and die. Soon, only the small circle around the Ascendants would remain alive, all about them would be dark.

'Listen to me, Gorian,' said Arducius. 'You don't need to do this. You can't understand what you are doing. You can't mean it. You are one of us. An Ascendant.'

'And I have ascended further, my dear brittle brother. I am sorry for your pain but it will fade. Everything I do, I must do. It is the work of Gods to create paradise for their people.'

'You are no god.'

Arducius looked to his left. Ossacer had regained consciousness and was propped up by a tree that clung to life because of his presence alone. He was a hand's breadth from the touch of the dead.

'Am I not, Os-sick-er?' A chuckle that rumbled through the ground. 'You fought me. You are stronger than I thought. But you have not limitless power. That is what I have. We must become the elements to control them. A God must have absolute power.'

'It is you who is sick,' said Jhered. 'And it is you who will die.'

Gorian blinked and looked at Jhered. A sigh whispered through the dead surrounding them and across the grass beneath their feet.

'You are mortal and I can snuff you out if I wish. Look about you. My people await my command. Even the great Exchequer Jhered cannot hold back so many.'

'So what are you waiting for. What do you want?'

'Come to us, Mother. Then he will let me go. He promised.'

Kessian's words hung in the air. The sound of innocence. Mirron's chest heaved and she broke down again.

'No, no, my love, no. He is lying to you. Don't believe him, fight him. Please.'

Jhered was with her again, trying to comfort her. His eyes were on the dead briefly but they came to rest on Gorian. Arducius felt a pulse in the life map. He had seen it before. Desire.

'But it is what must happen,' said Gorian. 'We must be the family we always should have been. The one destined to rule this earth. And we can be merciful. Those we loved might be spared. Mirron. Come to me. Come to us.'

'Don't you move a muscle,' said Jhered. Mirron had reacted, made to reach out. 'He'll kill us all.'

'But I won't if Mirron comes to me,' said Gorian. The gentleness had deserted him now. This was far more like the Gorian of old. 'We will not harm you then. Would you deny Mirron the touch of her son?'

Mirron sagged in Jhered's embrace. She said something to him that Arducius couldn't catch. He let her go with his arms but not his eyes. Mirron turned to look at Arducius and at Ossacer who had dragged himself to Arducius's side. And in her eyes was all the loss and desperation of the world. All her desires for her son clashing with her loneliness and leaving a void that only his touch could fill.

'No, Mirron, don't do it. You can't do it.' Arducius felt Ossacer clutch his arm and the both of them reached out to her, beseeching her to come to them.

'For the good of all, sometimes one must go,' she said.

'Not to him,' said Ossacer, words strangling in his throat. 'He will deceive you. He never stopped deceiving you.'

'I will not desert my son.'

Jhered turned his head. His expression said he understood but he did not. Whatever words Mirron had spoken, he had misconstrued.

'We must live if we are to fight,' he said.

Arducius shook his head. 'This will not be life.'

Mirron stood and took in a deep breath. Gorian and Kessian were watching her. Gorian's eyes betrayed his triumph, Kessian's his yearning.

'Mirron?'

She turned one last time. 'It will be all right, Ardu. I promise.'

Gorian was beaming, triumphant.

Mirron smoothed her hands down her fire-cleaned skin and wiped imaginary hair from her face. She walked the short distance to Gorian and laid a hand on his head.

Chapter Sixty-Seven

859th cycle of God, 12th day of Genasfall

'It's not working, it's not working!' Yola's voice was a screech, desperate and lost. She was crying even as she tried to Work. 'I can't force the map out, it won't connect.'

The catapults on the walls of the palace were sounding. Onager stones whistled away to land amongst the dead marching down the processional approach. Panic had consumed the courtyard. Citizens were still trying to batter their way past their fellows to gain entrance even though flight into the parks was by far the safest option.

The security around the fountain had increased. The rest of Iliev's squad were on station and Vasselis stood with them too, bringing over a hundred Ascendancy guard with him. Palace guard were in amongst the citizens, trying to direct but it was a task doomed to failure. Others were still trying in vain to close the gates.

Iliev looked down on Yola and felt her despair. The other two Ascendants were looking to her for guidance but she could offer none. She was the hope of everyone in the palace, everyone left alive in Estorr for that matter, and the knowledge was too much for her.

'The dead are at the back of the crowd,' rumbled Kashilli. 'We should face them.'

'No,' said Iliev. 'Our place is here, defending the innocent. Keep your promise. Stand your ground.'

'You are scared, little one.' Kashilli was speaking to Yola. 'But we will not let you fall.'

'You don't understand. I can't reach the dead and I can't make the map work and I can't save anyone and no one can help me.'

Vasselis stepped into the fountain pool and crouched by Yola where she knelt in the cold water. She responded to his touch. Vasselis handed her a cloth which she put to her face.

'Dry your eyes, Yola, you are already wet enough.' Vasselis sat down, the water covering him to his midriff. 'I always like to be comfortable before telling a story.'

Yola giggled.

'A story?' hissed Kashilli. 'I can tell him one of those. Coming through the gates right now.'

Iliev put a finger to his lips. Vasselis continued.

'When my son was young, your age actually, he wanted to do great deeds and win battles and save everyone. Just like the heroes of the old Conquord, or so we read. But the truth is, we can never do that. The task is too much for any one person. A legionary can only defend those he stands next to. A surgeon can only save the one lying on the table. It is the same for all of us. We can only hope to save the one we love the best and then hope that they in turn can save another. And in the end, that is what my son did. He saved the one he loved more than life itself. And in so doing he set a chain in motion. You are here because of it. And so am I. Don't think of saving everyone here, Yola. You know who you love. Who you would die to save. Save that person and that person alone. Not such a big task, now is it?'

Yola gazed up at him, tears shining on her face and her eyes sparkling. She shook her head. And then she turned and looked at another of the Ascendants. The boy. He raised his eyebrows but Yola merely smiled.

'Let's try again, shall we?'

Iliev patted Kashilli on the back.

'Here they come. Be ready. They're like dogs on a scent and we're standing in front of their quarry.'

Kashilli rolled his shoulders and circled his head on his bull neck. 'Let them come.'

Citizens spilled away from the gates and a gap opened up in the courtyard. Arrows flew into the open maw of the Victory Arch. People hurled stones, knives, anything that came to hand. Nothing stopped the dead. The dull thud of their feet and the mould that spread out before them forced people further and further back. There was screaming, so much that it hurt the ears.

In front of Iliev on the ground, the guards were edgy, beginning to look over their shoulders.

'Stand,' said Iliev. 'Stand with the Ocenii. Be heroes for the Conquord this day. Keep your spears level and firm. You can hold them back.'

Iliev became aware of a sluicing sound behind him. He risked a glance over his shoulder. Water was cascading over the three Ascendants, drawn up from the fountain pool around them. It covered them in a second skin. The air crackled with power. Next to Iliev, Kashilli was bouncing his hammer in his hands, growling. Nature and power clashing. Man in the middle.

The dead marched towards the fountain. The front line was ordinary citizens and a scattering of militia. They barely looked dead but for the sick taint to their skin and the mould that covered their clothes. At their feet, the disease spread more slowly than it had. Like the force driving it was weakened or looking elsewhere. Kashilli had seen it too. He grunted. Iliev knew what he was thinking; the odds had evened just a little bit.

The living ran away where they could, leaving the fountain exposed to the dead who surrounded it completely. Squad seven were atop the lip. Ascendancy guard on the ground. And they would not stand for long.

'Kashilli, a dying wish?'

'Steady ground under my feet,' he said. 'And the freedom to swing one last time.'

Iliev nodded. 'Then let's do it as one. Squad seven! To the fore. Move!'

Kashilli and Iliev leapt over the ranks of guards and landed between spears, pushing them aside. Squad seven filled in around the fountain, one thin line of the Ocenii. Kashilli did not pause. He ran to the dead, whirled the hammer two-handed over his head and swept it through a rotting body, smashing through ribs and spine, smearing the corpse into two others.

Iliev dropped to his knees and chopped his axe into the knees of a dead citizen and his hammer in to the ankle joint of another. Both stumbled and he bounced backwards, dashing skulls as they fell, chopping into hamstrings on his way to the next.

The press was enormous. The dead just moved on. Those under attack did not stop and though the Ocenii could make holes in the line, they were quickly filled in. Step by step, they were pushed back. Kashilli brought his hammer down again, destroying another citizen.

Kashilli took a pace back and swung low to high, catching a dead under the ribcage and catapulting him up over the heads of those behind. Squad seven battered and hacked, chopped and kicked. Perhaps they slowed the advance. Perhaps they didn't. Iliev found he didn't care. It felt like buying time and if he was to die, it would not be standing still.

Iliev backed up another pace and felt the point of a spear. The dead closed. A festering hand reached out to touch him.

He heard a woman scream.

The dead man's hand froze.

The penultimate flask hit the stairway. Dead were smeared aside. The stone grumbled again. There was a sharp crack and dust billowed into the air. The stairs wobbled. They juddered and began to fall backwards, spilling dead from them.

'Yes!' Davarov punched the air.

And they stopped falling, wedging against the causeway behind. The gap was three feet. Nowhere near far enough.

'Shit,' said Roberto.

The dead on the upper half climbed without looking back. Davarov swung his long blade, feeling it bite deep and shove three Tsardon back on to the ground of the compound. The numbers did not seem to have diminished at all. Behind them, dead were beginning to reach the roof. The living were being pressed back but they had no place to go.

'We have to make it move sideways, bring it down into the compound,' said Roberto.

'Fine,' said Davarov. He decapitated a dead and kicked his body off the top step. 'I'll fetch a hammer and chisel and get started.'

'One flask might do it,' said Roberto. 'Right down at the base.'

'What about here at the top? Take out these eight steps and they can't jump the gap. Too high and too wide.'

Dead were regrouping. A handful came up the first half of the stairway. The first of them stepped straight into the gap and fell back to the ground, rising immediately to try again. The next up did not. They stopped, gauged the distance and jumped. Roberto shook his head. It was as he feared. Dead but not rendered stupid. Those that came after, learned from those before.

'Well, we can't fight down there, it'd be suicide.'

'It's the only way to slow them,' said Roberto.

'Got any bright ideas?'

'Yes.' It was Harban. He snatched the flask from Roberto's grasp. 'Make it a good shot.'

'I do not intend to throw it. Return the surviving Gor-Karkulas home for me. It is legacy enough.'

Roberto grabbed at Harban, understanding his intention and feeling a chill steal through him. 'No way. No way.'

Harban shrugged him off. 'The only way.'

Harban ran and jumped from the roof of the fort. Roberto watched him fall. It was thirty feet and more to the ground. He landed on the heads of the dead, using them to break his fall but he must have broken bones too. Ignoring the dead moving up the stairs to him, Davarov stared down too.

Dead surrounded Harban. Swords rose and fell. Harban was struck in the back but he did not stop. Another blade caught his left leg. He cried out but within it, his determination was undimmed. He shoved his way to the base of the stairs, dropped to his haunches and cocked his arm to strike the flask against the base of the steps.

'Down!' yelled Roberto.

Mirron was astonished at the purity of the power running through Gorian and his net of roots. She shuddered as they enveloped her. She felt no pain as they pierced her. She flushed with the energy. She felt whole, finally connected at the core to the workings of the earth and of God. She exhaled in a shivering sigh.

'I can feel you, Kessian. I can feel you.'

It was release. All her tensions and anguish flooded away with the touch of him through the life map Gorian had created. Exhilaration consumed her. Ecstasy embraced her. Kessian's scent, the touch of his hand, the feel of his hair and the brush of his lips. It was all there.

Mirron tried to move but the case of roots had stolen around her completely.

'You do not need to move, my love,' said Gorian. 'Everything you could ever want is here. All you need do is reach out with your mind.'

'It is so clean, so pure what you have created,' she breathed. 'It's incredible.'

'I have dismissed disease from us. It is the breath of my people but it is not good enough for Gods.'

'It was killing you, wasn't it, Father?'

'Yes, Kessian, it was. So we got rid of it, me and you. And now here we three are, together as one. And we can stay like this forever.'

Mirron could still move her head. She turned it and swivelled her eyes. Jhered, Arducius and Ossacer were there. Her brothers clung to each other, barely able to meet her gaze. And Paul ... Paul was the anxious father waiting to see if his daughter had made the right choice.

'It's all right,' she said. 'It really is.'

Mirron delved down below the purity of the three of them and the glade. Down to where the sick energies roiled and curled. Down through the strands of energy Gorian sent there to fuel his Work. The dead and the wave and the thousands of threads that fled away south and east to those walking in distant places. She reached out with her lifelines and caressed the strands, felt their power and the barricade that held back the disease. A perfect circuit.

'It *is* perfect, isn't it, my love?' said Gorian. 'You need never worry that we will be harmed. We are too strong. It is the way of Gods.'

'Mirron?'

'Paul, it is wonderful. And you are free to move. No one will harm you.'

Jhered nodded. He took a pace or two towards them and stopped, just beyond arm's reach.

'Is that truly your wish?' said Gorian, his voice filling her mind. Memories of the Genastro Falls, of snow in Westfallen, of beautiful blond locks, muscle and the gentle caress of his touch on her skin. 'They will forever seek ways to harm us.'

'They have no wish to hurt me,' said Mirron.

'Then their wish is my wish. Go, my brothers. Go, Paul Jhered.'

'Kessian?' said Mirron.

'Yes, Mother?' Her son's voice warmed her skin, made the roots cling harder.

'Remember your little sailing boat in our house?'

Joy and love sprang through the energy map. 'My favourite toy.'

'But not important now,' said Gorian, an edge to his voice.

'And would you like to see it again? To see it sail its figure of eight?'

'With all my heart,' said Kessian.

'Then you shall,' said Mirron. 'And all you have to do is close your eyes. And close your mind.'

'No!' Gorian fed fear into the energy map. The roots tightened. 'You will not do that.'

'Ah, but Gorian, my dear stupid brother. A son always does as his mother asks.'

Mirron's hand gripped harder onto Gorian's skull. She felt Kessian's mind go blank. The well of his stamina closed to Gorian. She felt down with her mind to the sickness and disease, coiling down Gorian's energy strands. Down here, the power buffeted her but she was strong. She formed a strand of her own and buried it deep, deep into the mire of the rotting earth. And she sucked it up inside her.

A crawling darkness flooded inside her. She could hear Gorian shouting, feel his mind trying to tear her strand from the depths of the earth. Kessian was crying. Roots surrounding them snapped and withered. Mirron fed the rot, mould and disease through her body. She felt her organs cry out in pain. She felt her blood thicken and slow, clogging her arteries. She felt her breath come hard and painful in her chest.

Mirron would not stop. She sucked it more and more while Gorian bucked and twisted, trying to escape. But his Work had become his prison. She fed all of it through her hand and down into the top of his skull, pouring it over his brain and dousing his mind.

'Did you really think I would let you take my son, you bastard? Did you really think it would make me love you and want to be with you? Deluded fool. You are no god, and you are no Ascendant. Your deeds bring shame to our calling and you must be removed.'

Her strength failed quickly. With every mote she possessed, she clung on. And she shouted lest the one she really loved should not hear her.

'Now, Paul. Now!'

The dead were screaming and shrieking where they stood. The cacophony made any thought difficult. But Jhered had moved close enough and her words carried to him. The web of roots that bound all three of them was cracking, splitting and falling away. Loose strands flailed in the air. Gorian was raging. Jhered could see his face, purple and black under the pressure of Mirron's Work. And he could see her too. Eyes closed, face deathly white, only standing because the remaining roots held her upright.

'Hang on, Mirron. Hang on. Don't you give in now.'

A root caught him across the face and pitched him over backwards. Blood flowed from the cut deep in his cheek. Jhered wiped his hand across his face, got to his feet and hurled himself at the root web. Beneath his hands it was slimy, difficult to grip with the rot setting in and the decay rippling through it.

Jhered tore at the outer roots, making a hole big enough for his hands. He buried them in the writhing mass, clutched on to an arm and pulled. Pulled hard. He used all his weight and dragged. The roots gave way. He fell back hard, clutching the body to him. He hugged it so hard and he never wanted to let go.

'It's all right, Kessian. It's all over now.'

Jhered opened his eyes. The roots were sliding from Gorian and Mirron. Her hand was still gripping the top of his head and he had his hands around her throat, trying to drive the life from her. His whole body rippled with sickness. Sores burst from his skin, showering stinking pus into the air. He screamed, a tortured, agonised sound that tailed off to a whimper.

Jhered went to lay Kessian down but the boy clung on.

'It's all finished now,' said Kessian.

Gorian's hands dropped from Mirron. Hers came away from his head and the two of them fell side by side on to the grass. Jhered stared round at the dead. They were still standing. But not as one. There was wavering and he was sure they were looking at each other, confused and frightened.

Kessian rolled off Jhered and the two of them stood. Arducius and Ossacer were already by the other two. Jhered joined them, Kessian running to Mirron's still form. Gorian remained alive but only just. His hands were clawed and his arms drawn up to his chest. His body convulsed and his skin was covered in red blemishes, boils and open sores. Gorian's face was swollen and dark, his lips a mass of blood and his mouth black. But his eyes stared at them all with that startling power that he had always possessed.

'It didn't have to be this way, Gorian,' said Ossacer. 'This was never the path the Ascendants should have taken.'

'Always ... hate ... us.' Gorian's breath bubbled at his ruined mouth. 'Never. Accept.'

'Not now,' said Arducius. 'Not after what you have done.'

Jhered looked at Arducius askance. There was no mockery in his face. Only regret. Ossacer put his hand out and grasped Gorian's left ankle.

'You should have let us help you,' said Arducius. 'Before it was too late. Now all we can offer you is peace at the very end.'

Gorian's body relaxed, his eyes closed and his head fell to one side, a thin line of drool dripping on to the grass. Ossacer removed his hand.

'And what about Mirron?' asked Jhered.

Ossacer set those blind eyes on him and they filled with his tears as a kaleidoscope of colour rippled across them.

'Oh, Paul, you know it is already too late for her.'

Jhered closed his eyes and sank to his knees. He didn't even register the extraordinary sound of the dead falling back to the embrace of God.

'She can't be gone,' he whispered. He shoved Gorian's body aside and caressed her warm cheek with the back of his hand. 'Not now we've won. Not now there is a future for her.'

The four of them clustered around Mirron. Kessian was leaning against Jhered who put an arm around him and held him close. Arducius, his eyes wells of sorrow and his physical pain forgotten, let his tears fall on her still body. So pale, so beautiful. So close to life.

'Ossacer, you must be able to do something,' said Jhered. 'She can't be gone.'

'I can't raise the dead,' said Ossacer, his voice a broken croak. 'You wouldn't want that.'

Jhered paused and his eyes flicked to Gorian. 'No. I wouldn't want that.'

'She is with God now,' said Kessian. 'The true God.'

Jhered drew him even closer. 'Yes, she is, Kessian. And on this day we can all be thankful for that mercy.'

He cleared his throat and let a trembling breath escape, trying hard to retain control.

'We should probably go back to the barrier, what's left of it,' said Arducius.

Jhered nodded. 'Yes. Yes, you're right. Although right now, I feel like nothing more than sitting here forever.'

'But we have to go and face our fate,' said Arducius. 'We Ascendants, that is.'

'A fate that Mirron's action has surely changed,' said Jhered. 'You have to believe that. Another chance to become accepted.'

'It doesn't matter that Ossie and I believe it. And of course we do.

But what is right for the Conquord? And it can't be the enduring risk of this happening again.'

Arducius gestured around him at the thousands of fallen dead. The ruined land beyond the tiny glade.

'I just don't know that we deserve another chance.'

Chapter Sixty-Eight

859th cycle of God, 12th day of Genasfall

And the woman's scream was joined with tens of thousands of others. A blaring howl that echoed from every wall and clawed up to the sky. It bounced from the arena, mourned across the docks and set birds to flight from the palace's highest roofs. The cry sheared through Iliev's head. He dropped his hammer and his axe and clamped his hands over his ears.

Kashilli fell to his knees, groaning, his mighty hammer cracking cobbles when it fell from his nerveless fingers. The fountain's water thrashed behind them, the living were shouting for the pain to stop and the Omniscient and Ocetarus looked on them and blessed them all.

The wailing ceased. In front of Iliev's nose, the hand of the dead man dropped to his side. Iliev stared at him. He was an Estorean citizen. Middle-aged and through the mould, appeared to have been well-dressed. The dead man stared back. It was a deeply unsettling feeling. He blinked and opened his mouth as if to speak but nothing came.

Iliev reached out to him. The dead man closed his lids on a mind full of fear and confusion, exhaled a breath that sounded like relief and fell into Iliev's arms.

'It's all over,' said Iliev. 'You can rest now, my friend. Rest now.'

The sound of the dead dropping to the ground across the city and throughout the palace courtyard reverberated for what seemed an age. Some stayed on their feet longer than others. A few even took a few tentative steps before the Omniscient reached out to them and took them back to his embrace.

The silence in the palace courtyard was complete but for the trickling of the fountain at Iliev's back. He laid the dead man down and turned, rising as he did so. He laid a hand on Kashilli's shoulder.

'Come on, Trierarch. On your feet.' Iliev looked at the three Ascendants, Vasselis and Hesther Naravny. Yola was lying flat on her back, floating in the pool. 'What happened?'

Vasselis shrugged. 'Yola?'

'I don't know,' she said. 'I can't explain it.'

'So why were you screaming, little one?' asked Kashilli. 'Had me worried there for a moment.'

'Well . . .'

'I think you're being too modest,' said Hesther. 'Look at what you've done.'

Yola sat up in the fountain and wiped her hands through her hair. 'You don't understand. I didn't do anything. I wasn't ready to release the Work when I felt something coming at us from everywhere. It was through the ground and went through all the dead. I thought it was going to be the end of us all. So I screamed.'

Iliev laughed. 'A sensible reaction, young Yola.'

'But possibly the best news of all,' said Vasselis. 'Because if these dead have fallen and something came through the trails under the ground to do it, Gorian might have been beaten. Our Ascendants, the true Ascendants have surely defeated him.'

'Dead?' asked Hesther.

'We can only hope,' said Vasselis. 'We can only hope.'

Kashilli was massaging his chin and staring out over the dead and through the gates.

'Tell you something though. Dead or not, he's left one bastard of a mess to clear up.'

Roberto and Davarov embraced one another long and hard. Weapons were dropped from hands. Breath could be taken and screaming muscles could relax. All around them, the few survivors on the roof of the fort were congratulating each other on their survival. But there was no triumph here. There could only ever be relief.

'They did it, then,' said Davarov.

'If you really want something done, make sure Paul Jhered is in charge,' said Roberto, stepping back.

'Not just him, though,' said Davarov.

'Well, I'll believe that when I hear about it. All I know is that an Ascendant has caused all the pain and death you see around you. If other Ascendants have killed him, all well and good. Don't expect me to shower them with gifts.'

Roberto walked to the stairway and looked down to the ground.

'Harban? Still conscious down there?'

Harban raised the hand that clutched the flask. 'But it hurts, Ambassador.'

'It would have hurt more if you'd bashed that thing against the concrete,' said Davarov. 'Stay where you are, we'll get you away from there. Patch you up somehow.'

'With what?' asked Roberto. 'There's nothing here but us for mile upon mile.'

Davarov gazed over the fort's crenellations and into Atreska.

'I wonder how far the wave went,' he said. 'How much of my country has he ruined?'

'We'll measure it as we walk across it,' said Roberto. 'What a fucking mess. Are you coming with us, Julius?'

He sighed and began to walk down the steps. He jumped the space to the bottom half, stepped around the dead and continued down to the causeway.

'You never used to swear,' said Davarov.

'Julius changed all that. Wants me burned, you know.'

'Does he?' Davarov looked over at Julius.

Julius spread his hands. 'There was a difference of opinion. I think I understand the ambassador's point of view now. I don't agree with it, but I understand it.'

Roberto smiled at him. 'Thanks for standing with us. You made a difference, Julius. Kept the faithful believing.'

But it was hardly enough. Roberto pushed a hand through his hair and could feel nothing but a swelling of grief. He was wading through the flotsam of friend and enemy, none of whom should have died today. The number was uncountable. Unthinkable. But it would be a number they would one day know.

He felt sick. Flanked by Davarov and Barias, with the handful of other survivors trailing in their wake, they picked their way slowly towards Harban-Qvist. None of them could find any more words. Down here, the sheer scale of the crime was brought into sharp focus.

Away across the compound and out towards the camp, bodies lay, carpeting the rotted earth. A haze rose from the scene. Surrounding them more closely, thousand upon thousand of Tsardon dead. Every one of them covered in mire. Every one of them at peace at last. Roberto started to count. He couldn't help it. Twelve thousand Tsardon. Fifty thousand refugees. Something like four legions of Conquord troops, administrators and engineers.

And that was just here at Neratharn. How much further had Gorian's influence spread?

'Your God have mercy on you all,' said Roberto.

Davarov spat on a Tsardon corpse.

'Don't pity them. They brought this on themselves. My people had to stand here.' He kicked at the body. 'These bastards were uninvited.'

Roberto saw the hatred burning within Davarov and chose not to rebuke the big Atreskan. But there had to be a different view here. All were the victims of the crime perpetrated by Gorian Westfallen, the Ascendant. Roberto followed Julius over to Harban. They made a space among the bodies and Julius checked over his wounds.

'They're only serious if they get infected,' he said. 'Leg is superficial, back is a bit nasty.'

'Infection is all the rage here,' said Roberto. 'Come on, let's get him into what passes for open ground and wash these cuts out. Someone must have some clean water on their back.'

Davarov and Roberto chaired Harban out of the compound and into the camp areas which were a little clearer of dead. There was nowhere clean to lay him down so Roberto spread his cloak in the slime. They used another as a pillow. Harban was placed on his side.

'Thank you,' said the Karku.

'Least we can do,' said Roberto. 'Julius? All yours.'

'Hey Roberto, look.'

Davarov was pointing away to the west. Figures were moving in the haze, resolving slowly. There were six of them. No, eight. Two were being carried, apparently dead or unconscious. They moved terribly slowly. Two hung on to one another and it was unclear who was in the worse condition. Ossacer and Arducius. Arducius was wearing nothing but a cloak. There was a child who had his hand on the body of one of those being carried by a man who had to be Paul Jhered. He didn't work out who the other two were until they were much closer. One of them carried Gorian's body.

'Well, there's some good news for you at least, Harban.'

The Karku winced as Julius patted at the wound in his back. 'The mountain still stands. That is enough.'

'And two of your priests have been saved by Paul Jhered.'

Harban smiled. 'If you want something done . . .'

'So it would seem.'

Roberto walked a few paces towards Jhered and his charges. The Exchequer held Mirron in his arms. He had no need to speak.

'I am so sorry, Paul. I know how much she meant to you.'

Jhered nodded. 'She made the ultimate sacrifice, Roberto. Whatever you might think about the Ascendants, remember that. She saved us. All of us.'

'All we have done is stop a mass slaughter, perhaps a genocide, that should never have been allowed to begin. And we all standing here carry blame for that,' said Roberto.

'No one could know what Gorian would do,' said Arducius.

Roberto shrugged.

'Mirron was our sister. And she died to stop this. Sacrificed herself so that we could all live,' said Ossacer.

Ossacer looked terrible. His hair was lank and his face crumpled with old age that was the result of a Work and choked with the pain of his loss.

'And you expect me to be grateful?' Roberto gestured around him, feeling a rising frustration. 'Take a look, Arducius, Ossacer. Take a long look. Seventy-five thousand and more were breathing the border air as the day dawned. Twenty of us will see the sun go down. Count us, count us.'

'I understand how you feel, believe me,' said Arducius. His face was white with pain. His breath came in anguished gasps. 'And yes, I do expect you to be grateful. Not because she stopped the devastation, for which we all carry blame as you say. But because she, Mirron Westfallen, laid down her life to save all that she could. Including you.'

'The problem is that this whole catastrophe was so eminently avoidable,' said Roberto. 'An Ascendant caused all this. It is the least I expected that an Ascendant should finish it.'

'Mirron died,' said Ossacer.

'And so did my brother.' Roberto forced himself to unclench his fists. 'We all lost people we love. This is a result. It is not a happy ending, if indeed it is an ending at all. After all, Ascendants still live and with that comes risk. Particularly from the progeny of Gorian, I would say.'

'This will never be allowed to happen again,' said Arducius. 'On that you have my word.'

'Damn right, it won't,' said Roberto. 'But how that is guaranteed will be up to my mother and me. Not you.'

Roberto stared at Arducius and Ossacer, expecting a response but it was plain they were both too exhausted and, in Arducius's case, too injured to argue further. Roberto looked at Gorian in the arms of the Karku priest.

'You can drop him in the filth he created now. I've seen all I need to see.'

'*Hark's Arrow*'s in the bay at the Gaws,' said Jhered.

His voice was small and quiet. His face was lined, etched with all he had seen. Roberto thought he looked old for the first time.

'Assuming she survived the earth wave,' said Davarov.

'I have no doubt she did. I ordered her anchored in the bay. She'll have ridden it like an ocean swell.'

'There's so much to do here, Paul,' said Roberto. 'How can we leave it like this?'

'What can we few really achieve if we stay?' countered Jhered. 'This place is dead. It's gone. We need legions to clear it and rebuild. And who knows if anything will ever grow here again. You need to get home. See your mother. Give her the news she must hear from you and you alone.'

Roberto's shoulders sagged. His emotions boiled within him. The grief was back as keen as ever.

'Duty. There's always some damned duty to perform. Dear God-surround-me, Paul, how do you tell your mother that her youngest son is dead? Poor Adranis. So much greatness snuffed out.' Roberto snapped his fingers and turned his gaze on Arducius and Ossacer. 'How do I do that?'

They didn't answer him. And that was probably as well.

'I think it is time we all left this place to the peace of God,' said Julius Barias quietly. 'We can do no more good here. Only deepen our anger and our hate. And we must not do that.'

Roberto stared at the Speaker. He nodded.

'Come on,' said Jhered. 'Let's get Harban up and get going. I need to put my back to this place.'

The flames still gorged on the flesh of the innocent. The fire spat from the sky tearing bodies asunder. And Mirron still sucked the sickness of the earth through her dying flesh to end the misery.

Arducius could not dismiss the images just as he could not dismiss his guilt. So vast were the crimes committed in the name of the Ascendancy that no act of contrition would ever suffice. He, like Ossacer, spent much time in prayer and contemplation. But no answers were to be found there. The Omniscient would not turn their way.

And out there on the dark quiet deck, Roberto Del Aglios stared at the black smoke billowing from every beacon they passed. Another death to set at the feet of the Ascendancy.

'You're awake, aren't you?'

Ossacer's voice came from his left. It was thick from where he had been crying quietly.

'That isn't a deduction requiring any ability,' replied Arducius. 'I am always awake. As are you.'

'I could have saved her, you know,' said Ossacer.

'No, you couldn't, Ossie. We've been through this a thousand times. Maybe if you were undamaged you could have slowed what was travelling through her. But you sampled the sickness. You saw how quickly it ravaged her. Nothing could have prevented her death.'

'But I did nothing,' said Ossacer.

'Rubbish. You saved us so we could fight Gorian. What greater act could you have done? It was I who did nothing. Just broke my bones when we could least afford it.'

From the darkness came a dry chuckle.

'Listen to us. Fighting over who did the least. What are we both trying you avoid, do you think?'

'Inevitability,' said Arducius.

'Is that what it is?'

'How do you twine the threads of a life so torn? Where trust is lost so completely that the thought of forgiveness makes you nauseous. Roots will have to regrow. The flower must bloom afresh.'

'Not just us, though. The Order too,' said Ossacer.

'Oh yes. The damage done to the Order is incalculable. But to the Ascendancy it is surely irreversible.'

'Eternally?'

'I don't know, Ossie. But in our lifetimes I cannot see any hope, can you?'

'Mirron didn't die so we would run away.' Ossacer's voice was a whisper.

At the mention of Mirron's name, the tears burst from Arducius's eyes, the dam of his emotions breached so effortlessly. They said nothing more while the sniffs and sobs held sway, each trying to regain enough control to begin again. Eventually, Arducius had to speak though he was so raw that it hurt his throat.

'I miss her so badly,' he said.

'Me, too.'

'But she wouldn't want to leave us prey to persecution and hate.'

'So what will we do?' asked Ossacer and at once he was the scared teenager Arducius had always protected.

'I don't think we have a choice. You've seen the way Roberto looks at Kessian. You know what he's thinking and what he fears more than any of us.'

'Poor boy,' said Ossacer. 'The only innocent one on board and orphaned so young. I'm glad Paul is taking care of him.'

'But he won't forever. Paul Jhered belongs to the Advocacy, not the Ascendancy.'

The *Hark's Arrow* moved easily through calm waters, a natural wind at her stern. The warm winds were blowing down from the great northern deserts. The heralds of solastro. The sky was clear. Stars sparkled. Dawn was coming, casting the land below the eastern horizon into the deepest dark of night.

Roberto stared at the mountain tops and the beacon towers that marched the length and breadth of the land. His land. The fires were bright against the night and the smoke billowed heavenwards. Black smoke. The only feature that would not resolve to a lighter shade when dawn kissed Estorea once more.

He had kept his grief private. Jhered too. But the two of them had stood together a great deal on this dreadful journey home. And in those times he had been thankful like never before for the Exchequer's huge strength of character and will for the Conquord to survive and prosper.

They had found time to laugh and to reminisce. But in the quiet of his cabin and now out here alone for once, Roberto was left to regret the fact that Jhered had known his mother much better than had her own son.

Soldier, and now diplomat. So keen to be away from the cosseted centre of power and now, how little he understood of the art of rule. And how he would need his friends about him.

Advocate.

Him. Roberto Del Aglios. And after him, no succession. Not yet.

Roberto stared over the rail into the dark Estorean coastal waters. The sail was full behind him and the deck crew quiet. He could see the flecks of foam thrown from the bow and hear the water ripple away behind. It was mesmerising.

'I've watched Ascendants stare into the deeps contemplating jumping but was never worried. But you, Roberto, you *can* drown.'

'No need for concern, Paul. Just searching for inspiration.' Roberto raised his head and looked round at Jhered. 'And wishing this barrel would travel a little faster.'

Jhered joined him at the rail. He was unshaven and bore the same marks of tiredness they all shared. Jhered was wearing trail clothes but not his cloak. Mirron's body was wrapped in that before being sealed in a long crate in the hold. Ossacer's ministrations ensured that the odours of decay were kept at bay.

'This barrel is the fastest trireme the Conquord possesses,' said Jhered. 'And it could go faster.'

'No,' said Roberto. 'I will not have a devil wind rush me to my mother's grave.'

'And yet you are desperate to arrive,' said Jhered.

Roberto dropped his chin to his chest and leant hard on the rail.

'Yes, I am. But scared of what I might find and what I might see.'

'Herine picked her closest friends well,' said Jhered. 'When crises occur, that inner group you hate so much are discarded and those she knows can save her Conquord are called upon. Things were already ugly when I left but Vasselis, Gesteris and Kastenas were with her. Your sister too. They were preparing for invasion.'

'So how can she be dead when evidence tells us others in power are not? She was always so strong. So ... healthy. Vital. I swear, Paul, if she felt the touch of the walking dead, I will execute the whole Ascendancy.'

Jhered said nothing. They'd been through this before. No agreement, only understanding and sympathy.

'The fact is, I'm terrified by the thought of what we'll find when we row into the harbour. We have no idea who is alive and who is dead. We don't know where anyone is and they have no idea that you, I and Davarov survived.'

'The plague of the dead was vast,' said Jhered. 'Expect the worst.'

Roberto's chest constricted further. 'I do.'

'But at least we know some form of government is resident on the hill. The black smoke tells us as much.'

Roberto nodded, feeling a little relief at last.

'And they did respond to the victory flag we flew from the Gaws beacon,' he said.

'I'm just sorry I had no birds to send word of your survival, my Advocate,' said Jhered.

'And we'll have none of that, Exchequer Jhered. Not if you are to stand with me in the basilica.'

'There must always be acknowledgement of the chain of command.'

Roberto smiled at last. 'You never change, do you?'

'No.'

Roberto looked out towards the distant harbour of Estorr. 'I wonder how many still live?'

'Two days and we will know.'

At least they found time to decorate the harbour. Flags flew. Flowers adorned every hanging and nestling space. Fresh paint gleamed. The horns sounded the arrival of the Advocate. Yet the dockside was hardly straining at its polished seams. And there was reserve to the fanfares and cheers. Hardly a surprise. Most of them wouldn't know whether to cheer or to cry. At least there was genuine relief at Roberto's arrival.

But the air still stank of ash and the surface of the water both within and without the harbour was covered in a film of oil and dust. All the paint in the world couldn't disguise the damage the city had suffered. Jhered had warned Roberto what to expect but his information was out of date. Estorr had been invaded and she had been badly hurt.

The *Hark's Arrow* rowed sedately to her berth. Roberto, Jhered and Davarov stood at the prow. Roberto searched the faces and figures of the welcome party and at last a little joy entered his heart. There, standing beside Arvan Vasselis, was Tuline.

'The Omniscient still knows mercy,' he breathed.

Barely had the gang plank struck the dockside than Roberto was pounding down it. Protocol could burn. He ignored everyone else, enveloping his sister in an embrace that breached the floodgates of his relief and his grief.

Nothing and no one else existed for Roberto in those moments when Tuline shuddered against him, grasping him as if to let go was to lose him forever.

'I will never leave you alone,' he said. 'Just you and me now, Tuline.'

Roberto felt Tuline freeze in his arms and he cursed himself for the idiot he surely was. Tuline looked into his eyes.

'Where's Adranis?'

'Oh, Tuline, Tuline, we have lost so much.'

Chapter Sixty-Nine

859th cycle of God, 5th day of Solasrise

'This crown does not sit easily on my head,' said Roberto. 'And I should not have had to bear it for many years yet.'

Roberto Del Aglios, Advocate of the Estorean Conquord, brushed a fallen strand of ivy from the bust of his mother where it stood in the formal palace gardens. It had been her favourite place and, following his commissioning of the piece on his return to Estorr, Roberto had never considered another place for it. He couldn't bear the walk to the Principal House to visit her grave. This was the best he could do for the moment.

'And yet it fits you just as it did Herine. Perfectly.'

Roberto turned. He brushed down his formal toga and walked the marble path back to the colonnaded walkway, his sandals slapping on the polished stone.

'Hello, Paul.'

'Got some reports for you,' he said, waving a leather satchel.

'Do I want to hear them?' Roberto gestured they walked up to the state room. He enjoyed the view. Estorr's slow but beautiful rebirth.

'Well, you be the judge, but things are going according to plan. Elise Kastenas has confirmed that the Neratharn site is clean of bodies. Marcus Gesteris is heading into Tsard to take back Khuran's ashes. He's under Sirranean guard so he ought to be safe enough. Similarly, the Gosland border is reformed. The fort is clean. We've heard nothing from Gestern yet and we should not expect good news. That country was almost wiped clean. Katrin Mardov was surely a victim. You need to visit there. The Gatherers are going in mid-solasfall. Why don't we make it an Advocacy tour as well?'

Roberto shrugged. 'If you think I should.'

'Come on Roberto, this is you now. It's what you do.'

'Excuse me if I don't love it all right away, eh?'

'Fifty-three days and counting since Neratharn and the earth wave, my Advocate. Time moves on.'

Roberto held up his hands. 'I know, I know. And don't call me that. You know my name. I don't need you to be formal with me of all people. Even caught Davarov at it the other day.'

'He should be in Atreska,' said Jhered.

'He knows. But I'm not forcing anyone who survived Neratharn to do anything they don't want to do.'

'Except . . .'

'No, no. Their decision, Paul. I didn't say a word.'

'You didn't have to. Your expressions can be magnificently eloquent. And they knew any other decision would leave your position untenable with the citizenry and the Senate.'

'And praise the mystique of Sirrane that means both citizen and senator agree with what we're doing.'

The two men walked to the balcony. Estorr was resplendent. The sun was hot, the fields swelled with crops to the west and every tile glared red, every wall shone white. It was a fitting epitaph for his mother. The city, her city, lived on. Though it was quiet. More than fifteen thousand soldiers and citizens had perished in the brief invasion of the dead. And the hole they left was reflected in the hollowness of Estorr's mood. It would be a long time recovering, if it ever truly did.

Down in the courtyard, a line of carriages waited. Children were playing tag around the fountain. Roberto smiled.

'Just an adventure for them, isn't it?'

'For now. And only for some of them. The teenagers are none too happy, I can assure you. And it's one big voyage they all face. The excitement will soon wear off.'

'Is he here?'

'Waiting in the ante-room,' said Jhered. 'Shall I?'

'Please.'

Jhered strode over to the door to the ante-room and opened it. Arducius walked in. He looked whole and healthy though there was a tint to his eyes that told he would never forget, never quite shake the guilt he had assumed.

'Thank you,' said Roberto. 'I know I've said it already but you have done me and the Advocacy a great service. I am in your debt.'

'No, you aren't,' said Arducius. 'By the time we reached Estorr,

Ossie and I had worked out there was no other way.'

'Perhaps not.' Roberto almost regretted what had to happen. He had formed a new respect for Arducius in particular that had surprised him. 'And everything is ready?'

'Yes, yes,' said Arducius. 'The Academy is empty of books and papers. The trunks are packed and loaded and the strands all understand what is happening. Not all of them like it but they understand, I think.'

'And do you really understand yourself? Plenty of support hereabouts, not least from my new Chancellor.'

Roberto smiled. He still didn't know what had possessed him. It would be a relationship to rival the last one between Advocate and Chancellor. Arducius chuckled.

'Maybe but Julius Barias is all against fire for anything other than light and cooking and that's an element we treasure even more than before Mirron ...' He tailed off and glanced at Jhered for a moment, needing a change of subject. 'Disbanding the Armour of God is a brave move. Bringing the Order closer to the Advocacy, very wise—'

'Not a difficult decision, though, Arducius. The backlash was quite something to behold. There has been almost no dissension. Apart from the Speaker Council and Horst Vennegoor, as you might expect. But we'll see if this really brings state and Order closer together. I think my mother would tell you that a certain amount of distance and friction keeps both arms grounded.'

'But you are the Advocate,' said Arducius.

'Yes, I am and I will choose different battles within my government if I can. And one of them wouldn't have been with you. Not in the end. Part of me wants to keep you close where I can better control you. But I am no dictator.'

'The fact is, my Advocate, that the Conquord does not need the complication that accompanies us. Your own inner debate is apt evidence. I don't think the world will ever be ready for us. I know we speak about evolution but there's so much more still to learn. Perhaps nature should be allowed to take its course on this one. Perhaps the Ascendancy Echelon were wrong from the start. Best we take our leave until the Omniscient deems it the right time for natural-born Ascendants to appear.'

'And you think that'll happen?'

'I think it is inevitable,' said Arducius. 'But what we, the firstborn and our younger siblings represent is a continuation of the memory of Gorian and all that he did. I cannot live with that. Neither can Ossacer. And the young strands do not deserve to be tarred with it either. They, among all of us, are true innocents in all this. The Conquord must be allowed to return to glory with us as a chapter in history. But I hope they remember it was not always an unhappy chapter.'

'I can agree to that,' said Roberto. 'But how do I know that one amongst you is not another Gorian, eh?'

'Because I give you my word that it will not be allowed to happen. Kessian is Mirron not Gorian, believe me. None that are alive now may demonstrate such tendencies and live. And our child-rearing days are already over. The Ascendancy will diminish and fade. In a hundred years or so, all that will be left will be the books. And they will be in the safest of hands.'

Roberto held out his hand and Arducius took it.

'Your word is enough for me, Arducius. You at least are a good man. Your wisdom will be missed by the Advocacy.'

'But not my abilities.'

'No.' Roberto shook his head. 'Not those. Never those. Not for me.'

'Goodbye my Advocate.' Arducius thumped his right arm into his chest. 'My arm and heart remain yours.'

Roberto handed him a sealed roll of parchment that was lying alone on a small table.

'Arvan Vasselis will be there well ahead of you. Along with the Sirranean negotiator but just in case there's a problem, this should get you an audience with Tarenaq and Huatl. They are good people.'

'Thank you, my Advocate.'

'Have a safe voyage. I'm surprised you aren't going overland. It's a very long way round to Sirrane.'

'I think avoiding people is our primary concern.'

'And no one wants to see Gorian's legacy,' said Roberto. He tensed a little. 'You know we think it is a perfect circle, the ruined land? Almost eight thousand square miles where man nor animal will willingly tread and where nothing grows but a quartet of trees at its absolute centre. Quite a sight, I'm told.'

'It is a monument to a failed experiment that I have no desire to see. I can only say I am sorry so many times.'

'Yes, yes. And it could have been worse, eh?' Roberto managed a smile. 'Paul? I understand you are seeing the Ascendants to their ship.'

'That I am. Come on, Ardu, the tide will not wait.'

Arducius bowed his head to Roberto, turned and walked from the state room. Jhered patted Roberto's shoulder and followed him out. Roberto waited until the carriages had all left the palace under the last flag of the Ascendancy guard before returning to the gardens to speak with the bust of his mother.

The captain of the *Hark's Spear* was anxious to get away. The tide was on the turn and he wanted to make best use of the wind. But Paul Jhered was not quite ready. The rest of them were on board. Only Ossacer and Arducius remained on the shore, one foot on the gangplank.

'So this is it, then?' said Jhered. 'I find it a little hard to believe I am not just waving you off on some mission to a corner of the Conquord.'

'It's for the best,' said Ossacer. His eyes bored into Jhered. 'Don't feel loss. We are not lost.'

'I will never work out how you do that.'

'I know. And I will leave it maddening you because you would never really understand even if I told you.'

'Well, I will feel loss, Ossie. If anyone was my family it was the four of you. Two are gone and now I am losing the other two. Not a great record for a father.'

Ossacer laughed and it lightened Jhered's heart. But the laughter was short and the serious face that was his signature returned.

'I couldn't ever have stayed here. Every day wondering if the knock on the door will come dragging me to my death or sending me out to battle. The Ascendancy started out as a benevolent force and look at what we became.'

'I think that's a little unfair,' said Jhered.

They fell silent for a while.

'You should be coming with us,' said Arducius. 'If Mirron had still been alive, you would have come.'

Jhered nearly cracked then. 'Perhaps I would. Or perhaps you would never have chosen to leave. We'll never know. But my place is here, in the heart of the Conquord. It will always be my life and my destiny. And so here our family must go its separate ways. And that is a regret I will take to my grave.'

'Us also,' said Arducius.

Jhered pulled them into embraces, one after another, holding them close, patting their backs.

'Look after Kessian for me,' said Jhered. 'He is all that remains of Mirron.'

'And he is as close to our hearts.'

'I know. Safe journey. And be good. My crew will report and I don't want to be disappointed.'

The three of them laughed and Jhered waved them up the gangplank. It was raised almost immediately and the captain ordered the ship push out into the harbour. No fanfare, no civic farewell. Just a Gatherer ship rowing sedately out into the Tirronean Sea on a beautiful, Omniscient-blessed morning.

Jhered stood and watched until the ship was out of sight around the south fort. He smiled to himself, nodded and turned away, deciding a walk back to the palace was in order. Something inside him refused to believe that this really was the end of the Ascendancy, and of his work with those two fine young men. After all, the cork was pulled from the jug. Could it really be stoppered back up?

Whatever the will of the people, and their attitudes, Ascendants were alive and would still walk the earth. Hidden, maybe. Out of the reach of friend or enemy. But alive. Jhered wondered what that meant for the balance of the world and how the Omniscient would deal with them. As faithful disciples or as threats. A conundrum that only a God had the authority to solve and there was some real satisfaction to be found in that thought.

Jhered turned and looked back out past the harbour. A small white cloud was floating out beyond the south fort. It was travelling against the wind and was the shape of an upturned mouth. He laughed out loud, turning a few heads.

'You cheeky little bastard.'

Jhered swung about a final time and walked back up the hill towards the palace, his Advocate, and the rebuilding of the Estorean Conquord.

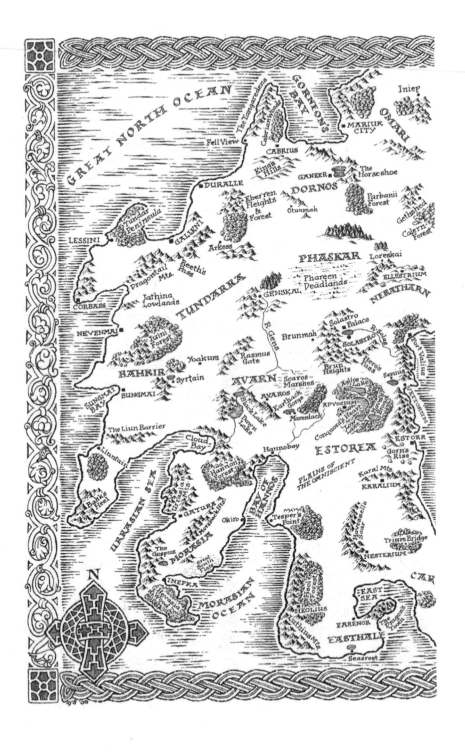

THE
ESTOREAN
CONQUORD

Scale (approx.)
500 Miles